The VOICE the REVOLUTION & the KEY

What Readers Are Saying

Fantastic! As I read, I seem to forget *The Voice, the Revolution and the Key* is classified as "fiction." Thank you, Jenny, for creating an accurate image of Patrick Henry for us as we read your well-crafted words. Patrick Henry would agree: *Bene factum, et tibi gratias ago, fidelis scribæ!* (Well done, and thank you, faithful scribe!)

—**Patrick Henry Jolly,** Fifth great-grandson of Patrick and Sarah Henry, East Claridon, OH

I appreciate Jenny L. Cote keeping the spirit of Patrick Henry's 'voice' alive and igniting a revolution of interest in early American history with the next generation. Thank you Jenny, for your passion and inspiration!

—**Hope E. Marstin,** Chief Operating Officer, Red Hill, Patrick Henry National Memorial, Brookneal, VA

The Voice, the Revolution, and the Key recounts actual history as seen through the eyes of fictional animals. Patrick Henry's illustrious life has been thoroughly researched and is presented in an engaging manner. Jenny L. Cote introduces the young reader to this congenial, highly principled, and deeply religious man through imagined conversations based on documented events. It's time to put those social media devices aside and learn about the man who initiated our country's march to independence.

—**Dr. Robert Bluford, Jr.,** Chairman, Historic Polegreen Church Foundation, Richmond, VA

Jenny L. Cote provides a wonderful platform for understanding our country's rich history. In a time when looking back helps us interpret the present and comprehend the future, Jenny's books are an important addition to any library. She furnishes young readers with a fun, accurate, and easily digestible way to learn.

—**Chuck Schwam,** American Friends of Lafayette, Gaithersburg, MD

Jenny has taken spiritual, mystical, and historical elements and has woven them into a fascinating story that is sure to capture the interest of readers of all ages. Her research on Mr. Henry is exceptional.

—**Raymond Baird,** 73, Richmond historian, Manakin Sabot, VA

Patrick Henry's eloquent words are as applicable today as they were when he spoke them, and, under Jenny L. Cote's deft handling, are now resurrected to new life. Oh how I pray that Cato's words, Patrick Henry's words, Cote's words will inspire young men and women to love God, live with integrity, and fight for liberty.

—**Lisa Hockman,** Grant writer, Roswell, GA

Those who read this account of Patrick Henry's life will have a rebirth of patriotism in their hearts and will value the freedom that our American nation affords us. This book is for adults as well as for children and youth.

—**Dr. Paul Mims,** 79, Minister, Cornerstone Baptist Church, Cherry Log, GA

I have read all of Jenny's books to my own children and introduced them to my students. Yet I was so excited to read *The Voice, the Revolution, and the Key*, as it includes one of my favorite time periods—the Revolutionary War. The lives of George Washington, Patrick Henry, and others are opened up to the reader, giving more light to their actions and their characters. I cannot wait to see how Jenny continues her tale!

—**Liz Hamilton,** 3rd Grade Teacher, Providence Classical School, Williamsburg, VA

Jenny's ability to weave a story that is fascinating to readers—whether they be 8 or 89—is absolutely miraculous! All of the characters come alive.

—**Edith Poindexter,** 89, Long Island, VA

KIDS & TEENS

I have always loved history, but I had no connection with the people I read about; they were little more than words on a page. After reading this book, I no longer suffer from that problem. I was there with the characters. I felt their every hope and fear, and when I turned the last page I knew Patrick Henry, George Washington, and Marquis de Lafayette as if I had walked alongside them. Jenny L. Cote's writing lays bare the mystery of our founding father's lives to reveal their great personal faith, and in doing so, displays the biblical foundation upon which they built every stone of our country. In a way that no mere history book could, it reveals the true vitality of God's hand in the shaping of our country.

—**Madison Franks,** 15, Homeschooled, Idalou, TX

The Voice, the Revolution, and the Key takes the American Revolution and puts a great twist on the telling of the story so the reader can't put it down.

—**Adam Walters,** 11, Waller Mill Elementary School, Williamsburg, VA

Throughout *The Voice, the Revolution, and the Key*, little teasing tidbits of information are carefully placed, creating major suspense and so many questions such as how, where, what, when, and huh! Amazingly, Mrs. Cote takes all of the questions and creates a beautiful tale of tragedy and suspense.

—**Laelah Credeur,** 13, Lafayette Christian Academy, Lafayette, LA

The Voice, the Revolution, and the Key shows the American Revolution through the eyes of the Order of the Seven and Patrick Henry, a man that most people only know for seven courageous words, not for his amazing life or for his steadfast faith. Jenny L. Cote instills the ideal of liberty in her readers, making them feel as if they might one day be willing to say, "Give me liberty, or give me death!"

—**Katie Wyrick,** 12, Homeschooled, Niota, TN

The imaginative author strikes again! The interaction between the characters peppered with her wit and humor made me feel like I was actually within the story myself. I learned so much more about Patrick Henry than I had ever known before. Clearly, God's hand was upon him to help shape and change the course of the beginning of our nation. I highly recommend this book.

—**Abbagael Sullivan,** 12, Homeschool (Dream Big Academy), Sebastian, FL

Jenny L Cote's newest book, *The Voice, the Revolution, and the Key,* is a perfect blend of historical fiction and mystery. I learned an amazing amount of facts about Patrick Henry that I had never heard before. At the same time, I was racking my brain trying to find the piece of the puzzle that would help me see through the shroud of mystery that surrounded almost everything. Personally, I believe that of all the books that Jenny L. Cote has written so far, this is the most captivating.

—**Andrew Buckner,** 13, Homeschooled, Clearwater, FL

This book is AMAZING!!! I liked it from the very beginning. It all starts from when Patrick Henry and his friends were little kids, which leads the readers to really know their personalities and how they continued to develop as they grew up. This book vividly presents Patrick as kind, resilient, bold, hardworking, compassionate, and a courageous freedom fighter.

—**Evangelina Thornton,** 11, Edlin School, Herndon, VA

Yet again Jenny has outdone herself; this book is a work of art! I love all of these books, but this is her best so far. The faith, adventure, and intrigue that Jenny weaves into the seemingly simple story of Patrick Henry is astounding.

—**Hope Thompson,** 14, Homeschooled, Cinnaminson, NJ

In this brilliant historical novel, Jenny L. Cote takes you through the lives of our founding fathers and the words that started the Revolutionary War. You will experience their emotions, and gasp and cry and smile with them. It is a real page turner!

—**Faith Boustany,** 11, Atlantic Shores Christian School, Chesapeake, VA

The Voice, the Revolution, and the Key is a rollicking, energetic, fast-paced ride that is full of twists, turns, and historical facts. While all the characters are lifelike, Patrick Henry in particular jumps off the pages to make his "Liberty or Death" speech. It is a fascinating take on the years preceding the American Revolution.

—**Jenni Ervin,** 16, Homeschooled, North Branch, MI

Once again, we found ourselves wishing the book would never end! We love how she connects characters from previous books. Like all of the series, it 'totally takes the biscuit'!

—**The Miller Family** (Elijah 13, Korban 12, Simeon 10), Homeschooled, Three Hills Alberta, Canada

The Voice, the Revolution, and the Key is split into four acts that span 32 years. The plot progresses smoothly, and shows how America gradually began to see itself as a nation. There is some mystery ("the fiddle has a riddle"), some drama, and humor too. The story tells us about Patrick Henry's family and his life as a kid. Patrick Henry perseveres! This book was a "Shuccshessh!" I give it five stars.

—**Joseph Geaney, IV,** 11, Jacksonville Lighthouse Charter School: Flightline Upper Academy, Cabot, AR

I was so excited to read Jenny L. Cote's new book! It is such a gripping story that it kept me turning the pages, and I learned a lot that I didn't know before about Patrick Henry and the Revolution. I am so looking forward to the next book in the trilogy!

—**Zachary Huckel,** 10, Homeschooled, Adelaide, South Australia

Jenny L. Cote describes every character so well, I feel like I really know each of them! I learned that not only was Patrick Henry a great speaker, he was a kind brother, a self-taught lawyer, a patient husband, a loving father, a passionate patriot, and above all, a devoted Christian. I learned all about what life was like in colonial days, from the food the colonists ate and the clothes they wore, to the festivals they celebrated and the churches they attended. I love how Jenny L. Cote describes everything in glorious detail, and I adore each member of the Epic Order of the Seven.

—**Emily Gwaltney,** 15, Homeschooled, Morgantown, WV

I really enjoyed this book as a Christian and as a reader with historical interests. I can't wait for the next one!

—**Connor Stevens,** 15, Valor Christian High School, Lone Tree, CO

You will simply devour this book. With its intriguing beginning, charming middle, and beautiful ending, *The Voice, the Revolution, and the Key* certainly will leave you more than hungry for the next installment. *Je ne peux pas attendre!* (I can't wait!)

—**Georgia Ferry,** 13, Homeschooled, ShellMera Pastaza, Ecuador

The Voice, the Revolution, and the Key is the best historical fiction book we have ever read. We love the way Jenny L. Cote brings the Epic Order of the Seven into the American Revolution. We read Jenny's latest novel while we were studying the Revolutionary War at school. Jenny's story really brought to life the events we were learning about in our class. We hated for the story to end! If you are looking for a history-filled book that contains action, humor, and a touch of mystery, then this is just the book for you.

—**Emily Newton,** 11 and **Ashlyn Newton**, 11,
Cottage Hill Christian Academy, Irvington, AL

Being a Canadian, I wasn't much interested in American history, because I found it boring. The only enjoyment I got in learning about American history was through Adventures in Odyssey. But Jenny opened up a new love for history through this book. Although I won't be jumping into a textbook for fun anytime soon, I will be opening Jenny's books for any questions I ask about the Patriots. Thank you, Jenny! Your book was a complete shuccshessh!

—**Alyssa Bueckert,** 15, Homeschooled, Taylor, British Columbia, Canada

The Voice, the Revolution, and the Key is Jenny L. Cote's magnum opus. Each and every novel she's written in this series is connected and masterfully comes together in this EPIC adventure. Everyone who studies the birth of our nation needs to read this book! It is going to be very, VERY difficult to wait for the next two installments in this series, which will also be on the American Revolutionary War. So, I say, "Give me the next book, or give me death!"

—**Kira Dewey,** 14, Homeschooled, Orlando, FL

In France with the young Marquis, in the wilderness with Patrick Henry, or on the battlefield with George Washington, Mrs. Cote describes what it takes to make a revolution, and the price at which it comes. She shares the stories of some of the most forgotten hopes and ideas that set the Revolution in motion. This is not a boring history lesson; this is an exciting and thrilling HIStory lesson as seen through the eyes of Max and Liz. Another EPIC adventure with all of our favorite characters. Well done and very much appreciated. Thank you Mrs. Cote!

—**Hannah Huffey,** 12, Homeschooled, Johnson, AR

And she does it again! Jenny L. Cote brilliantly weaves together the rich sound of America's beautiful voice with her wonderfully whimsical characters who leave their paw prints across the pages of HIStory. So come along laddies and lassies, and join the crew in yet another adventure! HUZZAH! This is definitely her best book yet!

—**Anna Davis,** 13, Homeschooled, Chesterfield, VA

I am a HUGE history fan, and this book really hit the mark. I expected this book just to be another Christian faith-based historical novel. *The Voice, the Revolution, and the Key* is so much more. Get ready to feel Patrick Henry's struggle with freedom and the independence of his nation while staying true to his faith.

—**Reagan Lengefeld,** 12, Fellowship Christian School, Roswell, GA

Woven with care and packed with history, Mrs. Cote has spun a tale of emotion, leading the reader to more fully understand the lives of our forefathers.

—**Abigail Gilbert,** 14, Westminster Academy, Germantown, TN

I loved this book. I loved the way that it was an in-depth history lesson. I look forward to many more books and will be DEVASTATED when the series ends! I feel like I am very close friends with all the characters: Max, Liz, Big Al, Nigel, Kate, Clarie, Gillamon, and even Cato!

—**Madeline Wright,** 10, Regents School of Austin, Austin, TX

I have loved all of Mrs. Cote's books, and *The Voice, the Revolution, and the Key* is no exception. It's so exciting to follow Max, Liz, and their friends on their epic adventures to important times in HIStory and feel like I'm actually there watching all of the people I've only studied about in school.

—**Luke Highfil,** 12, Neuse Charter School, Clayton, NC

Jenny L. Cote outdid herself on *The Voice, the Revolution, and the Key!* I picked up the book with a vague understanding of Patrick Henry's role in the American Revolution and put it down with a love for him and his contribution to American Independence. As I read, laughed, and yes, cried, I was reminded of what I have known all along: that Jenny L. Cote's books are a thrilling, enlightening, and entertaining ride, from the very first word to the last.

—**Kiara Kalmey,** 17, Commonwealth Charter Academy, Waynesboro, PA

Jenny L. Cote blends humor, history, and faith beautifully in *The Voice, the Revolution, and the Key.* I love how the characters' personalities are different but all used to honor the Maker.

—**Andi Bradsher,** 12, Homeschooled, Roxboro, NC

EPIC ORDER OF THE SEVEN

The VOICE the REVOLUTION & the KEY

JENNY L. COTE

LIVING INK BOOKS
Writing Worth Reading

Epic Order of the Seven®

The Voice, the Revolution, and the Key

Copyright © 2017 by Jenny L. Cote

Published by Living Ink Books, an imprint of AMG Publishers, Chattanooga, Tennessee

Print Edition	ISBN 13: 978-0-89957-795-1
ePUB Edition	ISBN 13: 978-1-61715-361-7
Mobi Edition	ISBN 13: 978-1-61715-365-3
ePDF Edition	ISBN 13: 978-1-61715-363-1

Scripture quotations are taken from the Holy Bible, New Living Translation, copyright ©1996, 2004, 2007, 2013, 2015 by Tyndale House Foundation. Used by permission of Tyndale House Publishers, Inc., Carol Stream, Illinois 60188. All rights reserved.

Scriptures taken from the Holy Bible, New International Version®, NIV®. Copyright © 1973, 1978, 1984, 2011 by Biblica, Inc.™ Used by permission of Zondervan. All rights reserved worldwide. www.zondervan.com The "NIV" and "New International Version" are trademarks registered in the United States Patent and Trademark Office by Biblica, Inc.™

Scripture quotations taken from the New American Standard Bible® (NASB), Copyright © 1960, 1962, 1963, 1968, 1971, 1972, 1973, 1975, 1977, 1995 by The Lockman Foundation. Used by permission. www.Lockman.org

Scripture quotations are taken from the Good News Translation in Today's English Version– Second Edition. Copyright © 1992 by American Bible Society. Used by Permission.

Scripture quotations are taken from the King James Version (Authorized Version), which is in the public domain.

EPIC ORDER OF THE SEVEN is a trademark of Jenny L. Cote.

Cover and internal illustrations by Rob Moffitt, Chicago, Illinois.
Internal images shutterstock.com
Interior design by Katherine Lloyd, theDESKonline.com.
Editing by Rich Cairnes, Walworth, Wisconsin.
Proofreading by Rick Steele, Chattanooga, Tennessee.

19 20 21 22 23 MAR 7 6 5 4 3

Printed in Canada.

To Edith Poindexter

You were the one who first took me
to see Patrick Henry at Red Hill.
Thank you for being my "MizP" all these years,
and especially for telling me about the chair.
With you around, there's always enough blue
in my sky to knit a cat a pair of britches.

Love you good.

This book contains fact, fiction,
fantasy, allegory, and truth.

. . . He marked out their appointed times in history . . .

—Acts 17:26

CONTENTS

PART THREE: DESPAIR NOT THE TRAGIC (1759–65)

PART FOUR: LIBERTY OR DEATH (1765–75)

Acknowledgments

Patrick Henry took out a fresh piece of parchment, picked up his quill, looked me square in the eye and with a broad grin declared, "IF THIS BE GRATITUDE, MAKE THE MOST OF IT!"

Okay, so he really didn't do that. (Fiction author.) But I'm sure Patrick Henry was the first to give credit where credit was due, and so must I. I've labored on this book for a decade, so my thank-you list must therefore be longer than seven little words. But even if I had seven *million* words, they would be woefully inadequate to fully express my gratitude to those who have made this book possible.

God

You knew when I happily ran around the battlefields of Yorktown as a toddler that I would someday write the story of the American Revolution. Thank you for allowing me to grow up immersed in the place where America herself was a toddler and grew to Independence. Thank you for ensuring that I would be raised as a proud Virginian by my godly, history-loving parents, Dr. Paul and Janice Mims. I will ever be Your most humble and obedient servant to command.

Richard Schumann

You have no one to blame but yourself for ten years of relentless questions from me. I'll never forget that warm day behind the Governor's Palace in Colonial Williamsburg when I first heard your voice. You took the stage, removed your tricorn hat, bowed and introduced yourself to the audience. I was mesmerized as you brought the Voice of the Revolution to life for me for the very first time with your staggering knowledge, brilliant humor and wicked wit. Chagrined that I didn't remember more about Patrick Henry other than seven little words, that day I determined I would learn every other word he said. Thank you for patiently teaching me those words across these many years, for helping me with plot lines running through multiple books, and for supporting me in so many ways. I'm happy that you were not only my Revolutionary muse, but also became my dear friend. Had I missed seeing you that day, I undoubtedly would have missed a major turning point in my life. Gasp! Imagine what could have happened if I'd met *Jefferson* first! I'll always be your devoted scribe. And you'll always be "my Henry."

Mark Schneider

You, too, have only yourself to blame for inspiring me to write the story of the Marquis de Lafayette (and Banastre Tarleton, for that matter). There must be something magical about that stage behind the Governor's Palace, for that is where you also first brought the Marquis to life for me. I knew nothing of America's favorite fighting Frenchman before your enthusiastic portrayal, but I knew in an instant that he would be the colorful lens through which my readers could watch the Revolutionary War unfold. Of course that led to my having to research in Paris and Chavaniac in the south of France because of you (wait... *merci beaucoup!)* Alas, being the brilliant military historian you are, you would soon fall prey to not only my Lafayette research, but also to my barrage of ancient Roman military questions for my earlier books. You even morphed from a Frenchman to a Roman in my mind's eye. I'm forever grateful to you for allowing me to pattern my Roman Centurions after you and your precious son, Armand. Thank you for your tireless assistance, your treasured friendship, and for keeping me from writing like a girl in battle scenes. You turned my world upside down, dear friend, and I'm forever grateful.

Epic Historians and Historical Sites

Whenever kids ask me what the best part is about being an author, I always answer with an enthusiastic, one-word answer: "RESEARCH!" I've amassed nearly two hundred books in order to write this trilogy on the Revolution, but books alone are insufficient to drill down to the nitty gritty details of history. You have to go see where history happened, so I have. I've been to every place Patrick Henry ever step foot, and I've travelled to France multiple times to research Lafayette. ("I *have* to go back to France," I cried with the back of my hand dramatically draped over my forehead. "It's for the *children!"*) You also need to pick the brains of historians who know the subject inside and out. I'm grateful to an endless list of epic historians and historical sites that have endured my questions, my repeated visits and even my "slipping behind the curtain" moments when I should have remained seated in the audience. I know some have moved on, and I will miss naming many others. So please forgive my faulty tribute of gratitude.

Mark Couvillon (Interpreter at Colonial Williamsburg, Curator of Red Hill, the Patrick Henry Memorial Foundation, and author of *Patrick Henry's Virginia* and *Patrick Henry, the Demosthenes of His Age*) You can answer every question that could possibly be asked about Patrick Henry! I literally could not have written this book without your keen memory and knowledge about not only Mr. Henry, but also the most obscure details of the eighteenth century. I've worn your books ragged and burned up your phone with my numerous, lengthy texts. Wonder Twin huzzahs and thanks, Mark!

Mrs. Edith Poindexter/
Red Hill Patrick Henry Memorial Foundation

Thank you "MizP" (Retired Curator-Geneologist) for first touring me privately through Red Hill, serving as a key information resource, for allowing me to turn you into Patrick Henry's horse, and for being my dear friend. And thank you, my Red Hill Family, for patiently waiting for me to write this book, and including me in Living History Days. I hope this book will have you overrun with new visitors in the coming years! I truly feel like I come home every time I pull into Red Hill, for it's not just the place but the *people* who make Mr. Henry's beloved homestead so very special. Much love to you all: Hope Marstin, Myra Trent, Bruce Olsen, Patrick Henry Jolly, Scott Brown, Melissa Carwile, Bonnie George, Wanda Holt, Betsy Hanmer, and Sandra Crews.

Colonial Williamsburg is my epicenter for research and I'm grateful to countless individuals and friends who work and/or live there, and have helped me over the years: Michael P. Monaco, Lee Ann Rose, Bill Rose, Dennis Watson, Mike McCarty, Alex Morse, Adam Canady, Rodney Pressley, Nick Alsop, Jonah Stephens and George Morrow. Specific thanks to: Marianne Martin, Special Collections Department of the J.D. Rockfeller, Jr. Library, who permitted me to see Patrick Henry's hand-written Stamp Act Resolves, and other documents from Patrick Henry and the Marquis de Lafayette.

Virginia Historical Society, for allowing me to see Patrick Henry's spectacles.

Mr. Christopher K. Peace, Va House of Delegates, 97ᵗʰ District Thank you for connecting me with Dr. Robert Bluford, Jr. and inviting me to get involved with the Education Advisory Council of the Polegreen Historic Church Foundation.

Dr. Robert Bluford, Jr. Founder and President of Polegreen Historic Church Foundation, author of *Living on the Borders of Eternity,* the story of Samuel Davies. Thank you for touring me through Polegreen, Rural Plains, Studley, and the Pine Slash Honeymoon Cottage. Your book was an invaluable resource for me as I wrote Patrick Henry's young years and explained the Dissenter movement in Hanover County. Thank you for being my friend and my unwitting, innocent "partner in crime" that day we accidently set off the alarm at Rural Plains. Who knew they had installed a security system?

Mrs. Lois Wickham, Curator for Hanover Historical Society Thank you for touring me through Hanover Courthouse, and to Jennifer E. Schero, Curator of Education, Hanover Tavern for making the arrangements.

Sandy Satterwhite, Ann Reid, Lynwood Barthurst, and Lynn Price at Patrick Henry's Scotchtown Thank you for providing multiple, excellent tours of Scotchtown. Ann, thank you especially for allowing me the privilege of writing Sallie's death scene in the room where it happened. That will ever be a highlight of my writing career.

Wendy and Mark Rada, owners of Mt. Brilliant Thank you for allowing me to frequently walk Patrick Henry's childhood home site and to visit the grave of John Henry.

Sarah F. Whiting, Executive Director, and Raymond Baird, Tour Guide, St. John's Episcopal Church, Richmond, VA I am eternally grateful for the privilege of sitting in St. John's Church on the 241ˢᵗ anniversary of Patrick Henry's Liberty or Death speech to write that scene. Thank you for granting me such a once-in-a-lifetime honor. Ray, I appreciate your kindness and for touring me through St. John's more than once. And I think Cato the eagle did a flyover just for us on March 23, 2016. Thank you for letting me ring the bell to open the Second Virginia Convention!

John Slaughter, Group Superintendent, Southern Campaign of the American Revolution Parks, National Park Service I'm so grateful to Mark Schneider for introducing us at Cowpens! Who knew "Banastre Tarleton's" introduction would lead to the creation of Epic Patriot Camp? I'm so very thankful for that encounter, and honored to partner with you, Katherine Lynn and the NPS. I look forward to inspiring the next generation of patriots every summer.

Anthony Melita, Revolutionary Tours, Philadelphia, PA Tony, you made the history of colonial Philadelphia and the First Continental Congress live for me. Thank you for the amazing private tours of Philadelphia, Brandywine, Paoli Battlefield and Valley Forge. Your passion for history is as electrifying as Ben Franklin's kite!

Comte Gilbert de Pusy Lafayette, Paris, France What an incredible honor it has been to know the sixth great-grandson of the Marquis de Lafayette! I appreciate your time in Paris and in Normandy, as well as your friendship. I hope my words bring honor to your illustrious ancestor and to your esteemed family name. *Merci, mon ami et* VIVE LAFAYETTE!

xxiii

Family and Friends Thank you for your love, encouragement, prayers, feedback and inspiration while I researched, travelled, spoke and wrote: My husband Casey and son Alex, my parents Dr. Paul and Janice Mims, my EPIC muse Claire Roberts Foltz, my EPIC sales manager Laura Brunson and my EPIC critique team and friends: Lisa Hockman, Lori Marett, Beth Woods, Hannah Woods, Julia Slaughter, Dave Trouten, Francine Locke, Michelle Cox, Carl and Donnalynn Davis, and Doug Peterson.

Publishing and Publicity Team

An EPIC thank you to the people who take what comes out of my pen and turn it into something so beautiful to hold and read! Illustrator Rob Moffitt, Editor Rich Cairnes, Proofreader Rick Steele, Interior Designer Katherine Lloyd, Literary Agent Paul Shepherd, Publicist Kelly Oliver, and the AMG Publishing Team: Steve Turner, Amanda Jenkins, Donna Coker, and the support staff.

Readers

You are making history for me! Thank you for your prayers, encouraging notes, letters, pictures, cards, e-mails, Tweets, Instagram and Facebook posts. They make me smile, and you encourage this author's heart more than you could ever know. I'm honored that you love the books and that they inspire you to fall in love with history. I always welcome your feedback at jenny@epicorderoftheseven.com. I'll keep writing as long as you keep reading!

With Epic Love,

CHARACTER PROFILES

ORDER OF THE SEVEN

Max: a Scottish terrier from (where else?) Scotland. Full name is Maximillian Braveheart the Bruce. Short, black, with a large head, always ready to take on the bad guys. Faithful leader of the team who started with their first mission on Noah's Ark in *The Ark, the Reed, and the Fire Cloud*. Loves to mess with Al, "encouraging" him to work on his bravery. Immortal.

Liz: a petite, French, black cat from Normandy. Full name is Lizette Brilliante Aloysius. Brilliant, refined, and strategic leader of the team, beginning with Noah's Ark. Loves the study of history, science, the written word, culture, and languages. Prides herself on knowing the meanings of names, and simply adores gardens. Immortal.

Al: a well-fed, Irish, orange cat. Full name is Albert Aloysius, also called "Big Al" by his close friends. Hopelessly in love with his mate, Liz, since Noah's Ark. Simple-minded, but often holds the key to gaining access to impossible places, and figuring out things everyone else misses, including deep spiritual truths. Lives to eat and sleep. Afraid of everything. Immortal.

Kate: a white West Highland terrier, also from Scotland. The love of Max's life ever since they 'wed' on the way to the Ark. Has a sweetness that disarms everyone she meets. Is also a fiery lass, unafraid to speak her mind. Always sees the good in others, and sticks up for the underdog. Immortal.

Nigel P. Monaco: a jolly, British mouse. Possesses impeccable manners and speech. Wears spectacles and is on the same intellectual level as Liz. An expert Egyptologist who joined the team in *The Dreamer, the Schemer, and the Robe*. Taught Liz all about Egypt, giving her the endearing title "my pet." Travels quickly via carrier pigeon and has an affinity for music. Immortal.

Gillamon: a wise, kind mountain goat from Switzerland. Moved to Scotland, where he raised Max (an orphan) and served as his mentor. Died before the Flood, but serves as a spiritual being who delivers mission assignments from the Maker to the team. Can take any shape or form, and shows up when least expected.

Clarie: a sweet little lamb from Judea. Shepherds gave her to Mary and Joseph as a gift for Baby Jesus in *The Prophet, the Shepherd, and the Star.* Died enabling the family to escape to Egypt without harm and joined Gillamon as a spiritual being member of the team. Serves as all-knowing guide in the IAMISPHERE when the team goes back in time to observe historical events. Can take any shape or form.

Open your ears to what I am saying,
for I will speak to you in a parable.
I will teach you hidden lessons from our past—
stories we have heard and know,
stories our ancestors handed down to us.
We will not hide these truths from our children
but will tell the next generation about the
glorious deeds of the Lord. We will tell of his power
and the mighty miracles he did.

—PSALM 78:1–4

PROLOGUE

JEWELS IN
HER CROWN

NEW YORK CITY, MARCH 17, 1944

L iz sat on a bench in Battery Park, gazing out across the Hudson
River, her golden eyes fixed on the upraised arm of the Statue of
Liberty. A gentle breeze brushed her cheek, and she closed her
eyes, smiling at the thunderous voice that forever echoed in her mind.
*"They see a land in which Liberty hath taken up her abode—that Liberty,
whom they had considered as a fabled goddess, existing only in the fancies
of poets. They see her here, a real divinity—her altars rising on every hand,
throughout these happy states . . ."*

Liz opened her eyes, squinting against the sun as her gaze drifted to
the statue's patina crown. *"Liberty, the greatest of all earthly blessings—
give us that precious jewel, and you may take everything else."* The sleek
French cat sighed deeply as the voice continued to remind her of what
was at stake when it first uttered those words. *"When the American spirit
was in its youth, the language of America was different: Liberty, sir, was the
primary object."*

"Liberté is once again the primary object, *mon* Henry. Much is at
stake now, just as it was then," Liz said aloud to herself, scanning New
York's bustling harbor filled with ships of war. She slowly curled her
slender black tail up and down as she studied the determined face of
this once fabled goddess. *"Ma chère amie,* how many jewels are in your
crown after all these years? You will no doubt earn many more as you
bid these brave soldiers *adieu.* They will once more return the gift of

liberty to my beloved France."

"I tr-r-ried ta tell ye, Big Al. Thr-r-ree hot dogs were plenty," came Max's scolding voice. The Scottish terrier shook his head at the clearly miserable orange cat waddling along next to him. "But no, ye jest *had* ta make it four."

"Aye, that on top of two pretzels," added Kate, the white Westie, sharing a knowing look with her mate, Max. She then spotted Liz sitting on the bench and trotted along ahead.

". . . and three helpin's of cotton candy," Al groaned, clutching his belly. His groan was followed by a loud, drawn-out belch.

Liz turned and wrinkled her brow at hearing her mate make such a disgusting sound at such a moment for reflection.

"Sorry ta disturb ye, Liz," came Kate's soft voice as she jumped up next to the black cat. "I can tell ye be in one of yer thinkin' times."

Liz smiled at her longtime friend. "It is quite alright, *chère* Kate. Did you have fun at the parade?"

Kate's sweet face brightened. "Aye, the St. Patrick's Day Parade were a grand time!"

Al let go another long belch and proceeded to fall onto his back, moaning and rubbing his fluffy orange belly. Sitting crooked atop his head was a green hat with the words, *Kiss me, I'm Irish*. "One day off to celebrate me favorite holiday, and I make meself miserable."

"Daft kitty," Max growled. "Ye think ye'd have learned yer lesson with this holiday, after 180 years of celebr-r-ratin' it."

"I jest can't help meself," Al whined. He peeled off a clump of green shamrocks that were stuck to his fur and held them up in the air. "Liz, I brought ye these."

Liz and Kate shared a giggle. Liz cleared her throat. "*Merci*, Albert. You always think to bring me something green."

"This time it's somethin' green an' or-r-range," Max joked, seeing Al's orange fur stuck to the bouquet of shamrocks.

"At least his bouquet looks like Ireland's flag then," Kate suggested. She leaned over to whisper to Liz, "I still think the edelweiss he brought ye on the way ta Noah's Ark were the best flowers ever, lass."

"I daresay, even a British mouse such as myself feels Irish after today," Nigel interjected with a chuckle as he joined the group. He straightened the gold spectacles atop his nose. "I find it quite fascinating that this parade's observance honoring St. Patrick began in this very city fourteen years before America declared her independence from my homeland."

"The bagpipes always be me favorite thing aboot the parade," Max offered.

"I like seein' all the humans dressed in green," Kate added happily, wagging her tail.

"Please don't say green," Al moaned, pulling his hat over his eyes.

Nigel pretended to jab an imaginary sword into Al's belly. "I am pleased to report that we saw a statue of George Washington as we wended our way through the streets of New York."

"Ah, *oui*, Nigel," Liz answered with a nod, "the 'Sword of the Revolution.'"

"An' we also saw a statue of Thomas Jefferson," Kate offered.

Nigel turned his imaginary sword into a pen and proceeded to write on an invisible parchment. "Right! 'The Pen of the Revolution.'"

Liz wrinkled her brow and returned her gaze to the Statue of Liberty. "But 'the Voice of the Revolution' remains eerily silent." She jumped down from the bench and walked over to the water's edge. Waves from passing ships splashed against the seawall, sending a spray of mist onto her fur.

Max and Kate walked up behind her, sharing looks of empathy for their feline friend. Kate put her paw on Liz's shoulder. "Ye're thinkin' aboot *yer* Patrick."

"Aye, not Al's Patrick," Max added quietly. "Ye're thinkin' aboot yer Henry, aren't ye, lass?"

"*Oui,* my Patrick Henry," Liz said with a nod as she lifted a paw toward the Statue of Liberty. "The people of this land do not even realize that without him, *she* would not be here."

"I thought she were here because of Lizertas," Al offered, now sitting up in spite of his enlarged belly and lifting the hat from his eyes.

The animals all gazed out at the towering statue, allowing the memories to flood back into their minds. The history they shared with Lady Liberty stretched back not just decades, but centuries.

"If there ever was a time for Americans to embrace all that this celestial goddess embodies, it is now," Nigel declared, jumping up onto the seawall next to Liz. "At least for this Second World War, our beloved homelands are once again on the same side of the conflict."

Liz smiled sadly. *"Oui, mon ami.* It was difficult to have such tension between our countries for a time." The petite cat leaned over and kissed the little mouse on his head. *"Je suis très heureuse* to be allies once again."

"Aye, an' with the br-r-rave American lads joinin' in ta help the Fr-r-rench, too," Max added.

Kate wrinkled her brow with a determined expression as she recalled the words of the American soldiers who arrived to fight for France in World War One. "Lafayette, we are here!"

Liz nodded fondly. *"Oui,* the Marquis de Lafayette would be happy to see his adopted country once more coming to the aid of France."

Nigel grinned and preened his whiskers. He then paused and put his spectacles atop his head, wearing a determined look on his face. "Does this remind you of your Henry, my pet? 'Give me liberty, or give me death!' Nigel exclaimed with a fist raised high in the air before dramatically plunging his imaginary sword into his chest.

Liz smiled and giggled. *"Oui, mon cher,* Mr. Henry." She placed her paw over her heart and batted her eyes.

Suddenly a transport ship full of soldiers glided past the Statue of Liberty. Young men lined the railing of the ship to gaze up at her resolute face. Just as they carried the pictures of their wives' and girlfriends' faces in their pockets, so, too, did they wish to carry in their memories the face of America's sweetheart. They would need to draw strength from her chiseled features to take with them as they headed to England to prepare for war against Germany.

"Some of those lads will never see her again," Max said. A low growl rumbled in his throat. "Those Germans will be waitin' for them."

"I forgot all aboot the Germans today!" Al cried, putting his paws up to his mouth in fear. "The worst o' the worst be them Nazis. I hate Nazis!"

Kate's eyes filled with tears. "They're all jest young boys! How can they defeat such a strong enemy?"

"We are not weak if we make a proper use of those means which the God of Nature has placed in our power . . . the battle, sir, is not to the strong alone. It is to the vigilant, the active, the brave," Liz said, quoting the Voice. "May the jewels in America's crown always grow as she answers your resounding voice, Mr. Henry."

"Aye, if only the humans would r-r-remember Patrick Henry's words when they look at Lady Liberty," Max suggested.

Al waddled over to join the others on the wall. "Sure, ye'd think that'd be easy for them to do, especially with reminders like 'Give me liberty or give me death' then."

"Seven little words. That's all they remember about Mr. Henry," Liz lamented. "Hmmm. Seven."

"What a travesty, seeing how he said infinitely more words than that," Nigel added, shielding his eyes against the sunshine as he spotted an incoming pigeon.

Al gazed at Lady Liberty and held up his paw, punctuating the air as he counted out loud. "Seven. The lass has seven points on her crown. Jest like there be seven of us." He turned and looked at Liz with his goofy grin. "And jest like yer Patrick's seven little words."

Liz's eyes lit up and she kissed Al on the cheek, causing him to melt. "Brilliant, *cher* Albert! *Oui!* Seven!"

"Jolly good, old boy! *Seven*, like Mr. Henry's words, and *seven*, like HIS Majesty's animal team!" Nigel cheered with a fist of victory raised high in the air as the pigeon landed next to him. "Speaking of which, back to the mission at hand. It is time for me to catch my flight so I may get aboard the *USS Nevada* bound for England." The little mouse stood in front of Liz and Kate, taking each of their paws in hand for a farewell kiss. "Stay strong, fair ladies. Until we meet again."

"Bye, Mousie," Kate replied. "Be safe then."

"*Bon vol,* Nigel," Liz said. "It looks like you are back to flying on pigeons instead of eagles."

Nigel gave a jolly chuckle. "I shall reserve an eagle for when we achieve victory in Europe. Besides, my team of pigeons is shaping up to be a formidable team of informants."

"Aye, keep up the good spy work, lad," Max added with a salute. "I guess we all need ta get back ta our places in this mission. Ye, too, Big Al. Back ta Germany."

Al's lower lip trembled. "Ye mean, I have to go back to that evil lad with the funny moustache," he paused with a gulp, "in his cursed Eagle's Nest?"

"*Whether this will prove a blessing or a curse, will depend upon the use our people make of the blessings which a gracious God hath bestowed on us.*" Liz perked up as the last words penned by Patrick Henry suddenly came to mind. "What was it that Gillamon tried to tell me before that pivotal day with my Henry?" Liz asked aloud, her heart beating wildly as her mind finally filled with understanding—after all these years. "Of course! The eagle's nest!"

But she wasn't thinking about Germany, 1944. She was thinking about Virginia, 1743.

PART ONE

FIDDLING AROUND

DOWN TO
THE LETTER

Bravo, *mon ami!* Liz exclaimed to Nigel. The little mouse was beaming. "Tonight's performance was *magnifique!*"

The animals were gathered in the home of George F. Handel, following the London premiere of his new oratorio, *Messiah,* at Covent Garden Theatre. Handel had long since retired for the night, so Max, Liz, Kate, Al, and Nigel quietly made their way to Handel's composing room per Clarie's instructions. Their Italian stick bug friend, Shandelli, had also turned in, exhausted from the day's events. The Order of the Seven had successfully completed their mission of helping Handel compose the most important piece of music that would ever be written. The mission was so vital it had even entailed revisiting the life and passion of Christ with a trip through the IAMISPHERE. A celebration was in order now that the mission was complete.

Candles illuminated the room where the magic of *Messiah* had come to pass. Max and Kate brought meat scraps from the butcher shop across the street, which was their assigned station for the Handel mission. Liz brought an assortment of cheeses, including Nigel's favorite, a sharp white cheddar. Clarie delivered a sweet array of biscuits and cookies. And Al just enjoyed everyone's contributions.

"Thank you, my pet. It was one of the highlights of my life," Nigel replied with a paw tenderly touching his mouse-sized violin. "Not only was Handel himself pleased, but the king of England was pleased enough to stand during the Hallelujah Chorus."

"And THE KING of Kings was the most pleased of all, applauding

3

your faithful work," Clarie interjected. Clarie, a sweet white lamb, was one of the two spiritual being members of the Order of the Seven animal team. She could take any shape or form, and served as a guide and messenger from the other spiritual being and team leader, Gillamon. Tonight she was dressed in the finery of a proper British lady, wearing a silk dress that matched her blue eyes and a fashionable white wig with a single curl dangling onto her shoulder. She had attended the concert as "Lady Clarie."

Nigel's eyes welled up behind his golden spectacles, and he wiped away a tear of joy while nodding with a smile. He had been given the honor of helping to secretly inspire Handel with his mouse-sized violin while the famed composer slept. "Indeed, my dear. To know that I had pleased the Supreme Maestro was the most important outcome of the whole evening."

"Aye, he weren't pleased jest with the whole evenin' but with the whole *mission* then," Max added. "Clarie, lass, I assume we'll be leavin' the butcher shop an' headin' ta our next mission soon."

Al's eyes got as wide as the salami slices that were stuffed in his mouth. "LEAVE the butcher shop?!" he mumbled before swallowing hard and picking up the last slice. "Can't we make this mission last a while longer? Or at least stay in London for the next one? I'd *hate* to think of what would happen to that poor butcher without us there to keep his shop clear of beasties."

Kate shook her head at the ever-hungry feline, who was a greater threat to the butcher than the rats. "It sure be thoughtful of ye ta think aboot the *poor* butcher, Al," she remarked in a sarcastic tone, tapping Al's belly.

"Always thinkin' with yer stomach," Max murmured.

Clarie giggled. "Be careful what you wish for, Al. You just may get it."

Al grinned and held up the salami. "I'm up for the challenge, lass."

"I'm glad to hear that, Al," Clarie said with an impish grin, reaching for the round piece of savory meat. "Then may I have this last slice, please?"

Al clung to the salami with both paws. Clarie frowned and tugged against the stubborn cat, who held onto the meat with all his might.

"Drop the salami, Albert," Liz scolded. "Do not be so selfish!"

Al's lower lip quivered as he reluctantly let go of his prize. "Thank you, Al," Clarie said as she pried the salami from his paws. She then placed on the floor the program from tonight's *Messiah* concert, which contained the *libretto,* or words, from the composition. Clarie placed the salami on the 'O' of the words 'Sacred Oratorio.'

"Lass, the salami be *savory,* not sacred," Al protested. "Can't ye see that it belongs in me mouth, and not on the ora-oreo?"

Clarie ignored Al's complaint and sat down on the floor with the animals, her blue dress spread out around them. She grinned, wrapping the dangling curl from her white wig around her finger as the animals gathered in close around the *libretto.* Suddenly the salami began to ripple as if it were being cooked. Liz glanced over at the others and smiled. She knew what was about to happen. "Time for us to see Gillamon, no?"

Suddenly the salami bubbled and turned into a red wax seal imprinted with the words *ORDER OF THE SEVEN.* Clarie held out one hand to the Seven seal and placed her other hand on Al's back. "Would you like to do the honors, Al?"

Al looked questioningly at Clarie. "Ye know how nervous I get goin' in there, lass, but seein' how me salami made the seal, maybe the inside won't be as scary this time." The orange cat timidly walked across the *libretto* and held up a paw over the wax seal, gazing around with uncertainty at the others.

"You can do it, old boy!" Nigel cheered. "Just swipe that iron claw across the seal and break it."

Al popped out his iron claw and a goofy grin appeared on his face. "Me secret weapon." He closed one eye and got ready to break the seal. "Here goes nothin'!"

As Al's claw broke the seal, a beam of light seventy stories high encircled the animals. The IAMISPHERE swirled around them with a rushing wind, and the animals were frozen in place by the blazing light and supernatural power of this time portal. They tingled from head to toe as they saw the moving panels of scenes from all points in history playing before their eyes. The IAMISPHERE was the unseen realm of how the Maker observed time—past, present, and future—all happening at once. As the wind began to subside and the blinding light to diminish, standing there before the animals was their wise leader, Gillamon.

"Welcome, everyone," the majestic mountain goat greeted them. Gillamon never failed to make the animals immediately feel at ease with his calming voice and warm, blue eyes. "This has been a date

5

to remember. Well done, all. And to you, Nigel, I give my heartfelt congratulations."

Nigel bowed with his foot extended and a paw draped humbly across his chest. "Thank you, my dear friend. I daresay, March 23 is a date I shall not soon forget!"

Gillamon grinned broadly. "Indeed you most certainly will not. This date will soon be punctuated by another pivotal moment in history. You are about to embark on a mission that will connect more dates and layers of history from previous assignments than you could ever have imagined."

"*Bonsoir,* Gillamon," Liz greeted him with eyes full of expectation. "How so?"

The wise leader smiled with that familiar twinkle in his eye, filled with veiled anticipation and knowledge he carefully imparted to the Order of the Seven on a need-to-know basis. Gillamon didn't know everything that would happen in the future, but was granted far more insight than he was allowed to divulge. "Let us review your newly completed mission." He pointed to various scenes from Handel's life, which swirled in the panels behind him: Handel playing musical instruments as a young boy; Handel as a young man walking through the Forum in Rome, where he purchased the "star coin" and then composed his first work; Handel being passed over by King George II as Master of the King's Musick; Handel receiving the *libretto* for *Messiah,* which Liz had helped Charles Jennens to write; Nigel playing the violin in Handel's ear as he slept; the Dublin premiere of *Messiah* and the scene from tonight's London premiere.

Kate pointed to the last panel. "There be ye an' Clarie sittin' in the audience with David Henry!"

"Indeed, little Kate. And I'm pleased to let you know you will continue to be assigned to David Henry for a time before you are moved to another key human in this mission, but he has not yet been born," Gillamon replied. "You and Max did well to arrange for David Henry's marriage to Mary Cave, which led to his position with the *Gentleman's Magazine* here in London. As you know, each mission involves helping one primary human to fulfill his or her life's purpose, but there are many supporting humans who need to do *their* part in fulfilling the Maker's ultimate plan. You, little Kate, are always crucial working behind the scenes with these supporting humans." Another scene appeared of David Henry sitting down at his desk. He lit a candle and set out a quill, paper, and ink. "And tonight, he is writing a letter that will impact the primary human for your next mission."

"Who, Gillamon?" Max asked. "Ye always kill me with yer suspense, lad."

Gillamon touched his hoof to another panel and a wooded scene appeared with a little boy sitting next to a creek, holding a fishing pole. The animals gathered around the panel to stare intently at the sandy-red-headed, barefoot young boy. He just sat there, staring at his line, not moving. The birds were singing, and he would occasionally look up to the trees and listen for a moment, but then return his gaze to his motionless fishing pole.

"Um, Gillamon, the lad ain't doin' anythin'," Max noted, wondering, what could be so important about this boy.

Gillamon didn't reply, but kept his gaze fixed on the scene.

"*Au contraire,* he is observing everything around him," Liz suggested, studying the boy closely.

Gillamon smiled. "Precisely."

The brilliant French cat's tail curled slowly up and down as she studied the scene. "And if I'm not mistaken, the boy is sitting next to a black willow."

"A black willow! Those be deadly!" Al cried with a paw up to his mouth. "Gillamon, we need to jump in there and save the lad from that dreaded beastie!" The worried cat looked over at Max and shoved him forward. "Max here is perfect for the job. Go save him, lad!"

"Black *willow,* Albert—not black *widow,*" Liz corrected him. "The *salix nigra* is the largest species of willow tree in North America. It provides many benefits to humans and the animal kingdom, like charcoal for gunpowder, and nectar and pollen for honey bees." Liz was an expert in flora and fauna, and had long adored gardening as her favorite hobby.

"Daft kitty, it be a *tr-r-ree,* not a spider," Max corrected, bonking Al on the head. "An' ye be as br-r-rave as ever, volunteerin' me for the dangerous part of a mission."

Al grinned a toothy, sheepish grin. "Well, it still sounds dangerous with bees buzzin' aboot."

"Aye, yer 'enormous flyin' beasties,'" Max answered with a sarcastic tone, referring to the first time he met Al in a forest, hiding from bees.

"I say, and if *I'm* not mistaken, that looks like the colony of Virginia,"

7

Nigel noted, pointing to the scene. "I remember our time there with great fondness, venturing in the woods with Pocahontas."

Liz perked up. "*Oui*, it *is* Virginia! And I would surmise that the little boy is none other than Patrick Henry!"

"Well done, Liz and Nigel," Gillamon said. "It is indeed Virginia, and that is David Henry's little cousin, Patrick Henry. You two will soon depart to join him on the banks of the Totopotomoy Creek, along with Max."

"Sorry ta be parted from ye, me love," Kate said, nudging Max with her nose. "I'm sure it won't be for too long then."

"See, ye be goin' to the boy next to the black willow on that Hippopotomos Creek," Al said, slapping Max with the back of his paw. "Gillamon, ain't I goin', too? I like fishermen. Peter were the best human I ever had."

"*Totopotomoy* Creek, named for an Indian chief, Al," Clarie corrected him. "I thought you wanted to stay here in London. I said to be careful what you wish for."

"Clarie is right, Al, for you shall go to live with another boy here in London," Gillamon answered, pointing to another scene from the life of Handel. The composer leaned over to speak to a young boy dressed in the finest red silk breeches and coat Al had ever seen.

"Who's that lad?" Al asked. "Do he like to fish?"

"That is the next king of England, King George III," Gillamon replied. "I do not know if he likes to fish himself, but you will suffer no lack of food with the bounty in the palace. Your mission will primarily be to gather intelligence."

Max snickered and whispered to Nigel, "The kitty needs all the intelligence he can get."

"How *does* he do it, I wonder?" Nigel chuckled back, shaking his head good-humoredly at their dear friend. While not the brightest member of the team, Al nevertheless gained access to places and information that made the others marvel. "The old boy always gets the posh palace assignments: Pharaoh of Egypt, Nebuchadnezzar of Babylon, and now, the king of England."

Al sat up excitedly. "I get to live with the *KING?!* Hooray, another palace!" he cheered, but then frowned. "I'll miss me lass, though." He enveloped Liz in a smothering hug.

"I . . . shall . . . miss you, too, Albert," Liz struggled to say. She wriggled free of Al's embrace. "Gillamon, what exactly are we supposed to do with young Patrick Henry?"

Gillamon walked over to look Liz in the eye. "Liz, Patrick Henry will primarily be *your* human, and your mission will be to help him find his voice. His voice will alter the course of history. Although you may not know it, I have been preparing you for this one assignment for centuries. You will delight in seeing exactly how as time goes on."

Liz's golden eyes widened, and she placed a paw over her racing heart. "I am honored, Gillamon, and I shall guide my Henry to the greatness for which he is destined. I've long had a feeling about this boy, ever since I first read his father's letter to David, announcing his birth. His name means 'noble ruler of the house.' But what house will he rule?"

Gillamon smiled and turned to Max, not answering Liz's question. He liked for his team to figure things out for themselves. "You, Max, will provide protection for Patrick, but also for other important humans who will come into this revolutionary mission. The Enemy will ever be lurking about, both in human and other forms."

"AYE!" Max readily responded. The black fur bristled along his stocky little body, his short tail was erect, and his triangular ears were pointed up, alert to the slightest hint of danger. A low growl entered his throat. "I'll be r-r-ready at all times."

"Revolutionary? Whatever do you mean, old chap?" Nigel wanted to know.

"It is time to birth a new nation, and I'm afraid yours and Liz's homelands will be on opposite sides of the conflict for a time," shared Gillamon.

"But this is nothing new," Liz quipped. "When are England and France ever *not* at war, *mon ami*? It is more unusual for our homelands *not* to be fighting than engaged in battle!"

"Hear, hear," Nigel agreed, preening his whiskers. "What a devilish shame that the humans can't be as civilized as we animals."

"This time, the war will be different," Gillamon suggested. "Nigel, you shall begin your mission with Patrick Henry, but will eventually escort an Englishman back here to London. But first you will assist him with a science experiment that will impact the outcome of the war. Dr. Benjamin Franklin is a printer and an inventor."

"Jolly good! An Englishman, a printer, *and* an inventor? I say, I already like this mission," Nigel enthused. "I shall be high as a kite with this thrilling assignment!"

Gillamon shared a knowing look with Clarie. "You have no idea, my little friend. His experiment will be a key to unlock the door to another nation. As usual, we will also call upon you to be a go-between for communications on this mission. Clarie and I will fulfill numerous roles as well in the coming years."

Liz gazed at young Patrick Henry and his fishing pole. "Gillamon, you mentioned that this mission will involve multiple layers of dates and history from our previous missions. What do you mean?"

Gillamon once more put his hoof up to a series of panels that swirled into view. There were scenes from past missions with Noah, Joseph, Isaiah, Jeremiah, Daniel, Jesus, the Disciples, Paul, Constantine, and even the little monk Telemachus. "Your new mission has been foreshadowed throughout every one of these *past* missions. But there are two historical layers of special importance," the mountain goat explained. He once more touched the panels and a series of them came into view.

10

"I say, there's the Roman centurion Marcus Antonius, when he commissioned the Libertas statue to be carved back in Jerusalem!" Nigel exclaimed. Since the Romans would carve Libertas with a liberty-loving cat at her feet, Liz stood in as the cat model for the sculptor while Marcus's wife, Julia, posed as the goddess.

Al leaned over and put his head dreamily on Liz's small frame. "Ye be the most beautiful model ever, me love. I think we should call it the Lizertas statue."

"Merci, cher Albert," Liz replied with her shy smile.

"An' there I see the Libertas statue when Marcus's lad, Armandus, sent her ta R-r-rome with his family on the ship," Max added, pointing to another scene many years later. The animals watched the scene of Armandus's two little boys, Julius and Theophilus, running down the dock in Caesarea after talking with Paul.

Al caught a glimpse of another scene, still many *more* years further in time. "Sure, and there be Julius Antonius meetin' our ship when his mum, Bella, and his nephew brought the Lizertas statue from Rome to Gaul." Al licked his chops as he saw himself trotting down the dock toward a basket of fish. Julius hugged his nephew, Leonitus, and placed his Roman centurion's helmet on the boy's head. Leonitus went chasing after Al, wielding a fish as if it were a sword.

"Gaul—now finally known by the humans as France," Liz thought out loud, her tail swishing back and forth as her mind was racing. "There is meaning behind this statue, no? Libertas, the goddess of liberty. She represents freedom and hope for life lived in the pursuit of happiness. Freedom, beginning in Jerusalem and spreading around the globe." Liz wrinkled her brow as she thought this through. Suddenly it dawned on her. "Liberty is also coming here to America. Is that right, Gillamon? But from France? I do not yet understand this."

"Precisely, Liz. But you will, with time," Gillamon answered the curious cat. "In order to figure out the importance of the Libertas connection, you will first need to figure out the importance of the Plutarch connection."

Another scene came into view with Liz sitting on the desk of the ancient Greek historian, Plutarch. He was writing a series of books, called Parallel Lives, about the way good and bad influences impacted the lives of famous Greek and Roman men. Back in Rome, Gillamon himself had given Liz the assignment to ensure that Plutarch wrote about one particular Roman, named Cato, in his book.

11

Liz studied the scene of herself as the soft glow of the oil lamp danced off her black fur. Spread across Plutarch's desk were rolls of fresh parchment and scrolls of his work. A small, ivory figurine of the Greek goddess Nike, or "Winged Victory," also sat on his desk.

"I r-r-remember how ye made that big Winged Victory statue lass come ta life when we were travelin' with Paul in Gr-r-reece," Max recalled.

"*Oui,* and you told me we would see that statue again in my beloved France," Liz added. Her head was spinning with the many scenes and layers of history to connect in her mind. "Gillamon, there is so much to try to put together, no?"

Gillamon nodded. "As I said, there are many layers of history and past missions coming together for the mission ahead. The Maker leaves His mark on every page of history, doesn't He? Even on the pages of those who don't follow Him. Why do you think it is called HIStory?" The mountain goat put his hoof onto a scene of an eleven-year-old boy crying over the loss of his father. "Each of us will be witness to a unique point in history because of a unique generation of world leaders. Most of them are just children now, or have not yet even been born. Take note how important one generation of children can be. Marvel at each child and the power they have to change the history of the world for the good (or bad) of all. You will see that what goes into the first part of life goes throughout *all* of life." Gillamon gazed at the boy who sat alone, wiping his eyes. "It is time for me to leave you and attend to one of those children now."

"The poor dear," Kate said sadly. "Who's the wee lad, Gillamon?"

"His name is George. George Washington," Gillamon replied, catching the perplexed look on Liz's face. "Liz, you will connect all the dots for this mission *down to the letter*, just as you always do. When the time is right, I will give you the clues you need. For the moment, just focus on Plutarch, and remember what I told you long ago." With that, he stepped into the scene with young George Washington and was gone from the IAMISPHERE as the scene faded from view.

Liz returned her gaze to the scene of Plutarch writing at his desk. She watched her image lean over and read what Plutarch had just penned, quoting Alexander the Great: "Remember, upon the conduct of each depends the fate of all."

Never had this been more true for the Order of the Seven.

12

David Henry lit the candle on his desk and reached for his Bible. As he flipped through the Old Testament, then the New, he smiled to see the passages he had heard sung tonight in Handel's *Messiah*. Isaiah. Haggai. Zechariah. Malachi. Matthew. Luke. *Ah, and here we are—John.* He found John 1 and began to read:

> In the beginning was the Word, and the Word was with God, and the Word was God. The same was in the beginning with God. All things were made by him; and without him was not any thing made that was made. In him was life; and the life was the light of men.
>
> And the light shineth in darkness; and the darkness comprehended it not.
>
> There was a man sent from God, whose name was John. The same came for a witness, to bear witness of the Light, that all men through him might believe. He was not that Light, but was sent to bear witness of that Light. That was the true Light, which lighteth every man that cometh into the world. He was in the world, and the world was made by him, and the world knew him not.
>
> He came unto his own, and his own received him not.

But as many as received him, to them gave he power to become the sons of God, even to them that believe on his name: Which were born, not of blood, nor of the will of the flesh, nor of the will of man, but of God.

And the Word was made flesh, and dwelt among us, (and we beheld his glory, the glory as of the only begotten of the Father,) full of grace and truth.

David paused a moment and thought about what that meant. The Light—Jesus—came into the world, and the world didn't understand Him. It took a while for the world to begin to understand Him. And the world began to understand the Light from the voices of those who told His story. And that was all He asked His followers to do. Simply tell His story.

He read another passage further down. "I am the voice of one crying in the wilderness, Make straight the way of the Lord."

John the Baptist was that voice. And that voice was silenced by evil men who didn't want to hear what he had to say. But even when John was killed, others rose up to keep speaking about the Light, and all the Light represents. The twelve disciples started a movement that turned the world upside down. They spoke boldly and unashamedly about Messiah. And the world persecuted them for it. But other voices rose up, and have been rising up for more than seventeen hundred years to speak boldly about the Light of the world: Messiah.

Messiah. Handel's is yet another voice risen to speak about Messiah through music. And the world has sought to silence that voice.

David smiled as he thought to himself, *What the world doesn't understand is that the VOICE will never be silenced. Truth cannot be held back. It always will be victorious, if spoken boldly. God has given me a platform and a voice to speak the truth, and I intend to use it whenever I can, just like Jesus' cousin, John.*

John. Suddenly he thought about *his* cousin. *I must tell John about this!* He took out a fresh piece of paper, dipped his quill in the ink, and wrote a short letter. He then sealed it with wax and locked it in a metal box containing outgoing correspondence.

When David blew out the candle and left the room, the rat's glowing red eyes narrowed from the open window. *Looks like I'll be sailing to the colonies,* the rat thought with a grimace, *along with that letter.*

13

Conquering Scots
and Rising Tides

L and ho!" a sailor cried from the crow's nest high atop the mast towering over the ship's deck. He pointed happily to the faint glimpse of land on the blue horizon as the ship's crew erupted into cheers of "Huzzah!" The sailor smiled and gazed through his spyglass while the crew ran to the railing to view their long-awaited port of call.

"Finally!" Max exclaimed, wagging his tail as he and Liz also peered through the railing of the ship. The sea spray tickled his nose as the ship clipped along at a brisk pace, slicing through the deep Atlantic waters toward the entrance to Chesapeake Bay. "Eight weeks at sea be long enough."

"I couldn't agree with you more, old boy!" Nigel cheered, jumping on the Scottie's back for a peek. The salty sea spray quickly covered his spectacles. "Oh, bother!" The little mouse put the spectacles atop his head and squinted at the horizon. "I shall have to take your word for it that Virginia is indeed out there."

Liz placed her dainty paw on Nigel's small form. "It *is* Virginia, *mon ami!* We will soon enter Chesapeake Bay, and will then glide up the York River to make port. It is good to be back in these waters, no?"

"Aye," Max chimed in. "At least this time the humans know where they're goin'. When we explored all them r-r-rivers an' cr-r-reeks with John Smith more than a century ago it were a never-endin' journey of twisty-turnin' waters," he recalled. "There were no gold, jest water, water, everywhere!"

"Ah, but there *was* gold, just not the kind the early explorers expected," Liz suggested. "The humans call this eastern area of Virginia the 'Tidewater.' The water levels rise when the tide comes in, keeping the soil rich with nutrients. So while Virginia did not have the gold the first explorers sought, it had rich *land* that the early planters turned into 'gold' by growing tobacco."

"Right you are, my dear. Riches are not always seen with the naked eye," Nigel agreed, jumping down from Max's back. He reached his paws out in front of him to wipe off his spectacles on a nearby sailor's wet breeches, but to no avail. "It is good to be back in these waters. And although a long ocean voyage was required, I must say I am glad we had this time at sea to study up and be prepared to meet our human subjects."

"*Oui,* nothing thrilled me more than to learn that the Henry family originally came from my home of Normandy, France!" Liz replied. "To know that Patrick's ancestor invaded England with William the Conqueror and was listed in his *Livre des Conquérants* makes me love this assignment all the more."

"He may have started out as a Norman who was landin' in England, lass, but the Henrys then made their way ta *me* home of Scotland," Max pointed out. "Knowin' the lad be good Scottish stock fr-r-rom Aberdeen makes *me* happy aboot this assignment, too."

Nigel lifted a finger to conclude the matter, staring in a direction *away from* the animals, as he still couldn't see clearly. "AND, Patrick's *mother* came from the Winston family line of Bristol, England. They are an ancient and honorable family that originally came from *my* home of Wales. So there you have it. Our human is a splendid specimen of fine French, Scottish, *and* English bloodlines."

Max winked at Liz and gave a proud, definitive nod with his large, square head. "The Henrys may not be r-r-rich but they have wha' matters—a gr-r-rand r-r-reputation in Scotland for their good sense an' smarts."

"But of course this is just like I was saying about gold, no?" Liz replied. "Proverbs 22:1 says, 'A *good* name is to be more desired than great wealth, Favor is better than silver and gold.'"

"'Rich and poor have this in common: The Lord is the Maker of them all,'" Nigel followed, quoting the next line of the Proverb. He crossed his little arms over his chest with great satisfaction, unknowingly with his back to Max and Liz, who chuckled at the proper little mouse.

A sailor squatted down next to them, holding out a dry handkerchief. "Here, Nigel. Dry your spectacles." It was Clarie, now in disguise as a courier. She wore dark gray knee breeches, a red shirt, a navy blue coat, silver-buckled black shoes, and a black tricorn hat. Her brown hair was pulled back in a short braid that trailed down the nape of her neck. "When we disembark from the ship at Yorktown I'll get a horse with large saddle bags so I can carry you the sixty-odd miles from the Tidewater to the back country of Hanover County. As I've shared with you, Patrick Henry's family lives on a 600-acre tobacco plantation there called 'Studley.'"

"Ah, yes, Hanover County, so named as a sign of affection for King George I, the first ruler of the House of Hanover," Nigel noted as he cleaned his spectacles and smiled. "Much better! Thank you, my dear. Always better to see things clearly."

Clarie's attention was diverted when out of the corner of her eye she saw something scurry across the deck. Her hand instinctively went to her pocket. "I couldn't agree more," she told her small friend.

"Now, then, let us review the society that has grown up since we first helped the humans to found this colony. Virginia has three classes of citizens, following the English model: upper, middle, and lower class. Of course, Virginians view this as terribly proper and quite natural to accept one's station in life," Nigel explained, pacing about the deck and twirling his paw in the air for emphasis. "The upper class is made up of aristocrats with wealth and prestige, who are well-educated, well-connected, and quite the polished gentlemen and ladies. They own most of the land and hold positions of power in this new world. In the 1600s *they* were the ones who developed expansive plantations in the Tidewater of Virginia, *ergo* they are known as 'the Tidewater elite.'"

"*Oui,* they are the fancy humans with luxurious tastes in clothes, possessions, and lifestyles," added Liz. "The middle class also own land, but are merchants, planters, tradesmen, artisans, and the like. They make up half the people in Virginia and have many different person-alities, interests, and habits. I believe this variety makes them far more interesting humans to be around."

"Aye, an' far more *fun* instead of those stuffy, puffed-up types," Max added. "So who's on the bottom r-r-rung of the ladder?"

"The lower class is made up of those who do not own property. They are the laborers, tradesmen apprentices, and indentured servants, who sell themselves as workers for several years in order to gain passage to America," Liz answered.

"An' with which gr-r-roup will we find Patr-r-rick Henr-r-ry?" Max wanted to know.

"Right in the middle, old boy. In Hanover we shall find quite the rugged, less refined sort of dwellers on the edge of Virginia's frontier. They are the proud Scots/Irish from the rugged regions of Britain's empire. I daresay, I expect that Patrick's middle class family will be more like the common people of the region rather than the refined, wealthy Tidewater elite in Williamsburg. The Tidewater aristocrats have long held positions of power in governing the colony of Virginia, and I'm afraid do not properly appreciate those 'not of their kind.'"

"Uppity English types," Max huffed. "No offense, Mousie. We saw those same types givin' Handel a hard time in London."

"No offense taken, old boy," Nigel replied. "Unfortunately, the British have long held the upper hand over the people of their Scottish and Irish dominions, and never seem to let them forget it."

"While this is true, Clarie explained to me that John and Sarah Henry have made a strong name for themselves in Hanover," Liz pointed out. "While they are not the fancy, Tidewater elite sort of people, for their rural society you could say they are regarded as the 'upper class' of their middle-class world. Sarah's ancestors were the frontier farmers who conquered the backwoods on the northern edge of the Tidewater and rose to become the highly intelligent, influential leaders in that rugged region. Her family has owned vast amounts of land and held positions of importance in the area for generations. They are educated, and musically and socially inclined, so John was well received when he arrived from Scotland with his solid background from King's College, no?"

"That's right, Liz," agreed Clarie. "John has become one of Hanover's most influential men. He is the chief justice of the county court, colonel of the militia, and a vestryman of the Church of England, so he is very well connected. Yet he started with very little. He came over from Scotland to help his friend and fellow Scotsman, John Syme, to manage Studley and to survey the land. Tobacco is Virginia's most important crop, but it gobbles up the nutrients in the soil every few years, so planters are always in search of new land. And those who find the land get the first chance to snatch it up and hopefully make money when it sells. John Henry started out well, but sadly John Syme died

17

after only a few short years. Happily, however, John Henry then married Mr. Syme's widow, Sarah."

"So that's how John came ta own Studley an' became a tobacco planter?" Max asked. "Does he have a gr-r-reen thumb like ye do, Liz?"

"No, according to Clarie he unfortunately has not been a huge success as a planter, and has not chosen the best of overseers to help him run the plantation. But John Henry does provide for the needs of his growing family," Liz said. "Patrick has two older brothers and several little sisters."

"John is first and foremost a *scholar,* so it has been hard for him to try to be a success as a planter," Nigel added. "As we have seen with humans across time, it is important for them to find the thing they most enjoy, and that the Maker created them to do."

"Hmmm, if Patrick is to have a voice that speaks of important things, he first must *learn* of important things. Perhaps we can help father *and* son," Liz thought out loud. "Perhaps I can find a way to encourage John to pour his superior education into Patrick so *he* is well grounded, no?"

"Well, first things first, lass," Max said, wagging his tail as the ship entered the mouth of the Chesapeake, giving a view of land and ships of all sizes sailing toward the York River. "Let's get *our* paws well gr-r-rounded on land then. I'm r-r-ready ta get off this ship!"

That's when Max saw something scurry across the deck near where they were gathered at the railing. A low growl entered his throat. "I jest saw a r-r-rat."

Clarie nodded. "We're being stalked. I didn't want to alarm you before now, but that rat has been following us since London. He is after David Henry's letter."

"Rats?!" Nigel exclaimed as he grimaced and shivered. "How revolting!"

Clarie frowned. "I didn't want to tell you this, Nigel, but that is the same rat who destroyed your first violin."

Nigel's eyes widened with disgust. His cheeks puffed and his whiskers quivered as he balled his paws into angry fists. "If I get my paws on that . . . that . . . evil vermin, I will . . . will . . ." but Nigel was at a loss for words.

"Steady, Mousie," Liz told him as she spied the pair of red eyes staring at them from a darkened space between two barrels. Her fur rose on end and her tail switched back and forth. "Clarie, what should we do with this stalker?"

"I say let me handle this before we get off this ship!" Max growled, running to the barrels and sniffing around. "I see ye in there, wee r-r-rat! How dar-r-re ye think aboot comin' after us after wha' ye did ta Mousie's fiddle!"

Clarie stood and stretched out her back, extending a calm hand to the eager Scottie. "Be my guest, Max."

With that Max growled and barked wildly at the barrels, scratching at the wood and pushing his large head into the small opening between them. The small, brown rat came darting out under his belly, but Max moved quickly and locked his strong jaws onto the rat's tail.

"Don't do it! Don't trow me o'er to the fisherman's daughter!" the rat screeched in a shrill cockney English accent. "I was jest followin' orders!"

"An' I'm not aboot ta let ye follow any more of 'em!" Max kept his jaws clenched as he made his way to the railing. "We know ye're up ta no good! Ye've been followin' us since London but this be where ye get off!" Max proceeded to hurl the rat over the side of the ship. "Good r-r-riddance, ye vile beastie!"

"Well done, *mon ami!*" Liz exclaimed as the rat went flying through the air and splashed into the white seafoam of the ship's wake.

Nigel punched Max in the shoulder with an appreciative jab. "Good show, old boy! I shall forever be in your debt." He then turned to Clarie. "Why didn't you tell us about the vile beast, my dear?"

Clarie took off her tricorn hat and wiped the sweat from her brow. "There was no need. I knew what he was up to, and it only would have made for a more difficult voyage for you. There will always be rats out to ruin things. But remember, even when they do, the Maker always turns their bad around for our good." She reached into her pocket and lifted out Nigel's tiny violin with a grin.

Nigel clasped his paws behind his back and smiled. "As much as I relished seeing that revolting creature flying through the air, especially after what he did to my violin, I must admit that you are right. If he hadn't destroyed my first violin, I never would have had the far grander instrument in your hand, made from the most priceless of objects."

Liz put her paw on Nigel's back. "This is true, no? And whenever the Enemy tries to destroy something or someone, it is always because

19

he feels *threatened*. This must mean that David Henry's letter will inspire my Henry in ways we do not yet realize."

"Keep a watchful eye. There will always be other rats to take the last rat's place," Clarie warned, looking around them on the ship. "Rats of all shapes and sizes—and species."

"Aye," Max agreed with a nod. He spied the tiny rat bobbing on the waves in the growing distance behind the ship. "R-r-rats can swim a half a mile an' tr-r-read water for thr-r-ree days, so at least this beastie will be kept busy while we deliver that letter."

FOREST-BORN
DEMOSTHENES

HANOVER COUNTY, VIRGINIA, MAY 29, 1743

Sunlight danced through the green canopy of hardwood trees as the gentle spring breeze moved the branches lazily up and down, giving occasional glimpses of the vibrant blue sky above. The forest was alive with the sounds of birds calling to one another, bumble bees buzzing from flower to flower, barking tree frogs croaking out the day's news, and, close by, the rushing waters of the Totopotomoy Creek.

The smell of honeysuckle wafted through the air, and young Patrick Henry breathed in the sweet fragrance. It made his mouth water. "I can almost taste the air," he smiled and said aloud to himself as he walked along the well-worn path leading to the creek. "Better to taste it for real." He followed his nose until he found the honeysuckle vine covering a patch of wild shrubs. He set his fishing pole down and reached over to pluck a bloom. He pinched off the end of the bloom and carefully pulled out the nectar onto his tongue. He nodded. "Sweet." He pulled off several more blooms to enjoy, tossing the flower remnants onto the ground. He then pulled off a section of the vine and stuck it in the knapsack draped across his chest. "The girls will like these."

Patrick picked up his fishing pole and balanced it across his right shoulder as he kept making his way to the creek. Soon he came to a fallen tree that blocked his path. He used his left hand to help himself climb on top of the moss-covered log. He stood there for a moment with a fist on his hip, looking all around from the top of the log as if he were king of the forest. Although no other human was around, the

21

boy knew he was hardly alone. He stood there and smiled, closed his piercing blue eyes, and listened.

"Wha's he doin'?" Max whispered. He, Liz, and Nigel were sitting by a cluster of ferns growing along the bank of the creek. They had been following Patrick since he entered the forest.

Liz didn't reply, but just studied the barefoot young boy. He was commonly dressed in brown knee breeches and a white, open-collared, long-sleeved shirt. Liz cocked her head and smiled at the boy's charming features. His sandy-red hair was messy and untied so it fell to his shoulders as he held his head back to listen to the symphony of sounds coming from the forest. His face was rather long and thin, with a nose that was straight and sharp like the ancient Greeks, but dotted with freckles.

"Sweet-sweet-sweet, sweeter-than-sweet, chip! Sweet-sweet-sweet, sweeter-than-sweet, chip!" a bird called overhead.

Patrick kept his eyes closed and pointed to the sound of the bird. "Yellow warbler." He then opened one eye and saw the tiny bright yellow bird with a touch of light olive coloring on its back. "Yes!" he exclaimed with a smile. He closed his eye again and continued to listen.

A nasally bird sounded off in the opposite direction, *"Chuck, chuck, chuck, churrrrrrr!"*

Patrick pointed right to the bird. "Red-bellied woodpecker." He peeked to see the black and white barred feathers and red crown of the woodpecker that humorously poked its head around the tree at him before taking off in flight.

"By Jove, he's right!" Nigel declared.

Then a rapid-fire chorus of birds sounded as Patrick blindly pointed and named each and every one:

"Yank-yank, yank-yank, yank-yank!"

"Nuthatch."

"What-cheer, cheer, cheer; purty-purty-purty-purty!"

"Cardinal."

"Bob-WHITE! Bob-WHITE!"

"Even *I* know that one," whispered Max.

Patrick gave a sarcastic grin, not bothering to open his eyes. "Too easy. Bobwhite."

Just then a faint cry was heard above the canopy of the forest. It wasn't bold or powerful, but rather high-pitched and soft.

"Bald eagle," Patrick said, opening his eyes and gazing up at the majestic eagle soaring high above him. He followed the eagle as it made long, wide circles that gradually grew smaller the closer it came to the tops of the trees. In its beak it held a massive stick. Patrick jumped down from the log and went running down the path, continuing to glance up and follow where the eagle was headed. He wanted to see where it would land.

Max, Liz, and Nigel quietly followed along behind him, darting around shrubs and trees. Patrick was fast and seemed to know every boulder and rock in his way, careful to avoid getting tripped. Soon he came to a clearing where the creek widened. Patrick stood on a large rock and watched as the eagle landed in a tall tree on the other side of the creek. The boy spied what he was looking for. The eagle was building a nest. "I knew it! I knew you lived around here." His eyes scanned the branches leading up to the top of the tree. "I bet I could climb up there to see that nest."

"The lad likes ta talk even though no one's ar-r-round," Max noted as they stayed behind a tree on the bank.

"Perhaps he wants to talk to the birds, no?" Liz suggested. "And who better to teach him how to try? The time has come, *mes amis*. I am going to meet my Patrick Henry." The petite black cat put her cute curlicue-tipped tail high in the air as she sauntered out to the rocks.

23

"We'll stay here for now, my dear," Nigel whispered.

Patrick threw his line into the clear water of the creek and leaned back on a rock to keep staring at the eagle in the nest. Liz proceeded to jump from rock to rock, walking right past him as if she didn't even notice the boy was there. She found a sunny rock with the water rushing past her tail. She looked up and spied a tiny white and black chickadee sitting on a low-hanging branch nearby.

"*Bonjour*, my friend," Liz meowed to the little bird. "I wonder if you would be so kind as to have a conversation with me. My name is Liz, and the Maker has sent me to befriend this young boy. He is very fond of birds, and I wish to encourage him to not only recognize your voices, but also to learn to *speak* to you. Think of it as a voice training exercise if you will."

"Hello, Liz," the little chickadee chirped in reply. "I'd be delighted. I'm Pip. I've seen this boy here at the creek quite often. What should we talk about?"

"*Merci*, Pip. Why don't you tell me about the creatures that live in the area," Liz suggested.

"Oh, there are too many to name!" Pip answered in her high-pitched chirp. "Here in the creek are fish of all sorts, of course. Brown trout, catfish, minnows, sunfish, perch, and smallmouth bass, just to name a few. Lots of salamanders and lizards, bullfrogs, box turtles, slugs, and snails, too."

Patrick sat forward and wrapped his arms around his knees with a curious smile on his face as he observed this sleek black cat meowing. "Where did you come from, little cat? Are you . . . trying to talk to that bird?" Liz kept her back to Patrick while she continued her conversation with Pip.

"And of course, I assume the usual bugs frequent this wet area, no? Flies, mosquitoes, mayflies, stink bugs, dragonflies, ticks, jumping spiders, etc.," Liz offered, her tail slowly curling up and down.

"Yes! But we have the bad creatures here as well," Pip continued. "Be careful with the cottonmouth snakes and the black widow spiders about."

Liz smiled, thinking of Al mistaking the black willow tree for a black widow spider. She missed her funny mate. *"Merci* for the warning. Indeed, they are both quite dangerous."

Patrick looked from the cat to the bird and back to the cat again. "You're a cat, you know. How can you talk to a bird?"

Liz turned and gave him a coy smile. *"And you are a human, yet this does not keep you from talking to me, no?"* she meowed in reply. She walked over and rubbed her cheek across his foot. *"Bonjour, Patrick. Although you do not know it, I am here to help you find your voice,"* Liz meowed. *"You already listen extremely well, so learn to speak the language of those you already study."*

Patrick wrinkled his brow at this meowing cat that seemed to be trying to talk to him. "I wish I knew what you were saying," he told her.

"Oui, *it would make* my *work much easier as well,* mon ami, *for I can understand you perfectly,"* Liz meowed. *"But it has never stopped me from helping humans before, so we shall learn to communicate in other ways, no? You shall soon see."*

Liz sat down next to Patrick's leg. He set his fishing pole on the rock and petted her silky coat as she resumed her conversation with Pip. "What large animals have you seen at the creek, Pip?"

"We have a resident beaver, and river otter, raccoon, possum, skunk,

24

fox, and weasel that stop by," Pip replied. "Of course they are large to *me*!"

Liz giggled. *"Bien sûr.* Of course they are, for you are quite small. What about the truly grand animals that come to drink at the creek?"

"We have mainly deer, but every now and then we see a wolf, a bobcat—or worse—a panther," Pip answered.

Patrick listened to Liz and Pip banter back and forth. "Chickadee-dee-dee," he sounded. "Funny, this bird's voice sounds like its name."

Liz turned and purred in approval. "Bon! *Try again. The more you try to mimic the birds, the more you will relate to them. And of course, the better your diction will be as you listen closely to each syllable."*

"Chickadee-dee-dee. Chickadee-dee-dee. Chickadee-dee-dee," "spoke" Patrick with a grin at the little bird, not realizing he was following Liz's instructions.

Pip hopped to a closer branch. "He's trying to speak chickadee, Liz!"

"Oui, he is a fast learner, no?" she replied. "Please continue."

"Hello, Patrick. I know you can't understand, but thank you for trying to talk to me," Pip chirped, cocking her head to stare at the boy. *"I think you're a smart boy."*

Suddenly Patrick heard the bobwhite again. He shrugged his shoulders and called out with perfect inflection, emphasizing the second syllable in a higher pitch, "Bob-WHITE! Bob-WHITE!" He grinned at himself.

Liz smiled and batted her eyes affectionately. *"C'est magnifique,* Patrick!"

"You're a funny little thing, the way you like to talk," Patrick said. "I don't know where you came from but I think you should come home with me."

"This is the idea, no?" Liz meowed back with a grin.

Max came bounding out on the rocks, barking as something was pulling on Patrick's line. Patrick jumped in surprise at both the barking dog and the movement of his pole. He lunged forward and landed chest-first on the rock, catching the end of the pole before it fell into the water. He pulled back on the line and hauled a dangling catfish out of the water.

"I got one!" Patrick cheered. He sat down cross-legged on the rock and held the fish in one hand. He then pried the hook out of its mouth, careful to avoid the catfish's sharp, barbed "whiskers." He cast a glance

25

at Liz and then looked the fish in the eye. "Any last words, fish?" He laughed at himself and held the fish out for Liz. "He's not talking but I bet you speak catfish, huh, little cat? I'll take this one home for you." He pulled a string from his knapsack to carry the fish.

Max came up next to Liz and Patrick on the rock, wagging his tail. "Hey, boy! Now where did *you* come from?" Patrick asked, giving Max a gruff pat on the head.

"If you only knew, Monsieur Henry," Liz meowed in reply. *"Allow me to introduce Max. He will, of course, be coming home with us, too."*

"You're a sturdy little dog," observed Patrick, looking at Max and then at Liz. "It looks like you two know each other. I guess I'll need to take you both home." He wrinkled his brow. "I'll have to convince my mother to let me keep you though. Hmmm . . . we could use a dog around the house to keep the raccoons from stealing the chicken eggs, since we lost our last dog. And you're *Scottish,* too. That should help." The boy smiled, standing up and putting his hands on his hips, thinking this through. "And it *is* my seventh birthday, after all."

"Seven?" Liz's eyes brightened with this news. *"Joyeux anniversaire, Patrick! How did I not know this? May 29 is a special date I will need to remember."*

"Aye!" Max barked. *"Happy birthday, lad! We'll be on our best behavior for yer mum, then."*

"Come on, let's get back home," instructed Patrick. "Father told me Uncle Patrick was stopping by for my birthday today, so I have to clean up a bit. It's not a good idea to smell like fish with him around."

"My Albert would disagree, cher ami," Liz jested.

With that, Max and Liz followed Patrick Henry, while Nigel scurried along behind them, staying out of sight. And waiting for them at Studley would be a courier delivering all the latest mail including, of course, a letter from John's cousin, David, in London.

4

Settled
at Studley

"How beautiful!" Liz exclaimed as they walked along the lane leading to Studley Plantation. Two rows of thickly grooved fifty-foot trees with blackish bark lined the avenue. Bright green leaves filled branches heavy-laden with blooms of fragrant white flowers. "I have long adored the *Robinia pseudoacacia*, but of course you know it better as the black locust tree."

"Aye, of *course* we do, lass." Max shared a knowing grin with Nigel. Liz knew the scientific as well as common name of every tree, flower, and plant under the sun, it seemed. She assumed everyone else would want to as well.

"He's back!" came the voice of a little five-year-old girl running up the lane. Her flowery print dress kicked up around her heels.

Patrick smiled as his little sister came to greet him. "Hi, little Jane! You seem excited."

"Mother is getting everything ready, and the courier just got here, so Father is looking through the mail, and Uncle Patrick is with him, and they are going to . . ." Jane gushed out before putting her small fingers over her mouth. She was dying to say more.

Patrick tilted his head as he studied his little sister's face. He smiled and leaned in close. "What are you trying *not* to tell me?"

Jane's eyes widened and she pulled her head back. "No-o-othing," she replied innocently. But she knew her actions betrayed her words. She had a secret she was dying to tell.

Patrick grinned, knowing it likely had something to do with his birthday. He reached into his knapsack and pulled out the honeysuckle vine. "I brought you something, Jane. Here, taste this." He proceeded to pull off a bloom and pinched off the end to release the sweet nectar.

"M-m-m!" Jane's hazel eyes brightened as she tasted the sweet honeysuckle. "Just wait 'til you see what Uncle Patrick brought *you* for your birthday!" Her face fell as she realized she had made public her secret.

Patrick laughed and winked at his little sister, handing her the rest of the honeysuckle. "It's alright, little Jane. I'll keep your secret."

She giggled, and then noticed Max and Liz walking along behind Patrick. "Where did *they* come from?" she inquired happily, squatting down to pet them. Nigel had scurried over to the tall grass. He knew humans didn't appreciate his presence. They sadly assumed he was more like the rats he abhorred rather than the refined, educated creature he was.

"Bonjour, *Jane,*" Liz meowed, rubbing against the little girl's knees while Max wagged his tail and smiled.

"They were down at the creek. They just came out of nowhere," Patrick explained and pointed to Liz. "And this little cat likes to talk."

"Are you going to keep them?" Jane wanted to know, following along after Patrick, who was again walking up the path.

"That's the plan," he replied, thinking about the argument he would need to make to his mother. "But don't spoil *my* secret yet, alright, little Jane? You run along and I'll be there in a minute."

"Alright!" Jane giggled, putting a finger up to her mouth. She skipped along ahead as her big brother had asked. "But remember to stay out of the kitchen!"

They soon came to a two-story brick house covered with whitewashed wooden clapboards. A one-story wing extended from the house, and nearby were several smaller outbuildings including a kitchen, dairy, stables, barn, and granary. Patrick breathed in the woodsy smell of the boxwood hedges and grazed his fingers along their small, dark green leaves. Nigel darted under his feet and into the boxwoods, peeking to see what awaited them on the other side of the hedge. The plantation was a beehive of activity, with everyone milling about at their various chores. Smoke curled from the chimney over the kitchen, and they could hear the cows mooing as they passed the barn.

"I bet you're thirsty. I know *I* am," Patrick told Max and Liz. He stopped at a wooden table outside the barn and set down his knapsack. He then ran over to the well and turned the crank handle to pull up a bucket of water. He dipped a wooden gourd into the bucket and gulped down the cool, fresh water, wiping his chin with the back of his sleeve. Patrick then refilled the gourd with water and walked just inside the barn, setting it on the ground for Max and Liz. "Here you go."

Patrick then ran back over to the table, where he filled a small basin with the rest of the water. He took out a knife from his knapsack and hurriedly cut up the fish into several pieces. He rushed back to the barn and put the fish onto the hay next to the gourd and took some dried beef from his pocket to set down next to the fish. "You two stay here for a while. I'll be back."

Max and Liz did as instructed and looked around the barn, while Patrick made his way back over to the table, where he washed his hands and face in the basin of water. He hurriedly dried off with a small cloth and tied his hair back with a black piece of string, thinking all the while about what he would say to his mother about the animals.

Patrick's sixteen-year-old half-brother John was helping his nine-year-old brother William unload a wagon of wooden crates filled with goods they had picked up in the nearby trading town of Newcastle. Two little girls younger than Jane, Anne and Sarah, ran around excitedly while their mother, also named Sarah, instructed the boys where to take items they unpacked from the crates. She was soon expecting another baby, and held yet another one-year-old little girl on her hip. Sarah put a hand to her aching back and bounced the toddler, who was whining, kissing the fussing child on the forehead.

"Can I help you, Mother?" Patrick asked as he walked up to his mother and the busy scene of children and chores. He clapped his hands together once and then held them out to take the toddler from his tired mother.

Sarah smiled and cupped Patrick's chin tenderly in her hand. "There's my birthday boy." She handed over the toddler, who happily reached her tiny arms out to Patrick. "Yes, please hold Susannah for a moment." As Patrick took Susannah into his arms, he made a funny face, causing her to immediately stop fussing. He proceeded to lift her high in the air and twirl her around, causing the toddler to giggle uncontrollably.

Sarah called to one of their slaves across the yard, "Peter! Please bring some fresh eggs from the barn. Hopefully the chickens have laid plenty more this morning after that pesky raccoon got into the chicken coop yesterday." She then turned to her older boys. "John dear, please take this crate to the kitchen." She picked up a jar of molasses and handed it to William. She put a hand on his back and whispered in his ear, "Bill, take this to Rose and please tell her I'll be there shortly to check on things." Sarah was a sturdy, handsome woman with strong features and a cheery disposition. Her voice was firm as she called out orders to everyone, yet her manner was gentle as she interacted with her children. She was very intelligent and knew how to run her household efficiently. And as was the habit of her Winston family, she gave to her Henry family endearing nicknames, including Patrick, whom she called "Pat."

"I say, what a handful the Henrys have with all these children!" Nigel said to Liz, who joined him in the boxwood hedge. "I count three boys, four girls, and one on the way."

"Our Patrick is so good with his little sisters, no?" Liz added with a smile. "He clearly loves them, as every big brother should."

"Indeed, and I'm quite impressed with Mrs. Henry," Nigel answered. "She clearly runs a tight ship."

"Pat, did you catch any fish at the creek?" Sarah asked, stretching out her back once more.

"I caught one," he answered, still making funny faces at Susannah.

Sarah smiled at her son. His thoughtfulness and care of his little sisters made her proud. "I'm glad. Did you see any wildlife?" She reached out to take Susannah back into her arms. "I've been concerned about you going out there alone lately. The Merediths spotted a panther last week."

That little cat looks like a panther, Pat thought. He brightened as he considered that this might be a perfect lead-in. "Sam told me his father saw that big cat. I spotted a bald eagle building a nest." He hesitated and then added with a grin, "And actually I did see a panther, but it was a small one."

Sarah's eyes widened in alarm, so Patrick quickly held up a hand and explained. "It was only a little black cat, Mother. And I think I might have a solution for the panther and the raccoons. There was a little black dog with her, too—a terrier. A *Scottish* terrier. Father told me he had one when he was a boy. Since they keep varmints away, I figure he could chase off a panther in the woods with me, too. And the cat can keep the mice under control around the barn."

Nigel and Liz exchanged humorous looks. "The boy has no idea of the truth with which he speaks," chuckled Nigel, bowing to Liz. "I am your humble servant to command, *petite* Madam Panther."

"*Merci,* Nigel." Liz smiled. "I am happy that Patrick could use us to make his argument. He certainly has the ability to make things seem reasonable."

Patrick's mother tilted her head. "I see. And where are your little panther and her Scottish friend right now? In the barn?"

Patrick pursed his mouth to keep from grinning and nodded. His mother always seemed to know things. "Can I please keep them, Mother? I promise to take care of them." He put a hand on his mother's arm and looked up at her hopefully with his penetrating blue eyes. "It *is* my birthday."

Sarah smiled and kissed Patrick on the cheek. "Very well, Pat. Happy birthday! Go get them and show them to your father and uncle. They've been waiting for you in the garden. The courier brought the mail and should be just leaving. A letter arrived from Cousin David, so we'll get to hear the latest news from London."

Patrick wrapped his arms around his mother with joy. "Thank you, Mother!"

With that he ran back to the barn and called for Max. Liz sauntered out from the boxwood hedge and together they made their way across the yard. Coming around from the garden was the courier walking his horse to the front of the house to head off to his next destination. He tapped a finger to his tricorn hat. "Good day, young Master Henry."

"Hello, sir," Patrick answered.

"My, what fine animals you have there!" he said as he squatted down to scratch Max under the chin. "What are their names?"

Patrick shrugged his shoulders, petting the courier's horse. "I haven't named them yet. I just got them today."

"Well, why not give them grand names, for fun? This fine dog looks like a 'Maximillian' if you ask me," he suggested with a wink to the animals. "And this beautiful feline looks like she could be an 'Elizabeth,' like the beloved queen of old Elizabethan England."

Patrick chuckled. "Those are pretty fancy names, much too fancy for me. But my mother always uses nicknames for us."

"Max and Liz, perhaps?" the courier suggested with a sly grin.

Patrick nodded. "That sounds more like it, sir."

"Very well, then it's settled. I must be on my way," he said, putting

31

his foot into the stirrup and climbing up onto his horse. "Farewell, young Mr. Henry. Take care of Max and Liz. I'm sure they'll be good friends who will also take care of you."

The boy looked at Max and Liz and smiled. "I think so, too." He lifted a hand in farewell. "Goodbye, sir." As the courier galloped away, Patrick grinned and started running toward the garden. "Come on, Max and Liz! Let's see what came in the mail!"

"That worked out well, thanks ta Clarie's quick thinkin'," Max whispered to Liz with a big grin as they followed Patrick. "It's always nice when we can actually go by our r-r-real names then."

Liz giggled. *"Oui,* Maximillian. Everything has worked out well. We are settled at Studley, and our mission can now truly begin."

"Hear, hear, a splendid beginning at Studley!" Nigel cheered as he came alongside them. "I do look forward to this next encounter. What*ever* could have come in today's mail, I wonder?"

"Mousie's actin' cheeky," Max joked.

"Occupational hazard, old boy," Nigel replied with his jolly chuckle. "The humans have no idea the game is ours."

32

GREAT AWAKENINGS

John Henry filled the end of his white clay pipe with tobacco while he listened to his brother, the Reverend Patrick Henry. Young Patrick was named for this beloved uncle who had followed John from Scotland and had become the pastor of St. Paul's Parish here in Hanover County. They sat on opposite wooden benches in the shady garden on this warm Virginia afternoon. Reverend Henry was sharing the latest news about some of the local Dissenters who chose not to attend the required services at his Anglican church.

"I tell ye, John, this Samuel Morris and his 'Morris Reading House' will only stir up more trouble for the Anglican church," Uncle Patrick fumed in his Scottish brogue. "Once he shared the printed sermon of that Methodist preacher, George Whitefield, the people can't get enough of this 'New Light' teaching. Whitefield's preaching has taken America by storm, and I fear that the church will lose control of maintaining social order and the civility of the people. The established church is what keeps morality and decency in line, not this 'Great Awakening!' From what I hear, the people become an emotional mob as they hear these sermons and are struck ta the heart, crying out, 'What shall we do?'"

Patrick entered the garden and immediately noticed that his father and uncle were having a serious discussion. He knew he needed to respectfully remain quiet and not disturb them, so he sat down on a tree stump to listen. And learn.

Max and Liz stayed behind young Patrick, lying down in the cool grass. Nigel stayed hidden between them.

"Wha's the parson r-r-ramblin' on aboot?" Max asked. "I thought America were the place of fr-r-reedom for humans ta worship as they please. Weren't that the main reason why the humans came over ta the colonies?"

"Not necessarily, old boy," Nigel answered. "It is quite the complicated situation."

"You see, while some of the thirteen colonies were indeed founded for religious freedom, this was not the case for them all," Liz offered. "Virginia was the first colony, founded in 1607, but it was a business venture by a group of investors known as the Virginia Company. It had nothing to do with religious freedom."

"Max, allow me to help you understand all of this by rewinding history a bit," Nigel offered, adjusting his spectacles. "Right. England has been a Protestant country since it broke away from the Roman Catholic Church under the rule of King Henry VIII in 1534. He formed the Anglican Church and appointed himself as the sole, rightful ruler of this new Church of England. Many English Christians *dissented,* meaning they disagreed with either the beliefs or practices of the church. It was quite the nasty business! Sadly, those Catholics who still believed the pope was the head of the church were treated harshly."

34

Max frowned. "Wha' a mess!"

"Oh, it gets far worse, I assure you! While the English Catholics were persecuted, some of the English Protestants wanted to change, or *reform,* the Anglican Church, and became what are called *Puritans.* Other English Protestants wanted to completely break away from the Anglican Church and set up their own churches, and they became known as *Separatists.*"

"*Oui,* so then the Separatists *also* were persecuted in England and fled to the Netherlands," Liz interjected. "A group of them made an agreement with the Virginia Company to settle in Virginia, where they could practice their religion however they chose, calling themselves *Pilgrims* because their journey to America served a religious purpose."

"Right, but in 1620 their ship, the *Mayflower,* unintentionally landed not in Virginia but much farther north, in Plymouth," Nigel went on, pointing up. "This land was, of course, not within the territory and laws of the Virginia Company. But the Pilgrims decided to stay where they were and eventually founded the colony of Massachusetts in 1629."

"As each new colony was founded by various leaders and for different reasons, the thirteen colonies developed entirely separate identities with different stances on the practice of religion," Liz explained. "Massachusetts and Rhode Island were formed *purely* for religious freedom. Connecticut, Pennsylvania, Maryland, and Georgia were formed *in part* for religious freedom, but also for other reasons such as selling land and trade. And the rest of the colonies—New Hampshire, New York, Delaware, New Jersey, North Carolina, South Carolina—were founded solely for reasons *other* than religious freedom."

"Which leads us back to the issue at hand in the colony of Virginia," Nigel continued. "Virginia is a royal colony, and *by law,* Virginians are members of the Anglican Church, or Church of England. They are required to both attend worship and pay taxes to support the state church. This money pays the salaries for the clergy, builds and repairs church buildings, and supports the poor, orphans, and others in need. Virginia does not have an Anglican bishop, but the state church is governed by Virginia's General Assembly.

"Unfortunately, many of the ministers appointed to the churches across Virginia are rather dull, and do not inspire the people, who are forced to listen to their boring sermons," continued Nigel. "Sadly, some of them are even poor *moral* examples, as they engage in behavior unbefitting a shepherd. Of course, Reverend Henry does not fall into this last category, as he is an honest man of faith."

"The people do not want such dry sermons that have no depth or personal meaning," Liz lamented. "I believe this Great Awakening movement sweeping across America is a *good* thing, no? The people are *hungry* for the hopeful teachings of Jesus!"

"And, they are *hungry* for the freedom to practice their faith however they choose," Nigel added.

"Aye, but the *power*-hungr-r-ry humans have made a mess of things!" interjected an agitated Max. "Jesus an' his disciples made it so simple when they first set up the church. We saw it firsthand." The Scottie frowned. "Wha' aboot that Whitefield pr-r-reacher then? He must be one of them Dissenters."

Liz nodded. "This is true, Max. All the Protestant faiths that are not part of the Anglican Church are considered Dissenters—Methodists, Baptists, Lutherans, Presbyterians, Quakers, and any others. So here in Virginia these groups are looked down upon and are discouraged from meeting. But with so many immigrants bringing these faiths to Virginia anyway, trouble is brewing for the state church. George Whitefield and other preachers are delivering the kind of sermons the people long to hear. So even though they are required to attend the Church of England, many are choosing to disobey. They may be fined or even *imprisoned* for doing so."

"And Virginia's leaders are walking a fine line of tolerating some of these new preachers and groups who apply for permission to preach the way they do," Nigel further explained. "The law requires Dissenters to officially tell the courts they wish to dissent. They *can* practice their faith on a limited basis, but there *is* a catch."

"*Oui,* only those who are part of the Church of England can hold political office," Liz added. "So you see, if you wish to worship freely, you may to a degree, but you then have no right to govern at any level."

"And Dissenters still have to pay the taxes to the local parish church, even if they choose not to attend," Nigel added, crossing his arms over his chest. "Like I said, it is a *nasty* business."

"Let me get this str-r-raight. Humans can go ta *jail* for missin' church where they don't even want ta go. An' Parson Henry thinks *he* has a r-r-right ta be upset if they don't like his pr-r-reachin'," Max stated, finally understanding what the mess was all about. "This be daft! It sounds jest like how the R-r-romans wouldn't allow the Chr-r-ristians ta worship. At least there be no lions in coliseums here in America for the leaders ta thr-r-row the Dissenters to."

Liz frowned as she pondered Max's words. "No real lions, *mon ami.* But the *British* lion is very real, and seeks to silence some Christians. There is no freedom of religion in this colony."

"I understand your concern, brother, and I agree with ye, of course," John Henry said, also with a Scottish accent. He puffed on his pipe and leaned over to rest his elbows on his knees. "I've also learned that a Reverend William Robinson, a *Presbyterian,* so captured the hearts of the people of Hanover with his recent preaching that they gave him a large amount of money as a gift. He refused ta accept it, but they would not take no for an answer." He sat back and rested his arms on the back of the bench. "Robinson said he would only accept the money if he could use it ta educate a young minister ta send back ta them here in Hanover. A Samuel Davies, I think, was the name he gave them."

Uncle Patrick wrinkled his brow. "I see. So now the Presbyterians will have not only a reading house but a *preacher* ta go along with it as well!"

Just then, Patrick's mother joined the men in the garden. As she did so, the men cleared their throats and stopped talking. But Sarah had heard every word as she approached.

"And I suppose that means the world is coming to an end, is that right?" she said with a flash of exasperation in her voice. "The Presbyterians are *fine* Christians and I happen to agree with what they teach."

"Yes, I know your father Isaac is one of their Dissenting followers," Uncle Patrick said, holding up a hand to stop her from launching an all-out attack. "Let's not debate this now."

"Agreed, especially on young Patrick's birthday," Sarah whispered, leaning over to look the men in the eye with a stern expression. "Let's keep this a day of happy celebration, not a day of religious war."

"I couldn't agree more, Sallie," John answered, slapping his knee and sitting up straight to conclude the matter for that day.

The animals looked at one another in surprise. "Patrick's father and uncle agree with the Anglican church while Patrick's mother sides with the Dissenters," Nigel remarked. "I say, this issue of religious freedom is playing out right in Patrick's own family!"

"With the lad caught in the middle," Max added.

Liz curled her tail up and down as she studied young Patrick. "I wonder which side he will choose."

"Where is my birthday namesake?" Uncle Patrick asked.

Patrick stood up from the stump but didn't move. "Here I am."

Sarah turned and smiled to see Patrick and the dog and cat next to him. "Come here and introduce us to your new little friends."

Patrick picked Liz up to carry her over to the adults. Max followed along behind, wagging his tail. "I found these animals when I was fishing at the creek today. I've named this cat 'Liz' and this dog 'Max.'" He looked his father in the eye. "Mother said I could keep them."

"That I did." Sarah gave Liz a tender pat on the head. "Hello there, Liz. Aren't you a pretty little thing?"

"Bonjour, *Sarah Henry*," Liz meowed. *"I admire your zeal to speak your mind with these men. Kate would call it 'Lassie Power.'"*

"She likes to talk," Patrick said with a grin.

"And look what we have here! A fine Scottish terrier!" John Henry exclaimed, giving Max a rigorous scratch on the head. "Patrick, do you remember our Scottie back in Aberdeen?"

"Aye, there was never a finer breed!" Uncle Patrick replied, standing to hug his nephew. "I'm glad for ye, lad. Happy birthday, Patrick."

37

Patrick closed his eyes and smiled. "Thank you, Uncle."

"I told Patrick there was news from David in London," Sarah said, sitting down next to her husband on the bench and searching through the stack of mail on the table. She found what she was looking for and handed the sealed envelope to him. "John, why don't you read us his letter?"

"Of course," John replied, taking the letter and breaking the seal.

Patrick sat on the ground with Max and Liz, who shared a grin as John started to read aloud:

From David Henry, LONDON, England   23 Mar 1743

To John Henry, Hanover Co, VIRGINIA

Greetings, Cousin:

I trust this letter finds you and yours well and prospering. I have just returned from a most miraculous evening. The great composer George F. Handel gave a sublime London debut of his new Sacred Oratorio, called Messiah. I must say I was moved greatly by the words comprised of prophetic texts from Isaiah and others, and the gospel accounts of our Lord. It truly is the most remarkable music I have ever heard, and I pray that one day you will be able to hear it performed in the colony of Virginia.

His Majesty, King George II, was in attendance. He surprised the audience when he stood during an especially powerful part called The Hallelujah Chorus. I have obtained a copy of the libretto which was printed for the audience and will enclose it herewith. I can only surmise that even the great king of England recognized the King who is Sovereign even over his own rule. I pray our king never forgets this truth. As Isaiah's words about Messiah were powerfully relayed in song: the Government shall be upon HIS shoulder.

Despite the glory of the evening, I must tell you that Mr. Handel has experienced a backlash of persecution for this work, and who knows if it will ever become an oratorio that is played beyond a small number of performances this season. Handel went against London's religious elite, who criticized his choice of venue for such a sacred work, namely Covent Garden Theatre. How preposterous to attack such a magnificent, godly work for something so completely meaningless!

A gentleman sat next to me in the performance, a Mr. Gillamon,

38

and as we discussed Mr. Handel's situation, he reminded me of John 1:5. If Messiah himself was misunderstood and persecuted when he came into the world, why should his followers not also be misunderstood and persecuted? In fact, our Lord said that this would indeed happen. I have been pondering those followers across time who have given voice to the truth, and have come to realize something important.

If only one voice of faith will rise up and speak (or sing, or write, using whatever gift the Lord has given him,) the history of the world will be changed.

I have been inspired to contemplate what my one voice can do, and will do in this world for the good. I wish to impart that same thought to you, my cousin. You are over in the New World. Perhaps your one voice will change the history of America. Or even that fine young son of yours, young Patrick. Perhaps his one voice will rise up and change history. Time will tell, as it always does.

I pray you to give my best to your family, and may our Lord bless your endeavors.

Your Humble Servant,

David Henry

Sarah beamed and leaned over to put her hand on Patrick's back. "How wonderful that cousin David mentioned you specifically, Patrick!"

"Aye, and what an inspiring word for ye ta hear, especially on yer birthday," John added, handing the letter to Patrick. "I want ye ta keep this letter and read it from time ta time, Patrick. I think it will be a good reminder that ye can achieve great things."

Patrick took the letter in hand and put his finger on the line where he saw his name. He was just learning to read, so while he did not understand every word, he could pick out his name. He didn't say anything, but smiled and nodded.

"*Your voice will indeed change the history of America!*" Liz meowed in exclamation.

"I believe the cat has your tongue," Uncle Patrick quipped with a chuckle. "Perhaps Liz will be like your 'Aaron,' who served as Moses' voice when he could not speak to Pharaoh."

Patrick smiled and stroked Liz, who was purring on the ground next to him. "Perhaps."

"*I am well qualified to do so, no?*" Liz meowed.

"Aye, seein' how ye spoke ta Pharaoh himself, lass," Max whispered to Liz.

"What an extraordinary story of the king of England standing during this concert," John remarked, looking over the libretto David had included with the letter.

"You should have been there to see it in person, old boy!" Nigel squeaked from under the bench as he listened in. He quickly covered his mouth so he would not be heard. Max dipped his head and spotted the little mouse, and winked at him.

"Aye, it must be an extraordinary musical work," Uncle Patrick echoed. "I do hope we can hear it ourselves one day."

"But how tragic that Mr. Handel has experienced persecution for his work from the *religious elite,*" Sarah noted with a convicting tone, staring right at the men. "Here Mr. Handel is expressing the *same* Scripture preached by the Church of England, but in a different manner than the established church is used to, so he is *persecuted* for it."

Uncle Patrick and John squirmed in their seats. It was a rather convicting scenario to hear, especially since they were just having a similar discussion about the Dissenters, who were doing the same thing here in Virginia. The Dissenters simply desired to express their faith in a way that went against the British Lion's way of doing things. The tension hung in the air like a cannonball. Liz beamed at Sarah's 'lassie power.'

Patrick remained quiet and didn't comment on this exchange between the adults. But David's words echoed in his mind: *I pray our king never forgets this truth. As Isaiah's words about Messiah were powerfully relayed in song: the Government shall be upon HIS shoulder.*

Sarah allowed the invisible cannonball to accomplish its work and then clapped her hands, smiling broadly. "Well, no more squabbles today. Time to celebrate!"

"Aye!" Uncle Patrick exclaimed, relieved to change the subject. He stood up and hurried over to retrieve something from behind a small tree in the garden. "Close yer eyes, Patrick. And hold out yer hands."

Patrick did as he was told and sat back on his heels with his eyes closed.

Sarah squeezed John's hand with joy as Uncle Patrick placed a brand new musket in the boy's outstretched hands. John smiled. "Open yer eyes, Patrick."

Patrick couldn't believe his eyes. "A musket! Is this mine?"

40

"Aye, yer very own gun," John answered happily. "Yer Uncle Patrick and I had it made just for ye. It's time ye learned ta shoot."

"Thank you! I can't believe it!" Patrick exclaimed, standing to hold the gun and stare down the barrel.

"It isn't loaded," Uncle Patrick told him, gently pushing the gun to point toward the ground. "But always practice safety and never point it at anyone."

"Unless ye *mean* ta shoot them!" John jested.

Sarah playfully hit John in the shoulder. "I hope he'll only ever have to use it for hunting! And who better to teach him how to hunt than my brother Bill?" She stood and leaned over to speak in Patrick's ear. "Uncle Langloo will have to take you hunting soon. For now, you'll have Max *and* a gun to guard against that panther."

"I sure will," Patrick replied with a grin, running his hand along the beautiful brown wood of his new gun. "I love my new musket."

Sarah cupped her hand over her mouth and called out to everyone waiting outside the garden behind the boxwoods. "You can bring it in now!"

Uncle Patrick took the musket from Patrick to hang on to for the moment.

The sound of cheering filled the air, as all the Henry children came running into the garden, followed by a group of servants. Jane held the hands of her little sisters as they ran over to surround Patrick, smothering him with hugs. Then they turned their attention to Max and Liz, who were smothered with other pets. William carried little Susannah and handed her to his mother. "Happy birthday, Patrick!" everyone exclaimed.

The oldest son, John, carried a wooden plate that held a birthday cake, and placed it onto the table in front of him. "Happy birthday, little brother!"

Patrick's eyes grew wide at this sudden surprise. "For me?"

"I didn't tell you *everything,*" Jane said, giggling as she hugged her big brother.

"So *that's* why I wasn't allowed near the kitchen today," Patrick said. "I wondered why mother said I could skip my chores and go fishing."

Rose held a lantern and started using a lighting wick to light the seven skinny beeswax taper candles placed on the cake. "Happy birthday, child. I hope you like this cake. I made it 'specially for you. Apple cinnamon with molasses."

Patrick leaned over and hugged Rose. "Thank you, Rose! I know I will!" She was a slave who had been with the family for more than a decade, and was very dear to all of them, but was especially dear to young Patrick.

"What happy thought will you wish to come true?" Sarah asked her son as he got ready to blow out the candles.

Patrick thought a moment and grinned but didn't say a word. He stole a glance with Liz and gave her a wink. He took in a deep breath and blew out the candles as his family applauded.

John Henry picked up his fiddle and started playing a lively Scottish tune, while Rose cut the cake for everyone. The girls giggled and danced as John and William each picked a little sister for a partner. Sarah bounced little Susannah on her knee, while Uncle Patrick and the servants clapped in time with the music. Max barked and jumped around happily with the children.

"Can I have this dance, little Jane?" Patrick asked.

Jane giggled. "Yes, big brother!"

42

Liz crawled under the bench to sit with Nigel as the family celebrated. There on the ground next to them was David's letter. Although they had traveled with Clarie to deliver this letter to Virginia, none of them knew what was actually in it until today.

"This has been a happy day, *mon ami*," Liz told the little mouse. "I never imagined that what David wrote back on March 23 would be so perfect for this specific day of May 29. He did not realize he actually penned prophetic words about my Patrick!"

"Quite so, my pet. The power of your Patrick's future voice must be one we cannot yet even imagine," foretold Nigel, preening his whiskers. "No wonder the Enemy wanted to keep that letter from reaching Virginia. He wanted to keep that prophecy sound asleep."

Liz grinned as she watched Patrick twirl Jane around the garden. "*Oui,* so now it is time for Patrick's voice to have a great awakening of its own."

BACK IN ST. ANDREW'S DAY

Gillamon stood in the IAMISPHERE with Clarie, both taking their respective natural forms of a mountain goat and a lamb. The wind encircled them, blowing Gillamon's goatee around his chin. They were looking at panels of time from long ago.

"I want to show you something before we arrive in Hanover for St. Andrew's Day," Gillamon told Clarie, his blue eyes twinkling with delight. "It is easy for the humans to forget why they celebrate the way they do, but the Order of the Seven must always understand the layers of history converging at key points in time." He touched his hoof to a panel where John the Baptist stood with two of his followers on the banks of the Jordan River in Israel. They were in a deep discussion:

"So when Isaiah wrote, 'The government will be upon his shoulder,' he showed that Messiah will be a ruler," John the follower said. "That much is clear."

"Indeed, Isaiah says just a few verses later, 'Of the increase of his government and of peace there will be no end, on the throne of David and over his Kingdom, to establish it and to uphold it,'" Andrew added. "Messiah will definitely be a King."

John the Baptizer saw Jesus coming in the distance and was in awe of the presence of the Holy Spirit clearly on his cousin. He kept his eyes on Jesus but answered his two followers, Andrew and John. "Yes, he will be a King. But he will also be the final lamb needed to take away the sin of the world . . ." John trailed off, taking a few steps forward and meeting Jesus' gaze. They locked eyes, and Jesus smiled, but kept on walking.

43

John pointed his finger at Jesus and said in a loud voice, "Behold, the Lamb of God!"

Andrew and John quickly turned to see whom John the Baptist was talking about. They had heard him speak of the One who had come to him for baptism—the true One they should follow as Messiah. It was this kind of teaching that had attracted these men and their friends. This man John the Baptist wasn't trying to build a religious empire for himself, but was simply preparing the way for the One whom men should truly follow. So Andrew and John were prepared, ready at a moment's notice to follow John the Baptist's lead. Immediately they ran after Jesus. John the Baptist crossed his arms and nodded his head in approval as his two followers left him. *This is how it should be,* he thought to himself. *They are yours now, Jesus.*

Jesus heard the two men running up behind him. He turned and stopped. "What are you seeking?" he asked simply.

Andrew and John looked at one another, not sure who should speak first. "Teacher," Andrew finally blurted out awkwardly, rubbing his hand on his brown tunic. "Where are you staying?"

John nodded enthusiastically in agreement. Jesus smiled, fully aware these men wanted to know far more than simply Jesus' place of lodging. "Come and see."

Together the three men walked across the countryside toward the place where people coming to see John the Baptist stayed. A tiny village of huts and makeshift camel-hair tents was off the main road, a short walk north of where they were. They got to know each other as they walked along.

"I'm Andrew, son of John, originally from Bethsaida," Andrew started.

"Ah, so you don't live there now?" Jesus asked.

"No, my brother Simon and I now live in Capernaum," the young man replied, feeling a little more comfortable. "We're fishermen."

"So are we," John interjected. "I mean, my brother James and I. We're fishermen, too."

"Fishing is an important job. It feeds many," Jesus affirmed. "Do you enjoy it?"

Andrew shrugged his shoulders. "It's hard work, but good work. Simon is the one who handles all the business. I just do what he asks."

Jesus looked at John. "What about you, John?"

"We're sons of a fisherman, so it's a family business," John explained. "I do sometimes wish for more in life."

"When you're doing what you were truly made to do, then work takes on a new meaning," Jesus noted. "It becomes your passion."

"And what is *your* passion?" John asked Jesus.

Jesus stopped and put his hand on John's shoulder. "To seek and save those who are lost."

John glanced at Andrew, and the two men shared a look full of anticipation.

"John the Baptist told us you were the promised One for whom Israel has waited," Andrew related with growing excitement.

"He said we should follow you now," John quickly added.

"John speaks truth," Jesus said. He locked eyes with Andrew and John and they shared a brief moment of understanding. The fishermen didn't even know how to respond. They were walking down the road with a man who was possibly the promised Messiah, foretold by prophets and expected for hundreds of years by the people of Israel. How could they respond?

45

Suddenly they heard Max barking. Jesus smiled, turned, and pointed to a tent up ahead. "Ah, here we are."

Jesus led them to the tent where Gillamon sat just outside with a small fire, baking more bread. He stood when Jesus, Andrew, and John came up to him.

"This is where I'm staying. Please, meet my friend," Jesus stopped and said, giving a knowing look at the old man, "Gillamon."

"Shalom. Please, sit and I will serve you," Gillamon offered as they gathered around the fire.

"Thank you," Andrew and John answered in unison, sitting down with Jesus.

"I see you have many animals," John said as Liz came up to him, purring and rubbing her cheek on his blue tunic.

"Bonjour," Liz meowed. John smiled and petted her head.

"Yes, they are my friends," Gillamon answered warmly, handing the men some bread. Al came into the midst of them, batting at the bread. "But watch out for this orange one. He'll eat anything in sight."

Max and Kate came up wagging their tails and sat next to Andrew. Nigel peeked out from Clarie's saddlebag. The animals were excited to witness the beginning of Jesus' ministry with these young men.

"I say, they don't look like rabbis," Nigel whispered in Clarie's ear as he scurried up onto her head.

"Remember what Ahura said about Jesus," Clarie whispered. "Expect the unexpected."

Clarie smiled at seeing herself whispering to Nigel. "How well I remember that day. Andrew was the very first disciple to meet Jesus. And he was the one who introduced Peter to Him."

"Indeed," Gillamon replied, touching another panel:

"Teacher, may I please go get my brother?" Andrew asked. "I want him to meet you."

"Of course," Jesus replied. "I'll be here until tomorrow."

Andrew got up quickly. "It can't wait until tomorrow. I'll be right back!" He ran off down the road, leaving Jesus there with John and Gillamon.

Andrew ran to the tent where he and his brother were staying. There he found Simon lying on his mat, with his eyes closed. Simon was a big man, with wild, curly, black hair, and dirt all over his deep red tunic.

"Simon, get up!" Andrew said, kicking his brother's foot.

Simon opened his eyes and kicked Andrew back forcefully in the shin. "What is it?!" he scowled, scratching his thick black beard.

"Ow!" Andrew rubbed his shin, and squatted down next to Simon. "We've found Messiah!"

Simon's scowl turned into a look of surprise. Andrew grabbed his hand and pulled Simon to his feet. "Come on, get up! Come and see!"

"Do you remember what Jesus told Andrew when he called him to be one of the twelve disciples?" Gillamon asked, touching another panel later in time.

"Andrew, you appreciate the value of a single soul," Jesus smiled and said with his hand on Andrew's shoulder. "You pay attention to people and details, and were the first to introduce me to your brother Peter."

"Nothing escaped Andrew's attention," Clarie recounted, smiling at the dear apostle. "That's why he was able to spot the little boy with the lunch. Of course, Al helped him." Gillamon chuckled while touching another panel.

Al was now climbing all over the little boy, pawing at his knapsack. The boy's face was red from laughing so hard. Andrew squatted down next to them.

"Hi," Andrew said, pulling Al off the boy. "I see you have a lunch there. With our cat crawling all over you like this, I'll guess you have fish."

The little boy sat up and happily opened his pouch. "Yes, two fish, and I have some barley loaves, too." He reached in and eagerly grabbed a loaf. "Want some?"

Al meowed, reaching his paw up to the boy. *"O' COURSE I DO!"*

Andrew laughed, placing his hand on the boy's shoulder. "No, but I know someone who does. Can you come with me to see Jesus?"

"Sure!" the little boy answered eagerly, standing up. He took Andrew by the hand, and together they walked over to Jesus. Al was trailing along behind, staying close to the boy.

Andrew stood behind the little boy and placed his hands on the lad's shoulders. He wore a chagrined look on his face but offered, "Here is a boy with five small barley loaves and two small fish, but how far will they go among so many?"

Gillamon's smile faded, and his face grew solemn as he touched a panel much further in time. Peter was reading a letter. "Andrew was always faithful to do what Jesus asked, no matter the cost."

Tears welled up in Clarie's eyes. "I'll never forget that day."

To Peter: Greetings in Christ

Our Lord prepared us for the troubles we would face as we boldly shared the good news of his saving grace to a hostile world. He never promised us that we as the bearers of the good news would be triumphant—only that the gospel itself would be. The Enemy seeks our destruction, and to keep us from fulfilling the commands of Jesus to take the gospel to the ends of the earth.

You were with me when I lost my brother, James, early on in Jerusalem as the first of the twelve to be martyred for Christ. It grieves me to have to now share with you that your brother Andrew has been lost as well. After ministering in the far northern regions of Scythia, he was sentenced to death by the Roman governor of Patras in Achaia. Andrew did not wish to be executed in the same manner as our Lord, and requested a different cross. So they bound him with ropes to a decussate, or X-shaped, cross. He suffered a prolonged dying process, but ultimately we know he entered paradise with Jesus. I am certain my brother James immediately welcomed your brother Andrew there.

Please know that the brothers and sisters here in Ephesus are keeping you lifted in prayer as you receive this difficult news. Stay strong, Peter. May our Lord continue to bless you as you faithfully serve him in Rome. - JOHN

48

Peter sank to his knees and let the parchment fall from his hand onto the floor. He wrapped his arms around himself, weeping bitterly.

Gillamon lifted his chin and nodded with a resolute smile. "Andrew's reward was immediate, of course, as he indeed entered paradise. And the work he did was also rewarded here on Earth." He touched another panel some thirteen hundred years later. Scottish warriors dressed in kilts were cheering and waving blue flags with white X-shaped crosses. Robert the Bruce, king of Scotland, had just defeated Edward II of England at the Battle of Bannockburn.

"So Andrew became known as St. Andrew, and was chosen as the patron saint of Scotland. Scotland's flag bears Andrew's X-shaped cross," related Clarie, now smiling at the scene of Robert the Bruce celebrating their victory for independence. Max barked happily in the background, running around the proud Scots, who petted him as he wagged his tail and congratulated them. "Maximillian Braveheart the Bruce was happy that a Bruce became king of Scotland, especially on that victorious day for the Scots."

"Aye," Gillamon agreed with a chuckle. "And shortly after that victory came The Declaration of Arbroath, proclaiming Scotland's independence from Britain. Of course it was largely symbolic, but that declaration will have a big impact on Patrick Henry and others in the near future."

Clarie's eyes widened. "There are so many layers of history happening here, Gillamon! If only the humans realized the thread connecting Andrew, Scotland, and Patrick Henry."

"Perhaps some of them will, one day when scribes write of this history," Gillamon replied. "All of HIStory is related."

"Patrick is very much like Andrew. He's a fisherman, he follows Jesus, and nothing escapes his attention," Clarie noted.

"And one day, Patrick will also be the first one to speak up when it matters," Gillamon replied, looking at scenes of celebrations in Scotland and Virginia. "But for today, his family will join their fellow Scots to celebrate Scotland's national holiday: St. Andrew's Day." He pointed to a panel showing the town square of Hanover, Virginia. Down from the Hanover Courthouse was the Old Field where people were busily setting up tents, tables laden with food, and areas for contests and horse races. "We need to get ready ourselves, Clarie. Shall we?"

49

"Aye! A fun day awaits us all," Clarie enthused. She spotted John Henry steering the horses that pulled their family wagon. It was full of excited children and baskets of food.

"But no one will enjoy it more than Patrick," Gillamon said with a smile, putting his hoof into the scene.

The wind started to pick up around Clarie and Gillamon, swirling around them with such force that they began to change shape.

"Don't forget the black case!" Clarie shouted above the wind.

Gillamon nodded. "I have it in hand. After you, little one."

In an instant they were in Virginia, walking down the streets of Hanover.

Magical Meetings

Abundant sunshine took the chill off this late November Saturday. But the excitement, not to mention the piping hot food and drink, provided just as much warmth to the crowds milling about the Old Field in Hanover. Aromas filled the air with crackling fires used to roast savory chickens and sides of beef. Tent after tent covered tables overflowing with food from seemingly every kitchen in Virginia: ham biscuits, cheese wafers, corn pudding, three-bean relish, melon balls, spoon bread, curried shrimp, oyster fritters, plum pudding, roasted artichokes, brandied peaches, ploughman's pastry pies, sweet potato muffins, Sally Lunn bread, almond macaroons, cranberry-orange bread, lemon tartlets, gingerbread, apple pies, pumpkin pies, and cherry pies. Mugs were filled to the brim with cider, ale, rum punch, and wassail, and were lifted high and often in toasts to St. Andrew, to Scotland, to King George, and to the bountiful harvest celebrated by this cheerful community of Scottish immigrants.

"It's a good thing Al ain't here for St. Andrew's Day," Max said as he, Liz, and Nigel jumped off the back of the Henry wagon. "I don't think the lad could survive tastin' even jest one bite of everythin' here."

"Right you are, old boy." Nigel breathed in the aromas and wiggled his whiskers. "It's quite the tantalizing cornucopia of delicious offerings. No doubt Al would become as miserable as on the day Andrew discovered the boy's lunch of loaves and fishes. It's surprising that the disciples even had twelve baskets of leftovers with Al in attendance at *that* banquet."

Liz smiled at the memory. "That was a magical day, no? Andrew was the 'founder of the feast,' so to speak. And today, our very same Andrew is celebrated here on the other side of the world with *this* feast."

"I'm pr-r-roud that me homeland of Scotland adopted the lad as their favorite saint," Max added happily, gazing up at the flag of Scotland bearing St. Andrew's cross, flapping in the breeze.

"Today will be a magical day, too," added a tall, middle-aged man dressed in the finery of a Tidewater gentleman. His breeches and coat were made from fine black silk, and he wore an elegant red waistcoat, white shirt, and a white ruffled cravat. His brown wig was well made, and tied back with a black silk ribbon. His black tricorn hat was adorned with gold piping, and his fine black shoes were adorned with gold buckles. He wore a magnificent red wool cloak that matched his waistcoat, and held a black carrying case. He leaned on a maple walking stick ornately carved with a mountain goat as the handle.

Max knew immediately who it was. "Gr-r-rand ta see ye, Gillamon! Ye be lookin' like a r-r-real gentleman."

"Why thank you, Max," he replied, holding out his arms and bowing with a foot extended toward the little animal trio. "I thought I would become Tidewater gentry for this festive occasion."

"*Bonjour,* Gillamon. You look quite handsome. Is 'Lady Clarie' with you?" Liz asked, looking around him.

51

"Of course," Clarie answered, coming up to them in a beautiful blue taffeta gown, white lace neckerchief, and apron. She wore a royal blue cloak, fashionable wide-brimmed hat, and white satin shoes. She wrapped her finger around the single brown curl dangling on her shoulder and smiled. "I thought I might be overdressed, but there are humans of all sorts here today, including the fanciest types."

Although St. Andrew's Day was celebrated by those of Scottish ancestry, people from all backgrounds came to enjoy the festival—the rich, middle class, poor, whites, blacks, and Indians. The common folk wore homespun clothes of linen and wool, frontiersmen wore buckskin pants and fringed coats made of deerhide, the wealthier class wore fancy suits and gowns made of silk, and the Indians wore colorful costumes adorned with beads and feathers. They arrived at the Old Field on foot, on horseback, in plain one-horse gigs, in large two-horse wagons, and in fancy enclosed carriages. The frontiersmen carried their guns, and the women carried babies and baskets of food. People greeted old friends and made new ones. Children ran around, filling the air with laughter.

"This is a happy day, of course, but what will make it magical, Gillamon?" Liz asked, watching Patrick helping to lift his little sisters down from the wagon.

"The humans have created fanciful myths about how young ladies can meet husbands at the St. Andrew's Day festival," Gillamon answered at seeing the young Henry girls giggling with laughter. "Let's just say that for this particular St. Andrew's celebration, myth may become reality for some. Magical meetings lie ahead today that will also impact young Patrick."

Liz followed his gaze. "Patrick has many little sisters who will need to someday find husbands, but they are much too young for this now, Gillamon! They are but children, no?"

"Too young to marry, but not too young to *meet*," Gillamon replied, leaning in with a wink. "Remember that for the Maker, all time is happening at once, so these humans may be children in our eyes, but the Maker already sees them as the adults they will become."

"I jest want ta see the r-r-races an' contests," Max enthused. "Patr-r-rick's been pr-r-racticin' with Sam for the footr-r-race. They agr-r-reed ta split the plate of gingerbread cakes if either of them wins."

"Jolly good fun ahead!" Nigel cheered. "I was reading in the *Virginia Gazette* this morning about the day's events and the brilliant prizes to be had: a splendid hunting saddle for the winner of a horse race, a fine hat to be boxed for, a pair of silver-buckled shoes to be wrestled for, a handsome pair of shoes to be danced for . . ."

"A fine pair of silk stockings to be given to the prettiest maiden . . ." Clarie interjected, twirling her curl.

"And a fine fiddle to be *played* for," Gillamon added, pulling out a beautiful violin from his black case to hold up for display on an empty table. He lifted Nigel from the ground so he could see. "Nigel, would you do me the honor of helping me judge the competition? No mice or men here have your experience of playing or can appreciate this fine instrument as can you."

Nigel's whiskers quivered with excitement as he walked around the violin. "What an exquisite specimen!" the little mouse exclaimed, running his paw along the wood. "Carved in the Flemish style, dark chestnut with brown over golden ground finish, an artificial flame exquisitely stained on the back." He then inspected the bow. "The bow is well made with the finest horsehair. Now for the violin strings. May I?" He leaned over and plucked the instrument, closing his eyes in delight at hearing its perfect pitch. "I say, if I weren't so small I would wish to enter the contest myself! Some lucky chap will go home happy today with this piece."

Clarie lifted Nigel's mouse-sized violin from her silk handbag. "Well, you can at least play along if you wish."

"Splendid! Thank you for bringing my violin, my dear," Nigel cheered, taking his tiny violin from Clarie. "This will take the biscuit to once more join in the musical revelry!"

Gillamon chuckled, pointing the bow toward the excited mouse. "Very well, Nigel. You can hide in the fold of my hat."

"Is this fiddle goin' ta somcone in particular?" Max asked.

"That will depend on the fiddlers," Gillamon said evasively with a grin. "But this violin and bow, as with Nigel's, were made with *special* parts. It is no ordinary fiddle."

Liz furrowed her brow. "Gillamon, I feel I have only 'fiddled' with Patrick's voice by teaching him to mimic the birds. You told me I am to lead him to find his voice for this mission. You said to think about Plutarch and that I would figure things out down to the letter, but I am at a loss, *mon ami.* Might you have a way to help me know what to do next?"

"There is always a way, Liz." Gillamon smiled tenderly at the curious cat and leaned over to softly pet her behind the ear. "As with learning to use any instrument, developing a voice takes time." He glanced over at the fiddle and then back at Liz. "But once the fiddler gets the hang of it, magical music will come forth."

Liz smiled and nodded. *"Merci. Je comprends."*

Just then John Henry came walking toward them with Patrick, William, and John Syme, Jr. Gillamon scooped Nigel up into his hat and stood up.

"Now what have I told ye that we Scots always need ta remember?" John stopped to ask the boys.

"Play hard!" Patrick answered first with a chuckle and a hand raised high.

John smiled and leaned in, mussing Patrick's hair. "Aye, after ye've *worked* hard."

"Never back off from a fight," William added.

"That'll serve ye well in the wrestling match today," encouraged John, putting William in a headlock as the boy laughed, gripping his father's arm.

"Never waste a penny, and always be fair in your dealings with others," John Syme added.

John Henry reached in his pocket and flipped a coin in the air toward his teenaged stepson. "Aye, I know ye'll spend this wisely for yer brothers."

John Syme gripped the coin and kissed his balled fist. "Thank you, Father!"

"Ye boys have a good time today. Patrick, run a good race. William, remember the Indian grip that your Uncle Langloo taught you. We'll all be there ta root ye on. Then I'll take John ta visit with some of the county men and attend the horse races. We'll all meet up later for the fiddling contest."

"You should enter that contest, Father," Patrick insisted. "The winner gets a new fiddle!"

"Not just *any* fiddle, young man," Gillamon pointed out. "*This* fiddle." Patrick's eyes widened as Gillamon held out the violin for him to touch.

"It's beautiful," Patrick said, running his hand along the wood. "I wish I had a fiddle, especially one like this."

54

"Good day, Sir. I don't believe we've had the pleasure," John said, bowing respectfully. "I'm John Henry and these are me sons, Patrick, William, and John Syme, Jr."

Gillamon returned the gesture. "A pleasure to make your acquaintance, Mr. Henry. I am Mr. Gillamon and this is my kin, Lady Clarie, recently from London, by way of northern Virginia. We've been invited to judge the fiddle competition and have brought this special violin from England as the prize."

Patrick remembered the letter. "Mr. *Gillamon?* Were you at the *Messiah* concert in London when the King stood?"

Gillamon and Clarie exchanged looks of feigned surprise. "Why, yes we were, young man. How ever did you know that?" Gillamon asked.

"Our cousin, David Henry, wrote to us about the concert, and mentioned your name. He said he sat next to you," Patrick explained happily. He studied Clarie's blue eyes and squinted. There was something familiar about her.

"My, what a small world indeed!" Gillamon exclaimed, sharing a wink with Max, who shook his head with a humorous chuckle. It never got old to play this game with humans.

"Extraordinary!" John exclaimed, putting his hands on Patrick's shoulders. "Patrick will have ta write David about meeting ye here, of all places. Mr. Gillamon, where are ye and Lady Clarie staying?"

"From here we must travel on to Williamsburg, leaving right after the fiddle competition," Gillamon explained, packing the violin back in its case. "In fact, I must go meet with my contact for that event."

"I see. Please know ye're always welcome if ye ever come ta Hanover again. We live nearby," John offered.

"On Studley Plantation," Clarie added, immediately blushing as she realized she was blowing her cover.

"Why, yes. How did you know?" John asked.

"Your reputation precedes you, of course! You are well regarded by those we've met here in Hanover," Clarie answered, giving a quick curtsy. Patrick cocked his head and studied her, noticing beads of sweat on her brow.

"Most kind, Lady Claric," John replied with a bow. "We will leave ye with it, and look forward ta seeing ye later this afternoon."

"Indeed, a pleasure to meet you all," Gillamon replied, tipping his hat before offering his arm to Clarie. "Shall we, my dear?"

55

As they walked off, Patrick noticed Clarie reaching down to pet Max and Liz. It was as if she knew them.

"Come on, Pat! Let's get ready for the footraces," came the voice of a boy four years older than Patrick. It was Samuel Meredith, Patrick's best friend. He was tall and lean, with light brown hair and dark brown eyes. He put a finger to his tricorn hat in greeting as he ran up to them. "Good day, Mr. Henry, William, John."

"Hi, Sam! I'm ready," Patrick answered. "See you later, Father."

"Good day, Samuel," John answered. "Ye boys run fast. We'll see ye at the race."

"Good luck, Pat!" William called. "You run for cakes while I wrestle for shoes."

"Good luck, Billy!" Pat called behind him in reply. Sam was running ahead of him. "Sam, wait up!"

The boys ran in the direction of the footrace being staged for boys in two categories, ages seven through ten and eleven through thirteen. Max and Liz followed after the boys.

And a shadowy figure hiding behind a tree followed after them as well.

LIFE LESSONS AND FIERY FIDDLING

"I think our chances are good to win, Pat," Sam said as the boys raced to a pile of pumpkins. He stopped and turned, seeing that Patrick lagged behind. He put his hands on his knees as he leaned over to catch his breath. "Sorry, Pat. I want to be warmed up for the race."

Patrick caught up to Sam, resting his hands on his hips to also catch his breath. "Well, my chances wouldn't be good against you, Sam! I sure am glad I'm racing against the younger boys."

Sam smiled and stood, putting his hand on Patrick's shoulder. "You always run faster than those boys at school! So do I, so I think our chances are good." Max and Liz came running up behind them. Nigel scurried behind a pumpkin. "They follow you everywhere, don't they?" Sam said with a laugh, squatting down to pet Max and Liz.

"Aye, they do," Patrick answered proudly. He looked over to see the crowds gathering to watch the first footrace. A man was showing the boys where to line up. "I better get over there." He spied his mother and the Henry girls standing near the front of the crowd. "Come on, Max and Liz, you and Sam can stand with Jane and the others."

"Aye!" Max barked happily as they trailed along behind. They went to stand over with Sarah and the girls. John Henry and the boys were making their way over as well.

"Do your best, Pat!" Sarah encouraged him, bouncing new little baby Lucy on her hip.

"I'll try, Mother," Patrick answered with a grin. He took off his hat and quickly handed it to Jane. "Hold this for me, little Jane?"

"Sure thing, Pat," Jane replied, taking his tricorn hat in hand. "Sallie and I are cheering you on!"

Jane had a little friend with her named Sarah Shelton, whom they all called "Sallie." Her family lived near the Henrys in a house named Rural Plains. Sallie had a pretty, round face that was framed by dark brown hair tucked into the white cap tied under her chin. The girls wore daisy-chain necklaces they had made.

"I hope you win," Sallie spoke up happily. Her deep brown eyes lit up with the excitement of the race set to begin.

Patrick winked at Jane and Sallie. "Thanks, girls." He ran over to the starting line and looked down the row of a dozen boys, all close to his age.

He knew some of the boys from school, but some were from out of town. One very thin boy named Jimmy didn't go to school, as he was from a poor family in the area who couldn't afford to send him to the common school. His father had been an indentured servant who worked the tobacco fields belonging to a wealthy farmer. Patrick met Jimmy one day on the road in front of Studley. He frequently rode with his father in the back of a cart carrying hogsheads of tobacco three miles north to Page's Warehouse on the Pamunkey River. From this grand Virginia river port, the tobacco was inspected and sent downriver on ships, eventually reaching the Chesapeake Bay and then crossing the Atlantic to England. Europe couldn't get enough of Virginia tobacco.

57

St. Andrew's Day was a day for setting work aside, when everyone could simply come and enjoy a day of fun. On this day, these boys who lined up to race were not rich or poor. They were just boys.

Patrick quickly assessed his competition and what he knew of their running speed. "Good luck, boys," he offered, catching Jimmy's eye with an affirming nod. Jimmy smiled back. Patrick planted his feet and spied the finish line where a man stood with a flag.

"I hope the lad wins!" Max told Liz and Nigel, who stayed hidden. *"R-r-run like the wind, Patr-r-rick!"* he barked.

"Hear, hear! We must cheer him on to victory!" Nigel exclaimed with his tiny paw raised high. "I dare say, the anticipation of this event reminds me of the thrill awaiting the chariot races in the Circus Maximus!"

Liz smiled to see Patrick's sisters and Sallie all holding hands as they excitedly jumped up and down.

"Here they go!" shouted Sam, as the racing judge lifted his hand to start the race. "Watch, Jane! Your brother will win this with no trouble at all!"

"Go, Pat, go!" Jane cheered.

With that, the man quickly lowered his arm, and the boys were off and running. Patrick sprinted ahead as the crowds broke out cheering. He stayed several yards ahead of the pack, when behind him he heard two of the boys arguing.

"Don't shove me!" shouted a small boy. It was Jimmy.

"Get out of my way, urchin!" replied the boy doing the shoving, a bully known by the name of Enoch. He pushed Jimmy hard enough to cause him to trip over his feet. Jimmy fell face first into the dusty path and had the wind knocked out of him.

Patrick heard Jimmy land with a grunt and looked back over his shoulder to see Enoch grin. The bully was closing the gap between them. In a split second, Patrick peeled back and ran to where Jimmy lay curled in a ball, gripping his stomach.

"Are you alright, Jimmy?" he asked, helping the boy sit up.

Jimmy nodded, wiping his eyes. "Just . . . hard . . . to breathe."

Patrick's face turned red, and he watched in anger as Enoch raced ahead of the other boys, reaching the finish line. The bully lifted his arms in victory.

Patrick fumed. "Come on, Jimmy. I'll help you." He helped Jimmy to his feet and walked him back over to the crowds.

"Thanks, Patrick," Jimmy said in a barely audible voice. "I hoped I could win."

Patrick clenched his jaw and patted him on the back. "You'll win next time, Jimmy." He knew that, for Jimmy, it wasn't just about winning a prize, but bringing home a food gift he could share with his family.

Jane, Sallie, and Sam came up to Patrick as he walked back over to join them.

"What happened?" Sam asked in surprise.

"Enoch made Jimmy trip and fall," Patrick explained. "He's no winner. He cheated."

Jane clenched her fists and shot an angry glance over to see Enoch strutting around. "Why, that no-good bully!"

Sam put his hand on Patrick's shoulder. "You're a good lad, Pat. I'll go win the next race for us both."

"Thanks, Sam," Patrick said with a nod.

As Sam turned to go run his race, Jane skipped along after him. "You can do it, Sam!"

Sallie stood behind a moment and smiled at Patrick. She didn't say a word, but removed the daisy chain necklace around her neck and slipped it over Patrick's head before quickly darting off to go rejoin her family, who were leaving the field.

"Thanks, Sallie," Patrick called after her, smiling at Sallie's kind gesture. He had forfeited the race and the prize to help the underdog, but had received a garland of victory from the little girl.

The man judging the race hadn't seen what happened. He handed Enoch the gingerbread cookies. Enoch bit into one and smiled, carrying his prize off the field to keep all for himself.

But the shadowy figure stood camouflaged behind a row of trees. And he had seen everything.

———

"Fiddlers! Time to take the stage!" shouted the man organizing the fiddle competition. A huge crowd was gathered around the wooden stage for the most popular event of the day. There on the table was the beautiful violin Gillamon had brought as the prize for the best fiddler. Gillamon and Clarie sat together behind the table, scanning the crowds. People were celebrating with great merriment. It had been a wonderful day.

59

Patrick threw his head back laughing as he walked along with his family, who praised him for his gallant effort of helping little Jimmy during the race. All was well now. Sam had indeed won his race, and they feasted on the gingerbread cookies, sharing them with everyone, including Jimmy. William sported his new silver-buckled shoes after winning the wresting competition for his age group. The Henry boys took care of their little sisters and they gathered near the stage, eager to see who would win the prized fiddle.

Max and Liz jumped up onto a stack of barrels so they could see the stage. While the humans watched the big fiddlers, Max and Liz would be watching the tiny fiddler sitting in Gillamon's hat. Liz smiled as Nigel waved his bow once he spotted them.

"Mousie's got his fiddle, I see," observed Max with a big grin.

"*Oui,* Nigel is the happiest mouse in Hanover today," Liz told him. She blew a kiss to Nigel, who bowed in reply.

A group of nineteen fiddlers were gathered at the base of the stage, one shy of the maximum allowed in the contest. The man conducting the event announced the rules. "Each fiddler will get to play one song, and our judge, Mr. Gillamon, will be awarding the prize to the best player based on both skill *and* the applause of the crowd. After the prize fiddle is awarded, the winner will play a tune for the crowd to end this St. Andrew's Day! So enjoy the music, dance a jig, and cheer on your favorite fiddler!"

With that, the crowd erupted in cheers! The first fiddler stepped up onto the stage and stomped his foot four times to set the rhythm before he broke into playing a lively Scottish tune. Men kicked up their heels and grabbed partners, as the crowd started dancing to the contagious highland music. Others shouted from their seats on wooden barrels and clinked pewter mugs of ale, while others clapped in time with the fiddler. It was impossible to remain still with the Celtic tunes of Scotland filling the air.

Patrick danced around, kicking up his heels as his sisters clapped their hands in time to the music. One at a time he'd grab a sister by the hands and twirl her around in a lively jig. Max wagged his tail and "barked" his applause, Liz bobbed her head, and Clarie clapped her hands. Gillamon tapped his foot in rhythm while keeping a roving eye on the audience, as Nigel played along in Gillamon's hat.

A few of the fiddlers soon stood out as crowd favorites. Nigel gave a running report to Gillamon on the performances he deemed most worthy.

As the final fiddler finished his performance, the man announcing the competition held up his hands to quiet the crowd. "Do we have a winner?" he shouted with a broad smile, holding his hands wide.

"Not yet!" came a bellowing voice from the back of the crowd. A big, burly man with a thick, scruffy beard parted the crowd, as he held a fiddle high above his head. He was dressed in the rugged attire of a frontiersman, and people murmured and cleared a path for him as he walked toward the stage. The fringe on the man's caramel-colored buckskin shirt dangled from his outstretched arm, and a black, broad-brimmed hat was pulled low over his eyes. His large boots echoed heavily on the wooden steps as he climbed to the stage. The man running the event stepped aside and the mystery fiddler nodded to him and to Gillamon.

Immediately the man put the fiddle under his chin and stomped out the rhythm to set the pace for the liveliest tune anyone had yet heard. His bow blazed across the fiddle with such speed that soon it began to shred, its horse hairs sticking out in all directions. The crowd was spellbound, clapping out the energetic rhythm as this fiery fiddler caused their spirits to soar all the way to Scotland and back. No one even danced. All they wanted to do was focus on the magic of this moment.

Nigel's mouth hung open, and he held his violin down by his side, unable to keep up with the fiddler. Gillamon shared a knowing look with Clarie and clapped along with the crowd. Max and Liz looked at one another in amazement. And Patrick Henry thought he had died and gone to heaven to hear such playing. He stood on tiptoe to try to get a glimpse of the fiddlemaster, but it was hard to see him with the people crammed together in front. He studied the reaction of the people and their expressions of frenzied delight. The scene of a crowd set ablaze was immediately pressed onto his mind.

When the fiddler pulled his frayed bow across the strings of his fiddle for the final note, the crowd erupted with whooping and hollering, cheers, and wild applause. The man overseeing the competition held up his hands and shouted, "I think *now* we have a winner! Mr. Gillamon, do you agree?"

Gillamon stood and straightened his waistcoat and murmured under his breath, "Nigel? What say you?"

61

"There simply IS no contest, old boy! This fiery fiddler takes the biscuit and *then* some! Bravo, I say, bravo!" Nigel cheered, ducking under the folds of Gillamon's hat.

"I'm glad to hear it, Nigel." Gillamon lifted the violin and bow from the case and bowed, handing it to the mystery fiddler. Gillamon locked eyes with the man he had been expecting. "Congratulations, Sir. The prize is yours."

The man set his fiddle and frayed bow on the table to take the prize fiddle and bow in hand. "I'm much obliged, sir." He turned and held the prize up in the air to the raucous applause and cheers of the audience.

"Play 'Strip the Willow'!" called out someone in the crowd. Immediately the crowd echoed the request and divided into two rows to dance the favorite Scottish country reel.

The man lifted the brim of his hat and pointed the bow right to Patrick Henry. "This is for you, Pat! Let me break in this fiddle for you."

Patrick's eyes got as wide as gingerbread cakes when he finally recognized the mystery fiddler. "Uncle Langloo!" he exclaimed. It was his mother's beloved brother, who would disappear for six months out of the year to go hunt deer and live in the rugged mountains with the Indians. Patrick had hoped to see him for his birthday back in May, but the elusive uncle never showed. While Patrick was named for his Uncle Patrick, William was named for this uncle, William "Langloo" Winston. But Patrick and this uncle shared a love for the freedom of exploring the adventurous outdoors that gave them a special bond.

Uncle Langloo tore into the new fiddle, igniting the crowd by honoring their request. He stomped his foot and played "Strip the Willow" while couples danced the country reel in front of the stage.

"Mother! Did you hear that? Uncle Langloo won that fiddle and is giving it to *me!*" Patrick shouted in disbelief above the noise of the crowd.

"I'm happy for you, Pat!" Sarah hugged Patrick and laughed with joy, shaking her head good-humoredly, as Langloo stomped his foot at the edge of the stage, playing with a big grin while winking at her and Patrick. "That's my brother Bill!"

When the song was over, Patrick ran to the steps, and Langloo enveloped his nephew in a smothering hug. "Hi there, Pat. I may be late but here you go. Happy birthday!"

Patrick took the fiddle in hand with a look of awe and inexpressible delight. "I can't believe it! Thank you, Uncle Langloo!"

"You deserve it, lad. I saw the good you did out there in that race today," Langloo told him with a broad smile. "Never forget the lesson of doing the *right* thing even at the expense of getting a temporary *good* thing. You stuck up for that boy, putting him ahead of yourself, and he'll never forget it."

Patrick tightened his mouth and nodded. "Thanks, Uncle. I couldn't leave him in the dirt like that."

"He's not the only one who'll never forget your good deed," added Langloo, touching Sallie's victory garland still around the boy's neck. "I hear you got a musket for your birthday. When you're a little older I'll take you hunting with me in the wilderness. I'll show you how to play your fiddle and shoot your gun." He leaned in close and looked his nephew in the eye. "In addition to doing the right thing, those are two of the most important things a man needs—a fiddle to woo a lass, and a gun to provide for her and protect her with." He gave Patrick a hearty wink.

Patrick threw his head back laughing. "Thanks, Uncle Langloo! I can't wait to go with you!" Together they turned to join Sarah, John, and the rest of the Henrys, who celebrated Patrick's prize and the joyous reunion with their favorite uncle.

Max and Liz shared a grin and looked over to see Gillamon give them a bow and a wink. "Gillamon knew all along who'd end up with the fier-r-ry fiddle," Max told Liz.

Liz studied Patrick fondly, smiling at his good fortune on this day of magical meetings, life lessons, and fiery fiddles. *"Oui,* and I believe Gillamon also knows about other prizes my Henry appears to have won today. But I wonder what Gillamon meant about this violin not being an ordinary fiddle."

"I guess we'll soon find out," Max replied.

FIDDLE A RIDDLE

Max, Liz, and Nigel sat together by the hearth of the Henry home. The family had gone to bed after enjoying a lively time with Patrick playing on his fiddle. His little sisters laughed and danced around the room until they were exhausted.

"The lad's impr-r-rovin' all the time, I have ta give him that," commented Max, rolling over onto his back for a good stretch.

"Yes, but how I wish I could personally instruct him as I once instructed my blind harp student, Benipe, back in Egypt," Nigel remembered with a sigh. "Young Patrick could truly make even greater progress under my tutelage. Then again, my expertise lies more with the violin."

"*Oui,* but Rome was not built in a day," Liz reminded the mouse, running her paw along the beautiful wood of Patrick's fiddle. He had left it sitting on a stool by the hearth. "Neither is the fiddle mastered in a day."

Nigel walked across the wood, wiping off smudges here and there. "I wish I could play this beautiful instrument myself."

Max wrinkled his brow and rolled over onto his belly. "I've been meanin' ta ask aboot this. Wha's the difference between a violin an' a fiddle anyway?"

"Absolutely *nothing,* I assure you!" Nigel exclaimed. "It is quite the misunderstood terminology. 'Violin' and 'fiddle' both refer to the same instrument; however, the type of *music* played determines what the instrument is called."

"Scottish folk music is an example of 'fiddle music,' as it is played in an informal setting and usually by common, everyday humans," Liz explained. "Fiddle music is livelier, and serves well for country dancing."

Nigel nodded eagerly in agreement, clasping his paws behind his back. "Yes, yes, yes, whereas the *baroque* music of Mr. Handel is an example of 'violin music.' It is much more refined and appropriate for formal concerts."

"Kind of like the difference between the fun Scots and the stuffy Tidewater types, aye," Max replied. "I'll take the fiddle music over that br-r-roke violin music any day."

"That's *'baroque,'* not 'broke,' old boy," Nigel corrected him as he adjusted his spectacles.

"I knew wha' I were sayin', Mousie," Max said with a grin. "Either way, I think the lad is gettin' the hang of playin' his fiddle."

Liz's ears perked up and began to tingle. "What did you say, Max?" Her tail swished back and forth quickly. "Something is coming."

"What do you mean, dear girl?" Nigel asked as he took hold of the fiddle's tuning pegs.

"Gillamon said, 'Once the fiddler gets the hang of it, magical music will come forth' . . ." Liz started to say before quickly catching her breath. She now felt a tingling sensation all over.

Max's fur rose on end and he stood up, a low growl rumbling in the back of his throat as he looked around the room. "Somethin's here alr-r-right. I can feel it." The fur on Nigel's head stood straight up, and his eyes got wide as he held onto the fiddle's tuning pegs. "Mousie! Yer head looks like a tiny pineapple!"

A source of warm energy held on to Nigel's paws to the point he couldn't let go of the pegs. "I believe the 'something' is Patrick's fiddle!" Suddenly the fiddle began to glow with a golden hue, as if the red stain were on fire. Nigel's whiskers curled, and his back legs lifted off the stool as if he were in flight. He began to chuckle uncontrollably. "I'm quite unable to let go, but this is extraordinary!"

"I'll save ye, Mousie!" Max reached over and gently took Nigel's back paws into his teeth to free him from the fiddle, but then he also was lifted off the floor. The Scottie's wiry black fur stood on end, and he spoke through clamped teeth. "So this is wha' flyin' feels like! No wonder ye like it, Mousie!"

Liz's eyes glowed and widened to watch this unusual phenomenon. All she could do was laugh at the hilarious sight: Nigel holding onto the tuning pegs while flying in mid-air, and Max clamped onto his back feet, also flying with his legs behind him, but unable to let go. The fur

65

on both of their heads stood on end. *"C'est incredible!* I do not know exactly what to do at the moment!"

"Perhaps use the bow!" Nigel chuckled. "See if it will somehow break the energy force!"

Liz picked up the bow and pulled it across the strings, playing a discordant set of notes. Immediately Max and Nigel fell to the floor, as whatever held them suspended from the fiddle suddenly let go. The three friends quickly huddled together to see an inexplicable thing. The notes Liz had played became physical, black musical notes floating in the air above Patrick's fiddle.

The musical notes magically grew larger, and glowing words appeared inside them:

Good evening, little ones.

Max, Liz, and Nigel looked at one another in stunned silence, mesmerized by the floating, glowing musical notes. After a moment the notes rose to the ceiling and evaporated without a trace.

"Gillamon, ye weren't lyin'!" Max exclaimed. "This ain't no ordinary fiddle!"

"Bonsoir, Gillamon!" Liz exclaimed, in awe of what was happening. But there was no response. The violin sat there glowing but no more notes appeared.

Nigel scurried around the violin, careful not to touch the tuning pegs. "This is extraordinary! I believe we must use the bow to produce the magical message-bearing notes."

"Oui, but we may wake the humans," Liz cautioned him. "Nigel, what if you used *your* bow? I believe it would make a much softer sound."

"Brilliant!" Nigel answered before scurrying into his hole in the corner of the room. A moment later he returned with his violin bow. He jumped up onto the fiddle, but then hesitated, looking back at Max and Liz.

Liz lifted a paw and whispered. "Gently, *mon ami."*

The little mouse nodded and carefully lowered his bow to a single string. He squinted as if expecting another flow of power, then slowly pulled his bow across the string. Magically, a series of notes rose from the violin into the air, once more filled with glowing words:

Now you're getting the hang of it, Nigel. Keep playing.

"This takes the biscuit, old boy!" Nigel exclaimed, as he continued to slowly pull his bow across Patrick's fiddle. "I don't think we've ever seen anything like this."

"Actually we kinda have, Mousie," Max recalled. "Wha' aboot Gillamon's talkin' scr-r-roll back durin' the Isaiah mission?"

Nigel's eyes widened. "By Jove, you're right. Words also magically appeared on that scroll. And sometimes they became talking or musical words. Good show of remembering, old boy!"

"Gillamon, is it time to help Patrick truly find his voice?" Liz asked. "You said I would figure things out 'down to the letter,' but I never imagined musical notes. I thought David Henry's letter was what you meant."

It has always been time, Liz.
There are many layers of meaning for you to discover.
David's letter was just the beginning.

"If I may, musical notes *are* indeed letters," Nigel interjected. "A, B, C, and so forth."

Liz nodded. "*Bien sûr,* this is true, *mon ami.*"

Nigel continued to draw his bow across Patrick's fiddle and a stream of notes emerged:

Heed the fiddle's riddle.
Once these things take place, Patrick's voice
will be forever etched in history.
When you've reached the end, something new will begin.

"Hang on playin' for a minute, Mousie," Max suggested, turning to Liz. "Ye better wr-r-rite this down, lass."

"*Oui,* down to the letter!" Liz exclaimed. "*Un moment.*" She ran over to John Henry's desk to look for a blank piece of paper.

Nigel ceased playing, and the notes stopped coming from the fiddle. "This is terribly thrilling!" he told Max.

Liz dipped a quill in the inkwell. "I am ready. Please proceed, Nigel."

"Right!" Nigel resumed his playing, and the word-filled notes drifted into the air once more, disappearing once they reached the ceiling.

A voice in the wilderness,
A voice in the past,
A voice in the present wakes eternity en masse.
A voice in the tavern,
A voice in the court,
A voice in the house makes seven words, two short.

A voice that is hungry,
A voice unified,
A voice that is dying on the out- and inside.
Despair not the tragic, each pain is a key
To unlock the next door for the voice to be free.

Liz hurriedly wrote down each letter of the riddle as fast as she could before the notes dissolved into thin air. After the last words of the riddle disappeared, the notes ceased and the fiddle stopped glowing.

"Do you believe it is safe for me to stop?" Nigel asked, continuing to draw his bow across the strings.

"Aye. Gillamon's gone then, Mousie," Max replied with a grin. "Looks like you're gettin' the hang of playin' the fiddle, too."

"I never knew I had it in me," the little mouse replied, preening his whiskers. "That was quite an unexpected tune."

Liz jumped down from the desk and brought the riddle over for Max and Nigel to read. She wrinkled her brow as she studied the fiddle's riddle. "An unexpected tune with unexpected notes. At least now we have clues to guide us more specifically on this mission."

68

"Wha's first, Liz?" Max asked.

Liz studied Patrick's now silent fiddle. "There is always more than meets the eye, or in this case, meets the ear. Nigel, what was it you said about notes?"

"Do you mean my referring to notes as letters? A, B, C, *etcetera*," Nigel answered.

Liz smiled. "If I am going to figure this out down to the letter, then that is where we must begin—where letters are taught."

Liz and Nigel sat on the schoolmaster's desk of the one-room common schoolhouse early the next morning. They arrived before the humans so they could hide in the rafters and observe the classroom. The school was built with rough-hewn logs and furnished simply with this desk for the teacher and hard, backless benches for the students. A woodburning stove sat in the corner but was thankfully no longer needed since the warmer days of spring had arrived. But with the warmer weather came the increasing challenge to keep Patrick Henry's attention. He wanted to be anywhere but here. With summer approaching, parents needed their children home to help with the tobacco crops and other chores. Patrick was tasked with picking worms off the underside of tobacco leaves, which he much preferred to sitting on an uncomfortable bench inside this schoolhouse for seven hours.

The schoolmaster did little more than have the students memorize and recite segments of *The New England Primer*. While it was an excellent resource to teach ABCs, reading, writing, and sound moral and religious principles, it lacked the depth of knowledge Liz sought for her pupil. The children also were taught basic counting but, to Liz, such math was too simple. Patrick was put in a room with twenty to thirty other students, depending on whether families needed their children home to do chores on any given day. Children ranged from ages five to fifteen, with the youngest students sitting in the front and the oldest students sitting in the back of the classroom. That put Patrick right in the middle. He always tried to get a seat on the end of the bench so he could at least look out the window. He would watch for birds, wishing he were out soaring with them, or at least talking with them.

"Patrick needs lessons that will make him *think*, not just lessons to recite," opined Liz, her tail swishing back and forth. "My Henry will simply need more education beyond what is provided here, but he shows so little interest in school. I doubt that John Henry will think it worth sending Patrick to university in Scotland or even to the College of William and Mary in Williamsburg as do the gentry class, even if he could afford it."

"No wonder young Patrick drags his feet whilst coming to school," Nigel agreed. "I must admit I believe he would have preferred attending the school back in Egypt. At least he could have sat comfortably on the floor before the master. Ah, what a splendid school that was! Do you recall those days, my pet?"

Liz smiled. *"Bien sûr!* How could I forget them? That is where you taught me how to read and write in hieroglyphs, no? It is also where you first called me your 'teacher's pet,' *mon professeur."*

Nigel preened his whiskers, relishing the memory. "Quite right! You were the finest pupil I ever had." He gave a jolly chuckle and adjusted his spectacles as he turned his attention to *The New England Primer*, flipping through the pages of illustrated ABCs.

A   In ADAM'S Fall We sinned all.
B   Heaven to find; The Bible Mind.

C CHRIST crucify'd For sinners dy'd.

D The Deluge drown'd The Earth around.

E ELIJAH hid By Ravens fed.

F The judgment made FELIX afraid.

G As runs the Glass, Our Life doth pass.

H My Book and Heart Must never part.

J JOB feels the Rod,—Yet blesses GOD.

K Proud KORAH's troop Was swallowed up.

L LOT fled to Zoar, Saw fiery Shower On Sodom pour.

M MOSES was he Who Israel's Host Led thro' the Sea.

N NOAH did view The old world & new.

O Young OBADIAS, DAVID, JOSIAS, All were pious.

P PETER deny'd His Lord and cry'd.

Q Queen ESTHER sues And saves the Jews.

R Young pious RUTH, Left all for Truth.

S Young SAM'L dear, The Lord did fear.

T Young TIMOTHY Learnt sin to fly.

V VASHTI for Pride Was set aside.

W Whales in the Sea, GOD's Voice obey.

X XERXES did die, And so must I.

Y While youth do chear Death may be near.

Z ZACCHEUS he Did climb the Tree Our Lord to see.

"I find it quite surreal we had the privilege of working behind the scenes in the lives of nearly every one of these alphabetized Bible heroes, save Adam," Nigel remarked. He put his paw on Liz's shoulder. "Although I wasn't there, you, Max, Al, and Kate were indeed there for Noah."

Liz put her dainty paw on the 'N' phrase. *"Oui,* Noah did view the old world and new, as did we. That was the very beginning of our life's work for the Maker. So much has happened through time since then." Liz shook her head, scarcely able to take in the history she had experienced. *"Bon.* I am pleased to see the children at least learning their ABCs this way, no?"

"And three cheers for this 'Lesson for Children,'" Nigel said, pointing to the next part. "These pupils are receiving solid instruction on how to behave."

Pray to God. Call no ill names. Love God. Use no ill words.
Fear God. Tell no lies. Serve God.

Hate Lies. Take not God's Name in vain. Speak the Truth.
Spend your Time well.
Do not Swear. Love your School. Do not Steal. Mind your Book.
Cheat not in your play. Strive to learn. Play not with bad boys.
Be not a Dunce.

"You are right, *mon ami,*" Liz replied. "And I too appreciate these verses and instructions for the children." She pointed to the next section:

Good children must,
Fear God all day, Love Christ alway,
Parents obey, In secret pray,
No false thing say, Mind little play,
By no sin stray, Make no delay,
In doing good.

Our Saviour's Golden Rule.
BE you to others kind and true,
As you'd have others be to you:
And neither do nor say to men,
Whate'er you would not take again.

The Sum of the Ten Commandments.
WITH all thy soul love God above,
And as thyself thy neighbour love.

Learn these four lines by heart.
HAVE communion with few,
Be intimate with ONE,
Deal justly with all,
Speak evil of none.

"Quite the *superb* wisdom for children to absorb like little sponges," Nigel said. He pointed to another prayer written out for children. "I fear that while this is a comforting prayer for all children at bedtime, our young Patrick struggles *not* to quote it every day at school," he quipped with a chuckle.

Now I lay me down to take my sleep,
I pray the Lord my soul to keep,
If I should die before I wake,
I pray the Lord my soul to take.

71

"If Patrick could lay himself down to sleep in school, I am certain he would," Liz giggled. "These are all wonderful lessons and prayers for the children to learn. But where is the mathematics? The Latin? The Greek mythology and culture? The history of ancient Rome and its Republic?" Liz lamented.

"And Rome's emperors, including that horrid, cheeky beast, Nero?" Nigel added. "The nerve he had, fiddling while Rome burned!"

Liz's ears perked up. *Fiddling.*

Nigel sighed and paced about on the desk, lifting a paw in dramatic woe. "Oh, if only we were permitted to give young Patrick our *eyewitness* accounts of Rome's architectural marvels, the Greek tragedies performed in the grandeur of the theater of Ephesus, or the sublime writings of Plato, Socrates, Livy, and Plutarch!"

"Fiddling *with* Plutarch," Liz pondered, swishing her tail as she thought this through. "Patrick needs both. I think I know what the first two fiddle riddles mean."

"Brilliant! Do enlighten me, dear girl," Nigel urged, twirling his whiskers.

"Gillamon said Plutarch would be important for influencing Patrick's voice, so in order for Patrick to be influenced by Plutarch, he of course must *read* Plutarch," Liz explained. "If he is to have a voice that will change the world, he needs to know about the world out there to be changed. And what better teacher is there than history, especially the history of ancient Rome?"

"Ah, yes. *Historia vitae magistra;* history, the teacher of life. Indeed, there is much to learn from the good side of Rome, such as their brilliant ideas for government. But Patrick must also understand the dark side of Rome. The mighty Roman Empire was a formidable foe to the fledgling band of Christians out to change their world." Nigel held a finger up in the air. "But with the help of the Maker, the Christians persevered against tyranny and the impossible odds stacked against them!"

"*Exactement!*" Liz cheered. "John Henry received a stellar education at King's College back in Aberdeen, and he surely can pour his classical education in history into Patrick and William. I will arrange for John Henry to discontinue Patrick's studies here so he can instruct him at home. Of course, he will need the right set of books in his library, including *Plutarch's Lives.*"

"Brilliant idea, my dear. So that answers the 'voice from the past' riddle with Plutarch," Nigel enthused. "And the fiddling? Uncle Langloo did promise Patrick he would take him hunting and teach him how to play his prized fiddle when he was older."

"*Oui!* I believe that the 'voice in the wilderness' riddle means training time with Langloo," stated Liz. "I overheard Sarah say that Langloo was returning soon to Hanover for supplies. Such a trip into the wilderness will not only refresh Patrick's mind and spirit before introducing him to Plutarch, but I believe there are many lessons out there for him to learn."

Nigel preened his whiskers, approving of Liz's plan. "Jonathan Edwards recently said, 'It is God's manner of dealing with men, to lead them into a wilderness before he speaks comfortably to them.' As a boy Edwards loved to explore the wilderness, as does Patrick. He had an affinity for flying spiders of all things! But Reverend Edwards is right. Before the Maker uses His messengers, they always seem to require a time of wilderness training."

"This is true, no? We saw this firsthand in the wilderness with Moses, Paul, and, of course, Jesus Himself," Liz agreed. "*Bon.* I will make arrangements for John to teach Patrick at home. You and Max can go with Patrick and Uncle Langloo for the 'voice in the wilderness' part of the riddle."

"Splendid. How do you propose to approach John Henry with your riddling suggestion?" Nigel asked.

Liz gave a coy grin. "By fiddling with my preferred instrument, of course—an anonymous letter."

A Voice in the Wilderness

P atrick opened his mouth to speak but Uncle Langloo quickly silenced him, holding a finger to his mouth. The big man then slowly lowered his hand to the musket leaning against his leg, closed his eyes, and listened. They were crouched down, hiding behind a dense thicket of green brush, in the shady cover of the canopy of hardwood trees. Beyond them was a babbling creek, and all around them the forest was alive with activity. A mosquito buzzed around Patrick's ear, and he slapped his neck to kill it, frowning as he looked at his fingers. The mosquito had drawn first blood.

Patrick wiped his hand on his brown breeches and watched his uncle intently. He had quickly learned there was always a reason for even the smallest actions his uncle made. Since Langloo spent so much time with the Indians, he had learned how to stealthily blend in with the forest. He knew what he was doing, and was well equipped to protect them. On his belt Langloo carried a hunting knife and a hatchet. Draped over his shoulder were a carved powder horn and a leather satchel. For a week now he had taught Patrick how to load and fire his gun. *Always keep your powder dry and your gun loaded and at the ready at night, Pat.*

They hunted deer, wild turkey, and even possum. Langloo taught Patrick how to clean and prepare their kill, how to build a fire, make a shelter, and even how to make a delicious stew with the meat and some vegetables they brought with them. They slept out under the stars, listening to the owls and the tree frogs. Uncle Langloo told Patrick endless stories of his adventures in the wilderness. He taught him how to tell a good joke, and of course taught him how to play his fiddle. Patrick had never been so happy or had more fun. He didn't want this adventure to ever end.

Patrick looked at Max, smiled, and put his finger up to his mouth as had Uncle Langloo. They could hear the distant call of a crow getting closer. Soon it was joined by calls from other crows, all drawing nearer and varying in pitch and sound. Suddenly one of the crows belted out a staccato of caws. Langloo opened his eyes, touched Patrick on the leg, and softly said, "That's an alarm. There's a predator nearby. Come with me."

"Aye, I can smell it," Max growled.

Patrick's heart started pounding and he swallowed hard as he picked up his gun and followed his uncle down the path. Max stayed at his heels to guard from any threats behind them. Langloo kept his gaze on the path as they slowly crept along. They came to a patch of disturbed leaves in the mud. Langloo squatted down, taking a stick to clear away the leaves. "What do you see?"

The young boy leaned over and saw animal tracks in the mud. "Looks like a deer with those two toe tracks."

"Not a deer, lad," Max growled, peering over the tracks with his large head in the way. Patrick smiled and mussed Max's head to get him to move.

Langloo took a stick and pointed to the outsides of the tracks. "Good guess, but not quite. See how these tracks are blunt and rounded? Deer tracks are sharp and pointed. This is a wild boar. Pay attention to the smallest details to identify things correctly."

"I see," Patrick replied, studying the tracks. "The smallest details make the difference."

His uncle walked on, searching for what he suspected might be in the area. Soon he stopped again and knelt down. This time there were two sets of tracks. "What do you see?"

Patrick took his time and studied the tracks in detail. He wrinkled his forehead and pursed his lips as he thought about his answer. He wanted to get it right. "I think this time it *is* a deer. Its hooves are sharp and pointed."

"Very good, Pat. What about the other ones?" Langloo quizzed him, pointing to the other set of tracks.

"It looks like Max's paw prints. Is it a dog?" Patrick asked, petting Max. "Are those your prints, boy?"

Langloo smiled. "At first glance it does look like Max's paw prints, but let me show you why it isn't a dog. Do you see claw marks anywhere on top of the four small toe prints?"

"No, just the paw pad marks," Patrick answered.

"Dogs can't retract their claws when they walk, so their toenails make a mark," Langloo explained, pointing to the track in the mud. Max walked over and made some fresh prints in the mud to illustrate. "There, now you can compare this one with Max's print. See the difference? Look at the shape of his large back heel toe. Now look at the mystery paw print. See how the top of it is squared off, and the bottom of it has three rounded lobes? Max's heel toe is rounded like an arch at the top and doesn't have three rounded lobes on the bottom."

"Yes, I see it clear as day! So it's not a dog," Patrick answered. *"Cats* can retract their claws when they walk. Is it a cat?"

Langloo nodded. "A *big* cat. It's a panther and it's tracking that deer. The alarm caw of the crow back there could have been signaling that this panther was on the ground. Or it could have meant there was a predator in the sky, like an eagle. Crows have at least twenty different calls, so as you study them, try to see whether they are talking about on the ground or in the air." He stood up and wrinkled his brow, looking around them. "One thing is for sure. That panther is nearby."

"Aye, he's aboot fifty yards away," Max barked, bristling his fur on alert and looking in the direction of the big cat.

"I think Max can smell it," Patrick said nervously, also looking around. "Should we try to hunt it down?"

"No. Never provoke or kill one of God's creatures unless it's for food, but always be ready to defend against attack," Langloo replied. "That cat doesn't want to mess with us, so let him be. Just the same, stay close to me and let's head back to camp. We need to get the fire going before sundown."

As the humans walked away, Max turned his gaze up to the trees and nodded. Nigel waved from a tree branch where he sat with his crow friend named Harold who had agreed to be his transport for this hunting excursion. "Well done in sounding the alarm about the panther, old chap!" Nigel told the crow. "I'm quite relieved Patrick and his uncle have averted an untimely meeting with that hungry feline. Although Max is standing guard on the ground, it's best if he also can avoid tangling with the 'tiger.'"

"No problem, Nigel," Harold answered, fluttering his wings to stretch his feathers.

"Pardon me, but my 'crow' is a little rusty. Besides announcing the panther below, what was it you were telling your fellow birds of a feather whilst we were in flight?" Nigel asked.

"Oh, I had to explain to my friends why I had a mouse on my back so they wouldn't try to eat you," Harold answered. "We'll eat anything, you know, but since you're working for the Maker, you're off the hook."

Nigel grimaced and smiled nervously. "Yes, I see, very well. Thank you for preventing that most distressing scenario." He climbed onto the crow's back. "Shall we follow them back to camp?"

"Sure thing," Harold answered, taking off. "That panther is still around. Look down there. Nine o'clock."

Nigel looked down and saw a panther slinking through the woods but in the opposite direction of Langloo, Patrick, and Max. "Oh, dear. I do hope that big cat keeps walking the other way." He leaned over and patted the crow on the shoulder. "That's a good chap. Keep sounding the alarm."

While Langloo gathered dry wood, Patrick dug a fire pit about two feet square and one foot deep. He then took two heavy, forked sticks and stuck them in the ground on either side of the pit. Max brought him a third heavy stick that he placed on top of the forked sticks to finish their cooking rack. "Thanks, boy. That should do it." Patrick stepped back to wipe the sweat from his forehead. He then quickly slapped another mosquito that was about to bite him on the arm.

"Now that's one of God's creatures I think it's *alright* to kill whenever you see one," Langloo said with a laugh, dropping a pile of wood.

"I hate mosquitos," Patrick complained, examining his arm for bites. "But they must love me. Why did God have to make mosquitos?"

Langloo nodded, stacking the larger sticks in the fire pit, while Patrick placed some dry scrub brush and tiny dry twigs around them at the base. "I don't think mosquitos bit before man was tricked by that snake in the Garden. Otherwise, Eden wouldn't have been much of a paradise."

Patrick laughed. "Speaking of snakes, I keep expecting to see one in the firewood like the one that bit Paul. But I haven't seen one this entire trip."

"*Aye!*" Max barked. "*I were too late ta get the snake that bit Paul, but that'll never happen again on my watch.*" Little did Patrick and Langloo know that the reason they hadn't seen any snakes around their camp was that Max had gotten to all of them first.

Langloo smiled and took out some flint from his satchel. He struck it a few times to ignite a spark onto the scrub brush and carefully blew the small flame to get the fire going. "Nature doesn't appreciate us invading its territory. The Indians taught me that. They respect all of nature." The fire started to crackle and the inviting smell of the burning wood mixed with the scent of the pine trees around them. "The smoke will help keep those pesky mosquitos away." The burly man stood and pointed to the smoke mingling with the growing evening mist. "Always wait to build your fire until the mist comes so you won't give away your position to other unwanted pests—the *human* kind."

Patrick sat with his arms wrapped around his legs and watched the rising smoke. "That's really smart. Did the Indians teach you that, too?"

Langloo stoked the fire and added a few more sticks until it grew hotter. "Yes, they've taught me many things. They are an intelligent, ancient race of people and they were here in America long before the white man. There is much to learn from them. But before you can learn from them, you must earn their respect. Treat them well, and they will respond in kind."

"I thought they were all savages until you started telling me about them," Patrick confessed to his uncle, poking a stick into the fire. "I've heard the Indians have done terrible things to white men out on the frontier."

"That's the problem men have of judging people who are different from themselves based on the actions of a few who *have* acted like savages," replied Langloo, sitting down with a grunt next to Patrick. "If you don't take the time to see for yourself and get to know those different from you, you can't possibly understand them. It's easy to misjudge others. Worse yet, men make it *convenient* to misjudge sometimes. All men are capable of doing evil to others, no matter the color of their skin. That's one thing that makes all men equal. We're all fallen sinners and will bite others, just like the mosquitos."

Patrick nodded thoughtfully as he listened. "I've never thought about it that way. I've heard father and Uncle Patrick talk about how the rich Tidewater types don't understand the people out here on the frontier. They think we're not as good as them because we don't dress or act as they do," Patrick said.

"Aye, an' I bet those uppity breeches say they play the violin while ye only play the fiddle," Max grumbled.

Langloo chuckled softly and leaned in. "If you ask me, I think those fancy breeches types look silly with their powdered wigs and frilly shirts. I'd hate to live like they do, trying to impress people all the time with their social rules!" He held out his arms with his dangling fringed buckskin shirt. "I like the way *I* dress. I'm comfortable, and I can move easily out here in the forest. I'd like to see one of them fancy breeches try to survive one night out here in the woods!"

"I agree, Uncle! I don't care about all those fancy clothes." Patrick and Langloo shared a laugh. "But remember Mr. Gillamon, who brought my fiddle to the festival? I really liked his red cloak."

"Gillamon's the best dressed goat there ever were, lad!" Max cheered with a happy whine.

"Well, it's more important to be comfortable in your own *skin*," Langloo offered. "If you are confident about what you believe and think, men will care more about what you have to *say* than what you *wear*. But learn to appreciate the opinions and ways of others. You don't have to agree with them, but always hear them out. Earn their respect by trying to understand them. Then you'll earn the right to be heard. But be ready to back up why you believe the words you speak."

The fire popped, and sparks shot up into the air. Langloo and Patrick sat silently for a moment, staring at the fire. Patrick pondered all these things, slowly petting Max. Langloo stood up to put an iron hook on the cooking rack, and then hung a small cooking kettle full of hearty stew. He stirred the stew with a wooden spoon and then sat back down with Patrick.

"It's kind of like tracking," Patrick responded. "Every animal leaves its own mark that tells us about itself. But people leave their mark in how they act. That bully at the St. Andrew's Day race left a bad mark, so no one likes or respects him. No one would want to follow him anywhere. And I guess it's like how birds communicate, too. They have different voices that may sound like gibberish, but they really are saying something. If you want to understand what the crow is *saying*, you have to understand what he is *seeing*, is that right?"

Harold and Nigel sat listening in a tree above the campfire. "I have to give it to the boy. He's almost as smart as a crow," Harold cackled.

Nigel rolled his eyes and put his paw over the bird's beak. "Please allow me to hear Uncle Langloo's response, old boy," he whispered.

Langloo slapped his hand on his knee. "Exactly, Pat! Listen and learn about what is important to others. Pay attention to what makes people react so they will pay attention to you. Never lie or twist your words. Indians can *instantly* tell if someone's words and actions don't match. Always speak truthfully and honestly, even if it's not what others want to hear. But learn to persuade those who see things differently than you by touching their hearts as well as their minds." He handed Patrick the spoon. "But also keep *your* mind open to learn from others, as long as it doesn't go against what the Good Book teaches. There's a lot of different things in that stew, but when all those tastes come together, it makes for good eating." Langloo took a twig and put it into the fire to light his pipe. "There wouldn't be squash or corn in that stew if it weren't for the Indians teaching the white men how to grow it. Nor would there be tobacco in my pipe."

80

An' the Order of the Seven introduced the Indians ta the white men, Max thought with a wide grin. *Ye're welcome for the tasty stew then.*

Patrick stood up and slowly stirred the stew. Uncle Langloo had a way of explaining things that made sense. "Sometimes I don't know what to think about things. Father and Uncle Patrick think one way about the church, but mother and your father Isaac think another way. I love and respect all of them, but who's right?"

Langloo puffed on his pipe for a moment to think about his response. "Sometimes it's not that doing something is right or wrong, but *how* it's done that causes the most conflict. Just because people disagree about how things should be done doesn't mean they are any less passionate about it." He leaned forward on his knees and gestured with his pipe as he spoke. "Both sides of our family believe in Christ, but disagree about how to worship him. The Indians and the white men both love this land, but disagree about how to live off of it. Indians respect the forest and don't want the land cleared of trees. White men want to clear the trees so they can provide food and respectable homes for people. Indians think there is already plenty of food in the forest. The white man clears the land to then raise plants to feed cows, pigs, and chickens to then kill for food. To the Indians, the white man's way is wasted energy and work." He paused and took another puff from his pipe. "In order to find out what *you* believe, learn all you can about all sides of the issue. Educate yourself. Listen to others. Above all, ask the good Lord to guide you to the right course, and He will. But at the end of the day, you must find your own voice, Pat."

Max looked up to the trees and shared a grin with Nigel, who clapped his paws together. "Brilliant! This is just what we were hoping to hear!"

"I was hoping to hear them play the fiddle again," Harold crowed. "I like that music."

Patrick didn't answer his uncle, but lifted the spoon to taste the stew. He shook his head. "The stew's not ready yet. It needs more time to cook." He sat back down cross-legged next to Langloo, poking the fire with a stick.

"Kind of like your voice," Langloo chuckled warmly. "You're young, lad. That kettle voice of yours still needs lots of ingredients put into the pot. Give it time. Young Indian warriors have to do the same. And when they figure things out, they get rewarded. Let me show you something." He got up and walked over to his leather satchel. He took out a piece of cloth and unfolded it to reveal an eagle feather.

Patrick stood up, and Langloo put the feather into his hands. The boy held up the feather to examine it in the glowing light of the fire. "A real eagle feather!" He ran his fingers along the soft white quill tipped in brown. "There's an eagle's nest near the creek at Studley, but I've never got close enough to see a feather such as this."

"Indians revere the eagle above all creatures, and treat it with awe and respect. They believe that of all the birds, the Creator chose the Eagle to be the leader. It is the master of the sky because it can fly higher and see better than any other bird," Langloo explained. "They believe the eagle's perspective is different from that of any other creature because it stays close to the Creator in His realm of the sky."

"What a splendid analogy for any God-fearing creature!" Nigel enthused.

Harold made a gagging, cackling squawk. "We crows like it better closer to the ground where the action is. High flying makes us too dizzy in the head."

"Clearly," Nigel murmured under his breath.

"For Indians, to hold or wear an eagle feather, because they are hard to come by, causes the Creator to take notice of men," Langloo continued. "Whenever someone receives an eagle feather it means they are being shown gratitude, love, and the highest respect. Indians receive them for acts of bravery, but they can only be earned one at a time."

Patrick's eyes got wide. "One at a time? I've heard Indian chiefs have big headdresses *filled* with these feathers!"

Langloo nodded. "Yes, I once saw an old Indian chief who had won enough honors to have a double-trailed bonnet of feathers that reached the ground. An Indian would rather part with his horse or even his tee-pee than lose his eagle feathers. That would dishonor his tribe."

"How did you get this eagle feather, Uncle?" Patrick asked, in awe of the story. "Did you do something brave?"

Langloo smiled. "I helped some Indian friends defend their camp from an attacking tribe. You see, even the *Indians* fight between themselves! But this is what I want you to learn, Pat. Indians communicate their thoughts, their ideas, and their history through symbols such as this eagle feather. Sometimes such an object can say more than a book's worth of words."

Patrick pulled the eagle feather through his hand, as Langloo jumped up onto a stump, making sweeping gestures with his hands and speaking with a booming voice.

82

"The Indians also use hand motions to tell stories of their battles and victories. Act things out, Pat. And learn to project your voice to grab the attention of your listeners. Sometimes it's not just *what* you say, but *how* you say it," Langloo explained. He jumped down from the stump. "I have no doubt you will figure out both the 'what' and the 'how' with your voice and your actions someday."

Patrick wrapped his arms around Langloo for a hug. "Thank you, Uncle. I hope so." He handed the feather back to his uncle. "And I'd like to earn a feather one day as you did."

Langloo smiled and tapped the top of Patrick's head with the feather. "You will. But be patient as you grow up. The Good Book talks about eagles and waiting. Look it up sometime. And while you're waiting, study that eagle that lives nearby you. I'm sure he could teach you a thing or two."

Patrick smiled and nodded. "Yes, Sir. I'll do that."

"For now, let's eat," suggested Langloo, tasting the stew again. He tapped the spoon on the rim of the pot and then used it as an imaginary violin bow. "After supper you can play your fiddle for me and all the birds of the forest."

"If I play well enough, maybe an eagle will drop a feather to me as a reward," Patrick quipped.

Harold pulled out one of his feathers with his beak and tossed it in the air and shouted with a grating voice, "Here! Take one of mine!"

Nigel put a paw to his brow and shook his head at the annoying crow.

Uncle Langloo squinted with one eye. "You've gotten the hang of it, but you're still a little squeaky on that fiddle, Pat. Remember, some day you'll woo *lassies* with that fiddle." He gave his nephew a playful wink. "That alone will be a feather in your cap."

"Right, then. That will be all for tonight, my good fellow," Nigel said, patting Harold on the shoulder. "It's time for me to rejoin my colleague on the ground. Thank you for your assistance today, and especially for preventing your friends from ingesting me."

"Sure thing, Nigel. Anytime," Harold replied, flapping his wings to take off.

"Ta-ta," Nigel told the crow as he scurried down the tree. He joined Max by the fire to share some of the stew Patrick placed on the ground for his supper. "I thought I would try another bird for this wilderness excursion, but I doubt I will ever enlist a crow again."

Max snickered. "Aye, cr-r-rows may be smart, but they're obnoxious."

"Not to mention *dangerous*. They're a ravenous gang of thugs," Nigel answered. "Perhaps I should trade in my crow for an eagle. Our young Patrick was quite taken with the story of the eagle feather."

"Aye. It may be time ta finally meet that eagle in the woods near Studley," Max agreed.

"Splendid suggestion! Perhaps he would agree to become my new transport. With the height and speed eagles reach, I could cut my travel time in half when I depart for my journey up north to Philadelphia," Nigel replied. "But for local travel, I shall likely resume my traditional pigeon transports. It's quite easy to find a flight on a pigeon any hour of the day." The little mouse nibbled a carrot from the stew. "I think a dash of cumin or perhaps some minced garlic would add a bit more flavor to the stew, don't you agree?"

Max laughed at the little mouse. "Mousie, I think ye're more of a city mouse than a country mouse. City pigeons, flavored cookin', books, an' violins be more yer speed."

Nigel preened his whiskers and chuckled. "I quite agree, old boy.

But what do you make of our young Patrick? Do you think the 'voice in the wilderness' objective has been reached with this trip to the untamed frontier?"

Max stared at Patrick and grinned. "Aye. He's gotten ta str-r-retch his legs as well as his mind aboot wha' a voice should say, an' sometimes even *not* say. Now for the lad ta str-r-retch his mind. I'm sure Liz will have John Henry r-r-right where she wants him."

Nigel and Max looked at one another and exclaimed at the same time, "In the past!"

PLUTARCH'S NINE LIVES

Liz was in a deep sleep. Her eyes moved rapidly behind her eyelids, and her whiskers twitched. She was dreaming about an encounter she had with Gillamon in the IAMISPHERE long ago in Rome. It was July 4, AD 64, two weeks before Nero would fiddle while Rome burned. Liz was distraught about the animals locked up in the Circus Maximus. The Romans killed them for sport in their bloody games to entertain the masses. Gillamon was showing her panels in time that pertained to her mission, but once that was complete, she was then to go on mission to help a man by the name of Plutarch.

"I need to show you another leader whose conduct affected others in the past, but will also affect millions more in the future," Gillamon, touching another panel, told Liz. A man stood in the Roman Senate, talking for hours on end. "This is Cato the Younger. He was Julius Caesar's worst enemy."

"His worst enemy?" Liz wondered. "But he is dressed in a toga, not in a military uniform."

"Indeed. He opposed the policies of Julius Caesar, fighting to preserve the Roman Republic while Julius positioned himself to take over Rome as dictator. Cato's battlefield was for the freedom of the people, and he led them both in speech and militarily until his back was up against the wall in Utica. In fact, he was so passionate about his battle for freedom, that when surrender to Julius Caesar became unavoidable, Cato drew a sword and killed himself."

"You mean he chose death if he could not be free?" Liz

wondered, shaking her head as a scene of Cato drawing his sword swirled before them.

"Yes, for Cato, it was either liberty . . . or death," Gillamon answered. "Remember what you see here, for just as you've inspired Luke to write down the story of Jesus, you will need to inspire a man by the name of Plutarch to write down the story of Cato. He will also write about Alexander and many other men in history, and how their conduct affected the fate of all. But Liz, you must help these characters live forever in the pages of history when it comes time for Plutarch to pick up his pen. The voice of a future leader depends on it."

A clap of thunder shook the house and awakened Liz with a start. She sat up and looked around. The humans stayed asleep. Rain pelted the windows, and the wind boomed against the chimney. Liz's heart was racing, and her mind had to remember where she was. *Studley Plantation, Virginia, 1745. Patrick Henry.* The last words of Gillamon echoed in her mind. *The voice of a future leader depends on it.* Liz looked out the window. "The voice of my Henry depends on it," she said aloud to herself.

She had been sleeping in the alcove of a window and could see a spring storm sweeping through the trees. Drops of rain ran down the glass, and she slowly traced them with her paw as she thought out loud. "Gillamon's riddle: a voice in the past. At the beginning of this mission he said, *'In order to figure out the importance of the Libertas connection, you will first need to figure out the importance of the Plutarch connection.'*" Liz's eyelids began to get heavy again. She yawned, stretched out long and hard, closed her eyes, and leaned her head against the windowpane. As she started drifting back to sleep, another thought entered her mind. *Cato,* oui, *but with Gillamon there is always more than one connection.* Soon she was asleep, this time dreaming she was back in the Greek city of Chaeronea.

The wind was blowing furiously outside, but inside, the soft glow of the oil lamp danced off Liz's black fur as she gazed at the aging Greek historian, Plutarch. Spread across his desk were rolls of fresh parchment and scrolls of his work. Liz sat next to a miniature ivory statue of the Greek goddess Nike, or "Winged Victory," that also sat on his desk. Plutarch was hunched over, trying to finish the end of a sentence, but he was running out of ink. His pen was skipping across the bumpy parchment.

"I'll be back, my little muse," Plutarch said to Liz, scratching her under the chin affectionately. "I need to refill my inkwell once more. I have accomplished much today. With this last biography I now have eight lives in my book."

As Plutarch left his desk, Liz slipped a piece of parchment into his *Symposiac,* a record book of conversations with family and friends while sitting around the dinner table. He used this book, along with letters, speeches, and collected quotes, as resources to write about the lives of great heroes from history. Plutarch was starting a new genre of writing: biographies. But as he explained to his friends, *"My design is not to write Histories, but lives, and the most glorious exploits do not always furnish us with the clearest discoveries of virtue or vice in men; sometimes a matter of less moment, an expression or a jest, informs us better of their character and inclinations, than the most famous sieges, the greatest armaments, or the bloodiest battles whatsoever."*

87

Plutarch's credo was that a man's true character was revealed in his private life rather than in his public deeds. In his research he also discovered that men are defined by their most peculiar traits, so those were the very things he sought to uncover when writing life stories. He was out to show the *consequences* of men's actions, not so much the actions themselves. He wanted to inspire men to follow the good deeds of heroes, while urging them to avoid the bad deeds of history's villains. But all the while he cautioned that these biographies he wrote were dependent on the fallible memory of others: *"The true history of these events is hidden from us."*

Liz had supplied Plutarch with information on several characters including Alexander the Great, Demosthenes, Cicero, Pompey, Agis, Mark Antony, Julius Caesar, and Brutus. But now, she supplied the primary character for Plutarch per Gillamon: Cato the Younger. She stretched out long and hard with her front paws before her like the Sphinx. When she pulled herself up to stretch out her back leg, she accidentally hit the miniature statue of Winged Victory, sending it falling to the floor.

"Quel dommage!" Liz exclaimed as a piece of the statue broke when it hit the hard marble surface. She jumped off the desk and

sat among the broken pieces of ivory there on the floor. Plutarch came running back into the room, wondering about the crashing noise.

"Je suis désolée! *I have broken her wing!*" Liz meowed. Her face filled with sadness. She wrapped herself around Plutarch's legs. "It was an accident, *mon ami.*"

"Did you do this?" Plutarch frowned and squatted down next to her. "Ah well, I am to blame. This statue was too large to sit on my desk with everything else piled there." He sighed and picked up the ivory fragment of Nike's broken wing. "Some things do not last. Even victories. The large Winged Victory of Samothrace statue was carved after a victorious naval battle to remind the Greek warriors that victory is fleeting. Men must remain vigilant to protect what they have fought hard to win, or it will fly away." He furrowed his brow. "The Greeks learned that costly lesson when Rome overtook them." He gave Liz an affectionate pat and left the broken statue on the floor while he sat back down at his desk. He placed the ivory wing fragment next to his scrolls.

Liz sighed with relief and smiled at Plutarch. He had a gentle spirit and special affection for animals. He wrote, "The obligations of law and equity reach only to mankind, but kindness and beneficence should be extended to the creatures of every species."

"Merci, mon ami," Liz meowed, jumping back onto his desk where Nike once stood. *"I hope my accident will not distract you from your next writing assignment. Your ninth life must be Cato."*

Plutarch lifted his *Symposiac,* and out fell Liz's inserted paper. He cocked his head and started to read. His muttering lips moved as he read the quotations she had provided about Cato. He didn't question where he obtained this paper, for he had spent decades collecting documents such as this. Plutarch knew about Cato the Younger, having already written about his great-grandfather, Cato the Elder, but he was selective about who he chose to put into his book. He leaned forward, and a line on Liz's paper caught his attention. He read it out loud:

"When Cato had seen to the safety of his men, he knew Caesar was coming with his whole army to defeat him. But Cato felt that he had got the victory and had conquered Caesar in all points of justice and honesty. It was Caesar who ought to be looked upon as one surprised and vanquished; for he was now convicted and found guilty of those designs against his country, which he had so long practiced and so constantly denied." Plutarch continued to read Cato's story of how, in the end, he took his own life rather than be beholden to a tyrant for his acts of tyranny.

"Cato was the last, true citizen of Rome's Republic before it fell to a tyrant," Plutarch said, leaning back in his chair. Liz sat there staring at him with golden eyes, purring. He turned his gaze to her and then to the broken statue of Winged Victory on the floor. "Indeed, nothing lasts, not even the Republic of Rome. Cato will be the ninth character in my book."

"This was the plan, no?" Liz meowed with a coy grin.

Plutarch took out a fresh scroll and started writing:

CATO THE YOUNGER

THE family of Cato derived its first lustre from his great-grandfather Cato, whose virtue gained him such great reputation and authority among the Romans, as we have written in his life. This Cato was, by the loss of both his parents, left an orphan . . .

89

Liz smiled as Plutarch's pen took off in writing the story of Cato the Younger. While she studied what he wrote by the light of the oil lamp, she didn't see the pair of eyes peering in the window to study *her and Plutarch.* Suddenly another crash sounded, this time from outside.

"Now what?" Plutarch grumbled, scraping back his chair and getting up. Liz followed him outside to investigate.

There on the terrace was a broken Grecian clay urn with a pink oleander shrub sprawled out in the scattered dirt. Plutarch looked all around but didn't see anything that could have knocked the urn off the pedestal where it sat. He put his hands on his hips and shook his head. "More brokenness. Must have been a strong gust of wind. I'll have my servant tend to this later." He turned to go back inside and called back to Liz, "Stay away from that plant, little muse. It's beautiful for my terrace, but poisonous to cats."

"Oui, of course it is," Liz muttered, being an expert in flora. *"Nerium oleander,* in the dogbane family *Apocynaceae.* All its parts are toxic." Although it was dark, a swath of light escaped the open doorway. Liz was curious about how the oleander fell so she

walked around the fallen plant, careful not to touch it. Suddenly she spotted paw prints in the dirt on the terrace near the outside steps leading to the courtyard below. She furrowed her brow. *Some creature was just here.* Just as she walked over for a closer look, a gust of wind came up and scattered the dirt before she could identify the paw prints. Liz shielded her face from the blowing dirt, careful to not get any of the toxic oleander in her eyes.

BOOM! A crash of thunder woke Liz from her dream. She inhaled quickly and looked around the darkened room, remembering again where she was. The rain continued to pound the window, and an eerie feeling came over her. She shook her head, needing to clear her mind from these ancient dreams. "Perhaps something to read. I need to inspect John Henry's library for copies of *Plutarch's Lives.*"

Liz jumped down from the alcove and walked across the wooden floor. Lightning flashed, briefly lighting up the room from the window. She made her way over to a small bookshelf and traced her paw along the spines, reading the titles. *"Bon,* here we are. *Plutarch's Lives,* Volume 1. But where is Volume 2, which contains Cato the Younger?" She tipped Volume 1 forward from the shelf to see if perhaps the missing volume was behind it. When she did so, a folded note with a red seal fell onto the floor.

90

"What is this?" Liz asked herself. She read the outside of the note:

Your presence is requested at Kew Palace in London.

Then she looked at the seal. It was the signature red wax seal for the Order of the Seven. "This has been a strange night, no? Rome, Greece, and now London." She then smiled and licked her paw to brush back the fur on her face. "I must look my best for my love. I am coming, *cher* Albert."

Liz poised her open claw over the seven seal and swiped across the wax, disappearing from the room and into the IAMISPHERE.

A Tragedy in London

L iz walked through the green grass along the banks of the Thames, breathing in the fresh air and thinking about the long history she had with this river. She, Al, and Clarie had stood on the banks of the Thames when their Roman centurion, Armandus Antonius, was sent here to scope out the land, to collect engineering, trade and military intelligence, and to strengthen the bonds of the Rome-Britannia alliance. Liz smiled, recalling Armandus's words to Roman-appointed King Verica and a group of his tribesmen: *"My men and I have studied the water here and found it to be narrow enough to build a bridge, but deep enough for Roman ships to enter and make port."*

"If only you could see Londinium now, Armandus," Liz said out loud. "Your bridge made London not only the center of power of the Roman Empire in Britannia, but now the center of power for the entire world."

It was also here on the banks of the Thames ten years ago in 1735, that Liz, Al, and Nigel had begun their mission with George F. Handel. They stowed away on a boat at the Royal Palace of Hampton Court to follow the king's courier to deliver the bad news to Handel. King George II had passed him over as the new Master of the King's Musick. But that shattering disappointment was the open door they needed to eventually inspire his masterpiece, *Messiah*.

Liz gazed at the path leading into the beautiful gardens of Kew Palace. King George II and Queen Caroline had lived here early on in their reign, but preferred Kensington Palace in London or summers at Hampton Court Palace. Their oldest daughters Anne, Caroline, and Amelia now lived here at the red brick Kew Palace while their oldest son, Frederick, Prince of Wales, lived across in the White House on the palace grounds. Frederick and his father the king had a bitter falling out, so he kept his distance from the royal court at the other palaces. He was heir to the throne, but his father wished it otherwise.

Prince Frederick and Princess Augusta were happy at the White House here at Kew, enjoying country life and raising their many children, including their oldest son, George. Gillamon had said that George would someday be king, and Al's mission was to gather intelligence while living in the palace. As Liz walked along the fragrant path filled with colorful flowers of every variety imaginable, she sighed with delight for Al, yet wished she could be here with Al always. How she adored gardens! *Someday, cher Albert, we shall have another garden together. You must be so happy living here, without a care in the world in this garden paradise.*

Suddenly she heard Al screaming at the top of his lungs. "Albert!" she cried, starting to run in the direction of his voice. Soon she came upon a lush, green, open space, and there she saw Al being chased by a dog. She stopped in her tracks to assess the situation, but soon started to giggle. Al's short, pudgy legs took him as fast as they could. His pursuer's legs weren't much longer, although they were indeed fast. Al was being chased by a fawn and white-colored Corgi nipping at his heels. True to form for this Welsh herding dog, the Corgi was running in semicircles behind Al, nipping at him from side to side. Liz knew Al wasn't in danger. He was just being herded for sport.

Liz jumped up on a stone wall and sat there, amused at her mate. *This is good exercise, no?* she thought, as Al led the Corgi zigzagging across the grounds. When they came near, Liz cupped a paw to her mouth and shouted, "If only Henriette were here to rescue you, my love!" She hearkened back to the obnoxious French hen she assigned to protect Al from an angry Spanish bull who chased him on the way to Noah's Ark.

Al's eyes grew wide and a big grin appeared on his face as he spotted Liz sitting there on the wall. "Liz!" he shouted happily. He immediately stopped in his tracks and turned to face the Corgi, who rushed up to him and bit him on the nose. "OUCH! Stop it, Molly!" he cried, swatting the dog back on the nose and pointing to Liz. "Me Liz has arrived!" He held his other paw over his aching nose.

Molly panted heavily, allowing her large tongue to hang out the side of her mouth. Her large rounded ears shot out diagonally from a head that looked much too large for her elongated body and stubby legs. "Why didn't you say so?" she asked with a beautiful Welsh accent.

Liz jumped down from the wall as Al ran over to envelop her in a smothering, welcoming hug. "Liz! Are ye really here, lass? I'm so happy to see ye!"

"*Bonjour,* Albert. I'm happy to see you, too," Liz replied, looking over Al's shoulder at the Corgi. "You have a new friend."

"Aye, that's Molly. I can't get her to stop chasin' me," Al replied with a frown and a hoarse whisper, still breathing hard.

"It must be your irresistible charm, *mon cher,*" Liz said with a kiss on Al's cheek as Molly came up to them. "*Bonjour,* Molly. I am Liz. *Merci* for keeping Albert in such good shape."

"Good day, Liz. It comes naturally to me," Molly giggled. "Al told me you were coming today. Welcome to Kew."

Liz saw that Molly's collar had a printed copper plate attached. "May I?" she asked as she leaned over to read the inscription. "*I am His Highness' dog at Kew. Pray tell me, whose dog are you?* The humans have given you quite the humorous collar."

93

"My master had it engraved when he gave me to Prince Frederick," Molly explained. "He was a poet."

"Aye, the Pope's a poet, and he knows it," Al said with a nod, still rubbing his nose.

"He *knew* it," Molly corrected him, "but Alexander Pope died last year. He used to visit Kew frequently, and was good friends with Prince Frederick."

"I am sorry to hear this, Molly," Liz replied.

Al's eyes widened. "But that's why ye're here, lass! There's a special play Gillamon wants ye to see tonight in London. Molly's Pope wrote a little ditty at the beginnin' of the play, so they be havin' a special performance in his memory." He leaned over and smiled. "And *I* get to take ye on a date to the theatre."

Liz looked puzzled. "While I am very happy to go on a date with you, Albert, this is very curious. I wondered why I needed to come to London, but why would Gillamon bring me from America to see a play?"

"From America?" Molly asked with big eyes. "That's a long way to come!"

"Kate will be there, too," Al explained with a whisper. Then turning to Molly, he pointed over at a large bird walking in the distance. "Look, Molly. The pheasant's out for a walk!" Molly took off running and barking after the beautiful bird. "It's easier to jest send her chasin' after somethin' than to explain how ye got here, lass."

"Good thinking, Albert," Liz complimented him with a smile. "How unusual to see a pheasant here."

"Oh there be all sorts o' beasties here at Kew," Al replied. "Little George's mum loves gardenin' and even made a menagerie of animals for her wee lads and lassies to enjoy. There be talk aboot them even gettin' a kangaroo."

Liz's eyes widened. "A kangaroo in London? I look forward to seeing the menagerie. But I am looking forward most of all to seeing Kate tonight. Do you get to see her often?"

"She stops by every now and then. Kate's David Henry were friends with the Pope, and the Pope were friends with the lad named Addison who wrote the play," Al explained.

"You mean Alexander Pope, not *the* Pope," Liz replied. "Albert, where is the play to be performed?"

"In the very same place we got to see Mousie play along with Handel on his fiddle," Al replied.

"*Bon!* At Theater Royal, Covent Garden!" Liz exclaimed. "How exciting to return to the same theater where we saw *Messiah*'s London debut! What is the name of the play we will be seeing?"

Al wrinkled his forehead and scratched his head. "I don't remember it all, but ye may get sad, lass. It's some sort of tragedy aboot a dog like Kate, I think. At least it sounds like it."

Liz wrinkled her brow, perplexed about the subject. "While I am here in London, I need to find a book for my Henry before his father begins his schooling at home. Perhaps we can go to a bookstore before our theatre date?"

Al shook his head. "No, lass. I've got a better idea. Our date can start *now.*"

"What do you mean, Albert?" Liz asked, tilting her head with a grin.

"Follow me." Al wore a happy smile and trotted off across the green grass toward the red brick Dutch style palace. "We're goin' to a school fit for a little king."

Liz gaped up at the shelves of books that ran from floor to ceiling in the royal library. "I must be in heaven! There are hundreds of books here. *C'est magnifique!*"

Al held up his pudgy paw. "Welcome to little George's schoolroom."

"*Le petit prince* has a happy place to learn, no?" Liz exclaimed as she walked along a row of books. "Oh, if only my Henry could have access to all these books."

"Well, I can help the lad with one he needs, anyway. They must have a couple of each book here, so little George won't miss lendin' one to little Patrick. Besides, every royal palace has a library, so they got lots of extras," Al said. "Who be the writer ye need?"

"Plutarch," Liz replied happily, watching Al as he jumped up to a second-tier shelf.

"L-M-N-O-P," Al chanted until he found the right section. "And what be the name of the book?"

Liz curled her tail up and down expectantly. "*Plutarch's Lives,* Volume 2."

"Is this writer a kitty?" inquired Al as he looked along the spines for the right title.

Liz giggled. "No, why?"

"Well how many lives do this Plutarch have? Kitties have at least nine," Al answered. "Of course, *we'll* never run out of lives, lass."

"And I am happy for that," Liz answered.

"Plutarch!" Al shouted, as he located the books. "This lad has lots of lives up here, lass."

Liz clapped her paws. "*Bon!* But I only need one."

"*Plutarch's Lives,* Volume 2, got it! Watch out below," Al exclaimed, tipping back the book. It fell to the floor with a thud.

Liz ran over to the book. "*C'est ça! Merci,* Albert! This is exactly what I hoped to find." She kissed him, and he started purring wildly.

"Ye're welcome, me love," Al said dreamily. "Anythin' for me lass."

Suddenly they heard footsteps coming down the hall. Al's eyes widened. "Uh-oh. They must have heard me drop the book."

Liz looked quickly around the room. "What shall we do?"

"Hurry!" Al scooped up the book under one leg and went running on his other three legs down the hall. "Follow me, lass!"

Together they hurried outside and hid under a finely trimmed hedge in the garden. "That were close!" Al exclaimed.

95

Liz nodded rapidly and spied two young boys running by. "Albert, is that he? Is that *le petit prince,* George?"

"Aye, that's him," Al answered. "The future king of England himself."

"Amazing to think he and my Henry are just boys now," Liz answered.

"And they'll both be readin' Plutarch," Al declared as he thumped the book with his paw. "Now that's what I call gatherin' intelligence."

"I look forward to seeing what they do with what they learn," Liz replied. "I suppose we must leave the book here until nightfall. So how shall we get to the theater from here?"

"In style," Al announced with a flirty grin. "Only the best for me lass."

———

The clip-clop of horse hooves echoed like a symphony off the busy cobblestone street of Drury Lane. Carriages lined the street with the elite of London society, who were being dropped off at the Theater Royal here in Covent Garden. The excited buzz of the people dressed in their finery grew to a frenzy as the gold and black carriage of Frederick, Prince of Wales, arrived. Out stepped the Prince and the Princess onto a red carpet laid out for their welcome. While the humans were busy eyeing the royals, Al and Liz peeked out from their hiding place behind a small trunk on the back of the Prince's carriage. Kate spotted them immediately.

"Over here!" Kate called, wagging her tail happily. She was standing next to a carriage parked by a side alley. Liz and Al jumped off the carriage and ran over to the white Westie. "Welcome ta London, Liz!"

"What a joy to see you, *mon amie!* And for such an exciting evening as well," Liz replied, kissing Kate on each cheek. "So your David Henry will be here?"

"Aye, an' Gillamon has arranged for him an' Clarie ta sit next ta David as they did at *Messiah,*" Kate said happily, wagging her tail.

"It's almost like *déjà vu* all over again," Al mused.

"*C'est magnifique!* Did Gillamon tell you he and 'Lady Clarie' met John Henry and my Patrick at the St. Andrew's Day festival in Virginia?" Liz asked.

"Aye, he told me all aboot the fiddle he brought for Patrick, an' the riddle Mousie fiddled with it," Kate answered. "Gillamon said it be a magic fiddle!"

Al's eyes widened. "Hey, diddle, diddle, a magic fiddle? Maybe I could play it then, jest like the rhyme!"

"If you come to Virginia during this mission, I will see that you get to do just that, Albert," Liz assured him with a pat on his cheek.

Al grew excited at the thought. "If I be the cat with the magic fiddle, that means I can make a cow jump over the moon!"

"An' I'll laugh ta see such a sport," Kate added with a giggle.

Just then a carriage pulled up in front of the theater. When the footman opened the door, out stepped a man in a magnificent red cloak, followed by a beautiful lady in a blue dress.

"Look who has arrived," Liz said, pointing to the carriage.

Gillamon took Clarie by the hand and glanced over at the animals, smiling and touching his elegant hat with a finger in recognition as they walked into the theater.

Liz mouthed, *"Bonsoir."* Her eyes lit up with excitement. She couldn't wait to see what this play was all about.

"Shall we sneak in like we did last time?" Kate asked, looking down the alley that led to the back stage door.

"I know the way!" Al exclaimed with a paw pointed up in the air. He ran ahead to the back door and jumped up to release the latch, hanging on the door while it swung open. "After ye, lassies." Liz and Kate looked at one another and smiled.

"I must say I like this royal treatment, Albert. Palace life suits you, *mon cher*," Liz teased with a coy grin, as she and Kate stepped inside.

"Jest usin' me royal charm, lass," Al replied with a goofy grin.

Once Kate, Liz, and Al were hidden in the very top of the theater on a rafter, they scanned the audience to spot Gillamon and Clarie sitting on the tenth row in the center. Prince Frederick and Princess Augusta sat in one of the royal boxes with gilded, plush arm chairs and the balcony decorated in ornate red and gold. The audience was buzzing about the presence of the royals, looking up to steal a glimpse of them seated high above the theater. Liz then noticed the Roman columns decorating the stage.

"Kate, Albert could not remember the name of this play, but said it was a tragedy. Do you know what it is called?" Liz asked.

"Aye, it's called *Cato,*" Kate replied.

Al slapped the railing. "That's right! Kate-o! See, I knew it were like Kate's name."

97

Liz's eyes widened. *"Cato!?* There is a play about Cato? I hoped I would find a copy of the story of Cato in *Plutarch's Lives* while in London, but I did not know about this play!"

Kate grinned. "It's not a new play. Gillamon said Joseph Addison wrote it way back in 1712, an' the humans have loved seein' it for more than thirty years. He said they even present it in the colonies."

"Why have I not heard of this play in Virginia?" Liz wanted to know, her tail swishing excitedly to learn this news.

"Maybe because ye're not in a big city like me and Kate here in London. Gillamon said ye, Max, and Mousie be livin' in the country," Al posited, drawing surprised looks from Liz and Kate. He was right.

"Bien sûr, this is true, Albert," Liz answered with a wink. Al grinned happily.

"Before *Cato* were first performed back in 1713, Addison asked his friend Alexander Pope ta write a few words ta open up the play," Kate explained. "Tonight's performance is dedicated ta Pope."

"That's nice of them to honor the Pope like that," Al remarked absentmindedly.

"Aye, an' the same Joseph Addison who wrote this play *also* founded *The Spectator* that later became *Gentleman's Magazine* where me David Henry is editor now," Kate added.

Liz then spotted David Henry making his way down the aisle. "Speaking of which."

"Mr. Gillamon? Lady Clarie?" David Henry asked, checking his ticket and slipping into his seat next to Gillamon and Clarie. "Why, this is a delightful surprise to see you once more at the theater!" He tipped his hat to Clarie and reached out his hand to Gillamon.

Gillamon reached over and shook David's hand with a warm smile. "Indeed, what a coincidence, Mr. Henry. It's a pleasure to see *you* again also."

"We had the privilege of meeting your cousin John when we were in Virginia," Clarie added. "His son Patrick made the connection from the letter you sent about the *Messiah* concert."

"Yes! Young Patrick wrote to me about the chance meeting he also had with you. And he was thrilled to receive the fine fiddle you brought from London," David added. "John tells me the boy practices it continually."

"I'm delighted to hear it," replied Gillamon with a knowing grin. "So, have you seen *Cato* performed?"

"Oh, yes, many times," David answered. "I'm certainly indebted to Mr. Addison's work, both for the magazine and for this inspiring play. But I came tonight in honor of Mr. Pope's memory so I can write an article for *Gentleman's Magazine.*"

Gillamon nodded. "We learned that *Cato* is becoming popular even in the colonies, although not yet performed by such a large theater company as in London. The religious community in America has long considered plays to be frivolous and a waste of time, and the characters to be of questionable morals. However, *Cato* appears to be causing even the most rigid types to warm to the idea of seeing Plutarch's hero come to life."

David raised his eyebrows and nodded. "I doubt my cousin John has seen it, although being the scholar that he is, he knows his Plutarch."

"Given that Mr. Pope also translated Homer's *Illiad* and *Odyssey,* perhaps Mr. Henry would be more inclined to read any of Mr. Pope's work, including his introduction for *Cato,*" Gillamon suggested.

"Mr. Gillamon and I discovered that many in America do enjoy reading the plays even if they never see them performed," Claric quickly offered, letting their unspoken suggestion linger in the air for a moment.

The audience started to applaud, as the curtain rose to reveal a scene from ancient Rome.

David leaned in to Gillamon and Clarie with a smile. "I will have to write to John about this evening as well—about seeing you both again, and, of course, about *Cato.*"

Gillamon smiled and nodded. As David turned his gaze toward the stage, Gillamon turned to lock eyes with Liz, also giving her a smile and a nod.

"Shhhhh, the play's startin'!" Al said, clapping his fluffy paws together. He was spellbound at seeing a Roman actor dressed in a toga take the stage, welcoming the audience. "I haven't seen a human dressed like that in years. It's almost like *déjà vu* all over again."

"And now, to honor the memory of Mr. Alexander Pope, I will recite for you his Prologue for *Cato: A Tragedy*:

> To wake the soul by tender strokes of art,
> To raise the genius and to mend the heart,
> To make mankind in conscious virtue bold,
> Live o'er each scene, and be what they behold;—
> For this the tragic muse first trod the stage,

Commanding tears to stream through every age;
Tyrants no more their savage nature kept,
And foes to virtue wondered how they wept.
Our author shuns by vulgar springs to move
The hero's glory, or the virgin's love;
In pitying love we but our weakness show,
And wild ambition well deserves its woe.
Here tears shall flow from a more generous cause,
Such tears as patriots shed for dying laws:
He bids your breasts with ancient ardor rise,
And calls forth Roman drops from British eyes . . .

For this the tragic muse first trod the stage, Commanding tears to stream through every age . . . Liz repeated in her mind as the actor continued reciting the prologue. *He bids your breasts with ancient ardor rise, And calls forth Roman drops from British eyes.*

———

100

Cato captured Liz's complete attention. She didn't say a word as the play moved on from scene to scene showing the Roman statesman and his band of Roman exiles in Utica making a last stand against the tyrant, Julius Caesar. Soon they came to *Act the Second, Scene 4,* and her unbroken attention was about to break.

Juba put a hand humbly over his heart:

"Cato, thou hast a daughter."

Cato lifted a hand to stop the young man:

*"Adieu, young prince: I would not hear a word
Should lessen thee in my esteem: remember
The hand of fate is over us, and heav'n
Exacts severity from all our thoughts:
It is not now a time to talk of aught
But chains or conquest; liberty or death.*

Al leaned over and whispered to Liz, "What's 'aught' mean?"

Liz blinked as Al broke her undivided attention to *Cato.* "Aught means 'anything.' Cato is telling Juba that now is not the time to talk about the young man's love for Cato's daughter. Greater things are at stake at the moment."

"Like if they should surrender to that tyrant lad, Julius Caesar," Al answered, nodding thoughtfully. "So they shouldn't be talkin' aboot anythin' but liberty or death."

Suddenly the scene of Gillamon in the IAMISPHERE in Rome came rushing back to Liz's mind. She had just dreamed about this scene of the real Cato the night before. *"Yes, for Cato, it was either liberty . . . or death,"* Gillamon answered. Liz shot a glance down at Gillamon, who stared up at her with a twinkle in his eyes.

In that moment, she figured out more of the riddle. She leaned over and whispered to Kate, "A voice from the past! *C'est ça!* The Plutarch connection with Patrick Henry *has* to mean not just the story of Cato in *Plutarch's Lives* but the story of Cato in Addison's play."

"Aye, since Gillamon brought us here tonight, that makes sense," Kate whispered back. "I can see young Patrick readin' an' learnin' aboot Cato, but how can a play help him then?"

"Je ne sais pas." Liz wrinkled her brow and stared down at Gillamon sitting next to David Henry. "The layers of history continue to unfold, just as Gillamon said."

"At least ye know more than ye did before, lass," Kate encouraged her happily. "Ye'll figure it out."

"Oui, mon amie. But there is one thing I know for certain." Liz stared at the actor portraying Cato on the stage, now with a drawn sword on the table next to him. "It will have something to do with 'liberty or death.'"

101

ANOTHER CATO:
ANOTHER TRAGEDY

I t were inspirin' . . . in an uncomfortable sort of way," pondered Al as he, Liz, and Kate walked out into the alley behind the Theater Royal.

"Cato were a hero the way he took care of his family an' friends so angry Caesar wouldn't hurt them when he arrived with his army," Kate added. "Still, it were sad when he died."

Liz nodded. *"Oui,* the loss of life and liberty is not an easy thing to see."

"But at least Cato comes back to life for the humans every time they perform the play," Al pointed out as he jumped from cobblestone to cobblestone as if he were playing a game of hopscotch.

"Cato comes back to life, hmmmmm . . ." Liz repeated aloud.

When they reached the corner there was a flurry of activity with fancy carriages lining up to transport their distinguished guests home from the theater. "I guess ye best hide on the prince's coach ta get home," Kate suggested.

"That won't be necessary," came the voice of Gillamon. "Hide under my cloak and come get in my carriage. All three of you. We're making a side trip."

Liz, Kate, and Al looked at one another with excitement before doing as Gillamon instructed. As his carriage pulled up, the footman eagerly opened the door. Gillamon held out his cloak to cover the steps as the animals climbed into the ornate carriage. The footman closed the door and tapped on it to signal the driver to take off.

Gillamon rested his hands atop his decorative cane. "How did you like the play, little ones?"

"It were tragic, jest like the humans said it would be," Al told him, batting at the dangling fringe that swayed as the carriage took off.

"A tragedy, *oui,* but it was a splendid way to bring the historical character of Cato to life for humans. Hearing him speak helps them to understand who he was and what he did," Liz added.

"I wanted you to see the play for yourself, and understand the impact it has had on humans for decades," Gillamon told her. "You may be interested to know that Addison started writing *Cato* back in 1687 when he was just a student at Oxford. He never meant for it to be brought to the stage, but as you can see, the play is wildly popular, and will soon grow even more so in the colonies. Clarie and I have arranged for David Henry to write to John about it."

"Wait, Gillamon, where is Clarie?" wondered Kate, looking around the carriage.

"She is driving the carriage," Gillamon answered with a smile. "We need to make a secret stop so I let my usual driver go for the night."

"Where are we goin', Gillamon?" Kate asked.

Gillamon leaned in. "To the Tower of London."

Al's eyes filled with fear. "No! Not the Tower! Ple-e-e-ease don't send me to the Tower! Humans go in there . . . and some never come out alive!" He started panicking, holding his head out the window to get some air.

"Oh, Albert, only a few humans have been executed there," Liz told him, putting her paw on his back. "More have been executed on Tower Hill, but even those horrible deaths are not as common as the humans make it sound. The Tower is a prison, but also a royal palace, armory, and even a treasury to hold the crown jewels, no? And my fellow Norman, William the Conqueror, built the Tower after he invaded England."

"Aye, but more dogs an' cats have died there than humans," Kate said with a growl. "Ta feed the lions."

Liz's eyes grew wide. "What do you mean?!"

Kate furrowed her brow. "When the Romans died out from Britain, some Roman habits didn't die with them. The humans have a menagerie of animals at the Tower, an' the Royals allow the common humans of London ta come see them. But while the Romans offered the games for free at the Colosseum, the humans of London have ta pay with either three half-pence, or," she paused with a gulp, "bring a cat or dog ta be fed ta the lions."

Liz's face filled with horror. "I did not know this! Gillamon, is this true? Why would you take us there?"

"Indeed, what Kate says is true," Gillamon answered with a frown. "There is another tragedy besides *Cato* happening in London. These exotic animals have been brought here to London as royal gifts from other nations. For the king of England to own such rare animals is a sign of power, for it shows the king's influence around the world."

Al jumped down to cling to Gillamon's legs, shaking with fear. *"Déjà vu,* jest like Rome," he whined with a muffled voice.

"It's like a mini-Noah's Ark inside the menagerie," Kate offered. "There be lions, tigers, leopards, jaguars, cheetahs, hyenas, bears, elephants, baboons, zebras, llamas, macaws, cockatoos, cranes, pelicans, owls, sea eagles, raccoons, alligators, boa constrictors, anacondas, rattlesnakes, an' even a Japanese civet, jest like our friend 'Bang' from the Animalympics in Rome."

"Do this civet have fireworks, too?" Al asked, looking up. "Maybe he could set 'em off so all the beasties could escape."

Gillamon looked Liz in the eye. "Do you remember your anguish in Rome, about the animals used for sport by the Romans?"

"Oui, I just dreamed of this last night. It was the same night you told me about Cato for the first time," Liz answered somberly.

"Well, just as you had one night to free the animals of Rome, you will get to free one creature tonight," Gillamon explained.

"Why jest one?" Kate asked sadly.

"The escape of this one creature must be so secret that the humans never know why we are really there," Gillamon explained. "The Tower is heavily guarded. Sadly, if we tried to free all the animals, they would likely be killed to prevent their escape into the streets of London. But take heart, Liz. Although these animals are sometimes used for games, most of them are used simply for display, so at least their lives are not all in danger."

"Aye, some animals even have nicknames, like a Virginian horned owl named 'Hopkins,'" Kate added. "The lions there be named Marco, Phillis, Nero, Jenny, an' Nanny."

Liz's eyes brimmed with tears. "It saddens me to think about these animals locked up away from their homes. Kate mentioned a Virginian horned owl, so there are creatures from America in the Tower?"

"Yes, animals have been brought to the Tower from many countries, including America." Gillamon picked up Al to stroke his fur for comfort. "And we shall free one of those American creatures tonight. The sea eagle Kate mentioned is a baby bald eagle. He fell out of his nest in Philadelphia before he could learn to fly. Some British explorers found him and brought him back to England on a ship. He is growing quickly, but is not learning how to be an eagle."

"*Quel dommage,*" Liz replied with a paw to her chest. "This is sad for the eaglet, but why save this one, Gillamon?"

"I need you to take him back to Virginia with you. Max and Nigel will soon return to Studley with Patrick Henry. Uncle Langloo encouraged Patrick to study the family of eagles there. Patrick will not only help this baby eagle, but one day, this eagle will return the favor," Gillamon explained.

Liz was puzzled. "But how can I bring him with me through the IAMISPHERE? He will know about our secret time portal."

Gillamon reached into his pocket and pulled out a small black bag. "He won't see where he is, and he won't remember the instantaneous passage. You will arrive in the forest at Studley, just as Patrick returns. Nigel already has plans to chat with the eagles there. All will be well, Liz."

"*Je comprends.* I will do as you say, Gillamon," Liz replied.

The carriage stopped, and Clarie jumped down to open the door. She was in the form of a young man dressed in the livery of a gentleman's coachman. "We're here."

"So how are we supposed ta break him out?" Kate asked.

Gillamon set Al on the opposite seat and threw his cloak over himself for a moment. When he lifted it, his clothes had changed into those of a Yeoman Warder (a royal guard). He smiled, and lifted a set of keys. "I'll walk right in and get him."

"Ye mean we get to stay here?" Al asked with a voice trembling in relief. "We don't have to go to the Tower ourselves?"

Gillamon chuckled. "Yes, Al. You and Kate can stay here with Clarie, but tell Liz farewell. I will send her back to Virginia from the Tower."

"And I'll take you two back home," Clarie offered, mussing the fur on Al's head. "Liz, I'll see you soon."

Al's lip trembled. "Sure, and I don't like that option either." He gave Liz a hug. "I loved havin' ye with me for a day, but sorry our date turned out so tragic, lass."

105

"Au contraire. I would not call it tragic, *mon cher.* Borrowing a book from the royal library, seeing a play at the theater, and helping a creature to escape the Tower of London? I would call a date such as this *exciting."* Liz kissed Al on the nose, making him break out in a goofy grin. "À *bientôt."*

Gillamon carried Liz down the stone-walled corridor that was illuminated with torches hanging on the dank walls. He looked behind him and whispered in Liz's ear. "The other guards thought I was bringing you as food for the lions."

Liz smiled coyly. "If they only knew that this was really a prison break." Her smile faded as they passed the animals locked up in cages. *"C'est tragique,* Gillamon. I wish we could free them all."

"I know, but at least we will give liberty to one," Gillamon responded, stopping as they came to a darkened cage.

Liz looked up and saw a small eagle with his brown head drooping as he leaned against the wall with his yellow talons curled under him. Soft, downy feathers were scattered around him. He had grown long brown feathers speckled with white. "Gillamon, he looks so sad!"

"He will die if he stays in this prison," Gillamon replied, setting Liz down on the stone next to the cage.

"Liberty or death," Liz said quietly.

Gillamon opened the cage and reached in to get the bird. The eaglet didn't even try to fight against him. "Don't be afraid, little one. We're getting you out of here and taking you back to America."

The eaglet's eyes moistened and his small voice cracked. "Home? You're taking me home?"

"Oui, I will take you there myself, *mon ami,"* Liz told him, her eyes also welling up with tears. "My name is Liz. Can you hide in this black bag for a little while until we carry you out of this prison?"

The eaglet nodded his head and stepped into the bag Gillamon had opened for him. Gillamon closed the top of the bag. "We'll leave by a different gate," he told Liz. "Walk along beside me, and I'll distract the guards while you slip out underfoot. Where we're headed is dark, so I don't think they'll see you."

Liz nodded and followed Gillamon down the darkened corridor. As they walked along, they passed a cage where Liz noticed a flea-bitten, forlorn female gray cat. Her ear was torn, and one eye was puffy. Her heart fell to see a fellow feline in such a sad state. She locked eyes briefly with the cat, who looked at her with great hopelessness.

When they turned a corner, a guard stopped Gillamon. "You, there. I haven't seen you here before."

"I'm on temporary assignment," Gillamon explained.

"Well, we need a new guard," the other guard said, revealing a missing upper tooth. "The other night guard died on the spot. They think it was something he ate."

As Gillamon carried on a brief conversation with the guard, Liz looked up at Gillamon and then sneaked back around the corner to the cage where the sad cat was locked up.

"Shhhhh, be very quiet. I'm going to help you escape," Liz told the cat.

"You're saving me?" the astonished cat whispered with a Greek accent. "The humans are going to feed me to the lions in the morning."

Horrified, Liz listened to make sure Gillamon was still talking to the other guard. She furrowed her brow. "Liberty or death. I must not permit that to happen!" As she fiddled with the lock, she looked into the eyes of the cat. "I am Liz. What is your name and how did you get here, *mon amie?*"

"My name is Kakia," the cat replied in a hoarse whisper. "The humans named me when they threw me on a ship from Greece so I could kill the rats on board while they transported a lion for the British king." She spat. "*Misó tous anthrópous*—I hate humans."

"I can understand your hatred for humans," Liz whispered, fiddling with the lock. "I almost have it. If only Albert were here with his iron claw." Finally she opened the lock. "You are free! Hurry now, and get away from this place."

Kakia escaped the cage and looked Liz in the eye. "*Efcharistó*—thank you! Where should I go? Where are *you* going with that human?"

Liz bit her lip. She knew she couldn't take Kakia with her. "Go down to the wharf behind the Tower and escape on a ship to America. You will be safe and happy there. Come quietly and follow me out the gate." They turned the corner, and Liz stopped to make sure the coast was clear. She pointed to Gillamon and hesitated. "He is not what you think. We are helping another creature to escape, a baby eagle. I do not have time to explain."

107

Kakia looked around Liz to the black bag Gillamon was holding. *"Ýpoulos*—sneaky. I like it. Thank you again, Liz. I won't forget this."

Gillamon tapped his foot, and Liz knew she needed to hurry.

"Go, Kakia!" she said as she pushed the cat. Kakia ran out the gate and into the night. Liz slipped out after her and waited for Gillamon.

"Good night then. I'll see you later," the other guard told Gillamon.

Gillamon put a finger to his hat. "Ah, of course, thank you. Good night." He stepped out the gate and the guard locked it behind him. Gillamon then carried the eaglet out of the Tower of London.

———

Gillamon scrolled to find the panel of Studley Plantation. They had entered the IAMISPHERE as soon as they were clear of the main Tower gate. There wasn't time for Liz to tell Gillamon what had happened with Kakia, and she figured it didn't matter anyway.

"Clarie will act as courier and deliver the copy of *Plutarch's Lives* that you picked up for Patrick at Kew," Gillamon told Liz as he handed the black bag to her. "There is also a note from a very pleased Mr. Gillamon, who hopes Patrick will put as much practice into his studies as he puts into his fiddle."

Liz beamed and gently cradled the bag. *"Bon!* That will be the perfect encouragement for John Henry to tutor Patrick at home. I will not have to write an anonymous letter after all."

The baby eagle cried from inside the bag. "Shhhhh, do not cry, little one. Just a moment more and I will have you back to America," Liz assured him, listening to the eaglet's soft cries. "Gillamon, what is his name?"

Gillamon smiled warmly as he prepared to send her back to the forest at Studley. "He doesn't have one."

Liz wrapped her paws around the black sack and lifted her head with honor and determination as Gillamon hit the panel. "His name will be 'Cato.'"

14

WILLING TO SOAR

A warm breeze enveloped Liz as she gently placed the black bag onto a moss-covered rock by the Totopotomoy Creek. "There, now. You are safe, Cato," she said as she opened the bag for the eagle to step out.

Cato squinted against the bright sunlight and flapped his wings as he stepped onto the rock. He looked around to see the creek and the lush green canopy of trees overhead. He breathed in the fresh air of freedom and smiled. "America! Thank you for rescuing me, Liz."

Liz gazed into the clear waters of the rushing creek. Her tail whipped back and forth as she studied some fish. She tried to catch one that swam by, but missed. "If only Albert were here. You must learn to catch fish on your own." She looked up at the eagle's nest high above them. "You also must learn to fly. You are a little over two months old, so the time for flight is close, no? But normally you would learn from up there."

"It's scary up there," Cato softly told Liz. "I fell out of the nest while my parents were off hunting for food. I peeked too far over the edge, and fell through the branches to the ground."

"*C'est tragique!* That must have been terrifying," Liz replied. "Then the humans found you and carried you away, and have fed you ever since."

"I don't know how to fly, or feed myself," Cato said with a dejected voice. "But I'm hungry."

"I hope that eagle will teach you how to do these things," Liz replied, pointing up to the eagle's nest. "When my friends arrive we will know more. For now I need you to trust me, Cato. I know a very kind human who will help you."

"I trust you, but the only humans I have known have been cruel to me," Cato replied, furrowing his brow. "They made me an orphan when they carried me away."

"Patrick Henry is a young boy who loves nature, especially birds," Liz explained. "We are on mission from the Maker to help Patrick, so I know he will help you. Do not be afraid of him when he arrives."

"If you say so," Cato answered, staring up at the eagle's nest. He ruffled his feathers and turned his gaze back to the ground.

Patrick Henry hopped over a fallen log and then jumped up on top of a boulder. He spread out his arms. "Now we're back in *my* forest, Uncle Langloo!" He cupped a hand over his mouth and called, *"What-cheer, cheer, cheer; purty-purty-purty-purty!"*

Langloo smiled and walked along the trail with Max following close behind. Nigel flew above on a pigeon. "Does Mr. Cardinal ever answer you back?"

Patrick laughed and jumped down to join his uncle on the path. "Sometimes, but I don't know if he's talking to me or not. We're almost to the open area of the creek. I'll show you the eagle's nest!"

Together they hiked along the path, brushing against the ferns that sprouted new green growth. Max looked up to see Nigel circling overhead. He smiled and thought, *Mousie's had a better flight home on his pigeon instead of on that obnoxious cr-r-row.*

As they neared the wide creek opening, Patrick spotted Liz and the bird next to her, and he was filled with alarm. "Uncle! It looks like a hawk is going after Liz!"

"Wait a minute, Pat." Langloo put a hand out to stop his nephew from running. "Before you rush into things, make sure you understand what is really going on. That's not a hawk. It's a young bald eagle."

"How do you know?" Patrick asked, easing a bit to see Liz sitting comfortably with her tail curled around her legs next to the bird.

"Young bald eagles are brown with white mottled coloring in their feathers, so they look like hawks at this age. They don't get their white head and tail feathers until they're about four or five years old," Langloo explained. "Golden eagles have a yellow band behind their necks. This young fella doesn't. He's got the right head shape and yellow talons. His beak is black now, but it will turn yellow as he grows. Looks like he might have fallen out of his nest."

Patrick's eyes widened, and he followed his uncle, cautiously walking toward the bird so as not to scare it. "He must have fallen out of *my* eagle's nest! Can't his parents come get him and carry him back to the nest?"

"No. Eagles can only carry about half their own body weight." Langloo shook his head, squatting down a few feet away from the bird. "You see, Pat, baby eagles gain weight and get big in a few short weeks. Then the nest starts getting crowded, so the mother eagle starts to 'stir the nest.' She'll take some of the sticks and move them so they point in toward the eaglets instead of out. It starts to get uncomfortable for the babies in there. But this is part of the process of encouraging the young eagles to leave the nest. She'll hover over them, flapping her wings to show them how it's done, and pretty soon the young eagles start trying to flap *their* wings on their own. When it's time, the mother will push the young eagles to try to fly, and they may fall far before they get the hang of it. The parents will fly with the young ones, and might be able to swoop under them for a moment, but ultimately, it's up to the young eagles to figure it out." Langloo pointed at Cato. "This eagle is going to have to make it from the ground and learn how to fly by himself. This won't be easy."

111

"Won't animals come after him?" Patrick asked, holding his arm around Max, who came to sit next to him.

"Eagles don't have natural enemies except for man," Langloo explained. "An occasional raccoon or horned owl might bother eaglets in the nest, but eagles are at the top of the food chain and are generally left alone by the animal kingdom. But being on the ground like this, a big cat could get to him if it wanted to tangle with those talons."

"Max could scare a big cat away, or I could shoot it with my gun," Patrick offered determinedly.

"That's true, but you can't camp out here for two more weeks or so. Your mother would kill me," Langloo said with a chuckle. "But you can check on him every day and help feed him some fish."

"Alright, I can do that!" Patrick said excitedly. He hurriedly grabbed his fishing pole and walked cautiously around the bird. He looked at Liz, who stayed where she was near Cato. "Hi, Liz. Did you miss me? Who's your new friend here?"

"Bonjour, *Patrick. This is Cato,*" Liz meowed in reply. "*Cato, this is the boy I was telling you about. He is going to catch a fish for you.*"

Cato kept a cautious gaze fixed on Patrick and hopped around on the rocks, nervously fluttering his wings. He watched as Patrick baited the hook and quickly had a fish on the line. Patrick grabbed the fish with one hand and pried the hook out of its mouth with the other. He squatted down and slowly tossed the fish over to the eagle. "Here you go."

The eagle looked at Patrick and then at the fish flopping around on the rocks. He then hopped over and grabbed the fish with his talons and tore into it.

"He's eating it!" Patrick cheered.

Langloo stood up and put his hands on his hips. "Well, that's one problem solved. He's hungry but looks like he's in good shape. And he's not injured."

"What do we do with him now?" inquired Patrick.

"We have to leave him here, and hope for the best, Pat," Langloo replied. "If you can catch him some fish now and then, that will help, but he has to learn to do this on his own."

Patrick looked up at the eagle's nest. "If only I could speak eagle."

Langloo pointed at the eagle devouring the fish. "Looks like you already speak his food language anyway. We best get going before dark sets in. You can check on your eagle tomorrow."

"Take care of him, Max," ordered Patrick as Max hopped back over the rocks to reach him. Patrick squatted down and mussed the fur on Max's head. "You can protect him 'til I get back."

"*Aye!*" Max barked.

As Langloo and Patrick headed toward the house at Studley, Max walked over to sit with Liz. Nigel came in for a landing nearby, and scurried over the rocks to join them.

"*Bonjour,* Max and Nigel. Welcome back," Liz said. She then whispered, "I shall explain everything later, but Gillamon called me to London while you were away. He and I rescued this baby eagle that had been captured in Philadelphia and sent to the king's menagerie in London. Gillamon told me to bring him back here. He needs to learn how to be an eagle. I named him Cato."

"Good day, my dear," Nigel replied, kissing Liz's outstretched paw. He turned to address the eagle. "Welcome, young Cato. You have been given a splendid name. I am Nigel." His face fell as he saw the sharp beak and talons of the young eagle. He stepped behind Liz. "But please understand that I shall *not* be part of your diet."

112

Liz giggled. "Cato, Nigel is part of our team on assignment for the Maker, so please *do* try not to eat him."

Cato nodded. "Alright, I won't. Nigel, did you teach that pigeon how to fly?"

Nigel chuckled. "Of course not, dear boy. That pigeon learned to fly on her own. I merely enlisted her for a ride. But I shall endeavor to help you in any way I can."

"An' I'm Max, lad," the Scottie said, wagging his tail. "I'll help keep ye safe fr-r-rom any bad beasties while ye're on the gr-r-round."

Cato spread his wings and flapped them, showing his wingspan, impressive even at his young age. "Thanks, Max. I know I'm supposed to fly, but can't."

"Alas, 'tis a dreadful thing to be grounded," Nigel consoled him.

Max turned to Liz. "So ye went ta London while we were away? Did ye see me Kate?!"

"*Oui,* and she sends her love," Liz answered. "I saw Al and Clarie as well."

"I'm intrigued about your trip across the pond, although I am surprised you left without me," Nigel said.

Liz wore a coy grin. "When the mouse is away, the cat will play, no?"

"*Touché,* my pet!" Nigel responded with a jolly chuckle. He walked over to observe Cato's wings. "I say, you are growing into your feathers quite nicely. Nothing damaged, so you should have no trouble with liftoff."

"Nigel, could you fly up to the eagle's nest and inquire about his assistance?" Liz asked, and then leaned in to whisper to the little mouse. "You can tell him Cato was traumatized when he fell out of the nest. He's afraid to fly."

"Understood," Nigel whispered back. "I shall make haste and go chat with our local eagle now." He flagged down his pigeon to pick him up.

"I told Mousie it were time ta meet that eagle," Max said. "We've got lots ta share with ye, too, lass. Patr-r-rick learned all aboot eagles an' Indians. The lad's got his heart set on earnin' an eagle feather by doin' somethin' br-r-rave."

Liz observed Cato's helplessness on the ground. "He may get that chance very soon."

113

"They're back!" Jane exclaimed, as Patrick and Langloo stepped inside the house. She rushed up to give her big brother a smothering hug. "I missed you, Pat! But shoo! You need a bath."

"I guess I do!" Patrick said with a laugh. "I missed you too, little Jane." Anne, Sarah, Susannah, and Lucy surrounded him with hugs before holding their noses to tease him. He held his nose and said in a pinched tone, "I missed all of you, too."

"There are our wilderness explorers!" Sarah exclaimed, walking over to embrace them while she carried one-year-old Mary on her hip. "I'm so glad to see you both. Did you have a good time, Pat?"

"I sure did!" Patrick roared. "Just wait 'til I tell you everything I learned with Uncle Langloo!"

"He's a natural out there," Langloo added. He leaned over to kiss Sarah on the cheek. "Thanks for letting me take your boy into the wilderness, Sallie."

Sarah placed her hand on Patrick's back. "Well, I'm just relieved you're both back safe and sound. Your father, John, and William are out inspecting the fields, but should be back soon."

"Mother, by the creek there's a young bald eagle who fell out of the nest! He can't fly yet so I caught him a fish," Patrick told her. "I need to check on him first thing in the morning to make sure he's alright. He's not injured, so hopefully he'll be able to fly soon."

Langloo took off his black hat and pulled his fingers through his thinning hair. "He looks to be about two months old."

"Will he be able to fly?" Sarah asked hopefully, bouncing Mary.

"That will be up to him," Langloo replied.

Nigel could see an eagle sitting inside the massive nest mounted in the top of a pine tree. The nest was eight feet across and four feet deep, made with huge sticks and twigs carefully wedged together to support the one-ton nest. It appeared it had recently been used to raise some eaglets, as there were some downy hatchling feathers spread about. The eaglets were gone, and so was the mate, as eagles remain alone except during mating season.

"I say, bald eagles are quite the handsome birds, but they always look so serious with those permanently furrowed brows," Nigel pointed out to the pigeon with a chuckle. "Please do a fly-by and I shall announce our intentions, my dear."

"Sure thing, Nigel," the pigeon replied, circling above the nest while Nigel waved to the eagle, who watched the curious mouse riding atop a pigeon.

"Hallo!" Nigel called. "May I have a word with you? I'm seeking some guidance for a young eagle who sadly fell from his nest and then fell victim to humans. He is afraid to fly and needs assistance."

The bald eagle cocked his head and ruffled his feathers. "Come."

"Right!" Nigel leaned over and petted the pigeon. "My dear, please put me down on that large branch sticking out from the nest, and then you may take your leave. I shall request transport from this fine fellow back to the creek."

The pigeon did as requested and Nigel walked along the branch toward the nest while the massive eagle stood to stretch, revealing his six-foot wingspan. The eagle towered over Nigel, wearing a stern expression. *Oh, dear, for a mouse this is rather like walking right into the lion's den!*

"So Big Al helped ye get inside ta see the play?" Max asked. Liz was filling him in on her trip to London. "Mousie's gonna be jealous when he hears wha' ye did in London, especially since he had ta be out in the wilderness dealin' with those cr-r-rows. He's more of a city mouse, ye know."

Liz smiled and pointed to the sky. "It looks like our city mouse has just upgraded to a first-class flight."

A magnificent bald eagle soared high above them, circling the creek to inspect the scene below. He didn't flap his wings, but caught the warm thermal currents to coast through the air. His white tail feathers were spread out, and his yellow talons were tucked under his body. They could see Nigel sitting on the dark brown feathers of the eagle's back, waving as the eagle descended toward the creek. When the eagle neared the ground, he pulled back his wings and thrust his feet forward to brake for landing. Nigel slid down the side of the eagle's long feathers and stood in front of him.

"That was the most exhilarating flight of my entire life! Brilliant! Utterly stupendous!" Nigel exclaimed. "If I thought flying on pigeons took the biscuit, then flying on eagles must take the baguette!"

Nigel held out a paw to Max and Liz. "These are my colleagues." Then he held out a paw to Cato. "And this is Cato."

The eagle ignored Max and Liz and slowly walked over to Cato, who was in awe of the handsome, older bird. The eagle didn't say anything but slowly walked around the eaglet, giving him a thorough examination. Finally he leaned right into Cato's face with his sharp bill and piercing yellow eyes. "Do you have what it takes to be an eagle?"

Cato looked nervously at Liz and then back at the eagle. "I'm an orphan, but I hope I do."

"You *hope* you do?" the eagle challenged. "You need to decide if you're going to be an orphan or an eagle."

Cato furrowed his brow, puzzled. He didn't answer, but looked at the ground.

"Flap your wings," the eagle instructed him.

Cato furiously flapped his wings, but to no avail. "I can't lift off. It's hard! And it's so high up there!"

"Of course it's hard, and of course it's high! But an eagle that doesn't use his wings has no purpose," the eagle said gruffly, touching Cato's wings with his own. "You have healthy wings that are ready to fly." He leaned in closer to Cato's face. "But are you willing to face the fear of falling in order to feel the thrill of soaring?"

Cato stood there speechless, trembling from the intimidating stare and tough questioning from this eagle. The eagle stood erect and looked down at Cato. No one said a word.

"The Maker made you to fly, and you are ready. But until you trust Him and choose to soar, I can't help you." He took off without another word, and soared back into the sky.

"Wait! What do I need to do?" Cato cried. He furiously flapped his wings, trying to lift off. He rose a bit, but then landed in the water. He swam to the bank and climbed out onto the rocks. He shook off his feathers and turned his gaze to watch the eagle catching thermals high above him.

Max, Liz, and Nigel looked at one another, speechless.

"I explained the situation thoroughly to that eagle, yet he was so hard on the poor boy!" Nigel fumed.

Max growled. "How dar-r-re he! I were an orphan, too, an' Gillamon helped me. Why won't that eagle help the lad?"

Liz studied the eagle as he flew higher and higher, screeching above them into the pink sky of the sunset. She then looked at Cato, who kept trying to flap his wings. "I believe he just did exactly that."

TEACHING CATO

rowing rays of sunlight poured into the room as Liz sat on the bed next to Patrick. He softly petted her as he searched for verses on eagles as his uncle had suggested. He was waiting for sunrise to head out to check on Cato. Max and Nigel had stayed with Cato last night, making sure nothing got to him. While they were upset with the gruff eagle's treatment of Cato, Liz helped them realize that since he couldn't push Cato physically from the nest, he would have to push him mentally from the ground.

Cato was used to others doing everything for him, but now he needed to do things for himself. And as the eagle told him, he could either choose to be an orphan, remaining a victim of his circumstances, or he could choose to be an eagle, and rise above those circumstances.

"Hast thou not known? hast thou not heard, that the everlasting God, the Lord, the Creator of the ends of the earth, fainteth not, neither is weary? there is no searching of His understanding. He giveth power to the faint: and to them that have no might he increaseth strength. Even the youths shall faint and be weary, and the young men shall utterly fall: But they that wait upon the Lord shall renew their strength; they shall mount up with wings as eagles; they shall run, and not be weary; and they shall walk, and not faint," Patrick read from Isaiah 40. He flipped back in his Bible and read from Deuteronomy 32. "Like an eagle that stirs up its nest, that hovers over its young, He spread His wings and caught them, He carried them on His pinions."

Patrick closed his Bible. "Uncle Langloo said an eagle can't carry its young if they fall, since they are too heavy. But here God says *He* can."

"Oui. *The Maker carried the young nation of Israel when they were helpless,*" Liz meowed, referring to the text.

Patrick sat up and pulled on his breeches, thinking out loud. "So God stirs up the nest as we grow to make things uncomfortable so we'll *want* to fly." He put on his hat and smiled. "But then he'll catch us if we fall. I'd say that makes him a better father than an eagle." He scratched Liz under the chin, picked up his fishing pole and gun, and headed out the door.

Liz smiled, seeing the impact that Langloo, the young eagle, and Scripture had on Patrick, helping him to understand God and life. Such life lessons were important in forming his character. But now other lessons would be added to the mix. *Go help little Cato while I wait for your other Cato to arrive, my Henry. Today will be an important day.*

—————

Patrick smiled when he saw his faithful dog Max lying on the bank of the creek next to the eagle. His back paws were spread behind him and he rested his head on his front paws as he watched the eagle dipping his beak into the water.

118

"Hey, boy," Patrick said quietly so as not to startle the eagle. He squatted down next to Max and gave him a pat. He set his gun and his fishing pole on the rocks. "You're the best dog I ever had. You watched our eagle all night. Here you go." Patrick handed Max some dried beef and a leftover biscuit.

Max gobbled it up and wagged his tail. *"Thanks, laddie."*

The eagle flapped his wings and squawked. *"I'm hungry!"*

Patrick studied Cato while he baited his hook. "I bet you're hungry, too. Let me see if I can catch you a fish." He threw his line into the creek and the cork bobbed along on the surface.

"We're going to have to get you off these rocks, little eagle," Patrick said, looking up at the trees. "If you're going to learn to fly, you're going to need to start on the ground and work your way up. Uncle Langloo told me last night that baby eagles just hop in place on the nest when they start to learn to fly. Then they move to branches and hop from branch to branch to get used to the feeling of air under their wings. Since you can't start out in a nest, I figure you could at least start out on some low branches."

"Brilliant!" Nigel cheered, chewing on an acorn. He was hiding behind a rock nearby.

"Aye, that'll work," Max said. "He's a smart lad, Cato."

Cato brightened. "That doesn't sound hard. Or scary."

Patrick held his pole and stood on the rock to spy out some potential trees with low-hanging branches. "I'll go look for a good tree after I catch you a fish."

Suddenly they heard a screech coming from the air and all looked up quickly. The bald eagle was diving toward the creek.

"Look! There's the eagle!" Patrick announced excitedly, pointing to the sky.

"Aye, the jerky eagle," Max huffed.

Cato's eyes were glued on the eagle. He watched as the big bird came in low to the creek and snatched up a fish from the water with his talons. *"He caught one!"* Cato cheered.

Max grumbled to himself, *"For himself, I'm sure."*

The fish wriggled back and forth as the eagle rose to then make a wide circle over them.

"He's coming back!" Patrick exclaimed, pointing at the eagle as he began a rapid descent toward them.

"EAT!" the eagle screeched as he dropped the fish on the bank next to Cato. *"AND LEARN!"*

Patrick's jaw dropped. "He must be your father, little eagle!"

"Well, I'll be," Max remarked in a surprised, hushed tone. *"Liz were r-r-right. He r-r-really do care aboot the lad."*

Cato hopped over to the fish and clamped his talons over it while he tore into his breakfast. Tears filled his eyes as he realized the gruff eagle was going to help him after all. He had been tough yesterday to prod him on to try harder. *"I'm going to learn, I promise!"*

"If your father is going to feed you, it means I don't have to worry about that," Patrick said, wedging his fishing pole in between some rocks. "Now to find you a good tree."

Nigel scurried over to Max and whispered, "Jolly good turn of events! That eagle isn't as bad as we thought after all."

Max nodded. "Aye, the eagle lad came thr-r-rough."

As Patrick walked along the tree line by the creek, a pair of eyes followed him from behind a thicket on the other bank.

"Bonjour, mon amie," Liz greeted Clarie as she arrived at Studley on horseback. She was once again the courier delivering mail from London.

119

Clarie looked around to see if the humans were about and then got down from her horse to speak with the petite cat. "Hi, Liz. I'm here with your book and letters from Gillamon and David Henry. How goes it with little Cato?"

"*Bon!* Max and Nigel spent last night with him, and now Patrick has gone to check on him. I thought you might come today, so have stayed behind to see the response to these letters," Liz explained. "Nigel brought the local eagle down to speak with Cato, but he was quite stern. Cato needed to be pushed to *want* to learn how to fly and how to become an eagle. But Clarie, I wonder if he can learn to fly without the heights and the winds to teach him. Couldn't you simply carry him up to the eagle's nest while you are here?"

"Lifting Cato up from the ground would ultimately only keep him there," Clarie answered. "This eagle has an extraordinary destiny in front of him, and must learn in extraordinary ways to overcome the hardships he has experienced. Patrick will help him more than any of us, so trust what the Maker has allowed to happen in young Cato's life, and trust your Henry as well."

120

Liz smiled. "As usual, you have stirred up my imagination with intrigue for what is to come."

Clarie kissed Liz on the head. "For now, enjoy what is to come today with these letters." She held up the letters and the package from Gillamon and winked at Liz. "You coming?"

"But of course! I would not miss this for the world," Liz replied, following Clarie up the path to the house.

———

"What's the latest news from David?" Sarah asked, as she and John looked through the mail. Liz jumped up on a chair next to her.

"You will not believe this! David saw Mr. Gillamon at the theater while attending a performance of the play *Cato* by Joseph Addison."

"*It was* magnifique!" Liz meowed. She grinned to herself. If these humans only knew she had been there, too.

"How uncanny," Sarah marveled, petting Liz. "Liz seems just as surprised as we are. I'm not familiar with this play. Do you know of it?"

"I haven't seen it but it was showing in London long before I left Scotland for America," John answered, scanning David's letter. "David said the play continues ta be wildly popular in London, and he was there for a special performance honoring Mr. Alexander Pope, who wrote the prologue." John dropped his hands to his lap. "Hmmmm. Mr. Pope also translated the *Iliad* and the *Odyssey.*" He glanced over at his bookshelf, realizing he had never shared those books with his boys.

"What else does he say?" Sarah asked.

John resumed reading the letter. "Let's see. He says the play has also been performed here in America. Mr. Benjamin Franklin has even printed copies for Mr. William Parks, owner of the *Virginia Gazette*, who has them for sale in Williamsburg." He raised his eyebrows and pursed his lips. "Did ye know that David worked with Mr. Franklin when he was in London as a journeyman printer? I'm sure David never realized Mr. Franklin would become such a success in Philadelphia."

"Indeed! What a small world!" Sarah exclaimed.

Liz's eyes grew wide. *David Henry knows Benjamin Franklin? I did not know this!*

"David said the play portrays the heroic Roman patriot Cato in a way that people in our day and age can truly grasp. He encourages us ta get a copy of the play ourselves. He goes on ta say he hopes we are all well, and sends his fond regards."

121

"How lovely to hear from David," shared Sarah, picking up the package from Gillamon. She removed the attached letter and handed it to John. "I'm not sure who this is from."

Liz's eyes danced with excitement as John opened the sealed letter. He held it up and rustled it in the air.

"Now we have a letter from Mr. Gillamon in London," John Henry exclaimed to Sarah. He scanned the contents of the letter with his finger. "He concurs that he saw David at the Theater Royal. How extraordinary that both letters arrived on the same day!"

Liz stifled a giggle. *If you only knew, monsieur.*

"Mr. Gillamon writes, '*I was pleased to hear that young Master Patrick is practicing his fiddle with great determination. Your lad has potential. From what I gather, he seems to have a most tenacious memory. Your cousin shared that you studied at King's College in Aberdeen. May I assume that you will impart your wealth of knowledge in schooling young Patrick? To that end I enclose one of my favorite works for his study that includes the subject of Cato, upon which the play was drawn. I trust he will practice his Plutarch with as much vigor as his fiddle.*'" John walked over to Sarah. "What book did he send, my dear?"

Sarah held up the book and then handed it to her husband. *"Plutarch's Lives,* Volume 2. What a kind gift from that kind gentleman!"

"Aye. Most kind, indeed." John walked over to his bookcase to scan the spines of books on the shelves. He stopped at *Plutarch's Lives,* Volume 1. "How fortuitous! I only had 23 of the 46 lives for study."

"Oui, *now you have a complete set of Plutarch, compliments of* le petit prince," Liz meowed.

He paused and turned to look at Sarah. "I have so much ta offer our boys, if they'll choose ta embrace it. What do ye think about my tutoring Patrick and William at home, withdrawing them from school?"

Sarah smiled and stood up to go hug her husband. "I can think of no one better to give them the education they need."

John smiled and kissed Sarah on the head. "I don't know what path either of the boys will take in life. Studley meets our needs, but I won't be able ta produce enough ta send the boys ta university. I've tried ta teach them farming, but ye and I both know it's not what I do best."

"And farming may not be what William and Patrick are called to do," Sarah added. "But if you give them a strong education, they'll figure out their own paths with time."

"Agreed." John pulled a Latin book from the shelf and blew off the dust. "I'll begin with this. I don't think Patrick will shed any tears about leaving school."

Sarah laughed and tapped the Latin book. "He won't shed tears about leaving the common school, but I'm sure he'll shed a few when he starts being drilled by his new taskmaster."

"Non operae pretium est elit," John said with a chuckle. "Nothing worthwhile comes easy."

"Veni, vidi, vici," Liz said with a coy grin, and her curlicue tail lifted in the air as she sauntered out of the room.

I came, I saw, I conquered.

———

Patrick sat back down on the rocks next to Max, while Cato finished his fish. "I found a tree. Now to get him over to it." He frowned for a moment and looked at the young eagle. Then he looked at Max. "I have an idea, boy. I need you to act like an eagle for a minute." He proceeded to take off his shirt.

Max's eyes widened. *"Wha' in the name of Pete is the lad thinkin', Mousie?"*

Nigel held out his upturned paws and shrugged his shoulders.

"Alright, Max, put this on." Patrick proceeded to slip his shirt over Max's head and pulled it along Max's back. Patrick chuckled, lifting up the sleeves and making them "fly" on either side of Max. "Look, little eagle! You're going to flap your wings like this . . ." he put his hands under Max to lift him in the air, ". . . and you're going to fly!" He zoomed Max around in midair with his shirt sleeves flying behind him.

Nigel fell over backward laughing. "A flying Scottie! I never thought I'd ever see the day!"

Max grumbled, "Watch it, Mousie!"

Cato giggled but was watching and listening carefully to what Patrick was saying.

"But you're going to need to let me help you get up to a branch," Patrick continued. He set Max back down on the rocks and took the shirt off his back. "Good boy. Thanks, Max."

Max shook vigorously from head to tail. *"Jest doin' me duty."*

Patrick held up the shirt and walked slowly over to Cato. "I need you to trust me to pick you up, little eagle."

Cato ruffled his feathers and flapped his wings, unsettled at the boy's approach. *"What do I do? The last time a human grabbed me I ended up in a cage."*

"Not to fear, young Cato," Nigel exhorted the nervous eagle. *"Our valiant Patrick will not harm you."*

"Steady, lad. Do as he says," added Max. *"Ye saw him carry me ar-r-round in his shirt, so now ye do the same."*

A shadow passed overhead, and Cato looked up to see the eagle flying above him. *If I'm going to learn to fly, I have to learn to trust.* He closed his eyes and swallowed back his fear. He then sat calmly while Patrick approached.

"Easy," Patrick said. "I'm not going to put you in the shirt, just wrap it around you so I can hold you." He slowly approached Cato, who allowed him to gently drape his shirt over his back. The boy's heart was racing, and beads of sweat dripped down his face as he carefully put his hands under the eagle's chest. "I've got you. Easy now." He slowly stood and held the bird close to his chest. "I can't believe I'm actually holding

123

a bald eagle!" he murmured quietly under his breath. He wanted to scream with excitement.

He walked over to the tree he had picked out, Max and Nigel following along. There was a large boulder next to the tree.

"Alright, here we go, little eagle. I'm going to climb up this boulder so I can get you close to the lowest branch," explained Patrick. He carefully climbed in his bare feet up onto the boulder and stood where the branch was just over his head. He exhaled slowly, uncertain if this would work. "Easy now. I'm going to put you up on the branch. Steady." Nigel clung to Max's front leg as they held their breath.

Cato flapped his wings into Patrick's hair and eyes as the boy carefully placed him up on the branch. Patrick squinted as the eagle flapped, and carefully pulled his shirt off the bird.

"Ye did it!" Max barked.

Patrick balled up his shirt and held it to his mouth as he waited to see what the eagle would do.

Cato's heart was racing as much as Patrick's. He flapped his wings, exhilarated to be just ten feet off the ground.

"I say, can you jump in place, dear boy?" Nigel shouted.

"I think so," Cato replied with a squawk to Patrick's ears. He flapped his wings and used his legs to jump off the branch. He hovered for just a moment and then lighted back down on the branch.

"Bravo! You're doing it!" Nigel cheered with a fist of victory held high.

"That's a lad! Keep flappin'!" encouraged Max.

"He's doing it! He's doing it!" Patrick exclaimed, grabbing either side of his head with his hands. He danced around on the boulder. "Huzzah! He's doing it!"

"See if ye can hop up another br-r-ranch!" prodded Max.

Cato set his face like flint and looked up at the next branch above him. He flapped and flapped and flapped and hovered in place but couldn't lift himself any higher. He was getting tired. He stopped a moment to catch his breath.

"Did you see that, boy?" Patrick exclaimed, squatting down to give Max a big hug. "The little eagle is trying to fly!"

Cato started flapping again and lifted off, but as he did so he went tumbling to the ground.

"Oh, no!" Patrick cried, quickly getting up to go check on the bird.

124

"*Are ye alr-r-right, lad?!*" Max barked, running around the side of the boulder.

Cato sat there on the ground, a bit dazed and shaken by the fall. Memories of falling through the branches came rushing back to him and for a moment he felt paralyzed.

A loud screech sounded from the heavens above as the eagle called down to Cato, "*GET UP! TRY AGAIN!*"

Cato turned his gaze at the soaring eagle modeling for him what he wanted to be—what he was *meant* to be. *An eagle that doesn't use his wings has no purpose.* The wise eagle's words came crashing into the young eagle's mind. *Do you have what it takes to be an eagle? Are you willing to face the fear of falling in order to feel the thrill of soaring?* The young eagle closed his eyes, took a deep breath, and then opened them, for the first time with an angry determination he had not felt before.

As Patrick reached out to once again put his shirt around the young bird, Cato squawked and flapped his wings furiously against him. "*NO! Let me try!*"

Patrick held his hands up and backed away. "Easy."

125

Cato flapped and jumped in place on the ground. He flapped and flapped until he got enough lift to land on the boulder. Exhausted, he stopped and folded his wings. But inside, his heart was beaming. For the first time, he had lifted *himself* up from the ground.

And that small beginning was enough to make him want to try again.

CATO TEACHING

TWO WEEKS LATER

Patrick rested his chin in his hand and slid his elbow down onto the wooden table. Spread out before him was a book on Latin. He could hear frogs calling to one another outside. He sighed, wishing he were outside on this warm summer evening with the eagle instead of stuck inside with his nose in a book. The dancing light from the flickering candle inside the glass globe caught his attention, and his gaze drifted from the book to the lamp.

"Perfer et obdura; dolor hic tibi proderit olim," John Henry said as he saw Patrick sitting there, clearly not excited about his work.

Patrick sat up straight and smiled weakly at his father. "What does that mean, Father?"

"Be patient and tough; someday this pain will be useful ta ye," John translated, sitting down next to him, placing a skinny booklet on the table. He smiled and leaned over to tap the Latin book. "Studying ancient languages and history is vital ta understanding our world today."

Patrick wrapped his arms around the chair back. "How?"

"Man hasn't changed throughout history. Oh, the clothes we wear, the languages we speak, and the places we live change, sure, but the heart of man remains the same," John explained. "If ye learn the behavior of men and nations across time, ye'll see the same patterns repeated again and again. Ye'll come ta understand human behavior, and that will help ye predict what men might do."

"So the past will help me figure out the future?" Patrick asked, gliding his hand over the candle to make the flame dance.

"Aye, that it will." John rested his arms on the table next to Patrick.

"Ye'll find that just as this lamp gives light ta the room, the experiences ye gain from yer own life history will give light ta *yer path."*

Patrick nodded but didn't respond. He continued to stare at the light. "I just wish it were easier to learn."

"Has it been easy for yer eagle ta learn how ta fly?" John asked him.

Patrick smiled and gave a singular laugh. "No. He's been trying hard for two weeks."

John leaned back with a knowing grin. "And is he making progress?"

"Yes," Patrick answered hesitantly. "He's slowly reaching the higher branches of his learning tree."

"And when he finally lifts off from that tree, it will no longer be his tree of learning, but his tree of *libertas.* Liberty. For he will be free ta soar as he was meant ta do. Liberty is a precious jewel, Patrick. Always remember that." John smiled and put his hand over the glass globe. The heat from the flame licked at his fingers. He grimaced and quickly pulled back his hand. "The flame is hot. See for yerself."

Patrick looked at his father with a grin and then tried to do the same. He rested his hand on the heat of the flame but quickly pulled it back. "Ouch!"

John smiled and patted Patrick on the back. "What kind of lessons do ye remember most, Pat? The ones that are easy or the ones that are hard and maybe even cause ye a little pain, like that flame?"

The boy twisted his mouth as he thought about his answer. "Well, for math I most remember the harder problems because I have to spend more time figuring them out."

"Maybe that's why ye like math more than any other subject," John offered. "We tend ta care more about what we've had ta struggle with and then conquered. So, as ye struggle ta learn the hard things, ye'll better remember them. Including *Latin*." John mussed Patrick's hair and stood up.

Just like the eagle learning to fly, Patrick thought. He smiled. "Alright, Father. I'll keep trying."

"*Capta est optimus mundus creatus vitas hominum historia,"* stated John with a raised finger. "'The world of man is best captured through the lives of the men who created history.' Plutarch said that, and tomorrow we start studying the great men of Greek and Roman history."

Patrick's eyes lit up. "Do we get to read the book Mr. Gillamon sent?"

"Aye, and I'll let ye and William each choose one of the lives ta present an oral report in a month or so," John answered. He then picked up the small booklet on the table. "Consider this extra credit reading material ta go along with yer Plutarch. This just arrived today from Williamsburg."

Liz's heart raced wildly in the corner of the room as she saw Patrick pick up the booklet.

"*Cato: A Tragedy,*" Patrick read. His eyes grew excited with anticipation. "This is the play cousin David wrote us about! The one he saw with Mr. Gillamon."

"Aye. But remember that this is a *play*," John emphasized. "*Ficta voluptatis causa sint proxima veris,* which means, 'Fictions meant ta please should approximate the truth.' I challenge ye ta read the account of Cato in Plutarch and compare it with the play. See if fiction approximates the truth."

"I will, Father," Patrick said, looking at the cover of the play. He squinted to read the small print. "B. Franklin, Philadelphia."

John leaned over to hug Patrick. "Time for bed. *Longissimus dies cito conditur.* Even the longest day soon ends."

Patrick quickly flipped through the pages of his Latin book and looked up at his father with a big grin. "*Dormi bene.*"

John raised his eyebrows and smiled. "Excellent! Good night ta *ye.*" As Patrick climbed into bed, John leaned over to blow out the candle. "Did ye ever name your eagle, Patrick?"

"No. I guess I should have by now," Patrick answered. "I'll think of something."

John smiled at his son and blew out the candle. "*In absentia luci, tenebrae vincunt.* 'In the absence of light, darkness prevails.'"

Sic infit, Liz thought with a grin in the dark.

"So it begins."

ONE MONTH LATER

"He's halfway up the tree now!" Nigel exclaimed, holding his paw to shield his eyes from the sun. Cato was slowly jumping his way branch to branch up the tree, and was able to fly from the boulder on his own to the lower branches. "Good show, Cato!"

"Aye, an' he can even catch his own fish now," Max added, running ahead of Patrick to join Nigel and Liz, who were already at the river early on this summer morning. "I bet even the gr-r-ruff old eagle be smilin' aboot that now."

"You see? That old eagle knew what young Cato needed at the time." Liz sighed with satisfaction. "I did not know if he could make it at first, but he has chosen to be an eagle and rise above his circumstances. I am very proud of Cato."

"And how remarkable it is that young Patrick even chose to name Cato 'Cato,'" Nigel quipped. "If he only knew he was simply repeating history, as the young eagle was already so named."

"Aye, but the lad still has ta take off. Stayin' on br-r-ranches ain't tr-r-rue liberty for an eagle," stated Max, looking up into the tree.

"*Oui,* you are right, Max. For this to be a liberty tree, Cato needs to be completely free of it, no?" Liz added.

"Max!" Patrick called, walking into the clearing with his gun slung over his shoulder and his fishing pole in hand. "Where are you, boy?"

"*Here, lad!*" Max barked, running over to meet Patrick.

"There you are," Patrick said with a smile, leaning down to muss Max's fur. "How's Cato doing today? Do you think he's ready to take off yet?"

I hope so, lad, Max thought.

Patrick stopped to put a hand up to his brow and gaze up at the eagle in the branches. He smiled, seeing the young bird still there. "Well, it's all up to him at this point. I'm going fishing." He walked over to the bank and set his musket down on the rocks. He took his fishing pole, baited the hook, and walked to the water's edge to cast his line into the slow-moving current.

Just then, Cato flapped his wings and lifted off from the branch to soar to the creek with a confident screech. His wings were still somewhat awkward, but he made his way over to the creek, spotting a fish and plunging into the water with a splash. He hadn't yet learned how to grab a fish and take off, so he held on to the fish in his beak and swam to the other creekbank.

Max, Liz, and Nigel cheered while Patrick cheered, "Huzzah!" for Cato's catch. Patrick then looked down at the squishy mud between his toes and suddenly noticed a set of animal tracks on the muddy bank. He frowned. *That's a panther.* He quickly lifted his gaze to trace the path of the tracks and saw they disappeared at the water's edge. He glanced across to the other side of the creek just as he heard a sound that made the hair on the back of his neck rise. A panther came leaping out of the woods and was headed straight for Cato.

Patrick dropped his fishing pole and staggered back to retrieve his musket. Max started barking wildly down at the water's edge to warn Cato, and ran up and back along the bank, frustrated to be on the wrong side of the creek. "Get out of there, lad! A big cat be comin' for ye!"

The panther was closing in fast. Cato saw the big cat heading his way and his heart started pounding out of his chest. He spread his wings, and staggered back a step, paralyzed with fear.

Patrick's hands were shaking as he loaded the musket ball into his gun and poured the gunpowder into the pan. He cocked his gun, lowered it to take aim, and just as the panther was about to reach Cato, he fired! A sickening, guttural growl rose from the big cat as it was hit in the leg. It stumbled but quickly got up and disappeared back into the woods.

130

Smoke from the gunshot swirled around Patrick's face, but as it dissipated he saw a beautiful sight. Cato had lifted off the ground and was soaring up into the sky.

"He did it! The young boy finally flew!" Nigel exclaimed, hugging Liz.

Tears filled Liz's eyes. "It took facing liberty or death to make Cato fly."

Max ran up to Patrick and nuzzled the happy young boy whose eyes brimmed with proud tears. *"Alis aquilae,* Cato."

On eagle's wings.

ONE WEEK LATER

"Ab initio," John Henry said, looking over the top of the book at Patrick and William as he paced in the front of the room. The two boys looked at one another and then started reciting a list of phrases. Stacks of books had been placed on a wooden table where Patrick and William sat in their father's study: Greek, Latin, and French language guides, mathematics, English grammar, and classic literature including Plutarch, Virgil, Livy, and Homer's *Illiad* and *Odyssey.*

"Wha're they sayin' with all this str-r-range talk?" Max whispered to Liz.

Liz smiled. "John Henry is teaching Latin to the boys. *Ab initio* means, 'from the beginning.'"

"I say, have I missed anything?" Nigel asked, joining Max and Liz.

"Nothin' that I can make out, lad," Max answered with a frown.

"*Bonjour*, Nigel. John is reviewing a new list of Latin terms before going to today's history lesson," Liz answered. "*Plutarch's Lives* is on the agenda for today. William is to review Plutarch's account of Julius Caesar, and Patrick is to review Plutarch's account of Cato!"

Nigel adjusted his spectacles. "Splendid! At last, *historia vitae magistra!*"

"Now Mousie's doin' it," Max grumbled. "Can't ye speak in words I know?"

"Nigel said the Latin phrase, 'history, the teacher of life,'" Liz translated. "This is a special day, no? I have been waiting to see what Patrick gleans from Cato. *Both* of them."

"*Ita vero.* Thus, indeed," Nigel replied. "It will be the greatly anticipated conclusion of the 'voice from the past' riddle."

"Patrick, why don't ye go first, since yer character was first in the historical timeline?" John asked. "Remember I want ta hear what ye learned most about this character. You can use segments of Plutarch verbatim, if you wish, as long as ye relay what was most important ta ye."

Patrick nodded, stood, and gathered his paper. "My report is on Cato the Younger," he started, clearing his throat. "He was the great-grandson of Cato the Elder, and was left an orphan, together with his brother, Caepio. He began to learn slowly at first, but once he started learning, his memory was strong and determined. Plutarch said, 'and such in fact, we find generally to be the course of nature; men of fine genius are readily reminded of things, but those who receive the most pains and difficulty remember best . . .'" Patrick paused and shared a grin with his father before resuming his report, "'. . . every new thing they learn, being, as it were, burnt and branded on their minds.'"

Liz sat enraptured with every word that rolled off Patrick's tongue. Her heart thrilled at observing the Plutarch connection branded on his mind.

"Cato was very obedient, and he would do whatever he was commanded; but he wanted also to ask the reason and inquire the cause of everything. He loved his brother above all," Patrick said, looking at his brother William, who rolled his eyes at him with a big grin. "Cato

131

devoted himself to the study, above everything, of moral and political doctrine, and he pursued every virtue, especially justice. He learned the art of speaking and debating in public but would never recite his speeches before company. He said, 'I will begin to speak, when I have that to say which had not better be unsaid.'

"Plutarch writes, 'His speech was straightforward, full of matter, and rough, at the same time that there was a certain grace about his rough statements which won the attention; and the speaker's character, showing itself in all he said, added to his severe language something that excited feelings of natural pleasure and interest. His voice was full and sounding, and sufficient to be heard by so great a multitude, and its vigor and capacity quite indefatigable, for he often would speak a whole day and never stop.'

"Cato loved discipline and showed bravery, courage, and wisdom in everything. He was given command of a Roman army and his men loved him. Whatever he commanded them to do, he did himself. He was more like a common soldier than an officer." Patrick stopped and took a breath. "When his time of service was over, Cato's men gave not only prayers and praises, but tears and embraces, and they spread their clothes at his feet and kissed his hand as he passed. This was an honor that Romans at the time were scarcely paid, even to a very few of their generals.

"He was a man of honesty and brought integrity back to the Roman treasury by exposing corrupt practices. He never missed an assembly of the people, or sitting of the senate; being always anxious and on the watch for those who lightly, or as a matter of interest, passed votes in favour of this or that person. Cato gained a great and wonderful reputation and many times refused to hold office, as the demands were many. But some offices he sought with danger, that he might defend the liberty of the people and their government.

"As Julius Caesar rose to power and threatened the Roman Republic as a tyrant, Cato warned the people that he would do so if not stopped. He said, 'If you had believed me, or regarded my advice, you would not now have been reduced to stand in fear of one man, or to put all your hopes in one alone.'

"Cato tragically ended his life rather than live under the tyrant, Julius Caesar," Patrick reported and then paused to conclude. "What I have most learned about Cato is to always speak the truth boldly and without fear, for the cost of liberty lost is high . . ." Just then Cato flew by the window, and Patrick smiled. ". . . But the jewel of liberty gained is worth the price."

132

PART TWO

RUMORS
OF WARS

PEACE, PEACE, WHEN THERE IS NO PEACE

HANOVER, OCTOBER 1745

I had no CHOICE!" Uncle Patrick fumed, pacing angrily behind the garden bench. "If I hadn't allowed him *inside* my church, he would have preached *outside* in the churchyard, and then my entire congregation would have gone over ta him."

"So the great George Whitefield blazes across the colonies in his Great Awakening movement, and sends word he's coming ta none other than Hanover County, asking ta speak at St. Paul's Parish," John Henry said, lighting his pipe. "What did ye tell him?"

"Well, I didn't say yes or no, but invited him first ta come meet at my home on Saturday and discuss what he would speak about," Uncle Patrick offered, then blew his nose. "Pardon, I'm still getting over this fever and cold."

"Sorry for yer malady, brother." John took a puff on his pipe and nodded. "Yer request sounded reasonable."

"But Whitefield didn't have the courtesy of even *replyin'* ta my request!" Uncle Patrick blurted out, raising a hand in the air and letting it drop to the back of the bench. "Yesterday he just showed up at St. Paul's and by the time I got there, a great crowd of people had already gathered. All I could do at that point was ta allow him entry ta speak inside, but on the condition that he first read from the Book of Common Prayer."

"Well, he abided by yer request. He is an ordained Anglican minister after all, and knows how ye do things at St. Paul's," John answered.

"Aye, but when the Anglican Church in England didn't assign him a

135

pulpit, he just started preaching in parks and fields on his own, and people en masse actually started ta come hear him!" Uncle Patrick added, gesturing wildly with his arms. "Ye heard that little cross-eyed preacher yesterday. His big voice can be heard over 500 feet away. He has become nothing short of a celebrity in the colonies."

"Aye, over half the colonists have either heard or read his sermons by now, this being his third trip ta America," John added.

"And he just *had* ta come ta Hanover!" Uncle Patrick ranted.

John pointed at his brother with his pipe. "I heard that even Benjamin Franklin was so moved by Whitefield in Philadelphia that he helplessly emptied his pockets when the preacher asked for support for an orphanage in Savannah."

Uncle Patrick shook his head and gripped the bench with both hands. "I simply do not understand the effect he has on people."

"I do!" Sarah said. She plopped down on the bench with her arms crossed over her chest and an impish grin on her face. "His *Method of Grace* sermon was beyond inspiring yesterday. I'm so glad Patrick got to hear him. Your namesake was *mesmerized*, dear brother-in-law."

136

The younger Patrick sat within earshot of the adults, listening to the Scottish burr of his father and uncle in a heated discussion, once more about religion. He had brought his fiddle outside to play, but stopped behind the hedge when he heard their voices. Max and Liz sat next to him and he quietly petted them as he closed his eyes and thought back to yesterday morning's events at his uncle's church.

Patrick sat with his parents up in the new gallery built for the use of gentlemen justices, vestrymen, and their families. He leaned over the railing above the main floor and looked down in awe at the crowd hanging on every word of this thirty-one-year-old maverick preacher. The people packed into the church until there was no standing room, and the air grew so hot with their breath that steam formed on the ceiling. Whitefield held the people captive with his hypnotic voice, which he could raise or lower at will. Patrick was awestruck by what came out of the small man's mouth. His words were burned into Patrick's memory:

"Today's text is Jeremiah 6:14: "They have healed also the hurt of the daughter of my people slightly, saying, 'Peace, peace, when there is no peace.'"

"As God can send a nation or people no greater blessing than to give them faithful, sincere, and upright ministers, so the greatest curse that God can possibly send upon a people in this world, is to give them over to blind,

unregenerate, carnal, lukewarm, and unskilled guides. And yet, in all ages, we find that there have been many wolves in sheep's clothing, many that daubed with untempered mortar, that prophesied smoother things than God did allow. As it was formerly, so it is now . . .

"The prophet Jeremiah gives a thundering message, that they might be terrified and have some convictions and inclinations to repent; but it seems that the false prophets, the false priests, went about stifling people's convictions, and when they were hurt or a little terrified, they were for daubing over the wound, telling them that Jeremiah was but an enthusiastic preacher, that there could be no such thing as war among them, and saying to people, 'Peace, peace, be still,' when the prophet told them there was no peace. The words, then, refer primarily unto outward things, but I verily believe have also a further reference to the soul . . ."

"How many of us cry, Peace, peace, to our souls, when there is no peace! How many are there who are now settled upon their lees, that now think they are Christians, that now flatter themselves that they have an interest in Jesus Christ; whereas if we come to examine their experiences, we shall find that their peace is but a peace of the devil's making—it is not a peace of God's giving—it is not a peace that passeth human understanding . . ."

Patrick opened his eyes when he heard his father's voice. "I must say that Whitefield's historical faith comment was rather brilliant. He was clever ta make that illustration with Caesar or Alexander." The boy's sharp memory raced back to that part of the sermon.

"My friends, we mistake a historical faith for a true faith, wrought in the heart by the Spirit of God. You fancy you believe, because you believe there is such a book as we call the Bible—because you go to church; all this you may do, and have no true faith in Christ. Merely to believe there was such a person as Christ, merely to believe there is a book called the Bible, will do you no good, more than to believe there was such a man as Caesar or Alexander the Great."

Patrick's memory was interrupted once more, this time by the alarm in his uncle's voice.

"I'm telling ye these itinerant preachers manage ta screw up the people ta the greatest heights of religious frenzy, leaving them in this state for ten ta twelve months until another enthusiast comes along!" Uncle Patrick argued. "My congregation grows more and more unsettled by this Dissenter movement against the Anglican Church. What good can come from it?"

137

"What *good* can come from it? Did you see the response of the people when Whitefield implored them to choose grace?" Sarah shot back with her hand in the air. "I've never seen so many hearts moved to want genuine salvation through Christ!"

Patrick's mind filled with the crescendo of Whitefield's imploring voice, his warm smile, and his outstretched arms beckoning the people to embrace true peace:

"Would you have peace with God? Away, then, to God through Jesus Christ, who has purchased peace; the Lord Jesus has shed his heart's blood for this. He died for this; he rose again for this; he ascended into the highest heaven, and is now interceding at the right hand of God."

"Well, I'm not going ta take this invasion of my church lying down!" Uncle Patrick exclaimed with a huff. He picked up his black tricorn hat and positioned it firmly on his head. "The Dissenters of Hanover, including yer father, dear sister-in-law, had better heed the law if they know what's good for them. Isn't that right, *Sheriff* Henry? I'll see myself out." With that he bid John and Sarah good day and left Studley.

"What's that supposed to mean?" Sarah asked John.

John loosened his shirt collar uncomfortably and got up from the bench. "I have ta uphold the law, dearest Sarah. No matter how close it hits ta home." He cleared his throat and walked back inside the house.

"Peace, peace," Patrick said in a hushed tone. "But there is no peace." He furrowed his brow, got up, and walked away toward the woods.

Max, Liz, and Nigel stayed behind, allowing Patrick to be alone.

"I daresay, Uncle Patrick's parting words sounded like a declaration of war!" Nigel exclaimed, adjusting his spectacles.

"Aye, an' Whitefield jest pr-r-reached aboot peace in the lad's own church," Max added. "Kate an' me were with Jeremiah when he wr-r-rote those words, warnin' Jerusalem that the Babylonians were comin', but the people wouldn't listen."

"*Oui,* and Jeremiah was right about the war to come. King Nebuchadnezzar did destroy Jerusalem and carry the Jews off into captivity," Liz remembered. "Although sad in many respects, those years with Daniel in Babylon were exciting."

"Exciting and *vital* to laying the groundwork for the Wise Men to find Messiah so many years later," Nigel added with a finger pointed in the air. "How utterly brilliant, the way the Maker weaves time and events together!"

"Aye, so Jeremiah were talkin' aboot a *r-r-real* war," Max added. "Whitefield were talkin' aboot a war within."

"I submit that both kinds of wars are equally real," Nigel suggested. "What do you suppose Uncle Patrick meant by that 'Sheriff Henry' comment?"

"Do not suppose that I have come to bring peace to the earth. I did not come to bring peace, but a sword,'" Liz said. "Do you remember when Jesus said that to the twelve disciples the first time he sent them out on their own?"

"Indeed. He followed with Micah's prophetic words: *'A man's enemies will be the members of his own household,'"* Nigel added.

"Aye, but he were warnin' his followers aboot those comin' against them who didn't believe in Jesus," Max added. "The Henry an' Winston families be on the *same side.* They all believe in Jesus, jest not how ta worship him. They're daft ta be *fightin'!"*

"Ah, but such has been the case with warring religious groups across time: the Jews and the Christians; the pagans and the Christians; then sadly, the *Christians* and the Christians, Protestant and Catholic alike." Nigel clucked his tongue and clasped his paws behind his back, shaking his head. "What a sad lot these humans are to allow the Enemy to get between them! And how dreadful that the war for religious freedom must rage right under the Henrys' roof."

Liz watched young Patrick slowly walk away from them, thinking about the things he had heard. "My Henry has learned that even though Christians may cry 'peace, peace,' sometimes there is no peace between them when it comes to running God's house."

"Meaning no peace between Uncle Patrick and John Henry on one side and Sarah Henry and her father Isaac Winston on the other," Nigel added. "This could turn into quite the nasty business."

Liz saw Patrick's fiddle lying there. The boy had been in such deep thought he left the instrument behind. She placed her dainty paw on the fiddle, recounting the next part of the fiddle's riddle. *"A voice in the present wakes eternity* en masse. Hmmm." She looked over at Max and Nigel. "Uncle Patrick used those very words, *'en masse.'* There must be something in the midst of this 'holy war' that will help my Henry find his voice. What else could this part of the riddle mean other than the Great Awakening, no?"

"Of course! I believe you are correct, my pet," Nigel agreed, wiggling his whiskers. "Whitefield started a movement that is leading masses of people to wake up in deciding their eternal condition."

"Do ye think hearin' Whitefield jest one time were enough ta do the tr-r-rick for the r-r-riddle?" Max asked.

"When have Gillamon's words ever meant only one thing? There are always multiple layers of meaning to his riddles," Liz replied. She looked at the fiddle. "Nigel, I do not suppose you have your bow handy, do you?" She ran her paw along the velvety stem of a pink gerbera daisy growing there next to her. "Never mind."

Liz broke off the flower stem and pulled it across the strings of Patrick's fiddle. Up rose the softest of musical notes with glowing words inside them.

Hello, little ones.
How fitting to be played with a flowery flourish
on this glorious spring day.

Nigel's jaw fell open, watching the magical notes rise and disappear into the hedge. "I never would have imagined a flower stem could play a fiddle! Brilliant!"

Only this fiddle, Nigel.
You've done well solving the first two parts
of the fiddle's riddle.
Each part builds on the one before, so everything that happens
for Patrick's voice will gain momentum from here on out.

"*Merci*, Gillamon. We were just discussing the next part of the riddle, 'a voice in the present wakes eternity *en masse.*' Are we correct to assume it involves the Great Awakening?" Liz asked, continuing to pull the daisy stem across the fiddle.

Indeed it does. But Whitefield's voice was only
Patrick's wake-up call. Of course we arranged for
Whitefield to choose Uncle Patrick's church to coincide
with another battle coming in the Henry household.
When that matter is resolved,
a more permanent voice will arrive in Hanover.

"I say, could it be Samuel Davies?" Nigel asked. "I recall John Henry mentioning his name as a young pastor in training who would come to the people here."

Precisely.
Clarie and I will escort Samuel Davies
safely to Williamsburg,
where the governor will give him a legal license
to preach here.

"If he's legal then the humans can go hear him pr-r-reach without gettin' in tr-r-rouble," Max said happily. He then shook his head in disbelief at the absurdity of the situation. "I can't believe those words jest came out of me mouth."

Davies will impact Patrick's voice
more than any other,
but he will do far more in the process.
You must see that his voice is heard clearly
by everyone in the Henry family,
including Uncle Patrick.

"We've been most distressed by this religious war in the Henry household," Nigel remarked.

"Aye, they're *all* supposed ta be on the same side—Jesus' side!" Max added.

Paul and Barnabas were also both on Jesus' side
before their argument split them apart.

"*Oui,* which led to a greater spreading of the gospel than had they stayed together," Liz recalled. "I remember how troubled we were about that war between the apostles at the time, but it all worked out better than we could have hoped."

Despite the warring between believers,
the Maker always brings good from it.
And in Patrick's case, this war is
exactly what his voice needs.
But many battles lie ahead before a truce.

The daisy stem wilted and the notes ceased coming from the fiddle.

"That's it, then," Max said. "No more notes."

"No more notes for now." Liz twirled the daisy stem in her paw and grinned. "But when the time comes to trade in my daisy stem for a quill, the pen will be mightier than the sword in this war between the Henrys."

141

A VOICE IN THE PRESENT

HANOVER, APRIL 1747

The sound of a horse coming up the entrance road to Studley caught Sarah's attention. She had been nervously waiting for word about her father, Isaac Winston. He and three other men had been indicted by the highest court in the colony of Virginia, and had to appear at the General Court in Williamsburg to answer charges.

Isaac had permitted a dissenting minister to speak without a license in his home at Laurel Grove in October 1745, the same month George Whitefield fanned the flames of religious fervor in Hanover County. Other charges included non-attendance at the Anglican Church, and helping Samuel Morris to build several reading houses in the area for the purpose of reading religious material. Sarah's dissenting father, Isaac, had actually stood before her magistrate husband John in Hanover courthouse to pay fines for not attending church.

A war of silence raged in the Henry household that night.

Sarah set her mending down and stood from her seat on the porch when she recognized her brother, John, riding up the lane. He smiled and waved his hand happily.

"Please let this mean good news," Sarah said to herself, hurriedly running down the stairs.

John jumped off his horse with a big grin and leaned over to kiss his sister on the cheek. "All is well, Sallie. Father only had to pay twenty shillings plus court costs. No jail time required," he reported.

Sarah put her hand over her heart and closed her eyes with relief. "Thank goodness."

"Father and the others had to stand before Governor Gooch and his council, but our friend Peter Fontaine was on the jury and confirmed that the services held at Laurel Grove were not riotous, nor did they go against the teachings of the Church of England," John explained.

Sarah tightened her fists. "It infuriates me that Father had to stand before anyone save his LORD! Still, I'm relieved to hear this news."

"I've got more happy news from Williamsburg," John added. "Remember when that preacher William Robinson came through here a few years ago and the Dissenters begged him to take a donation? He said he would only take it if he could use it to help the education of Samuel Davies in Pennsylvania. Well, before Father's appearance in court, that young minister Samuel Davies stood before the governor, and although he was opposed by Attorney General Peyton Randolph, he was granted a license to preach at four meeting houses! He calmly presented his case, drawing from the Toleration Act of 1689, so he honored the law and used proper procedure to secure his license. He'll be the first non-Anglican minister in Hanover County, and he's going to be preaching only four miles away from Studley!"

143

"Samuel Davies is coming to Polegreen Meeting House?" Sarah exclaimed. "When does he arrive?"

"He'll be preaching this Sunday," John answered with a wide smile. "But Sallie, I want you to know that when Davies learned about the case against Father and the others, he remained in Williamsburg to be with them. He started ministering within minutes of receiving his license."

"How wonderful!" cheered Sarah, clasping her hands with joy. "I know he and Father made fast friends."

"Yes, and Reverend Davies wants to come here to Studley to meet you and John," John continued. "Father explained the tense situation of John's position as magistrate and sheriff of Hanover, his brother's position as priest at St. Paul's, and your attendance at Polegreen Meeting House. Davies has such high respect for the law, for the church, and for the family that he wants to set everyone at ease and start off on the right foot here."

"What a breath of fresh air he will be, to all of us!" Sarah exulted with a sigh of relief, grasping his arm to take him into the house. "We need his calming influence. Blessed are the peacemakers."

Liz sat with Nigel next to a lilac bush, listening in on their conversation. "How would you like to deliver a note this afternoon?"

"Do you mean via airmail, my dear?" Nigel quipped, preening his whiskers. "I'd be delighted."

———

"There must be four hundred people here!" Patrick exclaimed as he pulled on the reins to stop the horse. The eleven-year-old boy was taking on more and more responsibilities, including driving his mother and sisters in the carriage. Today he had the privilege of driving them to church at Polegreen. "Look! There's Sam Meredith and his family. They're here, too!" He waved over at his friend Sam in the distance.

People were arriving by foot and on horses, carriages, gigs, and wagons lined up and down the road. It was a beautiful spring morning, and given the lack of rain over the past few days, the roads were dry and easy to travel for both man and beast. The sun was rising bright in the blue sky overhead. Birds darted to and fro in the trees that provided shade in the grassy area where the people gathered and excitedly greeted one another on this happy morning. Eleven o'clock was the appointed time for the service to begin, as it was the midway point of the twice-daily feeding for the farm animals. This allowed people enough time to travel to worship and back.

"Here, Pat, please take Mary," Sarah said. She handed the three year-old girl to Patrick as the others climbed down the side of the carriage. She held a blanket out to her nine-year-old daughter. "Jane, please take this, and watch out for Lucy." The girl did as she was asked.

Patrick clapped his hands once and smiled. "Come here, little Mary." He set her gently on the ground, and then offered a hand to his mother to help her down from the carriage. "I wonder if we'll be able to hear Reverend Davies, especially if he's inside."

"Only eighty people can fit inside the building, so he'll have to speak outside," Sarah answered, taking Mary by the hand. She smiled broadly, looking around at the crowd gathered to hear the new pastor. "What a wonderful beginning, to outgrow the building on his first day!"

"I see Grandfather Ike over there!" Anne cheered, pointing to a tree where Isaac Winston was waving them over.

"After you, little girl," Patrick told her with his hand at her back. He followed his sisters over to his grandfather and as Jane spread the blanket out for all of them to sit, he shook Isaac's hand.

"Good morning, Pat. I'm glad you're joining us today," Isaac said with a wink and a smile. "You're going to learn a lot from Reverend Davies, so pay close attention. He's a great man."

"I will, Grandfather," Patrick answered, smiling. Just then Sam Meredith came up to him.

"Hi, Pat," greeted Sam, then tipped his hat to all the family members there. "Good morning."

"Hi, Sam. Want to go fishing later?" Patrick asked him.

"Sure!" Sam answered. He saw Jane straightening out the blanket and smiled. "Hi, Jane."

Jane smiled a bashful grin. "Hello, Sam. Have you seen the Sheltons here? I'd love to see Sallie."

"There she is," Patrick answered for Sam, spotting Sallie about twenty yards away, sitting with her family and another little friend. He smiled and waved at the dark-haired girl, who returned the wave and the smile. "Who's that with her?"

Sam looked where Patrick pointed. "That's Elizabeth Strong. Her family is new to the area, and she and Sallie have become fast friends. I think you'll like her, Jane."

145

"I want to meet her!" Jane said. "Mother, may I go say "Hi" to Sallie?"

"Not now, Jane. They're getting ready to start the service," Sarah answered, gesturing to the front of the crowd. "You can go say "Hello" afterward."

Samuel Morris was calling the people to attention. In order for them to be able to see and hear the pastor, they had positioned a flatbed wagon near the entrance to the building.

As Samuel Morris welcomed everyone and recounted the long wait for the arrival of Davies, Max and Liz peeked out from the burlap sack where they hid in the corner of the Henry carriage.

"Looks like Davies is already surpassing expectations!" Liz cheered. "I cannot wait to hear him speak."

"He don't look too healthy, lass," observed Max with a frown as the slender, frail-looking pastor climbed up into the flatbed wagon to speak. He was nearly six feet tall, and dressed in the black gown and white wig of a parson.

"Sadly, Davies has tuberculosis," Liz answered with a frown. "And he is only twenty-four years old. But the Maker has allowed this for a reason, no?"

The shadow of a bird passed overhead, and Nigel came in for a landing. The pigeon perched on the side of the carriage and let the little mouse hop off before taking flight back up to the trees.

"Reverend Henry appears to be missing quite a few members of his flock who have wandered over to this grassy pasture for worship this morning," Nigel reported.

"That'll make the laddie madder than a hor-r-rnet's nest," Max noted.

"It will be quite the showdown at the Henry household this afternoon, I assure you," predicted Nigel. He patted Liz on the shoulder. "I delivered your 'invitation' to Reverend Henry as requested, my dear."

"*Merci*, Nigel," Liz replied. She pointed to Davies, who started to speak with a loud baritone voice that immediately captured the crowd's rapt attention. "Samuel Davies has finally arrived in Hanover. Let us hope that Armageddon does not arrive this afternoon as well."

———

146

"I really liked him. Did you see how he kept the people listening to every word he said?" Patrick asked as he gently snapped the reins to urge the horse along. "He had a lot more depth to his sermon than I'm used to hearing, no offense to Uncle Patrick."

"None taken," Sarah answered with a satisfied grin. "Tell me what you heard that impressed you most, Pat. Can you give me the main points of his sermon?"

"Sure I can," Patrick answered. "The main point of the sermon was that the Lord is the Supreme Ruler over the entire world. No earthly kingdoms can compare to His, so the people of the earth should be glad, like it says in Psalm 97."

Sarah raised her eyebrows, impressed with all that her son had soaked up from the sermon. "My, my, Pat, you were really listening."

He grinned and looked over the horse's head, which bobbed up and down as the animal clip-clopped down the road. "I always listen. And I remember everything."

"Oh, really?" his mother asked playfully with her head tilted to the side as she repositioned Mary on her lap. "Can you recite some of Davies's sermon?"

Patrick cleared his throat and adjusted his tricorn hat with a grin. He held the reins with one hand and lifted his other hand as if to make a suggestion. His tone was matter-of-fact, and he wore a pleasant expression. "Wise and good rulers are a huge blessing to their subjects. In a government where wisdom sits above everything; and where justice and fairness are balanced; where liberty and property are safe and secure; where motives are kept in check; where helpless innocence is protected," he said with a gesture to his sisters, "and where there is order—then, peace and happiness flow through the land as does . . ." he paused and gestured to the Totopotomoy ". . . a creek." His little sisters looked over at the flowing creek as the sun danced off the water. "In such a land, every heart is happy, and every face looks cheerful." He smiled, placed his hand over his heart and nodded, willing his mother and sisters to agree with what he was saying. His little sisters bobbed their heads up and down, following his lead and smiling.

His expression then turned sour, and he lowered the pitch of his voice. "But, on the other hand, 'Woe to you, oh land, when your king is a child.' That is—weak, ill-advised, thoughtless, and bad-tempered. Solomon's wise words of caution have come true time and again throughout history." He looked back at his little sisters, who were enthralled with his speech. He frowned and emphasized every point with a finger pointed at each sister. "Empires have fallen, liberty has been chained, property has been invaded, the lives of men have been randomly taken away, and misery and despair have come in like a flood—when the government has been entrusted to the hands of childish tyranny!"

147

Sarah looked back at her daughters, whose eyes widened as if they were guilty of spreading the destruction of a tyrant. She smiled and then gazed at Patrick, who shook his head sadly and continued.

"It has frequently been the unhappy fate of nations to be enslaved to such rulers. But such is the sad state of all human governments because they are run by flawed humans. Without the guiding hand of the supreme King, this world would fall into confusion," Patrick went on with a flourish of emphasis as he gazed up at the heavens with an upturned palm. "We sometimes hear of wars and rumors of wars, of thrones tottering, and kingdoms falling, and of nations raging like the waves of a stormy sea. In these times, as says the psalmist, we can say, 'The LORD reigns, he is robed in majesty and is armed with strength. The world is firmly established; it cannot be moved. Your throne was established long ago; you are from all eternity.'" As he quoted the Psalm, he kept his hopeful gaze upward as if speaking directly to God.

Patrick paused and let a moment of silence hang in the air before resuming his "sermon." "Sometimes the desires of foreign countries or even of tyrants in our own land may threaten our liberties, as a cannon aimed and ready to fire against the church of God," he began again, slowly raising the urgency in his voice, "while every believing heart trembles in fear." He lifted a hand triumphantly to the heavens. "But the Lord reigns! Let the earth, and let the Church, rejoice!" Patrick then balled his fist and gave a triumphant glance toward his mother. "He will overrule the revolutions of the world for her good; and the united powers of earth and hell shall not prevail against her!"

"Amen!" exclaimed Jane in the back of the carriage.

Sarah and Patrick exchanged a smile. He was making Davies's sermon understandable for his sisters.

"Because the One who is wisest of all sits at the helm, He can steer the feeble vessel of His church through the raging, stormy seas! He sometimes may seem to lie asleep—but in the middle of extreme danger, He will awake and still the winds and the sea with His command, 'Peace, be still!'" Patrick held out his hand as if calming raging waters all around the carriage.

148

"Men may form powerful political schemes in defiance of God, 'but God frustrates the plans of the crafty, so their efforts will not succeed. He catches those who think they are wise in their own cleverness, so their cunning schemes are stopped.'" Patrick pulled on the reins to stop the horses, and held them loosely in his hand for the perfect pause of emphasis. "Solomon wrote that the hearts of men, yes of kings, 'are in the hand of the LORD . . .'" He then snapped the reins and steered the horse to turn left. ". . . and He turns them wherever He will.'"

Patrick stopped speaking and looked forward to the road ahead. Sarah sat in stunned silence at hearing her son take the words of Reverend Samuel Davies and restate them in his own expressive language. Patrick's face then broke out in a big grin and he looked at his mother. "How was that?"

Liz smiled and whispered softly beneath the burlap, *"C'est magnifique,* my Henry."

———

"You should have heard him!" Sarah exclaimed happily.

"Yer new itinerant preacher?" Uncle Patrick asked with a huff.

Sarah leaned in close to him. "No, dear brother-in-law, your namesake *nephew.*" She smiled and sat back in her seat. "Patrick took Davies's sermon—and might I remind you, he is *not* an itinerant preacher but a minister licensed by the governor of Virginia—and made it his own. He kept the message the same, but restated it in such a way the girls could understand what Davies had preached. Patrick simplified it for them. And he enunciated every word with perfect diction," Sarah recounted, exaggerating each word for emphasis.

John raised his eyebrows. "Patrick has one of the most amazing memories I've ever seen. He can read something one time in an assignment, and remember it when I later quiz him on the subject."

"So he remembers what he hears and what he reads," Uncle Patrick stated. "We just need ta make sure that what he is hearing *and* reading are proper."

"Well, I plan to take Patrick with me to hear Reverend Davies as often as possible," Sarah told him.

"He will also continue ta go with me ta St. Paul's ta hear his uncle," John interjected quickly, gesturing to his brother Patrick. "Patrick can then decide for himself which form of worship is best."

149

They heard Max barking out in the front of the house. "Oh, that must be Reverend Davies now," Sarah guessed, standing with a broad smile to go welcome him.

Uncle Patrick's face flushed, and he leaned in to John as Sarah walked away. "Davies? He's here? Now? Her note didn't say anything about Davies being here today!"

John shrugged his shoulders.

Liz and Nigel shared a look of uncertainty as Sarah escorted Samuel Davies into the parlor. Nigel whispered, "The rumors of wars may no longer be rumors. Here he comes."

"Right this way, Reverend Davies," Sarah said. John and Uncle Patrick stood and cleared their throats.

"May I introduce Hanover's newest addition, Reverend Davies?" Sarah said happily. "This is my husband, John, and my brother-in-law, Reverend Patrick Henry."

"It's an honor, and please, call me Samuel," Davies said with a warm smile and a hand extended to the men.

"Reverend, uh, *Samuel,*" repeated John, shaking his hand. Davies's grip was surprisingly firm and the young minister looked him squarely in the eye. "Welcome ta the Henry home."

"Thank you, Major Henry," Davies said. "I am honored."

"Samuel," Uncle Patrick said coolly, next taking Davies's hand. "I understand you had quite the turnout this morning at Polegreen. On the lawn, no less. How very . . . quaint."

Davies held out both hands and humbly answered, "Why the Lord would allow me to speak for Him to such a large crowd, I do not know, but I am grateful. The far more important thing is that the people came to hear the Word of God, not to hear Samuel Davies."

"Please, sit," Sarah offered as she proceeded to pour cups of tea for the men.

Uncle Patrick raised his eyebrows, taking his cup and saucer in hand with a frown. "The people can hear the Word at St. Paul's but many chose to indeed go hear you, Reverend Davies. The pews in my parish were dotted with noticeably absent members today."

Davies clenched his jaw and nodded gently. "Reverend Henry, I wanted to come meet John and Sarah's family today, as I understand the tensions that have surrounded the Henry and Winston families. But I was also hoping especially to meet you at some point soon. So I'm delighted you are here today so I can speak my heart plainly to you."

150

Uncle Patrick sipped on his tea and gave a skeptical, "Oh?"

Davies nodded and held out his open hands. "I wish to make it clear from the start that my purpose is not to try to take *any* of your parishioners away. I will never speak ill of the Anglican Church or of you, as I've regrettably heard that some of the Dissenters have done. My respect for you, a fellow servant of the Lord, is far too great," he shared. He then turned to John and said, "As is my respect for the law and for the Crown. My goal is to answer the call of ministering to the numerous lost souls in Hanover, and to do my part in reaching whatever small portion the Lord may bring to me. And I will do so within the boundaries of the law, down to the letter. Besides, there are far more lost lambs and sheep than either one of us could ever hope to shepherd alone, don't you agree, Reverend Henry?"

Uncle Patrick set his cup and saucer on the table and straightened his waistcoat. "There are indeed many who are lost among us, but I would like ta know why ye think ye have a better message and way of reaching them than the Church of England."

"Not better, just *different,*" Davies answered energetically. "Just as Paul and Barnabas disagreed on how to go on mission and therefore parted ways, we might disagree on how to deliver the good news, but in the end, our goal is one and the same—to reach those who are lost."

John shared a quick glance with his brother and cleared his throat. "I think my brother and I both are concerned with how other preachers have stirred the people into an emotional frenzy and disrupted the community. Can ye assure us ye will not do the same? I am charged with keeping the peace in Hanover."

"As am *I*," Davies quickly answered. "While the people's hearts may be stirred by the Lord, I am not one of those preachers who will tell them they must prove their faith through an outward show of emotions. I believe the actions of a heart devoted to God show themselves in how we treat one another." He stopped and held out his hand. "I am here to offer my pledge of working side by side with you, not against you," Davies promised. "I give you my hand of friendship, and I hope you will accept it."

John nodded slowly and leaned forward to shake his hand. "Very well, Samuel. I appreciate yer words and yer offer."

Davies smiled and shook John's hand, then turned to Uncle Patrick, who breathed in deeply and pursed his lips. The skeptical reverend extended his hand. "I am not convinced, but I shall give ye the benefit of the doubt."

Davies shook his hand and nodded. "I'm happy to take that as a starting point, Reverend Henry. Thank you for listening."

Sarah noticed Patrick standing in the doorway and motioned for him to join the adults. "Pat, come in. I want you to meet Reverend Davies."

Patrick walked over and bowed slightly to the minister. "Nice to meet you, Reverend. I enjoyed your sermon today."

Sarah put her hand on Patrick's arm and proudly added, "He even recited parts of your sermon on our drive home."

Davies smiled and stood to take Patrick's hand. He placed a hand on the boy's shoulder. At six feet, he towered over the boy. "I am honored, young Master Henry. You are a fine lad. Perhaps you will grow up to be a minister such as your Uncle Patrick."

Patrick smiled and nodded humbly. "I'm not sure what I want to do, sir."

"'I know the plans I have for you, saith the Lord,'" Davies said. "Jeremiah 29:11. And He'll show you exactly what they are with time."

151

He smiled and patted Patrick on the back. "Now, I do not wish to take up your family Sabbath so I will be going. Thank you for allowing me to visit, and I look forward to seeing you again soon."

The men stood and politely shook hands as Sarah got up. "I'll show you out, Reverend."

"Call me Samuel, please," Davies requested again firmly as he followed her out of the parlor.

"If you ever do choose to become a preacher, Patrick, make sure you preach inside the sacred walls of a church and not outside like some commoner," Uncle Patrick said with a jab to Davies's morning service. He grinned at John with a smug expression.

Without a moment's hesitation Patrick answered very matter-of-factly, "Jesus preached outside."

The smug expression melted off Uncle Patrick's face as his nephew exited the room, calling for Max to go fishing with him at the creek. Liz stifled a giggle and Nigel preened his whiskers jubilantly over Patrick's quick thinking.

John swallowed a laugh. "Brother, I think ye might have met yer match today."

"Ye mean with that Davies?" Uncle Patrick answered with a harrumph.

"No," John replied with a grin. "With yer nephew."

High and Mighty

Watch your step! We're almost there," Patrick called back. The twelve-year-old jumped from rock to rock ahead of his friends. A pleasant breeze rippled through the tall green trees of the forest, bringing a welcome relief from the heat of recent days. A tiny hint of fall was in the air today. A discussion among friends about fall led to talk of pumpkins, which then led to pies, which then led to a Christmas goose, which then led to migrating birds, which then led to Patrick's eagle. He was proud of having "taught an eagle how to fly," as he phrased it, but the friends were a little skeptical. Not that Patrick ever lied, but since none of them saw him do such an amazing thing, they wondered if he might be exaggerating things. They knew he was an expert at bird calls, but teaching an eagle to fly was a bit much.

Jane, Sallie, and Elizabeth took their time, lifting the hems of their skirts so as not to get them muddy from the trail along the creek. Elizabeth Strong had become good friends with both Jane Henry and Sallie Shelton, and the trio was inseparable at the common school. Samuel Meredith and Patrick's brother William brought up the rear, carrying their muskets and telling the girls about the latest bucks they had shot while out hunting.

"Mine was at least an eight-, maybe even a *ten*-pointer," William claimed loudly. "He was huge!"

"Too bad he got away, Billy," Sam teased, jabbing the younger boy in the ribs. "Mine was six points, but he was big. Lots of meat on that buck. I cleaned him myself."

"So where is this eagle of yours, Pat?" Elizabeth wanted to know, wrinkling her nose at the thought of deer hunting and cleaning. "Do you speak eagle as well as chickadee?"

"He's around. You'll see," Patrick answered. He stopped on top of a big rock, looked back, and saw the girls following along. Sallie looked up and smiled. He returned the smile and noticed a vine hanging down over the bank. He reached for it and swung out over the creek in an arc to land back on the bank with a thud in front of the girls. He winked at them and then cupped a hand to his mouth. He tried to screech like an eagle but his changing voice cracked and came out sounding like chalk on a blackboard. The girls giggled, and he shrugged his shoulders.

Max, Liz, and Nigel trailed along behind the young people. "It would appear our young knights seem eager to impress these fair maidens," Nigel posited with a grin. "Ah, youth!"

"My Henry has become quite the daredevil," Liz added. "I hope he does not get in the habit of showing off. Or of boasting."

"He's jest havin' fun, lass," Max assured her. "We laddies like ta show off for our lassies, like when Al went ta get yer edelweiss in the Alps. Ye gotta admit that's wha' made yer heart first flutter for the daft kitty." He placed his big head in her face with a knowing grin. "Come on, lass. Ye know it did."

A shy grin grew on Liz's face. *"Oui.* It was very brave for Albert to get me that beautiful little white flower."

"So r-r-relax," suggested Max with a confident nod. "It's jest wha' we knights do."

"Is that he?" Jane asked, pointing to the bird circling high above them.

Patrick turned to see what she was pointing to. "No, that's a red-tailed hawk, little Jane."

"How can you tell the difference?" Sallie asked.

Patrick smiled broadly. *Perfect,* he thought. He then launched into a mini-lecture on the differences between birds of prey. As they reached the wide opening of the creek, Patrick said, "So the bravest of Indian warriors can wear a train of eagle feathers down his back."

"Do you have an eagle feather?" Sallie asked him.

"Yeah, Pat, if you trained an eagle, it seems like you would have gotten a feather," Sam said with a twinge of a challenge in his voice.

Patrick frowned and put his hands on his hips. *No, I don't have a feather. But I want one.* "I know where to get one." He pointed up to the eagle's nest high in the tree above them. Before anyone could say anything, he jumped up on a boulder, and hopped from one rock to another to get to the other side of the creek. He put down his musket and made his way quickly to the tree that contained Cato's nest.

The girls' eyes widened, and they put their hands up to their mouths in awe of what Patrick was getting ready to do. Sam and William sat down on the rocks and casually rested their muskets next to them. "This should be interesting," William muttered. "Pat can climb, but not that high."

"I do not like this, *mes amis,*" worried Liz with a frown. "That is too far up for him to climb!"

Max and Nigel looked at one another. "Looks like the lad jest r-r-ran off without thinkin'."

"Oh, dear," Nigel agreed.

Liz kept her worried gaze glued on Patrick, who was now climbing from branch to branch. The wind was beginning to pick up speed. She ran ahead of Max and Nigel to the creek.

155

Cato circled over the creek when he noticed movement down below. He saw Patrick and his friends, Max, Liz, and Nigel. He then noticed Patrick hurriedly crossing the creek to disappear into the greenery of the forest. Soon a gust of wind gathered together the upper branches of the trees, as if pulling back the curtains on a window, and his extremely keen eye spotted movement.

Little did anyone on the ground realize that the real threat was not looming at the top of the tree, but in the branches close to where Patrick stopped to catch his breath. A panther sat there waiting for him. Cato turned to make a rapid descent.

"There's the eagle!" shouted Sallie as she saw the white head and brown body of the majestic bird. She pointed to the bird. "He must be calling to Patrick!"

Sam and William looked at one another in disbelief. "Well, who would have thought . . ." Sam started to say.

Cato came swooping by the branches, screaming at the panther. "Don't you dare touch him!"

The panther gave a sinister laugh and answered the eagle, "This time he doesn't have a gun."

But the others do! Cato thought as he turned to circle back over the others. He screeched repeatedly, *"PANTHER! GET PATRICK OUT OF THAT TREE!"*

The friends all noticed the commotion with the bird. Sam looked down and saw the fresh tracks in the mud and his face fell. He looked up in the tree and saw what Cato had seen. A panther was sitting in the branches and Patrick was heading right for it. "Pat! Get out of that tree! Panther!" he cried.

Patrick heard Cato screeching and his friend calling, but Sam's voice was muffled with the wind that was now picking up in intensity. He looked back to his friends on the rocks. The girls were screaming, jumping up and down hysterically, and the boys were shouting and waving their arms frantically. *What are they yelling about?* He looked down and realized how high up he was, yet he still had a long way to go to reach the eagle's nest. *I was foolish to think I could reach the nest. Maybe they're telling me to stop. They're right.* He then heard Max barking in alarm. Patrick lifted his gaze and there ten feet above him was a panther. Instantly panic filled him, and he broke out in a sweat as his heart began to pound.

"Coming up for your precious feather, boy?" the panther growled, opening his mouth wide in a threatening show of teeth. *"I knew you'd try it eventually. Stupid boy! Trying to be so high and mighty."*

"Do something!" the girls screamed. Liz joined them, meowing in terror.

Max ran ahead over the rocks, barking his head off as he made his way to the other side of the creek. Sam and William grabbed their muskets and followed the little dog. "Stay here!" William told the girls.

Patrick started to climb down backward as fast as he could while the panther crouched to jump down to the next branch. Sam and William reached the other side of the creek and started making their way to the tree, following Max, who was way ahead of them.

"We can't shoot at the panther!" William shouted. "We might hit Pat!"

Cato made another pass and screeched, *"Patrick! I'll try to harass the cat. You're going to have to jump!"* The eagle soared upward, then quickly circled back. *If only the boy spoke eagle!* he thought to himself. Cato came in above the branches and got as close as he could to the panther, continuing to screech, talons protruding, but the big cat was too well protected by the foliage as he followed Patrick down the tree.

Patrick looked down to see how far he was from the ground. *Still too far!* he thought as he continued as quickly as he could from branch to branch.

Max barked, *"Jump, lad! Jump!"*

Sam cocked his musket and took aim at the panther, keeping his gaze on the big cat while his friend slowly made his way toward the earth. "Get ready to get him out of there, Bill," he said as calmly as he could.

"I'm ready," William answered. He held his gun up to use as a club if need be.

As Patrick got within a safe distance to jump, the panther lunged toward him, causing him to slip and fall just as the cat reached the branch. He landed with a hard thud and cried out just as Sam fired. A sickening growl came from the cat as it leapt from the branch and landed in the cloud of smoke, screams, and barks. William ran over to swing his musket at the cat but it darted off into the woods, choosing to fight another day. Max took off after it.

Sam and William dropped their guns and ran over to Patrick, who lay on the ground, writhing in agony and struggling to breathe. He held his upper left arm with his right hand and curled up in a ball.

"Pat!" William shouted in a panic.

157

"I think it's . . . broken," Patrick struggled to say as the boys surrounded him. He closed his eyes tight and bit his lip against the pain.

"That was close, but the cat is gone," Sam said, exhaling in nervous relief.

"Here, we'll help you up," William replied as he and Sam carefully cradled Patrick and slowly helped him to stand. He winced in excruciating pain.

"Sam, take the guns and get over to the girls," William instructed. "We had better get out of here before that panther returns."

———

Max ran as far as he could until he realized he couldn't keep up with the speedy panther. He stopped in his tracks and panted heavily, looking all around to see if he could see a trail of blood. He wasn't sure if Sam had hit the big cat or not. He gazed up to see Cato circling overhead. "Thank goodness ye sounded the alarm, laddie," he said softly to himself. He then frowned. "That big cat wasn't jest sittin' there. It were *waitin'* for Patr-r-rick."

Just then Max smelled something wafting through the air. He lifted his nose, and a low growl instinctively rumbled in his throat. "I've smelled that foul stench before."

"Max, you must hurry back to Studley!" came Nigel's voice from a pigeon overhead. "Our Patrick has broken his collarbone and everyone is in hysterics. Now Patrick is worried that you have been claimed by the panther. You need to show him you are alright so he can calm down, old boy!"

Max took a step forward and thought he saw movement about thirty yards up ahead. He frowned and answered Nigel. "Aye, I'm comin'." The Scottie turned around to hurry back to Studley.

Behind a thicket, the same eyes that had been watching Patrick for three years narrowed angrily as Max trotted away. "A broken collarbone does nothing. It should have been his *neck,*" murmured a low voice. The being heard the groans of the panther lying in a cluster of ferns. The big cat was wounded, but not mortally. Sam's bullet had simply grazed its shoulder. *No more failure from this one.* The source of the evil voice walked over to where the panther lay.

"Poor *you,*" the voice said in a mocking tone. "You only suffered a shoulder injury as did the boy. Pity."

"I tried to get him again, really I did," the panther answered nervously.

"Of *course* you did!" the voice said, cackling with a sarcastic, sinister laugh. "THREE TIMES, NO LESS!" the voice screamed. It paused to quickly change its tone from anger to that of icy contempt. "That's enough. For you," the voice calmly said as it leaned in close over the big cat, filling the panther's eyes with fear. "Something to ease the pain?"

158

HONEY TO THE BONES

arah winced as she tightened the linen sling around Patrick's neck to hold his arm in place. It hurt her to see her son in so much pain. He tearfully groaned, and she dabbed a soft cloth on his forehead to wipe away the sweat and grime caked on his face from his fall onto the hard dirt. "There now, the bone is set. Close your eyes and try to rest."

"I was so foolish." Tears leaked out of Patrick's eyes onto the flat pillow. "And now Max is missing, and who knows if the panther got him?! Please, Mother, we have to make sure he's alright. If anything happens to him . . ." He caught his breath with a wave of pain.

"Shhhhh," Sarah said softly, wiping away his tears. "I'm sure Max is fine." She looked back to the doorway where all Patrick's little sisters were huddled together. They were worried sick about their big brother. Sarah smiled at them and motioned for them to stay where they were so as not to disturb Patrick. "Your sisters are here checking on you, Pat."

"We love you, Pat!" they whisper-shouted.

Patrick tried to lift up his head to answer them but felt a sharp jab of pain and stayed where he was. "Thanks, little girls." His voice was broken and exhausted.

Liz made her way through the legs of the girls and jumped softly onto the bed, slowly walking over the blanket to inspect Patrick's arm. She frowned, seeing his condition and the pain written all over his face. *"Je suis désolée, mon Henry,"* she meowed softly. *"But I am relieved you suffered only a broken collarbone. Do not worry about anything. I will stay with you until you are healed."* She curled up by him so he could feel her presence next to his leg.

Sarah smiled at Liz. She told her son, "You have a little nurse to stay with you while you rest."

Patrick closed his eyes and placed his hand on Liz's soft fur to feel her purring next to him.

Suddenly Max barked outside, and Patrick opened his eyes. A grateful lump rose in his throat, and his lip trembled happily through tears. "He's alright. Oh, he's alright."

"Now you can rest easy," Sarah said soothingly, cupping Patrick's cheek in her hand. "You are safe. Max is safe, and Liz is here. I'm going to let you sleep." She kissed his forehead and stood to leave. "Call out if you need me. I'll have William and John sleep elsewhere tonight so you can have it quiet and still in here."

"Thank you, Mother," Patrick whispered back. "And I'm sorry."

"Shhhhh, no more talk. Rest," Sarah answered. She shooed the girls out from the doorway and closed the door behind her.

Patrick inhaled deeply and softly petted Liz. "Thank God you're here, and that Max is safe."

160

"I will be here when you awaken, mon cher *Henry,"* Liz answered softly.

Soon Patrick drifted off to sleep, and so did Liz. It was only twilight, but they both felt as if they had lived a thousand lifetimes in the course of one terrifying afternoon.

—————

Nigel and Max sat outside under the window by Patrick's room. "I'm tellin' ye, that weren't no ordinary cat. It were after the lad," Max told the mouse.

"It certainly seems that way, despite the unwise decision the boy made to climb the tree," Nigel agreed. "Thank goodness Cato saw what was happening. I conferred with him about the incident, and he was most distressed about it."

"Well at least Patr-r-rick's safe now," Max stressed. He hesitated, furrowing his brow. "When I were out there chasin' after that panther . . . I smelled somethin' str-r-range."

"What kind of strange, old boy?" Nigel queried, straightening his spectacles.

"Like somethin' I haven't smelled in thousands of years," Max replied.

Nigel's eyes widened. "Do you mean like the dank tombs of ancient *Egypt?*"

Max looked Nigel in the eye. "No, Mousie. Even earlier than that."

———

"Good afternoon, John," Samuel Davies said as he pulled on the reins to stop the horse drawing his gig. He came to a complete stop, and John walked over to greet him. "I've come to check on Patrick. I was so sorry to hear about his accident."

"Good day, Reverend," John answered. "That's very kind of ye."

Davies climbed out of the gig and shook John's hand. "How is he?"

"He's in a lot of pain," John answered with a frown, staring at the ground, shaking his head. "With him being such an active lad, I think the boredom might be an even worse malady for him in the coming weeks. There's only so much Latin and Livy a sick lad can take."

Davies folded his hands in front of him and nodded. "Yes, I can imagine. Such an injury requires rest and no movement, especially for the first couple of weeks. I hope I can give him some words of encouragement."

"We appreciate ye coming ta see him, Reverend," John replied. "Pat has such respect for ye, especially after all ye went through with yer recent losses. It takes a great amount of strength ta lose a wife and baby in childbirth, and keep on with yer responsibilities in the midst of it all."

Davies tightened his mouth and nodded humbly. "The Lord is my strength." He stopped and lifted a hand to Sarah, who came out to greet him. "Good day, Sarah. How is our patient?"

"He's very *im*patient, Samuel," Sarah answered, wiping her hands on a towel. "Pat will be so happy to see you."

Davies looked at John and Sarah. "Before we go in, I wanted to let you know that some men found that panther deep in the woods yesterday. It was dead."

"Oh, what a relief to hear that!" Sarah said, placing her hand over her heart.

"So Sam's musket ball got it?" John asked.

"From what they could tell, the ball only grazed the cat," Davies answered. "The strange part was that it appeared as if the panther had been poisoned."

John and Sarah looked at one another in surprise and then to Davies, asking in unison, "Poisoned?"

161

"Evidently," Davies answered. "Perhaps the beast got into some bad mushrooms or met up with a snake."

"Well, I'm just glad it's dead and will no longer be a danger to the children," Sarah answered. "Let's go in, and you can tell Patrick."

The minister nodded and touched his hat, bowing slightly. "John."

John nodded and touched his hat in respect. "Reverend."

Davies put his hand on John's arm. "Call me 'Samuel,' please."

John smiled. "Aye, very well. *Samuel.*" The two men shared a grin and then Davies followed Sarah inside.

"Pat, you have a visitor," Sarah announced, as she led Davies into the room.

Patrick used his good arm to position himself higher in the bed. "Who is it?" Davies appeared behind his mother, and Patrick smiled. "Reverend Davies!"

"Hello, Patrick," Davies responded with a smile as he walked over to the bed. "How are you today?"

"I'm bored, sir," Patrick answered honestly. "I've been in this bed for a week, and I just want to be well."

"I'll leave you two to chat," Sarah told them with a smile as she left the room.

"Waiting on things is hard. But when you're waiting on the right thing, it's always worth it," Davies said, pulling up a chair. He spotted Liz. "And who is this?"

"That's Liz," Patrick answered happily. "She hasn't left my side since I got hurt."

"Good friends do that. They stay by your side through the hard times as well as the good times," shared Davies, giving Liz a scratch under the chin.

"*I am pleased to finally meet you in person,* Monsieur *Davies,*" Liz meowed.

"She's a very talkative cat," Patrick told Reverend Davies with a grin. "My dog Max is outside."

"Patrick, I wanted to let you know they found the panther dead in the woods," Davies reported, "so you won't have to worry about that threat anymore."

Patrick's eyes widened with relief. "That's great news, Reverend! Sam has always been one of the best shots around."

"Well, this time Sam only grazed the big cat. The men who

found the panther related that it looked as if it was poisoned," Davies explained.

Poisoned? Liz thought. For some reason her thoughts ran back immediately to ancient Rome. Al had witnessed the poisoning of Emperor Claudius.

"Poisoned? How could a panther be poisoned out in the middle of the woods?" Patrick wanted to know.

Davies shrugged his shoulders. "I'm not sure, but let's talk about you. Your mother said you met that panther while climbing a tree." Patrick lowered his gaze, and a look of shame came over his face. Davies tilted his head. "Do you want to talk about what happened?"

"I was foolish," Patrick replied softly. He shook his head and then raised his gaze to look into the face of his pastor. "Can I tell you something? I told my parents the truth, that I was climbing a tree when I saw the panther, but I didn't tell them *why.*"

Davies nodded. "You can tell me anything, Patrick."

"I was climbing the tree because I was showing off," Patrick admitted. "I've bragged about how I trained an eagle to fly. I may have helped the little eagle, but I didn't really train him. He learned to fly on his own. And I wanted to get an eagle feather since Indian warriors earn them for doing brave things. I guess I wanted everyone to think I was smart and brave, too. So I said I could climb that tree to reach the eagle's nest and get a feather. If I hadn't been so hasty and proud, none of this would have happened."

163

Davies leaned over and rested his elbows on his knees. *"'Pride goes before destruction, a haughty spirit before a fall'* the sixteenth Proverb tells us. In your case, it was a *literal* fall out of a tree. Thank you for sharing the truth, Patrick." He leaned back in his chair. "Pride is the deadliest thing you could ever play with. Learn this hard lesson now, and it will save you more aches and pains throughout the rest of your life."

"Why deadly?" Patrick asked.

"Pride is why God cast Lucifer out of heaven. He was the most beautiful, most promising, most powerful, and most gifted angel that God had created. But he wanted to be all powerful and have all the praise. He wanted to be God," Davies explained. "Most of the heartache in this world can usually be traced back to pride, for it causes men to do the most selfish of things. Anytime men want to be a 'god' of their world, pride is always at the root of it. Lucifer uses the very thing that caused him to be cast out of heaven as his favorite weapon to cause men to stumble as well."

Patrick lifted his hand to touch his collarbone and thought a moment. "That makes sense."

"Throughout history it has always been the same. The heroes God used to do great things first had to be emptied of their pride," Davies explained. "You see, Patrick, before God's heroes can be of any use to Him, they must no longer be of any use to themselves."

Patrick nodded and was quiet for a moment. "I asked Sam and the others not to share what I was really doing in that tree. I've learned my lesson about bragging," confessed Patrick. "I never want to make it about me anymore."

"You want to *earn* that eagle feather, not take it," Davies added with a smile. "Trophies are hollow if they aren't won honestly."

"Thank you, Reverend Davies," Patrick said with a smile. "Your words are helpful."

164

"*The heart of the wise instructs his mouth, and adds persuasiveness to his lips. Pleasant words are a honeycomb, Sweet to the soul and healing to the bones.*' Those verses are also in the sixteenth Proverb," Davies said. "It means that intelligent people *think* before they speak; what they say is then more persuasive. And kind words are like honey—sweet to the taste and good for your health. Healing to broken bones such as yours." He smiled and pointed to Patrick's shoulder. "Always remember the opposite of this is true. Fools don't think before they speak, and mean words are hurtful to the bones."

"I think I need to learn that Proverb by heart," Patrick said with a smile.

"*I am enjoying this 'sweet talk' very much, no?*" Liz meowed, thrilled to hear all these wise words pouring into her Henry.

"Told you she likes to talk," Patrick said with a chuckle. Then he wrinkled his brow, thinking about the harsh words he had heard about Dissenters in his own household. "Reverend Davies, can I ask you about something else that has bothered me for a long time?"

"Absolutely, Patrick," Davies replied, petting Liz.

"How do you handle it when men say mean words about you and your Dissenter preaching?" Patrick asked.

"I take comfort from the fact that I am hemmed in and surrounded by a power far greater than men," Davies answered with a smile. "It matters not what men say about me, but it matters tremendously what I say or don't say about them or to them. Remember the Presbyterian tenet of our faith: God alone is the Lord of the conscience, and hath left it free from the doctrines and commandments of men; and that the rights of private judgment, in all matters that respect religion, are universal and inalienable."

"What does inalienable mean?" inquired Patrick.

"Inalienable means something that can't be taken away," Davies explained.

Patrick thought a moment. "Which is right? What the government says or what God says?"

"My first allegiance is to God, then to government," Davies said. "But God created the authority of government. Isaiah wrote that 'the government shall be upon his shoulder.' He commands us to obey such authority, as long as it does not conflict with his primary law of commandments. So I've had to balance the two in how I conduct myself in coming to Virginia."

"What about when members of your own family disagree?" Patrick wanted to know. "Father and Uncle Patrick say I should be Anglican, but Mother says I should be Presbyterian."

"You need to find your own voice in this, Patrick," Davies encouraged him. "What do *you* say you should be?"

"I'm both, but I'm neither. I'm not a Presbyterian or an Anglican," Patrick answered. "I'm a *Christian*. And that to me is the most important thing to be."

"I think that is a *fine* way of looking at it," Davies replied happily. "You know, while the Great Awakening movement has caused conflict across the colonies, it has also unified hearts around one cause. Isn't it interesting that the first time the colonies have ever come together for anything has been for the Great Awakening?" He leaned in and smiled. "Jesus unified a continent."

Patrick raised his eyebrows. "And *that's* a fine way of looking at it, too!"

Davies smiled and petted Liz again while he looked around the room. He saw Patrick's fiddle sitting there. "I hear you are quite the fiddle player. I would love to hear you play."

Patrick sighed. "I don't know when I'll be able to play it again." He pointed to his shoulder.

"What about the flute?" Davies asked him.

"I've never thought about that. I'm a fiddle player," Patrick replied.

"That doesn't mean you can't learn to play the flute, too," Davies suggested with a smile, getting up from the chair. "Wait here a moment."

"I'm not going anywhere. Doctor Henry's orders, meaning my mother," Patrick replied.

Davies chuckled and left the room.

"I see why you like him, mon ami," Liz meowed. *"And I see why Gillamon said you would learn so much from him."*

Davies quickly returned and held in his hands an ebony wooden flute with six finger holes. "I just so happen to have a flute with me, and I wish to give it to you as a get-well gift."

"For me?! Oh, Reverend, thank you!" Patrick exclaimed happily as Davies put the instrument into his hand.

"It was given to me by a friend, but I have never played it. I am unable to do so with my condition," shared Davies. "I need to save my lung power for my preaching. So I'd like you to have it if you'll promise to learn to play it."

"I will! Thank you so much!" Patrick said excitedly, putting the flute to his lips and blowing into the hole, making a squeaking sound. He and Davies shared a chuckle. "It will take me time to learn."

Davies held out his hands and looked around the room. "And how fortunate for you that you have plenty of *that,* young Mr. Henry."

"That I do," Patrick replied with a broad grin.

"Well, I shall leave you with it, and I hope to see you able to return to worship soon," Davies said. "And Patrick, I will keep your confidence in what you shared with me today. No one has to know how or why you broke your collarbone. You've benefited from a lesson learned, and that is all that matters."

"Thank you for everything, Reverend Davies," Patrick said, holding up the flute. "And for the flute."

"You're welcome. You can play it at Polegreen when you're well," Davies replied with a smile.

"I will!" Patrick replied. "Good-bye and thanks again."

Davies leaned over and gave Liz a final scratch under the chin. "Take good care of Patrick now, Liz."

"This is why I am here, no?" Liz meowed in reply.

Davies chuckled and left the room. Patrick proceeded to put the flute up to his mouth and moved his fingers along the six holes to learn the notes. He paused and smiled. He was so happy to have something new to do, and his spirits rose from his talk with Davies.

'*A voice in the present wakes eternity* en masse,' Liz thought to herself. She smiled as she watched Patrick. *Davies is not only living up to the riddle, but he has sweetened it, with honey to my Henry's bones.*

167

21

GOD'S RIDDLE

CHRIST CHURCH, PHILADELPHIA, PENNSYLVANIA, APRIL 27, 1749

Benjamin Franklin made his way down the center aisle to the front of Christ Church and stepped into his rented pew, number 70, eight rows from the pulpit. As he took his seat he gazed up at the magnificent brass chandelier hanging above his right shoulder. Its wrought iron stem was attached to the soaring ceiling by a cable chain, and its twenty-four tiered, S-shaped arms each held two candles that cast a welcome, warm glow across the beautiful sanctuary. Although it was morning, the dark sky outside boded an approaching storm. The forty-three-year-old Franklin studied the flickering candle-light and silently calculated the longevity of the forty-eight burning candles against the length of the coming sermon: *I pray the light will outlast the pulpit's occupant.*

Although he attended church now and then, Franklin did not have a great interest in organized religion. His father had wanted him to be a minister, but lack of funds yielded only two years' worth of schooling for the young Franklin, and at the age of ten his education and life path were his alone to make. He loved to read and at the age of eleven picked up *Plutarch's Parallel Lives* as well as *Pilgrim's Progress*, both of which became numbered among his favorite books. His curiosity about how things worked led him on a never-ending journey of discovery, scouring newspapers as well as the world around him to learn all he could. His first invention was a pair of swim fins, which he made when he was eleven years old, for his hands.

Young Benjamin also dabbled in writing, penning a ballad after the capture of Blackbeard the Pirate when he was twelve. At fifteen, his father sent him to apprentice with his brother James, who founded and published the *New-England Courant*. He longed to write for the newspaper, but had a difficult relationship with his mean brother, who would not allow him to do so. This didn't stop Benjamin. He posed as an old widowed woman named 'Silence Dogood' and wrote fourteen letters that he slipped under the door of the print shop at night. The readers of Boston loved the witty and opinionated woman, but when Benjamin finally revealed himself as the author, his brother was furious. He eventually left Boston and found his way to Philadelphia to work in a print shop there. Soon he was duped into travelling to London in 1724 to buy printing supplies on a false promise of help to set up his very own print shop, and found himself stranded there without a job. It was then he met young David Henry, another young man struggling to become a printer in London. Neither of them knew that their friendship would one day electrify the world.

But Gillamon knew. Not everything, of course, only that they needed to meet. So he had arranged for Benjamin Franklin and David Henry to work together as journeyman printers for one Samuel Palmer. Franklin eventually headed home to Philadelphia and rose through the ranks of the printing world in America until he purchased the *Pennsylvania Gazette* in 1729, and became the official printer for the Colony of Pennsylvania a year later. In 1732, he began publishing the wildly popular *Poor Richard's Almanack*, selling ten thousand copies a year throughout the colonies. Meanwhile David Henry rose in the British printing world to become editor of the most widely read paper in the world, *Gentleman's Magazine*. Of course David had help, courtesy of Max, Kate, and Nigel, who arranged for him to meet and marry the sister of Edward Cave, founder of *Gentleman's Magazine*. The Order of the Seven had encircled these two men all their lives to help them meet and realize their purpose. Now Gillamon couldn't wait until Franklin met the next human connected to their mutual mission—David Henry's cousin, Patrick Henry.

Benjamin Franklin believed in one supreme Deity, and that the most acceptable service to God was doing good to man. He believed in the value of churches in bringing good and encouraging virtuous behavior in the community, but he cared not which religion a church claimed. Although his wife Deborah was a member here at Christ Church, and his children had been baptized here, most Sundays found Franklin reading and writing on his own. But today he ventured out against the dark skies of Philadelphia to warm his rented pew. It was always prudent for the famous printer of the *Pennsylvania Gazette* to be seen at church, if anything to be a walking advertisement to remind the parishioners of his work. He had made a fortune printing and selling George Whitefield's sermons when the preacher came through Philadelphia during the Great Awakening. He was now moving on from the printing business to other pursuits, namely his science experiments and higher learning for others. He was looking for investors to fund the establishment of a college. He reasoned that Pennsylvania needed to have an academy on par with Harvard, William & Mary, Yale, and Princeton, so he published a pamphlet on *Proposals Relating to the Education of Youth in Pennsylvania.* When he heard that a wealthy visitor from London was in town, he took the chance he could meet him at church.

Franklin's smiling eyes met others seated around him, and he nodded politely as he settled into his red velvet cushioned pew. He looked up to the balcony and the soaring arched windows to appreciate the beautiful architecture of this sanctuary, now five years old. The magnificent brick Christ Church was missing a steeple, and Franklin thought the cityscape of Philadelphia, the largest city in budding America, needed one. After all, the bells could ring out news for the city and the lanterns serve as lighthouses for approaching ships in the harbor. *Churches are such practical things,* he thought.

The bronze, 350-pound Great Bell rang from the small wooden belfry outside, signaling the top of the hour and the call to worship, as it had done since 1702 when it arrived from Whitechapel Foundry in London. Franklin sat listening to the peal of the bell, silently calculating in his mind, *Forty-seven years times fifty-two Sundays times the eleventh hour equals roughly twenty-seven thousand rings. Of course one must consider the other occasions for bell ringing to get a full count of times the clapper has struck the bell . . .*

Franklin's thoughts were interrupted as music for the worship service began. He adjusted his spectacles and rested his hands atop his walking stick held between his black and gold-buckled shoes. His receding hairline was compensated for by its length. His grey-streaked, shoulder-length hair danced around the neckline of his blue satin coat as his head kept time with the punctuated notes of the organ's staccato rhythm. He gazed out the window at the trees blowing in the wind in the courtyard, and soon saw rain drops pelting the glass. The spring shower was coming full force now, enveloping the church. Franklin frowned at the storm. *If this bad weather continues it will delay my experiments this week.*

"Today we have a special guest visiting from London, who has made a gracious contribution to our church building fund," the rector announced, jarring Franklin's attention back to the pulpit. "I have granted his request to read this morning's Scripture, which is remarkably appropriate for this morning's weather." He lifted his arm and smiled at the visitor who approached the pulpit. "Mr. Gillamon, if you'd be so kind."

Gillamon left his red cloak in the pew as he made his way up the few steps to reach the pulpit. He bowed his head humbly. "I thank you, Reverend, for this honor." He looked around the room, and his eyes landed briefly on Benjamin Franklin. "The reading of today's Holy Writ comes from Job, chapter 38." A rumble of thunder echoed in the distance and an imperceptible smile crept onto Gillamon's face. "Hear now the word of the Lord:

171

> "Then the Lord answered Job from the whirlwind: 'Who is this that questions my wisdom with such ignorant words? Brace yourself like a man, because I have some questions for you, and you must answer them. Where were you when I laid the foundations of the earth? Tell me, if you know so much. Who determined its dimensions and stretched out the surveying line? What supports its foundations, and who laid its cornerstone as the morning stars sang together and all the angels shouted for joy? Who kept the sea inside its boundaries as it burst from the womb, and as I clothed it with clouds and wrapped it in thick darkness? For I locked it behind barred gates, limiting its shores. I said, 'This far and no farther will you come. Here your proud waves must stop!'"

Franklin's mind was energized by God's rapid-fire questions aimed at Job. He would mentally pause at each question, attempting to seek an answer. *Seas are bound by land, but currents run through them from one land to the next . . .*

> "Have you ever commanded the morning to appear and caused the dawn to rise in the east? Have you made daylight spread to the ends of the earth, to bring an end to the night's wickedness?

As the light approaches, the earth takes shape like clay pressed beneath a seal; it is robed in brilliant colors. The light disturbs the wicked and stops the arm that is raised in violence. Have you explored the springs from which the seas come? Have you explored their depths? Do you know where the gates of death are located? Have you seen the gates of utter gloom? Do you realize the extent of the earth? Tell me about it if you know!"

I wish I knew the extent of the earth! Franklin answered in his mind. *I wonder if a corked bottle set afloat could travel on those sea currents around the world. A message tucked inside the bottle could relay such an experiment . . .*

"Where does light come from, and where does darkness go?" bellowed Gillamon's voice, bringing Franklin's attention back to God's riddling conversation with Job. "Can you take each to its home? Do you know how to get there? But of course you know all this! For you were born before it was all created, and you are so very experienced! Have you visited the storehouses of the snow or seen the storehouses of hail? I have reserved them as weapons for the time of trouble, for the day of battle and war. Where is the path to the source of light? Where is the home of the east wind?"

At that moment a boom of thunder shook the church, and a deluge of rain pattered on the roof. "Who created a channel for the torrents of rain? Who laid out the path for the lightning? Who makes the rain fall on barren land, in a desert where no one lives? Who sends rain to satisfy the parched ground and make the tender grass spring up? Does the rain have a father? Who gives birth to the dew? Who is the mother of the ice? Who gives birth to the frost from the heavens? For the water turns to ice as hard as rock, and the surface of the water freezes.

"Can you direct the movement of the stars—binding the cluster of the Pleiades or loosening the cords of Orion? Can you direct the constellations through the seasons or guide the Bear with her cubs across the heavens? Do you know the laws of the universe? Can you use them to regulate the earth? Can you shout to the clouds and make it rain?"

Gillamon paused, and the darkened sky lit up with a flash of lightning. He looked right at Benjamin Franklin. "Can you make lightning appear and cause it to strike as you direct?"

Franklin raised his eyebrows. *What an intriguing thought!* He turned his gaze to the rain-streaked windows as the storm continued to rage outside. *Wouldn't that make for quite the philosophical amusement?*

"Who gives intuition to the heart and instinct to the mind?" Gillamon continued, keeping his gaze on Franklin. The corners of his mouth turned upward, as he could see the wheels turning inside the brilliant inventor's mind. "Who is wise enough to count all the clouds? Who can tilt the water jars of heaven when the parched ground is dry and the soil has hardened into clods?" He kept reading to the end of the chapter but Benjamin Franklin wasn't listening.

Gillamon finally took his seat and, outside, the Great Bell rang out, as the storm raged around Christ Church. Ever since St. Thomas Aquinas declared that "the tones of the consecrated metal repel the demon and avert storm and lightning," churches had rung their bells during storms. For centuries, God-fearers believed that lightning was the expression of God, but that the bells of a church could ward off the dreaded scourge. Gillamon smiled at Franklin, whom he could tell was already in his mental laboratory, hard at work.

How can it be that so many churches have been struck by lightning while the bell ringers were ringing the bells, even killing some of them? Franklin thought to himself, furrowing his brow. *The lightning seems to strike steeples of choice and at the very time the bells are ringing.* He looked up at the cross of Christ in the large window over the pulpit. *I cannot imagine God would randomly punish his followers in such a way. If God makes lightning appear and causes it to strike as He directs it, He must be using His own laws of nature to do so. And those laws of nature are as constant and steadfast as their Creator.*

Franklin glanced over and met Gillamon's knowing gaze. He nodded and smiled and then looked out the window as another flash of lightning lit up the sky. '*Can you make lightning appear and cause it to strike as you direct?*' he recalled God's question posed to Job. *Churches— God, bells—metal, steeples—sky. I am not Job, but I believe it is now time to try some other trick to answer God's riddle.*

173

A Brilliant Move

The fresh fragrance of spring filled the air on this sun-drenched Sunday. Max, Liz, and Nigel walked through the fields of Studley Plantation, waiting for Patrick's return from the church service at Polegreen.

"So is the new house finished yet, Mousie?" Max asked.

"Not yet, but Cato and I did a flyover yesterday and it's coming along splendidly," Nigel answered. "It's a charming English-style house with a solid brick foundation for the story-and-a-half structure. I took the liberty of inspecting the roof and was quite impressed to see the hand-hewn oak framing."

Liz noticed a butterfly flitting around them. "I look forward to seeing the new Henry *château!* I was most pleased when I first walked around the *petite* mountain where their new home could sit. It reminded me of my home in France." She winked at Nigel. "I am pleased that John Henry pursued our 'anonymouse' suggestion to build on that property, *Monsieur* Monaco. You make a delightful travelling surveyor on paper, no?"

"Indeed! I rather liked posing behind the quill as a Frenchman traveling through the Virginia countryside." Nigel chuckled and preened his whiskers excitedly. "My dear, the landscape is lovely, just like your beloved Norman countryside. Six hundred thirty acres of rolling land that gently slopes downward more than half a mile to the South Anna River."

"But it's a shame the Henrys have ta leave Studley," Max replied. "That *we* have ta leave Studley. Movin' twenty miles away will take us far from the forest an' Cato."

"Max, I assure you Patrick will be *thrilled* with the adventure of new fishing spots and swimming holes," Nigel assured his canine friend. "There's a whole new forest of tall trees with wild game for him to hunt and birds for him to talk to."

"You see Max, John Syme, Jr., has come of age, and Studley by right of inheritance is his land," Liz explained. "So John Henry must honor the way things are and move the family."

The butterfly landed atop Max's nose. Suddenly Clarie interjected, "Things never stay the same, Max, and lots of changes are in the air. You'll be leaving Patrick Henry soon as it is. Gillamon has new instructions for all of us."

Liz smiled. *"Bonjour,* Clarie! What do you mean? Where will Max go?"

"For now, you and Max will both move with the Henrys to their new home twenty miles from here," Clarie answered. "Keep up your watch care of Patrick in the new forest and get him settled in his home. His time to enjoy this new home will be short-lived, however. He is growing up and the time for deciding what he will do with his life is at hand. He will soon take the next step to find his voice."

175

Liz wrinkled her brow. "Hmmm, the next part of the fiddle's riddle says 'a voice in the tavern.' Does that mean he will work in a tavern? How can this be a career choice that will lead him to greatness?"

"You'll see. Sometimes young people have to experience failure as they figure out the right path over time," Clarie explained with a knowing grin. "Speaking of time, Patrick cannot know that you are immortal, so in the coming years you and Max both will need to leave him for a while. Max, you will go on assignment to help Gillamon watch over George Washington."

"Weren't he the lad who lost his father at the beginnin' of this mission?" Max asked.

"Yes, he's now seventeen and has just received his surveyor's license from the College of William and Mary," Clarie reported. "In the near future, he will head to the Ohio country and will need your protection. Nothing, and I mean NOTHING, can be allowed to harm George Washington. Know that when the time comes, you and Gillamon will be very busy in making sure no harm reaches him."

"Aye, lass, ye can count on me," Max stated determinedly. "Wha' aboot Patr-r-rick's pr-r-rotection?"

"There is no threat to him for the time being," she assured him. "Liz, when the time comes for you to 'leave' Patrick's sight, you will actually still remain near him, but he must not know it. When you later 'reappear,' he will think you are simply a different black cat who resembles his beloved 'Liz.'"

"This makes sense, no? My brilliant Henry of course would figure out that something was amiss if his pets kept living for years on end," Liz answered.

"If I may, back to the current situation with the Henry move. What about Patrick's ability to hear Samuel Davies on Sundays?" Nigel asked. "Twenty miles may be short as the eagle flies, but not for humans over country roads. It would be too far for them to drive to Polegreen Church once they move."

"We arranged for Davies to be granted a license to preach in the Ground Squirrel Meeting House, only three miles from their new home, so Patrick will be able to continue learning from Davies at that location," Clarie told him. "But Nigel, you need to leave for Philadelphia. It is time to start your mission with Benjamin Franklin."

176

Nigel clapped his paws. "Jolly good! How I've looked forward to this mission. I say, should I enlist Cato as my transport?"

"Yes, in fact Cato is *meant* to be your transport, for this will be the first of many flights to Philadelphia," Clarie answered. "Gillamon set things in motion with Ben Franklin today at Christ Church. When Franklin established the first library in Philadelphia, a merchant in London named Peter Collinson became his contact for ordering books. They soon discovered a mutual love for scientific discovery. For the past couple of years Franklin has been corresponding with Collinson about his experiments with electricity in the laboratory. But as of today, Ben will begin a whole new quest of discovery to learn about electricity and *lightning*. Nigel, you must see to it that he writes to Collinson about these new ideas, taken from his journal notes. Al and Kate will figure out a way to then get those letters to David Henry. It is *vital* that Ben's work be published for more eyes to see than just Mr. Collinson's."

"Brilliant!" Nigel cheered. "Is that all? A simple mission of correspondence?"

Clarie smiled. "Hardly, Nigel. The letters are just the beginning. You will then need to help Ben figure out how to actually conduct his experiments."

Nigel's eyes widened, and his whiskers wiggled. "How *utterly* thrilling! What bliss to delve into the world of scientific discovery! Splendid!"

"I think Mousie's excited," Max teased with a chuckle.

"Clarie, I was fascinated to learn that Benjamin Franklin and David Henry know each other," Liz added. "It seems with this mission there are many connections taking place over in London."

"Yes, we have been setting things in place for quite some time, but you'll be happy to know that it was Al who came up with the brilliant idea to connect these men even further," Clarie replied. Liz beamed. *"Bon!* What was my Albert's idea?"

"It involves Nigel's favorite composer," Clarie answered with a grin.

"Mr. Handel?" Nigel exclaimed.

"Yes, Mr. George F. Handel himself. As you know, part of your mission to help Handel write *Messiah* was so it would become the most famous music ever written or performed. Since *Messiah's* initial debut in London, it has not been performed much in seven years. So as Kate was working on a way to promote *Messiah,* Al had an idea to help hurting children at the same time," Clarie explained. "Peter Collinson is not only a scientist who corresponds with Benjamin Franklin, but he also established the Foundling Hospital for Children in London. Al suggested the idea of Handel performing *Messiah* to help raise money for the children, so Gillamon and I will soon set things in motion to make that benefit concert happen."

177

"Jolly good show!" Nigel cheered. "I must say I am delightfully surprised that Al suggested this, since music is not his *forte.*"

"Music, no, but children, *oui! C'est magnifique!* My Albert is much smarter than he lets on," Liz beamed proudly. "I presume that in addition to Peter Collinson, David Henry will be there."

Clarie nodded. "Yes, Kate will see to it that David publicizes the event in *Gentleman's Magazine.* This benefit concert will finally not only be the key to *Messiah's* success, but will be the first key on the ring to unlock future success for Franklin, Patrick Henry, and ultimately America."

"Wha' a br-r-rilliant move with that kitty an' me bonnie lass!" Max cheered with a grin, wagging his tail.

"Stupendous!" Nigel welled up with emotion. "How glorious for Handel's *Messiah* to finally get the attention it deserves while helping the orphaned children of London."

"So Handel, Henry, and Collinson will all be connected to this event . . ." Clarie started to say.

"*Ergo,* Henry and Collinson will then be connected for publishing Franklin's electric letters!" Nigel quickly interjected. "My dear, this is a brilliant plan!"

"I understand the keys for helping Handel and Franklin, but how will any of this help my Henry and America?" Liz asked with a puzzled expression. "How can this be?"

"Time will tell, Liz," Clarie replied with a smile. "It always does. In the meantime, why don't you come up with a name for the new Henry plantation—your 'little mount' as you call it? Since it was your brilliant idea, feel free to put your name to it. You can help John Henry 'come up with the name himself.'" She winked at Liz and flew off.

Liz smiled shyly as she watched the butterfly flitter into the air. "Hmmm . . . Mount Lizette. No, this is much too obvious, no?"

"Clarie said it were yer *brilliant* idea, lass," Max added with a grin.

Nigel tapped a finger on his chin. "Right! Isn't your maiden name Lizette *Brillante,* my dear? And didn't the Henry ancestors originate from your home of Normandy, France?"

Liz's eyes lit up with delight. "*Oui! C'est magnifique!* Perhaps a name that speaks to their Norman roots?" she answered. "*La Montagne Brillante,*" she said softly, pondering a minute longer.

"But the Henrys be Scottish now, lass," Max reminded her. "Scots wouldn't dare name their house after the Fr-r-renchies. Ye better translate it then."

"*C'est vrai,* Max," Liz answered. She broke out in a wide grin. "Then the name will be . . . Mount Brilliant."

PHILADELPHIA, APRIL 29, 1749

"I was so little when they took me away to London that I don't remember much about this place. I've never seen anything like this before!" Cato exclaimed, as he and Nigel soared over the city of Philadelphia. Wide, dusty streets and broad thoroughfares framed the bustling city below, with occasionally paved narrow back streets and alleys peeling off to reach row upon row of merchant buildings. "What kind of fat, red trees are those?"

Nigel smiled and patted the eagle on his shoulder. "My boy, those are not trees but *buildings*. The humans make them with the wood from trees and also with hard, red objects called bricks." Nigel scanned the busy harbor filled with tall ships unloading cargo. "Welcome back to your hometown of Philadelphia! Of course *this* Philadelphia is nothing like the original I visited in Asia Minor, I assure you." He chuckled warmly and pointed to the Pennsylvania State House. "Why don't you land on that tall red building, just there?"

"Sure thing, Nigel," Cato replied, coming in for a landing on the roof.

Nigel preened back his windblown fur as he hopped off Cato's back. "May I commend you for your superb flight from Virginia? We have broken the mouse air travel barrier, by travelling two hundred miles in just two days! Well done, old boy!" He bowed with one foot forward.

"At your service!" Cato said, spreading his wings and bowing graciously back to the little mouse. "Do you know where Ben Franklin lives?"

Together Nigel and Cato walked to the edge of the roof of the State House and looked at the city streets below. "From Clarie's instructions, I believe I shall find him in that direction," Nigel answered, pointing down the street. I shall proceed to his house and take up my abode there for the time being, enlisting pigeon transport while in the city. I hope you enjoy the seafood here during our stay. I've heard it is simply delectable!"

"I think I'll go fishing now," Cato replied, eyeing the harbor in the distance. "How long do you think we'll need to stay here in Philadelphia?"

"I imagine at least a year, possibly more. So, settle into a new nest on the outskirts of town, and make yourself at home as a Philadelphia eagle in the City of Brotherly Love," Nigel said, patting his wing. He waved to a pigeon flying by, flagging her down. "I shall find you when there is news to report; otherwise, you'll know where to find me." He walked up to the pigeon, who had landed on the roof. "Good day, my dear. I am Nigel P. Monaco, on assignment for the Maker. Would you be so kind as to transport me to the home of Mr. Benjamin Franklin?"

"I'd be delighted, Nigel," the pigeon replied with a sweet smile. "I'm Phoebe. It's an honor. Climb aboard."

Cato smiled and shook his head good-humoredly as the little mouse flew away on the pigeon. "That charming mouse sure knows how to get

179

around." The bald eagle then lifted off the roof and headed toward the harbor.

———

Oil lamps were scattered all around the study of Benjamin Franklin. Nigel scurried among the shadows cast on the floor by the lamps' flickering light against objects of all shapes and sizes. Never had Nigel seen such a wonderland of inventions, some completed and some in process. Franklin sat in a rumpled black robe, stocking cap, and slippers, mumbling as he dipped his quill in the ink to feverishly scrawl his latest theories across the yellowed parchment of his journal. ". . . electrified clouds pass over . . . high trees, lofty towers, spires, masts of ships . . ." he continued. Nigel couldn't make out what the inventor was saying for the next few minutes, until he made a loud exclamation.

"A TURKEY! Ha!" he said out loud to himself, as he neared the end of his entry for the night, chuckling as he wrote. When he finished writing he set his quill down and stretched out his back with a satisfying groan. "Ahhhhh, I can smell it now." He chuckled, yawned, and then blew out the oil lamps. "Early to bed, early to rise, makes a man healthy, wealthy, and wise."

Nigel waited until Franklin had left the room before he relit the lamp on the desk. "Let us see what have you penned, Mr. Franklin." He turned the pages of the journal until he found the part about the electrified clouds. He ran his paw along the page, nodding as he read, explaining to himself aloud what Franklin had hypothesized. "Brilliant! So the water vapors in a cloud can be electrically charged, with the positive and the negative charges separating in electrified clouds. Then as they pass over tall objects, they draw the electrical fire, and the whole cloud discharges. Dangerous therefore it is to take shelter under a tree during a thunder gust."

Nigel scanned further through the details of Franklin's hypothesis. "Now what was it you wrote about a turkey?" He soon found the journal entry:

Chagrined a little that we have hitherto been able to produce nothing in this way of use to mankind; and the hot weather coming on, when electrical experiments are not so agreeable, 'tis proposed to put an end to them for this season, somewhat humorously, in a party of pleasure, on the banks of the Schuylkill. (The river that washes one side of Philadelphia, as the Delaware does the other; both are ornamented with the summer habitations, of the citizens, and the agreeable mansions of the principal people of this colony.)

Spirits, at the same time, are to be fired by a spark sent from side to side through the river, without any other conductor than the water; an experiment which we some time since performed, to the amazement of many. A turkey is to be killed for our dinner by the electrical shock, and roasted by the electrical jack (an electric device I invented that rotates the turkey) before a fire kindled by the electrified bottle; when the healths of all the famous electricians in England, Holland, France, and Germany, are to be drank in electrified bumpers, under the discharge of guns from the electrical battery.

181

Nigel's eyes widened. "He's going to *electrify* a turkey for a barbeque! Oh dear, I best make sure that Cato does not attend, should Mr. Franklin wish to choose a bald eagle over a turkey."

———

MOUNT BRILLIANT, APRIL 1750

"Come on, I know you can do it! You're the most athletic boy I know," encouraged Patrick, giving skinny Jonah a playful nudge. He dug into his pocket and pulled out a few pennies to hold out to the servant. "If you climb up that tree, say ten feet, I'll pay you for your trouble."

Jonah's brown eyes widened at the challenge. This would not only be fun, but profitable as well. "You got yo'self a deal!" The young boy ran over to the tall pine tree and wrapped his hands around the trunk.

Patrick raised his hand to stop him. "Uh, FEET first, remember?"

Jonah's bright smile lit up his face as he laughed at himself. He squatted down to the ground and did a handstand to get himself into position.

Patrick grinned and crossed his arms on his chest. "Up you go!"

As he stood there watching Jonah, Patrick's cousin Charles Dabney snickered and jabbed him with his elbow. "You're making him climb up that tree, feet first?"

"Not *making* him, I'm *paying* him to do it," Patrick replied. "Jonah does fun stuff like this all the time."

Max and Liz stood back, watching the hilarious scene. "At least he's not askin' Jonah ta untangle knots he made on purpose in his fishin' line jest ta see the lad work the knots like a puzzle."

Liz giggled. "My Henry has developed quite the mischievous streak, but it is all in good fun, no?"

George Dabney, Charles's older brother, stood with his mouth open, watching Jonah climb the tree feet first. "Well, I'll be!"

Patrick held out a hand to Jonah. "Didn't I tell you he could do it?" He walked over and stood under the tree. "Good job, Jonah! Better get down now before all the blood rushes to your head."

Jonah shimmied back down the tree and did a flip to land on his feet. He held out his hand and Patrick slapped the coins into his palm. "Until the next trick, Mr. Henry!"

"You never know when that will be." Patrick winked at his friend before turning to his cousins. "Charles, George? Ready to go canoeing?"

The South Anna River was high from recent rains. The three cousins would easily be able to slip their dugout canoe into the fast-flowing river.

"I'm kind of hot," Patrick said as he took off his hunting shirt and checkered pants, leaving them on the bank. He slid a paddle into the canoe. "You two ready?"

"I am! Let's go fishing," Charles enthused, placing his fishing pole in the canoe. He and George and Patrick got behind the canoe, and together the three teenage boys shoved the heavy wooden vessel into the river.

Once they got settled, Patrick handed the paddle to George. "I'm going to relax for a while in the sunshine." He draped his arms over the bow and rested his head back on the rim of the canoe. He closed his eyes and breathed in deeply, enjoying the sun on his face. "What a perfect day!" The three boys drifted along, and Patrick listened to the birds in the trees. He lifted a finger and pointed to the various birds, keeping his eyes closed as he named their species and exactly where they were chirping. "Cardinal. Goldfinch. Wren."

"You really know your bird calls, Pat," George complimented him, looking toward the birds as Patrick blindly pointed to them.

Patrick pointed to his ear. "Just take the time to listen. And learn."

After a while, the boys reached a deeper spot of the river that was a great swimming hole. "I'm glad you're closer to us now at Mount Brilliant, Pat," Charles said, as he threw a line into the water.

Patrick kept his eyes closed and smiled. "Me, too. I like it here. Good fishing in the South Anna." He opened one eye to peek and see where they were. A big grin appeared on his face and suddenly he arched his back over the canoe and slipped into the water backwards, causing the canoe to tip over. "Good swimming, too!" he said, laughing as he bobbed to the surface.

Charles and George went flailing into the chilly river as the tipped canoe tossed them into the water, fully clothed. "PAT!"

"Oops, sorry!" Patrick said with a mischievous grin. He dove under and surfaced again, squirting a fountain of water out of his mouth. "I've been gone too long. I need to get back to the house." He grabbed his fishing pole, swam over to the riverbank, and climbed out of the water. "I have to get to father's class. You boys alright to get the canoe back?"

Charles slapped the surface of the water at Patrick. "Yeah, sure, we'll get the canoe back. See you later, Pat."

Patrick grinned and ran back to retrieve his dry clothes to head home.

George and Charles pushed the canoe to the riverbank so they could right it and dump the water out. They stepped out and felt the weight of their soggy, dripping clothes.

George frowned as he looked at Charles. "That's the third time Patrick has *accidentally* tipped the canoe. Have you noticed that he always seems to end up with dry clothes while we're left sopping wet?"

A look of realization came over Charles's face. He put his hands on his hips and shook his head at the ground, laughing. "Brother, I think we've been had by our sly cousin. We'll have to get him back somehow."

183

Max rolled on the ground laughing while Liz giggled at the soggy boys. "I have ta hand it ta yer Henry, lass. He's one sneaky, funny lad!"

Liz's eyes glimmered with delight, as she watched Patrick hurriedly slip on his dry clothes and laugh to himself before running back home to get to class. "Brilliant, *mon* Henry."

⎯⎯⎯⎯

"So after twenty years of war, and after defeating King Edward II at the Battle of Bannockburn, isn't it reasonable ta see how King Robert the Bruce and the Scottish people would have thought they would be left in peace?" John Henry said, pacing about in the front of his study as Patrick and William sat at their desks in his makeshift classroom. He held up his hand and wagged his pointer finger. "But the English king would not give up that easily. The Scottish Wars of Independence raged on. In addition ta the military war, there was a war of *ideas* with the Pope, who had excommunicated Robert the Bruce for murdering a rival ta the throne on the altar steps of a Franciscan abbey. The English king then inflamed the people ta action when he encouraged the Pope ta excommunicate *all* the people of Scotland from the church."

184

"Aye, I r-r-remember this mess," Max huffed. He and Liz were sitting quietly in the corner for today's tutoring session after following Patrick back from the river. "R-r-robert the Br-r-ruce were unjustly tr-r-reated, despite wha' he did! I should know. I were there!"

"Steady, Max," Liz whispered softly, putting her paw onto Max's bristled fur. "I know how sensitive you are about the memory of your namesake."

"So the Declaration of Arbroath was Scotland's response to the Pope?" William asked, as he and Patrick looked over the famous April 6, 1320, document printed in Latin in their history book.

"Exactly, Bill. It was a letter ta the Pope, signed by fifty-one nobles, asking him ta reject the claims of the English king," John Henry replied. "Read it over and tell me what ye see as the main points in this Declaration."

"It says that Scotland had always been independent, even for longer than England, and that Edward I of England had unjustly attacked Scotland, adding the atrocities of war," William began. "But Robert the Bruce had delivered the Scottish nation from such peril."

Patrick read an excerpt: ". . . *for, as long as but a hundred of us remain alive, never will we on any conditions be brought under English rule. It is in truth not for glory, nor riches, nor honours that we are fighting, but for freedom—for that alone, which no honest man gives up but with life itself."* He looked up at his father. "This document put the will of the people above the king, who had long been regarded as appointed by God. The king could be replaced if he didn't uphold the freedom of the Scottish people."

"Very good, Pat. The Scottish people understood the value of that precious jewel of liberty," John replied. "So what is the most important thing you've learned from this document?"

Patrick thought a moment, dragged his fingers through his still damp hair, and sat back in his chair. "That man has a right to freedom, and it is his duty to defend it with his life," he answered. He then leaned forward with a piercing gaze at his father and put his hand onto the book. *"This* is a declaration of independence. The Scottish people stripped the jewel of liberty from the king's crown and put it back where it belonged—in the hands of the people."

"Yer Henry may have fun with tr-r-ricks an' tippin' canoes, but the lad's got a str-r-rong head on his Scottish shoulders," Max said happily.

"Oui, my Henry is brilliant both in his humor *and* his seriousness," Liz agreed quietly.

Max smiled and looked at the lanky teenager in his checkered pants, bare feet, and hunting shirt. "Then I think ye named this place well, lass. He's livin' up ta yer name."

Liz sat there admiring her teenage protégé. *"Merci.* But he hasn't reached the peak of Mount Brilliant quite yet."

185

KEYS TO THE FUTURE

PHILADELPHIA, MARCH 2, 1750

Clarie sat in the darkened corner of Benjamin Franklin's study, watching Nigel, who mirrored the inventor-printer as he put the finishing touches on his letter to Peter Collinson in London. Clarie stifled a giggle of delight to see the mouse and the man exhibit the same tendencies: adjusting their spectacles, murmuring, and nodding as they read by the soft glow of the oil lamps. While Benjamin worked at his desk, he couldn't see Nigel behind him on a table where the mouse read the last of several pages going to Collinson, spread out for the ink to dry. *If there ever were a human version of Nigel, it would be Benjamin Franklin,* thought Clarie.

Franklin picked up the last page of this second letter to review, referencing his journal to make sure he had included all his notes. He gave a definitive nod and read the last sentence aloud:

> *Let the experiment be made.*
> *Your humble servant,*
> *B. Franklin*

Franklin leaned back to stretch out both arms and gave a big yawn. He stood up and Nigel darted behind a stack of books as Franklin walked over to gather up all the pages he had written. He proceeded to fold and tie the pages with some heavy twine, melted a glob of red sealing wax onto the knot, and embossed the letter with a brass seal bearing the initials "B.F." He straightened up and sighed as he looked at the bundled letter, which would go out in the next day's post. "Well *done* is better than well *said.* I hope my next letter will not just be about theory but actual experiment, Mr. Collinson." With that he left the room.

Nigel scurried out of his hiding place after Franklin had gone, and tried to peek inside the multiple folds of the sealed letter. Clarie joined him on the table, once again in the form of a blue butterfly. "Looks as if the second letter is signed, sealed, and ready to be delivered to Collinson."

Nigel jumped at the butterfly's sudden appearance. He placed his paw over his heart. "You startled me, my dear! Yes, the letter is ready to go, but unfortunately Franklin sealed it before I could read the final page. But everything is there from his journal, and after a little anonymous coaxing, it is done. Mr. Franklin was a bit hesitant to share his theories, even with Collinson. But his idea of putting a tall metal rod atop a tower or steeple to actually draw the electrical charge from a cloud is *brilliant!* He is obviously eager to test his hypothesis to see if it holds true, but he doesn't wish to be embarrassed if it does not. Benjamin Franklin is not the first scientist to wonder if lightning could be electricity, but no one has ever spelled out how the theory might be tested, much less made a rallying cry to find out for certain."

187

Clarie alighted on the wax seal of the letter. "Sometimes the key to opening new doors for the future is a voice bold enough to say what others are thinking but are too afraid to speak."

"Indeed," Nigel agreed, cleaning his spectacles on a cloth sitting there. "It would appear that Patrick Henry isn't the only one who needs to use his voice in this mission."

"Well, while I get these letters to London, you can help Franklin figure out how to put his words into action and conduct his experiment here in Philadelphia," Clarie instructed him.

Nigel furrowed his brow, placed his paws behind his back, and proceeded to pace back and forth across the table. "There is a slight problem, my dear. Although there are plans to erect a steeple on Christ Church and a tower on the Pennsylvania State House, there are currently no spires in Philadelphia to get the height we need to reach the clouds." He stopped and wrapped a finger around his whiskers as he thought out loud. "How does one get a metal rod up into the clouds without a tower?"

"I'm sure you'll figure something out," Clarie replied. "Perhaps Cato might have an idea."

Nigel's eyes widened. "By Jove, you're right. An aerial survey of Philadelphia may yield a solution we have not considered."

"Just keep Cato away from Ben's end-of-season turkey fry while you're flying around," Clarie joked.

Nigel roared, holding his belly. "If our dear Mr. Franklin could harness a turkey to fly while holding a piece of metal, he would most certainly perform a mid-air turkey fry, thereby killing two birds with one *rod*—his lightning experiment *and* his main course!"

FOUNDLING HOSPITAL CHAPEL, LONDON, MAY 1, 1750

"Here it comes, lass!" Al whispered to Kate, whipping his tail back and forth while he crouched low, anticipating the climactic moment. Kate's face beamed with her perky grin and she wagged her tail.

188

As soon as Handel pressed the keys of the organ to play the first four notes of the *Hallelujah Chorus*, the crowd rose to their feet, following the tradition of King George II when he stood at the London premiere of *Messiah* seven years earlier.

"Jest look at this crowd! They love it!" Kate exulted. She and Al were watching the concert from high above in the rafters of the newly built chapel of the Foundling Hospital. There was standing room only for this benefit concert. People pressed near the opened windows outside to hear the magnificent music of George Frideric Handel pouring out into the streets of London. "If this don't make *Messiah* popular, I don't know wha' will. We'll need ta make this benefit concert for the children's hospital an annual tradition."

"Aye, and we should have this concert every year, too," Al answered, oblivious to what Kate had just said.

"Now ta the next part of tonight's mission," Kate said, scanning the audience. She spotted Peter Collinson and David Henry sitting near each other, compliments of Gillamon, who sat between them. "Ye're sure ye put Ben Franklin's letters in Collinson's left coat pocket?"

Al's eyes widened, and a look of fear overtook him as he put a paw up to his mouth. "Oh, no!"

Kate furrowed her brow. "Don't tell me ye forgot! We've got ta get those letters into me David Henry's hands tonight!"

Al put his paws on his left hip, then his right hip, then back to his left hip. "I'm sorry, lass. If it were supposed to be in his left pocket, I messed up. I think I put 'em in his right pocket, but I can't be sure. I were tryin' not to be seen."

Kate softened. "As long as the letters be in one pocket or the other, that'll work. Once Gillamon introduces Peter an' David, then mentions meetin' Franklin in Philadelphia, one thing will lead ta the next. Jest wait 'til Peter an' David figure out they both be good friends with Ben."

Al crossed both pairs of legs and his eyes. "Here's hopin', lass!"

After the concert, right on cue, Gillamon struck up a conversation with the gentlemen about their mutual acquaintance, Mr. Benjamin Franklin. As they started chatting, Peter Collinson felt the lump in his right coat pocket.

"I thought I had left these letters on my desk, but amazingly, here they are!" Peter Collinson exclaimed, pulling them out to show to David Henry.

189

"May I see them?" David asked, eagerly scanning the contents.

Collinson smiled and clasped his hands behind his back. "The Royal Society was extremely impressed with Ben's theories on electricity and lightning. Our motto is *Nullius in verba*—meaning 'take no one's word for it.' The Fellows of the Society are determined to verify all statements with facts proved by experiment."

"Do you think our friend would object to my printing some excerpts in the next edition of *Gentleman's Magazine?*" David asked.

"If there is one thing I know about our mutual friend, Benjamin Franklin believes that such discoveries are meant for the benefit of all," Peter replied with a smile. "I think he would be happy to share his theories, as I did already with The Royal Society."

"This is extraordinary!" David exclaimed. He placed his finger on a sentence that had caught his eye. "Ben says that, 'houses, ships, and even towns and churches may be effectually secured from the stroke of lightning by their means. This may seem whimsical, but let it pass for the present until I send the experiments at large.' May I borrow these letters for my article?" David asked, thumbing through the pages.

"Perhaps we need to publish these letters in their entirety. I will discuss printing a complete pamphlet with Edward Cave."

"Please do! I will write to Benjamin and tell him of your plans," Peter replied. He turned to Gillamon. "My, what a momentous evening this has been, Mr. Gillamon! First, this spectacular evening for Mr. Handel's music and the Foundling Hospital. Now, this connection with Mr. Henry. Truly remarkable!"

"Indeed, I would say it has been an *epic* evening," Gillamon replied, shooting a glance up to Kate and Al with a knowing grin.

PALACE OF VERSAILLES, FRANCE, FEBRUARY 4, 1752

King Louis XV walked along the opulent Hall of Mirrors with its seventeen mirror-clad arches reflecting the seventeen arched windows overlooking the magnificent palatial gardens. He slowed his pace to study a dark cloud creeping across the grey winter sky. He frowned at the stormy weather and the now-still fountains, longing for the warm, sunny days of spring with flowering gardens full of music, flowing fountains, and delightful parties. He was tired of bad weather and sneered at the dark cloud, today's nemesis for his mood.

The king of France entered the lavish room where his royal court awaited him. The walls were lined with his fanciful courtiers, men and women dressed in colorful silks and powdered wigs, who immediately bowed before the king. He raised his hand in acknowledgment and took a seat in his red, plush royal chair. He was not in the mood to listen to the requests of those seeking money, power, or prestige today.

Standing there before him were three men who bowed low and with exaggerated movements, trying hard to ingratiate themselves with the king. Louis sighed as his aide approached him with an ornate silver tray, bearing a beautifully quilled document. "Sire, if it please the king, these men, Messieurs de Buffon, D'Alibard, and de Lor, wish to present a proposal for a scientific experiment. They have translated an exciting document from America." The king picked up the document:

Expériences et Observations sur l'électricité faites
à Philadelphie en Amérique par M. BENJAMIN
FRANKLIN et communiquées dans plusieurs lettres à M. P.
COLLINSON, de Londres, F.R.S.

190

"I have heard of this *Monsieur* Franklin and his *Poor Richard's Almanack*," the king recalled as he flipped through the document. "A printer and a scientist who now proposes what?"

The three scientists looked at one another nervously, excited about sharing the possibilities with the king. Suddenly a rumble of thunder was heard outside. Comte de Buffon cleared his throat and spoke up, "Taming lightning, sire."

Clarie, dressed in her blue silk gown to blend in as one of the ladies at court, smiled in the back of the crowd, wrapping her finger around the single curl that dangled onto her shoulder. The king sat up excitedly, eager to hear about Benjamin Franklin's proposed lightning-rod experiment. An animated conversation ensued, turning the king's foul mood into one of giddy anticipation. Clarie beamed, proud of the scientists she had handpicked to translate into French Benjamin Franklin's 86-page pamphlet printed by Edward Cave in London. They had outlined how they would conduct the experiments here in France, a land filled with soaring steeples, towers, spires, and plenty of lightning. They discussed Franklin's experiment:

191

> *On the top of some high tower or steeple, place a kind of sentry box big enough to contain a man and an electrical stand. From the middle of the stand, let an iron rod rise ... upright 20 or 30 feet, pointed very sharp at the end. If the electrical stand be kept clean and dry, a man standing on it when such clouds are passing low might be electrified and afford sparks, the rod drawing fire to him from the cloud ...*

With a broad smile, the king of France held up Benjamin Franklin's document and exclaimed, *"Laissez faire l'expérience!"*

Let the experiment be made!

MAY 20, 1752

Gillamon and Clarie stood in the IAMISPHERE gazing at a scene from the village of Marly, on the outskirts of Paris. It was 2:00 p.m. on May 10, 1752, and a dark storm cloud passed over the 40-foot rod the French scientists had erected on top of a sentry box, just as Benjamin Franklin instructed. A retired French soldier lifted an insulated wire and immediately drew sparks, causing the crowd to erupt in awe and cheers of celebration.

"See? It worked just as Ben predicted!" Clarie reported happily. She quickly pointed to another panel. "In the excitement another man grabbed the wire and the experiment was repeated six times." She then pointed to several panels showing the same experiment in different settings. "Since then, it's been repeated dozens of times all over France! King Louis was so excited he had his French scientists immediately send a *personal* letter to the Royal Society of London with a message of gratitude to Ben!" Clarie was giddy with excitement as she next pointed to the panel from today. A very proud Peter Collinson smiled broadly and read aloud the letter from France:

> *"The Grand Monarch of France strictly commanded his scientists to convey 'compliments in an express manner to Mr. Franklin in Philadelphia for the useful discoveries in electricity and application of the pointed rods to prevent the terrible effects of thunderstorms.' M. Franklin's idea has ceased to be conjecture. Here it has become a reality."*

192

Gillamon's silky white goatee blew in the wind of the IAMISPHERE as he gazed at the exuberant Peter Collinson, who tonight sat at his desk, writing a letter to share the exciting news from France with his friend Benjamin Franklin. "And with that first spark, Benjamin Franklin became an international celebrity and a hero of France." He turned to look at Clarie, his blue eyes twinkling with delight. "The key is now firmly in the door of France. Well done."

"I can't wait to go tell Nigel!" Clarie exulted. "He won't need to wait weeks for the good news to arrive from London."

But Gillamon stopped her. "Don't tell Nigel just yet that Mr. Franklin's experiment worked in France."

Clarie's lamb eyes grew wide. "Why not?"

"If we do, we'll prevent Benjamin Franklin from becoming a hero in America." Gillamon turned to gaze at a panel showing Nigel and Cato soaring over the city of Philadelphia. "Besides, I would hate for Nigel to miss all the fun flying his way."

THE KEY TO OUR SHUCCSHESSH

PHILADELPHIA, JUNE 4, 1752

Nigel shook his head as Cato circled over the city, sighing at the spire-less skyline of Philadelphia. The mouse told the eagle, "I have grown just as impatient as Mr. Franklin. Two years have passed and still no steeple or tower has been erected to test his theories on lightning!"

"Maybe they will figure out how to do the experiment in Europe," Cato suggested.

"That is the hope, old boy, but it would be a dreadful travesty for the scientist not to experience the thrill of seeing his brainchild delivered by his own hands," Nigel lamented. He saw Benjamin Franklin locking the front door of the Pennsylvania State House, having finished his business for the day, evidently the last man to leave. He had been elected to the Pennsylvania Assembly and was given a key to the State House, which he slipped into his coat pocket. "Please set us down on the State House roof, Cato."

Cato pulled back his wings to come in for a landing. Nigel hopped off the eagle's back and started pacing back and forth. "Let's go over this again from the top. Right. We've scoured the countryside for anything that could work as a tall tower, and all we found were trees. These of course, are easy for us to reach upon your eagle wings, but unless Benjamin Franklin grows wings of his own, he cannot reach the top of a tree to install his lightning rod." He lifted a hand to point to the eagle. "Although you have bravely suggested flying with metal in your talons, there is the issue of your safety, as well as Mr. Franklin not observing the

193

experiment close-up, as it would be conducted by the animal kingdom on his behalf."

At that moment, a green lizard went running by Cato and Nigel across the roof, followed by something that swooped over them, causing them to duck.

"Whoa!" Cato said, lifting his wing. "What was that?"

Nigel looked all around them on the roof and saw nothing. "I say, I have no idea."

Suddenly the green lizard came darting back toward them, and Nigel could see that in his mouth he carried a small key attached to a string.

"I say, what*ever* are you doing?!" Nigel demanded as the lizard almost ran into him.

"Can't explain!" the lizard answered through gritted teeth. It looked up in the air over him, and Nigel turned his gaze upward to see what was after the little reptile.

A flying squirrel came barreling into Nigel, and together they went tumbling across the roof.

"Shorry little moushe!" the flying squirrel exclaimed with a pronounced whistle through his teeth. "Almosht had the shneaky little monshter!" He smiled widely and held out his paw to help Nigel up. Nigel couldn't help but grin at the adorable, funny, brown-and-grey striped squirrel. He had unusually large, round, black eyes, round ears, and large buckteeth. "I'm Abraham Shamuel Penn, but you can call me Ashpen for short. That's *A.Sh.Penn.* Shee how I did that with my initialsh? Clever, huh?"

Nigel took Aspen's paw and stood to his feet, preening his whiskers to regain his composure after being assaulted by a flying squirrel with a speech impediment. "Well, Abraham Samuel Penn—*Aspen*—I am Nigel P. Monaco, and this is my colleague, Cato."

Aspen saw the bald eagle and hid behind Nigel, who wasn't much larger than the tiny squirrel. "He won't eat ush, will he?"

"Of course not, old boy!" Nigel replied with a chuckle.

"We're on mission for the Maker, so rest easy, little guy," Cato added. "I promise not to eat you."

Aspen smiled, showing his pronounced teeth. "That'sh a relief! The Maker, you shay? That'sh big shtuff!"

Nigel had to withhold a giggle. Just listening to the squirrel was enough to make him want to burst out laughing. "Indeed, so why are you chasing the green anole lizard?"

"Me and Leonard like to play hide and sheek with shtuff," Aspen replied. "He'sh hiding sho I'm sheeking."

Cato and Nigel looked at one another and had to quickly look away to muzzle their mutual mirth. Cato's feathers shook from his silent laughter. Nigel wiped away his tears of amusement and cleared his throat with a broad smile. "I see. Well, we don't wish to keep you from your game."

Suddenly Leonard came running by again. "Ha-ha! You'll never get the key!"

"Shaysh you!" Aspen replied, running quick as a flash up to the top of a stack of crates where he jumped and spread out his arms to reveal his 'wings.' He soared over the running lizard, spread out like a white, flying square with a tail. His silky skin flaps stretched from his wrists to his ankles, and he wiggled his hands and feet in opposite directions to control his descent. His feathered tail helped him steer until he landed directly on top of the lizard, wrapping himself completely around his little green friend. "Gotcha!"

195

Together the tiny friends started laughing and rolling around the roof. Aspen finally let the lizard go and Leonard held up the key by the string. "You win! Let's play again."

"What does the key go to?" Cato asked.

"Shome old shed in a field," Aspen answered, picking up the key and twirling it in the air.

Nigel stood there with his jaw hanging open, staring at Aspen, who proceeded to jump off the roof and glide away with the key dangling from his foot. Cato nudged him with his yellow beak. "Nigel? You alright?"

The corners of Nigel's mouth slowly turned up into an awestruck grin. "By Jove, I believe I have an idea. We don't need a tower or a *shteeple.*" He looked at Cato. "All we need is a kite."

FIELD OUTSIDE PHILADELPHIA, JUNE 6, 1752

Twenty-one-year old William Franklin held onto his hat against the blustery wind and looked up into the darkening sky. He carried a thin metal wire and a Leyden jar, a container to collect electrical charges.

"Father, it appears as if the weather is cooperating. But why are we coming out here in the middle of nowhere?"

Benjamin Franklin walked briskly ahead of his son, looking around them to make sure no one was about. "If we're going to fly a kite, we need an open field. And as I wish to keep this experiment a secret for now, you and I shall be the only witnesses." In his hands he held a kite made from a silk handkerchief with two cedar cross sticks. On the top of the upright stick he had attached a sharp, 12-inch pointed wire. Silk twine was tied to hold the kite, and at the end of the twine was attached a silk ribbon. And on the silk ribbon dangled the key to the Pennsylvania State House.

Cato and Nigel flew above father and son. "This storm is intensifying," observed Cato, feeling the drop in temperature. "It won't be safe for us up here much longer."

"Agreed, my good fellow," Nigel answered, looking up at the angry skies. "Once they enter the shed, you may land atop the roof."

"Why do they have to stand inside to fly the kite?" Cato asked.

"Because the silk ribbon must remain dry to act as an electrical insulator so the current may be gathered into the key," Nigel explained.

"If you say so," Cato answered with a grin. "Science is not my gift. How did you help Franklin figure all of this out with the kite and the key?"

"It took some doing, but the old boy figured out the pieces he needed with a few simple clues placed on his desk," Nigel answered, preening his whiskers proudly.

A clap of thunder sounded and Benjamin and William hurried to the shed. "Quickly! Help me launch the kite before it starts to rain," Benjamin ordered, as he gave the kite to William, who held it in place while his father got the twine ready. He nodded, and William released the kite, which quickly lifted into the air. Benjamin smiled to see his homemade silk kite take flight. "Get inside the shed and put the wire and the Leyden jar on the ground." He let the twine take the kite up higher to reach the swirling clouds. Drops of rain began to fall and Benjamin backed into the shed. "Now, attach the wire from the key, and stick it into the Leyden jar."

William did as he was told and together he and his father stood in the doorway of the shed. "Now what?"

"We wait," Benjamin replied.

Rain began to splatter Nigel's spectacles as Cato landed on the roof. "Oh, bother!" the mouse exclaimed, removing his spectacles and squinting. "I shan't be able to see a thing!"

Cato smiled and lifted his wing to shelter Nigel. "Here, Nigel, get under my wing."

Nigel scurried under the eagle's outstretched wing and wiped the rain off his spectacles onto Cato's silky feathers. He replaced his spectacles and smiled broadly. "Brilliant! Thank you, old boy! I shall be able to see everything beneath the shelter of your wing."

"You're welcome. Now what?" inquired Cato, ducking his head under his wing with Nigel.

"We wait," Nigel answered.

The wind picked up and started blowing the rain, but quite a bit of time passed with nothing happening. Benjamin frowned. *Perhaps this won't work after all,* he thought, starting to despair. He gazed up at the storm clouds and thought back to God's riddling questions for Job. *God in heaven, if it pleases you and in your goodness to mankind, please make lightning appear and cause it to strike my kite as you direct.*

197

Suddenly the kite lurched against Benjamin's hand. He looked down and saw that some of the individual strands of twine holding the soaring kite stood on end. "Look, William!" he exclaimed. He then moved his free hand close to the key, and felt a mild shock against his knuckle. He quickly pulled back his hand and shook it. "It's working!"

"It's working!" Nigel cheered. He ran to the edge of the roof and peered over the side as the rain now began to drench the twine. He could see sparks starting to stream from the key to Franklin's hand.

"Huzzah! It's working indeed, Father!" William cheered, gripping his father's shoulder as the electrical charges filled the Leyden jar.

"I *knew* it! I *knew* lightning had to be electricity!" Benjamin exclaimed excitedly. He looked up at the heavens. *Thank you for helping me to solve your riddle!*

While the men shouted their huzzahs below, Cato chuckled at the exuberant little mouse dancing on the rooftop with his rain-splattered spectacles. *Now it's Nigel's turn to be high as a kite.*

"Thank you, Maker, for sending that funny-sounding, key-toting, flying squirrel to knock me down!" Nigel exclaimed with a jolly chuckle at the top of his lungs. "He was the key to our shuccshessh!"

THE ART OF PERSUASION

Patrick Henry plopped down to stretch out on the long, burlap bag marked SALT that rested on the wooden floor. He had just unloaded the final crate of goods from the wagon by himself into his general store. He wiped the sweat from his brow and exhaled, trying to cool down on this hot summer day. His brother William hadn't shown up for work today, as had occasionally been the case since they opened two months earlier. After sleeping late, he was likely out fishing or hunting, or hanging out with friends. Although Patrick was the younger of the two Henry boys, the sixteen-year-old was the more responsible one to mind the store.

After spending a year as an apprentice with a Scots merchant, learning how to sweep floors, stock shelves, and wait on customers, John Henry decided that Patrick and his brother could make a living as merchants themselves. Since sending them to college was not possible, their choices were either farming or trading goods with those who did the farming. The Piedmont region of Virginia was dotted with Scotsmen who set up small trading houses along the network of rivers. They aligned with the many local Scots tobacco farmers and conducted business directly with merchants in Glasgow, Scotland, trading tobacco for other goods like food, clothing, and household items. In this way the small Scots farmers could bypass the large, elite Tidewater tobacco planters and ship their tobacco directly to Great Britain. While the Scots farmers made more profit this way, this angered the Tidewater planters who lost money from not overseeing the shipping of the Piedmont tobacco to England and collecting a fee.

John Henry rented a small storefront in Hanover County by the

Pamunkey River at the crossroads of Newcastle Road and Old Church Road. Anyone crossing the river would have to go right by the store, and as long as they stocked an ample supply of goods that people needed, and Patrick and William worked hard, business could be good.

Patrick and William cleaned the store, installed a long wooden counter, painted the walls, hung shelves, and nailed hooks on the walls to display merchandise. They painted a sign for the outside that read, HENRY BROS. TRADERS, and hung it after they had filled the shelves with the small stock of goods that John Henry purchased to get them started. As they began trading with the locals, the size and variety of their merchandise would grow. Customers didn't just pay for goods with money, but also in tobacco, fruits and vegetables, wild game, fur pelts, and whatever else they had or managed to make that other people needed. The Henry Brothers would then turn around and sell or trade those goods with other customers. If customers didn't have money or goods to trade, they would ask to purchase items on store credit, with a promise to pay for their merchandise as soon as they could.

Tobacco was the main crop in Virginia, and most tobacco farmers had to wait and see how the harvest went in order to settle their debts. If they had a good year, they could easily pay back their debts. If the crops failed due to drought or worms, their debts would pile up. Just as the Henry Brothers set up shop, so also did a drought in the tobacco fields of Virginia. Patrick's kindhearted nature led him to listen to the struggling farmers who gave numerous excuses as to why they couldn't pay. He didn't have the heart to turn down anyone who needed help.

On the bright side, Patrick and William were able to move back into Studley Plantation with their half brother, John Syme, Jr., so they wouldn't have to pay for a place to live while they got on their feet. Patrick was also able to see his childhood friends and even go hear Reverend Samuel Davies at Polegreen Meeting House again. Things looked promising for the young Henry boys to make their way in the world, but time would quickly tell if the hopes of their father, and their hard work, would pay off.

Patrick looked around the store from his vantage point on the floor, lying on the salt bag. He sighed, thinking about how he'd like to be doing something other than selling another pound of sugar, a box of nails, a dozen beeswax candles, and two yards of ribbon to customers today. He closed his eyes, smelling the blended aromas of bayberry soap,

199

smoked ham, and tobacco, and remembered the conversation he had with his father before they opened the store. *"Remember, Patrick, as you enter the world of business and dealings with men, put to good use our family creed to guide you. Do you remember it?"*

"To be true and just in all my dealings. To bear no malice nor hatred in my heart. To keep my hands from picking and stealing. Not to covet other men's goods; but to learn and labor truly to get my own living, and to do my duty in that state of life until which it shall please God to call me."

Patrick sat up and blew a raspberry. "Time to labor truly to get my own living." He stood up and walked behind the counter to set out the stack of periodicals that had arrived to sell in the store. They carried newspapers like *The Virginia Gazette,* and because of the wildly popular *Poor Richard's Almanack* published each year by Benjamin Franklin, they also carried *The Pennsylvania Gazette.* Patrick smiled as he picked up the magazine he was most proud to carry, his cousin David Henry's *Gentleman's Magazine.* Customers were always eager to hear the latest news from London, and although it took a few weeks to reach the colonies, the store filled with happy readers who spent time talking about the latest news from the Old World.

The door creaked open. "Good morning, Pahtrick," came the lilting Virginia drawl of a middle-aged man with deep smile lines around his eyes. He tapped his wooden walking stick across the floor as he entered the store.

"Good morning, Mr. Poindexter! How are you today?" Patrick answered happily.

"If I were any bettah, I'd be you," Jack Poindexter answered with a grin, pointing at Patrick with his long white clay pipe. His given name was John, but everyone called him Jack. The Poindexters were among the oldest families in Virginia. Jack's grandfather, George Poingdestre, migrated from Normandy, France, to Virginia in 1657. As a merchant and planter, George owned ships with Nathaniel Bacon and participated in Bacon's Rebellion. He purchased land in Middle Plantation and served the first vestry of Bruton Parish Church in Williamsburg. Jack carried on his grandfather's esteemed reputation as a landowner and was one of the founders of Louisa County. Everyone knew and loved Jack. He had a son Patrick's age, named Joseph Poindexter.

"I don't know about that," Patrick chuckled with a broad smile. "How is your mare doing? Isn't she foaling soon?"

200

"Any day now. Give me a block for May, please," Jack said, pointing to a block of salt in the corner. He put a few coins on the counter. "I'm hoping for a filly. I'm always partial to girls."

Patrick set the salt block on the counter and picked up the coins to put in his money box. "I hope you get your filly." He reached over and lifted an apple from a wooden bowl. "Here, give May a treat for me."

"Why thank you, Pahtrick. I'm sure she'll enjoy it," Jack answered, putting the apple in his pocket. "I see the new papers are here."

Patrick smiled and patted the stack of periodicals. "Yes, sir! I was just setting them out. The new *Gentleman's Magazine* is here. You know my cousin, David Henry, is the editor."

"And you're not proud a bit, are you?" Jack teased with a wink. He rested his elbows on the counter as Patrick set the paper in front of him. "Let's see what news he's chosen to share with us." He puffed on his pipe and lifted his eyebrows as he read aloud a notice that immediately grabbed his attention:

"The Grand Monarch of France strictly commanded his scientists to convey 'compliments in an express manner to Mr. Franklin in Philadelphia for the useful discoveries in electricity and application of the pointed rods to prevent the terrible effects of thunderstorms.' M. Franklin's idea has ceased to be conjecture. Here it has become a reality."

Patrick's eyes grew large. "Mr. Franklin was commended by the king of France?!" He leaned over to read the excerpt of the French experiment. "And he's figured out a way to tame lightning?" He looked at Mr. Poindexter in awe. "What do you suppose will come of this?"

Jack nodded and kept reading. "Great things, Pahtrick. Great things."

The door creaked open again and in came a farmer in his late twenties, covered in dirt and looking forlorn. His clothes were worn, and his face was streaked with the grime of already a full day's work before noon. He nodded at Patrick meekly. "Good day."

"Good day, Mr. Smythe," Patrick replied, walking from around the counter. "What can I help you find?"

The man looked over at the section of tools. He hesitated and pointed to a hoe hanging on the wall. "I'm in dire need of a new hoe. We're working as fast as we can to move the tobacco plants. The horn worm destroyed half of our crop last week," Mr. Smythe explained in a defeated tone. He clenched his jaw and fought back the emotion in his voice. "I . . . I know I already owe you a great deal, but I don't . . . that is . . . I mean to say . . . could I take that hoe on credit?"

Patrick felt badly for the struggling farmer who was working as hard as he could to battle the elements of drying fields, worms, and a race against the clock. He gave him a reassuring smile and put his hand on the man's shoulder. "I'm sorry to hear of your troubles, Mr. Smythe. That wicked horn worm is a tobacco farmer's worst nightmare." He reached up to lift the hoe and brought it down to the floor. "I know you'll pay me when you can."

Mr. Smythe nodded quickly and his eyes brimmed gratefully. "Thank you, Mr. Henry. I'll do my best to pay you from my harvest."

Patrick smiled and he lifted the hoe, walking to the door. "Let's get this in your wagon."

Jack had been quietly observing Patrick's compassionate handling of his customer. He locked eyes with the farmer as the man followed Patrick outside. Mr. Smythe nodded and looked to the floor, as if ashamed of his financial situation. Jack smiled and returned his gaze to the *Gentleman's Magazine.* He turned the page and thought, *David Henry isn't the only Gentleman Henry in this store today.*

"Do you see what I mean?" Liz whispered to Nigel as they listened in on the conversation from the crawl space below. A shaft of light peeked through a space in the floorboards above them. Nigel and Cato had just returned from Philadelphia, and Liz was showing the mouse Patrick's new venture with the store. "My Henry's large heart is wonderful, no? But it may lead to failure for the store if he is not paid for all the goods he gives on credit."

"I see what you mean, my dear," Nigel said with a concerned expression. "But on a happy note, I am delighted to see Patrick carrying his cousin's magazine! How thrilling to see those words about Mr. Franklin travel all the way to Virginia!"

"Oui! Come, let's go and you can get me caught up on everything," Liz replied. Together they left the crawl space and made their way down to the Pamunkey riverbank. Nigel told Liz about their adventures with Benjamin Franklin, flying the kite and the exhilaration of it all. Liz told Nigel all about life at Mount Brilliant, Patrick tipping canoes, and how she helped him return to Hanover by finding the location for the store.

"I am so very pleased, *mon ami!* I know that you and Cato enjoyed such an exciting adventure," Liz said. "I am sorry you missed seeing Max. He left to go help Gillamon on his mission with George Washington. George's brother Lawrence is close to death, and this will be very hard for him, no?"

"How dreadful to lose one's sibling," Nigel lamented.

"*Oui,* George even travelled to Barbados with Lawrence where they hoped the tropical climate would help his brother," Liz said. "Sadly, it did not. George even suffered a bout of small pox while on the island."

"Oh, dear!" Nigel replied. "Well, I suppose the bright side is that George will now be immune to that horrid disease. I assume you heard the tragedy of the other George—'Al's George'? His father Frederick died of injuries sustained from a blow to the chest in a game of *cricket* of all things."

"*Quel dommage!* So fourteen-year-old George is now the next heir to the throne of England, and sixteen-year-old Patrick is a merchant," Liz replied. "Many things are changing now in this mission."

"Have you been able to discover what benefit Patrick's job as a trader will yield?" Nigel wondered. "The riddle's next clue references 'a voice in the tavern,' but this store is clearly not a tavern."

203

"I do not know what the tavern riddle means yet. But so far, Patrick has developed a love of reading, which is happy news! He reads every paper, magazine, and novel he can. He just started reading *Robinson Crusoe,*" Liz reported. "But when he is not reading, he is listening. The conversations do get quite lively in the store. The humans discuss what is going on with farming, politics, and lately the land out west. There is much debate about the endless miles of rich land waiting to be explored and developed."

"Ah yes, the vast land that belongs to the *king* back in England," Nigel remarked. "Land the colonists are not given the freedom to have."

"*Oui,* this of course does not sit well with the younger generation. They wish to go claim and develop this land," Liz answered. "They have heated arguments with older men still very loyal to the king. So, Patrick is hearing both sides of many issues from the common people of both generations. I have noticed he does something quite clever. Instead of learning the voices of birds, he is now learning the voices of men. He is no longer tipping canoes, but he is tipping conversations."

"How so?" Nigel asked.

"When several customers are in the store, Patrick will suggest a particular scenario and ask them what they believe is the proper course of action. He usually suggests something that he knows will spark a debate. Then he watches to see what they say and then asks *why* they believe the way they do," Liz explained. "I can tell that Patrick is entertained by studying their arguments, as if he is trying to guess what they will say before they say it. I have also heard him amuse different groups of customers with the same story, but telling it differently each time."

"As if he is testing out which delivery receives the best reaction from his listeners, no doubt," Nigel noted. "My dear, it sounds to me like the store is a new classroom—one for studying the art of persuasion."

"Which of course is important in order for Patrick to find his voice, no?" Liz added. "Well, while he is trying to persuade others, someone else is trying the art of persuasion on *him.*"

"Oh? Who would that be?" Nigel asked.

Liz grinned. "Little Sarah Shelton, who is not so little anymore."

⸻

204

Due to the heat of the morning, Samuel Davies decided he would hold the Sunday service outside under the shady trees at Polegreen. Fourteen-year-old Sarah Shelton sat on a blanket with Elizabeth Strong, scanning the crowd.

"He's not here yet, Sallie," Elizabeth teased.

"Who?" Sallie replied, trying to act innocent.

"You know very well 'who,'" Elizabeth replied. *"Patrick.* Have you gotten to see him much since he moved back to Studley?"

Sarah smiled, and her cute dimples appeared. "Only a couple of times here at Polegreen, but never for long. He's always seated somewhere else during the service. I visited his store with my mother, but he was busy loading someone's wagon, so William waited on us." Suddenly her heart leapt as she heard the gallop of a horse and saw that it was Patrick Henry. She watched him climb down from the saddle and lead his horse to a fencepost where he tied the reins. He slowly walked up to the crowd, looking for a place where he might sit.

"Well, what are you waiting for?" Elizabeth inquired, nudging her friend.

Sarah took a deep breath and got to her feet. She lifted her hand to get Patrick's attention, and he smiled. She waved him over to join them.

"Good morning, Sallie," Patrick said, taking her hand. He then leaned over to take Elizabeth's hand. "Hello, Elizabeth. It has been a long time since I've seen you two." He clasped his hands behind his back, acting much more mature than the girls remembered.

Sallie's heart was racing. "Would you like to join us?"

"Thank you," Patrick replied, taking a seat on the blanket.

"Have you climbed any trees lately, Pat?" Elizabeth teased, breaking the ice for Sarah.

Patrick chuckled at himself. "No, not lately. It's hard to believe that four years have passed since I broke my collarbone."

"I'll never forget that scary day," Sallie blurted out, putting her hand over her heart. "I hope you *never* try anything like that again. I couldn't bear it."

Patrick tilted his head and studied the pretty young girl for a moment. "Why, Miss Shelton. I didn't know you cared."

Sallie blushed and was saved by the voice of Samuel Davies calling the church service to order. It was all she could do to concentrate on the sermon. After the service, Patrick said his hurried goodbyes in order to travel over to his Uncle Patrick's house for lunch. *Lunch,* Sallie thought with a grin. *A barbeque would be even better.*

205

AUGUST 1752

Before, as I walked about, either on my hunting or for viewing the country, the anguish of my soul at my condition would break out upon me on a sudden, and my very heart would die within me, to think of the woods, the mountains, the deserts I was in, and how I was a prisoner, locked up with the eternal bars and bolts of the ocean, in an uninhabited wilderness, without redemption. In the midst of the greatest composure of my mind, this would break out upon me like a storm, and make me wring my hands and weep like a child. Sometimes it would take me in the middle of my work, and I would immediately sit down and sigh, and look upon the ground for an hour or two together; and this was still worse to me, for if I could burst out into tears, or vent myself by words, it would go off, and the grief, having exhausted itself, would abate.

But now I began to exercise myself with new thoughts: I daily read the word of God, and applied all the comforts of it to my present state. One morning, being very sad, I opened the Bible upon these words, "I will never, never leave thee, nor forsake thee." Immediately it occurred that these words were to me; why else should they be directed in such a manner, just at the moment when I was mourning over my condition, as one forsaken of God and man? "Well, then," said I, "if God does not forsake me, of what ill consequence can it be, or what matters it, though the world should all forsake me, seeing on the other hand, if I had all the world, and should lose the favour and blessing of God, there would be no comparison in the loss?"

Patrick was so engrossed reading *Robinson Crusoe* that he didn't look up when Sarah Shelton and her mother entered the store. He leaned over the opened book and mindlessly rolled his flute back and forth on the counter. Sarah and her mother looked at one another and grinned. Finally, Sarah cleared her throat.

"Have you met Friday yet?" Sarah asked, stopping the flute, mid-roll.

Patrick started and looked up in surprise, snatched from the world of being a castaway on a tropical island and thrust back into the reality of being a merchant in a store. "Good day, ladies. Please excuse me," he said, chagrined as he got to his feet. Puzzled at Sarah's question, he asked, "Have I met Friday? Today is Wednesday, so not yet."

Liz giggled and whispered to Nigel from their hiding spot. "He does not realize that 'Friday' is a book character, not a day of the week."

"Indeed! I must say I am impressed that Miss Shelton has read *Robinson Crusoe*," Nigel answered.

"Didn't Reverend Davies give you this flute?" Mrs. Eleanor Shelton asked. "I seem to remember you playing this at Polegreen."

"Yes, ma'am, he did. And yes, I did," Patrick answered Mrs. Shelton, watching Sarah out of the corner of his eye. She picked up a bar of lilac soap, and he noticed how she smiled at the lovely fragrance. "What can I help you with today?"

"We need a pound of sugar, one jar of molasses . . ." Mrs. Shelton replied.

"And two yards of this blue ribbon, please," Sarah quickly added, holding up the end from a bolt. "For my new shoes and hat."

Patrick walked over with a pair of scissors and measured out the ribbon. He instinctively leaned over slightly to smell her perfume. She was dressed in a bright, flowery dress, and he had never seen her look so lovely. She turned and walked over to the candles. "Mother, shouldn't we pick up some candles as well? It will likely get dark before our guests leave."

"Of course, Sarah," Mrs. Shelton answered while picking out some needles and thread.

Sallie picked up a box of candles and set them next to their other items on the counter. "We're having a barbeque at Rural Plains on Saturday. We have a lot of baking to do. Homemade apple pies, and even vanilla ice cream." She let the delicious idea linger in the air for a moment, picking up his flute.

"Ice cream, too?" Patrick replied, putting their items into a small crate. His mouth watered. "I'm sure it will be a festive time."

"Why won't she ask him to attend the barbeque?" Nigel asked Liz.

"Wait, *mon ami.*" Liz grinned at Sallie. "She has clearly changed her tactics."

"How much do we owe you, Patrick?" Mrs. Shelton asked, spying the copies of *The Virginia Gazette* sitting on the counter. She smiled and tapped the stack. "I'm pleased to see my father's newspaper in your store, Patrick." Her father, William Parks, was the printer in Williamsburg and had founded *The Virginia Gazette.*

"Of course! No store worth its salt would be complete without Mr. Park's paper, Mrs. Shelton," Patrick answered, totaling the amount and handing her a bill of sale.

"I seem to remember that you play the fiddle even better than the flute," Sallie said.

"Yes! It's my favorite instrument," Patrick eagerly answered. He hesitated and then added, "I could come play for your barbeque, if you like."

"And . . . done," Liz muttered with a coy grin.

"Why, that would be wonderful, Pat," Sallie answered with smiling eyes as her mother paid for their goods. "Thank you for offering."

"Yes, of course you *should* come be our guest, Patrick," Mrs. Shelton added. "Saturday, six o'clock."

"Thank *you,*" Patrick answered happily. "And thank you for your purchases, Mrs. Shelton. Let me help you out with these things."

As they walked outside, Nigel turned to Liz. "So the persuader has been persuaded . . ."

". . . into thinking it was his idea to attend the barbeque," Liz finished his sentence with a grin.

PUPPY LOVE

SHELTON PLANTATION, RURAL PLAINS,
HANOVER, AUGUST 1752

The fragrance of magnolias was heavy in the air around the Shelton home, seemingly growing stronger as the air cooled and the summer sun softened and melted into the pink sky. The red brick house on the hill overlooking the Totopotomoy Creek had been home to the Shelton family for thirty years, but they had owned the 5,000-acre tract of land since King James I granted it to them in 1609. Not only were the Sheltons among the longest-landowning families in Virginia, they were one of the most respected.

Laughter and music wafted through the air along with the scent of magnolias as everyone enjoyed the simple delights of sumptuous food, punch, and country dancing. Patrick stood at the top of the brick steps playing his fiddle and stomping his foot as couples danced a reel on the front lawn. Never had the Sheltons enjoyed such lively entertainment at one of their barbeques.

After nearly an hour, Mr. John Shelton walked up the steps and exclaimed, "Aren't we glad to have Pat back in Hanover?" The guests applauded and cheered the fine young man who had grown up in their midst. "Thank you, Pat, for coming to play for us tonight. Welcome back."

"Thank you, sir, for your kind hospitality," Patrick replied, taking a bow.

"Please, go enjoy yourself," Mr. Shelton said kindly. He leaned in and whispered, "They're serving the pie and ice cream now."

"Thank you, Mr. Shelton. Right away, sir!" Patrick said, making his way down the steps. People greeted him and thanked him for his lively playing and asked about how his family was doing over in Mount Brilliant. He soon put his fiddle back into the case and headed to the dessert table.

Sallie stood there holding a huge piece of warm apple pie topped with vanilla ice cream. "I think someone has earned this."

"I'll fiddle for pie any day of the week," Patrick assured her, eagerly taking the plate. "Thank you, Sallie."

"We can sit over here," Sallie said with a smile, leading him to a table with chairs over by a crepe myrtle tree. Candles were lit as dusk set in and the stars were starting to faintly appear in the sky. "You're right. You *do* play the fiddle better than the flute, if I must say."

Patrick nodded, unable to respond with a full mouth. "It's my favorite," he mumbled.

"It's good to enjoy what you most love to do," Sallie replied, looking up in the sky. She was dressed in a beautiful green satin gown, with her hair pinned up and dressed with fresh flowers.

"What do you most love to do, Sallie?" Patrick asked her, catching her off guard.

This, she immediately thought. Suddenly she turned at hearing the barks of a puppy. "Oh, no, Nelson!"

Sallie quickly got up and ran to the little puppy frolicking in the grass, chasing a squirrel up a tree. The puppy jumped around excitedly, barking at the squirrel. The dog was solid black from his neck down along his back to the white tip of his wagging tail, which looked like the end of a pendulum rapidly swinging out of control. He had a perfectly straight, white neckline, almost resembling a bald eagle wearing a black set of puppy ears and eye mask. His nose, chest, and forelegs were white, and he stretched up the tree trunk, yipping at his desired conquest.

Patrick set down his plate and joined Sallie under the tree with Nelson. He squatted down to pet the puppy, who lavished him with kisses before turning his attention back to the squirrel. "What a *cute* dog, Sallie!"

"Isn't he? I found him wandering near the creek. I don't know where he came from, so I brought him home," Sallie recounted. "I named him 'Nelson.'"

Patrick smiled at Nelson and immediately loved his feisty spirit. He looked up the tree at the squirrel, who puffed up his cheeks, shaking his tail erratically and chattering in alarm at the pursuing hound puppy.

"You want that squirrel, Nelson?" He reached down and lifted the puppy in the air, causing the squirrel to scamper up the tree.

Sallie clapped her hands and laughed. "It looks as if you two make a perfect pair."

"Mother wrote me that Max disappeared soon after I left Mount Brilliant. I thought he'd be happier staying there. I don't know what happened to him," Patrick said, nuzzling the playful puppy who licked his face happily. "I've been sad about that. I miss him." Nelson playfully nibbled Patrick's fingers. "I'm sorry, Pat. I know how special Max was to you," Sallie said, putting her hand on his shoulder. "He was your dog all through childhood. I know he was about your best friend. What about Liz? I know *she* was special to you, too."

Patrick swallowed his emotion. "Liz also disappeared. I try not to think about losing her, too. But I know that pets don't live forever. That's part of life. The price we pay for loving pets or people is the pain we feel when we lose them." Nelson lunged for his neck with fresh kisses. Patrick smiled and threw his head back laughing.

Sallie watched Patrick and Nelson, smiling at the pair of fast friends. *I wasn't expecting this,* she thought. *Patrick is in love. Puppy love.*

NOVEMBER 1752

"Nelson needed a home, and was more than happy to be Max's stand-in for this season in Patrick's life," Clarie explained to Liz and Nigel.

"Well, he has certainly played the role of Cupid well," Nigel chuckled. "Patrick and Sallie appear to be quite the happy couple struck by his arrows of love."

"They are very young, but they have known each other since childhood. I am happy this is one part of Patrick's life that is going well." Liz's smile faded and she furrowed her brow sadly. "I am afraid his store is going to fail, with farmers unable to repay their debts after the weak harvest."

Clarie smiled. "Patrick's store was never about selling salt and ribbon. It was merely another classroom, and the key to open the next door on his life's journey."

Liz smiled. "I wonder what will be next for my Henry to find his voice." She looked at Clarie and knew what she was going to say. Clarie smiled and looked up through the floorboards of Patrick's store. "Time will tell. It always does."

"That Ben Franklin flew a kite and figured out that lightning is electricity! He wrote how to do it right here!" a customer exclaimed, poking his finger in his upraised copy of the October 19 edition of *The Pennsylvania Gazette:*

> As frequent Mention is made in the News Papers from Europe, of the Success of the Philadelphia Experiment for drawing the Electric Fire from Clouds by Means of pointed Rods of Iron erected on high Buildings, &c. it may be agreeable to the Curious to be inform'd, that the same Experiment has succeeded in Philadelphia, tho' made in a different and more easy Manner, which any one may try, as follows . . .

Patrick held up the newly arrived *1753 Poor Richard's Almanack.* "And he put his experiment to good use."

> How to secure Houses, &c. from LIGHTNING.

It has pleased God in his Goodness to Mankind, at length to discover to them the Means of securing their Habitations and other Buildings from Mischief by Thunder and Lightning.

After a lively discussion about Ben Franklin's exciting new discovery, Patrick smiled as he spotted one of Franklin's witty quotations printed in the *Poor Richard's Almanack:*

> A Pair of good Ears will drain dry an hundred Tongues.

He read down to another quotation and raised his eyebrows at another good testing quotation. He looked around the store and summed up his audience, predicting who would react exactly as he anticipated. "Gentlemen, what think you about this?

> The Good-will of the Governed will be starv'd,
> if not fed by the good Deeds of the Governors.

─────

DECEMBER 1752

Patrick picked the horsehair off his black coat and knee breeches, and straightened his tricorn hat. He took a deep breath and exhaled, then made his way up the path to the front door of Rural Plains. He could hear the music and laughter inside the house that beckoned him with its cheery yuletide warmth. Fresh wreaths of holly and ivy adorned each window, hung by the red ribbon bought at his store. White candles, also from his store, lit up each window. And on the front door hung a magnificent pine wreath adorned with sticks of cinnamon, dried oranges, and sprigs of red berries. In his hand he carried a gift for Sallie—he fervently hoped she would like it.

Mr. Shelton heartily greeted Patrick, and the family and friends gathered in their home echoed his Christmas greetings to the young man who had been calling frequently on John Shelton's daughter.

Sallie smiled and greeted Patrick as they melted into the gaiety of the Christmas celebration. They sipped mulled cider, enjoyed a bounty of delicious food, and toasted the good health of each other. Sallie's mother played the pianoforte, and everyone basked in the glow of the candlelight and the beauty of the music.

Patrick looked at Sallie, lovely in her Christmas gown, with brown ringlets of hair kissing her cheeks, and her dimples showing as she smiled with glee from the joy of the evening. "I have something for you," he whispered in her ear.

She looked up at him with an excited smile and together they left the room and crossed the hall to a side room. He handed her the wrapped gift in simple brown paper and green ribbon, but with a sprig of mistletoe stuck in the bow.

"What have you brought me, Mr. Henry?" Sallie asked, as she handed him the mistletoe and the bow. She opened the box, and her jaw fell as she lifted the beautiful brush and looking glass. Patrick looked at her sideways, trying to gauge her reaction. She took in a deep breath and held up the ornately carved mirror, shaking her head happily. She ran her hand along the soft bristles of the brush. "Oh, Patrick, they are beautiful! I *love* them, thank you!"

"You do?" he asked her. "I'm glad. I had them sent from London." He didn't bother to tell her this gift had cost him all the spare money he had. "Happy Christmas, Sallie."

She embraced him in a warm hug. "Happy Christmas, Patrick." She leaned back and whispered. "I have something for you, too." She set his gift down on a chair and held up her hands. "Wait here and close your eyes."

Patrick stood smiling with his hands crossed in front of him and closed his eyes as he had been told. He heard a chorus of applause as Mrs. Shelton finished playing another song. It wasn't long before he heard Sallie's voice approaching him. "Keep your eyes closed."

"They're closed," Patrick assured her.

Within a brief moment, he felt the unmistakable paws of Nelson against his leg. He opened his eyes, and there was the lanky puppy with a big red bow around his neck. He knelt down and Nelson covered him with kisses. He looked up at Sallie in surprise. "You're giving me Nelson?!"

"Yes, but this Christmas gift does come with a condition," she told him with an impish grin.

Patrick rose to his feet. "What is that, Miss Shelton?" he said, lifting her hand to tenderly kiss it.

Sallie smiled and looked around to make sure no one was listening. She whispered in his ear, "The girl comes with the dog."

Patrick looked at Nelson, who sat there gazing up at him with big eyes, huge red bow, and wagging tail. Patrick winked at the puppy as he hugged the girl. "I'll gladly take both."

Baptism by Ice

WILLIAMSBURG, VIRGINIA, OCTOBER 26, 1753

Governor Robert Dinwiddie paused to look out the window overlooking the Palace Green that stretched from the red brick Governor's Palace all the way to the bustling Duke of Gloucester Street. Merchants were busy selling their wares, craftsmen worked to build furniture, forge iron, and weave yarn, and the taverns and coffeehouses were filled with people exchanging the latest news in this bustling capital city. The colony of Virginia was thriving, but danger lurked along her frontier. The governor clasped his hands behind his back and frowned. *Something must be done, and soon,* he thought.

When he first had heard last spring that 1,500 Frenchmen were building two forts in the Ohio territory claimed by the British, he immediately wrote to inform the king. The French were moving down from Canada and into that valuable land. If the British didn't do something about it, that rich territory could slip through England's hands.

Five years earlier the king had awarded a group of Virginia investors called the Ohio Company a land grant of 500,000 acres in the Ohio Valley between the Kanawha and Monongahela rivers. Founded principally by brothers Augustine and Lawrence Washington, the Ohio Company enlisted investors for the venture, including Governor Dinwiddie himself. As part of the grant, they were required to construct a fort to protect the settlement of the land at their own expense. The Ohio Company hired surveyors to discover the best area to settle families, and were currently building roads and small trading forts. The most prized area for settlement was at the forks where the Allegheny and Monongahela Rivers joined to form the Ohio River. This was the gateway into the Ohio Valley, and the Ohio Company held the keys to the gate. The French, however, were trying to pick the lock.

With the colony's welfare as well as his personal interests on the line, Dinwiddie wanted to build strong British forts to keep the French out of the area. King George II instructed him to first warn the French to leave the area, then, if necessary, "repel force by force."

As the two greatest powers in Europe, Great Britain and France had been competing for land and wealth for centuries. They, along with Spain, had claims to stretches of land in North America that resembled a three-piece puzzle. The British possessed the coastline of thirteen colonies that extended west to the Ohio Valley, as well as land stretching north to Hudson Bay in Canada. The French claimed the territory west of the colonies, from New Orleans all the way up to New France, cutting through a section of British-held Canada. Spain claimed everything west of France's territory, plus Florida. As the American colonies began to expand further west, they pushed up against French-held territory, and tensions began to rise. It was only a matter of time before a spark would ignite military conflict between the French and the British.

215

Meanwhile, the native American Indians had to choose sides. Whoever secured Indian support and made the best trade deals would have ultimate control of North America. Unlike the British, the French cared mainly about trading furs, not in taking over Indian land, so they had strong relations with many Indian allies. The most powerful Indians in the East were the nations of the Iroquois Confederacy, or Iroquois League—Mohawk, Seneca, Cayuga, Onondaga, Oneida, and Tuscarora—also known as the Six Nations. They were masters at playing the French and the British against one another, but when the British put pressure on them in the 1750s, they gave up certain rights, and became reluctant British allies.

After receiving the king's instructions, Dinwiddie sent two men with a message to the French to leave the area, but they failed to reach the frontier outpost. He next called the Virginia General Assembly to meet in a special session in Williamsburg on November 1 about this mounting crisis. But as he gazed out the window, an untried young militia major rode up the Palace Green towards the Governor's Palace. Dinwiddie recognized him immediately. At more than six feet tall, he was hard to miss.

When the young man's brother had died the previous year, the governor appointed him as a major in the Virginia militia. Although he didn't have any military experience, the twenty-one-year-old was well acquainted with the rugged frontier, having worked as a surveyor. He was eager to prove himself worthy of the rank given him, and to honor the memory of his brother, Lawrence. Dinwiddie was about to hear the reason for his visit today. His name was George Washington, and he was here to volunteer to take the Governor's letter to the French.

━━━━━

DECEMBER 25, 1753

Kate put her paw around Al, who held his paws up to his eyes, afraid of what was to come. Gillamon had sent word for them to join him and Max at a crucial moment with the George Washington mission. Gillamon wanted Al to see what was happening in America so when he "gathered intelligence" in the palace in London, he would understand what all the talk was about. Gillamon also needed Al's skills as well as Kate's abilities to help out for a brief time in Ohio. While Al dreaded leaving the cheery Christmas comforts of the royal palace in London to enter the harsh, bitter-cold, dangerous wilderness of Ohio, Kate couldn't wait to get there. She and Max hadn't seen each other in years. It only took a brief moment in time before Kate and Al stepped out of the panel of the IAMISPHERE into the snow-covered land of the Ohio Valley.

216

"AHHHH! Sure, and that's cold!" Al shouted as his paws hit the icy ground. He rapidly lifted up his opposite fore and back paws about a dozen times, trying to get used to the shock of the freezing cold. "And to think a minute ago I were walkin' on soft red carpets and eatin' puddin'."

Max stood there with snowflake-covered black fur, smiling. He didn't even notice Al ice dancing in the background. All he could see was Kate.

"Max!" Kate exclaimed happily, running over to him. They nuzzled and embraced with such warmth that the cold around them vanished. "Oh, me love, I'm happy ta see ye! Especially on Christmas."

"Mer-r-ry Christmas, me bonnie Kate," Max answered. "A dog couldn't get a better gift than this."

"Welcome to Ohio," Gillamon greeted them. He was in his natural mountain goat form, so was warm and toasty in his heavy wool coat. "Merry Christmas."

"I were a wee bit merrier in the warm palace," Al whined. "I were about to eat dessert."

Gillamon chuckled. "I'm sorry for your suffering, Al."

"Listen, ye spoiled kitty!" Max scolded. "Me an' Gillamon have tr-r-raveled in nothin' but fr-r-reezin' rain an' a r-r-ragin' snowstorm for the past month pr-r-rotectin' George Washin'ton! We've cr-r-rossed mountains on muddy r-r-roads filled with savage Indians, an' all this after George were sent away by the Fr-r-renchies with a big fat 'NO!' An' here ye be complainin' aboot missin' yer sweeties?!"

"Steady, Max," Kate said, calming her mate. "It sounds like a terrible journey! Wha' happened with George Washington?"

"Well, he started out with Governor Dinwiddie's letter from Williamsburg on October 31," began Gillamon. "He had gathered a group to travel with him, including a French translator and friend, James Van Braam, four Indian traders, and Christopher Gist, a surveyor and guide with the Ohio Company. Along the way, Washington met with Iroquois Indian Chief Half-King."

"Why'd Washington meet with only half a king?" Al asked, shaking his soggy paw. "What happened to his other half?" He furrowed his brow, trying to imagine the scene.

Max rolled his eyes. "Indians have nicknames with special meanin's, lad. This Indian chief's important because he's fr-r-riends with the FULL king of England."

Gillamon nodded. "The support of these Indians will be crucial if tensions with the French lead to fighting. Washington needed to make sure these Indian friends would remain on the side of the British if it comes to war."

"George also met up with some Fr-r-rench deserters an' gathered intelligence aboot men an' forts up and down the Mississippi River," Max added.

"French dessert-ers?" Al asked hopefully. "Can I meet with them to share some intelligence, too? I know a lot aboot desserts."

Max ignored Al and turned to Kate. "George keeps a journal an' wr-r-rites down in lots of detail everythin' he hears. So now he knows all aboot the Fr-r-rench positions if it comes ta war."

"So will it come ta war?" Kate asked, worried.

"That will depend on what Governor Dinwiddie does with the French commander's letter," Gillamon answered. "French Commander

217

Jacques Legardeur de Saint-Pierre politely met with Washington, even wining and dining him. But he sent Washington back to the governor with a letter saying the French have no plans to leave Fort Le Boeuf or any part of the Ohio territory where they are planted."

"Le Boeuf? There's a fort o' beef? Where's the beef?" Al asked, brightening. He then furrowed his brow with a dutiful expression. "Gillamon, I hereby volunteer to go stay with the French commander and keep an eye on things there." The big cat broke out into a goofy grin and whispered to Kate, "With French desserts and beefy forts, this place is soundin' better all the time."

"Actually, Al, I have something far more important for you to do elsewhere," Gillamon answered. "And as soon as you're finished with your mission, you can head back to London. Kate will follow you there later."

"Alright, no beefy fort," Al replied with a disappointed frown. "Where do ye want me to go?"

Gillamon got right in his face. "To the Murdering Town."

Al's eyes widened and he cried before attempting to run off, slipping on the ice. "Not alright! Not alright! Not alright!"

218

DECEMBER 26, 1753

George Washington stuffed his regular clothes into his pack after changing into a "match coat," skins matched to wrap around his upper body, and an Indian walking dress: a knee-length coat, belted at the waist with hip-length leggings and moccasins. He took his journal, which detailed this harrowing journey, the letter from the French commander, and other important papers, and secured them in the pack along with other provisions. He put the pack on his back and picked up his gun. "You ready, Gist?"

"Just about," Gist replied, also putting on the warm Indian dress. "Van Braam should be able to get the horses and men to some decent shelter by nightfall. I'm not so sure about us, though."

Washington and Gist were now on their own to travel by foot through the snowy and icy conditions to reach Williamsburg. The horses were too weak to carry the heavy baggage on through the deep snow, but Washington was anxious to make it back to the governor as quickly as he could. So he gave money and directions to Van Braam, who was to take the horses, baggage, and supplies, and make their way toward Virginia at a slower pace. Washington and Gist would find other horses to take them to Williamsburg once they crossed through the woods and over the Allegheny River.

Washington exhaled icy breath and secured an old hatchet to his belt. "I want to make it past the Murdering Town and head on toward the Indian village of Shannopins after that."

Gist picked up his pack and gun. "I sure hope that place doesn't live up to its name while we're passing through."

———

DECEMBER 27, 1753

"What am I doin' here, and why did Gillamon need *me?* Max be the one who's been protectin' George Washington," Al whispered fearfully to himself. He was crouched behind a cluster of boulders along the snowy road.

219

"Gillamon says that if ye live up ta yer name of 'noble, famous warrior' by helpin' George Washington, ye'll help young George do the same," Kate had told him before she left with Max. "It must be somethin' important. Ye can do it, Al! We're goin' ahead up the trail ta make preparations with Gillamon. I'll see ye back in London."

Al peered over the boulder and saw George and Gist trudging through the snow-covered road toward him. An Indian guide had come alongside them, offering to help lead the men through the territory. Al thought through all that Gillamon had told him about George Washington—how he had overcome losing his father as a boy, then losing his brother Lawrence, and how hard he was working on this mission to prove himself a capable soldier and leader for the governor. Al thought of 'his spoiled George' back in the comfort of England and he frowned, ashamed of how spoiled he had become, too. "Come on, kitty. Be brave, for America's George."

The Indian guide seemed to be looking around nervously, glancing back at George and Gist. He went up the trail ahead of them as if he were looking for something and ducked behind the cluster of boulders near where Al sat. He quietly cocked his gun and Al's heart started racing as he realized what the Indian was getting ready to do. Al saw that

George and Gist were now only about thirty feet away. His paws went up to his mouth. "Oh, no! That Injun's gonna shoot! Maker, help!"

The Indian took aim, and Al took off running.

Al didn't know what he was going to do, so he figured he would just do what came naturally. George and Gist were now only fifteen feet from the Indian, who was ready to fire. Al instinctively sprang with his back paws and jumped up to reach the Indian, sinking his iron claw into his arm, causing the Indian to fall back as his finger pulled the trigger. The bullet went whizzing high over George's head and together he and Gist ducked. Al scampered off as George and Gist quickly got up and ran toward the Indian, who was on the ground holding his arm. They took him into custody and hurried him away with them in case there were other Indians in the area who also wanted to murder them.

Al lay on his back, breathing heavily from the scary moment, and smiled at his iron pointer claw. He rarely used it, but today it had saved George Washington from the Indian sniper. "Well, I didn't get the beefy fort mission, but there were no murder in this town today." A seven seal suddenly appeared on the rock next to his head and he grinned. "But I do know where I can get some beef *followin'* this mission." He clawed through the seven seal and entered the IAMISPHERE, returning to London, to his George, and to the royal kitchens of the palace.

220

ALLEGHENY RIVER, TWO MILES ABOVE SHANNOPINS, DECEMBER 29, 1753

"I expected the river to be completely frozen, but it looks like it's only frozen about fifty yards from each shore," Washington told Gist, scanning the icy river running through this frigid wilderness. Chunks of ice bobbed along rapidly through a middle channel of the whitewater river. "The frozen river must have broken up above here with all those chunks floating downstream."

Gist plopped down on a fallen log, exhausted from the past three days. They had kept the Indian sniper with them until 9:00 p.m. that night and let him go. They then kept walking the rest of the night to get out of reach of any other Indians from the Murdering Town who might pursue them. After briefly resting they walked on until they reached the river. "There's no way to get across but on a raft," Gist warned. He rubbed the back of his neck and pointed to the hatchet. "At least we have one hatchet."

George lifted it from his belt and felt the blade, frowning. "It's not very sharp, but it will have to do. How many logs do you think we'll need?"

Gist sized up Washington's height and his own. "At least ten across and five underneath."

Max and Kate hid in the shadows. "Alr-r-right, lass. They're here safe an' sound. That kitty came through."

"I never doubted he would," Kate replied with a smile. She nuzzled Max. "I'm sorry Gillamon had ta leave, but I'm enjoyin' me Max time."

"Me, too, lass," Max replied. He looked at George Washington's large frame. "I hope the beavers finished workin'. Time's up."

———

Gist closed his eyes and wrapped his cold hands around his tin cup, breathing in the smell of hot coffee. He had built a fire and made a pot while George cleared an area by the bank to build their raft. Gist took a sip and looked up at the wintry sky, willing the sun to come out and warm the day.

George walked up to the fire and warmed his hands briefly. He then poured a cup of coffee and stood with a hand on his hip. "It's light enough now to find the trees we need for our raft."

"It will likely take us all day to build it," Gist replied, taking another sip of coffee.

"Then we'd best get started," George declared, downing his coffee, setting down his cup, and walking to the tree line.

———

"We can't thank ye an' yer family enough, Howard," Kate said happily to a plump, brown beaver.

"It was no-o-o-o trouble at*tal*," the beaver replied with a gravelly voice. He gave a big grin that showed his prominent buckteeth.

Howard, Max, and Kate watched George and Gist happily piling up the logs for their raft. They couldn't get over their good fortune! A family of beavers had felled ten trees in the night, leaving piles of fresh wood shavings around the stumps.

"With George only havin' a single, dull hatchet, ye helped make buildin' their r-r-raft easier," stated Max. "Now all they have ta do is chop up those felled trees, trim 'em, an' tie 'em together. It's still a lot of work, but now at least it's more doable. Thanks, lad." Max chuckled as Howard's wife and cute little beavers waved and disappeared under the water.

"We needed to make way for a new canal anyway. The wife wants to renovate the lodge and add a new room this spring. Besides," he said, yawning, "the family needed a night out after being cooped up inside for the past month."

"Ye remind me of a kind beaver friend we knew a long time ago. His name were Bogart, an' he loved ta carve little wooden figurines with his teeth," Kate told Howard, glancing at Max. "His figurines were like pieces of art!"

"Aye, Ark art," Max mumbled under his breath. Bogart had been on Noah's Ark with them, and kept his teeth filed with his carving projects.

"You don't say," Howard said, tapping his big teeth. "I'll have to see what kind of art these babies can carve for the kits. For now though, I'm heading to bed. If you need me you know where I'll be."

222

"Sleep well, Howard, an' thanks again," Kate told him, kissing the beaver on the cheek.

"Happy dr-r-reams, lad," Max added, as the beaver waddled away and slipped into the water to join his family back in the lodge. Beavers worked at night and slept during the day, so it was past his bedtime.

Kate and Max turned their gaze back to George and Gist. "How long do ye think it will take them ta finish their raft?"

"Hours," Max replied, looking up at the cold winter sky and then at the men. "It's their turn ta be the busy beavers."

———

The sun set behind the veil of clouds as George Washington sat on a tree stump to rest for a moment. He wiped his brow and took a sip of water from his canteen. He leaned an elbow over his knee as he examined the completed raft. "I didn't expect the river to not be frozen when we arrived, I didn't expect the felled trees, nor did I expect it would take us until sun-setting to finish the raft."

Gist stretched out his back and circled his arm to work out a sore shoulder. "Well, we'll be able to float over first thing in the morning."

George put the cap back on his canteen, shoved it in his pack, and stood to his feet. "No, we cross now."

Gist looked at George with surprise. "And I wasn't expecting *this!*"

"There's no reason we can't make a river crossing at night, even if it is icy. It's only 800 yards," the former surveyor told Gist, patting him on the back. "Let's shove off."

Gist exhaled and let his arm drop to his side. "Whatever you say, Major Washington." He gathered up his things and followed George down to the water's edge. Max and Kate looked at one another in alarm.

"This could be r-r-risky, lass," Max said. Let's follow along the riverbank an' keep an eye on them." They made their way in the darkness down to the riverbank.

George handed his pack to Gist, who tied it on the raft. He then shoved with all his might against the slippery bank, drenching his feet in the icy water as the edge of the ice gave way. The rickety floating platform slid into the turbulent river. The men took long sticks to use as setting poles to steer them amid the floating chunks of ice and debris. The makeshift raft teetered as George climbed aboard and got to his feet. The men slowly spaced themselves apart on opposite sides of the raft until they felt the right balance to keep things steady. In the darkness they could hear chunks of ice scraping along the frozen stretch of river near either bank. The swirling river sprayed them with its icy mist, and their feet and ankles were soaked.

"I don't like this," Max growled. "Go get Howard, Kate. Now!"

"Aye!" Kate exclaimed, running off into the darkness to the beaver lodge. As she ran off, Max made his way out to the water's edge.

The men painstakingly made their way halfway across the river, when suddenly they became jammed against a massive chunk of ice. The rushing force of water wasn't about to stop. It would either break up their raft or move them out of its way. George and Gist filled with fear as they battled the ice with their setting poles.

"We're going to sink!" Gist shouted against the roar of the white water. "This raft won't hold against this ice!"

"Steady, Gist," George shouted back with a firm voice. He was terrified on the inside but kept his calm on the outside for Gist. "Hang on! I'm going to put out my setting pole to try to stop the raft. Hopefully the ice will pass us by."

Just as George pushed with his setting pole, the rushing river violently pushed back against it, jerking and sending him falling into the icy clutches of the Allegheny River. Immediately his lungs contracted with the sub-freezing temperature. He gasped for air as he surfaced and heard Gist yelling his name. Gist got to his stomach and crept across the raft, stretching his arm out to try to reach George, ten feet away.

George could feel his muscles cramping against the cold. Every second seemed like an eternity as the ice water felt like a thousand needles sticking into his skin. Something pushed against George's foot as he struggled to swim against the rushing current. Within moments he was able to touch the tip of the raft with his fingertips and then grab hold of one of the raft logs. Gist grabbed his arm and pulled him up onto the raft. Together they fell back into a soaked, freezing heap. The adrenaline raced through their veins as they tried to calm down after their terrifying experience.

"Thank you, Gist," George gasped.

"What was that you said about there being no reason we couldn't cross an icy river at night?" Gist teased as he rested his head back on the raft to catch his breath. "I'll give you a couple of reasons now."

George patted him on the foot and tried to catch his breath against the shivering cold. *"Touché,* m-m-my friend." George's teeth chattered as he spoke. "N-n-now to get to the other side."

"I don't think they'll make it across in that raft tonight," Howard said to Max, who rode along on the beaver's back. "The river is freezing up."

"Aye. It's a good thing ye were there ta push George back ta the r-r-raft, but ye're r-r-right. They can't make the journey tonight," Max agreed, looking around. He spotted an island in the middle of the river. "Take me over ta that island, then go back an' push the r-r-raft in this direction. Then please br-r-ring Kate to me. Thanks, lad."

"No-o-o-o trouble at*tal,*" the beaver replied, swimming toward the island.

George and Gist fought against the angry river current with their setting poles, but it was no use. The ice was starting to back up. They were wet, freezing cold, and exhausted. They both knew they couldn't make it back to either side of the river.

"Keep pushing, Gist," George shouted, scanning the area around them for options. *Please, God in heaven. Help us!* Suddenly they felt the raft break free from the quickly freezing ice all around them. It was enough movement to set the raft drifting, and he soon saw that they were nearing an island. "Look! An island. We can at least get out of the river until daybreak."

224

Gist shouted, "Huzzah! We can make it!"

In short order the men wedged the raft against the shore of the rugged, tiny island and took their packs with them to the dry land. They both collapsed on the ground and wrapped their arms around their knees, catching their breath. "Thank you, God," George prayed silently.

"They're on land but not out of danger," Max whispered to Kate. They stood behind some trees on the tiny island. "We don't have a choice."

"Agreed, love. We've got ta keep them warm," Kate said. "Let's go."

Together Kate and Max walked out to the men who were shivering and huddled together.

George jumped as Max nudged his hand. "What is that!?" Max licked his hand and relief flooded him as he realized it was a little dog. "It's a dog! Out here on this island?"

"Two of them!" Gist answered as Kate came to nuzzle him. "They must have got out here when the river was frozen, then were stranded when it broke up."

"They just walked across the ice?" George surmised. "Hello, little fella." He picked Max up and held him against his chest, immediately feeling the warmth from the dog. Gist did the same with Kate.

"I wasn't expecting to get baptized with ice," George said, burying his face in Max's soft fur. "But neither was I expecting this."

Fr-r-rom now on, ye best expect the unexpected, lad, Max thought. *Happens ta me all the time.*

It was an agonizingly bitter night, but George and Gist huddled with Max and Kate under the trees and made it through until dawn, having fallen asleep from utter exhaustion.

225

———

DECEMBER 30, 1753

"Get up, lad!" Max barked, nudging George's leg. *"Get up an' get movin'!"*

George opened his eyes and quickly sat up, looking around him. He put his hand out to pet Max's head and finally could see him in the light of day. "Why, you're a Scottie." He looked over and saw Kate pulling on Gist's pant leg. "And you're a Westie."

Gist slowly roused and sat up. He shook out his hands. "I can't feel my fingers."

George frowned and reached over to inspect his hands. "Take off your gloves."

Gist did as he was instructed and the tips of his fingers were red and hard. "They're frozen."

"What about your feet?" George asked.

"My left foot feels alright, but some of my right toes feel numb," Gist answered. "I think they're frozen too."

"So is the r-r-river!" Max barked, running to the shoreline. *"Ye can walk out of here now!"*

"So is the river," observed George as he looked out at the now still Allegheny River. He smiled and put his large hand on Gist's back. "We can walk the rest of the way to the other side."

Gist rubbed his hands together, trying to get the circulation going. "That's good news." He got to his feet. "What about you, George? Are you alright? Anything frozen?"

Rays of sunlight peaked through the clouds and immediately lifted their spirits. George leaned back his head, closed his eyes, and smiled as the sunlight warmed his face. Amazingly, he was completely fine. Nothing was frozen, and he didn't even have a sniffle. "I'm fit as a fiddle. Are you able to walk on that foot?"

"I'll manage," Gist replied, petting Kate before getting to his feet.

"Then let's get out of here," ordered George, picking up his pack and gun and walking toward the frozen river. "Unless you'd like to wait for the river to thaw and try the raft again."

"You won't catch me on an icy river for a long time," Gist replied with a laugh.

Max and Kate happily trotted along in front of George and Gist until they were safely across the frozen river. When they reached the other side, the dogs ran off in one direction while the men walked away in another.

George smiled at the two Scottish dogs running away. "I do know one thing. If I ever have to cross an icy river at night again, I'll want a pair of Scots to go with me."

STARTING A WAR

Governor Dinwiddie held the reply letter from the French officer and clenched his jaw as he came to the heart of the matter. George Washington stood at attention while Dinwiddie read aloud the terse reply:

> As to the Summons you send me to retire, I do not think myself obliged to obey it; whatever may be your Instructions, I am here by Virtue of the Orders of my General; and I intreat you, Sir, not to doubt one Moment, but that I am determined to conform myself to them with all the Exactness and Resolution which can be expected from the best Officer.

"*I do not think myself obliged to obey it?*'" Dinwiddie repeated the Frenchman's words with an angry tone. He looked at Washington and shook the letter. "So the French refuse to leave the Ohio?"

"There is more to it than that, Governor. I was able to uncover the real motives of the French while they enjoyed an abundance of wine over dinner," George answered. "The French told me it was their 'absolute design to take possession of the Ohio, and by God they would do it.' I wrote all of this down in my journal." He cleared his throat. "What will your response be, sir?"

Dinwiddie tossed the letter onto his desk and sat back in his chair with a huff. "The Virginia House of Burgesses refuses to approve funds for an armed expedition against the French. That's why I had to just send a letter with you to begin with. Those Tidewater planters are not concerned about the frontier." He rubbed his chin and thought this through. "We need to *make* them concerned. We need to make all Virginia concerned. In fact, we need to make all *London* concerned about this French threat. I want you to make a copy of your journal, and have it to me in two days' time."

"Very well," Washington replied, bowing his head to the Governor. He turned to leave.

"And Major Washington?" Dinwiddie called after him.

Washington turned around. "Sir?"

"I'm pleased with your work in the Ohio, despite the French reply," Dinwiddie said. "Get me that journal. I plan to send you back with more than a letter this time. I plan to send you back with an army, *Lieutenant Colonel* Washington."

Washington smiled with the promotion from the governor. "Thank you, sir. I shall have my journal to you right away."

"Very well. You may go," Dinwiddie replied. He stood and walked over to his wall map of the Ohio Valley. "I think myself obliged to reply to the French," he muttered to himself in a mocking French accent as his hand traced the rich territory at stake in this looming conflict. "This time not with a pen, but with a sword."

FORT NECESSITY, GREAT MEADOWS, OHIO VALLEY, MAY 27, 1754

Max and Kate had kept themselves hidden, shadowing Washington's difficult journey back to Williamsburg in December and January. When Kate returned to London, Max returned to Hanover County to spend time with Liz and Nigel. Gillamon took the form of a Virginia militia soldier and he and Max then had quietly slipped in with the 159 men who had marched with Washington back out to the Ohio in April. Dinwiddie ordered the newly raised Virginia regiment commanded by Colonel Joshua Fry to dislodge the French, who had set up new forts in the area. The primary fort they needed to capture was Fort Duquesne, where the Ohio River split into the Allegheny and Monongahela. Washington's company of men were the first to reach the area and started work on a small fort named Fort Necessity. It was not to be their primary military stronghold, but a small defensive outpost as they scouted the area.

"Ye mean George Washington's a celebr-r-rity on both sides of the Atlantic?" Max asked as he and Gillamon climbed into the one-man canvas tent.

"Yes, after Governor Dinwiddie published Washington's journal in Williamsburg and London, his fame and reputation for bravery spread overnight," Gillamon responded, placing his gun on his lap to clean it. "Not only did the journal inform people of Washington's heroic journey to the Ohio, but it helped them understand the growing threat in the Ohio Valley."

"Seems ta me that when the Fr-r-renchies get their hands on Washington's journal, they'll see all the secr-r-rets George learned aboot their forts an' soldiers, too. I'd say Dinwiddie were *dimwitted* ta publish George's journal," Max suggested. A grin grew on the Scottie's face. "George didn't wr-r-rite aboot me an' Kate, did he?"

"No, he left that part out, Max," Gillamon replied with a smile. "But with his new rank and reputation, Washington has now been given his first taste of difficulty in raising a militia of men, and of gathering supplies, horses, and guns. All this is preparation for what he is ultimately being groomed to do."

229

"Well I jest hope he doesn't have ta cr-r-ross an icy r-r-river at night ever again," Max shuddered, stretching out on his stomach with his back paws behind him on the cool grass. "I thought the governor weren't allowed ta send an army out here."

"He found a way around that," Gillamon explained. "While the House of Burgesses was out of session, Dinwiddie convinced his General Council to authorize him to raise a force to drive the French out of Ohio."

"So wha's the plan now that George be here?" inquired Max.

"Things are going to get rough tomorrow, Max. You stay here while I go with Washington. Dinwiddie instructed him to 'act on the defensive' but if need be, 'make prisoners of or kill and destroy' anyone resisting the British control of the Ohio," Gillamon relayed. He stopped cleaning his gun and looked at Max. "The French not only took a British fort out here without a shot, but decided that they would tell the British that *the British* need to be the ones to withdraw from this area. They've sent scouting parties and a small French force of soldiers to relay their message."

Max furrowed his brow. "Sounds like fightin' words be comin'."

Gillamon looked out of the tent at an Indian messenger who hurried by. Washington wanted to cut the French off before their scouting parties could report their strength and location, so he sent seventy-five men to scout out the area. The Indian chief known as Half-King was also assisting Washington's men. They had just come upon a small French force in a glen by a rocky ravine fifteen miles away. The Indian messenger was telling Washington that Half-King and his Mingo warriors would lead him to the French camp. "More than fighting words are coming." Gillamon looked at Max with great seriousness. "War is coming."

———

MAY 28, 1754

The French soldier heard the birds chirping and the water rushing from the nearby stream. The sunrise was just beginning to make it light enough to see. He knew the refreshing coolness of the early morning would soon give way to the heat of the day. He sat up, rubbed his eyes, and saw that most of the thirty-five soldiers camped around him were still asleep. Others were beginning to stir. He stood to his feet and kicked a fellow soldier in the foot to rouse him. *"Réveillez-vous."* His friend grunted and kicked him back, rolling over for one more minute of sleep. The first soldier stretched and reached for his gun to walk down to the creek.

It was then he looked up to the top of the rocky ravine and saw the line of British soldiers standing on the rim with guns pointed down at the French camp. *"Voici! L'ennemie!"* he shouted, immediately alerting his fellow soldiers, who sprang into action. Suddenly shots rang out from above and below, with the British and the French firing on each other. The Indians were positioned behind the French, and screamed with blood-chilling war cries as they emerged from the woods.

Gillamon took his position next to Washington, ready to shield him from incoming enemy fire on his right wing. Bullets whistled by Washington's ear, and the smell and smoke of gunpowder filled the air. The explosive fire fight lasted only fifteen minutes. From the British raining down a barrage of fire from the top of the ravine, the French were overwhelmed and quickly surrendered.

"Report. What are our casualties?" Washington asked his officer as they hurriedly made their way down to the bottom of the ravine.

"One dead, three wounded, sir," the commander replied.

Washington tightened his lips and nodded. It was the first time

230

a man had died in battle while under his command. The weight of responsibility for the lives of his men settled heavily on his mind. "Tend to our wounded."

The French expedition's commander, Joseph Coulon de Villiers de Jumonville, lay wounded, and thirteen of his men had been killed. Washington's men quickly took twenty-one other French soldiers as prisoners. Washington and his translators started the process to accept the French surrender.

Without warning, Chief Half-King approached Jumonville and leaned over him with an intimidating stare. A stripe of black war paint swept across his eyes, and his head was bald except for his red, spiked mohawk. Around his neck he wore feathers and Indian medallions strung together with a thin leather strap. Jumonville gasped and stared into the menacing eyes of this Indian warrior. Half-King spoke in French to the wounded commander, *"Tu n'es pas encore more, mon père."* Thou are not yet dead, my father. The Indian warrior screamed, raised his hatchet, and with a war cry killed Jumonville.

231

The other Indian warriors echoed their chief with blood-curdling screams and began killing the French wounded and scalping the dead soldiers.

"HALT! PUT DOWN YOUR WEAPONS!" Washington shouted as his men rushed up to the Indians to make them stop the bloodshed. "THEY HAVE SURRENDERED!"

The Indians reluctantly stopped, then shouted their cries of victory over the horrific, blood-soaked scene. It was too late for all but one of the wounded French soldiers. The French had been massacred. One of the surviving Frenchmen held out a blood-stained piece of paper with a shaking hand and shouted with a trembling voice.

"What is he saying?" Washington asked his two French-speaking officers, Jacob Van Braam and William Peroney.

"He says they were on a diplomatic mission to deliver this letter from their French commander to the British, ordering us to leave this territory," Peroney replied, scanning the bloodied document. He handed the paper to Washington.

It was essentially the same type of instructions Washington himself had delivered to the French only a few months before. But he had delivered Dinwiddie's letter openly, peacefully, and even in a pleasant setting of dinner, wine, and candlelight.

Washington looked on with disgust at the scene around him as he took the paper in hand. He gritted his teeth angrily. "Then why were they hiding here in this ravine for these many days? If they truly were ambassadors, they knew where to find us. They should have come forth out in the open to announce their intentions, if what they are saying is true." He breathed in deeply and lifted his chin defiantly against the Frenchman. He shook his head and held up the documents. "You tell this man that we believe they were here to spy on our troops and report back to French command about our military strength. These papers are only a ruse to be used if they were caught." He looked around at the massacred French camp and shook his head. "No, they were spies, acting in a military capacity. We had the right to defend our camp against their forces." He handed the French document back to his translator. "Tell him every word I said."

As the men translated Washington's words to the captured Frenchmen, Gillamon saw the one Frenchman who had witnessed the battle, yet escaped capture, run off into the woods. He would quickly report back to the French commanders what had just happened. "So it begins."

232

FORT NECESSITY, 8:00 P.M., JULY 3, 1754

"Report," Washington demanded in an exhausted voice, wiping the sweat and grime of battle from his face with the back of his sleeve.

His commanders huddled in close to their commander and exchanged looks of despair.

"Sir, all the horses and livestock have been killed," one commander reported. "And with this constant rain, our gunpowder is wet. Most of the men's guns are jammed, and we have no hope of repairing them."

"A third of our men are dead or wounded," officer Mackay reported. "Some have been drinking. A group of men broke into the rum supply to drown their fear."

"Sir, the French have broken off the attack and called for a parley," Van Braam added.

"Why would the French wish to negotiate when they are clearly winning?" Washington wondered with a frown. It was over. He clenched his jaw and locked eyes with Van Braam. "Go. Discuss terms of our surrender with the French."

Following the 'Battle of Jumonville,' as it quickly came to be called, Washington had returned with his men to Fort Necessity to ready the fort for battle. He feared the French and their Indian allies would retaliate for his earlier attack on them. Washington pushed his men hard to fortify the small fort with deep trenches around the perimeter. Washington had written to Dinwiddie that the fort was strong enough "not to fear the attack of five hundred men." But the French had left mighty Fort Duquesne with six hundred soldiers, Canadian militiamen, and one hundred Native Indian allies to surround tiny Fort Necessity, led by Jumonville's brother, Captain Louis Coulon de Villiers.

When Colonel Joshua Fry died after falling from a horse, Washington was made the commander of all the Virginia forces. Reinforcements arrived, and the twenty-two-year-old commander assumed that the French would meet his four hundred men on the field of battle to fight in the traditional, European way. Following a heavy rain early in the morning hours, the French troops arrived at 11:00 a.m. and advanced on the fort in three columns. Washington's men lined up to fight and plunged into the trenches full of rainwater to mount their defense. The French began to fire from six hundred yards but when they got within sixty yards, they suddenly spread out to the hillsides surrounding the fort. They then mercilessly bombarded Washington's men for eight hours.

233

"What does it say?" Washington asked as he and his officers huddled around a small candle to read the poor handwriting on the rain-splattered paper that detailed conditions of surrender.

Van Braam shrugged his shoulders, clearly uncertain of exactly what the terms actually said. He rubbed his chin. "Uh, it say that you leave this fort tomorrow with no harm, as long as you return their French prisoners, and leave the area. They say you agree not to return for at least a year," he explained. "Also, you admit to the . . ." Van Braam squinted and tried to make out the terms of surrender, ". . . to the death? Uh, to the *loss* of Jumonville."

Washington raised his eyebrows in surprise and in relief. He looked at his subordinate officer Mackay. "These terms are quite generous. Very well."

Max and Gillamon looked on from a darkened corner. They had spent the day in the heat of battle, keeping French guns that were aimed at Washington from hitting their target.

"With Peroney collapsed from his injuries, Van Braam is the only one who speaks or reads French, but his English is very poor," Gillamon explained to Max.

"If only Liz were here ta explain ever-r-rythin'," Max whispered back.

Gillamon nodded and looked at the confused British officers huddled around the small candle as Washington signed the document. The young colonel then handed the quill to Officer Mackay to add his name. "Liz would tell them Washington just signed a document that will set off an entire war."

Max's eyes widened. "Wha' do ye mean?!"

"Washington actually just admitted that he murdered Jumonville, an ambassador on a mission of peace," Gillamon explained. "George Washington has just started the French and Indian War."

<hr />

HANOVER, JULY 1754

Liz and Nigel sat looking at the *Pennsylvania Gazette* and Benjamin Franklin's clever cartoon. While George Washington was busy tangling with the French on the frontier, the colonies were divided on whether to fight against the French and their Native American allies to keep control of the land on the western frontier. Franklin's striking word picture showed what the disunity of the colonies looked like against the growing French threat. Eleven colonies were represented by the eight segments of a dismembered snake. New England represented four colonies and Delaware was part of Pennsylvania. The struggling young colony of Georgia was left off the cartoon. It was transitioning from a charter colony for debtors with no governor to a royal colony.

Nigel and Cato had just returned from accompanying Benjamin Franklin to Albany, New York. Representatives from New England, New York, Pennsylvania, and Maryland met there to discuss plans for war and how to defend against the French.

"Franklin's plan was utterly *brilliant*," Nigel explained. "His Albany Plan of Union suggested one government for the colonies, to have an elected legislature with the power to raise troops, collect taxes, and regulate trade. But not a single colonial assembly approved the plan!" Nigel paced back and forth across the desk. "Benjamin said, 'Everyone cries, "a union is necessary" but when they come to the manner and *form* of the union, their weak noodles are perfectly distracted.'"

"Weak noodles?" Liz asked Nigel with a confused look.

Nigel pointed to his head. "Weak brains, my dear."

"Ah, I must remember this term, 'weak noodle,'" Liz replied. "But Benjamin is correct, no? The colonies have separate governments and assemblies and yet they need to find a way to provide for the common defense. It will be very difficult for the divided colonies to fight as one force."

235

"Meanwhile the French have one government, with one direction, and one purse," Nigel added. "My dear, I'm afraid our countries are at war."

"And my beloved France will fight against my Henry's beloved country," Liz replied with a frown. "My two loves are at war."

"Indeed." Nigel adjusted his spectacles. "But to quote your Henry's favorite book, *Don Quixote*, "Love and war are all one.""

LOVE AND WAR

RURAL PLAINS, HANOVER, OCTOBER 1754

Clarie and Max were back in Hanover with Liz and Nigel for the time being. The animals needed to regroup and get caught up on the news about their respective missions. They sat in a grove of trees, watching the humans starting to arrive at the Shelton home on this beautiful fall day. Today was to be a turning point in the life of Patrick Henry.

Nigel beamed as he rolled up and down on the balls of his feet. "I'm simply delighted to report that in addition to his worldwide fame, Benjamin Franklin has been given honorary degrees from Harvard and Yale. Also, the Royal Society of London awarded him the Golden Copley Medal for his discoveries on lightning and electricity. A tower was finally erected on the Pennsylvania State House, with a magnificent bell hung there to ring out over Philadelphia. Mr. Franklin promptly installed one of his lightning rods in the tower, so now when that bell rings in a storm, the building will be kept safe." Nigel preened his whiskers proudly. "Isn't it amazing what one single spark of electricity can do?"

"Bravo, *mon ami!*" Liz cheered. "I am very happy for Mr. Franklin."

"Aye, good for yer turkey-fr-r-ryin' lad," Max added. "Me George also ignited a spark, but for a war here in America."

"This war will not be fought just in America, Max," Clarie explained. "The spark that George Washington ignited in the French and Indian War in America will spread quickly. It will grow into a blazing fire to cover the entire world. France and Great Britain will fight in Europe and wherever they have imperial interests around the globe—America, Europe, India, even at sea and in the Caribbean islands all the way to Barbados."

"So George Washington started a *worldwide* war?" Max asked. "Well, if ye're goin' ta do somethin', ye might as well do it all the way, I always say. Mousie's Fr-r-ranklin an' me Washin'ton be famous now, but for different things." The Scottie shook his large head. "Poor George were so humiliated by his sur-r-render at Fort Necessity, an' Dinwiddie only made it worse. The militia soldiers deserted all the way back ta Williamsburg so Dinwiddie wants ta start a new army of Virginia r-r-regulars ta be over any militia. He offered George a command but with a lower rank so George said, 'No, thanks.' He r-r-resigned his commission an' went back home ta be a farmer. After all the dangers I've seen that lad face—Indian snipers, snow storms, r-r-rugged wilderness, icy r-r-rivers, battles, an' Fr-r-rench bullets—seems like farmin' will be a waste of a gr-r-rand soldier."

"My Henry will also now become a farmer," Liz added with a wrinkled brow. "It is not clear to see how he will ever become famous like Franklin and Washington, or how he will become the great leader that Gillamon says he will be."

"Is anything ever clear at first?" Clarie asked with a grin. "In addition to all you saw George go through, Max, he also developed smallpox on Barbados. I wanted to protect him from getting the virus, but Gillamon said in the long run the smallpox *would* protect him. I didn't understand it at the time, but now I see that the immunity George got from his illness has and will continue to protect him in war."

"This makes terribly good sense, my dear," Nigel noted. "By the way, how was it that you *knew* George would get the smallpox in the first place?"

"Gillamon said George was intentionally exposed to the virus," Clarie explained. "Some creature wanted the virus to kill him, but Gillamon didn't say what or who."

Max, Liz, and Nigel looked at one another in alarm. "So it's like he were *poisoned* with the virus," Max pointed out.

"What the Enemy intended for evil, the Maker intended for good, just as with Joseph," Liz marveled. *"C'est incredible."*

"Indeed. Attacks, illness, failure, suffering, and even sorrow are all tools in the Maker's workshop to chisel His chosen humans into greatness!" Nigel exclaimed, using an imaginary chisel to shape an imaginary statue.

"All three of your humans will experience highs and lows in the

237

coming hard years," Clarie added. "Always remember that failure and heartache, when wrapped in the blanket of grace, bring gifts to the soul that can't be experienced in any other way. Before the Maker uses anyone to any great degree, He must break them completely to empty them of themselves. Only in this way can great men truly depend on the Maker and accomplish great things for Him that they couldn't accomplish on their own."

"Again, as we saw with Joseph in Egypt, no?" Liz noted. "He had to be emptied of himself in slavery and prison before he was ready to be made the second highest ruler in Egypt so he could save the nations from drought and famine."

"Aye, hard times make ye slow down," Max added. "An' when ye slow down ye have time ta figure things out."

"Exactly, Max," agreed Clarie. "It's in the hard times that humans discover who they really are and what they truly are called to become."

"Since Patrick's store failed and closed, I know he must try something else. But I cannot see how farming will lead him to his voice," wondered Liz. "I was expecting the fiddle's riddle about the tavern to come next."

238

Clarie smiled. "Every phase of life is a stepping stone. George and Patrick may be farmers for now, but they won't use their plowshares for long."

Nigel frowned and quoted the book of Joel. "They will turn their plowshares into swords."

"Aye, war be comin'," Max added.

Liz shook her head and held up her paw as she heard laughter coming from the Shelton home. "Enough talk about war. I wish to talk about *love* on this happy day. My Henry is getting married!"

"Too bad yer Al can't be here, lass," Max said with a grin. "Ye know how he loves weddin's."

"How splendid it will be to witness the tender nuptials of the young couple," Nigel declared with his paw over his heart. "It is fortunate their parents finally agreed for them to wed, despite their reservations."

"*Oui,* Patrick is eighteen and Sarah is only sixteen, which is much younger than most couples, but they are in love," gushed Liz. "And this marriage made sense to help my Henry figure out his next step in life. Sarah's father has given them the Pine Slash farm, so they have a place to live and he has a new line of work."

"I'm happy for the lad," Max agreed. "Gillamon told me ta get back ta keep watch over George, so I'm glad Patr-r-rick has Nelson ta help him on the farm."

"I need to be going as well," Clarie added. "It's time for me to do some gardening in the south of France in preparation for Kate's next mission. She'll be with the family of Lafayette in their château called Chavaniac."

"Gardening in the south of France?" Liz perked up, wide-eyed. "Ah, *mon amie*, how I wish I could be there with you and Kate! But my place is here with my Henry. What kind of gardening will you be doing?"

"Rest assured my gardening will help your Henry someday," promised Clarie, drawing a puzzled expression from Liz. "The kind of gardening I'll be doing is more the master planning, not planting, kind—placing benches, fountains . . . statues."

"And I am to remain with Liz for the time being, correct?" Nigel asked.

"Yes, you will be with Liz and Patrick Henry until you rejoin Benjamin Franklin at a later date," Clarie explained. "Or until you're needed for any side missions that arise."

239

Just then a carriage pulled up and out stepped Uncle Patrick Henry. He tucked his *Book of Common Prayer* under his arm and walked toward the brick home.

"*Adieu, mes amis.* It is time for me to attend a wedding," Liz said, kissing Max and Clarie on the cheek.

"But ye'll be seen, lass," Max warned as Liz started walking toward the house.

Liz smiled and lifted her curlicue tail high in the air as she walked away. "*Oui,* this is the plan. How else can I give my Henry his wedding gift—*moi?*"

———

Sallie Shelton, Jane Henry, and sisters Elizabeth and Sarah Strong giggled as they fussed with Sallie's dress and hair. The other six Henry sisters—Anne, Sarah, Susannah, Lucy, Mary, and Elizabeth—sat around on the settee and chairs, excitedly watching the bride get ready for her wedding to their brother.

"I love your dress, Sallie," complimented Jane, brushing Sallie's hair with the silver brush Patrick had given her.

"Well, you can borrow it whenever Sam Meredith gets around to asking you to marry him!" replied Sallie. "It's only a matter of time."

Jane blushed and smiled. "I'm happy we've known our beaux since childhood. It's been fun, all of us growing up together."

Elizabeth Strong held Patrick's mirror for Sallie. "I wish Sarah and I could say the same. I don't know who we'll find to marry here in Hanover."

"You two are even younger than I am! Give it time," Sallie assured them with a smile, lightly pinching her cheeks for color as she looked into the mirror. "Maybe your husbands aren't in Hanover at all."

Elizabeth's sister, Sarah, handed Sallie a pin for her hair. "Maybe we'll need to go find them elsewhere."

"Or maybe," Sallie encouraged her with a smile, twirling a daisy to put in her hair, "they'll come to you."

240

Patrick sat on a chair in the parlor, wiping his sweaty palms on his trousers. Nelson nudged him with his nose and Patrick smiled. He petted the dog on the head and whispered, "This is our big day, boy. I'm glad I got the girl with the dog." Nelson wagged his tail happily.

"A word, Pat?" John Henry said, sitting down next to his nervous son. "I'm grateful ta John Shelton for giving ye the dowry of Pine Slash. Three hundred acres and six slaves is a fine beginning for ye ta farm." He frowned and leaned forward. "I wish I were in a better situation right now ta give ye something equally grand. I promise ta give ye fresh land further west in Louisa County as soon as I can."

Patrick put his hand on his father's arm. "Thank you, Father. Sallie and I will be grateful for your gift whenever it is convenient for you to give it. I'm sorry the store you helped Bill and me to start failed. I truly hope this time I can make you proud by making my way as a tobacco farmer." He furrowed his brow. "But I have to admit that I feel uncomfortable owning slaves. I know they are a necessary part of our existence as farmers, but it doesn't sit well with me."

John nodded. "I understand, Pat. It is an unfortunate reality, but I'm sure ye'll be kind ta them, as yer mother and I have always been ta ours. Besides, the work that lies ahead in clearing that sandy, pine-scrubbed soil ta farm will primarily fall on yer shoulders. Aside from the older woman, Esther, who can help Sallie with the kitchen and running the house, the others are very young and won't be of much use ta ye in the fields."

"Somehow that makes me feel better about this business," Patrick replied with a smile. He suddenly heard the voice of his Uncle Patrick among the other guests his mother was greeting in the foyer. "Uncle Patrick is here to perform our ceremony. Perhaps it's best that Reverend Samuel Davies is in London right now. I know mother would have wanted him here as well."

"Aye, the last thing we needed is a war in the middle of yer wedding," joked John with a chuckle.

Sarah Henry peered in the parlor with a wide smile. "Pat, I have a surprise for you."

William Winston peeked around his sister and leaned on the door-frame. "So the boy is really going through with it. He's going to settle down with that pretty little girl."

Patrick's face brightened, and he stood to his feet to rush over to embrace his uncle. "Uncle Langloo! I didn't know you'd be here! I thought you'd be off with the long hunters for the season."

Langloo gave Patrick a burly hug, patting his nephew on the back. "I wouldn't miss your wedding, Pat! I brought my hunters along with me. I told them the first thing to hunt was my nephew's happiness, then we'd go hunt deer. Besides, you'll need someone to fire up a fiddle for your wedding party while you're dancing with your bride." He leaned in with a wink. "Did you woo your pretty girl with that fiddle of yours like I told you?"

Patrick leaned his head back and laughed. "I sure did!"

"I want you to meet my long hunters in training for the season," Langloo said, holding out an arm to two young men dressed in frontier clothes. "Sorry none of us is dressed in fancy clothes for your wedding, but I knew you wouldn't mind. These are Benjamin and Samuel Crowley. They're from Halifax County. I acquired a fine horse from their father, Jeffrey, on the condition I take his boys with me on the long hunt to train them, just like I did you on our wilderness trips."

Patrick held out his hand to the young men. "I'm happy to meet you boys. You're in good hands with Uncle Langloo here. He taught me everything I need to know about hunting and surviving in the wilderness. Make sure he tells you all about the ways of the Indians."

"Thanks, Patrick," Samuel replied, shaking his hand. "We can't wait, especially for the Indian part!"

"Congratulations on your wedding," Benjamin added.

"Thank you, boys. Enjoy yourselves today, and be safe out there with this wild man," Patrick teased.

"You earn that eagle feather yet, Pat?" Langloo asked with a grin.

"Not yet, Uncle," Patrick replied. "Maybe one day. For now I've got to settle down and take up farming, so I don't think I'll be a warrior anytime soon."

Langloo put a hand on Patrick's shoulder. "You'll be a warrior in the tobacco fields, Pat. It'll be tough, but just do your best."

"Thanks, Uncle. Have fun out there in the wilderness," Patrick replied, pointing to Samuel and Benjamin. "And take care of these boys."

Langloo winked. "Don't worry. I'll show them how to track panthers and Indians, just as I did you."

"It's time to get started, Patrick," came Uncle Patrick's voice as he entered the parlor. "Are you ready?"

Patrick let go a quick breath and went to stand over by the fireplace with his uncle. "As ready as I'll ever be."

242

━━━

John Shelton wrapped on the door where the girls were getting ready. "Sallie? It's time."

The girls opened the door and there stood his beautiful daughter in her bridal dress, her hair pinned up with daisies and ringlets. "I'm ready, Papa."

John smiled. "How beautiful you look!" He kissed her on the forehead and whispered in her ear. "Are you sure you're ready? You can still back out of this. Just say the word."

"Papa! Of course I'm ready!" Sallie playfully scolded her father. "I know you and mother wish I were older, but Patrick and I are ready to start our life together. And I'll only be a half-mile down the road from you and Mama."

"Why do you think I gave you Pine Slash?" John teased. "I want to keep my girl close."

Sallie's mother, Eleanor Shelton, came into the room. "Time to go, Sallie. Patrick is waiting. Both of them."

The Shelton home was crowded with family members from the Henry, Shelton, and Winston families, along with their close friends from Hanover. The doors were opened to allow a fresh breeze. Liz walked right in the front door and went over to sit in the corner with Nelson while Nigel scurried behind a chair to keep out of sight.

"This is a happy day, no?" Liz whispered to Nelson.

"Hi, Liz," Nelson replied. "It sure is! Are you going to be with us at Pine Slash?"

"*Oui,* I plan to present myself to Patrick and Sallie there. It is time," Liz replied.

Sallie and her father walked down the stairs to the hallway as family and friends parted for them to reach the parlor. Patrick's heart was beating out of his chest as his lovely bride walked up to join him in front of the fireplace. Uncle Patrick smiled and placed his hand on his opened *Book of Common Prayer* to read the Marriage Ceremony. Patrick and Sallie faced one another. Patrick winked at Sallie and her dimples appeared with her bright smile.

"Dearly beloved, we are gathered together here in the sight of God, and in the face of this congregation, to join together this Man and this Woman in holy Matrimony; which is an honorable estate, instituted of God in the time of man's innocency, signifying unto us the mystical union that is betwixt Christ and his Church; which holy estate Christ adorned and beautified with his presence, and first miracle that he wrought, in Cana of Galilee . . ." Uncle Patrick began.

Liz's heart filled with joy as she remembered being at that wedding in Cana of Galilee. Jesus did as his mother asked, turning huge jars of water into wine and saving the day for the embarrassed young couple's family, who had run out of wine. Jesus loved weddings, celebrating young couples starting their new lives together.

"Patrick, wilt thou have this Woman to thy wedded Wife, to live together after God's ordinance in the holy estate of Matrimony? Wilt thou love her, comfort her, honour, and keep her in sickness and in health; and, forsaking all other, keep thee only unto her, so long as ye both shall live?" Uncle Patrick asked.

Patrick looked into Sallie's eyes with unspeakable love and he smiled. "I will."

"Sarah, wilt thou have this man to thy wedded Husband, to live together after God's ordinance in the holy estate of Matrimony? Wilt thou obey him, and serve him, love, honour, and keep him in sickness and in health; and, forsaking all other, keep thee only unto him, so long as ye both shall live?" Uncle Patrick asked.

243

Sallie grinned. "I will."

"Who giveth this woman to be married to this man?" Uncle Patrick asked.

"Her mother and I," John Shelton replied, kissing his daughter on the cheek and placing her hand in Patrick's. Patrick nodded to John with unspoken words of gratitude for the hand of his daughter.

Following the instructions of his uncle, Patrick next repeated his vow. "I, Patrick, take thee Sarah, to my wedded Wife, to have and to hold from this day forward, for better for worse, for richer for poorer, in sickness and in health, to love and to cherish, till death us do part, according to God's holy ordinance; and thereto I plight thee my troth."

Liz's eyes brimmed with happy tears as she now watched her Henry and Sallie stand at the threshold of their new life together. She breathed a silent prayer of blessing. *Just as you did in Cana, I ask that you also bless this young couple,* cher *Jesus.* S'il vous plaît, *fill them with a love that will never run dry despite the coming war and hard times they will face—till death they do part.*

244

As the ceremony continued, Samuel Crowley found himself unable to keep his eyes on Patrick and Sallie. It wasn't that he couldn't pay attention to the vows they spoke. It was because on the other side of the parlor he saw for the first time beautiful Elizabeth Strong. And all he could think about was how he wanted to someday say those same words to her.

PLOWSHARES AND SWORDS

POLEGREEN MEETING HOUSE, HANOVER, MARCH 5, 1755

"A powerful and treacherous enemy is making inroads upon our territories, our religion and our liberty, our property, our lives; and everything sacred or dear to us is in danger! We are preparing to make a defense; and our most gracious king has been pleased to send a considerable number of his ships and forces to oppose the unjustifiable attempts of our enemies. But unless the success of the expedition depends upon the providence of God, to what end do we humble ourselves before him, and implore his help? The thing itself, upon supposition, would be an incongruity, an empty compliment, a mockery.

Upon my return from England to Virginia, I met with Governor Dinwiddie," Reverend Samuel Davies began, setting down the Proclamation from Governor Dinwiddie that he had just read. "He informed me of the looming war upon our land and that General Edward Braddock will soon arrive with two regiments to protect our western borders. As the largest of all the colonies, Virginia will of course be part of this campaign. We must support this noble cause with our resources, our soldiers, and our prayers. Governor Dinwiddie asked that I support this Day of Fasting and Prayer by reading his proclamation and leading us all to the throne of God to pray for our nation. I thank you for joining me today. Before we bow our heads together to pray for our brave British and American forces, I would like to speak to you on the subject of war and God's divine providence."

Patrick Henry stood in the back of the crowd, hanging on every word Davies spoke. Sallie was six months pregnant and had remained home. He walked the half-mile from Pine Slash to Polegreen after already working many hours this Wednesday morning in his tobacco fields. His stomach rumbled, but he paid it no mind. He rubbed his calloused hands on his soiled trousers and felt chagrined to not be as clean and presentable as others gathered here. It didn't escape his attention how those in the upper reaches of society looked at him when they rode by his fields in their carriages—the son of a gentleman justice, failure as a merchant, and now working in his crop-worn fields alongside his slaves. He appeared to be no better than an indentured servant, working the land in back-breaking work with sunburnt skin, a sweaty brow, and filthy hands.

But Patrick felt an urgency to join with the others on this day of fasting and prayer, so he came just as he was, right from the fields. Rumors of Indian atrocities against families living out on the frontier set off an alarm in everyone here in Hanover. War was coming, and Patrick Henry knew he couldn't join in the physical fight with a sword, having a dependent wife and baby. But he could join in the spiritual fight on his knees in prayer. For now, his hands were occupied with the plowshare, and he would have to let other young men take up swords to fight the enemy. Uncle Langloo was right—his battlefield was the tobacco fields.

After their blissful wedding, Patrick and Sallie immediately got to work, she with the house and he with clearing the land. Their families had provided them with enough furniture, dishes, and livestock to get their small farm going, but they would soon have a new mouth to feed. As with every family here in rural Virginia, they planted corn, wheat, and oats to feed themselves and their animals. They had pigs, chickens, sheep, cattle, and two old horses. But the crop they planted to provide for their livelihood was tobacco.

Pine Slash had flat, clay soil surrounded by pine woods. The land had been overfarmed and its soil nutrients depleted except for some remaining sandy loam. Patrick had high hopes that once he cleared the land of the pine brush, stumps, and rocks, he would have a chance to produce the tobacco he needed to support his family. In January and February he prepared the seedbeds, clearing, burning, and hoeing the soil. He and his workers were in the process of planting the tiny tobacco seeds. Next they would rake the seed beds and cover them with

246

pine boughs to protect the infant plants. Come April they would spread the fragile seedlings to four inches apart. If his seedlings survived bad weather and the hungry tobacco flea beetles, Patrick would then transplant them to prepared fields in May. "Hilling" was the hardest part of the tobacco-planting process. Knee-high hills of soil were made and spaced four feet apart. Experienced tobacco farmers could prepare five hundred hills in a single day, but Patrick was still learning, so would move at a slower pace.

Of course, even if Patrick prepared the land the best he could, he was completely dependent on the rain to water it. He would have to wait until rain softened the soil to transplant the young tobacco plants to their final location. Until the plants reached knee-high, weekly tilling was necessary to kill weeds and keep reshaping the hills. After about two months, a series of continual steps then had to be taken for the tobacco to grow. The plants would be "primed" by removing two to four leaves growing at the base of the plant, and "topped" by removing the cluster of small compact leaves at the tip so the plant wouldn't use its energy to make flowers and seeds. Healthy plants now grew to three to four feet tall, and "suckers," or tiny shoots, had to be continually removed from the stalks. Even with all that toil, diseases and pests battled the farmer to destroy the tobacco. If the dreaded horn worm wasn't daily picked off and crushed underfoot in the blazing summer months, they could destroy a crop in less than a week. Hopefully by late August or early September, the six- to nine-foot plants would be ready for harvest. Now came the danger of harvesting before the plant was mature or when its peak had passed. If Patrick waited too long, an early frost could destroy the entire crop. An experienced tobacco farmer could look at the color and texture of the leaves and know the right time for harvest. Patrick would have to figure out this timing as best he could.

247

Once the tobacco leaves were harvested, they would be "cured" by hanging them on sticks to dry for four to six weeks. Mold was a potential threat to the leaves during this time, so Patrick had to know the right time to remove the leaves from the sticks and lay them on the floor of the tobacco barn to "sweat" for a week or two. After sweating, the leaves would hopefully have absorbed just the right amount of moisture, allowing them to be stretched like leather and be glossy and moist. If the leaves were too damp, they might rot during shipping. If they were too dry, they would crumble and be unfit for sale. Finally the leaves were put into large barrels called "hogsheads," which each held about a thousand pounds of tobacco. Hogsheads were loaded on ships, sent down the rivers of Virginia to Yorktown, and then out to the Atlantic for transport to Great Britain.

Only then could farmers like Patrick expect to be paid for this long, hard process of growing tobacco. Patrick had been on the other side of this timeline as a merchant, providing struggling farmers like Mr. Smythe with tools and supplies on credit that Patrick extended. Now he was the one in Mr. Smythe's shoes, but Patrick Henry couldn't bear the idea of being in debt. To Patrick, there was no greater prison than to be financially beholden to anyone. He was determined to pay his debts and do whatever it took to stand on his own two feet. Hanover County had produced four thousand hogsheads of tobacco last year, but each year told a different story. Time would tell how much 1755 would allow his small farm to yield.

Just as his father had told him, eighteen-year-old Patrick was the one doing the backbreaking work out in his fields, along with two of the slaves, who were even younger than he. The days were long, and he collapsed into the arms of his Sallie every evening, happy they were together despite the exhausting work.

"If the affairs of nations are at the disposal of the King of heaven, then how dreadful is the case of a guilty, provoking, impenitent nation!" Davies exclaimed.

Samuel Davies had recounted God's powerful acts in biblical times and through history, encouraging the people with God's undeniable ability to deliver them. However, deliverance would be dependent on the humility and pure hearts of the people who asked for his aid. Just as John the Baptist called people to repent, so, too, did Davies implore the people to repent in order for God to listen to their prayers.

"And, if this is the case, how may we tremble for our country, and fear the divine displeasure? We have enjoyed a long, uninterrupted peace in this land. We have not been alarmed with the sound of the war trumpet, nor seen garments rolled in blood. But what a wretched improvement have we made of this, and many other inestimable blessings? What a torrent of vice, irreligion, and luxury has broken in, and overwhelmed the land? What ignorance of God and divine things; what carelessness about the concerns of religion and a future state? What a neglect of Christ and his precious gospel—has spread, like a *subtle poison,* among all ranks and characters!"

Poison, Liz thought with a furrowed brow. She and Nigel were also in the crowd here at Polegreen. *There it is again, but this time a* spiritual *poison.*

"Now what shall we do in this dreadful case? Shall we put our trust in our military forces? Alas! What can an arm of flesh do for us, if the Lord Almighty deserts us? Let us confess our own sins, and the sins of our land—which have brought all our evils upon us. Let us be importunate and incessant in prayer, that God would pour out his Spirit and promote a general reformation; that he would direct our rulers to proper measures, inspire our soldiers with courage, and decide the event of battle in our favor." Davies's voice was reaching a crescendo.

"Patrick Henry is not only paying attention to the words Samuel Davies speaks, but how each person here is spellbound by his delivery," Nigel observed.

Samuel Davies lifted his hands, animating his sermon. "The interposition of Providence is frequently visible in the remarkable coincidence of circumstances to accomplish some important end in critical times. I am not enthusiastic enough to look upon every event as the effect of an immediate Providence, excluding or controlling the agency of natural causes. But when such things happen—must we not own that it is the finger of God?"

249

"*Oui,* as they should," Liz answered. "And more people besides those present need to hear this sermon. Just as he published George Washington's journal here in Virginia and in London, Governor Dinwiddie needs to publish this sermon for others to read."

"We have no ground for a lazy confidence in divine Providence; nor should we content ourselves in inactive prayers; but let us rouse ourselves, and be active," Samuel Davies exclaimed. "Let us cheerfully pay the taxes the government has laid upon us to support this expedition. Let us use our influence to diffuse a military spirit around us. I have no scruple thus openly to declare, that such of you whose circumstances allow of it, may not only lawfully enlist and take up arms, but that your doing so is a Christian duty, and acting an honorable part, worthy of a man, a freeman, a Briton, and a Christian."

A loud cheer rose up from the crowd, as Davies elevated the spirits of patriotic fervor in those gathered there. Men were ready to enlist for the cause.

"So far, the words of Benjamin Franklin and George Washington have been published on both sides of the Atlantic," Nigel said. "Are you suggesting the same now for Samuel Davies?"

"*Oui, mon ami.* I'll prepare the letter of suggestion to Governor Dinwiddie myself." Liz smiled at her mouse friend. "How soon can Cato fly you to Williamsburg?"

OHIO WILDERNESS, JULY 8, 1755

"He still looks r-r-rough, Gillamon," Max whispered with a furrowed brow, looking over a now restlessly sleeping George Washington.

Gillamon gathered the rags and basin he had used to help Washington's fever and severe headaches. He motioned for Max to follow him outside the tent. "The dysentery has taken its toll, but George is recovering, although weak," shared Gillamon with grave concern. "He'll need supernatural strength for tomorrow. And so will you. Get some rest now, Max. I'll be here when you wake."

Max yawned and stretched out next to Gillamon by his small fire. "Aye. At least it's only ten more miles ta r-r-reach Fort Duquesne. General Br-r-raddock plans ta make it all the way tomor-r-row, an' I'll be r-r-ready for a fight, Gillamon."

Gillamon nodded and gave Max a pet. "Good lad. Get some sleep."

Gillamon had arranged to become Washington's personal assistant for this expedition into the Ohio Valley to recapture Fort Duquesne from the French. Following Washington's surrender at Fort Necessity last year, the British government decided to drive the French from the area once and for all with the strength of its red-coated army. General Edward Braddock was given two regiments of British regulars who were stationed in Ireland. The British reasoned that since this force had kept the defiant Irish in check, they could easily rout any French and Indian opposition.

George Washington did not pick up his plowshare to farm for long. After Governor Dinwiddie's proclamation for a day of fasting and prayer, he soon desired a military position with the British army to go on this expedition to expel the French. But he knew that the British regulars looked down on the colonial militia, requiring their officers to report to lower-ranking British regular officers. George decided he

250

wanted to trade his blue militia coat for the red coat of the regulars, and pursued a royal appointment as a major with General Braddock. He soon learned that no rank above captain would be approved here in America, so he accepted an unpaid, volunteer position as aide-de-camp for General Braddock. He would be serving next to the most powerful British officer in America, and Washington hoped this would be the stepping stone he needed for a royal commission.

Although General Braddock had long served in the British army with limited combat experience, he was a walking textbook of European military training, and he did everything accordingly. Upon his arrival in America in March, he proceeded to demand provision of funding and supplies from four colonial governors for his army, in intense training at Fort Cumberland. Braddock's brash, arrogant manner, coupled with a sense of entitlement, alienated the colonial leaders. Thankfully, Benjamin Franklin interceded to provide some wagons and supplies for the 1,400 regular soldiers, 700 colonial militia, and handful of Indian scouts.

The lack of sufficient Indian scouts was not due to lack of supply, but Braddock's lack of respect, vision, and diplomacy. Not only did he look down upon the colonial "backwoods" militia fighters, but he considered the Indians as nothing more than territorial squatters who needed to vacate the Ohio, along with the French. He rudely told the Indians who offered their assistance that not only did the British *not* need their help in fighting the French, but they would need to leave their ancestral lands once the British took control of the Ohio. Braddock's arrogance and ignorance hung heavily in the air as Washington watched the offended Indians storm out of Braddock's tent. Washington knew firsthand what strong allies the Indians could be in rough wilderness fighting. He also knew the vicious enemies Indians could be if they sided with the French.

In order to reach Fort Duquesne, Braddock decided to build a road twelve feet wide and one hundred miles long through the wilderness. He pushed a four-mile-long column of 2,100 troops, 2,500 horses, and 300 wagons, plus 600 additional horses carrying provisions and pulling the 12 field guns and mortars. The sheer amount of food needed for the men as well as the animals was staggering. A small number of women accompanied the expedition to cook, launder, and provide nursing. Progress was painfully slow as men had to cut trees and build

251

bridges over muddy bogs and streams; sometimes they only traveled two miles a day. As with any military campaign, illness struck, and accidents occurred along the way. George Washington was among many who were afflicted with dysentery, but he pushed on as best he could.

At Washington's suggestion, Braddock split his column into two divisions to increase their speed. Braddock led the forward "flying column" of 1,300 lighter-equipped troops and left Colonel Dunbar to follow with the slower supply column of 800 men. Because progress was faster for the forward division led by Braddock, fifty miles soon separated him from Dunbar's support column.

Meanwhile, Indian scouts informed the French at Fort Duquesne that the British were on their way with men and cannons. The French only garrisoned 250 combined regulars and Canadian militia at the fort, but 640 Indian allies were encamped outside. The French understood the threat posed by the British cannon, so decided to strike the British as they crossed the last natural obstacle to reach the fort: the Monongahela River. The Indians were hesitant to fight such a large, well-armed British army, but French commander Captain Beaujeu knew exactly how to gain their confidence and respect. He dressed as an Indian, covering himself with war paint, and quickly rallied them to his cause. Together the French and Indians left Fort Duquesne and headed out into the wilderness to ambush Braddock's forces.

Gillamon watched Max sleeping, then looked around at the small fires dotted through Braddock's camp. He sighed and breathed a prayer for all the soldiers and the day that awaited them. He then gazed at Washington's tent and lifted up the weakened soldier sleeping inside. Not only would George Washington need supernatural physical strength tomorrow, he would also need divine protection to survive the coming attack.

JULY 9, 1755, MONONGAHELA RIVER

"Some talk of Alexander,
And some of Hercules
Of Hector and Lysander,
And such great names as these.
But of all the world's great heroes,

There's none that can compare
With a tow, row, row, row, row, row,
To the British Grenadier!

"The lads seem in gr-r-rand spir-r-rits today," Max shouted above the loud chorus of energetic soldiers singing along with the fifes and drums playing their signature marching song, *The British Grenadier.* He rode next to Gillamon in the officer supply wagon. British flags flapped proudly in the breeze, and the noisy military parade would soon announce to the French their approach.

Gillamon held the reins and looked up at the hills sweeping upward on either side of the road. "Yes, they fully expect to sing and march right into Fort Duquesne tonight. General Braddock shares their optimism, but brace yourself, Max." He looked down at the Scottie, his striking blue eyes growing serious. "Things are getting ready to happen. When the music stops and I give the word, move quickly and follow my lead. You know what to do."

Max furrowed his brow and growled. "Aye."

253

"After those little skirmishes with random French and Indian scouts along the way, I think word of our approach has sent the French fleeing," Braddock, chin lifted high, confidently told Washington. "With no sign whatsoever of the enemy today, I believe the French have already abandoned Fort Duquesne. We should be able to take the fort with no resistance." Together they sat on their horses on the banks of the river, watching the splendid red-coated column singing and marching ahead. George frowned and tightened his lip in response. "Why the concerned face, Colonel Washington? Do you disagree?"

"Sir, with all due respect," George replied haltingly, looking around them, "I believe this lack of enemy activity could be a bad sign. Things are *too* quiet. With your permission, allow me to take a group of experienced woodsmen to scout out the woods ahead of the column. The French and Indians do not fight like the British in open-field formation. They use the trees for cover and stealth, just as our militia have learned to do. With this narrow road, I fear we could be walking into a trap with little room to maneuver while using traditional volleys in a firefight."

Braddock clenched his jaw and pursed his lips. In an irritated tone, he pointed to the front of the column of men marching in twos. "Lieutenant Colonel Thomas Gage has 300 of His Majesty's finest grenadiers leading this column! We are *well* prepared for a fight, and do *not* need to use your primitive militia ways of disorderly conduct to achieve victory. Remember your place, Colonel."

Washington frowned at the general's blind pride. "Sir, I assure you that my advice is based on personal experience in fighting this enemy . . ." he began.

"And you were soundly defeated at Fort Necessity, were you not?" Braddock shouted back angrily, with a humiliating jab at Washington. He pointed to the back of the column. "Bring up the rear of the column, Colonel. Go, and do not test me again!"

Washington nodded respectfully and turned his horse to obey his commanding officer. He headed to the back of the column as ordered, which only added to his uneasiness. Braddock would listen to no one but himself and to the cadence of the fife and drum serenading him as he rode to his presumed victory.

Braddock snapped the reins of his horse and moved ahead to join in singing the triumphant song with his resplendent red-coated army:

254

"Those heroes of antiquity
Ne'er saw a cannon ball
Or knew the force of powder
To slay their foes withall.
But our brave boys do know it,
And banish all their fears,
Sing tow, row, row, row, row, row,
For the British Grenadier!"

French commander Beaujeu and his men soon came to a narrow path that rose through the woods to an opening that curved to the right, forming a natural trench. He decided to make good use of it, ordering his two hundred French and Canadian militia soldiers to make ready in the trench. He instructed the Canadian militia and three hundred Indian warriors to target the British officers on horseback, picking them off first to ensure the greatest chaos among the British. The French and Indians readied their muskets as Beaujeu held up his hand, preparing to give the signal to fire. It didn't take long. When Beaujeu saw the redcoats crest the rise, he dropped his hand and shouted, *"FEU!"*

The air filled with smoke and Colonel Gage saw some of his men suddenly drop to the ground. "Halt! Form up and prepare to fire!" he shouted. His men immediately formed a traditional firing line in the road and fired a volley, stunning the French and Indian forces. Commander Beaujeu was instantly killed by a British bullet. The French hesitated in dismay and some Indians began to scatter into the woods.

Instead of pursuing a vigorous bayonet charge to quickly overcome the stunned French forces, Gage ordered his men to fall back toward the main body of Braddock's forces. This allowed French Captain Dumas to rally his men, who began firing again from the trench. The Indians fanned out in the woods and on the hillsides, surrounding Braddock's army in a horseshoe attack.

Braddock raced to the front of the column, eager to prove his leadership in combat. But only chaos ensued as he shouted orders for his men to continue forming traditional European firing blocks. Some of the militia fled to the trees for cover and stealth, just as Washington had suggested to Braddock earlier. In the confusion, the British took their own for the enemy and fired into the trees, killing many of their own colonial soldiers. Over the course of two hours, Braddock rode around furiously waving his sword, shouting threats to the troops if they did not continually reform and attack. Men were screaming in agony and falling at every turn, and officers were being picked off their horses by Indian snipers, one by one. Braddock's horse was shot out from under him, so he mounted another. That horse was also shot out from under him. Then another. And another.

Washington raced his horse to the front of the column, dodging enemy fire and the bodies filling the road. Just as he reached Braddock's position, a sniper took aim and the bullet found its mark—it penetrated Braddock's arm, then entered his chest.

"NO!" Washington screamed as Braddock fell from his horse. At that moment, George's second horse was also shot out from under him. He fell to the ground unhurt and immediately got to his feet, running to Braddock. The British general lay in the road, blood quickly causing his white shirt to match the red of his brilliant coat.

Max was in position. As George ran to Braddock's aid, Max jumped to hit the sniper who had Washington in his sights, causing the shot to miss. Max ran from sniper to sniper, pushing them off balance while George crouched on the ground.

"QUICKLY! HELP ME GET HIM TO THE REAR!" George

255

shouted to some of the British regulars nearby. Two men responded, lifting the wounded general as Washington led them through the carnage to get their commander to safety.

When they reached a safe distance they placed Braddock in a wagon to take him back to the other support column. Braddock wore a look of shock. "Who would have thought it!" he wondered with a garbled voice as he clasped a bloodied hand over his chest. "We shall know better how to deal with them another time."

Washington gritted his teeth at the absurdity of Braddock's words. Had the general listened to George in the first place he would have known better *this time,* avoiding this ambush. "Get him to safety and medical care!" the lieutenant colonel ordered the men. When the wagon moved on, a white horse was suddenly standing there calmly in the road. George quickly mounted the horse and drew his sword as he raced back to the fight. In his haste he didn't notice that the horse now carrying him back to the heat of battle had striking blue eyes.

SOLDIER ON

Word quickly reached Hanover about Braddock's shocking defeat, and Samuel Davies prepared to address the nervous congregation. General Braddock had died four days after he was shot during his rout by the French and Indians. Two-thirds of his officers and men were either killed or wounded. George Washington was the only one on horseback who escaped injury, not even receiving a scratch. He wrote to his brother, Augustine, on July 18:

"By the all-powerful dispensations of Providence, I have been protected beyond all human probability and expectation; for I had four bullets through my coat, and two horses shot under me, yet escaped unhurt, altho' death was levelling my companions on every side."

On that fateful morning, George Washington rose weakened from his sickbed and spent the better part of twenty-four hours saving the remnants of Braddock's defeated army. When Braddock fell, Washington assumed command by default and rallied the survivors, leading them in an organized retreat to safety. Governor Dinwiddie lauded Lieutenant Colonel George Washington as the 'Hero of the Monongahela,' and rewarded him with a commission as 'Colonel of the Virginia Regiment and Commander in Chief of all forces now raised in the defense of His Majesty's Colony.' Twenty-three-year-old George Washington was given the task of defending Virginia's frontier with the first full-time

American military unit in the thirteen colonies.

While people across Virginia were glad to have Colonel Washington at the helm, the war had just begun, and it had started with a massive defeat. Reports of now-regular Indian kidnappings of settlers and atrocities to families on the frontier trickled in with those who had seen the carnage firsthand. Patrick Henry gathered along with 1,500 others at Polegreen Church to hear words of encouragement from Reverend Davies. Patrick was beside himself with concern for his family and his country. He had a newborn baby girl, drought was ravaging his tobacco crops, economic hardship would follow, and now the enemy had dealt a devastating blow to the British-American army. The threat of war loomed on Patrick's doorstep, just three hundred fifty miles from his home.

It had been four months since Davies had called the people together for a day of fasting and prayer. He didn't mince words when urging the people to repent in order to receive God's protection. Today he read from the prophet Isaiah, who warned the people about the invasion of Jerusalem. The people of Jerusalem had exclaimed, "Let's eat, drink, and be merry, for tomorrow we die!" and then heard Isaiah's stern words. The people of Hanover were now receiving a stern warning from Reverend Davies.

"The prophet Isaiah, at the foresight of this, feels all the generous and mournful passions of a patriot, a lover of his country, of liberty, and religion. However others were sunk into a stupid security all around him, and indulged themselves in mirth and luxury; he is alarmed and mourns for his country!" Davies exclaimed, gripping his heart. "O Virginia! O my country! Shall I not weep for you? My heart pounds within me, I cannot keep silent. For I have heard the sound of the trumpet; I have heard the battle cry!"

Davies continued a long discussion of having every individual examine his or her behavior and to seek the Lord for help. But then he turned his attention to the established clergy of Virginia, laying responsibility on them for not speaking boldly enough to warn the people of God's judgment.

"O Virginia! Your ministers have ruined you! I speak not of all; some of them, I hope, are an ornament to their profession, and a blessing to their country. But there is little, very little, practical religion to be seen in our land. I speak this in the anguish of my heart; for in the course of my ministry among you, you have never heard me speak like this before."

No one left while Davies preached for more than an hour.

"Let us not be too much discouraged. Our country is in danger of famine and the sword; but the case is not desperate. Do not, therefore, give it up as a lost case," Davies preached. "Our inhabitants are numerous; some parts of the country have promising crops; our army, we hope, is not entirely cut off; the New England forces are likely to succeed in their expeditions; and we have a gracious, though a provoked God over all. To have a Friend in heaven, a Friend who is the Lord Almighty, what a strong support is this! And what is that religion good for, which will not support a man under trials? Draw on the promise of Proverbs 18:10: 'The name of the Lord is a strong tower; the righteous runs into it, and is safe!'

"We have many reasons to fear; we are a sinful land; we are but poorly provided against war or famine: it is fit we should in our turn experience the fate of other nations, that we may know what sort of a world we live in. It is certain many will be great sufferers by the drought; and many lives will be lost in our various expeditions; our poor friends in the frontier counties are slaughtered and scalped. In short, it is certain, be the final outcome what it will, that our country will suffer a great deal; therefore, be humble. Be diligent in prayer for our army, and for the unhappy families in our frontiers. 'And may the Lord Almighty be with us, and the God of Jacob be our refuge.'"

He's right, Patrick Henry thought. *I've never heard him speak like this before, with such words about love of God and country in the same breath.* He looked around at the congregation. *And the people are hanging on to every word.*

259

━━━━━━

PINE SLASH

Samuel Davies slowly rode his horse up the dusty lane leading to the humble home of Patrick and Sallie Henry. After worship on Sunday, Patrick asked Davies to come visit their home. Patrick wanted Samuel to see Sallie and meet his new baby daughter. He also wanted to talk.

Davies frowned as he passed Patrick's dust-choked crops. By now the corn should have been tall and green with silk tassels emerging from the top of the husks, and healthy ears hidden beneath the leaves. But this corn was dwarfed, with curling leaves at its edges. The small tobacco plants were only four feet tall, with leaves parched from the lack of rain. Despite Patrick's continual toil in these fields, things looked bleak. It would be a miracle if he could fill even one hogshead come fall.

Up ahead, Davies saw a gray cat sitting there on the lane. He smiled and dismounted his horse to walk the rest of the way to the house. As he reached the cat, she stood and lifted her curlicue tail in the air. He reached down to pet her. "Why, hello there, little one."

"Bonjour, *Reverend Davies,*" Liz meowed.

Patrick came out of the house, tucking his clean shirt into his breeches when he noticed Davies and Liz in the road. He lifted his hand in greeting and smiled at Davies. "Welcome, Reverend Davies!" He hurried down the steps and to the lane. "I see you've met our cat."

"Good day, Patrick. Yes, I thought she was gray, but petting her I see she is . . . black?" Davies replied, brushing the dust off Liz's fur. "Didn't you have a black cat when you were young? I remember meeting her when you broke your collarbone."

Patrick put his hands on his hips and smiled at Liz. "Yes, her name was Liz. She disappeared after we moved, but the day Sallie and I married, this little thing showed up. I decided to name her Liz as well." Nelson came running up, barking. "And this is Nelson."

"Why, hello to you, Nelson," greeted Davies, giving the hound dog a scratch behind his ears.

"Please, come in. I want you to meet the princess of the house," Patrick said with a wink.

Davies tied his horse to the post, where there was a bucket of water, and followed Patrick up the steps and inside.

"Sallie? Reverend Davies is here," Patrick called.

Seventeen-year-old Sallie came walking in the small parlor holding a tiny baby girl with big brown eyes and rosy cheeks. "Good afternoon, Reverend," Sallie welcomed him. "Thank you for coming."

"Allow me to present our firstborn child, Martha," Patrick announced proudly, leaning over to kiss his daughter gently on the head. "We call her Patsey. Isn't she beautiful?"

Davies's eyes lit up with joy. "Yes, she is." He leaned over and placed his hand on the little bundle. "Hello, Patsey. What a blessing from God you are! The Lord has given you very special parents who will train you up in the way you should go." Patsey cooed and wrapped her tiny hand around Davies's finger. He chuckled. "She already has me wrapped around her fingers."

"She gets that from her mother, I think," Patrick joked with a laugh. "Let me get you something to drink. I know you're thirsty from your ride here. It's another hot, dry day."

"Thank you, Patrick," Davies answered, placing his hand on Sallie's shoulder. "Congratulations, Sallie. I look forward to seeing Patsey run around the grass at Polegreen someday. That is, if it ever rains again."

"Indeed, Reverend. That's all we pray for," Sallie said, putting Patsey up on her shoulder and bouncing her softly. "Excuse me a moment while I feed the baby."

"Of course," Davies responded with a courteous bow.

Patrick carried two tin cups of water into the room. "Please, let's sit outside where there's a breeze." Davies followed him out to the front porch, where they took their seats.

"I'm happy for your new family, Patrick," shared Davies warmly. "I'm sorry I was in London when you married. Those fifteen months in England and Scotland were long, but successful. I was able to raise funds for the College of New Jersey, and bring back Bibles and hymnals for the congregations here. I've started teaching slaves in the community to read; therefore, many of the books were for them."

261

Patrick took a sip of water. "I so admire you, Reverend. Thank you for all you do. Might my slaves also join you sometime? I would like nothing more than for them to learn."

"Of course, of course!" Davies enthused. "They are welcome to join the others."

"I hate their wretched condition," Patrick told the reverend with a frown, gazing out at his struggling fields. "We're all working together the best we can." He sighed. "I don't know if we'll make enough to get by. This drought is a farmer's worst nightmare." He clenched his jaw, lowering his gaze to the floor.

"And the seven thin ears devoured the seven rank and full ears. And Pharaoh awoke, and, behold, it was a dream," quoted Davies from Genesis. "The drought in Egypt didn't catch God by surprise. It was all part of His ultimate plan to bring good to the nation of Israel. What seemed like a nightmare for Pharaoh and the nations ended up being the means of deliverance for the people of God through Joseph. And Joseph's rise to power in Egypt led to the birth of a new nation."

"A nation born during four hundred years of slavery," Patrick replied.

"I've often wondered why God chose to do that."

"Yes, but that nation, Israel, was led to freedom and the Promised Land by Moses," Davies quickly added, with a finger raised in the air. "The drought that hit Egypt led to great things eventually, but it followed seven years of plenty. There's a lesson there for all of us. It is possible for our best years or experiences to be swallowed up by periods of failure and defeat, if we allow them to."

Liz jumped up next to Patrick on the chair and meowed, "*Joseph had to endure slavery, failure, hardship, and prison before he found his true purpose. You are so very much like Joseph,* mon *Henry. I loved him very much.*"

Patrick smiled and rubbed Liz under the chin. "This Liz talks as much as the first Liz." He thought a moment more. "Joseph and Moses eventually found their purpose and did great things. I'm trying to figure out mine, but I only have nine mouths to feed, not a nation as they had. If I don't make it as a farmer . . ."

"Some time later the brook dried up," Davies said, drawing a puzzled look from Patrick. "That's from I Kings. Elijah fled to the Kerith Ravine, where God fed him with the ravens and the brook for a season. But then a drought came, and he needed to move on to Zarephath. God knew that Elijah needed both seasons at Kerith—times of provision and times of drought."

"Why both seasons?" Patrick wondered. "What good came from the drought?"

"If Elijah had gone right to Zarephath, he would have missed the season of depending on God alone to feed him and give him the water he needed," Davies answered. "He learned things and gained wisdom that would make him a better prophet. He experienced the exact things experienced by the people to whom he would later minister. But his miracle awaited him at Zarephath." The young minister leaned over and looked at Patrick. "And it was the drought that dried up his creek and forced him to move on to his miracle."

Patrick took in a deep breath and sighed. "Are you saying this drought will lead me to a miracle?"

Davies smiled and shrugged his shoulders. "Only the Lord knows what this drought will lead you to, Patrick. I do know it will teach you things you can't learn in any other way. You will gain wisdom that will be invaluable in ways you don't yet understand. God brought good from the droughts for Joseph and Elijah, so trust in His promise that

He will also bring good to you, and take care of you in the meantime."

"God is indeed faithful to His word, and to His servants. But who am I? I'm just a young married farmer who failed at the last thing he tried, and now has a young family to provide for." Patrick wore a sad smile. "When I think about what is going on with this new war, I feel small. While I worry about rain and crops, other young men my age worry about fighting and death. I know my place is here, providing for Sallie and Patsey, but . . ." He looked up at Davies with searching eyes. "I wonder if I should be fighting for my country. Should I bring my sisters here to help at Pine Slash, or have the Sheltons take care of my wife and child? When I heard you preach for love of your country, my heart burned within me to do *something*. I love this land, and would gladly take up arms to defend her."

Davies leaned forward and put his hand on Patrick's shoulder. "I know that if you could, you would gladly go fight. Your faith and your patriotism are admirable, Patrick." He smiled. "But you are most needed here. Your hands are far from idle, my friend. You *are* doing something. You are praying for our country and our soldiers. And you are admirably protecting and providing for nine precious souls by the sweat of your brow. You must keep up the fight here, in order to help to survive and to grow that which is worth fighting for." Davies sat back with a wide smile. "Just as Joseph and Elijah pressed on while they waited for good to come from their struggles, you must soldier on through this season in life."

263

Patrick nodded and smiled. "Thank you, Reverend Davies. I needed to hear that."

———

OVERTON PLANTATION, HANOVER, AUGUST 17, 1755

It was a hot and sticky morning, but hundreds gathered under the trees on blankets with their families to honor Hanover's newly formed militia before they went off to war. A local planter named George Overton, who lived between Polegreen and Hanover Courthouse, had raised this company of volunteer militia soldiers, most of whom were Dissenters who worshipped at Polegreen. Overton funded and equipped the soldiers himself, and had called them to muster today at his plantation for a great send-off by family and friends with a picnic on the grounds. Reverend Davies was asked to give the farewell speech to encourage the men and their families.

A total of sixty volunteers, aged sixteen to thirty-eight, paraded through Overton's lawn to the beat of a drummer, muskets proudly resting on their shoulders. They marched to the front of the porch where Samuel Davies stood to address them. Once Captain Overton set them at ease, Davies lifted his hands in greeting.

"Britons, Virginians, Christians, Hanoverians, and neighbors, I am gratefully sensible of the unmerited Honour you have done me, in making Choice of me to address you upon so singular and important an Occasion: And I am sure I bring with me a Heart ardent to serve you and my Country, though I am afraid my Inability, and the Hurry of my Preparations, may give you Reason to repent your Choice. I cannot begin my Address to you with more proper Words than those of a great General, which I have read to you: 'Be of good courage, and let us behave ourselves valiantly for our people, and for the cities of our God: and let the LORD do that which is good in his sight.'"

264

"Governor Dinwiddie has given our Davies here quite the unexpected title for a preacher," Nigel reported as he and Liz looked over the crowd.

"*Oui,* the governor calls Davies 'the colony's best recruiter,'" Liz answered with a smile.

Nigel preened his whiskers proudly. "No doubt due to the effect his printed 'war sermons' have had on the colonists in Virginia. Good show, my dear."

Liz watched as Patrick held Patsey in his lap, with Sallie seated next to him on a blanket. "I know that Patrick wishes he could march off with his friends here from Hanover, but I believe Davies helped to settle his mind about plowing ahead in the fields."

"Quite literally!" Nigel quipped. "But it is splendid to see how the men of Hanover have answered the call to take up arms."

"Courage is an essential Character of a good soldier:—Not a savage ferocious Violence; Not a fool-hardy Insensibility of Danger, or headstrong Rashness to rush into it; Not the Fury of enflamed Passions, broke loose from the Government of Reason: but calm, deliberate, rational Courage," Davies declared.

"The People of Meroz lay at home in Ease, while their brethren were in the Field, delivering their Country from Slavery. And what was their Doom? *Curse ye Meroz, said the Angel of the Lord, curse ye bitterly the Inhabitants thereof, because they came not to the Help of the Lord, to the Help of the Lord against the Mighty."*

Our brethren are already in the field, just like the people of Meroz, Patrick thought to himself as Davies recounted the verses from the book of Judges about those who wouldn't take up arms when called. *We can't stand here idle!* He clenched his jaw, wishing he could enlist with this group of soldiers getting ready to head to battle, but the responsibilities to his young family kept him home. He prayed that Davies's words would inspire even greater numbers of men to enlist and help turn the tide in the war.

"I count myself happy that I see so many of you generously engaged in such a Cause; but when I view it in this Light, I cannot but be concerned that there are so few to join you," Davies continued. He spread out his arms. "Are there but fifty or sixty Persons in this large and populous County that can be spared from home for a few Weeks upon so necessary a Design, or that are able to bear the Fatigues of it? Where are the Friends of human Nature, where the Lovers of Liberty and Religion? Now is the Time for you to come forth, and shew yourselves. I may point out to the Public that heroic Youth Colonel *Washington,* whom I cannot but hope Providence has hitherto preserved in so signal a Manner, for some important Service to his Country."

265

Davies turned his gaze to the sixty soldiers heading off to war. "May the Lord of Hosts, the God of the Armies of *Israel,* go forth along with you! May *he teach your Hands to War, and gird you with Strength to Battle!* May he bless you with a safe Return, and long Life, or a glorious Death in the Bed of Honor, and a happy Immortality! May he guard and support your anxious Families and Friends at home, and return you victorious to their longing Arms! May all the Blessings your Hearts can wish attend you wherever you go! These are Wishes and Prayers of my Heart; and Thousands concur in them: And we cannot but cheerfully hope they will be granted, through Jesus Christ. *Amen."*

Immediately following his speech, a line of young men formed ready to also answer the call and join Overton's militia.

Godspeed. A lump formed in Patrick's throat as he breathed a silent prayer for his brave brethren. *Soldier on.*

FIRE TO THE FIDDLE

PINE SLASH, APRIL 1757

D o you see the pretty red bird?" Patrick asked, pointing to the cardinal sitting on the fencepost. He held onto two-year-old Patsey's ankle with his other hand. She was riding on his shoulders as he carried her on their early evening walk. "He says, '*What-cheer, cheer, cheer; purty-purty-purty-purty!*'"

Patsey giggled, loving to hear her father imitate the birds. She kicked her little feet. "Again."

Patrick smiled and bounced his daughter as he walked along next to the fence. "*What-cheer, cheer, cheer; purty-purty-purty-purty!*" he repeated.

The toddler held her head back and laughed. "Again!"

"*What-cheer, cheer, cheer; purty-purty-purty-purty!*"

Patsey continued to giggle and wrapped her small hands around her father's face. She leaned over and kissed the top of his head.

"That is the best thing to happen to me all day, little girl," Patrick said with a happy smile as they walked along next to the freshly made dirt hills prepared for the new tobacco seedlings. He sighed, praying that this year's crop would beat last year's dismal harvest.

"Bi-i-ig bird," came Patsey's voice as she pointed to the sky.

Patrick looked up and there soaring above them was Cato. "That is my bald eagle. And his name is Cato. At least, I like to believe it's my eagle. Can you say, 'Cato'?"

"Ca-to!" Patsey repeated, moving her feet happily against Patrick's shoulders.

"I taught him how to fly, Patsey. Would you like me to teach you, too?" offered Patrick. He pulled her down from his shoulders and held her by the legs while he supported her chest. "Stretch out your arms.

Here we go!" He took off running while Patsey giggled with delight, her little hands spread out into the air.

For a few stolen moments of joy, Patrick forgot the cares of his day. In addition to Patsey, he and Sallie now had a newborn baby boy. They named him John, after both of their fathers. Patrick was twenty-one now. Most of his friends were off fighting the French and Indian War. Uncle Langloo himself also joined in the fight after Indians attacked his house out on the frontier. Patrick's half brother, John Syme, Jr., Samuel Meredith, and West Dandridge were all off fighting for their country. Patrick remained behind fighting the drought that daily confirmed to him that tobacco farming was the worst profession he could possibly have chosen.

But Patrick loved his little family, and spent the evenings giving Sallie a breather to care for baby John while he played with Patsey. He loved taking her on walks, playing his flute or his fiddle, and just simply hearing her laugh. The sound of her voice made any problems of the day melt away.

Liz sat in the field watching Patrick and Patsey zoom around. She smiled, turning her gaze up to Cato. Nigel was up there riding with him so he could survey the crops and bring Liz a report from the air. Suddenly she heard a rustling in the bushes and a rat came barreling out, running a mile a minute.

"AH-H-H!" he shouted as he nearly ran into Liz.

"Stop! What is your business here?" Liz asked with a stern tone, stopping the rat in his tracks.

The rat fumbled for words, trying to come up with any excuse to keep the cat's attention on him, and not behind her. "Uh, nice evenin' we're havin', miss."

Liz's eyes narrowed, hearing the rat speak with a cockney British accent. "You are not from here. I shall ask you again. What are you doing here?"

The rat smiled weakly and swallowed as Liz slowly crept toward him. He kept looking around her and rambled on. "I'm on holiday. Yeah, that's it. A *holiday*. I always wanted to come see America!"

It suddenly dawned on her. "You are the rat from the ship that followed us from London! Max tossed you overboard."

"But do I hold a grudge? Not at all, love! In fact, I were glad for the exercise," the rat said, continuing to look back toward the house over

267

Liz's shoulder. "Swimmin's the best form of exercise, I always say. Of course, I haven't been swimmin' all this time. I've been tourin' 'round the colonies, takin' in the lovely sights and whatnot."

Suddenly the rat's eyes widened in fear as Cato came swooping down on top of them.

Nigel called out, "FIRE! HURRY, TO THE HOUSE!"

Liz quickly turned around and saw smoke rising from Patrick's house. While her back was turned, the rat scurried off. She immediately started running toward the house and yelled up to Cato and Nigel, "ALERT PATRICK!"

Cato soared up into the air and circled over Patrick and Patsey, who hadn't seen the smoke. He screeched with his high-pitched eagle voice, "FIRE! YOUR HOUSE IS ON FIRE!" The eagle then turned and flew in the direction of the house, circling it and continuing to screech.

Patrick looked up and saw Cato. His smile faded as he followed the bird to the see the stream of smoke coming from his house. "Oh, no! Dear God above, help!" He pressed Patsey to his chest and took off running toward the house.

The servants were running back and forth with buckets from the well, trying to douse the flames. Nelson was barking as Liz reached him.

"Is everyone safe?" Liz asked, out of breath. "Where is Sallie?"

"Yes, I was able to alert Sallie in time. She and the baby had fallen asleep," Nelson explained hurriedly. Sallie came walking around the house, holding John, crying at the top of his lungs.

"Thank the Maker." Liz closed her eyes in relief.

"Yes, but Patrick's fiddle is still inside," Nelson answered.

Liz looked at him and their eyes locked with anguished thoughts of Patrick losing his prized treasure. Before she could say a word, Nelson took off running into the house that was now engulfed in flames.

Patrick came running up to Sallie and together they held their children as they watched their home being destroyed by flames.

"Thank God, you are both safe!" Patrick said with a trembling voice, burying his face in Sallie's hair.

Sallie nodded and wept, pressing her fingers into his back. "Everyone is safe, but I saw Nelson run into the house before you got here," she shouted above the din of the children crying, the servants shouting, and the flames roaring. Patrick took one step toward the house and Sallie grasped his arm to stop him. "Pat, Nelson saved us . . . but you can't save him."

———

The rat stopped running and held his hand to his chest to catch his breath. He looked behind him at the night sky ablaze with fire. He smiled, his yellowed, pronounced front teeth showing. "I did it, aye!"

"You did *nothing,*" came a voice from the darkness.

The smile melted off the rat's face. He held out his hand in protest. "Don't ye see the flames?"

"You tipped over a lamp and made a cozy little fire. Oh, goodie," the voice sneered in a tone that made the hair on the back of the rat's spine stand on end. "No one DIED!"

"But . . ." the rat protested before his voice was permanently silenced.

"If I can't kill him, I'll do the next best thing," the voice said, its source growing a smile in the darkness. "I'll discourage him."

———

The unnatural, horrible stench of charred, burning debris filled the air. An occasional pop sounded as a smoldering heap breathed its last. Patrick and Sallie's house was burned to the ground. Nearly everything they owned was destroyed. They thankfully had each other. No one was hurt in the blaze. But the paltry ownings they had—wedding gifts mostly—were all but gone.

Patrick walked around the smoking rubble that was once his house, and clenched his jaw. He shook his head. *Could things get any worse? My crops barely yield enough to keep us fed. Now, this?*

Liz and Nigel sat solemnly outside the barn, tired from the long night. The humans had all collapsed on the soft hay, sleeping together in the haven where the cows lowed softly and the cries of the baby rose occasionally in the night air.

"How did the fire start?" Nigel wanted to know.

"According to the humans, it was an 'accidental fire,'" Liz replied. "But I have no doubt that the rat I encountered was behind it. Sallie and John were asleep. The rat likely thought Patrick and Patsey were inside as well."

Nigel's whiskers bristled with anger. "RATS ARE INDEED REVOLTING!"

"But this rat was a minion only. Used by one who wants to bring harm to my Henry," accused Liz, furrowing her brow. She and Nigel

269

shared a silent moment or two, before Buttercup the cow mooed, welcoming a new day. "The last night I slept in a stable with a baby and a cow was the night Jesus was born," Liz remarked with a bittersweet smile. "Joseph and Mary had nothing, but they had everything that night."

"They had everything that matters, my dear," Nigel agreed. "And despite the tragedy of last night, Patrick and Sallie also still have everything that matters."

Liz nodded but blinked back tears. *"Oui."* She lowered her head and began to sob. "Except for Nelson. He is lost."

Nigel patted Liz's back with his paw. "He was a valiant soldier—brave to save Sallie and baby John, and then to face the fiery inferno to reclaim Patrick's fiddle."

Together the two friends shared a quiet moment of grief.

Nigel then heard a shuffling sound behind him and turned his head. His grief quickly turned to joy. A lump filled his throat, but he crackled out, "Nelson is *not* lost!"

Liz opened her eyes and lifted her gaze to see the limping form of Nelson making his way over to them. "Oh!" she exclaimed, running over to the dog. "You are alive, *mon ami!* How happy I am to see you!"

Nelson managed a weak smile, then winced and stumbled. "I'm alive alright."

Nigel came rushing up to them. "Good show, old boy! What happened?"

Nelson looked at Nigel and squinted with one eye open. "I ran inside to get the fiddle. The flames surrounded me. I quickly started gasping for breath and became confused. I couldn't make out how to escape. I don't know how I got out of there. But I woke up under the old elm tree outside the overseer's cottage."

Liz's eyes brimmed with tears. "I see. I'm glad you are safe." She realized, however, that Patrick's fiddle was gone.

"The strange thing is," Nelson added, "the fiddle was also next to me. Maybe I carried it out. I don't know. But it's safe, too."

Liz's heart caught in her throat and happiness filled her heart. She nodded and blinked back her tears, now tears of joy.

"Incredible!" Nigel exclaimed, running off to check on Patrick's fiddle.

"I know you are exhausted, *mon ami,*" Liz said. "You must drink some water and get some rest. But first, please let Patrick know you are alive."

Nelson looked over and saw Patrick walking around in the rubble, his head lowered as he wiped his eyes with the back of his sleeve. "Will do," Nelson agreed.

Liz watched as Nelson walked over to Patrick, who dropped to his knees and enveloped the hound dog with fierce love and gratitude, as if he were Patrick's last friend on Earth.

———

ONE WEEK LATER

Reverend Samuel Davies and Patrick walked along the lane leading away from the scene of devastation and loss. They slowly meandered next to the tobacco fields without speaking, sharing the precious gift of silence close friends easily share, knowing that sometimes quiet moments carry the most comfort. Patrick stopped and leaned over to pull a weed up by the roots. He dragged it through his fingers, stripping it of its invading abilities.

271

Samuel held his hand up to his eyes to shield them from the sun. "Weeds arc dastardly things."

Patrick frowned and tossed the weed to the ground. "Aye. They are."

They walked a bit farther until Patrick was ready to speak. "Thank you for coming, Reverend."

"Call me Samuel, please," Davies implored, as he had often done with Patrick's father. "I came as soon as I heard. Rest assured that the Polegreen family will check in on you and Sallie and help you get back on your feet. And you *will* get back on your feet."

Patrick nodded and swallowed the lump in his throat. "We're grateful. Thank you for the food and clothes you brought us today."

"The Lord has promised to supply all our needs, and so He has. You have each other, you have food, and you have a roof over your heads," Davies reminded the young man.

"Indeed, the overseer's cottage is small and run down, but it will do," Patrick answered. "The Sheltons and the Winstons have brought us a bed, a table, a chair, and some cooking pots and utensils. I'll have to make some more items and patch the leaky roof."

One hundred yards away from the where their house had stood

was a vacant (until now) overseer's cottage. It was a white, one-story rectangular building with three rooms, an attic, and a half-basement. A six-foot chimney rose up from a fireplace that could heat two of the three rooms. It was crude, but it was better than the barn.

Patrick shook his head. "I don't understand why everything seems to be against me."

Davies didn't respond immediately. He leaned over and pulled another weed from the ground and held it up to Patrick. "The writer of Hebrews said, 'Guard against turning back from the grace of God. Let no one become like a bitter plant that grows up and causes many troubles with its poison.' We can easily become discouraged when things come against us, which quickly can turn us bitter against God and man. And bitterness is poison." He stopped and put a hand on Patrick's shoulder, and touched his heart. "Keep the weeds of discouragement and bitterness from taking root in your heart, Patrick. Joseph also didn't understand the ill treatment he received from his brothers and in Egypt. If anyone had cause to be bitter, it was he. But he was faithful and never turned back from the grace of God. In the end he finally understood his trials, and could see how God had been preparing him all along for what he was meant to do. If he hadn't been thrown in prison, he never would have been in the right place at the right time to stand before Pharaoh." He handed the weed to Patrick.

Patrick nodded and twisted the weed in his hands. "Wise words indeed, Reverend. Thank you for reminding me. I know that one day I will understand all this."

"Call me Samuel—*please*," Davies begged with a grin. "That's the spirit. And I hope to be here when your miracle finally comes."

Patrick smiled. "That makes two of us, *Samuel*."

OCTOBER 1757

Liz and Nigel sat by the fireplace, watching the embers slowly die. The family was sound asleep in the other room. Nelson wheezed as he slept in the corner of their room near the cradle. He hadn't been the same since the night of the fire, suffering from a constant cough after inhaling so much smoke.

"*Cher* Nelson," Liz whispered. "I wish there was something we could do for his cough."

Nigel straightened his spectacles. "It's a dreadful battle wound, I'm afraid."

"I also wish there was something we could do for Patrick. The harvest does not look good, *mon ami,*" Liz lamented. She gazed at Patrick's fiddle sitting on the footstool. "We haven't received a word from Gillamon in the six months since the fire." She got up and walked over to the fiddle. The fire had only enhanced its fiery stain. "Nigel?"

"Yes, my dear?" Nigel replied, looking at the way Liz was studying the fiddle. "Do you wish for me to see if Gillamon has a word for us?"

"*Oui,* even if that word is to keep waiting," Liz replied. "But I need to hear *something. Anything.*"

Nigel scurried to his little cubby hole and retrieved his bow. He held it up with a broad smile and climbed up the legs of the stool. The mouse slowly pulled his bow across the strings and a series of notes lifted from the violin into the air, filled with glowing words.

Good evening, little ones. I was getting ready to contact you.

Liz's eyes reflected the soft amber glow of the fire and the notes. "*Bonsoir,* Gillamon. This means there is something for us to do, no? Please tell me it is time for the next part of the riddle."

Yes, it is time for the Henry family to leave Pine Slash.

"*Bon!* But where are they to go?" Liz asked. "Patrick has no money."

To the tavern.

Nigel's jaw fell open as he continued to play. "My dear fellow, do you mean to suggest that Patrick Henry will take his wife and two small children to live in a *tavern?* Forgive me, but I cannot imagine that this will be a suitable environment for them!"

That's exactly what I'm suggesting. But not just any tavern.

Liz's tail curled up and down as she pondered this directive. Her eyes lit up. "You mean John Shelton's tavern, no? Hanover Tavern?!"

Indeed. Hanover Tavern. This will be the most important move Patrick will ever make. It will lead him to his voice.

Nigel frowned. "I suppose he can sing and play the fiddle for the guests and help Mr. Shelton run the business, but I am still quite befuddled by this move, old boy."

And while he does all those things,
he will slowly find his voice.
You must help Patrick figure out this move, Liz.

"I do not know how I will get him to leave, Gillamon," Liz answered. "Not that he does not *wish* to leave this place."

Help him to see that a place has been prepared for him.
You will figure it out.
And I will see you there.

Nigel continued to pull his bow across the violin, but no more notes appeared. "I believe he is gone, my dear." He stopped playing and draped his elbows over the fiddle. "I am still quite befuddled. A tavern?"

Liz's mind raced. *"Oui!* A tavern, and I believe I know how to get him there!" She looked at Nigel with a coy grin. "With a Bible."

———

274 Patrick rested his elbows on the rickety desk, holding his head in his hands as he glanced over his account book. The news was bad. *Only one hogshead of tobacco. That's all I have to show for this grueling year of farming. That will only bring in £10 at Page's Warehouse.*

Sallie and the children had long since retired for the night. Little Patsey was curled up holding the handkerchief doll Patrick had made her. The bed creaked as Sallie turned onto her side, softly sighing in her sleep. She subconsciously reached her hand to touch the tiny wooden cradle next to her on the floor where baby John slept soundly. She was exhausted from the day of cooking, cleaning, and taking care of the children and the rest of the household.

Patrick sat up and turned his head to see his small family sleeping there. While he was grateful his family was saved from the fire, and that they had a roof over their heads, he knew they couldn't stay here. Patrick needed to figure out what to do next, but he was at a loss at the moment. He took in a deep breath and slowly exhaled through his nose. *Oh, Sallie. You deserve so much more than what I've been able to provide.* He choked back his emotion. *I've failed as a merchant and a farmer. Even the house you brought to the marriage was lost to the fire. I've given you nothing.* He rested his head on his arms as he leaned over the table. *I'm so tired, and I don't know what else to do.*

Liz's eyes reflected the soft candlelight as she watched her Henry struggling. She had looked over his account book as well, and knew how bad things looked. But this would only help prod her Henry on to his next destination. Earlier in the evening she slipped a note in the new Bible Samuel Davies had brought him, marking a passage of Scripture. Patrick's Bible had been lost in the fire, so she anonymously requested that one be sent to Patrick from the many that Davies had brought back from London.

Liz walked over and jumped up onto the desk, rubbing her cheek on his hand. *"Cher Patrick, turn to the light that will always guide you,"* she meowed softly.

"Sweet Liz." Patrick's hand went to gently pet her as he lifted his gaze to see the small candle on his desk. He glided his other hand over the candle. A distant memory with his father played again in his mind.

"So the past will help me figure out the future?" Patrick asked, gliding his hand over the candle to make the flame dance.

"Aye, that it will." John rested his arms on the table next to Patrick. "Ye'll find that just as this lamp gives light ta the room, the experiences ye gain in yer own life will give light ta yer path."

Patrick nodded but didn't respond. He continued to stare at the light. "I just wish it were easier to learn."

"Has it been easy for yer eagle ta learn how ta fly?" John asked him.

Cato. His eagle not only learned how to fly, but even alerted him to the fire. *Wings like eagles.* Suddenly the verses from Isaiah came rushing into his memory and he reached for the new Bible on his desk. He opened it and turned the pages until he found Isaiah 40. He quietly read, "Hast thou not known? hast thou not heard, that the everlasting God, the LORD, the Creator of the ends of the earth, fainteth not, neither is weary? there is no searching of His understanding. He giveth power to the faint: and to them that have no might he increaseth strength. Even the youths shall faint and be weary, and the young men shall utterly fall: But they that wait upon the LORD shall renew their strength; they shall mount up with wings as eagles; they shall run, and not be weary; and they shall walk, and not faint."

I must wait for the LORD, Patrick thought to himself. *That's easier said than done.*

Just then he saw the piece of paper sticking out of the bottom of his Bible. He tilted his head and turned the pages to read the slip of paper and saw that it marked Psalm 66. His eyes fell onto verse 12:

275

Thou hast caused men to ride over our heads;
We went through fire and through water:
But thou broughtest us out into a wealthy place.

"We went through fire," Patrick read again quietly. "But thou broughtest us out into a wealthy place." He then saw what was written on the piece of paper:

We may not be certain about the next step we are to take,
but we can always be certain of God.
Remember John 14:1–2.

Patrick flipped the pages of his Bible to find the passage in John:

Let not your heart be troubled: ye believe in God, believe also in me.
In my Father's house are many mansions: if it were not so, I would
have told you. I go to prepare a place for you.

"Many mansions." He held the paper and looked at the candle as thoughts swirled in his mind. "Many *rooms* in my Father's house."

Patrick suddenly sat up straight, as an idea came to him. He looked over at Sallie. "Hanover Tavern."

Liz smiled as a faint glimmer of hope entered the eyes of her discouraged Henry. *I do not yet understand what this next place will bring,* mon *Henry, but it is time to solve the next part of the fiddle's riddle—a voice in the tavern.*

276

PART THREE

DESPAIR NOT
THE TRAGIC

THE LITTLE MARQUIS

AUGUST 1, 1759

Where's 'here' now?" Al asked. "Or should I say 'when'?"

"Nowhere yet, but ye can open yer eyes now, Al," Kate said, prying the orange cat's paws away from his eyes.

Al's paws moved from his eyes to pat down the rest of his body. He wore a goofy grin as he looked over and saw Gillamon and Clarie there to meet them in the IAMISPHERE.

"Welcome, Al." Gillamon's white goatee blew in the swirling breeze of this epic time portal. He smiled and lowered his gaze to Al. "Never fear, you are still in one piece."

"It never hurts to make sure, lad," Al answered with a broad smile.

Clarie shook her head and giggled. "Welcome to the next phase of your mission, Kate. You'll be heading to the south of France."

"This will be grand," Kate said happily, wagging her tail. "But I think it's funny that Liz the French kitty be watchin' over a Scottish lad, an' me the Scottish dog will be watchin' over a French lad. I know Liz wishes she could go with me."

"Well, she will be there, in a way," Clarie replied, sharing a knowing grin with Gillamon, who tapped a panel from their mission 1,700 years earlier. "Al, you're here to learn about your human for a future mission."

"That's good because I already know aboot me past ones," Al answered, looking up and pointing at the swirling panels of history. "There's one now!" The scene of the Roman centurion Julius Antonius in Gaul came into view. He was standing on the dock in Arles, welcoming his mother Bella and young nephew, Leonitus. They had sailed from Rome, bringing with them all their worldly possessions, including the statue of Libertas. Al ran along the dock with the young boy, seeking out a basket of fish. "That's when we went to live in me Liz's homeland o' France."

"But it were called Gaul then," Kate added. "Why are we seein' this panel again? Ye showed it when we first started this mission. Somethin' aboot the Libertas connection?"

"Correct, Kate. Follow the Libertas statue, and you will understand the connection," Gillamon replied. He tapped another panel showing an aerial view of a fortress-like French castle dating from the fourteenth century. It was framed by two rounded stone towers, and surrounded by a moat and exquisite gardens. "This is Château de Chavaniac in the Auvergne region of southern France. And it was here in this rugged area of volcanic mountains that the ancient Gauls made their defiant last stand against Julius Caesar in 52 BC. The mighty Roman army defeated them, however, and Gaul naturally became one of Rome's provinces. Over the centuries, Gaul became France, and the Latin spoken by its Roman conquerors blossomed into the romance language of French."

280

"The humans always be *way* behind us animals in figurin' things out," Al remarked with a definitive nod. "Liz were already speakin' French when I met her on the way to the Ark."

"An' like we Scots-Irish be best friends with the French. It may take a while for the humans ta catch up in how ta get along," Kate added with a grin. "So who will be me human in France?"

Gillamon zoomed in on the panel to the open window in the corner tower of the château. The sounds of a newborn baby filled the room. A young mother cradled him while lying in a beautiful bed canopied with red and white toile fabric. An elegant older woman smiled and wiped back the sweaty dark strands of hair from her daughter's face while her other daughter saw to the needs of her sister and newborn nephew.

"Kate, this baby boy is your human, born September 6, 1757, and baptized as 'the very high and very mighty lord Monseigneur Marie-Joseph-Paul-Yves-Roch-Gilbert du Motier Lafayette, legitimate son of the very high and very mighty lord Monseigneur Michel-Louis-Christophe-Roch-Gilbert du Motier, marquis de Lafayette, baron de Vissac, lord of Saint-Romain and other places, and of the very high and very mighty lady Madame Marie-Louise-Julie de La Rivière.'"

"Sure, try to say that fast five times," challenged Al, shaking his paws after trying to count all those names on his toes.

"That sure be a lot of names for such a wee one," Kate marveled, studying the beautiful baby's cherublike face.

"His Catholic mother wanted to include the name of every saint who might protect him in battle. Warfare is part of being a Lafayette," Clarie explained. "You can call him Gilbert or simply Lafayette. His father was born in this very same room."

"Gilbert Lafayette," Kate said. "I love the little marquis already. It looks like there's a lot of rooms in his father's château."

"Chavaniac has twenty rooms, and you'll soon be walking around them," Clarie answered with a smile. "And around the gardens as well, of course. There are many surprises in store for you."

"The wee lad's surrounded by lassies, but where's his father?" Al wondered.

Gillamon frowned and tapped on another panel, showing a tall, twenty-five-year-old French grenadier colonel preparing for battle. "Here he is. Gilbert's father has been away at war since before the baby was born. Such has been the legacy of this military family. Many Lafayettes have sired sons before going off to war, never to return."

281

"The Lafayettes come from a long line of knights. While they have only been tracing their family history since the year 1000, we of course know their lineage back to ancient times," Clarie added, sharing a knowing look with Gillamon.

"Indeed, the Lafayettes have chronicled their gallant history of fighting and dying for France, stretching back to the year 1000," lectured Gillamon. "The halls of Chavaniac are lined with portraits and armor from ancestors who fought in the Crusades and with Joan of Arc. The young marquis's maternal great-grandfather commanded the *Mousquetaires du Roi,* or the King's Musketeers."

"Mouseketeers? Mousie should try out to be one of them," Al suggested. "He'd be a *natural.*"

"*Mus*keteer, Al," Clarie corrected him. "A member of the king's personal guard of infantrymen."

"The young marquis's paternal great-grandfather was awarded the hereditary title of 'marquis' for military service to the king of France, which indicated he was a nobleman," Gillamon explained. "As the next Marquis de Lafayette, Gilbert will grow up hearing his family's tales of war and glory. He will also experience the sorrow that has been part of that legacy—including the loss of a father he will never know."

Kate's eyes filled with anguish. "Oh, the dear boy won't ever get ta meet his own father?"

Gillamon pointed to the battle scene in front of them. "Today the next casualty of war in the Lafayette legacy will happen at the Battle of Minden, in Prussia. More than forty thousand British, Hanoverian, Hessian, and Prussian soldiers are fighting more than fifty thousand French and Saxon soldiers today. And Gilbert's father is in the middle of the action."

"I'm sad for the lad," mourned Al with flattened ears. "All that fightin' in America came over ta Europe, jest like ye said it would. It's all the king talks aboot lately."

Gillamon pointed to another scene, of George Washington leading his Virginia militia to the final successful capture of Fort Duquesne under General Forbes in 1758. The French were finally driven from the Ohio back to Canada, and Washington had then returned home to Mount Vernon to marry Martha Dandridge Custis. For now, Colonel Washington would lay down his sword, and pick up his plowshare. "Yes, the war started by George Washington in the line of duty has become a world war. Sadly, it will take the life of Gilbert's father today."

"Can't we jump in there an' protect him before that happens?" Kate pleaded.

"Not this time," Clarie answered softly. "We are not allowed to intervene. All the days numbered for him are complete."

"But know that the Maker will bring good from this tragedy for the little marquis and for the coming new nation," Gillamon foretold, watching young George Washington riding his horse through his fields at Mount Vernon. "Gilbert will not always be fatherless. Neither will America."

"Kate and Al, take note of three other young men at the Battle of Minden, as this one battle will connect their histories with George Washington and the Marquis de Lafayette," Clarie told them, pointing to the scene. "You see that boy running across the field, dodging bullets?"

"Aye! He can't be any more than fifteen!" Kate said.

"Patrick Ferguson is his name. He's a brand new cornet with the Royal North British Dragoons, famously known as The Scots Greys. That means he is the lowest grade of commissioned officer in this British calvary troop," Gillamon explained. "He's from the same village in Scotland as John and David Henry, and like Patrick Henry, he loves his gun."

Kate looked up at Gillamon. "Aberdeenshire? Does David Henry know him?"

"Perhaps the families know each other, but more importantly, this man will someday know him," Gillamon said, pointing to a twenty-one-year-old British soldier. "That ensign in the elite Brigade of Foot Guards is named Charles Cornwallis. Someday he will connect all these men we show you here today. Al, you will be specifically assigned to Cornwallis at a future date."

Al cocked his head and looked at the young soldier. "I wonder what he'll be doin' out there in the future. He's jest a young lad now."

"They *all* are," Kate pointed out, watching young men falling to their deaths on the battlefield.

"And this," Gillamon said before pausing to point to a twenty-eight-year-old British captain, "is Captain William Phillips." The officer was shouting orders to soldiers manning the battery of eight cannons of the British Royal Artillery. They followed a precise drill to ready the cannons for firing. Gillamon frowned as Captain Phillips raised his hand, ready to give the command.

On the other side of the field in the French position, Colonel Lafayette's commander suddenly fell to enemy fire. Lafayette immediately stepped up to take his place, although he was dangerously exposed to the enemy. He shouted orders for the men to take cover.

Captain Phillips rapidly dropped his hand and shouted, "FIRE!"

The ball exploded out of one of the cannons with a boom in a burst of flame and smoke. As it sailed through the air, Gillamon saw where it was headed. He quickly stepped in front of the panel so Kate and Al couldn't watch. The sickening thud and screams made Gillamon shut his eyes and wince.

Kate's eyes brimmed with tears, and Al's paws went to his mouth in horror. Clarie looked down and sadly shook her head.

"Lafayette? Is he . . .?" Kate asked haltingly.

Gillamon nodded with a mournful expression. "The little marquis's father is no more."

"Then, I must get ta him," Kate said tearfully.

CHAVANIAC, FRANCE

The hot summer sun shone bright over the gardens of Château de Chavaniac. Kate ducked under the shade of a rose bush to get her bearings before she made her presence known. Clarie told her she would find the little marquis outside. Kate could hear the birds in the trees and the distant sounds of a cart rolling down the cobbled, narrow streets of the tiny village below. The Lafayette château was perched high on a hill overlooking the provincial town, visible to the stone houses clustered together below. To the simple village peasants with modest gardens bearing one fruit tree and a single goat or sheep, the Lafayettes were viewed as glamorous aristocrats living in their moat-surrounded château with sprawling gardens. But to the lavish, wealthy courtiers sitting in the ornate salons of Paris and royal halls of Versailles three hundred miles north, the Lafayettes were viewed as provincial country bumpkins. The Lafayettes were appreciated for their loyal military service to the throne, of course, but lacked the social graces acquired only by mingling with French royalty.

Gillamon explained that Lafayette's mother Julie would soon leave him in the care of her mother, Madame de Chavaniac, and unwed sister. In her grief the young mother would seek an escape from sorrow by fleeing to the gaiety of Paris. She would rarely return home, entrusting the rearing of her son to the Lafayette women she left behind. So the little marquis was orphaned by his parents from the beginning. But such was the typical life for many European children of nobility who were born from arranged marriages and raised by nurses and tutors. The boys were sent off to military school and the girls were married off at a young age. They may not have been his parents, but the little marquis would be raised by his grandmother and aunt who loved him dearly.

Lafayette's grandmother was beloved by the peasants in the village below for her kindness and generosity. She allowed them to hunt on her grounds to feed their families and to use any extra game to earn income at the local market. Madame de Chavaniac was sought out by the heads of other villages so they could consult her for her wisdom.

Kate breathed in the lovely fragrance of the roses and listened. She heard the sound of a fountain and the giggles of a child. "That must be him." She stepped out onto the open garden path and followed the sounds of water and laughter until she came across a beautiful scene.

The little marquis was barefoot and dressed in a long white shirt. His gorgeous red curls bounced as he splashed his small hands in the flowing fountain. He had large blue eyes, a fair complexion, and round, rosy cheeks. His grandmother and aunt sat on a bench and clapped as Gilbert entertained them with his water play.

"Why, he's a wee angel!" Kate said with her bright smile upon seeing the unusually handsome child for the first time. He exuded joy as he played vigorously in the fountain. "He's a happy lad. Time for me ta meet the little marquis."

Kate stepped out and wagged her tail as she trotted up to the toddler. She sat down next to him and instantly he spread out his arms, squatted down, and enveloped her in a smothering hug. *"Grand-mère! Une chienne!"* he exclaimed at seeing the little white dog. He made the sweetest sound as he rested his head on her soft fur.

Madame de Chavaniac looked at the dog and then at her daughter with surprise. "Where did this dog come from?" She walked over to Kate, who looked up at her with her irresistibly sweet face. Gilbert softly petted her back, speaking tender words of affection to the little dog in a lyrical voice. *"Bonjour, petite chienne. Bonjour, petite chienne."* Madame smiled as Kate gently licked her hand.

Gilbert hugged Kate again, and his grandmother's heart immediately melted to see the love he instantly had for the little dog. She looked around to see if perhaps one of the villagers had come on the grounds with the dog, but no one was around.

"Perhaps she came from the village?" Madeleine, the boy's aunt, asked, squatting down next to them to meet Kate.

"I do not know," Madame answered. "But I am sure Gilbert wishes to keep her. We will keep her until someone comes looking for her."

Just then Gilbert's beautiful mother, Julie, came walking outside and saw the happy commotion going on. She smiled and joined the ladies in petting Kate. "Who is this, Gilbert?"

"Mine!" Gilbert replied, hugging Kate again.

Julie laughed and petted Kate on the head. *"Bonjour."*

Kate looked Julie in the face and wished she could tell the young woman how sorry she was for her loss. There was no way the Lafayette women could know what had just happened this day on the bloody battlefield in Minden—that the senior Marquis de Lafayette had just died and Julie was the next Lafayette war widow. But when the word did come and Julie's smile faded into the despair of grief, Kate would be here for the little marquis.

"Come, *petite chienne!*" shouted Gilbert, running around in circles. He wanted Kate to chase him. She happily did so, and the Lafayette women looked on as Gilbert was swept away with joy.

As Gilbert ran away from the fountain, they came to a statue standing there in the middle of the garden. The boy's cherub face lit up with a smile and he squatted down next to the statue. *"Voila, petite chienne! Un chat!* Meow!"

Kate's eyes widened as she looked into the marble face of Liz staring back at her. She looked up and realized that this was the Libertas statue—the same statue that the Roman family of Antonius had brought to Gaul long ago. This statue had been handed down from generation to generation, having never left the family.

Gilbert laughed and ran back to the fountain, looking over his shoulder and calling for Kate to follow. She looked from Libertas to the little marquis and could not believe what she was seeing. The Lafayette knights didn't just date back to the Crusades, but back to the knights of Rome. Gillamon's words echoed in Kate's mind: *Follow the Libertas statue and you will understand the connection.*

The little marquis would never know his father. But he also would never realize that his distant father was a Roman centurion named Marcus Antonius whose toddler Armandus had run around this statue at the same age chasing Al, and laughing with the Son of God.

A VOICE IN THE TAVERN

A rosy-cheeked, middle-aged gentleman dressed in a green wool coat stood unsteadily to his feet. He clanked a fork against his half-empty pewter mug and shouted above the noise in the tavern. "The church bells of London have worn *thin* from their happy ringing to celebrate our British victories this year!" He leaned over the table, sloshing his ale as he emphasized every point. "We've routed the French in the *Ohio*, in *Quebec*, in the *West Indies*, in *India,* and on the *high seas!*"

The pewter plates and tin lanterns rattled as the gentlemen seated around him pounded on the table and shouted, "HUZZAH! God save the king!"

"A toast to King George!" the gentleman exclaimed, followed by the others, who all lifted their mugs. "Patrick, another chorus!"

"Gladly, sir!" Patrick Henry answered, as he hurried to the table and held his fiddle up to his chin with a smile. He pulled back his bow, and immediately the tavern filled with music and voices singing *God Save the King:*

"God save great George our King,
Long live our noble King,
God Save the King!
Send him victorious,
Happy and glorious,
Long to reign over us,
God Save the King.

O Lord, our God, arise,
Scatter his enemies,
And make them fall,
Confound their politics,
Frustrate their knavish tricks!
On him our hearts are fix't,
O save us all.

O grant him long to see
Friendship and unity,
Always increase:
May he his scepter sway,
All loyal souls obey,
Join heart and voice, huzzah!
God save the King!

"Hear, hear!" the table of rowdy gentlemen exclaimed, continuing to pound the table. They clapped and cheered as their leader took his seat. They wore wide grins, gave each other hearty back slaps and clanked their mugs of ale. Several of these men had fought together with the Virginia militia against the French and Indians out on the frontier. They lifted toasts to their many fallen friends who didn't return from war. The bond they shared after all they had been through together was as solid as the heavy table they pounded.

Patrick immediately moved into playing a lively Scottish jig and danced to the delight of the tavern patrons. Barefoot and dressed in his coarse Ozna linen shirt and checked pants, he moved from table to table, giving individual attention to his guests, who smiled and clapped along. The tavern was packed, with some guests playing cards, billiards, backgammon, and dice while others pored over the latest newspapers just delivered, announcing the latest glorious British victory and news from the colonies and abroad. Other guests huddled together and discussed business, trade, or legal matters to be addressed at Hanover Courthouse for Court Day on the morrow.

Court Day was held the first Thursday of each month in Hanover County, but the major cases were held in the Quarter Sessions of March, June, September, and December. Every county in Virginia had a county court overseen by eight or so judges, or "Gentlemen Justices of the Peace." Patrick Henry's father, John Henry, was one of eight justices

288

who served at Hanover Courthouse, including Patrick's half brother, John Syme, and several cousins. John Henry was not a lawyer, nor did he possess formal training in the law, neither of which was required. The county court was the local arm of colonial government, and performed many functions including the processing of wills and deeds, hearing small civil suits and trying criminal cases except for those whose charges carried the death penalty. The more important and serious cases were heard by the highest judicial court in the colony, the General Court in Williamsburg. As the colonial capital, Williamsburg was also where the three-tiered central government of Virginia, made up of the Royal Governor, his Council, and the House of Burgesses, conducted its affairs. The governor was appointed by the king of England, and represented the interests of the Crown, not those of the people. His council was made up of twelve men appointed for life who served as advisors and sat on the General Court. The House of Burgesses were elected representatives of the people—two from each county. Towns such as Williamsburg, Jamestown, and Norfolk could petition to also send one representative.

289

In addition to local cases, county justices also oversaw the building and maintaining of roads and bridges, as well as ferry operations. They regulated tobacco warehouses, granted licenses to taverns, collected taxes, and served on the board of elections. It was important that elections be efficiently organized, with qualified voters properly registered, and votes correctly counted and reported. Judges also were empowered to pass ordinances on matters covered insufficiently by the General Assembly. Justice John Henry and his colleagues were not paid for these services, nor were their expenses reimbursed. But these powerful positions were sought after for the social prestige and access to political advancement they yielded, including election to the House of Burgesses, or even gaining the governor's ear by appointment to his council. The royal governor appointed these judges for life, so openings were few and far between. When openings did come available, the tight-knit group of justices would submit three names for the Governor to choose a replacement. They were always from 'the best people' of the wealthy landed gentry or prominent gentlemen of the county.

Court Days transformed Hanover into a festival-like atmosphere, similar to the St. Andrew's Day celebration. People travelled from their farms throughout the countryside and gathered for business, legal matters, and fun. Merchants and peddlers lined the streets with their carts to sell their wares. There were horse races, horse trading, traveling entertainers, cockfights, prizefights, and plenty of betting. People also entertained themselves at the expense of those unfortunate enough to be locked in the stocks, standing in the pillory, or receiving lashes. They cast jeers at the minor offenders who were caught drinking too much, cursing too loudly, slandering too often, punching too hard, or attending church too infrequently. If you were at least fourteen years of age, you were expected to stand trial and pay your fine.

Hanover Tavern was a long, wooden building with a porch running across the front, located directly across the street from Hanover Courthouse. It served meals and drinks to guests downstairs and offered lodging for travelers upstairs. It was not proper for genteel women to frequent taverns except if the tavern was used for a dance or other special function. Taverns were the nerve centers of colonial life where the people gathered, swapped news, conducted business, and enjoyed themselves.

290

John Shelton had graciously allowed Patrick and Sallie to move with their children into the cabin attached to the back of Hanover Tavern in the fall of 1757. Patrick gladly volunteered to help his father-in-law run the tavern when he could, especially during Court Days. He tended bar, served meals, entertained guests, and made sure overnight lodgers got their money's worth of seventy-five cents for a bed with clean sheets.

Patrick still attempted farming at Pine Slash with an overseer, and had even tried opening another store with a clerk a mile from Hanover Tavern in the summer of 1758. He only brought in £10 during the hot summer months before the tobacco harvest, so after just a short year, the writing was already on the wall. Another devastating drought and miserable tobacco crop caused Patrick to relive the same scenario as with the first store, which his father had set up for him and William. Farmers racked up debts they couldn't pay, and Patrick knew it was only a matter of time before he would have to close his store. So he had failed as a farmer and now twice as a merchant, living with his family on the good graces of his father-in-law in a tiny cabin behind a tavern. But Patrick suspected that John Shelton had also once been beholden in some way to *his* father-in-law, William Parks, who previously owned Hanover Tavern, so Patrick thought they might share an unspoken bond in that regard.

The six-foot, blue-eyed, one-hundred-sixty-pound, twenty-three-year-old Patrick Henry kept his good humor as he interacted with a cross section of every sector of society during Court Days. Lawyers, judges, witnesses, and plaintiffs and defendants filled the tables before and after sessions in Hanover Courthouse. And while he filled their glasses, they filled his ears with talk of their cases. Patrick was fascinated by the legal process and especially enjoyed the intrigue of challenging cases they discussed. He frequently slipped over to the brick-arched Hanover Courthouse to watch attorneys spar in the arena of law. He couldn't wait to sit and soak up the courtroom drama tomorrow.

"Should I make an appearance, my dear, so you can show Patrick that you are earning your keep?" Nigel asked Liz. Together they sat behind a large barrel near the enormous fireplace in the taproom, watching Patrick busily tending to his guests. They had arranged for Patrick to bring Liz to live at the tavern by having Nigel scurry around so Patrick could see the little mouse. They had put on a good show of Liz "catching" Nigel and carrying him outside. Patrick was pleased that Liz kept Hanover Tavern "mouse free."

291

"The fact that you no longer show yourself is evidence enough that my services are valuable, no?" Liz replied with a coy smile.

"By Jove, you're right!" Nigel chuckled warmly. "But I suppose we shall both need to stow away in the carriage for the family trip to Mount Brilliant for Christmas. Although I pray Patrick's horse will be able to make the journey. His old gray mare clearly is not what she used to be."

Liz frowned. "*Oui,* my Henry needs a new horse. He needs many things, including finding his voice. I simply do not accept that his voice is limited to singing in the tavern. There must be more to the riddle than that." The sleek black cat's tail curled up and down slowly as she studied the charming young man listening intently to a lawyer he was serving. "Nigel, have you noticed how Patrick's face lights up as he discusses the court cases with the lawyers and judges who come in here?"

"Indeed I have!" Nigel replied. "He always has to pry himself off the bench in Hanover Courthouse to return to the tavern to help Mr. Shelton on Court Days. He clearly loves the intrigue and spectacle of courtroom drama. I was just privy to a conversation Patrick had outside Hanover Courthouse with several lawyers discussing that testy Two Penny Act business. The dastardly Virginia parsons have been up in arms about it. Patrick was riled up as they discussed the appalling behavior of the parsons, including that of his own Uncle Patrick!"

"Two Penny Act? But it was passed to help the tobacco farmers, no?" Liz asked.

"*Precisely*, my dear. Parsons are paid an annual salary of 16,000 pounds of tobacco a year, which normally runs two pennies per pound in years with a bountiful harvest," Nigel explained. "But with the pitiful harvests in 1755 and 1758, the price of tobacco *tripled*, which would in turn *cripple* the farmers who simply could not pay that much. The House of Burgesses twice passed the Two Penny Act as a temporary relief measure so farmers could pay with coin instead of tobacco, and at the normal two penny rate."

"This is logical. So what is the problem for the parsons?" Liz wanted to know.

Nigel's eyes narrowed and he rubbed his hands together. "*Greed* is the problem. Specifically greedy *parsons, of all things!* Rather than see this as a beneficial measure to help their suffering congregations, they see it as an outrage and a loss of money to line their pockets! So half of Virginia's clergy met and decided to send Reverend John Camm to London to ask the king's Privy Council to overturn the Act. They're awaiting the response from London now."

Liz's eyes widened. "This is preposterous! How dare those shepherds fight something designed to help their own flocks! And they have even gone over the elected heads of the House of Burgesses, right to the king!"

Nigel nodded. "They act more like wolves than shepherds, I'm afraid. But you should have heard Patrick discuss the controversy with the lawyers. He has quite the brilliant understanding of the case. And his passion is undeniable."

"*Oui,* being a farmer himself, he can personally relate," Liz agreed, her tail whipping back and forth. She was angry. "If anyone could champion such a cause and speak up for the tobacco farmers, it is my Henry."

Suddenly it dawned on her as she heard Patrick playing his fiddle and singing loudly so all the tavern could hear. *A voice in the tavern.*

"Nigel, do you suppose Patrick could be a lawyer?" Liz asked, watching Patrick entertain the guests. The people adored him.

Nigel's eyes lit up at the thought. "I actually think that would be a *brilliant* profession for him! Patrick certainly has the mind for it. But how would he achieve such a feat? He cannot travel to London for schooling, nor does he have the luxury of studying for years under an established lawyer. He would then need to travel to Williamsburg to receive a law license."

"He could teach himself, here in the tavern!" Liz answered, growing excited. "Together Hanover Courthouse and Hanover Tavern make one big classroom for studying law! Patrick can read law books, attend 'class' at the courthouse with actual cases, and then ask all the questions he needs as his professors come to *him* here in the tavern! When he is ready he can then go to Williamsburg for his license to practice law. But he can practice not just at Hanover Courthouse but at many other court-houses in the surrounding counties. *C'est magnifique!* I believe I have uncovered the fiddle's riddle! My Henry's voice in the tavern will not be as a singer of Scottish songs but as a lawyer!"

"My dear, it is quite an ambitious, lovely idea, but do you suppose it is possible?" Nigel asked, twirling his whiskers with a paw, studying the barefoot fiddler performing for the guests. "He clearly needs help to be transformed into a lawyer."

Liz looked at Nigel and batted her eyes. *"Mon ami,* after all we have seen on our missions? You would ask if something is *possible?* Shame on you!" she teased.

293

Nigel bowed humbly with his paw draped over his chest and his front foot extended. "My most sincere apologies, my pet. You are right, and you have indeed unlocked the mysterious riddle of the voice in the tavern!" He straightened up and preened his whiskers. "Now I see what Gillamon meant by Hanover being no ordinary tavern."

"All my Henry needs are some law books and a horse," calculated Liz. Just then Jack Poindexter opened the door of the tavern and looked around for a table, book under his arm. "We will need to contact Gillamon tonight about some law books. For now, I know someone who can help my Henry with a horse." She lifted her tail and made her way over to the table.

"Good day, Mr. Poindexter!" Patrick, towel over his shoulder and a platter of food in his hand, greeted the kind, older gentleman. "Table for one?"

"Pahtrick, it's always good to see you. Just one, but hopefully not for long," Jack replied with a smile and his thick Virginia drawl, pointing his walking stick with a wink. "There's always someone to talk to in the tavern before Court Day. Bring me a hot toddy, please."

"Indeed, sir! Have a seat by the window and I'll be right there," Patrick agreed, taking the food over to another table.

Jack sat down with a grunt, set his book on the table, and leaned his walking stick on the open chair. He rubbed his hands together and blew into them to warm up. Liz came over and rubbed his legs, purring. "Hello there," he said with a smile, reaching down to pet Liz on the floor. He chuckled as she wrapped her tail around his legs. Patrick came over, set a warm mug on the table, and Jack noticed his feet. "Why Pahtrick, aren't you cold in those bare feet? You do realize it is December, not July."

Patrick looked down at his feet, placed his hands on his hips and laughed. "Yes, but it gets quite warm in here on a busy day like today. I've never liked shoes too much. Besides, Sallie would rather me clean my feet than my filthy shoes after working in the tavern." Just then a loud shout arose as the group of celebrating men cheered another toast, sloshing their mugs onto the floor. Scattered all around them were scraps of food and mud they had tracked in from the street. "As you can clearly see."

294

Jack chuckled. "I see. If only my horses could go around shoeless," he said, tapping his book.

Patrick leaned over and read the title. "*No Foot, No Horse.* An Essay by Jeremiah Bridges. What's this book about?"

"It's a new book from London about the care of horses and their shoes. As you know, if a horse doesn't have good shoes, it's as worthless as no horse at all," Jack replied. "I always like to make sure my horses are well taken care of, *especially* their shoes. I just bought several new pairs from the blacksmith, including some for 'MizP.' You know she always enjoys the apples you send to her, Pahtrick."

"MizP isn't a filly anymore, is she? She's grown into a beautiful mare," Patrick answered with a bright smile. "I wish I could buy a new *horse* to attach to some shoes. Mine has ridden about as far as she can."

Jack frowned. "I know you've been through a rough spell these past couple of years, Pahtrick, what with losing your house, and the drought killing your crops." He put his hand on Patrick's arm. "I also know how you've continued to help other struggling farmers with your store; your generosity in turn has hurt *you.*" He looked around the bustling tavern. "Mr. Shelton was kind to let you stay here, but what do you think you'll do next?"

Patrick tightened his lips but smiled while shrugging his shoulders. "I'm not sure yet. But I need to figure out something soon. Responsibility is breathing down my neck. I've been waiting and trying to figure things out, but . . . nothing yet."

"I know you're not much of a drinking man, so I'm sure you're not even enjoying any of the spirits that you serve," guessed Jack as he held up his cup and took a sip of his toddy. He set it on the table and lifted his walking stick from the chair. "Sit a moment, Pahtrick. I want to share something with you."

Patrick did as he was told, and took a seat. He leaned in to listen carefully, as he always did with everyone.

"There once was a knight who was being chased by merciless enemies. They were breathing down his neck," Jack started, locking eyes with Patrick. "He was galloping along at a fast pace, but soon realized his horse needed a new shoe. What was he to do? Stop and replace the shoe for his mare, or keep going?"

Patrick thought a moment. "I would think he should try to push the horse on to escape the enemy. It would take too much time to replace a shoe."

Jack smiled and shook his head. "Not that much time. That knight knew the small amount of time invested to shoe his horse would be worth it, for it wouldn't take long for the enemy to catch up if his horse stopped running altogether. He wisely stopped at the blacksmith to care for his mare. And although he heard the thunderous approach of the enemy, he knew his horse could outrun them if she was well equipped." Jack sat back in his seat and took another sip.

"So what happened?" Patrick eagerly asked.

"Just as the enemy got within a hundred yards of him, the knight mounted his horse and galloped off faster than the wind," Jack explained. He held up a finger to Patrick. "The stop had actually *hastened* the knight's escape." He leaned in. "Sometimes the stops we don't want to take end up helping us run ahead of everyone else. You're just stopped right now, Pahtrick."

Patrick breathed in deeply and nodded, staring at the book. "No foot, no horse." He smiled, tapping the book. "Thank you for sharing that, Mr. Poindexter. I'm sure you're right."

"Patrick, another round, and bring your fiddle!" cheered the rosy-cheeked man in the green wool coat.

295

"I need to tend to the other guests," Patrick apologized, standing up, "and to figure out what else I need, besides a new horse." He smiled and patted Jack on the back. Turning to the other table, Patrick announced, "Coming right up, gentlemen!"

Liz jumped up in Jack's lap and purred. He smiled and petted her as he watched young Patrick happily go about serving others in his bare feet. "That knight has no foot *and* no horse."

Then give him one of yours, Liz meowed. *Give him MizP.*

Jack smiled and scratched Liz under the chin. "Aren't you the talkative cat? If only I knew what you were saying." He chuckled and set her on the floor.

Liz swished her tail and looked up at the horse owner with a determined face. *You soon shall, Monsieur.*

She lifted her curlicue tail and walked back through the noisy tavern. She grinned at Patrick playing his magic fiddle. He winked at her as he bowed low to play a couple of notes before turning to hold out his arms and let his voice fill the tavern with song. *Enjoy your singing while it lasts,* mon ami. *You will not be doing it much longer.*

Liz couldn't stay for the merriment. She needed to get to work making a Christmas list for her Henry, and she knew exactly how to deliver it.

HAPPY CHRISTMAS, MR. HENRY

Fresh pine boughs, spiced wassail, bayberry candles, and sumptuous food delighted guests with the magical fragrance of Christmas. Silver platters of Virginia smoked ham, succulent pheasant, roasted vegetables, warm breads, and sweet delicacies filled the bountiful table of this splendid country home belonging to Colonel Nathaniel West Dandridge. Wine filled the crystal goblets and rum punch filled the silver cups that were frequently raised to offer toasts of glad tidings, good health, and bountiful cheer.

The well-off country squire's home was also filled with the finest guests, stemming from Colonel Dandridge's excellent connections. This large landowner was married to the beloved late Governor Spotswood's daughter, Dorothea. The Governor's Palace in Williamsburg was actually built expressly for Governor Spotswood in appreciation for the fine role he played in governing the colony. Colonel Dandridge was also the uncle of Martha Washington, new bride of the 'Hero of the Monongahela,' victorious in the French & Indian War, Colonel George Washington. Everyone wanted to be included on the Dandridge guest list. The festive Dandridge parties were always the highlight of the Christmas season in the upper piedmont of Hanover County, and John Henry's family was naturally included, as they were counted as neighbors and friends.

Musicians filled the long hall with the sounds of the season on pianoforte and violin. Couples bowed and curtsied across from one another as they danced one reel and minuet after another, creating a moving palate of twirling, beautiful colors. Chandeliers cast a soft glow over the elegantly dressed ladies in their silk gowns and the dashing gentlemen in their finest satin breeches, coats, and shiny gold-buckled shoes. The men and ladies divided into two rows for the next reel. The first couple was to join hands and dance between the rows of clapping dancers, and then take their opposite places at the end of the row. The next couple would do the same, and so on until each couple had had a turn and ended up in their same starting position.

Patrick and Sallie clasped hands and danced up the center of the divided rows, having the time of their lives while the other dancers kept time with the music. Onlookers lined the walls, enjoying the lively dancers and whispering about which couples danced the best. Patrick clapped for the couples who followed as he looked around the room. He noticed a tall, skinny, red-haired, freckle-faced young man no more than seventeen years old standing off in a corner alone. He looked a bit awkward, and Patrick could tell the young man felt out of place. It was then that Patrick saw someone walk up to the awkward young man and shake his hand. It was a gentleman in a magnificent red cloak. He had seen that cloak before, many years ago. He suddenly realized who it was. It was Mr. Gillamon.

While Patrick finished dancing the reel with Sallie, Gillamon struck up a conversation with the awkward young man in the corner.

"Good evening to you as well, sir. My name is Thomas Jefferson," the young man said. "I'm pleased to meet you."

A servant came and offered to take Gillamon's cloak. He took it off and handed it to the servant, and caught Patrick's eye. He smiled and lifted a hand in greeting. Patrick returned the smile and the wave. He was eager to talk to this man who had been so kind to him as a child. But he had promised to next play the violin for the audience, so he would make his way over as soon as he could.

"Do you know that young man, Thomas?" Gillamon asked him, pointing to Patrick, who continued to dance around happily with his lovely young wife.

Thomas looked over and shook his head. "I'm afraid I haven't had the pleasure of meeting him. Who is he?"

Gillamon smiled. "His name is Patrick Henry, and he is an extraor-dinary young man. I highly encourage you to get to know him. I've

298

known him since he was a child. His parents live nearby, but he now lives by Hanover Courthouse."

"Oh, really? Where by Hanover Courthouse?" Thomas asked.

"In Hanover Tavern," Gillamon replied, drawing a perplexed look from the young man.

"Is he a . . ." Thomas whispered, looking around at the other fine guests gathered at the Dandridge party, ". . . a barkeep?"

Gillamon chuckled softly. "Only as a volunteer, to help his father in-law, who owns the tavern. You see, he lost his home to a fire, his tobacco farm failed, and his store is closing soon. Yet look how happy he is."

Thomas looked on as Patrick picked up his fiddle and started stomping his feet. The party guests quickly lined up to dance. Henry's fiery fiddling ignited a whole new level of excitement in the room, and more dancers joined in the fun, laughing with delight. "One would never know he carries such a burden. He appears not to have a care in the world."

"The true mark of a man's character," Gillamon added. Together they watched as Patrick worked the crowd. The people adored him. He made his way over to Gillamon and Thomas and smiled broadly as he played the last part of his merry jig before them. He ended with a triumphant note, his bow raised high in the air and the audience cheering wildly behind him.

"Happy Christmas, Mr. Gillamon! How grand to see you here!" Patrick exclaimed over the sound of the delighted crowd. "The fiddle still plays as good as ever!"

"Happy Christmas, Mr. Henry," Gillamon replied with a warm smile and a hand to his shoulder. "Of course it does, especially in the hands of such a first-rate fiddler. I'm happy to see you as well after all these years, Patrick. Through others, I've kept up with your journey. Allow me to introduce you to Mr. Thomas Jefferson."

Patrick and Thomas each bowed in a respectful gesture. "Sir, I'm honored to make your acquaintance," Patrick said.

Thomas smiled weakly. "The honor is all mine."

"I took the liberty of telling Mr. Jefferson here about your life journey to date, Pat," Gillamon said.

"I'm sorry about your house and recent woes, Mr. Henry," Thomas said.

299

Patrick smiled and waved him off. "Every life has trouble of its own. Mine will work out in the Lord's good time."

"Pat, another dance, please?" came Sallie's voice behind him.

"Ah, my lovely bride," he answered, putting his arm around her waist. "Sallie, I would like you to meet my old friend Mr. Gillamon, and my new friend, Mr. Jefferson."

"I'm delighted to meet you, Sallie," Gillamon said, taking her hand and bowing gracefully. She smiled and curtsied to the men.

Thomas bowed also, but without the charm of Mr. Gillamon. "Mrs. Henry."

"Patrick, might I be permitted to have this next dance with your lovely bride?" Gillamon asked with a smile.

"Of course! Please, sir. She is a splendid dancer," Patrick consented with a grin. "Sallie, I shall chat with Mr. Jefferson while you and Mr. Gillamon take the floor."

"Thank you, Mr. Gillamon," Sallie said, taking the older gentleman's arm as he led her away.

300

"You have a lovely wife, Mr. Henry," Thomas said as they watched the dancers line up.

"She is my joy and delight," Patrick answered proudly. "What about you? Has some fair maiden captured your heart?"

Thomas looked to the floor and shook his head. "No. I'm afraid I'm not very good with women. I never know the right things to say."

Patrick smiled and held up his fiddle. "Then speak with music. My uncle once told me to play the fiddle to woo women, and it worked!" he said with a wink. "Do you play?"

"No, I do not play the violin," Thomas replied stiffly.

"Then I encourage you to take up the violin," Patrick suggested. "Mark my words, it will give you an open door and the confidence to entertain and meet the ladies."

Thomas smiled. "Perhaps I will when I reach Williamsburg. I'm heading there after the Christmas season to attend the College of William and Mary."

"Splendid! You will no doubt receive a fine education. What course of study do you wish to pursue?" Patrick asked.

"I hope to study law under Mr. George Wythe once I have completed my primary studies at the college," Thomas replied.

"Law is a fine profession finally gaining prominence," Patrick replied, nodding and smiling as Sallie and Gillamon twirled near them. "I know it requires a great deal of study, but perhaps an even greater skill of oratory. You must be a splendid speaker."

Thomas looked to the floor again, clasping his hands in front of him. "Honestly, I am not. But while I do not possess a great skill for speaking, I do love studying books." He looked up and held his chin high. "I cannot *live* without books."

"I cannot live without people," Patrick replied. "I love to talk with people. To hear what they think, and to understand what moves them— what *words* move them."

"You clearly are at ease with people, as is evident even in the few moments I've known you, Mr. Henry," complimented Thomas enviously, watching people smile and nod happily at Patrick as they walked by. "And people are at ease with you."

Thomas looked over Patrick's clothes, which were simple and inexpensive while his own were made from fine blue silk stitched with elaborate gold trim. He wore expensive shoes of quality leather while Patrick's shoes were dull and well worn. Thomas came from a wealthy family in the western Piedmont region of Albemarle County. His father Peter had begun a life path similar to that of Patrick's father, John Henry. He also started out as a poor land surveyor and then married 'up' so to speak, both financially and in social status. Peter Jefferson married a Randolph, one of the finest families in Virginia. Unlike John Henry, however, Peter continued to prosper and amassed land and wealth, providing a comfortable lifestyle for his family and the ability to send his eldest son to college. Although seven years his senior, Patrick Henry did not possess what Thomas Jefferson did in terms of worldly treasures. Patrick's manners were not refined like his; but he was courteous, polite, and undeniably charming to everyone he met with his good cheer and witty humor. People were drawn to Patrick like a magnet. Thomas was more reserved and more at ease with "mankind" in general than he was one on one. Patrick Henry, on the other hand, didn't know a stranger. He treated everyone the same, from the poor worker to the elite guests gathered here at the Dandridge home. Patrick Henry had the gift of common touch, an ability to reach the common folks.

Gillamon and Sallie came up to them, their dance finished. "Thank you for a lovely dance, Mr. Gillamon. Now, if you will excuse me, I

301

noticed that my dear friend Elizabeth Strong just arrived, and I wish to go to her. I've learned she is recently engaged to Samuel Crowley! Do you remember, Pat? He came to our wedding with Uncle Langloo and met Elizabeth that day."

"That's wonderful, Sallie! I'm happy for them. Go to her, and I'll join you in a moment to say hello," promised Patrick.

The gentlemen bowed in unison as Sallie hurried off to see her friend. Gillamon dabbed a handkerchief on his brow, having worked up a bit of a sweat. "Patrick, she is a treasure! I'm so very happy for you. And she tells me you are a very proud father of two."

"Thank you. Yes, can you believe I have *two* children?" Patrick replied. "I never imagined I could be so blessed!"

Gillamon gave him a knowing smile. "Well, what have you gentlemen discussed while I was fortunate enough to dance with Mrs. Henry?"

"I was sharing that I'll soon begin my studies at William and Mary," Thomas replied. "Mr. Henry and I were discussing our interests. Mine is books and his are fiddling, dancing, people, and words."

Gillamon raised his eyebrows. "Ah, yes, the spoken word. The gift of oratory does not belong to everyone. I know you have been privileged to hear one of the greatest orators here in Virginia, Patrick."

"Yes, Reverend Samuel Davies is the greatest orator I've ever heard," Patrick replied. "I am also proud to call him friend. He has been a tremendous help to my family during this hard season."

"So, what do you plan to do next, Patrick?" Gillamon asked.

"I'm not sure, Mr. Gillamon," Patrick answered.

"Well, if you love words and speaking, I can think of three professions that call for the gift of oratory," Gillamon suggested. "Minister, teacher, or lawyer."

Patrick thought a moment and shook his head. "I do not think I have the ability to fill the pulpit or the professor's chair."

"I suppose that leaves law," Thomas added flatly.

Patrick raised his eyebrows and pursed his lips. "Indeed, so it does."

"If you'll excuse me, I need to give my regards to a family friend who just arrived," Thomas said with a bow.

"Certainly," Patrick answered as he and Gillamon nodded courteously.

"What do you think of that idea, Patrick?" Gillamon asked when Thomas was gone. "I know that in addition to your skill with words, you have a remarkable memory, which a lawyer also needs. Can you see yourself being a lawyer?"

Patrick smiled. "I haven't shared this with anyone, but as I sit in Hanover Courthouse and listen to those lawyers, I often feel I could do what they do. I like to anticipate what the reaction of the jury will be. I've gotten to where I can tell when a lawyer loses the jury with his argument or his delivery." He looked around and whispered to Gillamon. "Sometimes it's all I can do to keep my mouth shut when they come in the tavern afterwards to discuss the case, wondering why they failed to convince the jury."

"Ah, you are a good observer, a good *listener,* as well as a good talker. That is a rare combination, my friend." Gillamon smiled. "I believe you've found your answer, Patrick. Perhaps you will be like Cato, whose words moved Rome itself."

Patrick put his hand on Gillamon's shoulder. "I still have my copy of *Plutarch's Parallel Lives* that you sent to me. Thankfully it was at my father's house and not with me in the fire." He sighed. "Perhaps I will study law. I need to do something. I've been struggling for seven years to figure out my calling."

303

"*Seven* years." Gillamon leaned in and looked at Patrick with his twinkling, blue eyes. "Do you know what 'seven' signifies? Seven means complete. Perhaps your struggles are finally coming to an end, Patrick. I have a feeling 1760 could be your turnaround year."

Patrick clenched his jaw and fought back the emotion. "Mr. Gillamon, you've always been so kind and encouraging to me. Thank you."

Gillamon grinned with a twinkle in his eye. "I have a special interest in young people. And I believe in investing in lives, for they are the only things that eternally last."

"Indeed," Patrick replied. "Still, I don't know how I'd make becoming a lawyer a reality. I can't afford law school in London. I can't even afford college like Mr. Jefferson. And with my family, I couldn't spend time away studying under a lawyer in Williamsburg as can Mr. Jefferson."

"You can read, can you not?" Gillamon jested.

Patrick laughed. "Yes, of course."

"And you are continually surrounded by lawyers in the courthouse and in the tavern, are you not?" Gillamon asked. "Young Mr. Jefferson should be so lucky to have the number of lawyers at his disposal as do you."

Patrick raised his eyebrows. "You're right. I hadn't thought about it in that way."

"So teach yourself," Gillamon suggested. "And don't waste time worrying about what you don't know. Get on with it."

Patrick placed his hands on his hips with a growing resolve. "I like this idea more and more, Mr. Gillamon. Thank you. Now I suppose I'll need to borrow a couple of books."

Liz has already seen to that, Gillamon thought.

"Pat, come see Elizabeth and Samuel!" Sallie whispered from behind Gillamon. "Will you excuse my husband, Mr. Gillamon?"

"Of course, and please give my regards to the happy young couple," Gillamon replied with a bow and a broad smile. He watched Patrick heartily shake the hand of Samuel Crowley, congratulating him and Elizabeth. The young couple was so happy to soon start their new journey together. "I have a special interest in Samuel and Elizabeth, too."

304

—

MOUNT BRILLIANT, DECEMBER 24, 1759

Patrick and Sallie were enjoying a wonderful time with his parents at Mount Brilliant. It felt good to come home and for John and Sarah to get to visit with their grandchildren. Patrick saw Thomas Jefferson again at other Christmas gatherings, and the two young men quickly became friends. Upon returning home this afternoon, his mother had given him a package that had arrived. While Sallie was bathing the children and getting them ready for bed, Patrick sat in his father's study and opened the package. Inside was a letter. It was from Mr. Gillamon:

Dear Patrick,

I was pleased to visit with you at the Dandridge home. I believe you have discovered your true calling. And if the Lord has called you to it, He will equip you for it. I encourage you to read the fifth verse of the sixty-fourth Psalm.

Your seven years of struggle have prepared you for what is to come. Adversity builds manhood. The characteristic of the good or the great man is not that he has been exempted from the evils of life but that he has surmounted them. The best men always make themselves.

*Enclosed are some books to help you begin your studies.
May they serve you well. Happy Christmas.*
Your servant,
Mr. Gillamon

Patrick smiled and opened the package, pulling out two books. He ran his hand along the soft leather-bound copy of the English lawyer's 1623 bible of common law, *Coke upon Littleton.* This book would give him the foundation he needed to study the law, showing him how legal documents were written. He soon would understand how to draw up wills, mortgages, deeds, land grants, pleas, declarations, and any manner of other documents. Also included was a copy of Giles Duncombe's *Trials per Pais,* which was the most popular law book in the colonies pertaining to evidence and courtroom procedure.

"Thank you, Mr. Gillamon," he said softly. He then reached over and picked up his father's Holy Bible to look up the passage from Psalms:

Blessed is the man You choose,
And cause to approach You,
That he may dwell in Your courts.

305

Liz smiled from the shadows as she saw the expression on Patrick's face. The voice in Hanover Tavern would soon be speaking not just *to* the other lawyers, but *with* them—as one of them.

Patrick leaned on the doorframe holding a brass candle lamp and watched Sallie as she gently tucked John and Patsey into bed. She wore the long, white shift, or simple cotton gown, that she daily wore under her dress. Her hair was pulled back loosely with a ribbon, and a single curl dangled down her cheek. She smiled at their small children nestled together, gently patting the blanket they shared while she hummed a soft lullaby.

Patrick quietly walked over and sat on the bed, setting down the candle on the bedside table and stretching out to gaze at his little family. Sallie looked over at him and smiled, her dimples showing. How Patrick loved this beautiful woman! His heart thrilled with what he was about to tell her. He hoped she would be excited as well. When the children were sound asleep, she came over and climbed onto the bed, resting her head on his shoulder. She let go a slow breath and whispered, "Finally asleep after their Happy Christmasing today." She yawned and draped her arm across Patrick. "I will soon be asleep, also. And you, my love?"

"I'm afraid I will not be able to sleep tonight," Patrick answered with a grin.

Sallie lifted her head and looked at her husband. "Why not?"

"I've got some reading to do," explained Patrick. "Sallie, what if I told you I've decided to study to become a lawyer? Would that please you?"

Sallie's eyes grew wide with delight. "Would it please me? Of course it would! But how will you do this?" She sat up and he did as well, taking her hands in his.

"Mr. Gillamon sent me some law books that I'll start reading tonight," Patrick explained excitedly. "I plan to discuss this with father tomorrow. He will be able to lend me a book or two as well. When we return home I'll sit in the sessions at Hanover Courthouse, ask the questions I need of the lawyers I serve in the tavern, and come spring, I'll ride to Williamsburg for my examination. I've failed as a farmer and a merchant, but Sallie, *this* time I think I can succeed. I don't need anything besides a strong mind, so this time there will be no expense for us to get started. My office will be 'under my hat,' so to speak." He looked down and ran his thumbs along her delicate hands. "If you believe in me, I know I can do this. I hope to finally make you proud, *and* better provide for you and the children."

Sallie lifted her hand to cup Patrick's cheek. "Oh, my love," she cooed as she raised his gaze to meet hers. "You'll be *perfect.* But you are wrong about one thing, Mr. Henry."

Patrick cocked his head to the side with a frown. "And what is that, Mrs. Henry?"

"I'm *already* proud of you," she answered with her irresistible smile.

Patrick's eyes welled up and he happily kissed his bride, who had supported him through everything without fail. He leaned back and gave her an impish grin. "Then, Mrs. Henry, I stand corrected."

"Happy Christmas, Mr. Henry," Sallie said.

Patrick hugged Sallie as his heart filled with expectant hope. "Happy Christmas, indeed, Mrs. Henry."

36

SWEET ON MIZP

Patrick sat with his three law books sprawled out on the table in Hanover Tavern, twirling his wig that sat atop his head as he read. His family had long since gone to bed, and he took advantage of the peace and quiet to study. A few solitary candles were lit around him, giving the tavern a tranquil, almost romantic feel, which was a far cry from the daytime atmosphere of this lively place. His father had loaned him *Digest of the Virginia Acts,* dealing specifically with Virginia law, and he had the other two books Mr. Gillamon had sent him. The most challenging book of course was *Coke upon Littleton,* laid out in three columns: complex law in French/Latin, the English translation, and then a lengthy commentary on the first two columns. It made Patrick's brain hurt. Coke's advice to the reader was that one should read:

> no more at any one time than he is able with a Delight to bear away, and after to meditate thereon, which is the Life of reading.

"With a *delight* to bear away?" Patrick repeated before he blew a raspberry. This was difficult, complex material. Studying law would not be easy. He looked up and saw Liz sitting there on the table next to the candle. The soft glow of the light cast a silky sheen on her black fur, and her eyes caught the light as she stared at him, her tail curled around her legs. He smiled, scratched her under the chin, and pushed *Coke* aside while he reached for his book by Duncombe. "Liz, would you like to study with me? I'm sure you often need to reference the law in your day to day activities prosecuting mice. I'll read aloud for both of us."

He chuckled and opened the book to the introduction and cleared his throat.

"Without Victory at the Trial, to what Purpose is the Science of the Law?" Patrick began. He paused and looked up at Liz. "I like this author already."

"That is why I chose this book for you, no?" Liz meowed. *"Please continue*, mon *Henry."*

"If any Man be delighted in History, let him read the Books of Law, which are nothing else but Annals and Chronicles of Things done and acted upon from year to year, in which each Case presents you with a petit history; and if Variety of Matter doth most delight the reader, doubtless, the reading of those Cases, (which differ like Men's Faces), tho' like the Stars in Number, is the most pleasant reading in the World." Patrick paused and looked up at Liz. "I love history. It's one of my strengths." He waved his hand over the candle to make it dance. "I can study the law as if it were one of my history books, like Plutarch. *That* will help me." He smiled and picked up the book and began reading again.

Liz grinned and curled her tail up and down. *Bon. That is exactly what I hoped it would do.*

308

———

MARCH 7, 1760

Liz jumped up to walk along the top of the fence behind which Jack Poindexter kept his horses. A large brown stallion was eagerly chewing on a fencepost, drooling and mumbling, "Yummy post, yummy post, yummy post, yummy post."

"Pardon, but do you realize this behavior is not beneficial for your teeth?" Liz asked him.

The horse ignored her, continuing to chew and mumble.

"Don't try tuh convince Bill utherwise," MizP said in a low Virginia drawl, walking up next to him, shaking her head. "Telling this stump sucker not tuh chew this post is like trying tuh enter a battle of wits with an unarmed man."

Liz giggled to herself at hearing the dry wit of MizP. She smiled at the beautiful four-year-old horse, jet black except for a tiny white star on her forehead, just beneath the forelock of hair between her large brown eyes. "I am actually here to meet *you*, MizP. My name is Liz, and I am on mission for the Maker to help Patrick Henry."

"Pahtrick Henry? Now there's a kind young man. I always appreciate the apples he gives me. I've been tuh his store a time or two," shared MizP. "Jack speaks highly of him, although I understand the boy's merchant business isn't worth a plug nickel. But if the Maker has you helping him, I assume *he's* worth a great deal."

"*Oui,* he is a very valuable human!" Liz exclaimed happily. "He will play an important role in the history of this country. And he is indeed a kind, loving man, always eager to help others. But now Patrick needs help. He needs a good, strong, reliable horse. MizP, I have come to ask if you would volunteer to become Patrick Henry's horse."

MizP whipped her tail back and forth and lifted her gaze to stare at the petite black cat sitting on the rail. "Why me?"

"Because I know that you have been well trained and cared for by Mr. Poindexter. You are very smart, strong, reliable, and fast," Liz explained. "You are *très jolie* also, no? Very pretty."

"Well, I'm quite flahttered, Liz. I'd be happy tuh help Pahtrick, but how do we get Jack tuh let me go?" MizP asked.

"By escaping and showing up at Hanover Tavern," Liz explained, her eyes beaming with good-natured mischief. "Several times."

"How many times?" MizP asked.

"Seven," Liz answered with a smile, walking along the fence to examine the gate. "Do you have an idea of how you could escape?"

MizP thought a moment. "If you chase two rabbits, both will escape," she replied with a grin, nodding toward Bill, who was still eagerly chewing the fencepost.

"This be some sweet but sticky stuff," Max muttered through clenched teeth, holding the bucket of molasses. Max and Nigel had slipped inside Patrick's store to secretly get the molasses like every other customer of late: "on credit." Max had returned to assignment in Hanover for the time being to help Liz and Nigel, but stayed out of sight of the humans, along with Nigel. He continually shadowed Patrick, keeping an eye out for any signs of threats since Nelson needed to remain at Pine Slash.

"Indeed, molasses is the nectar of the colonies," Nigel answered,

309

riding atop Max's large head. "And the bread and butter of New England, I might add."

"Aye, for makin' their r-r-rum," Max replied. "Is this Fr-r-rench or Br-r-ritish molasses?"

"If Liz has a say in what molasses Patrick Henry sells, I am sure she would prefer the superior *French* molasses from the French West Indies, as the New Englanders do," Nigel replied. "Although I doubt Patrick smuggled his molasses like his northern counterparts."

"Why do those lads need ta smuggle their molasses?" Max asked.

"Why, because of that *dreadful* Molasses Act of 1733, old boy!" Nigel retorted, straightening his spectacles.

"We were in England when that happened, lad," Max said. "Ye best r-r-remind me."

"Very well, I shall explain this sugary, syrupy business," Nigel offered. "Right. Molasses is produced on sugar cane plantations in the Caribbean islands, known as the West Indies, and is used for cooking or for making rum. England owns Jamaica and Barbados. Spain owns Santo Domingo, the Dutch own the Netherland Antilles and France owns Martinique. Britain realized they were losing a great deal of money as the American colonies chose to import molasses from these competing islands, which produced better quality molasses at a lower price. The French West Indies also enjoyed trading lumber, cheese, and flour with the New England and Middle colonies, and offered the cheapest price, so they had a splendid partnership. Are you with me so far?"

"Aye," answered Max, enjoying the sweet bucket handle as he trotted along. "They had a sweet tr-r-rade goin'."

Nigel chuckled. *"Precisely.* Yet England's trade was *not* so sweet. So, with the Molasses Act, Parliament decided to force the colonies to buy British molasses by taxing all non-British molasses at six pence per gallon. The Act was not meant to raise money, but to regulate trade. As you can imagine, this would force the American colonies to either buy the inferior British molasses or destroy New England's rum industry with the high taxes on other molasses. So what did they do?"

"They decided ta smuggle their r-r-rum instead fr-r-rom the Fr-r-renchies," Max replied.

Nigel nodded. "And this smuggling led to bribing or intimidating the customs officials in American ports, to keep them from collecting the tax and to make them turn a blind eye to the smugglers' sneaky, sugary shenanigans."

"So England passed a law that the colonists have ignored?" Max asked. "An' the king hasn't done anythin' aboot it?"

"Not in almost thirty years," Nigel replied. "But the Molasses Act is set to expire in three years so we shall see what happens then." The little mouse looked up and saw Liz sitting on Jack Poindexter's fence post. He waved. "We are here, my dear. I do say, I'm looking forward to meeting MizP."

Max trotted up to Liz and set the bucket of molasses on the ground. "Hello, Liz."

"*Bonjour,* Max," Liz replied. "*Merci* for bringing the molasses."

"Glad ta do it, lass. It were a sweet job," Max quipped with a wide grin, licking his chops.

MizP came walking up to them. "Well, this must be Max and Nigel."

"Aye, Liz says ye be one gr-r-rand horse, lass," Max said flatteringly.

Nigel scurried up the fence to where Liz sat, and bowed to MizP. "A pleasure to meet you, my dear. I am most grateful for your decision to become Patrick Henry's horse. I look forward to riding on many adventures with you in the coming years."

MizP lowered her head to get a good look at Nigel. "You'll be welcome tuh stay on this high horse anytime."

"I shall take you up on your kind invitation," Nigel replied with a smile and a tender pat on the horse's muzzle. "Seeing as how I have received it right from the horse's mouth!" He chuckled and wiggled his whiskers.

"Wha's the plan for the molasses then?" Max asked.

"*Bon.* The molasses will be used to encourage Bill the horse to chew on a fence post in the far field," Liz explained, pointing to the distant fence. "I will teach him to raise the gate latch in order to reach the other post, allowing both him and MizP to escape. Bill will run to the far fence post covered in molasses while MizP runs off to Hanover Tavern."

"And since Jack Poindexter cannot chase two horses at once, he shall first retrieve the closest horse, Bill, whilst he sees the direction MizP runs as she wends her way toward the tavern," Nigel added.

"*Oui.* Jack shall find her with Patrick at the tavern and bring her home. Then we shall repeat this process until Jack is convinced to allow MizP to stay with my Henry," explained Liz.

311

MizP looked up at the cloudy sky. "There's enough blue sky tuh knit a cat a pair of britches so I think we've got enough time tuh get this done tuhday before it rains."

Liz and Nigel shot glances at one another and giggled. "I simply *adore* her phrases, Nigel."

"Indeed, she is quite the splendid word picture *artiste,*" Nigel agreed.

"We need to first put a dab of molasses on this gatepost, and then promise Bill more sweet stump sucking on the far fencepost," Liz explained.

Max looked at MizP's tail. "MizP, do ye want ta do the molasses paintin' honors?"

"Do goats stink?" MizP said with a wink to Max, dipping her tail in the molasses and brushing some on the gatepost.

"Aye, of course they do, lass!" Max answered. "Except for Gillamon, that is."

"That's what she *meant,* old boy, meaning 'yes,' she would," Nigel quipped. "I shall ride Max to the far post and apply the molasses there."

"*Bon.* Expect Bill shortly," Liz replied with a coy grin.

MizP walked into the barn to get Bill while Liz sat on the gate, ready to lift the latch. Max and Nigel trotted off to prepare the other fencepost.

"I know you're going tuh love this sweet post, Bill," MizP said, leading the horse to the fencepost. "Just give that gatepost a lick."

Bill did as instructed and his eyes widened with delight. "YUMMY POST!" He drooled and licked and chewed until all the molasses was gone. Liz and MizP shared a knowing grin.

"I gotta get more of that sweet stuff!" Bill exclaimed, licking the gate.

"Do you see the small black dog in the distance?" Liz asked him. "If you will simply use your nose to lift the gate latch like so, there is a post covered in this 'sweet stuff' near the black dog." She proceeded to show Bill how to lift the latch. "*Voila.*"

Bill licked his lips and gazed over to the fencepost Max and Nigel had prepared with molasses. "That's easy!" he whinnied with excitement and proceeded to gallop out the gate toward the sticky, sweet post.

"You can lead a horse tuh molasses," MizP drawled sarcastically, "but he'll chew it all on his own."

"A day is lost if one has not laughed," Liz observed with a giggle, climbing onto MizP's back. "Shall we be going, *mon amie?*"

Just then Jack Poindexter came walking toward the barn, seeing what had happened with Bill. He started running in Bill's direction, shouting, "That crazy stump sucker!"

"Time tuh beeline it tuh Hanover Tavern!" neighed MizP. With that, she galloped out the gate.

———

Patrick bit into an apple as he sat outside reading on the front porch of Hanover Tavern. He was holding the apple in his mouth and turning the page when he heard the clip-clop of an approaching horse. He looked up to see MizP heading his way. Liz had jumped off before they got within view. Patrick tucked the book under his arm and walked down the steps with a puzzled expression. MizP walked right up and stopped in front of Patrick, snorting a hello and sniffing the apple.

"MizP? What are you doing here?" Patrick wondered, looking around the horse for signs of Jack Poindexter.

"Get used tuh seeing me at your doorstep, Pahtrick," MizP neighed.

"Did you run off?" Patrick asked, patting the horse on her cheek. "I better get you back home."

MizP reached down for the apple and Patrick chuckled. "Alright, you can have the apple. Then I'll take you back home."

"There you are!" came Jack Poindexter's voice. He was riding Bill, who still licked his chops from the molasses smeared around his lips.

"Hi, Mr. Poindexter! MizP just showed up here by herself. Did she get out of the gate?" Patrick asked.

"Yes, MizP and this stump sucker Bill both got out," Jack explained. "Although why she came here, I have no idea."

"Well, here she is," Patrick said, handing the reins to Jack.

"Sorry for the trouble, Pat," Jack said. "Thanks for getting my filly."

"No trouble at all!" Patrick assured him. "And she just had an apple, so you know."

"Maybe that's why she showed up at your doorstep," Jack said with a chuckle. He noticed the book under Patrick's arm and pointed. "What are you reading there?"

Patrick held up his book and smiled. "I've decided to study law, Mr. Poindexter. I've been reading this winter and plan to go to Williamsburg for my law license this spring."

Jack raised his eyebrows. "Well, I think you've settled on a fine path,

313

Pahtrick." He leaned over with a grin. "Has the stop been worth it?"

Patrick nodded. "Yes, sir. It has. It's helped me to figure things out."

"Glad to hear it. Keep up the good work," Jack said. "We'll be going now. Thank you, Pahtrick."

"Thank you, and see you later, Mr. Poindexter," Patrick called. "Bye, MizP!"

"Not for long," MizP whinnied.

Liz came walking by with her tail in the air and looked up at MizP. "Bravo, *mon amie.* We'll do this again in a couple of days, no?"

"Looking forward tuh it, Liz," MizP answered with a wink.

MARCH 31, 1760

Patrick Henry sat in the courtroom of Hanover Courthouse, gazing over at the images of the distant monarchs, proud to be a British subject and to live under the noble rule of British law. Liberty was a fundamental right for British citizens, as was the due process of law. Hanover County was founded and named for King George I of Great Britain, who was also the Electorate of Hanover, his birthplace in Germany. As the namesake county of the British Sovereign, Hanover Courthouse proudly displayed portraits of King George I and King George II, copies of royal paintings made by some emerging American colonial painter.

Patrick watched his lawyer friend John Lewis examining a witness for a case, taking note of every detail and manner of procedure. Every legal document was read aloud for all to hear, so even the illiterate could understand and respond appropriately to the proceedings of the law with witnesses present. But Patrick equally studied the jurors and their non-verbal behavior, watching their emotional responses to the lawyers' arguments.

John Henry was the judge presiding over the court today. Patrick sat in back and watched his father rule in favor of John Lewis's client. *I wonder how father would handle me as one of his courtroom attorneys.*

Patrick stood and made his way to the door of the courthouse to wait outside for John Lewis, who had prepared a certificate of recommendation signed by all the justices serving Hanover Courthouse. Patrick would need to present this certificate to the four men in Williamsburg who were the chosen examiners for the colony of Virginia: George

Wythe, Robert Carter Nicholas, John Randolph, and his brother Peyton Randolph. Such a recommendation would show that Patrick was a valid candidate worth taking the valuable time of the most distinguished lawyers in Virginia.

"Congratulations, John. You were excellent in there," Patrick told him, pointing back to the courthouse.

"Thank you, Pat. I hope you were able to glean an insight or two to apply to your study," John Lewis replied. He reached into his satchel and pulled out the promised certificate. He handed it to Patrick. "When you go to see the examiners, present this certificate. Remember, you don't have to face all four men at once, and you only need two of them to sign your law license."

Patrick took the certificate in hand. "I'm grateful, John. Whom would you recommend I see first?"

"Definitely go to see George Wythe first, and use my personal connections to open your conversation," John answered. "Give him my regards and tell him of our friendship. Remember, Wythe started his law practice as the younger partner to my father, and he married my sister, Anne, God rest her soul. When Anne died in childbirth, he later remarried and moved to Williamsburg, but our family history will open the door for you. Wythe was also self-taught, just as you are, even though he did have an apprenticeship. He will likely give you the most sympathetic ear."

"That sounds like a solid plan. Thank you for your recommendations and your help," Patrick said. "Anything else I should know?"

"Besides the full scope of the law?" John teased, drawing a pained expression from Patrick, who still knew very little. "You have the gift of persuasion, so use it to win your case for being admitted to the bar even though you haven't been formally trained or served as an apprentice. And since you've never been to a big city like Williamsburg before, you should at least know the law when it comes to riding horses in town."

"There is a law for riding in cities?" Patrick asked, realizing how little specific law he truly knew.

John Lewis nodded. "Those who are caught riding a horse or driving a carriage faster than a man can walk are fined a day's wages of five shillings. Those unable to pay the fine are given ten lashes at the whipping post."

Patrick's eyes widened. "You mean I could get *fined* for speeding through Williamsburg on a horse?"

315

John chuckled and put his hand on Patrick's shoulder. "Aye, so be careful!" He then looked intently into the young man's face and pointed to the certificate in Patrick's hand. "You take that certificate to Williamsburg and bring back a signed law license. I know you can do it, Patrick."

"Thank you, my friend," Patrick replied. "I'll do my best."

"Very well. Give my best to Mr. Wythe," John replied. He nodded and touched his hat before turning to walk away. "Godspeed, but no speeding in Williamsburg!"

"I can guarantee that," Patrick called after him. Then, muttering under his breath, he added, "I don't know if I'll even *make it* to Williamsburg on my old horse. I'll likely enter the city on foot."

As Patrick started walking across the street to Hanover Tavern, he saw Jack Poindexter slowly riding Bill toward him. He waved, and Jack pointed to the front of the tavern. There stood MizP, once again escaped from his farm. Patrick shook his head and hurried over to grab the wayward horse's reins.

"Good day, Mr. Poindexter. Here she is again!" Patrick exclaimed. "How many times does that make now?"

"Seven," Jack said as he got down off his horse.

Liz sat on the front porch grinning, her tail curling slowly up and down. "But of course it does."

Gillamon's words echoed in Patrick's mind. *Seven means complete.* "I'm sorry about this, Mr. Poindexter. I'll stop feeding her apples if that will help." He reached out to hand the reins to Jack.

Jack crossed his arms and cocked his head to the side with a grin. "I'm afraid that won't do, Pahtrick. What kind of horse owner would I be to deprive MizP of her favorite Henry apples?" He took a step forward and pushed Patrick's outstretched hand holding the reins back toward his chest. "Besides, it is clear she wants to be here. I think MizP is sweet on you."

"Sir?" Patrick asked, puzzled.

Jack smiled. "I'm giving MizP to you, Pahtrick."

Patrick shot a quick glance at the beautiful black mare. His jaw dropped, and he looked at Jack in disbelief. "But, sir . . ."

"You've given to everyone else who has struggled all these years," Jack insisted, interrupting the young man with an upraised hand. "It's *your* turn to receive, Pahtrick. You need a good horse if you're going to go get that law license in Williamsburg." He put his hand on MizP's shoulder and softly stroked her. "I know you'll take good care of my filly. You've always been sweet on MizP, too."

"Thank you, Mr. Poindexter. I don't know what to say," stammered Patrick with a broad smile, overwhelmed with gratitude.

"Say you'll be my lawyer if I ever need one," Jack teased with a wink.

Patrick's emotion caught in his throat. He smiled broadly and laughed with joy. "I give you my word, sir!"

"Done," Jack agreed, shaking Patrick's hand. He turned and climbed back into Bill's saddle. He leaned over with a grin and pointed to the young man. "Now if MizP turns back up at my farm, then that will be *your* affair."

"Understood! Thank you again, Mr. Poindexter. I'll be forever in your debt," stated Patrick with a hand raised in farewell. Jack turned, lifted his hand, and trotted off back to his farm.

Patrick put his hand on MizP's cheek and gently stroked her long nose. He looked at the tiny white star between her eyes and smiled. "Well, MizP, I hope you'll be happy with me. Let's go get you an apple." As he led her around back to the barn behind the tavern, he smiled and then asked, "Would you like to ride to Williamsburg tomorrow?"

MizP caught Liz's eye, smiled, and neighed, *"Do goats stink?"*

317

37

WITH A WYTHE
AND A PRAYER

APRIL 1, 1760

Patrick slipped his three law books into his saddle bag draped over MizP's back, and tightened the strap. "That about does it, MizP." He smiled and patted her on the back.

"Not quite, Mr. Henry," Sallie said from the doorway of their cabin behind Hanover Tavern. Patrick turned and saw her holding a fresh loaf of baked bread and cheese wrapped in a cloth in one hand, and a few small apples in her right hand. "Even lawyers have to stop and eat, as do their horses."

Patrick kissed her on the cheek as he took the food in hand. "I'm not a lawyer yet, Sallie."

She pressed her forehead against his and stared into his eyes. "You soon *will be*. I'm praying for you, my love. I know you will go to Williamsburg as simple Pat Henry, and return to Hanover as Patrick Henry, Esquire."

Patrick kissed her tenderly and nodded. "Then if Mrs. Henry so declares it, so be it." They shared a chuckle. "It will take me two days to travel the fifty miles to Williamsburg. I'll spend a day standing before the examiners, spend that night, and head for home the following day. Do you and the children have all you need while I am away?"

Patsey and John came out and he knelt down to give them big hugs. "Good-bye, my little ones."

"We'll be fine. Go, Mr. Henry," Sallie insisted with a smile. "You should stop in and see Mr. Jefferson while you are in Williamsburg."

Patrick nodded. "I will, Sallie." He packed the food and climbed up into MizP's saddle. He blew a kiss to his small family. "I'll see you in five days."

Sallie picked little John up and he waved his father off. "Bye-bye!"

Nigel leaned over and patted Cato on the neck where they sat on the branch of a nearby pine tree. "He's off, old boy. To Williamsburg!"

"As the eagle flies," Cato said, looping above Hanover Tavern. Cato's shadow passed over Patrick, as he and MizP galloped out of Hanover.

———

"MizP, you look a bit like Bill with all this brown mud on you," Patrick said, brushing off the horse's legs on their last stop before reaching Williamsburg. They had camped overnight in the woods, travelled through swollen creeks and ruddy roads, and were both splattered with mud. Patrick looked down at his coarse brown breeches and coat, and laughed at himself. "I look a bit like Bill, too." He brushed off the mud from his clothes the best he could and climbed back into the saddle. "Alright, let's get into town, but we'll take it nice and slow once we reach the city limits. I don't want to get fined."

"You're driving, Pahtrick," MizP whinnied.

319

Soon Patrick saw the cupola of the three-story building of the college of William and Mary and a surge of excitement ran through him. Never before had he been to a large city, and he couldn't wait to see the beautiful streets of Virginia's capital. As they entered the city from the west, they passed the college and saw some of the eighty enrolled students walking about the campus. Patrick wondered if he would see young Tom Jefferson, but decided he would wait to find him until after his examination. Tonight he would clean up, study, and rest to be ready for tomorrow.

Passing the college, Patrick smiled to see the broad, one-mile-long Duke of Gloucester Street spread out before them. Horses and carriages kicked up dust down the busy street, and pedestrians darted in and out of the flow of traffic to cross to the other side. Patrick now understood why limits were placed on the speed of horses, so as not to plow through so many people. At the other end of the sandy street was the elegant brick H-shaped Capitol building, and all along the thoroughfare were tidy homes spaced apart on half-acre lots. Gardens with emerging spring flowers, shrubs, and orchards separated the houses, not only making the city beautiful but also serving as protection against fire. Midway down the street was the Bruton Parish Church on his left, and the Palace Green, where a few sheep grazed and people met one another in the beautiful stretch of grass leading to the Governor's Palace. Located on the eastern side of Palace Green was a theater to entertain the crowds during "publick times" when the courts were in session and the city swelled to capacity. No doubt the play *Cato* had been performed here many times.

On Patrick's right began the Market District with shops, inns, coffeehouses, and taverns. The Magazine sat in the heart of the area and housed the armory of weapons and gunpowder needed to protect the town. Across the street was the Courthouse and the public stocks where law breakers were humiliated and punished for their crimes for all Williamsburg to see. But all was quiet at the moment. Although Williamsburg's approximately one thousand residents milled about in what felt to them like an abandoned town, to Patrick the city bustled like the busiest of Court Days back home in Hanover.

Patrick smiled when he saw the sign hanging over the print and book shop of *The Virginia Gazette*. Sallie's grandfather, William Parks, had founded this weekly paper, which served as the colony's news source and was the ninth paper established in America after those in Boston, Newport, New York, Philadelphia, Annapolis, and Charleston. It served the Virginia General Assembly, printing summaries of important acts, announcements, and proclamations from the royal governor. Although *The Virginia Gazette* carried local news, it was also the source all Virginians read for news from London and elsewhere abroad. He was pleased to see the place where the papers were printed and then sent all the way to Hanover to be read around the tables of Hanover Tavern.

Various inns and taverns gave Patrick options for staying overnight here in Williamsburg: Wetherburn's, The King's Arms, and Market Square, to name a few. But the most acclaimed of all was the white, wooden, and black-shuttered Raleigh Tavern, located near the Capitol. A bust of Sir Walter Raleigh above the entrance greeted guests and reminded them of how Virginia was named by the dashing Raleigh in honor of the virgin Queen Elizabeth I. The Raleigh was the social epicenter of Williamsburg, where the wealthiest and most fashionable of gentlemen gathered. Downstairs was the lively taproom for gathering and games, billiard room, and the elegant Apollo Room with its long dance hall and grand fireplace. Above the fireplace in gilt letters was inscribed, *Hilaritas Sapientiae et Bonae Vitae Proles*—"Jollity, the offspring of wisdom and good living." Upstairs travelers paid sixpence for usually cramped accommodations. Patrick knew he wouldn't fit in with the bewigged social elites, so after passing the Raleigh and viewing the majestic Capitol, he turned MizP to circle back down Duke of Gloucester Street to take his lodging at the modest Market Tavern.

Nigel and Cato kept a close eye on Patrick's movements, and once the young man had arranged for MizP to be kept in the barn behind the tavern, Cato descended to drop Nigel off. The little mouse would be following Patrick's examination closely tomorrow in order to be able to report back to Liz everything that took place.

"Welcome to Williamsburg, my dear! How do you like it so far?" Nigel asked MizP.

"It's a far cry from Hanover, and from the likes of the fancy big wigs I see strutting around town, it's a far cry from Pahtrick, too," MizP replied. "If he tries tuh present himself looking like he's been sleeping in a pig pen with those muddy clothes, I doubt he'll impress those lawyers."

"Oh dear," Nigel worried. "He's never been one to care about his appearance."

MizP snorted and shook her head. "Well, he best start caring tomorrow if he wants tuh be taken seriously as an aspiring lawyer."

321

The incessant sound of the ticking clock in the study of George Wythe only added to Patrick's nerves. He had not slept much the night before, cramming in as much reading by dim candlelight as he could before attempting to sleep in the same room as another boarder who snored loud enough to shake the walls of the tavern. Patrick rose early to walk across the street along Palace Green to a handsome two-story brick home located just north of Bruton Parish Church. Patrick Henry took a deep breath as he looked up at the imposing house with its two chimneys. He then walked up the central brick steps and used the brass door knocker. A servant soon opened the door. He introduced himself, handing over his certificate of recommendation. The servant invited Patrick in and led him to wait in Mr. Wythe's study. Meanwhile, Nigel slipped in the open door unnoticed.

Patrick looked around the small study at the many scientific tools and law books that filled the desk, table, and shelves. He imagined

Patsey and John trying to pick up everything they saw in this room. But absent were children who could wreak havoc there. While George Wythe was only ten years older than Patrick, he and his wife had no children, having lost their only child in infancy. Wythe threw himself into law, learning, and serving in the House of Burgesses.

Nigel gave Patrick a good looking over and saw that his coarse clothes were wrinkled with some mud still evident on the back of his coat. His shoes were covered in a film of mud. His wig was unkempt, and his tricorn hat well worn. He had attempted to clean himself off, but MizP was right. Patrick would have a hard time making a good first impression with the well-groomed men he would face today. *Oh, dear.*

Soon Patrick heard footsteps creaking down the large wooden stairs, followed by footsteps walking through the hardwood foyer. Patrick's heart started beating fast and he wiped his sweaty palms on his breeches. He stood to his feet and soon there appeared at the doorway a kind, short man with an unusually round head and smiling blue eyes. Mr. Wythe was dressed in a fine burgundy-colored silk coat and weskit, or vest, with gold buttons, black breeches, a crisp white ruffled shirt, and shiny black shoes with gold buckles. He was clean, fresh, and dressed to perfection—a stark contrast to the young applicant who waited in his study.

"Good morning, Mr. Henry," Mr. Wythe greeted Patrick with the most gracious bow he had ever seen. "I'm pleased to make your acquaintance. I've read your certificate of recommendation." He returned the certificate back to Patrick, and tried to stifle a frown at the sight of the unkempt backwoods young man who stood before him.

"Good day, Mr. Wythe. It is an honor, sir," Patrick stuttered with a nervous bow. "Mr. John Lewis sends his warmest regards. And he recommended that I seek an audience with you first for my examination."

"Ah, yes, my brother-in-law, John. A good man, and a fine lawyer," Wythe commented, walking to his desk, where he took his seat and motioned for Patrick to do the same in the chair opposite him. He fumbled with some papers in his desk and took out a parchment document, an unsigned formal law license. "Here we are," he said, holding up the unsigned document. "I assume you know the procedure for securing a law license in the colony of Virginia. There is no written examination, only an oral interview to be given by myself and my three colleagues, but only two signatures are required for this license to be valid."

"I understand, sir," Patrick replied.

"Now then, tell me, where have you studied in preparation for this examination? Did you attend law school in London at The Inner Temple or Gray's Inn?" Wythe asked, folding his hands on his desk with an expectant smile. "Both are fine schools where Peyton and John Randolph attended."

Patrick hesitated a moment before answering. He cleared his throat. "Those are indeed fine schools, and I would have been quite fortunate to attend either one of them, but I did not go to law school."

"I see. Well, I have not seen your name on the rolls of William and Mary where I serve as a burgess. Might you have attended college up north at Harvard, perhaps?" Wythe asked hopefully.

"No, sir, no college," Patrick answered. "But my father, Judge John Henry in Hanover, was a graduate from Kings College in Aberdeen, and saw to my education."

Wythe tapped his finger subconsciously on the back of his hand. "No law school, nor formal college training, either. Where have you apprenticed then?"

"Nowhere formally, but I've spent a great deal of time conversing with attorneys who practice at Hanover Courthouse," Patrick explained.

A glimmer of hope appeared in Wythe's face. "Ah, so you are industrious to seek out legal experts. Good, good. I assume you assist them with their paperwork and trials on Court Days."

"Well, I do attend trials when I can, but mainly I talk with them when they come over to Hanover Tavern," Patrick answered.

"Come *over* to Hanover Tavern?" Wythe asked him.

Nigel put his paw up to his mouth, feeling the anxiety in the air. *This will not go over well.*

"Yes, sir, where I live with my family, and help my father-in-law, Mr. John Shelton, who owns the tavern," Patrick honestly explained. He was completely transparent about who he was.

Wythe sat back in his chair and folded his arms across his chest, continuing to tap his finger. "So you *work* there? You are a barkeep?"

"I *volunteer* there, sir. I have a farm nearby, as well as a merchant store," Patrick explained. "You see, my crops have failed to make ends meet, and my store will likely close soon as well," Patrick continued to explain honestly. "Our house burned down, and my father-in-law took us in during this difficult time."

"So you thought you would just try being a lawyer, is that it?" Wythe asked sarcastically and with an expression of disdain.

"Yes, sir," Patrick replied eagerly. "I'm fascinated by the law."

Wythe tapped his finger on his elbow and breathed in slowly through his nostrils, letting out his breath in the same manner. "So you have no formal schooling and you haven't apprenticed with a law practice. How exactly *have* you prepared for this examination today?"

"I've spent the winter reading *Coke upon Littleton*, *Digest of the Virginia Acts,* and *Trials per Pais."*

"The *winter?"* Wythe asked, leaning forward over his desk and wearing a look of disbelief. "Just *three* months?"

"Yes, sir," Patrick answered.

"And you wish to take your examination now, at the beginning of April?" Wythe asked, setting the law license back over on the stack of papers. "Is this some kind of April Fool's joke?"

Nigel planted his face in his palm and shook his head.

"Not at all, sir," Patrick answered back confidently. "I understand you were also self-taught, isn't that correct? You read law under your uncle in Prince George County, and passed the bar at the age of twenty?"

Nigel looked up, as did Wythe. Patrick had certainly done his homework.

"Yes, I did . . ." Wythe started to say.

"You evidently benefitted from the counsel of your *one* uncle," Patrick quickly inserted. "I have received individual counsel from no fewer than *thirty* attorneys, justices, and sheriffs, which has allowed me exposure to a broad spectrum of various points of view on numerous matters of the law. I have received the benefit of their counsel *and* their valuable time, which they saw worthwhile to invest as I embark on this quest into your profession." He leaned forward and smiled. "You were given the opportunity to practice under the excellent seniority of the distinguished attorney Zachary Lewis as you embarked on *your* law career. Mr. Lewis trusted you not only with his law practice, but with his *daughter.* Might I say what a sentinel compliment that is to your unwavering integrity? I have heard the high regard that he and others have for you, especially from Mr. Lewis's son, your brother-in-law, John. I am humbled that John has trusted *me* enough to sign the certificate of recommendation that validates the benefit of taking up *your* valuable time as well."

Nigel's jaw hung open. Patrick had spilled out his 'case' to be heard by Mr. Wythe, and by the looks of the distinguished attorney he was now ready to look beyond Patrick's physical appearance and his lack of education and training. Wythe sat there still, listening intently.

Patrick pointed to Mr. Wythe's finger. "It would appear you have decided to listen, as you are no longer tapping your finger. I've noticed that jurors who are either disinterested or frustrated by the arguments of the attorneys in court tap their fingers incessantly. Those who especially wish to leave the courtroom tend to tap their fingernails on the wood railing to make their frustration better known. If they simply inspect their fingernails, that indicates boredom or disinterest. Of course, they do not realize they are doing this at the time."

The ticking clock was the only sound in the room as Wythe sat there staring across the desk at this bold young man who had put him on the witness stand and cross-examined him about his career and current state of mind. Nigel looked from Wythe to Patrick and back to Wythe. Anticipation hung heavy in the air. Slowly a grin grew onto Wythe's face.

325

"You, Mr. Henry, have studied what transpires in the courtroom beyond the workings of the process of law," Wythe said. "Now let us see what you have learned from your three books in your wintertime reading. I will pose hypothetical case scenarios, and you will give me the primary position you would take, first as prosecuting attorney for the plaintiff and then as defense attorney for the accused."

Wythe spent the next hour grilling Patrick on the formalities of courtroom law. Nigel squirmed as he watched Patrick make a feeble attempt at answering him. Wythe had to repeatedly correct him and point out where his argument was weak. Finally, Wythe put both hands on his desk and declared, "Mr. Henry, you have spent three months reading three law books and it *shows!* It would be futile and almost painful to examine you further on your knowledge of the law, for I know it will be woefully inadequate."

Patrick didn't move a muscle, but kept his determined gaze on Wythe.

"But, I see potential in you, both in the art of persuasion, which you clearly have, and in your ability to analyze your subjects," Wythe offered. "If you apply that skill in the law books—and I mean more than *Coke* and two others—you just may have the aptitude to make it as a lawyer."

Nigel stifled a hopeful cheer as he saw Wythe reach over and pick up the law license once more.

"I'm going to sign this, albeit reluctantly," Wythe said. "I have the benefit of three others who shall determine if this paper has any value at the end of the day."

"Thank you, Mr. Wythe! Thank you greatly for this opportunity," Patrick exclaimed as Wythe dipped his quill in the ink, signed the form, and placed his seal into the glob of wax he poured next to his signature.

Wythe stood and handed the law license to Patrick with a smile. "I wish you the best of luck, Mr. Henry." He then walked him to the study door and pointed to his servant, who stood by the front door, to see him out. "Please give my best to Mr. Lewis."

Patrick took the license and bowed humbly. "I shall, I shall. Thank you again, Mr. Wythe. Good day, sir." He walked briskly to the door, and Nigel scurried out the back door next to the study as another servant entered the house from the garden.

Once outside on Palace Green, Patrick allowed his enthusiasm to bubble out as he muttered, "Thank you, Lord!" and picked up his pace to walk down the street to the home of Robert Carter Nicholas. "I only need one more signature!"

Nigel followed Patrick to his next stop at the beautiful white two-story home belonging to the conservative, esteemed lawyer and burgess, Robert Carter Nicholas. He was the near neighbor of the royal governor. Bounding up the front steps with confidence, Patrick eagerly knocked on the door with a broad smile and proudly presented his certificate of recommendation *and* freshly inked law license to the servant to gain entry. But as he began his interview with the quiet thirty-two-year-old man, he soon realized that Nicholas would not be moved as easily as Wythe. Patrick's boldness actually served as a deterrent, and once the lawyer heard of the disheveled applicant's lack of schooling and brief preparation, he quickly dismissed him. Patrick's shoulders sank as he realized that his assumed ease of getting another signature was premature.

Patrick walked to the head of Palace Green and stood in front of the elegant Governor's Palace. He looked up at the imposing iron gate that bore the royal crest of the king of England, while a stone lion and a stone unicorn each sat atop the two brick gate piers, proud symbols of the British Empire. The three-story brick Palace was enclosed by a brick wall and flanked by two one-and-a-half-story wings and multiple outbuildings including the stable, carriage house, kitchen, laundry, and scullery. A lush garden spread out behind the palace with ornately designed and trimmed hedges and topiary plants, thousands of flowers, and an intricate maze. Paths filled with crushed oyster shells wended through the angled walkways and under vine-covered arbors down to the canal, graced with blooming lily pads. Delicate weeping willow branches kissed the water as swans glided across the surface. More than twenty servants buzzed around the palace grounds and buildings to keep the governor's homestead operating in perfect harmony.

Patrick had never seen anything like this. *I can't imagine living in a place this grand.* He thought back to the tiny cabin where his family lived behind the tavern. It wasn't even his. *I don't need a palace. I just need a place that is my own; one that my family can call 'home.' But I'll never have a home of my own if I don't succeed here in Williamsburg. God, help me, please.*

Patrick furrowed his brow, straightened his hat, and turned to walk south along Palace Green to Nicholson Street. His naive enthusiasm now was turned to fierce determination. He would next go see Peyton Randolph and, with God's help, he would gain his second signature and be done with this difficult business.

327

BARELY PASSING
THE BAR

WILLIAMSBURG, APRIL 3, 1760

Nigel struggled to keep up with Patrick as he walked briskly down Nicholson Street to the impressive home of Peyton Randolph located in Market Square at the intersection of North England Street. Sir John Randolph (the only colonial born in Virginia to be knighted), had willed the deep red wooden home to his son, Peyton, who had lived there since a child, and now resided with his wife. The expansive home overlooked the green fields behind the Courthouse, the busy market area, and the traffic coming and going on Duke of Gloucester Street. Peyton was appointed attorney general for the colony of Virginia, just as his father before him. A cousin of Thomas Jefferson, Peyton was highly respected in Williamsburg and the House of Burgesses for his exemplary service to the colony. Peyton's younger brother John lived on the south side of town, but Patrick hoped he would not have to even see John Randolph for the examination. If he could get Peyton to sign his law license, Patrick would be able to skip the fourth interview and call it a day.

Patrick walked right up to the house and knocked on the front door. When he didn't get an answer, he listened and heard several voices coming from the back side of the house. He walked around the corner where the numerous outbuildings buzzed with activity. Two female servants argued over some matter in the two-story brick kitchen. One of the horses was acting up in the stable, a wheel had broken on the carriage outside the coach house, and a servant boy had accidentally knocked over a bucket of fresh milk in the dairy. In the midst of all this chaos, the heavyset Peyton Randolph barked orders to bring some sanity back to each area of trouble. This was clearly not a good time for Patrick to approach Peyton Randolph about his law license.

Don't do it, old boy! Nigel thought as he watched Patrick walk right through the middle of the busyness in the Randolph household and up to the man who was trying to bring order to his chaotic morning.

"Samuel! Run down to the wheelwright and ask him to come address this loose fitting iron immediately! I paid him handsomely for this new wheel, and I expect him to fix it posthaste! I have business to attend to in Yorktown and need to leave as soon as possible," Peyton ranted. Turning to the kitchen, he chided, "Betsey, I do not *care* who was supposed to buy the flour; you go to the market and get it this instant! Mrs. Randolph is expecting company for afternoon tea, and she must have her biscuits on schedule." He took out his handkerchief and dabbed his cheeks and double chin. As he turned to walk to the stable, there stood Patrick Henry in his way.

"Good day, sir. I am Patrick Henry, from Hanover County," Patrick told him, holding out his certificates. "I've come to see you about my law examination. Mr. Wythe has already given me his signature and I was hoping . . ."

329

Peyton shut his eyes and held up both hands, his damp handkerchief flapping in the breeze. "Good sir, I implore you! Please, do not speak another word!" he insisted with an agitated voice. He took in a deep breath, regained his composure, and opened his eyes, taking a good look at the bedraggled young man whose appearance was a walking picture of how his morning was going. He placed his hand over his heart. "I do not wish to be rude, but as you can clearly see, I must attend to multiple, urgent matters around the house. I am bound for business out of town, and I cannot attend to this matter today."

Patrick's face fell. "I understand. I could come back tomorrow if you wish."

"No, young man, I will be unavailable then as well," Peyton answered, taking a step toward the stable where he heard the voices of men trying to settle the upset horse. He stopped, turned, and looked Patrick in the eye. "You say you have a signature from Mr. Wythe? What about Mr. Nicholas?"

Patrick tightened his lips and shook his head. "Mr. Nicholas declined."

Peyton Randolph put his plump hand on the young man's arm. "Then go to my brother John, and tell him I said to see you today. I am sorry, but that is the best I can do. I wish you success. Please excuse me, as I have another urgent matter to address. Good day." With that, he quickly bowed, turned, and left Patrick standing alone in his courtyard while he walked into the stable.

Patrick blew a raspberry and left the chaotic house to walk toward the south side of Williamsburg. He had one more chance for a signature today. He couldn't afford to stay another night or two at the tavern, and he felt that coming back to see Peyton Randolph any time soon would be a mistake.

Well, Mr. John Randolph, it is now up to you, Patrick thought. *And I do not plan to take 'no' for an answer.*

———

Cato had followed Patrick and the tiny mouse scurrying along behind him, but Nigel was falling behind. Patrick was heading for the home of John Randolph, and had to pass the green behind the Courthouse, cross over Duke of Gloucester Street, pass the Magazine, and head down South England Street. Cato landed on the back side of the Magazine and called to Nigel, who turned and waved. Cato lifted off and scooped Nigel up gently in his talons.

"Thank you for the lift, old boy!" Nigel exclaimed. "I was getting rather winded from the jaunt to the next Randolph residence."

Cato landed in a tree above John Randolph's house and put Nigel on the branch. "So what happened? After all that time in the Wythe house, Patrick has zipped through the next two examiners. Does he have three signatures?"

"Only one, I'm afraid, from Mr. Wythe," Nigel reported. "Mr. Nicholas declined our Patrick, and Peyton Randolph is in the midst of putting out too many fires to bother with the aspirations of an unpolished, unknown country lad seeking a position at the bar. John Randolph is his last chance to get that law license signed today."

Cato frowned. "Then the human must cooperate. Patrick must have that signature!"

Nigel placed his paw on the eagle's wing. "Do not ruffle your feathers just yet, old chap. There is still hope. I must get down there and see what transpires. Please pick me up when we exit the house, and Cato, *pray.*" The little mouse scurried down the tree and the eagle remained in the branches, eagerly awaiting the outcome below.

Patrick stood at the front door belonging to John Randolph, Esquire, and whispered a silent prayer. *Lord, if you have called me to this, please, then help me accomplish it.*

A servant answered the door and Patrick mustered his most convincing smile and look of confidence. "Good day, my name is Patrick Henry. I have just come from the home of Mr. Peyton Randolph, who beckoned me to seek an audience immediately with his brother for my law examination. I have already met with Mr. Wythe who signed my license, followed by a meeting with Mr. Nicholas." He smiled and held up his certificate of recommendation and law license, but the servant curiously only took the certificate.

The servant smiled with her warm and comforting blue eyes. "Good day, Mr. Henry. Come in, and I will let Mr. Randolph know you are here." Patrick suddenly felt a faint sense of familiarity with this servant girl, as if he had met her before. Something about her eyes? She held open the door and took Patrick's hat. Nigel hid behind a column on the porch, and she caught his eye, nodding to the little mouse to come inside.

331

"By Jove, it's Clarie!" Nigel exclaimed happily under his breath. He saluted her and scurried inside as she shut the door.

Patrick stood in the foyer with his hands folded in front of him, looking around at the paintings adorning the walls, trying to appear interested. Inside, his stomach was churning. He could hear the servant speaking to John Randolph in his study.

"Excuse me, Mr. Randolph, but there is a Mr. Patrick Henry of Hanover County here to see you," Clarie explained. "He has just come from your brother's house with the request for you to please interview this young man for his law license. He has also met with and received a signature from Mr. Wythe. He comes highly recommended by the justices of Hanover." She proceeded to hand the certificate to John Randolph.

Nigel listened and wrinkled his brow. "Did she just say that Peyton signed his law license?" He shook his head and mumbled to himself as he repeated her words in his mind. He realized that she had not specifically said so, but it could be easily inferred that Peyton had already signed the license, along with Wythe.

Thirty-two-year-old John Randolph, one of the most well-educated attorneys in Virginia, lifted the certificate and gave it a cursory glance, nodding as he read the names of the Hanover justices. "He's just been seen by Peyton? Very well, please, send him in."

Clarie turned and went to the foyer. "Mr. Henry, please come in. Mr. Randolph will see you now."

Patrick smiled and entered the study of John Randolph. Clarie quickly shut the door as she left the room. She looked around and saw Nigel poke his head out from under the settee. She squatted down next to him. "Nigel, Patrick will need to fight for his life in there." She held up her finger. "Wait for it."

"What do you mean, coming in here looking like this?!" John Randolph roared from the other side of the door.

Nigel put his paws up to his mouth. "Oh, dear! MizP worried about Patrick's careless appearance."

"Sir, if you will please allow me a moment of your time," Patrick insisted.

"In order to serve the profession of law, one must uphold the *dignity* of the law. And one cannot do so if such little respect is paid to one's appearance," John continued, ignoring Patrick's pleas.

"I understand, sir, and I do not blame you for your admonishment of my travel-worn appearance," Patrick fired back. "Mr. Wythe was put off as well by my appearance, but he was able to set that aside as I explained my situation. Our time together ended well, with him affixing his signature on my license. Please, Mr. Randolph. I implore you to allow me this interview. Ask whatever you wish, and I shall answer you with the utmost respect in my voice, if not in my appearance. I assure you, I am no cunning Tom Bell or Bampfylde Moore Carew. And if I might be so bold to say so, Tom Bell fooled Williamsburg's most respected citizens with his fancy clothes and genteel manners. Yet he was not what he seemed to be, and made off with their money and possessions." Patrick held out his arms wide. "I may appear the opposite in finery of Tom Bell, but I assure you my motives and desire to become a respectable man of the law are sincere. Please, allow me to prove myself to you."

Nigel cupped his ear against the door. "He's thrown out the names of two notorious con artists, and is challenging Randolph to prove his character as true."

332

John sat back in his seat and rested his elbows on the arms of his chair, holding his chin with the tips of his fingers. He slowly shook his head as he studied Patrick. "Hmmm . . . Tom Bell. That scoundrel stole a watch belonging to a friend of my father. He stole *time,* Mr. Henry." He then leaned forward. "And you propose to do the same to *me* today. However, if my brother and Mr. Wythe saw fit to hear you out and signed your license, I suppose I should give you an audience, albeit brief. If anything, I am curious as to what they saw in you."

Nigel smiled and raised a fist of victory. "Huzzah, he's going to let Patrick stay! But he mistakenly believes that Patrick already has two signatures."

"Amazing how miscommunications like that can happen," Clarie replied with a coy grin. "But it's all up to Patrick now."

The interview was anything but brief. Over the course of the next few hours, John Randolph mercilessly grilled Patrick, first on municipal law, where he quickly discovered that Patrick clearly lacked knowledge. He moved to philosophy, the law of nature and of nations, policies of the feudal system, and finally to history, where a faint glimmer of hope shone on Patrick at this one area of strength in this interview. Patrick circled back to the topic of impostors and crimes, referencing Tom Bell and the notorious celebrity criminal Bampfylde Moore Carew, who had profited from his crimes by publishing his widely read memoirs in London. Patrick explained how, in ancient Rome, three impostors claiming to be Nero rose up following the Roman Emperor's strange and swift suicide in AD 68, leading to a discussion about the never-changing heart of man. "The clothes may change over the eons and across cultures, but man's depraved heart does not. Man's greed for money and power drives him to violate laws and norms of society to attain what he cannot possess by virtue of his own merit."

John Randolph grew more and more impressed with Patrick Henry and his ability to maintain a defensive posture for his opinions. He decided to lead him into a discussion of common law, but decided to be a con man himself, pretending to disagree with Patrick on an answer he gave that was absolutely correct. Patrick continued to object and defend his position, until finally John got to his feet.

"You defend your opinions well, sir," John Randolph told him with a frown and a gruff voice, "but now to the law and to the testimony. Follow me." He proceeded to open the door, and Nigel ran for cover

333

while Clarie stayed out of the way, pretending to arrange some flowers in a vase. Randolph led Patrick into his adjacent office library.

"Where are they going?" Nigel mouthed. Clarie shrugged her shoulders but tiptoed so she could stand just outside the room with Nigel.

Randolph opened the heavy, dark walnut paneled door into an elegant room that reeked with the prestige of this accomplished attorney. Patrick had just argued and defied the reasoning of one of the most respected attorneys in Virginia. An entire wall of this office was filled floor to ceiling with shelves stocked with law books. Patrick's jaw gaped as he looked up at the enormity of resources in print that covered every aspect of the law. He felt chagrined that he had thought his three books would be sufficient for him to prepare for this examination. He suddenly felt like a fool. Now John Randolph would with his expert knowledge destroy Patrick's pitiful attempts at argument. *How could I have been so foolish! What was I thinking?* He suddenly wanted to run out of Randolph's house and escape before he was humiliated. But he knew that humiliation would only follow him home to Hanover, where he would have to tell Sallie he had failed at his attempt to become a lawyer. The blood started draining from his face at the thought.

John Randolph lifted his ruffled-cuffed hand to the numerous law books and bellowed, "Behold the force of natural reason. You have never seen these books, nor this principle of the law . . ." he said as he opened a book to the matter Patrick had been defending. Patrick started to open his mouth to apologize, but John held up his hand to stop him. "Yet you are *right,* and I am wrong."

Patrick's face filled with surprise and his eyes widened. "Sir?"

A grin slowly grew on John's face. He bowed humbly. "And from the lesson which you have given me—you must excuse me for saying it," he said as he slowly looked up and down Patrick's ill-fitting, mud-splattered, country attire. He chuckled and shook his head. "I will never trust to appearances again."

Patrick was speechless as John Randolph pried the law license signed by George Wythe from his fingers. John chuckled as he walked back to his desk with Patrick following behind him in shock. With both hands John flipped back his coattails and took a seat. He dipped his fine feather quill in the ink and signed his name to the law license. As he held a stick of wax over a candle and placed a blob onto the parchment with his seal, he declared, "Mr. Henry, if your industry be only

334

half equal to your genius, I augur that you will do well, and become an ornament and an honor to your profession." He blew on the ink and furrowed his brow as he realized his was only the second signature on the license. He realized that he had assumed differently.

Patrick shook his head in shock and disbelief. John Randolph had just signed and sealed his law license, not dressed him down as he expected! He cleared his throat and fought to retain his composure. "Sir, I am most humbled and grateful. I promise to strive to indeed do honor to the profession of law. If I am able to become a fraction of the skilled attorney you are, I will have accomplished a great deal. Thank you for giving me this opportunity."

John Randolph stood and walked around his desk. He held the signed law license up in front of Patrick and once again steeled his expression before handing it over. "Since you were not able to study at the Inns of Court in London, I shall pass on to you the old saying given to up-and-coming lawyers there: 'A lawyer must have an iron head, a brazen face, and a leaden breech,'" John Randolph told him. He then smiled and handed over the license to Patrick. "Congratulations, Mr. Henry. You are now a licensed lawyer, approved by His Majesty and the Colony of Virginia."

Nigel exclaimed, "HUZZAH!" but quickly covered his mouth so he wouldn't be heard. He and Clarie exchanged excited glances of joy and she quickly moved to the front door, anticipating Patrick's departure. She cracked the door and Nigel slipped outside.

Patrick swallowed the lump in his throat and bowed before taking the license in hand. He held it up and smiled broadly. "Thank you, Mr. Randolph, for giving me this chance. I won't let you down, sir!"

"Very well. Good day, Mr. Henry," the famous lawyer replied, escorting Patrick to the door. "But it wouldn't hurt if you bought a new suit after you win your first few cases."

Patrick blushed and nodded as he put on his worn tricorn hat. "Good advice. Thank you again, sir."

With that, Patrick Henry walked out the front door, no longer the twice-failed merchant, failed farmer, and part-time barkeep. He would now go by a new title: Patrick Henry, Esquire, Attorney at Law.

THE POWER BEHIND
THE THRONE

HANOVER, APRIL 1761

G eorge is dead! George, the mighty, the just, the gentle, and the wise! King George, the father of Britain and her colonies, the guardian of laws and liberty, the protector of the oppressed, the arbiter of Europe, the terror of tyrants and France! George, the friend of man, the benefactor of millions, is no more! Millions tremble at the alarm. Britain expresses her sorrow in national groans. Europe re-echoes to the melancholy sound. The melancholy sound circulates far and wide. This remote American continent shares in the loyal sympathy." Patrick stopped reading and looked at Sallie, holding up the printed sermon:

"On the Death of King George"
Delivered at Princeton College, January 14, 1761
by Reverend Samuel Davies

"I wonder if Samuel knew he would die only a few short weeks after preaching this sermon." Patrick's mother Sarah had sent this sermon to Patrick, having stayed in touch with Reverend Davies after he left Hanover to go become president of Princeton College in New Jersey, requesting copies of his printed sermons. She had proudly written to their former pastor about Patrick's successful new law career, knowing he would be pleased to hear the happy news.

"Samuel was so young—only thirty-seven," Sallie answered sadly.

Patrick shook his head mournfully, and he stoked the fire as he and Sallie enjoyed a few quiet moments together before bed. "Although I was sad when he left Hanover, I was excited for the incredible honor he had been given to lead at Princeton. But I never dreamed we would lose him just eighteen months later."

"It comes as a shock to us all. He was a big part of our lives growing up, but I know Samuel had an especially big impact on you personally, Pat," Sallie replied with a sympathetic smile. "Didn't your mother make you recite his sermons on the way home from church?"

Patrick smiled fondly as he remembered those days. "Yes, she did. I'll never forget the very first sermon I 're-preached' on the way home." He cleared his throat and held up a hand in dramatic form. "Woe to you, oh land, when your king is a child. Empires have fallen, liberty has been chained, property has been invaded, the lives of men have been randomly taken away, and misery and despair have come in like a flood—when the government has been entrusted in the hands of child-ish tyranny!" He paced in front of the crackling hearth where Sallie sat eagerly listening to him as he tried to recall the words he had repeated on the way home from Polegreen. He looked up at the ceiling, as if replaying that day in his mind. He closed his eyes and thought back to the scene as he drove his mother and sisters home in the carriage. He opened his eyes and slowly allowed his voice to grow in urgency. "Sometimes the desires of foreign countries or even of tyrants in our own land may threaten our liberties, like a cannon aimed and ready to fire against the church of God while every believing heart trembles in fear." He paused and held his arms out wide. "But the Lord reigns! Let the earth, and let the Church, rejoice!" Patrick then balled his fist and leaned over to give Sallie an assertive nod. "He will overrule the revolutions of the world for her good; and the united powers of Earth and hell shall not prevail against her!"

Sallie lifted her eyebrows in surprised delight that he could remember something from so long ago. "Amen, Mr. Henry!" she exclaimed, clapping her hands. "You are quite a powerful speaker, sir. No wonder you have won so many cases in your first year. Perhaps you should be a circuit-riding lawyer *and* parson. MizP could take you to the churches as well as to the courthouses!"

Patrick wore a sad smile as he took a seat to gaze at the fire's dancing flames. Liz jumped up in his lap and he slowly stroked her fur. "Samuel Davies taught me what an orator should be."

"But I pray he was not a prophet in that sermon," Sallie said, drawing

337

a curious look from Patrick. "Our new King George is not much older than a child. He is only *twenty-two* years old, Pat. Yet he commands the most powerful nation on Earth."

"Time will tell, Sallie. We will see what the real power is behind the throne as his advisers instruct him," Patrick replied. "For now, British subjects are to mourn King George II before celebrating King George III with a royal wedding and a coronation." He lifted Davies's sermon, wrinkling his brow. "I'm actually more concerned over what dead King George did with one of the final decisions of his reign. Samuel Davies spoke too kindly about our departed King George on one point."

"What point is that?" Sallie asked in surprise to hear Patrick talk this way.

Patrick lifted the sermon to read the opening words. "King George, the father of Britain and her colonies, *the guardian of laws and liberty.*" He shook his head and set the sermon down on the side table. "Before he died, the king struck down the temporary Two Penny Acts passed by our Virginia House of Burgesses to help the people struggling from the tobacco droughts."

"People like *us,* you mean," Sallie added, "when tobacco was all we had to support ourselves."

Patrick frowned and nodded, looking at his hands that were no longer dirty and rough from working in his failing tobacco fields. His law practice had quickly grown to seventy clients with one hundred seventy-six cases in his first eight months alone. He wasn't rich yet by any means, but at least he was starting to get back on his feet. Half of his clients owed him money, as all Virginia struggled from the recent hard years for the tobacco growers. It would take time for him to make enough money to even buy a house for his family and to move away from Hanover Tavern. So for now, the sign hanging from the front of the tavern advertised his resident office: "Patrick Henry, Attorney at Law."

Patrick well understood the endless toil farmers currently faced in their fields for such little tobacco and income. Yet they were still required by law to pay their share of the 16,000 pounds of tobacco due to each parson, normally worth two pennies per pound. Parsons were not paid in physical tobacco, but in paper receipts for tobacco that had been delivered to the warehouses of Virginia for shipment to Great Britain. Because of the poor tobacco crops in 1755 and 1758, the price of tobacco had tripled to six pennies per pound. The Virginia House of Burgesses knew the struggling farmers needed help, so they passed the temporary Two Penny Acts so the people would only have to pay the parsons the usual average amount of two pennies, and they could pay with coin rather than in tobacco. The parsons would receive what they normally did each year, so they wouldn't lose their regular income. But the parsons weren't satisfied with that. They wanted to be paid the extra amount from the tripled price of tobacco. They wanted more money, despite the fact that it would come out of the pockets of their toiling parishioners.

"The Virginia parsons went over the heads of Governor Fauquier and our lawmakers all the way to London to claim that these temporary relief laws were an attack on the church. The bishop of London actually called the laws *treasonous!* They asked that the laws be made null and void from inception so they could get the money owed them, all at the expense of their parishioners. The king *did* strike down the law, but it is unclear if the law was made void from the date it was passed in Virginia, or from the date the king's royal quill declared it so in London," Patrick explained. "If void from its passing, the parsons can sue to get the extra money they seek. If void from the date in London, the parsons wouldn't be owed the extra money since the temporary law had expired by then. Battles are coming in the courts to determine the answer to that timing question: When were the Two Penny Acts made void?"

Liz studied the passion rising in Patrick's voice, realizing how the people had lost their voice in this battle with the king. They needed someone to speak up for them.

Patrick clenched his jaw. "Part of me is glad that Samuel Davies isn't here to see the ugliness happening in Virginia. The parsons and the Burgesses are fighting each other with words in pamphlets and newspapers, and now the parsons are starting to file lawsuits to get the precious back pay 'owed' to them after the king's ruling. Can you imagine, Sallie? Parsons suing their *own* people for money?! Samuel's heart would be broken if he saw this madness."

"And his *voice* would no doubt be heard loud and clear as he preached against the despicable behavior of these parsons!" Sallie added angrily.

"But would he have preached against the despicable behavior of the *king?*" Patrick added, drawing a look of shock from Sallie. "How can a king 3,000 miles away understand what his struggling subjects need?

That's why his governor and burgesses are in place, to know what the people need, and to act in their best interest! People in crisis cannot wait for months on end to send a request and receive a reply from the king on certain matters. What the Virginia Assembly did was right and just and timely to meet the crisis. Yet the king listened to greedy parsons over his own representatives in government. The king shut his ears to what the people needed in their time of crisis." He waved off his bold comments. "Well, Samuel's voice is no longer here."

Liz looked up at Patrick and forcefully swished her tail, *"But* your *voice is here,* mon *Henry. Just* listen *to you!"*

A disturbing thought occurred to Sallie, and she held her hand up to her face. "Oh Pat, is your Uncle Patrick involved in this mess?"

Patrick rested his head back on the chair, closed his eyes, and breathed out a deep sigh as he stroked Liz. "Yes, Sallie. My uncle, the Reverend Patrick Henry, is in the middle of this war between the shepherds and their sheep. And my father, Colonel John Henry, is as well. He'll be a judge to hear any lawsuits brought by the parsons that come to Hanover Courthouse."

340

Liz's golden eyes glanced over at Patrick's fiery fiddle that seemed to glow from the reflection of the fire. *A Voice in the Court.* Liz's mind started to race with the next part of the riddle. For the first time in this entire mission, Liz could finally see a showdown where Patrick's voice might be heard as it never had been heard before, and in a way that could make all Virginia sit up and take notice. *He was being prepared for this coming legal battle his entire life!* Liz thought excitedly.

Patrick had heard the arguments between the Anglican parsons and the Dissenters in his own household, so understood the tensions between the parsons and the people. He had seen the battle of church and state as Davies and the Dissenters struggled with following the law while pursuing religious freedom. He had experienced the agony of tobacco farming and the financial hardships his fellow farmers faced. With his failed store and now booming law practice, he personally understood the plight of the people wracked with debt from the poor tobacco harvests. And Samuel Davies had been the one to teach Patrick Henry how to move crowds to action with his own voice, speaking the truth boldly and with courage when it needed to be said.

For the first time in its history, England had made a move that infringed on the rights of her crown jewel, the colony of Virginia. Never before had Virginia seen the king declare one of its laws void from inception as the parsons so claimed. And if England stomped on Virginia's right to pass laws for the good of its people, this could lead to the early hallmarks of a revolutionary response.

Although she didn't see exactly how just yet, Liz knew one thing for certain: The new king of England would soon be hearing a voice in the court three thousand miles away, and that voice would belong to Patrick Henry.

WESTMINSTER ABBEY, LONDON, SEPTEMBER 22, 1761

"'George, be a *king!*'" Al said in a high-pitched lady's voice, pointing a chicken leg at Clarie and Gillamon. "That's what his mum told him. Ye should hear the sort o' stuff she tells the lad now that he has the throne." Al swallowed another bite of the delicious food and spoke with a full mouth, spitting morsels as he relayed his latest "intelligence" gathered in the palace. "She told King George that he should make the people *always* do his will, since it be the right o' kings to have their own way." The orange cat tossed back the cleaned-off chicken bone, licked his greasy paws, and purred with delight as he peeked back into the picnic basket. "What's for dessert?"

Gillamon and Clarie looked at one another with frowns as Al dug into their basket for a sweet bite. They had joined the hundreds of other happy British subjects sitting in the balcony of the soaring cathedral who were gathered here to witness the joyous, historic moment: the coronation of King George III and Queen Charlotte. All London buzzed with excitement, anticipating this grand event. Such was the clamor to get to Westminster Abbey this morning that carriages collided in the streets of London. People poured into the hall bringing baskets of food and wine they had brought to celebrate in Westminster Hall following the coronation. Al decided that "dining a-la-coronation was in order," so had already dived into Mr. Gillamon and Lady Clarie's bounty.

"Well, if he follows his mum's advice, King George III will be more interested in listening to those who tell him what he wants to *hear*, rather than what he needs to *know*," Clarie said.

"For lack of guidance a nation falls, but many advisers make victory sure," Gillamon said, quoting from Proverbs.

341

Clarie and Gillamon gazed over the railing as King George III sat in the coronation chair while the Archbishop of Canterbury, senior cleric in the Church of England, placed the golden crown of jewels on his head. Three cheers erupted from the people, exclaiming, "God save the King!"

Immediately trumpeters sounded their fanfare and the church bells rang out across the city while shots that were fired as salutes echoed off the stone walls of the Tower of London and filled the trees of Hyde Park with smoke. After a moment the archbishop raised his hands and offered a prayer over the king:

"God crown you with a crown of glory and righteousness, that having a right faith and manifold fruit of good works, you may obtain the crown of an everlasting kingdom by the gift of him whose kingdom endureth forever. Amen."

Suddenly the soaring music of George F. Handel's coronation anthem filled Westminster Abbey:

342

Zadok the Priest, and Nathan the Prophet anointed Solomon King.
And all the people rejoiced, and said:
God save the King! Long live the King!

Gillamon stroked his white goatee as he studied the group of men surrounding the king, all dressed in the finery of his royal court. "Time will tell if *this* king will listen to prophets or puppets who advise him of things to come with the colonies."

"I wonder who will be the true power behind the throne," Clarie added.

Al joined Clarie and Gillamon at the railing as King George removed his crown to take communion. When the king set down his crown, they saw the unmistakable shimmer of a jewel fall out of his crown and land on the royal blue rug behind the throne.

Al pointed at the lost jewel with a cookie. "I'm no prophet, but seems to me if this king don't keep his jewels glued to his crown, no tellin' what else he'll lose on his throne next."

Two Pennies for Your Thoughts

HANOVER TAVERN, NOVEMBER 5, 1763

MizP yawned wide and rigorously shook her black mane. "Well, I for one am *glad* to stay put tuhday. Pahtrick has kept me running across six counties for three years, lawyering in the courts and hunting all along the way. Sometimes we'll ride a hundred miles so Pahtrick can attend tuh a case. That young man simply will not stop for *anything.*"

"Ye mean ta tell me the lad *hunts* on his way ta court?" Max asked with a big grin.

MizP gave an exaggerated nod. "I've seen him walk right intuh court carrying his gun and still dressed in his grimy hunting clothes, leaving his fresh prize draped over my back until he could clean it for supper. But he is always ready tuh get right up and speak for his clients, not missing a beat. Still, I think he could look more presentable in the courtroom."

"That's a wee bit surprisin' but huntin' do sound like somethin' the lad might do," Max said. "He still loves his gun."

"You're getting this straight from the horse's mouth, so of *course* it's true," the black horse replied with a snort.

Max and Liz were sitting in the barn behind Hanover Tavern, getting caught up with MizP and her travels with Patrick Henry. Nigel was across the street in Hanover Courthouse, there to see and report back on the parson's case filed by Reverend James Maury. Patrick made sure to be home that day in order to sit in on the case. His friend John Lewis was defending the two Louisa vestry parish collectors, Thomas Johnson and Tarleton Brown, whom Maury was suing for back pay from the controversial Two Penny Act. Colonel John Henry was the presiding judge for the case, which would no doubt be a sentinel event here in Hanover County.

"I know you are tired, *mon amie,*" Liz told MizP. "Patrick has handled 1,185 cases over the past three years, so of course this pace has been very difficult, no? But I am so very glad you are his horse. He never could have done this work without you."

"Well, I'm sweet on Pahtrick so I'm glad tuh carry him where he needs tuh go," MizP answered with a grin. "Besides, Pahtrick has another baby tuh feed since little William was born, so he has tuh do double duty with providing for his family."

"That's an awful lot of cases, Liz!" Max exclaimed. "He must be an important lawyer by now."

"*Oui,* but his cases have all been quite small," Liz answered. "Patrick has never had to prepare for an important case with many people present. Certainly, nothing like what is happening across the street today. But I *know* it is time for him to do so. I am convinced that the next part of the fiddle's riddle has to do with Patrick using his voice across the street in Hanover Courthouse, but I do not yet know when or how. Something tells me it has to do with this Two Penny Act business. No one is as passionate or can understand this case better than *mon* Henry."

Nigel entered the barn, shaking his fist and talking a mile a minute. "A defeat! A resounding defeat for the poor souls in that malicious Maury's parish! Blast it all, for the first time the crown has squashed the people of Virginia, and John Henry of all people was the one who allowed it to happen!"

Liz furrowed her brow and placed her paw on Nigel's small frame. "Steady, Nigel. Calm down and please tell us what happened."

"I'm terribly sorry for my outburst, my dear, but this case is quite upsetting." Nigel took a deep breath and preened his whiskers to regain his composure. "Right. King's Attorney Peter Lyons represented Reverend Maury, and John Lewis defended Johnson and Brown against the claim that they must collect additional money from the parishioners to give Maury his 'fair' back pay. Lewis argued that his clients had paid Maury all that was due him under the Two Penny Act. Lyons *objected* and argued that the Act was void from the *beginning,* like the parsons are arguing in other cases." The little mouse put a paw to his forehead and shook his head. "John Henry and the justices then did the unthinkable! They *upheld* Lyons' argument. John Henry is therefore the first judge in Virginia to declare the Two Penny Act void from *inception*! Ergo, Maury will now be able to get his precious extra money!"

Liz put her paw up to her mouth. "This is shocking! I cannot believe it, Nigel! What is to happen next?"

"Judge Henry ordered a jury hearing for December 1 to determine how much money Maury will receive," Nigel explained. "John Lewis is withdrawing from the case, as it is hopeless to argue any further defense. This means that not only has Maury won his case, but all the other parsons out there will have a precedent to win their cases! This will be intolerable for the people of Virginia!"

"Those parsons are now armed tuh the teeth with reason tuh dip their hands in the pockets of their struggling parishioners," MizP whinnied.

"Maybe Patr-r-rick should have been the laddies' lawyer today," Max suggested with a scowl.

"Indeed, old boy. By the way Patrick was frowning and clenching his jaw during the case, I believe he was perhaps angrier than anyone else there," Nigel replied. "He walked with John Lewis back here to the tavern, and they're inside talking about the case now."

Liz's tail swished back and forth as she thought this through. "Did you say that John Lewis is giving up the case? He will therefore *not* be representing Johnson and Brown at the pending hearing?"

"Sadly, not," Nigel answered with a frown. "Johnson and Brown must go it alone and simply abide by what the jury decides in damages for Maury in December."

"*Au contraire,*" Liz answered as she got up and walked to the entrance of the tavern. "They shall not be alone. They will have a voice in the court, if I have my two cents' worth to say about it."

Patrick Henry and John Lewis sat together in a high-backed, darkened corner booth of Hanover Tavern, oblivious to the clamor of other tavern patrons who were clanking mugs of ale, calling for their server, or talking loudly about the news of the day. Patrick leaned his elbows on the table and kept his firm gaze fixed on John, who went 'round and 'round on how things went in court.

Liz jumped up on the bench next to Patrick, but he ignored her. She was eye level with the table and peered over to notice a few pennies of change sitting there next to John's pewter mug.

"Pat, I'm telling you, your father has just changed everything with his ruling! The other pending parsons' cases are either stalled in the General Court, waiting to see what happens in our lower courts, or they have been ruled in favor of the parishes," John explained. "Once the jury decides and awards the amount due to Maury, there will be nothing to stop every other parson from filing suit and getting their 'just rewards.'"

"I understand and am just as upset as you, John. But why won't you stay with Johnson and Brown to see it through to the next step?" Patrick asked. "Johnson is a good man. I represented him for two small cases earlier this year, and think highly of him and his family."

"If I didn't have any influence in today's court ruling, I most certainly will have none for the damages hearing," John said, sitting back in his seat with a sigh. "Parsons will no doubt come from all over the colony to be there for that ruling, and the weight of their presence will smother any hope for whoever tries to prevent a generous award. Did you see your Uncle Patrick Henry sitting there staring smugly at your father during court? I know your father is a staunch Anglican and sympathizes on a personal level with this case. I just don't believe there is anything more I can do for Johnson and Brown."

346

Liz stood on her hind legs and reached her paw over to the coins. She slowly pulled two pennies over to the edge until they fell onto the bench next to Patrick.

Patrick mindlessly picked up the coins and put them back on the table. He noticed they were two pennies. He slid the coins back over to John and said, "May I put in my two pennies' worth?"

"We *are* discussing the Two Penny Act," John replied coyly. "Go ahead."

Patrick smiled and leaned in again, the glow from the lantern on the table illuminating the side of his face. "I think you are wrong, John. Maury chose to file suit in Hanover County rather than in his home county of Louisa. Why? I think he was trying to get away from the influences of Louisa County, where Johnson has local power and popularity and is repeatedly elected to the Virginia House of Burgesses. Since a tiny portion of his parish resides in Hanover County, Maury was entitled to have his court day here. And I think he *knew* my father would feel sympathy for and pressure from my uncle to get the court to rule in his favor. But I think he underestimated something far more powerful for the next hearing."

John leaned in close over the table. "I'm listening."

"Maury underestimated the *people* of Hanover who will serve on that jury," Patrick replied with a feisty grin. "It is no secret that Hanover is full of Dissenters and the New Light Presbyterians Maury and the other Anglican parsons look down upon. I think Maury believes he and the other parsons can hold sway over any jury with the backing of the king and now the backing of the court. But if the *people* truly understand what is at stake in this case, and how their freedoms have been trampled on by the church *and* the state, they will be inclined to render harsh judgment in Maury's case. Never underestimate the power of the people when their liberties are threatened."

John nodded slowly and he furrowed his brow. "I see your point, but the court has already decided the law in this case, Pat. *Nothing* more can be done about it. The only judgment left to make is for the jury to agree or not agree with the simple math that King's Attorney Peter Lyons will present—the difference between what Maury was paid and what he *should* have been paid. Maury was paid £133 under the Two Penny Act, but since that law is no longer considered valid, he should have been paid £400. Technically that means Maury should now be paid the difference of £267. That's the only thing the jury must decide. I think it will be an open and shut case."

347

Patrick frowned and let go an exasperated sigh. "I wish you would reconsider. *Technically,* nothing is ever completely open and shut. All you need is a sliver of a wedge to open the case up to other possible outcomes."

"*C'est vrai!*" Liz meowed. She once again rose to her feet and this time swatted the coins so they went flying off the table, barely missing Nigel, who had been sitting beneath the table to hear their conversation.

"Liz!" Patrick scolded her. He shooed her off the bench and reached down to the floor to pick up the two pennies. He placed them up on the table and slid them back over to John. "Forgive my cat. Sometimes she can be a bit too determined."

John smiled and put his fingers on the two pennies. "Sometimes that's just the kind of sliver of a wedge a case needs—being a bit too determined. Just like you were when I sent you riding off to Williamsburg with your certificate to get your law license after only studying for three months. And look at what you've been able to accomplish ever since. Very well, Patrick. I have reconsidered." He slid the coins back across the table to Patrick. "Here is *my* two pennies' worth. I'm turning the parson's case over to you. You can defend Johnson and Brown's interests against Maury."

Patrick's eyes widened, and he put his hand over his chest. "Me? No, no, no! They need someone with more experience. I've never spoken in front of a large courtroom or for a case of such importance. And I would only have three weeks to prepare. Besides, I would have to make the case before my *father* and *my uncle.*"

John gave him an impish grin. "You only studied three months for your law degree. Surely three weeks is enough time to prepare for one case. Besides, since you've represented Johnson before, you already know each other, so he will feel comfortable with you. You can do this, Pat. I know it. Yes, your father and uncle will be on one side of the case, but you and the people will be on the other." He leaned in close. "And as you said yourself, never underestimate the power of the people when their liberties are threatened."

348

Patrick picked up the two pennies and gripped them in his hand. He took in a deep breath and let it go. "This was not my intention in talking with you today."

But it was mine, Liz thought on the floor.

The door to the tavern opened and John saw Johnson and Brown step inside. He held up his hand and waved the men over. "Here are your clients now."

"Very well," Patrick replied, standing up to greet the men.

Liz walked over to Nigel and the little mouse preened his whiskers happily. "My dear, it was brilliant of you to inspire them with *your* two cents' worth, although it was purely a subliminal suggestion."

Liz giggled. *"Merci, mon ami.* I believe my Henry will be the perfect voice in the court, not just for Johnson and Brown, but for *all* Virginians. Now for the difficult part." She looked back at Patrick already engaged in a lively discussion with the men. "To prepare him to argue against the parson's cause."

―――――

Liz and Nigel sat on Patrick's desk scattered with law books, case documents, and tobacco receipt records. Patrick had read late into the night and fell asleep resting his head on his desk for a moment. He had been rereading a 1760 pamphlet by Virginia Burgess Richard Bland, primary author of the Two Penny Act. Entitled *A Letter to the Clergy of Virginia*, Bland argued that in times of emergency, "the safety of the people is the supreme law," and it was the right of the people to take whatever steps necessary for their welfare in times of crisis, despite the views of the king. This was the higher law and was a fundamental right of British subjects as set forth in the English Constitution.

A copy of John Locke's book *On Civil Government* lay open next to Patrick. Nigel adjusted his spectacles and peered over to read what Patrick had marked. "See here," Nigel whispered so as not to wake him, "Locke is *brilliant* in his views of the powers of government and the joint obligations of the ruler and the ruled. He states the 'inalienable right' of the people to resist tyranny and oppression. I believe our Patrick has found the arguments he needs to use when he goes to court."

"Oui, he knows the law and the arguments well. But his problem remains that he has no business to argue against the law, as it has already been decided by the court. Decided by his *father."*

349

"His father indeed. You bring up another piece of this unfolding courtroom drama, my pet. Aside from the case itself, there is the *personal* side of this matter. After failing at everything he has tried, this is perhaps Patrick's last chance to prove himself to his father as a lawyer." Nigel crossed his arms with a frown. "This will be a tense, complicated business. Patrick's job is to convince the jury to keep the damages paid to Maury as low as possible, and that is *it.* So that does not leave much room for him to shine or impress his father."

"A sliver of a wedge," Liz recalled, thinking about what Patrick had told John he needed to find a different outcome for the case. "If Patrick hopes to impress his father and influence the jury, he will to have to say some things that will be both uncomfortable in front of his Uncle Patrick Henry, and unpopular in front of the court."

"Not just unpopular, my dear, but *treasonous,"* Nigel added as he and Liz shared a look of concern. "This will take great courage and a verbal boldness Patrick has never used before."

"And the boldness he needs will not come from even the most brilliant legal minds, but from the Maker. I believe he needs reminders of things to inspire such boldness." The two pennies John had given Patrick were sitting next to his Bible. Liz walked across the desk to flip the pages to Jeremiah 15 and placed her paw on the passage. "Do you remember what the Maker told Jeremiah when he was afraid to speak?"

Nigel came over to read the passage and nodded. "Ah, yes. The Maker ensured Jeremiah that he would triumph over those bullies and be His spokesman, but only if he trusted in Him."

"Bullies." Suddenly an idea came to Liz. *C'est ça! Merci,* Nigel!" She kissed the little mouse on the head and jumped off the desk onto the floor. "I have to send our Scottish terrier on an errand."

"You're welcome, my dear, but for what I am not certain," Nigel replied, scratching his head. "Where are you sending Max?" he hoarsely shouted after her.

"To find some *Calendula officinalis*," she called back over her shoulder. "Scottish marigolds!"

Patrick was dreaming about the day he and Davies walked through his dust-choked tobacco fields.

"Are you saying that this drought will lead me to a miracle?"

Davies smiled and shrugged his shoulders. "Only the Lord knows what this drought will lead you to, Patrick. I do know it will teach you things you can't learn in any other way. You will gain wisdom, invaluable in ways you don't yet understand. God brought good from the droughts for Joseph and Elijah, so trust in His promise that He will also bring good to you, and take care of you in the meantime."

Davies started walking away from him in his dream and Patrick reached out his hand, begging him not to leave. *"Please, Samuel! Tell me what to say! I'm afraid to speak the words I know I must."* The dust from the tobacco fields filled his throat, causing him to choke. He struggled to speak. *"What if I fail?"*

Samuel Davies turned around and looked at Patrick. *"What if you fail? Fail to speak or fail not to speak, Patrick? You must decide which will keep you from your miracle."* The Presbyterian minister turned and walked away from Patrick and soon vanished from sight.

Patrick awoke with a start at the sounds of newborn William crying. He could hear Sallie getting up to take care of the baby. His heart raced and he had to remember where he was. He sat up and rubbed his eyes. The faint images of his dream left him with a bittersweet feeling of having seen his mentor and friend again.

"What a dream! I must have fallen asleep late last night," he said to himself, seeing the faintest ribbons of sunrise outside. He picked up the pamphlet he had been reading. "No offense, Mr. Bland." He stretched his arms out wide and yawned. He shook his head and looked around his desk. He gave a curious smile to see the two pennies sitting on top of his opened Bible. He leaned over and read the passage they marked, from Jeremiah 15:

> The LORD replied: "Stop this foolishness and talk some sense! Only if you return to trusting me will I let you continue as my spokesman. You are to influence them, not let them influence you! They will fight against you like a besieging army against a high city wall. But they will not conquer you, for I am with you to protect and deliver you, says the LORD. Yes, I will certainly deliver you from these wicked men and rescue you from their ruthless hands."

Fail to speak or fail not to speak. Patrick furrowed his brow at the difficult decision he needed to make. *I know I must trust you to help me speak, Lord, but do I dare call the parsons 'wicked'?*

Patrick picked up the two pennies and a grin slowly grew on his face. "Perhaps 'rapacious harpies' would sound better." His smile faded and he felt the blood drain from his face. "But not in front of Uncle Patrick."

351

CAUSE FOR THE PARSONS TO SMILE

DECEMBER 1, 1763

They're perfect, Max! *Merci!*" Liz exclaimed, kissing Max on the cheek as she looked over the bunch of Scottish marigolds in the barn.

"Ye're welcome, lass," Max replied, trying to spit the unpleasant taste from the flowers out of his mouth. "Now will ye tell me wha' in the name of Pete ye plan ta do with them?"

Nigel picked up a flower to smell the fragrance. "I second that request."

"They look tasty tuh me," MizP chimed in, "if you're taking suggestions."

"Since daisies are not currently in bloom, I needed for Max to find these instead," Liz replied, starting to tie two of the stems together. "If I am right, these will help Patrick find his voice in the court."

Max and Nigel looked at one another, wide-eyed, wondering if Liz had lost her mind. "Maybe the str-r-ress of these past thr-r-ree weeks has been too much for the lass," Max whispered to Nigel.

Liz finished tying the two stems together and held them up. "*Voila!* Now if you will excuse me, I need to find the girls." She picked up the flowers in her mouth and went running to the house.

MizP looked down at a very confused Max and Nigel and stomped her hoof into the dirt with a snort. "Let it play, boys. Let it play."

Patrick Henry was pacing back and forth, mumbling to himself while he tied his white silk cravat around his neck. He was clearly nervous, as he kept messing up his knot and had to start over. When he pulled it off for the second time, he heard a soft knock at the door. He turned, and there stood his eight-year-old daughter, smiling with her hands behind her back.

"Patsey," Patrick said, smiling back.

"I have something for you, Papa," she said.

"You do?" Patrick answered, leaving his untied cravat around his neck and coming over to bend down and look into the cherublike face of his little girl. "What is it?"

"Close your eyes," instructed Patsey. Patrick instantly obeyed. From behind her back she pulled a laurel of marigolds she placed over his head. "You can open your eyes now."

The twenty-seven-year-old father opened his eyes and saw the Scottish marigolds his daughter had tied together for him. He wrinkled his brow, followed by a smile. "Why, thank you, little girl. It's beautiful. What's this for?"

353

"Mama said you have a hard day ahead in court, so we need to encourage and pray for you to help you win. She told me she once made you a daisy chain laurel to give you after you won a race," Patsey explained. "These aren't daisies, but I thought I'd make you a marigold laurel to give you *before* your big case today, since I know you'll win."

Patrick felt a lump in his throat at the loving gesture from his daughter and the sweet memory of the St. Andrew's Day race so very long ago. He cupped Patsey's cheek with his hand. "Thank you, Patsey. This means so much to me." He kissed her on the forehead. "But Mama gave me her laurel after I *didn't* win that race."

"But you stuck up for the little boy and did the right thing, even though the bully crossed the finish line," Patsey argued. "What could be a better way to win than doing the right thing?" The little girl kissed her father on the cheek and turned to go help with breakfast, leaving Patrick standing there speechless.

Liz wiped away a tear of joy as she watched this moment.

Sallie appeared in the doorway, holding baby William. She smiled and gently touched the marigold laurel around Patrick's neck. "I think our daughter just may follow in your footsteps, Mr. Henry. She made quite the argument for what it means to truly win. And I happen to agree with her. No matter what happens in court today, you know where we stand, my love."

"More importantly, she is following in *your* footsteps, Mrs. Henry." Patrick kissed Sallie and put his hand tenderly on baby William's small head. "Thank you, Sallie. Just knowing my family supports me will give me the strength I need, no matter what comes."

"Are you ready to go up against Thomas Jefferson's tutor?" Sallie asked.

Patrick winced. "Knowing Reverend Maury prepared Tom for William and Mary only adds to the pressure I feel having to come against the parson. I'm sure he is a fine man in many respects, and I realize he has eleven children to provide for. Part of me struggles with knowing all of this about Maury, but I must keep my focus on his behavior over this Two Penny Act business."

"And you *will* keep your focus, Pat, although not if you wear this into court today," Sallie reminded him with a smile, lifting the marigolds.

354

"I won't wear it, but I will certainly carry it with me," Patrick assured his wife, taking off the laurel and carefully placing it deep inside his large, buttoned coat pocket.

"I'll let Patsey know," Sallie promised, her dimples showing. "One thing is for certain about court today, Mr. Henry."

"What's that, Mrs. Henry?" Patrick inquired, fixing his cravat and putting on his coat before heading out the door.

Sallie winked. "This will be the nicest you've ever smelled in a courtroom."

Despite the early morning December chill in the air, the courtyard outside Hanover Courthouse was packed with people milling about who had poured in from the surrounding countryside. Farmers, merchants, and citizens from all other walks of life gathered in the usual festival-like atmosphere of Court Day, arriving on horseback, by carriage, or on foot. Some were dressed in their modest homespun clothes, while others donned the silk and satin finery of their wealthy station. As always, it was a melting pot of diverse Virginians, but this time they all had come for one common purpose—to see what would happen with the parson's cause.

There was, however, one group of people who *did* stand out in the crowd, and they were dressed exactly alike. Twenty black-robed and white be-wigged parsons gathered with heads together under the brick arches of the courthouse portico, speaking in hushed tones. They would occasionally turn and look at the crowd milling about, no doubt assessing who were potential jurors for Maury's case.

The people also occasionally turned and looked at the group of parsons, no doubt making comments about which parsons had traveled to be here, and about how much money Maury would get today. The court's decision in November had shocked the people of Virginia, and they knew it was the money in each man's pocket that was actually on trial today.

"Isn't that Reverend Alexander White, the parson who lost his jury case in King William Courthouse?" a spectator asked, rubbing his hands and blowing into them against the chill.

"Aye, and the parish has been in an uproar against us Dissenters ever since," came the Scottish burr of an angry parishioner, his icy breath rising into the cold air. He clenched his jaw angrily. "If he weren't a man of the cloth . . ."

Patrick Henry tucked his folder of papers under his arm and patted the coat pocket with his daughter's gift inside. He smiled, took a deep breath, and crossed the street from Hanover Tavern, scanning the crowds and already feeling the butterflies in his stomach from the audience he would face today. The brick Hanover Courthouse with its five Roman arches loomed in front of him.

"Pat!" came a welcoming voice as he started up the walkway. It was his best friend and now brother-in-law, Samuel Meredith, who had married his sister, Jane. He smiled and held out a hand. "Big day ahead."

"Sam, it's good to see a friendly face," Patrick replied, heartily shaking his hand. "Yes, and I think all Hanover County is here for the big day."

"Not to mention most of Louisa County and people from at least a dozen others," Sam answered as the two men looked around the courtyard. He put a hand on Patrick's shoulder. "I want you to know that I'll be serving as one of the justices today, along with your half-brother John Syme, Jr., and your Uncle Anthony Winston. Hopefully that will ease your nerves a bit to see us on the bench. I can't imagine how hard it will be to see your father up there as the presiding judge. Are you ready?"

"Thanks, Sam. I'm as ready as I'll ever be, except for one matter . . ."

Patrick answered, his gaze suddenly following the familiar black carriage belonging to his Uncle Patrick. The driver pulled on the reins as it came to a stop in front of the courthouse. "Hold this please, will you, Sam?" Patrick requested as he handed the file of papers to Sam.

Patrick hurried over to the carriage as the driver got ready to step down from his bench to open the door. "I'll handle this, thank you, sir," Patrick offered with a hand raised to the driver so he would remain seated.

Patrick put his foot up on the carriage step and leaned his arms on the open window, but did not open the door. His uncle beamed a wide smile. "Why good morning, Patrick! How kind of ye ta greet me."

"Good morning, Uncle. I had hoped you would not come to court today," Patrick spurted out with a furrowed brow.

Uncle Patrick was clearly taken aback. He narrowed his eyes and tilted his head. "Why is that, Patrick?"

"Because, Uncle, you know I have not yet spoken in public for a large case like this. I fear I will be too awestruck by your presence to do my duty for my clients," Patrick began, drawing a look of shock from his uncle. "Besides, sir, I need to say some hard things about the clergy, and I am very unwilling to give pain to your feelings."

Uncle Patrick gripped his bony fist tightly over the top of his cane and glared at Patrick with a stern expression. "Ye should *never* have taken this case, Patrick."

Patrick tightened his lips and forced a nod. "Well, it would seem the clergy thought me unworthy of representing their side of the argument. And I can find no moral principle that would require me to refuse a fee from the opposing side. I am working hard to build my law practice, Uncle."

Patrick averted his gaze for a moment and saw one of his former customers from his failed store, Mr. Smythe. He never would forget the day he allowed Mr. Smythe to take that hoe on credit. The struggling tobacco farmer was ashamed to have to ask for such help, but was so appreciative to receive it. Uncle Patrick was his family, but today helping Mr. Smythe and countless people like him was Patrick's priority. He turned back to his uncle. "Dear Uncle, my affections are always yours, but in this controversy, both my heart and judgment, as well as my professional duty, are on the side of the people."

Uncle Patrick lifted his chin and leaned back in his seat with a look of disappointment. "I see."

356

"Please, Uncle, I beg you to do me the favor of not attending court today," Patrick implored. "I ask you to please leave the grounds."

Uncle Patrick took in a deep breath and exhaled through his nostrils. "Very well, Patrick." He then leaned forward and held up his cane to accentuate his words. "But as ta yer saying hard things of the clergy, I advise ye ta let that alone; take my word for it, ye will do more harm ta yerself than ta them." His face then softened slightly. "As ta me leaving the grounds, I fear, my boy, that my presence could neither do ye harm nor good in such a cause. However, since ye seem ta think otherwise, and desire it of me so earnestly, I will leave."

Patrick smiled and reached in the carriage to squeeze his uncle's arm. "Thank you, Uncle." He stepped back from the carriage and called up to the driver. "Reverend Henry will not be staying. You may drive on, good sir." Patrick put a finger to his hat in thanks and bowed respectfully to his uncle. "Good day, Uncle."

The driver tipped his hat in acknowledgment and snapped the reins. As the carriage pulled away Patrick let loose a huge sigh of relief and shared a knowing look with Sam, who had stood by to witness the tense scene. *"Now* I feel as ready as I'll ever be, Sam. Let's get to court."

As Patrick and Sam headed up the sidewalk to enter the courthouse, Liz and Nigel scurried behind them and slipped inside unnoticed. Meanwhile, Max sat under a tree where Cato rested in the branches. Together they watched as Uncle Patrick's carriage drove away from the square.

"Good thing Patrick got his uncle to leave," observed Cato. "That will make things easier for him in court."

"Aye," Max replied as he kept his gaze on the carriage. He wanted to make sure Uncle Patrick stayed gone.

Suddenly the carriage stopped after it passed two men heading toward the courthouse on foot: Samuel Morris and Roger Shackelford. Uncle Patrick poked his head out the window and looked back at the two men with an angry stare.

Samuel Morris, the bricklayer, was the man most responsible for starting the Dissenter movement in Hanover County. He had built the very first 'reading house' and was Samuel Davies's closest supporter and friend at Polegreen Meeting House. Roger Shackelford was one of Reverend Henry's own parishioners and had the nerve to once call Reverend Henry "an unconverted wretch," and had been brought up on charges for allowing a Dissenter to preach at his house.

Uncle Patrick banged his hand on the outside of the door and called up to his driver. "Turn this carriage around and take me back ta the courthouse!"

"Looks like tr-r-rouble comin' back this way," Max growled.

"That Scottish uncle needs to learn to hold his horses!" Cato opined with a frown.

Max and Cato looked at one another. "Why don't ye occupy the dr-r-river while *this* Scottie slows down his horse?" Max growled and took off running toward the carriage while Cato lifted off into the air.

———

The courtroom benches were packed and people lined the grey-paneled walls as the room hummed with the expectant fervor of spectators ready to watch the proceedings. Nervous whispers rose to the wooden rafters high in the ceiling above. Light filled the room from tall windows to the right and left of the courtroom as well as the large door that remained opened onto the covered portico at the back of the courtroom. Two side doors led to the judge's chambers and the jury room.

At the front of the courtroom a wooden-spindled bar separated the spectators from the higher positions of the court. A single wooden step behind the bar led up to the area where the lawyers sat with their clients at their respective tables. Between the attorney tables the court clerk maintained a desk and the sheriff stood at attention during court proceedings. Beyond them, two more wooden steps led to an elevated platform where the presiding judge's bench sat in the center. To his far left was the jury box with benches to hold twelve jurors. To his immediate left and right were benches to hold the additional four to six attending justices.

Hanging on the wall behind the judge's bench was the royal coat of arms bearing its two supporters: the powerful crowned British lion and the sinister Scottish unicorn, which heralded danger to those daring to come against the throne. The mottos, *Dieu et mon droit* (God and my right), and *Honi soit qui mal y pense* (shame upon him who thinks evil of it) graced the royal shield between the two supporters. A large map of Virginia hung on the side wall and portraits of King George I, King George II, and the newly added King George III graced the courtroom to keep watch over the spectators and representative court of His Majesty's colony.

Liz and Nigel scurried through the legs of the spectators to slip under a low bench in front of the bar. From here they would be able to see everything that took place. Patrick Henry sat with Johnson and Brown at the right table, speaking in hushed tones. King's Attorney Peter Lyons sat with Reverend Maury at the left table, also going over last-minute details of the case. Suddenly the courtroom of spectators parted as the twenty black-robed parsons entered the room. They proceeded to pass the bar and walk right up to the benches to the right of the judge's bench. Since the courtroom was packed, they asked permission to sit where only lawyers were normally allowed. They desired to sit above the common area where everyone else was required to stay.

"What are they doing up there?" Nigel asked incredulously.

Liz wrinkled her brow. "Obviously making a statement."

The sheriff pounded his stick on the wooden floor. "Oyez! Oyez! The court will now come to order! The Honorable Justice Henry presiding! All rise." Immediately, everyone got to their feet while Judge John Henry entered the room with six justices in tow. Patrick took a deep breath, held his chin high, and locked eyes with Sam, who gave him an affirming nod.

359

Judge Henry looked around the courtroom at the standing room only crowd. "Good day. You may be seated." In the audience were several Virginia burgesses, several members of the Johnson family from Louisa County, and the citizens of Hanover and surrounding counties. He gave a cursory glance at his son, but turned his attention to the sheriff and lifted his outstretched palm. "Sir, if you will please call the first case."

"The case of Maury vs. Johnson is hereby called," the sheriff replied, handing an official document to the judge.

"Is counsel ready for trial?" Judge Henry asked the attorneys, who each responded in the affirmative. "Very well, Sheriff, you may summon a select jury for the case."

As the sheriff left the courtroom, the buzz of the spectators resumed while Judge Henry and the other justices filed out to wait in the judge's chambers.

"I do hope the sheriff is able to secure a jury sympathetic to our Patrick," Nigel stated.

Liz studied Patrick to assess how he seemed to be holding up as the case was getting ready to begin. The twenty parsons sat like vultures over the desk where Patrick sat with Johnson and Brown. *"Oui,* the other side of this courtroom needs a counterbalance for the scales of justice up there beyond the bar."

———

In short order the sheriff returned to the courthouse, and Judge Henry and the justices once more filled their benches. The sheriff filed in with his docket of prospective jurors, who waited behind the bar. He handed his list of jurors to the judge, who then instructed him to share it with each attorney.

Immediately, Reverend Maury scowled and whispered in the ear of Peter Lyons his displeasure with the list, looking back and pointing at the prospective twelve men.

"The nerve!" Nigel exclaimed, balling his fists. "That Maury just told Lyons that the sheriff pulled these men from the 'vulgar herd'!"

"Steady, Nigel," Liz replied calmly.

"Your Honor, my client objects to this list. It appears that the sheriff quickly paraded through an audience of gentlemen in Hanover Tavern but proceeded to select casual bystanders from the green outside," Lyons offered. "Reverend Maury only knows one or two of these men, and claims that none belong to the gentlemen class. Furthermore, the sentiments of many of these men are known to be for Dissenters and against the clergy."

Patrick Henry immediately shot to his feet and raised his hand. "Your Honor, these are honest men, and are therefore unexceptionable. The sheriff took care to excuse one gentleman selected who is unfit to serve as he is a churchwarden, so we can all be assured he has carried out his charge with integrity." He turned and looked over the men standing behind the bar, holding up his hand to them. "This jury holds only a minority of Dissenters, and is honored to have many gentlemen from prominent families, some who are large landowners and due greater respect than my opponent has shown them."

Judge Henry nodded. "The jury is approved. Sheriff, please swear in the jurors so we may proceed."

The parsons frowned while murmurs of approval rippled through the spectators, as the jurors stepped forward to swear their oaths on the Bible. Soon these twelve men took their seats in the juror's box: Benjamin Anderson, John Wingfield, George Dabney, John Thornton,

Samuel Morris, Brewster Sims, William Claybrook, Stephen Willis, Jacob Hundly, Roger Shackelford, John Blackwell, and Benjamin Oliver.

"You see? My Henry secured a promising jury with no trouble," Liz told Nigel. "Samuel Morris and Roger Shackelford are both up there! This is going very well so far, no?"

Nigel preened his whiskers. "I'm delightfully pleased to see those Dissenters as well as Patrick's cousin, George Dabney. Although Patrick tipped George's canoe, I believe he will keep Mr. Henry's defense afloat."

"The plaintiff's counsel may begin," Judge Henry announced as the court was finally in order.

Lyons stood and handed a series of papers to the sheriff, who then gave them to Judge Henry. "Your Honor, I introduce as testimony the bond of the defendants as collectors for Louisa County and the order of the vestry directing a levy to be made for the salary of Mr. Maury in 1759. I also offer the evidence of two witnesses, Mr. Gist and Mr. McDowell, the largest tobacco dealers in the county. They confirm that the 1759 price of tobacco in the county was fifty shillings per hundred pounds."

361

Judge Henry looked over the documents. "Very well, does the plaintiff's counsel wish to present any more evidence?"

"No, Your Honor, we have nothing further," Lyons replied, taking his seat.

"Does the counsel for the defense wish to offer evidence for this case?" Judge Henry asked, looking down at Patrick.

Patrick Henry looked through his folder and picked up a piece of paper that he then gave to the sheriff. "Yes, Your Honor. I have here the signed receipt of payment made to Mr. Maury in 1759 for £144, which was the value of the tobacco due him per the Two Penny Act passed by the Assembly." He turned to take his seat, announcing, "I have nothing further."

The people in the audience exchanged disappointed glances at each other. "That's it?" "He doesn't have anything else to add?" "This doesn't look promising."

Lyons again rose to give his attention to the jury. "Gentlemen of the jury, my opponent has presented a receipt for a woefully inadequate salary paid to my client, the Honorable Reverend Maury. According to the expert testimony I have submitted, the price of tobacco for 1759 should have yielded three times the amount paid to my client. Therefore, my client found it necessary to file suit for the difference in pay in order to receive what was *legally* due him. The defendant has no argument, for the Two Penny Law was struck down by the king as null and void, and affirmed as such by this court in November. This point must be made very clear. The matter of the law is *settled*." The tall, Irish attorney gripped the open edges of his waistcoat. "The only task before you, the members of the jury, is to make one simple calculation—the difference between the £144 already paid to my client, and the amount he is due, based on the actual value of tobacco for the year of 1759."

The Dissenters among the jury members looked at one another with frowns. Lyons scanned their faces and how they glared at the parsons, who sat in places of honor across the platform.

Lyons proceeded to smile and hold up his hand to the parsons. "Could there ever be such a high calling in society, as to care for the souls of the people?"

"He should have stopped with the evidence," Nigel whispered to Liz as Lyons walked over to stand before the parsons, showering them with praise for their good-heartedness and loving watch care over their flocks.

Liz studied Patrick as he listened to Lyons gush forth a sickening dialogue of attributes that none of the parsons sitting on his lofty perch possessed. The parsons lifted their chins in the air approvingly. "Lyons sensed the popular feelings some in the jury have against the clergy, so decided to paint them in a more favorable light."

"The attorney doth protest too much, methinks," Nigel quipped, quoting Shakespeare. "I believe this shall play right into our Henry's hands."

"*Oui,* for Patrick this case is about money supposedly due a group of wolves who profess to be shepherds," Liz replied. "He will not stand for such false praise and the trampling of the truth. It is time for *mon* Henry to find that sliver of a wedge to tear down Lyons's case."

Lyons finally took his seat, and all eyes were on Patrick Henry. It was time for his reply. Either he was going to bow to the accepted facts of the charge to the jury, or he was going to speak up against what was taking place. Curiosity was on tiptoe.

Patrick rose and cleared his throat. He looked up and felt the weight of the stares from the parsons seated above him. He felt their silent warning: *Do not cross the king. Do not cross the Church of England. Do not cross US!*

Patrick looked up at his father's intense gaze directed at him, and felt his silent admonition: *Do not fail again.* He nodded respectfully to the bench and swallowed uncomfortably against the thought.

"G-g-gentlemen," Patrick stuttered as he loosened his cravat. He turned around to see the audience leaning in with eager anticipation for his reply. He felt their silent plea: *Do something! Fight for us!*

"I wish to, I mean to say that . . ." he continued haltingly, clearing his throat again. His posture was slightly stooped and bent over.

A low murmur rippled through the room as embarrassing discomfort filled the courthouse. The people looked at one another and hung their heads. Some crossed their arms and shook their heads while wearing looks of crushing disappointment. Several even filed out of the room, waving their hands and muttering quietly, "Henry doesn't know what he's doing! His defense is worthless. We've come here for *nothing.*"

Patrick fiddled with his papers on the table, stalling as his mind struggled for the words he needed. "If it please the court . . ." were the only words he could utter. The intensity and the gravity of the moment caused his mind to go blank and his mouth to shut in silence.

Nigel and Liz looked at one another in despair.

Patrick's father sank down into his seat, clearly embarrassed as he watched his son failing once more, this time in front of the entire community. The twenty parsons wore smug expressions, sitting in their elevated seats in the courtroom, looking down their noses at Patrick and the people. Oh, but they were very pleased indeed! They were all smiling at seeing Patrick flounder and grasp for what to say. They knew they had finally won against these people who dared to come against them. Finally the Dissenters and anyone else defying the parsons' authority would be put in their place—under the heels of the parsons, mouthpieces of the king. Watching this pitiful attempt at opposition to their power filled them with delicious satisfaction. Patrick looked up and noticed one of the parsons elbowing another next to him. They looked to the back of the courthouse, triumphantly nodding and smiling at someone who had entered the room.

Patrick turned to see who it was. His stomach lurched, and he instantly broke into a sweat. It was none other than his Uncle Patrick.

363

A Voice in
the Court

Reverend Patrick Henry wore a look of disdain as he glared at the jury, wrinkling his nose at Samuel Morris and Roger Shackelford.

"Ce n'est pas bien! Uncle Patrick must have changed his mind," Liz cried in shock and alarm. She looked over at Patrick, and his knees looked as if they were about to buckle. "Patrick was already struggling to speak. Now this!"

"I simply cannot watch!" Nigel lamented, burying his face into Liz's fur.

Patrick gazed over at the faces of those fine men and the other Dissenters and citizens sitting on the jury. The distant strains of Samuel Davies preaching to the crowd of Dissenters and rallying Virginians to fight for freedom filled his mind. Samuel Davies—his pastor, friend, mentor, champion of liberty, an obedient citizen of the law despite the heavy hand of government controlling religious freedom, and his role model for being a brave man of God—this incredible man had come under such harsh treatment by Uncle Patrick and his father. Patrick's heart stirred afresh with anger at such injustice. But at the same time, he was torn over his love for his father and uncle and his sustained loyalty to the Anglican Church.

Patrick's upper lip and brow beaded with sweat. He reached into his pocket for a handkerchief to wipe his face and felt the soft petals of the marigold laurel. Suddenly images flashed across his mind in that moment: Jimmy falling into the dirt after the bully pushed him in the race, shouting *'Get out of my way, urchin!'*; seeing himself help Jimmy to his feet, *'Come on Jimmy, I'll help you.'*; Jimmy catching his breath, *'Thanks, Patrick. I hoped I could win'*; telling the boy who didn't just want but needed the food prize, *'You'll win next time.'*

Patrick looked up and saw Mr. Smythe standing at the very back of the room next to his Uncle Patrick, with dirt on his face. At that moment he looked just like Jimmy in Patrick's eyes. The struggling farmer's imploring eyes once more needed his help. Above Mr. Smythe's head on the wall hung the portrait of King George II. Patrick's eyes narrowed, and his anger started to rise as he realized that the parsons were no different than the bully who had shoved Jimmy into the dirt in order to take what he wanted as his prize. The parson bullies had shoved Mr. Smythe and the people of Virginia into the dirt, while the king bully stood at the finish line waiting to give them their money prize.

The words from Patrick's dream filled his mind. *Fail to speak or fail not to speak, Patrick? You must decide which will keep you from your miracle.*

At that moment the passage from Jeremiah filled his spirit:

"Stop this foolishness and talk some sense! Only if you return to trusting me will I let you continue as my spokesman. You are to influence them, not let them influence you! They will fight against you like a besieging army against a high city wall. But they will not conquer you, for I am with you to protect and deliver you, says the LORD. Yes, I will certainly deliver you from these wicked men and rescue you from their ruthless hands."

Patrick opened his eyes and lifted his chin. He suddenly felt a torrent of words starting to rise in his throat like the hot lava of a volcano seeking its fiery exit. Patrick clenched his jaw, threw down his handkerchief, and stood up tall and straight, striding confidently over to the jury.

Now, mon *Henry!* Liz thought as her heart caught in her throat. *It is time to find your voice in this court!*

"Gentlemen, isn't it a privilege to sit where you are sitting? You have the honor of upholding the laws designed to protect and provide for the highest good of those fortunate enough to call themselves Englishmen," Patrick began, smiling at the jury who nodded back. He lifted his arms and turned to the audience. "And isn't it a privilege to sit where *you* are? His Majesty's loyal subjects, free to observe the open and time-tested administration of justice for the highest good of the people."

The people quieted down and immediately felt privileged to be seated there in the room.

Patrick turned to his father and the other justices sitting high above the courtroom and bowed low and with deep respect. "The people are truly fortunate to have legal guardians who fiercely protect the law from being ill-used or manipulated for purposes that could bring harm to the people." Judge Henry and the other justices nodded in appreciation.

The parsons sat up tall and expectantly, awaiting their turn to receive due appreciation for their service for the good of the people. But Patrick simply gave them a pregnant stare and said nothing. After allowing them to squirm for an awkward moment, he turned and walked back to the jury.

Liz and Nigel clung to one another with renewed excitement.

"Yes, the law is one of our most prized possessions, for it provides safe boundaries for liberty, which is our most precious jewel," Patrick continued. He gave a nod of respect to some of the Assembly members seated a few rows back. "And laws are made by the trusted representatives of the people whom they have appointed to be their voice. Our noble Assembly has the time-honored tradition of tirelessly serving the people and enacting laws that see to their welfare. The Two Penny Acts were laws passed in order to provide for the highest good of the people. We all know that our tobacco fields have struggled in recent years from drought and worms that devoured the tender plants." Patrick gripped his fist and looked around the room, eliciting nods from the people. "This crisis choked the livelihood of those who simply sought to provide a roof over their heads and food on the table for their families."

Patrick paced back across the bar and locked eyes with Mr. Smythe with a smile. His face lit up as he saw that his hypnotic voice had the people hanging on every word. "These laws were temporary, meant to provide a sturdy bridge of relief to cross those troubled waters until better days could return to our fields. They were meant for the good of each and every person in this courtroom," he said, pointing to various individuals scattered across the room. Patrick then walked over to the jury and placed his hand on the railing. "Gentlemen of the jury, you have been told by my worthy opponent that your charge here today is simply a matter of mathematics. He says the law that our able assemblymen passed is null and void by the hand of the king, and that Mr. Maury is due *damages* for a lost opportunity of extra coin in his pocket. But I submit to you that the equation you seek is not as simple as it would appear."

The parsons frowned and looked for any sign of displeasure from the court. They saw none. Judge Henry looked at no one but his son.

"Before you proceed to your mathematics assignment, allow me a moment to present another equation which may help to refresh those of you whose skills may be rusty from boyhood," Patrick quipped, drawing soft chuckles from the jury. He then lifted his hand and pointed to the portraits of the kings. "We Englishmen live under the protection of our noble king. And we are therefore to be his loyal and obedient subjects. This is the equation: One protective king plus his loyal subjects equals the desired sum: freedom. Can the gentlemen of the jury confirm that my mathematics here are correct?"

The jury chuckled and nodded in agreement. Patrick smiled and playfully hit the jury box banister. "My tutor will be most pleased to know that all was not wasted on my mathematics instruction."

The audience joined the jurors in a humorous moment, and Judge Henry wore a slight grin from the reference to himself. Patrick gave his father a knowing nod.

Patrick then held out his hands as imaginary scales. "Government, then, is a conditional compact, made up of mutual and dependent covenants." He kept his hands in perfect balance as he looked around the room. "The king provides protection on one hand, and the people provide obedience and support on the other. A violation of either of these covenants by either party throws the equation off," he said, holding one hand low and one hand high, "and therefore removes the obligations owed by either party."

Patrick allowed that concept to resonate for a moment as he assessed the jury and his audience. Murmurs of agreement filled the room.

"We are separated by a vast ocean from our king, the House of Lords, and the House of Commons, but this equation must somehow be kept in check here in America for the king," Patrick continued. He looked up to the ceiling as he pondered his next question aloud. "How can a king three thousand miles away know what his loyal subjects need in times of immediate crisis? How can His Majesty swiftly respond to provide the protection he has agreed to for his part of the equation?" Patrick crossed his arms and tapped a finger on his chin as he thought this through, feigning he didn't know the answer. This allowed his audience to answer the question for him in their own minds.

Suddenly he snapped his fingers with a coy grin. "I have it! It must

367

be that for our colonial government, the Burgesses *represent* the House of Commons, our Council *represents* the House of Lords, and our Governor *represents* the King. Any law passed by His Majesty's *representatives* should therefore be deemed valid until the king decides to disallow it for some reason, should it not?"

Patrick's face then grew serious. "The Two Penny Act had every characteristic of a *good* law, made for the highest good of a people in a moment of supreme crisis—a law made for the *protection* of the people, which we have determined is the king's obligation in our equation."

Suddenly Patrick's voice filled with blood-chilling authority and boomed with such force that the people's hair stood on end. "The Two Penny Law could *not* be struck down by the king without violating the covenant he holds with his people! Such a disallowance by the king is a glaring act of misrule, and he has neglected the interests of this colony," Patrick shouted. He pointed his finger directly at the portrait of King George II. "He has not only voided a good law, but he has voided the entire equation for his loyal subjects. By this conduct the king, far from being the father of his people, has degenerated into a *tyrant!* He therefore forfeits *all* rights to his subjects' obedience to his ruling on the matter!"

At this point Mr. Lyons cried out to the parsons, "The gentleman has spoken treason, and I am astonished that your Worships can hear it without emotion, or any mark of dissatisfaction."

The parsons murmured their opposition while one or two cries of "Treason! Treason!" rose from the onlookers.

Nigel thrust his fists up high in the air. "Brilliant! He has turned from a defense attorney into a prosecutor, putting both the king and the parsons on trial!"

The shock and awe of the people paled in comparison to what was happening up on the judge's bench. One or two justices frowned their disapproval while Sam nodded vigorously in agreement. John Syme and Anthony Winston beamed with satisfaction but properly restrained their show of emotion. Patrick's father, however, did not.

Judge John Henry's eyes filled with tears as he watched his son ignite the entire courtroom with a voice that heralded the cry to protect that precious jewel of liberty. He didn't bother to wipe away the tears that flowed down his cheeks. His son was no longer a failure in his eyes, for Patrick clearly understood and embraced all his father had tried to teach

368

him. His son had finally found his life's calling and was pushing it to the limits of greatness.

Patrick pushed his spectacles atop his head, and his eyes flashed from blue to ebony as he gazed up at the smug parsons. He paid no attention whatsoever to the outbursts and cries coming from opposing voices in the courtroom.

Suddenly a distant memory echoed in Nigel's mind. *Something about a future human who would push his spectacles up on his head?*

Liz smiled as she watched his approach. "The parsons wanted to hear a word from my Henry. Now, they shall have it."

"And what about the established clergy who are *also* the king's representatives? The king is the head of the Church of England, is he not?" Patrick asked, as he nodded to the spectators, who had no choice but to agree with him. The courtroom fell into a deathlike silence, for he was about to take them into uncharted territory against the parsons.

"The only use of an established church and clergy in society is to enforce obedience to the laws," Patrick exclaimed, as his voice slowly rose in volume with each word. "When the clergy ceases to answer these ends, the people have no further need of their ministry, and may justly strip them of their appointments." Patrick punctuated the air with sweeping gestures and pointed an accusing finger at the parsons. "Our own clergy of Virginia in this particular instance have come against and defied the purposes of this colony's legislature! Instead of being seen as useful members of the State, they ought to be considered as *enemies* of the community!" He wheeled around and then pointed a finger directly at Reverend Maury as he stormed over to the jury box. "In this case before you," he told the jurors, "Mr. Maury, instead of receiving damages, very justly deserves to be severely *punished!*"

Liz and Nigel looked at one another in stunned silence over what was coming out of Patrick's mouth. Their jaws hung open in disbelief.

Patrick was nowhere near finished. "We have heard a great deal about the 'benevolence and holy zeal of our reverend clergy,'" he said in a lofty, mocking tone. "But how is this manifested?" his stern voice roared back. "Do they manifest their zeal in the cause of religion and humanity by practicing the mild and benevolent precepts of the Gospel of Jesus? Do they feed the hungry and clothe the naked? Oh, no, Gentlemen. Instead of feeding the hungry and clothing the naked, these rapacious harpies would, were their power equal to their will, snatch from the hearth of the poorest parishioner his last hoe cake! From the widow and her orphan the last milk cow! The last bed, nay, the last blanket from a woman with child!"

Immediately, the twenty parsons rose to their feet from the bench, stomped down the steps to exit the bar and filed out of the courtroom to the haven of the courtyard outside. The people murmured and cast glances of disgust at the retreating parsons. "You shall repent of this, Patrick! You shall repent of this yet!" Uncle Patrick shouted above the din of voices as he joined his fellow parsons for their hasty retreat out the door.

Patrick allowed a delicious silence to settle in as the "guilty" parsons he had painted with his fiery brush of accusing words stomped out. Unmoved, he faced the court and kept right on, not missing a beat from the visual protest of the parsons.

"The equation here, gentlemen of the jury, is not one of mathematics, but of freedom or bondage," Patrick continued. "A people who are denied the privilege of enacting their own laws are not free, but are under the oppression of tyranny. And unless you wish to rivet the chains of bondage on the necks of your fellow Virginians, I hope you will not bypass this opportunity to make such an example of the plaintiff. From this day forward let *your* decision serve as a warning to Mr. Maury and to his brethren not to dispute the validity of our laws!" He stopped briefly not to catch his breath, but to allow his hearers to catch theirs.

"Finally, gentlemen of the jury, we come to the 'simple mathematics' you must now conduct to uphold the dignity of this court and your sworn obligations," Patrick told them in a calm tone that brought the jurors back to the practicality of this situation following the emotional hurricane he had unleashed on them for an hour. "Under the ruling of the court, you must find for the plaintiff, but you need not find more than one *farthing.*" Patrick looked into the eyes of each juror and gave an affirming nod, willing them to do his bidding. "This will accomplish all that the defense desires."

No one spoke a word. The only sound in the courtroom were Patrick's confident footsteps as he walked back to his table and took his seat.

After a breathless moment, the people instantly erupted in cheers, as Lyons rose to his feet and attempted to break the spell that Henry had cast over the jury. It was no use. The jury quickly filed out of the room.

370

Maury and Lyons huddled in a feverish discussion. Judge Henry and Patrick shared a timeless moment of unspoken words as their eyes met.

Liz and Nigel swayed together in a joyous embrace. "He found his voice, *mon ami!*" Liz exclaimed with tears rolling down her cheeks. "Everything that was poured into *mon* Henry since childhood flowed out of him into the court of Hanover today! *Dieu est bon!*"

Nigel's whiskers quivered happily. "Oh, the exquisite justice of it all!"

Their celebration was abruptly cut short when suddenly the jury filed back into the room. It had taken them less than five minutes to reach a decision.

Judge Henry motioned for the sheriff to call the court to order. The sheriff pounded his stick on the floor. "The court will now come back to order!" The crowd immediately grew quiet.

"Has the jury reached a decision?" Judge Henry asked.

"Yes, Your Honor," Samuel Morris answered, rising to his feet to represent the jury. "The jury finds for the plaintiff the damages of," he paused and looked at Patrick with a smile, "one penny."

371

"I object!" boomed Lyons's voice. "This verdict is contrary to the evidence! Your Honor, I humbly request that the jury be sent out again." But it again was no use.

"Overruled. Clerk, please record the verdict of one penny to be awarded to Mr. Maury," Judge Henry quickly replied.

"I wish to move for a new trial," Lyons cried with an upraised hand.

"Denied," Judge Henry shot back.

"Then we implore an appeal to the General Court," Lyons pleaded.

"Granted," Judge Henry shot back. "This court is now adjourned."

This entire exchange between Judge Henry and Lyons had taken place amid the growing voices of the people, scarcely able to contain their excitement.

Patrick shook hands with his clients, rose to his feet, and walked over to Lyons and Maury. He dug into his pocket and retrieved a single penny. He placed the coin on their table while the two men looked on in stunned disbelief. "I believe this covers the damages owed to Mr. Maury and settles the matter for my clients. Good day, gentlemen." He bowed and then turned to walk back to his table. He winked at Johnson and Brown before escorting them down the one step back across the bar.

Instantly the people rushed over to Patrick, and with frenzied delight they picked him up and carried him on their shoulders out of the courtroom. People were shouting "Huzzah!" and embracing, crying, and laughing with uncontrollable excitement as they paraded their champion around the courtyard.

Tears of joy filled Patrick's eyes as he caught the glimpse of his small family standing across the street in front of Hanover Tavern. Patsey and John were jumping up and down excitedly, and Sallie blew him a kiss. He struggled to reach into his pocket while being jostled, but he gradually pulled out the marigold laurel, kissed it, and waved it high for Patsey to see.

Max sat there grinning as Liz and Nigel joined him in the courtyard. "Looks like the lad did a gr-r-rand job then," Max greeted them. "Wha' were the verdict?"

Nigel frowned and shook his head. "Unfortunately the jury awarded Maury *four times* the damages Patrick had recommended."

Max's eyes widened. "Four times?! Then why all the celebr-r-ratin'?"

Nigel broke out into a jolly chuckle. "Because Patrick had suggested they award Maury a farthing, which is one-quarter of a penny, old boy! He was brilliant!"

"So jest a penny for the parson?" Max answered happily. "Now that's wha' I call justice!"

Liz watched Uncle Patrick pulling away in his carriage. The driver looked up in the sky as Cato circled overhead. The man crouched down in his seat, as if expecting to be dive-bombed. "Max, you and Cato were out here. Did you see what happened with Uncle Patrick that made him decide to return to the courthouse?"

"Aye. When he were down the r-r-road a bit he saw them two Dissenter lads headin' this way, so he told his dr-r-river ta turn ar-r-round. He weren't aboot ta miss the case if those lads were put on the jur-r-ry then," Max answered, wearing a sly grin. "But me an' his horse had a wee discussion while Cato swooped down an' *encouraged* the dr-r-river ta take the long way back ta the courthouse."

"Splendid! Reminds me of my aerial dive-bomb maneuvers on pigeons," reminisced Nigel, preening his whiskers, "way back in the day."

"*C'est magnifique! Merci,* Max! This was quick thinking on your and Cato's part, no?!" Liz exclaimed. "No telling what would have happened if Uncle Patrick had tried to interfere with the jury selection."

"Well, I see that you discovered the fiddle's riddle about the voice in the court," came the voice of a gentleman standing next to the animals. They turned to see Gillamon dressed in the finery of a gentleman and wearing his magnificent red cloak.

"Gillamon! *Oui,* but this riddle took many years to solve," Liz pointed out.

"Aye, but we solved it then," Max added with a definitive nod. "It had a lot of movin' parts though."

"I say, but it was a thrilling turn of events that came together," analyzed Nigel. "The meeting of the man and the moment came together for *this* crucial point in history!"

Gillamon chuckled. "You all did remarkably well with your assignments. And yes, this is indeed a crucial point in HIStory. Speaking of history, do you realize that Patrick is the same age as Cicero and Demosthenes when they discovered *their* voices when arguing the law in the courts of ancient Rome and Greece?"

"It would seem that twenty-seven is the perfect age for an orator to find his voice, no?" Liz marveled. *"Mon* Henry has an exciting future ahead of him now!"

Nigel's eyes widened with realization as he saw Patrick's spectacles still sitting on top of his head as the people paraded him about. "By Jove, I've got it! Also speaking of history, you foretold something way back in our Egypt mission, Gillamon. If I remember correctly, you said, 'There will be one special human who keeps his spectacles pushed up on his head when he's bothered and determined about things. You will find him to be quite the exceptional fellow.'" The little mouse grinned and put his own spectacles atop his head. "It was Patrick Henry you spoke of, wasn't it?"

Gillamon smiled and nodded. "One and the same."

Liz looked over as the people set Patrick down on the ground. In the midst of the people back-slapping him with congratulations, she saw Patsey running across the street toward him. She ran into her father's arms for a tight embrace, and he then put the marigold laurel around her neck and kissed her on the forehead. Liz's eyes brimmed with happy tears. "You were right, *mon ami.* He is *quite* exceptional."

"I say, our Patrick used a mathematics analogy in court today, and it would appear that the next part of the riddle does as well," Nigel noted. *"A voice in the house makes seven words, two short.* I have no idea what

373

this could possibly mean, but it will undoubtedly be another intriguing quest for us to solve it."

Gillamon looked up to see Cato soaring above the happy events. Patrick was surrounded by family and friends who escorted him over to Hanover Tavern for a big celebration. "If you hurry, you'll catch your first clue in the tavern."

Liz and Nigel looked at one another with growing excitement and took off after the humans. *"Adieu,* Gillamon!" Liz shouted. "The next riddle waits for no one!"

Max sat with Gillamon a moment longer. "I'm glad ye stopped by for the happy day, lad. Can ye tell me how me lass Kate be doin'?"

Gillamon bent down to pet Max on the back, smiling while his blue eyes twinkled. "Why don't you go to France and see for yourself? You've earned a furlough to see your bonnie Kate. Besides, she could use your help with her Lafayette mission. Wolves have always been your specialty."

Max's face lit up with joy followed by concern. "Wolves? Aye!" he growled. "Take me ta Fr-r-rance, r-r-right now, lad."

With that, Gillamon covered Max with his cape and the two disappeared from the courtyard.

A pair of eyes narrowed from behind a hedge as they watched Gillamon and Max disappear. "À *bientôt,*" the voice hissed. "France it is."

374

SOLDIERS, SMUGGLERS, SUGAR, AND STAMPS

LONDON

LEO, NO!" King George III shouted as he picked Al up from the overstuffed red velvet chair that sat next to a tea cart of sweet biscuits. The king put the fluffy orange cat on the ornate rug and plopped down in the chair himself. He reached over and picked up one of the delicious treats and took a bite. Al remained by his feet, looking up at him with his big, green, sad eyes. King George pointed the biscuit at Al and said, "I told you to stay away from the sweeties, yet you disobeyed me." He took another bite and relished it, taunting Al. "Because you ignored my command, you now will have none."

"I jest can't help me sweet tooth!" Al meowed sadly.

"Your Majesty, it would appear your little British lion either does not realize you are king, or chooses to disregard your sovereign authority," Lord Grenville quipped, standing with his hands folded in front of him. He was the new Prime Minister of Great Britain, already the second man the king had appointed to lead his cabinet after taking the throne.

At the very start of his reign in 1760, King George III did as his mother instructed—he set out to "be a king" and picked those who would do his bidding. He immediately appointed his tutor and father figure, Lord Bute, as royal advisor and leader of his cabinet. The king made it well known that Bute would be the power behind the throne. Bute had not only formed George's view of history, law, and politics since the king was seventeen years old, but he quickly put the young king on a collision course with the world.

Together Lord Bute and King George began the irrational move to oust William Pitt, Great Britain's popular and effective prime minister who had led Britain to victory in the French and Indian War, and in the worldwide conflict known as the Seven Years' War. Bute and other advisors had convinced King George that William Pitt had "the blackest of hearts." Pitt resigned in 1761 after clashing with Bute on how to end the war, and King George immediately turned to Bute to form a new government. Bute oversaw the signing of the shaky Treaty of Paris to officially end the war with the French, but King George's mentor quickly failed at the task of governing. Bute became the most hated man on both sides of the Atlantic, and only lasted 317 days as prime minister. Rumors circulated that Bute still remained in the shadows, advising the king despite George's next move in appointing a new prime minister, George Grenville. Grenville had a way of irritating King George, but the king had to put up with him for the time being.

"If Leo does not know I am king by now, he never will," King George told Lord Grenville. "He's been with me for as long as I can remember. His tendency to get into places he shouldn't be and touching foods he shouldn't touch has always been part of his mischievous charm." The king leaned over and scratched Al under the chin with a chuckle. "I can never stay mad at him for long."

"Speaking of getting into places he shouldn't be, I regret to inform Your Majesty that the 1763 Proclamation Act forbidding the colonists from getting into places where *they* shouldn't be has not been well received," Grenville relayed.

"What, what?" King George exclaimed with his quirky favorite phrase. He tossed the rest of the biscuit onto the floor and shot up from his chair, marching over to the map lying on the table.

Al's face lit up and he looked both ways before he snatched up the sweet biscuit and ran under a settee to finish it off.

The king pulled his finger across the map, noting the line west of the Allegheny Mountains, beyond which the colonists were no longer allowed to settle. "After the blood, years, and expense it took to defeat the French and gain all this territory, I am not about to allow the colonists to ignite more conflicts with the savage Indians! With our troops in place, Britain will control *orderly* westward movement. And it will be done at a slow enough pace to keep the colonists near the Atlantic coast and dependent on our imported British goods."

Grenville nodded in agreement and pointed to the map. "Indeed, Your Majesty, but those colonists living on the frontier in Virginia and the Ohio regions especially resent such restrictions. They wish to pursue new land and participate in the lucrative fur trade. They say they do not need our troops to protect them from Indian threats." He picked up one of the lead soldiers sitting on the map and held it up for emphasis. "Stationing ten thousand British troops in the colonies to protect these new lands comes at a cost. And that cost is on top of the massive debt we have from the war, which has risen from £73 million to nearly £130 million."

This laddie is jest full of good news, Al thought, shaking his head and licking his chops. Out of the corner of his eye he thought he saw something scurry up the writing desk. He slowly waddled over to investigate.

King George crossed his arms over his chest and scowled with a pouting lower lip as he stared at the lead soldiers on the map. "What is the cost to keep our soldiers in the colonies?"

"Maintaining an army of ten thousand costs £220,000 per year," reported Grenville.

377

"The colonies have long been spoiled from being allowed to do whatever they wish. I do not *care* if they resent our troops being there!" King George shouted angrily, pounding the map and causing a couple of the lead soldiers to fall over. "*They* will pay for the British troops stationed in America, as well as their fair share of the war debt. It is the very least they can do after all the Mother Country has done for them."

"Parliament wholeheartedly agrees, Your Majesty. I have several ideas of how to get the colonies to pay their fair share," Grenville replied, seeing Al slink across the room. "Just as your Leo has a sweet tooth, so do the colonies, especially those in the north. They also sneakily get their hands on sugar."

"Explain," King George prompted, watching Al's tail whipping back and forth next to the writing desk.

"The colonists have ignored the Molasses Act for decades, choosing to smuggle in sugar and molasses from other countries besides Britain to avoid paying the taxes," Grenville explained, gripping a tight fist. "Our customs officials too often turn a blind eye, but I propose we now come down hard on these smugglers. Colonial juries usually find their smuggler friends innocent, so we must take these guilty criminals to vice-admiralty courts in Nova Scotia instead of jury trials in the colonial courts. Make the smugglers *prove* their innocence without their friends there to defend them. Plus, we can clamp down on smugglers by giving our officers full permission to enter their homes and seize their smuggled goods without first going to court."

King George raised his eyebrows. "These are firm measures, but I like what I hear. The colonists need to be *taught* obedience to the crown."

"I agree. And we shall teach the colonies to respect the authority of the crown by taxing them without their consent," Grenville continued with a firm nod. "What if we also passed a Sugar Act? We could *lower* the taxes on molasses to convince colonists to pay the tax instead of smuggling. We could also restrict colonial exports of items like lumber to Britain alone. That would immediately help to start raising money. But we need to make sure the colonies cannot issue their own money and only use British coin. Therefore, I propose we pass a Currency Act as well."

"These measures will place the colonies securely under our thumb as we control the colonial sweet tooth *and* raise money," King George answered, nodding slowly. "This has promise, but I wonder if these acts alone will be enough to pay for our soldiers and the American war debt."

Grenville frowned and crossed his arms. "I agree, Your Majesty. We need something more. Something that touches not just smugglers and merchants, but *every* colonist in America so every citizen pays his fair share. The Sugar Act is more for regulating trade as an external tax. We need a deeper tax—an *internal* tax."

Suddenly Al jumped up onto the writing desk, knocking over an inkwell. He was chasing a bug around the desk. The pest ran under a copy of *Gentleman's Magazine*. "I'll get ye, beastie!" he meowed.

"LEO, NO!" King George snapped, stomping his foot and clapping his hands together loudly. Startled, Al scurried off the desk, sending the newspaper flying onto the floor. He took off running out of the room before he got into any more trouble.

"Allow me, Your Majesty," Grenville said as he walked over to pick up the newspaper. When he gathered the paper into his hands, he slowly stood and turned to face the king, wearing a broad smile. He held up the *Gentleman's Magazine*. "I have another idea for raising money that will indeed touch every colonist. We've used it quite successfully here in

378

Britain, and I have no doubt it will work in the colonies as well."

King George walked over and took the newspaper in hand with a frown. Al's inked paw print graced the front page. "And what is that?"

Grenville lifted his chin with pleasure over his idea, pointing to Al's paw prints. "A Stamp Tax."

379

MOUNT BRILLIANT, NOVEMBER 1764

"OF ALL THE NERVE!" Nigel ranted, tugging on his whiskers as he paced back and forth. "Grenville actually proposed that the colonial agents agree *in advance* to the Stamp Act before they know what's in it? How preposterous! How idiotic! Who in their right mind would ever *suggest* such a thing? Just who does this cheeky Grenville think he is?!"

"Steady, Mousie," Clarie told the little mouse. "Grenville didn't even know all that would be in the Stamp Act when he first met with the colonial agents. He tried to get them to blindly agree to the proposed act to establish a pattern where Parliament could proceed with taxes without consulting the colonies."

Clarie had just arrived from London to give Liz and Nigel a full report on all that had transpired as a result of the passage of the Sugar Act and now the pending Stamp Act. The colonies were sending petitions and pamphlets, and had their agents in London meeting with Grenville to avoid the passage of the Stamp Act in a few months.

"So let me see if I understand this Stamp Act correctly," Liz recounted. "There will be a tax on *fifty-five categories* of printed items used in public such as newspapers, pamphlets, wills, playing cards, and dice. Stamps ranging from a half-penny to £10 must be purchased from a British official and placed on these items. This tax will naturally hit printers, lawyers, ministers, and merchants the hardest. But just think how it will also affect the rest of the people. *Quel dommage!* A marriage will not be *valid* without a stamp on the marriage license."

"Nor will any poor dead chap be *officially dead* without that horrid stamp affixed to his death certificate!" Nigel ranted. "This is madness!"

"Parliament is interfering with the colonies by taxing them directly, *and without their consent,*" Liz noted.

"That's right, Liz. The Stamp Tax is the major part of the Stamp Act, but there will be two other items slipped into it as well," Clarie explained. "A new clause will be inserted into the Mutiny Act that says Britain can station however many troops it needs here in the colonies. And the Quartering Act will require the colonists to locate and provide quarters for those British troops. Colonists also must provide the soldiers with supplies like candles, bedding, drink, soap, etc."

"The king and Parliament are ignoring the tradition of self-government for the colonies, reducing them to the status of women and slaves, who have *no voice* in government," Nigel lamented, putting one paw on top of the other as if building an imaginary fire. "My beloved homeland simply does *not* realize they are placing one log of trouble upon another here in America."

Clarie nodded. "And all it takes is the right spark to set that fire ablaze."

"This lawyer James Otis in Boston seems to have a smart head on his shoulders," Liz reported as she scanned some of the writings Clarie had brought with her. "He makes it clear that the colonies cannot be taxed without their consent. No taxation without representation. But of course this is not only logical, but is the constitutional right of Englishmen, no?"

"Yes, and as predicted, he and the people of Boston such as Samuel Adams have been protesting the Sugar Act, and now this proposed Stamp Act," Clarie agreed. "Virginia did not respond as urgently to the

Sugar Act, but the coming Stamp Act is a different story. And Patrick Henry will soon hear all about it from the Burgesses in Williamsburg."

"*Oui,* Colonel Nathaniel West Dandridge hired Patrick to present his case against Littlepage over an election dispute," Liz said. "He is to leave for Williamsburg soon."

"Nigel, you'll be happy to know that Benjamin Franklin has gone to London and will now join the colonial agents to try to talk some sense into Grenville and Parliament," Clarie informed the little mouse.

"That is good news, my dear. But I thought I was to accompany Franklin to London," Nigel asked in alarm, as if he had missed a date on the calendar. "Should I make haste and away across the pond?"

"You will, Nigel, but later. Mr. Franklin will remain in London for quite some time," Clarie replied. "Al has things well in hand—or paw, as it were. You need to remain here with Liz and Patrick Henry for the time being. You two still have the next part of the fiddle's riddle to solve."

"Very well. We are both still quite perplexed as to what the riddle could mean," Nigel told her, tapping a finger on his chin and looking skyward. "A voice in the house makes five words, two short."

381

"A *house.* Patrick is building a house in Louisa County!" Liz offered excitedly. "After John Shelton sold Hanover Tavern last month, Patrick's family needed to move. But ever since Patrick became the people's hero after the Parson's Cause case, he has more clients than he can handle, no? With Patrick's successful law practice he is finally able to afford to build a house."

"Right! Patrick sold his Pine Slash farm and acquired the 1,700 acres of land his father promised him as a wedding gift, called Roundabout Plantation," Nigel added. "Just yesterday our promising young lawyer bought lumber to build a house on the land, and I learned that his closest neighbor will be none other than *Johnson* from the Parson's Cause."

"*Oui,* this is why Patrick brought his family here to stay at Mount Brilliant while the *house* is being built." Liz's eyes were lit up with excitement. "Clarie, is this part of the fiddle's riddle?"

"Yes and no," Clarie answered with a grin. "It does have to do with the house in Louisa County, but that is not the house in the riddle. Did you pick up any clues during the Parson's Cause celebration at the tavern with Patrick's new neighbor?"

Nigel cleared his throat and adjusted his spectacles. "We did overhear

Johnson telling Patrick that he would be glad to help him gain a burgess assembly seat in Louisa County."

"But of course this requires him to own land in Louisa . . ." Liz suddenly stopped and locked eyes with Nigel.

"House *of Burgesses!*" Liz and Nigel exclaimed at the same time.

"That's it!" Clarie said.

"*Bon!* So this means that *mon* Henry will have a voice in the House of Burgesses," cheered Liz happily. "But there is currently not an open seat in Louisa County."

Clarie smiled. "All in good time. Before he dives into deep waters to speak in front of the most powerful men in the largest colony in America, he first needs to get his feet wet with a small group of them in Williamsburg. And he'll gain a single ally that he will need in the future."

"I see." Liz glanced up to see Cato circling above them. "Nigel, tell Cato you two will be flying to accompany *mon* Henry to Williamsburg. I shall need a full report on everything that happens there." The black cat got up and slowly sauntered off. "I will make sure MizP's shoes are ready for this trip."

WILLIAMSBURG

MizP shook her head as Patrick Henry walked toward the imposing Capitol, where the Virginia House of Burgesses was in session. He was dressed in well-worn, coarse brown clothes that should have been given away long ago. As usual, his shoes were dirty from their long trip, and several hairs were sticking out from his unpowdered brown wig. He was oblivious to the looks he received from the refined, well-dressed gentlemen he passed.

"Will that boy ever learn tuh take his appearance seriously?" MizP asked Nigel. "Heaven help him if he wants tuh join those burgesses, looking like something the cat dragged in."

"Have faith, my dear," Nigel answered cheerfully. He sat on the post where MizP was tied. Cato had dropped him off, and he waited with MizP until it was time to follow Patrick inside. The little mouse gave the horse a fond pat. "Perhaps he will be inspired by the splendid array of tidy, colorful clothes he shall see today as he dips his toes into these new waters."

"I wouldn't count on it," MizP replied with a doubting snort. "He's a fish out of water."

Nigel chuckled and scurried away down the dusty Duke of Gloucester Street after Patrick. He slipped under the feet of the polished and powerful Tidewater elite and into the hallowed halls of the Capitol. He stayed out of sight but kept an eye on Patrick, who walked around in awe of the grandeur of the two-story H-shaped building. The downstairs housed the ornate General Courtroom on the west side and the impressive long chamber for the burgesses on the east side. Upstairs was the Governor's Council Chamber and Committee Meeting rooms, separated by a bridge that symbolically joined the royal and colonial branches of Virginia.

Patrick stood at the doorway to the elegant, dark-paneled chamber for the House of Burgesses, which was patterned after the House of Commons in London. Rows of long benches covered in green velvet cushions ran the length of both sides of the elegant room. The benches curved to meet at the tall, ornate chair where sat Speaker John Robinson in his black robe and powdered wig to oversee the representatives. Between the facing benches on the floor sat the clerk's table, piled with parliamentary law documents and the silver mace that represented the power of the House.

383

The air itself was thick with the authority of the Tidewater aristocracy that had long held the political power of Virginia. Those belonging to the families of the Randolphs, Carters, Beverlys, Lees, Harrisons, Burwells, and Blairs held leadership positions in the House and the important subcommittees. But the most powerful man in the room was Speaker John Robinson, who had held the prestigious chair for thirty years. All it took was a look, a nod, or carefully chosen words for the round-faced speaker to keep the representatives in line with his unchallenged authority. Whatever he agreed to in the discussion of the representatives was passed, and whatever he opposed was dropped.

Burgesses were expected to work their way up through Virginia politics, serving at the county level before they attempted to hold the prestigious position of burgess. Newly elected burgesses needed to earn the right to be heard by the Assembly. They were expected to remain respectfully quiet while the old guard controlled the discussions. And although those from the backwoods and upper piedmont regions of Virginia technically held voices equal to those of the Tidewater elite, they knew that their opinions were not highly regarded, or even welcomed.

Patrick listened intently as the representatives discussed the resolutions that had been drafted to send to the King, the House of Lords, and the House of Commons in response to the coming Stamp Act. He frowned as he heard the men discussing the need to tone down the harshness of their words so they would not give any offense whatsoever to the king. *Tone them down? Their words aren't harsh enough,* Patrick thought to himself as he gazed up at the eyes of royalty watching the proceedings. As in Hanover Courthouse, reminders of royal authority kept watch over the burgesses. Life-sized paintings of the kings and queens of England hung on the walls over His Majesty's servants, their eyes seeming to follow the burgesses who moved about the room.

The business of the House moved on to other matters and after a while the assembly ceased discussions in order to break out into their various subcommittees. As they filed out of the room and walked up the wide staircase to their respective meeting rooms, the clerk notified Patrick to follow him. He respectfully bowed and swallowed hard as he climbed the stairs. He was about to enter a room with the most powerful men of Virginia. Nigel followed along and slipped in the room where the Committee of Privileges and Elections would hear Patrick present the case of Colonel Nathaniel West Dandridge and a dispute over the recent election for the House of Burgesses seat in Hanover County. Dandridge accused a man named Littlepage of using gifts, bribes, and "swilling the planters with bumbo" (serving too much rum punch) in order to buy votes and win the election. There sat Chairman Richard Bland and members Peyton Randolph, George Wythe, Richard Henry Lee, Edmund Pendleton, and George Johnston. Nigel cringed as he saw their expressions when Patrick Henry entered the room. They looked at the disheveled backwoods attorney and cast glances at one another as if a mistake had been made for such a man to stand in their presence and take up their valuable time.

Only George Wythe maintained a slight grin as he looked at Patrick's attire, shaking his head and muttering under his breath, "Just wait, gentlemen." Wythe remembered judging Patrick too quickly when he last came to Williamsburg for his law license. He was eager to see if the backwoods lawyer had studied to improve his knowledge even if he hadn't improved his attire.

384

Patrick began in the same way as he now did with every jury in front of whom he argued a case. The method that had served him well in the Parson's Cause he now used deliberately when arguing a case. He started off slowly, as if he were unsure of himself, lowering the expectations of his listeners. While his skeptical audience listened, Patrick Henry studied their reactions and read them like a book. Once he assessed his audience, his voice rose and his eyes gleamed until they were spellbound by his delivery of the facts through convincing arguments. Using humor or dramatic, perfectly timed pauses, Patrick kept his audience hanging on every word with his powerful voice.

By the time Patrick finished presenting his case, the most powerful men in the colony of Virginia were speechless. And George Wythe and Nigel sat grinning from ear to ear.

MOUNT BRILLIANT

"He was magnificent!" Nigel exclaimed after he and Cato landed in the field next to Liz and MizP following their return from Williamsburg.

"C'est bon! Then he won the case for *Monsieur* Dandridge?" Liz asked expectantly.

"I'm afraid not, no," Nigel answered as he preened his whiskers. "There simply was not enough evidence to sway the burgesses. But if truth be told, those gentlemen themselves have been guilty of winning elections in the same fashion, so perhaps they could not bring themselves to punish another burgess for 'swilling the planters with bumbo.'"

"I think those shabby clothes made Pahtrick's case melt like a snowman in July," MizP interjected with a frown.

Nigel gave a jolly chuckle. "It is true that Patrick did not impress the esteemed gentlemen at first, but he soon squelched their unspoken negative thoughts about his appearance. They were spellbound by Patrick's delivery, and while he did not win the case for Dandridge, he left an extremely positive impression they shall not soon forget. That George Johnston fellow made it a point to compliment Patrick's case."

Cato stretched his wings. "Most importantly, Patrick was in Williamsburg at the perfect time to hear all the news and rumblings about the proposed Stamp Act. You should have seen the city! It was packed with humans, and that's all anyone talked about. I sat in the trees all over town, listening to the people below."

Nigel wiped off a smudge from his spectacles. "Indeed, old boy. I do believe this trip set the stage for Patrick's involvement in the House of Burgesses, whenever that may be. He was none too pleased to hear how timidly the burgesses expressed their concerns to King George and Parliament. When they meet again in the spring, they hope to have a response to their resolutions from London, and I know Patrick will be eager to hear that response."

"In the meantime we need to get *mon* Henry elected as a burgess," Liz added. "But somehow a burgess seat must open up in Louisa County."

Cato's eyes widened excitedly. "I might know of a 'somehow!' I overheard Patrick as he walked to the Raleigh Tavern with Thomas Johnson and his brother William," Cato relayed. "It sounded as if William is ready to quit his seat as a burgess. Those Johnson brothers are tired of the uppity Tidewater elites controlling the House and not listening to them. But William said he won't step down unless he finds another political position in which to serve in Louisa."

386

Liz's eyes brightened. "Thomas and William are both from Louisa County. *C'est ça!* If William gives up his seat, Patrick can be elected to take his place! We must find some other job for William."

PARLIAMENT BUILDING, LONDON, FEBRUARY 6, 1765

Gillamon and Clarie sat above in the "Stranger's Gallery" of the House of Commons with other spectators, listening to Parliament's discussion over George Grenville's proposed Stamp Act. The House of Commons had gone over the details, and there was no debate over the specific items in the Act. The debate rather focused on the principle and wisdom about passing such an act. Did the colonies have "virtual representation" in Parliament as some claimed? Or did Parliament have the right to tax the colonies however they chose? How they voted on this move against the colonies could forever change the colonies' relationship with the Mother Country.

"If they only knew the real 'strangers' that sat here," Gillamon whispered with a soft chuckle as he looked around the prestigious chamber of the mightiest power on Earth. "This gallery was well named in our case."

Clarie smiled and whispered back, "It doesn't get any *stranger* than a mountain goat and a lamb sitting in the House of Commons." She and Gillamon had taken their refined human forms as usual, but this time Clarie was a man so as not to cause a stir with a woman sitting in Parliament. Below them was the chamber that had served as the model for the Virginia House of Burgesses, with rows of benches facing each other, the Speaker's chair at the head, and the clerk's table in the center. "It's been eleven months since Grenville first introduced this bill." Clarie looked around at Virginia agents Edward Montague and Benjamin Franklin, and other colonial agents sitting nearby, who were visibly upset at what was about to happen. "He gave these colonial agents time to suggest an alternative for raising money in the colonies, but didn't give them the information they needed to find a solution."

"Grenville didn't intend for the colonies to come up with another solution. He simply wanted to give the *appearance* that he did," Gillamon explained, watching Benjamin Franklin sitting there with a frown as he gripped his hands on top of his cane. "Now that the petitions are pouring in from Virginia and the other colonies to stop the passage of the Stamp Act, Grenville has exactly what he wanted to push this bill through. Grenville refuses to allow those petitions to be read and discussed in the House of Commons except for the convenient sentiment that Grenville is sharing with them—that the colonies say that Parliament does not have the authority to tax them. Upon hearing this, these members now see the passage of the Stamp Act as more a matter of putting the colonies in their place than just raising money."

"Although not all of them feel that way," Clarie suggested. "Lord Cornwallis surprisingly is one of the members who opposes the Stamp Act."

Gillamon leaned over and gazed down at the twenty-seven-year-old Earl Charles Cornwallis, made a lord after his father's death three years before. He had served bravely in the Seven Years' War, and as they watched him fight in the Battle of Minden, Gillamon had told Al that he would someday be assigned to Cornwallis. "Yes. What a paradox that is, given what is to come. But there is another who also stands with the colonies, having fought side by side with them in the French and Indian War." Gillamon pointed to a genteel looking Irishman with a distorting wound on his face. "Colonel Isaac Barré received a bullet in his right cheek that left him blind in that eye. He understands the passion

Americans have to fight for their land and their liberty. The words he says today will forever be *stamped* on American history."

"The tax intended is odious to all your colonies, and they tremble at it," Isaac Barré exclaimed, holding one hand on his hip and pointing a finger at the gentleman he argued against, Charles Townshend. "He thinks part of the regulation passed last year very wise in preventing them from getting the commodities of foreign countries. We know not however the real effect of this. We are the Mother Country, but let us be cautious not to get the name of *Stepmother.*"

A low murmuring rippled through the assembly as Barré took his seat.

Charles Townshend rose to his feet, spread his arms wide, and spoke in a scornful tone. "And now will these Americans, children planted by our care, nourished up by our indulgence until they are grown to a degree of strength and opulence, and protected by our arms—will they now grudge to contribute their mite to relieve us from the heavy weight of that burden which we lie under?"

"Hear, hear!" voices echoed as the majority of the members nodded in agreement.

Isaac Barré again rose from his seat in a huff. "They planted by your *care?* No! Your *oppressions* planted them in America. They fled from your *tyranny* to a then uncultivated and unhospitable country," he shouted, casting a hand toward the Atlantic. "They nourished up by your *indulgence?* They grew by your *neglect* of them!" He paused and looked around the chamber and slowly pointed a finger around the room. "As soon as you began to care about them, that care was exercised in sending persons to rule over them, in one department and another, who were perhaps the deputies of deputies to some member of this House sent to *spy* out their liberty, to *misrepresent* their actions and to *prey* upon them; men whose behavior on many occasions has caused the blood of those Sons of Liberty to recoil within them."

Gillamon and Clarie exchanged glances as those words hung in the air over Parliament while Barré paused for a moment. No one spoke a word.

"They protected by your *arms?*" Barré continued. "They have nobly taken up arms in your *defense*, have exerted a valor amidst their constant and laborious industry for the defense of a country, whose frontier, while drenched in blood, its interior parts have yielded all its little savings to your reward." He stopped and held a hand up to his eye where the bullet had taken his vision when he fought alongside the Americans in the French and Indian War.

"The people, I believe, are as truly loyal as any subjects the king has—but a people jealous of their liberties. Believe me, remember I this day told you so," admonished Barré as he looked around the chamber, "that same spirit of freedom which actuated that people at first, will accompany them still." He took his seat and received nods of respect from the few fellow members who stood with him to oppose the Stamp Act.

"Sons of Liberty," Gillamon repeated softly. "Barré has just unknowingly named the movement that will come against this Stamp Act—a movement the likes of which these pompous members of Parliament have never seen."

"But that movement first needs a push to set it in motion," Clarie said with a knowing look to Gillamon.

"The Sons of Liberty will first need a *voice* to sound the alarm and move them to action," Gillamon answered. "And once that voice speaks, nothing will stop the ball of the Revolution from rolling through the colonies and all the way to London . . . right through the middle of this chamber."

389

A VOICE IN THE HOUSE

H ow utterly depressing," Nigel wailed, shaking his head as he read a letter while Liz looked over the April 18 edition of the *Pennsylvania Gazette.*

Spread across the front pages of the paper was the full content of the Stamp Act with the news that the House of Commons had passed it in February. Official word of King George signing the Act into law on March 22 had not yet reached the colonies, but Liz and Nigel already knew. Clarie had told them everything that happened in London, and had forwarded a letter that Benjamin Franklin had written to a friend in America after doing everything in his power to prevent the passage of the Stamp Act.

"Dr. Franklin writes, *'The tide was too strong against us. The nation was provoked by American claims of independence (of the power of Parliament), and all parties joined by resolving in this Act to settle the point. We might as well have hindered the sun's setting.'*" Nigel put down the letter. "The dastardly deed is done. The cursed Stamp Act will take effect on November 1."

"But that's a whole six months from now," MizP noted. "Couldn't Pahtrick speak up against the Stamp Act before then?"

Liz continued to scan the paper, but answered with a frown, "Unfortunately, the next session of the House of Burgesses starts in only three days. And the two seats from Louisa County are still taken by the Johnson Brothers. I failed to come up with anything else for William to do. He should be departing any moment now for Williamsburg to join the session."

Nigel wrinkled his forehead. "Oh, why couldn't Patrick have been a burgess when he could have railed against this coming act *before* it was passed? Even if by some miracle he were elected a burgess this very day, the spring session will soon be underway in Williamsburg. Surely the House of Burgesses will read this dreadful Stamp Act news and quickly accept the fact that what's done is done so they can move on to other matters."

MizP snorted and stomped her hoof into the dirt. "Will you two listen tuh the words coming out of your mouths? You sound like the end of the world has already come and gone and you missed it! Now if Pahtrick is supposed tuh do something grand with his voice in the House about this Stamp Act business, then you best have faith that he *will*. If that riddle said he's going tuh speak five words, or two words, or whatever it may be, then I suggest you get on with figuring out how tuh help him get there tuh say them." She put her head down low to get eye level with Liz and Nigel. "Remember, those parsons thought it was a done deal, too, until Pahtrick got involved. It ain't over 'til it's over."

Liz and Nigel looked at one another, chagrined by the scolding MizP had given them.

"I am sorry, *mon amie*. You are right. We should not sit here and have a pity party over what we have not been able to do so far," Liz confessed, straightening up. "We have faced far greater seeming impossibilities in our lives, have we not, Nigel? We must proceed to help Patrick and see where his voice leads. The spring session of the House of Burgesses will last a month in Williamsburg."

"Agreed, my dear. My apologies, MizP. I feel rather small at the moment," Nigel added with a frown.

"Nigel, you *are* small," MizP teased the little mouse, leaning down to get in his face. "But only in your size. Not in your brains or your heart."

"I relish the compliment, my dear. Thank you." Nigel lifted his chin and smiled. "Right, well we must pursue Liz's idea to find something for William Johnson to do before he leaves for Williamsburg so Patrick can take his seat."

"Pahtrick also needs a new suit of clothes tuh go with that burgess seat," MizP whinnied.

Nigel wiggled his whiskers and grinned. "MizP, I truly appreciate your continued concern over Patrick's attire. He certainly could improve, but I don't think his dress will kill his chances of being heard."

391

"I don't care if I sound like I'm beating a dead horse—I hate that expression—over Pahtrick's appearance, but this time I'm putting my hoof down!" MizP shouted as she repeatedly stamped her hoof in the dirt. "If he becomes a burgess, he had better *dress* like one."

"Dead horse," Liz repeated as an idea suddenly came to her. "Kill his chances of being heard." Her eyes lit up with excitement. "Perfect, *mes amis!* I know exactly what William can do! *Merci!* Now I must go write a note about the job to *Monsieur* Johnson. Nigel, you and Cato can drop it off this afternoon. There is no time to waste!"

Liz ran off, leaving MizP and Nigel looking at one another in confusion.

MizP called after Liz as she ran off to search John Henry's study for pen and ink. "While you're at it, write Pahtrick a note telling him tuh buy a new suit before I carry him all the way tuh Williamsburg!"

———

WILLIAMSBURG, MAY 20

"Merci for bringing me, Clarie," Liz beamed. "I could not miss *mon* Henry's debut in the House of Burgesses!"

"Of course, Liz," Clarie answered. She was disguised as a gentleman in town on business during the busy Court Days of Williamsburg. She blended in with the six hundred visitors who had come to town filling the taverns, inns, coffeehouses, and marketplace. "Besides, you and Nigel need to act quickly on the fiddle's riddle once you figure out the rest. I will need to leave you soon to attend to other matters."

"Je comprends," Liz answered confidently. She smiled as she saw Patrick Henry proudly walking down Duke of Gloucester Street toward the Capitol. He was dressed in a crisp black linen suit with a fresh white shirt, a new tricorn hat, and polished black buckled shoes he had taken time to clean after the trip to Williamsburg. His clothes were not as fine or expensive as the genteel Tidewater elites, but they were respectable and neat. "Be still my heart! He looks so handsome in his new clothes!"

"I think MizP was even more excited than Patrick about the new clothes," Nigel chuckled, joining the two friends on the south side of the Capitol. "She certainly clip-clopped happily into town with her head held high."

"Well, her suggested note seems to have encouraged Patrick to invest in his appearance," Liz replied. "Sallie even insisted Patrick splurge and buy a new hat and shoes for his twenty-ninth birthday, which he'll have while he's here. She made sure his wig was in good order as well. She and the children are so very proud of him. I am, too. *Mon* Henry is a burgess at last!"

"And *your* note suggesting that William Johnson take the position of coroner for Louisa County worked out just in time, my pet," Nigel added.

"Coroner is obviously not a job most humans seek out, but it is necessary and it pays well for writing out death certificates," Liz replied.

"It is a rather *dead-end* job," Nigel quipped with a jolly chuckle.

"William was more than happy to give up his seat so Patrick could run in such a quickly scheduled election," reported Liz. "And it was wonderful to see more than forty of Patrick's family and friends with land in Louisa drop everything to travel from Hanover and come vote for him! The people simply adore him."

"That they do," Clarie agreed with a grin, pointing to the Capitol. "But just wait until he becomes a star inside those walls."

393

Liz purred and whipped her tail back and forth excitedly. "I do not wish to miss a moment of it! Shall we?"

Clarie picked Nigel up to put him in her pocket. She then picked up Liz to carry her under the folds of her cloak. Together they walked inside the Capitol to witness the swearing in of Patrick Henry, Esquire, as the new burgess from Louisa County.

———

LEWIS'S TAVERN, WILLIAMSBURG, TUESDAY, MAY 28

Once Liz and Nigel got their bearings in the assembly room, they quickly discovered that they could hide in the middle of the action, right under the clerk's table, which was covered with a long, green table-cloth draped to the floor. With the late spring heat, the windows and doors of the assembly room were opened early to allow fresh air to cir-culate before the sessions promptly began at 10:00 a.m. Each morning, Liz and Nigel easily slipped inside the chamber and under the table before the burgesses arrived.

After Patrick took the time-honored traditional oaths to be sworn in as a burgess on May 20, he was appointed to fill a vacancy in the

Committee on Courts of Justice, and took his seat among the sixty other men gathered in the chamber. Although there were 116 total representatives in the House of Burgesses, nearly half of them had either already returned home after three weeks of service, or had not attended the May session at all. Many of these men were planters and merchants who had to sacrifice their time and money to travel to Williamsburg. With the planting season well underway, many of the burgesses had to attend to their vast crops, such as Colonel George Washington at his sprawling plantation in northern Virginia, called Mount Vernon. Liz beamed when Patrick met George Washington for the first time, knowing it was because of Max's bravery that Washington was there at all.

As the close of the May session neared, each day saw a few more burgesses taking their leave and heading home. Most of the major business that needed attention had been covered at the beginning of May. Patrick listened to a myriad of routine business items like bills for building roads and unique items such as offering bounties on wolves or forbidding hogs to roam the streets in the new town of Richmond.

394

Nigel had been especially interested in hearing a petition from the organist for Williamsburg's Bruton Parish Church, Peter Pelham, who was requesting reimbursement of £50 for repairs he had made to the church organ. The mouse had so enjoyed spending time listening to Mr. Pelham practice his music that he opted to spend his nights snug inside the beautiful church. Mr. Pelham had been quite busy providing music at the Governor's Palace, as Governor Fauquier entertained burgesses and guests visiting Williamsburg. Never had Nigel been happier to be a "church mouse" and drift off to the melodious tunes of Bach, Handel, and Telemann.

Patrick Henry had caused quite the stir on his third day when he rose to speak for the first time in the House of Burgesses. The old guard of powerful members raised their eyebrows to see this new burgess who had been unusually elected without having first served in any other position in Virginia politics. This twenty-eight-year-old upstart shot straight to the top of the political arena, and was ignorant of the unspoken "rules" about how things were run. And he didn't really have any personal connections in the House of Burgesses, save Thomas Johnson. But Johnson had butted heads with the speaker in previous sessions, and was absent from this session. Although Patrick had previously impressed Wythe, Bland, the Randolph brothers, and

Edmund Pendleton when he applied for his law license and presented the Dandridge case, that was before he was in the House. If Patrick directed his talent for piercing argument at *them,* their first positive impressions of him would quickly fade and turn hostile. And that is exactly what happened. This new, young, unknown backwoods burgess did not keep respectfully quiet as was expected of him, but decided that his first words in the House would challenge the most powerful man in Virginia: Speaker John Robinson.

Robinson had proposed a bill to establish a Public Loan Office to supposedly help some planters who had gone into debt from the still-depressed tobacco market. Patrick loudly and forcefully opposed the bill on principle, arguing that it would pay the debts of a few wealthy planters at the expense of the public. Little did Patrick know that a dark secret lay behind the real reason for the bill. Speaker Robinson also served as the treasurer of the colony, and had already lent £100,000 in public money to some of his friends. This bill would help him float those secret loans with public money.

Although the bill passed despite his objections, Patrick's powerful 395 oration immediately established him as the bold new voice for the backwoods and up-country farmers against the Tidewater elite. Every one of them backed him, including George Johnston of Alexandria, to whom he had presented the Dandridge case in the fall. Johnston had a huge law practice and a plantation on the Potomac River in the upcountry of Virginia. But Patrick's voice also immediately gained him new enemies the likes of Speaker John Robinson and his protégé, Edmund Pendleton, the most skilled trial lawyer in Virginia. For the first time, there was almost a palpable change in the air of the Virginia House of Burgesses. The newer outsiders from the west and up-country were standing up to the older insiders from the east, and the voice of Patrick Henry was leading the charge.

Patrick spent the following days in the House and the following evenings in the company of George Johnston and his other new friends. They frequented one of the more quiet taverns of Williamsburg, away from the heavy gambling and boisterous drinking that was common in the other taverns like the Raleigh. Tonight Patrick met with a trio of them in Lewis's Tavern, discussing the one thing on the minds of all but also the one thing the Virginia House of Burgesses refused to talk about: the Stamp Act.

Littered about the table were the latest gazettes from the other colonies, and the outsider burgesses read by the soft glow of lanterns as they devoured the news. They were eager to see what the other assemblies up and down the Atlantic seaboard were doing about the Stamp Act.

"It seems that even Boston's James Otis, who touted 'no taxation without representation,' has given in to the passage of the Stamp Act," Patrick scowled, reading the news. "Otis *now* says that *'It is the duty of all humbly, and silently, to acquiesce in all the decisions of the supreme legislature. Nine hundred and ninety-nine in a thousand of the colonists will never once entertain a thought but of submission to our Sovereign, and to the authority of Parliament in all possible contingencies. They undoubtedly have the right to levy internal taxes on the colonies.'*" Patrick tossed down the paper in disgust and blew a raspberry. "Are all the other colonies simply lying down at the feet of England like this and giving up without a fight?"

"It appears so," answered John Fleming, a lawyer from Cumberland. "As this news trickles in from England, the colonial legislatures are sadly accepting the inevitable."

"Nothing is inevitable if you speak up," Patrick answered. "Why won't our burgesses even discuss the Stamp Act?"

"You missed the opening session, Patrick, but Speaker Robinson and the conservative members decided it would be best to put off any further discussion of the Act until we receive an official reply from England to these petitions we sent over in December," George Johnston explained. He tapped a copy of the Virginia petitions that the House had sent to England. They were filled with the humble pleadings of a submissive House.

Colonel Robert Munford from Mecklenburg wrinkled his brow. He was from the far western reaches of Virginia, and owned a plantation on the Staunton River. "Well, it appears a captain in Annapolis just arrived with the news that the Act has already passed. Look at this from the May 2 *Maryland Gazette*. They printed the entire Stamp Act along with news of its passage. King George signed it into law in March." He looked up at the men around the table with a frown. "It takes effect November 1."

"Not only do we have a speaker who wishes to postpone discussion about the Act until the next session," Patrick lamented, scanning the local paper, "he has kept our own *Virginia Gazette* from printing anything negative about the Stamp Act."

Munford shook his head and got to his feet. "Gentlemen, I have had enough for today, and shall leave you with it. I bid you good night."

Patrick, George, and John stood and shook hands with Munford, offering their evening farewells.

Patrick pushed his spectacles on top of his head and wrinkled his brow as he took his seat, continuing the conversation. "With this news, it is clear now that England has ignored our 'polite' petitions. And it will be too late to do anything about it if we wait until the next session!"

"Well, only a few short days remain in this session," John answered, nodding. "And we're down to only thirty-nine burgesses who've stayed in town."

"I think that many of the burgesses have already left town because they are *afraid* to take a stand and let their voices be heard. They know that if they speak words of protest or resistance against the Act, they could be seen as disloyal subjects or even *rebels,*" Patrick emphasized pointedly. He leaned back in his chair and tapped his finger angrily on the table. "Look at the moves Parliament has made against the colonies with the Sugar Act and now the Stamp Act: taxation without representation, home searches without warrants, quartering British troops in our homes that *we* must pay for, treating accused citizens as *guilty* until proved innocent, moving jury trials by peers at home to vice-admiralty courts far from home. If we remain silent, this will have far-reaching consequences, enabling the Crown to only further destroy our liberties."

397

John and George looked at one another in surprise and then to Patrick, silently willing him to do something. Suddenly Patrick stood up and screeched back his chair, leaning over to pick up the copy of the Virginia petitions. He read a line with a sarcastic tone: *"Nothing is further from our thoughts than to show the least disposition to any sort of rudeness."* He slapped the petition on the table. "Spineless! No wonder they were ignored!" He clenched his jaw and looked around the tavern at the common people who filled the tables. Not only were the original resolves written in the flowery language of the highly educated, refined burgesses in order to appease the Crown, they were written with words the common folk didn't use. The resolves didn't represent the voice of the people. "Stay here, gentlemen. I'll be back."

Liz and Nigel were huddled under a table nearby. "Now where do you suppose Patrick is going?" Nigel wondered.

"I am not certain, but you are the only one small enough to find out, *mon ami,*" Liz replied. "Go follow him."

"Right!" agreed Nigel as he darted out and followed Patrick Henry upstairs to his room.

———

As the two gentlemen waited for Patrick to return, Liz listened to their conversation. She beamed as she heard how they admired her Henry's zeal. They weren't sure what Patrick was up to, but they were eager to find out. Liz and Nigel had been waiting day after day for the discussion of the Stamp Act to begin, but no one in the House had been willing to step up and take action. They knew time was running out. The May session would soon come to a close, and the governor would not reconvene them until fall at the earliest. Or, if the burgesses did something rash or displeasing to the Crown, Governor Fauquier could dissolve the House of Burgesses for an even longer period of time. If the governor dissolved them entirely, not only could he delay the next session indefinitely, but each burgess would have to be re-elected to office all over again.

"My dear, you are in for a magnificent surprise!" Nigel exclaimed in a giddy voice when he rejoined Liz under the table. He preened his whiskers excitedly and pointed to the table as Patrick took his seat to rejoin the men. "*Seven* surprises to be exact."

Patrick set the original Virginia petitions on the table and held his hand above them. "Gentlemen, these resolves are what the House of Burgesses sent to the king. They were *ignored.*" He pushed the paper aside and then took out a leaf of paper he had torn from his *Coke upon Littleton* law book. On it he had written seven new resolves. "And these," he said with an assertive grin as his hand hovered over them, looking into the anxious eyes of the men, "will *not* be so easy to ignore."

398

IF THIS BE TREASON

A voice in the house makes seven words, two short. Seven words! *C'est ça!*" Liz exclaimed. "Patrick's seven *resolves* must mean the seven 'words' from the fiddle's riddle. But I do not understand the meaning of 'two short.'"

Nigel and Liz were reading over the preamble and seven resolves Patrick had penned against the Stamp Act. After a lively discussion that went well into the night, Patrick, John, and George all agreed they would boldly present Patrick's resolves in the House the next day. John Fleming wrote out a copy of Patrick's resolves for them to keep when Patrick turned in his copy to the clerk to record following a vote.

"See here, Fleming's copy is spread across two pages, with the first five resolves on page one and the last two resolves on page two," Nigel offered, pointing to the pages. The single candle flickered as Liz and Nigel read by the dim light in the tavern bedroom. The men snored loudly, exhausted after their draining day and night. "These last two are the most radical, so I can see why they suggested Patrick hold back from reading them should the first five prove to be too much for the old guard to handle."

Liz furrowed her brow. "Perhaps. But the first four resolves do not contain anything truly different than the original resolves the House sent to England. Patrick deleted the polite, pompous words of lawyers and restated them in more assertive, straightforward terms even common people can understand. *Mon* Henry knows how to speak the language of the people, *for* the people."

Nigel tapped the fifth resolve. "But the fifth has one word that will pose an issue for the pompous burgesses."

"Oui, it is the *'therefore'* the burgesses will need to get past," agreed Liz, "as there begins the language of forceful action."

"Even if they get past resolution number five, the shocking words in the sixth and seventh resolutions will launch a firestorm of debate like these burgesses have never heard," Nigel posited. Suddenly his eyes widened. "Fire. Great Britain has been stacking the dry logs of issues for quite some time against the colonies."

"And because these last two resolves could be the spark that ignites that fire, the old burgesses will do everything in their power to dampen them," Liz answered somberly.

———

WEDNESDAY, MAY 29, 1765

Patrick Henry, John Fleming, and George Johnston filed confidently into the assembly room just shy of the 10:00 a.m. bell that struck the hour and designated the official opening of the House of Burgesses. The friends each gave Patrick an affirming pat on the back as they took their seats. As the bell tolled ten times, Patrick removed his hat and tucked it under his seat. He smiled, thinking how Sallie insisted that he purchase the hat for his birthday. He was twenty-nine years old today. In a way he felt so much older than the days when he was a struggling merchant and failed farmer. But as he looked around the room, he knew how young he really was compared with the old guard burgesses who had sat for decades in their well-established seats of this powerful chamber. Patrick slipped a finger around his collar to loosen his cravat as he gazed up at the life-sized portrait of King George III staring down at him. His heart raced because of what he was about to do. It was one thing to oppose the Crown before a law was passed, but quite another to come against the king of England once his signature graced the parchment and he placed his signet ring into the glob of hot red wax to seal the law with royal finality. Patrick knew he was playing with treasonous fire. He closed his eyes as the words from Jeremiah once more filled his mind:

You are to influence them, not let them influence you! They will fight against you like a besieging army against a high city wall. But they will not conquer you, for I am with you to protect and deliver you, says the LORD.

Amen, Patrick prayed silently.

Liz peeked out from a narrow slit in the green tablecloth under the clerk's table. Her heart raced as well. *"Joyeux Anniversaire, mon* Henry," she whispered. How she wanted to run over and curl her tail around him affectionately to wish him happy birthday. "It is you who shall *give* a gift today on your birthday. You shall give the gift of liberty, *cher ami.* Know that you are loved, and you are able."

Nigel smiled and softly put a paw on Liz's shoulder. "He is ready, my dear. And the Maker will make him able indeed. Never fear."

Liz smiled. *"Merci,* Nigel. Now, we wait for the moment to come."

Speaker Robinson opened up the session and proceeded to oversee the morning's business. First the Treasurer's report was passed, and then a few other minor matters were discussed. When Patrick couldn't take the waiting any longer, he nodded to George Johnston, who rose to his feet.

"Mr. Speaker, I propose that the House immediately meet in the Committee of the Whole to consider the steps necessary to take in response to the impending Stamp Act," announced Johnston.

"Second," Patrick Henry offered with an upraised hand.

Speaker Robinson's face went flush. What he had tried to stall for weeks would wait no more. "All in favor, say 'aye'," Speaker Robinson announced, looking around the chamber at the scant representatives numbering only thirty-nine burgesses. "The motion is carried." He frowned, put his hands on his knees and lifted himself up out of the speaker's chair. He slowly removed his wig and robe and took a seat on the bench as an ordinary burgess. As was proper procedure, Attorney General Peyton Randolph took Robinson's place to preside over the meeting.

Suddenly the clerk, John Randolph, lifted the green tablecloth to place the silver mace under the table. This was to signify the informality of the meeting. Liz took in a quick breath and stepped back as the clerk nearly put the mace on her tail. She rested a paw over her racing heart and shared a knowing look with Nigel. "That was close!" she mouthed.

Peyton Randolph lifted his hand. "The Committee of the Whole is now in session. You may proceed, Mr. Johnston."

"I defer to my colleague, the gentleman from Louisa County, Mr. Patrick Henry," stated Johnston with an outstretched hand. The burgesses looked at one another in concern. They were expecting Johnston, not Henry, to address the committee.

"Thank you, Mr. Johnston," Patrick Henry began as he rose to his feet. He reached into his pocket and unfolded the paper of his resolves.

He glanced around the room and bowed respectfully to Speaker Robinson and the burgesses who sat up with heightened curiosity as to what he was going to do.

"With your permission, I would like to read this document pertaining to the impending Stamp Act," Patrick said, clearing his throat and taking a deep breath. "Given that the law will go into effect this November, I have prepared a statement and resolves in response."

The old guard burgesses looked at one another and murmured in alarm. They immediately fixed their icy gaze on Patrick.

"We do not need such further statements before we have received England's response to our petitions," Richard Bland insisted.

"Proceed, Mr. Henry," Peyton Randolph said reluctantly, knowing that Henry must now be heard in the committee.

Patrick held up the paper and gave one last look at Fleming and Johnston before he began. "Whereas, the honorable House of Commons in England have of late drawn into question how far the General Assembly of this Colony hath the power to enact laws for laying of taxes and imposing duties, payable by the people of this, His Majesty's most ancient Colony: for settling and ascertaining the same to all future times, the House of Burgesses of this *present* General Assembly have come to the following resolves:

"How dare he assume to speak for us?!" Robert Carter Nicholas muttered under his breath.

"*Resolved,* that the first adventurers and settlers of His Majesty's Colony and dominion of Virginia brought with them and transmitted to their posterity, and all other His Majesty's subjects since inhabiting in this His Majesty's said Colony, all the liberties, privileges, franchises, and immunities that have at any time been held, enjoyed, and possessed by the people of Great Britain," read Patrick, looking up briefly as he went on to read the second resolution.

"*Resolved,* that by two royal charters, granted by King James I, the colonists aforesaid are declared entitled to all liberties, privileges, and immunities of denizens and natural subjects to all intents and purposes as if they had been abiding and born within the Realm of England."

Nigel peeped out from under the green tablecloth to gauge the response from the burgesses. "So far so good for these first two resolves," he whispered. "The burgesses cannot dispute that when the explorers and colonists arrived in America, they brought with them all their rights as English citizens and that Virginia's two royal charters also promised these same rights to the colonists."

Patrick continued reading, now the third and fourth resolves: "*Resolved,* that the taxation of the people by themselves, or by persons chosen by themselves to represent them, who can only know what taxes the people are able to bear, or the easiest method of raising them, and must themselves be affected by every tax laid on the people, is the only security against a burdensome taxation, and the distinguishing characteristic of British freedom, without which the ancient constitution cannot exist.

"*Resolved,* that His Majesty's liege people of this his most ancient and loyal Colony have without interruption enjoyed the inestimable right of being governed by such laws, respecting their internal policy and taxation, as are derived from their own consent, with the approbation of their sovereign, or his substitute; and that the same has never been forfeited or yielded up, but has been constantly recognized by the kings and people of Great Britain."

Liz had to see for herself and peeked out from under the table to look into the faces of the burgesses. "They also must agree that taxation by the people or their chosen representatives is the true mark of British freedom, and that the people have only ever paid taxes voted on by Virginians alone," she echoed. People had begun crowding around the open doorway as word quickly spread about what Patrick was doing. "This is acceptable, so far. But here comes the 'therefore.'"

Patrick glanced over at John Fleming and George Johnston, who gave him firm nods of support. He then saw the crowd gathering at the doorway and spied young Thomas Jefferson. He then glanced over the old guard who scowled and seemed to dare him to take things one step further, leaning in expectantly and clenching their fists. Patrick lifted his chin high and read the fifth resolve:

"*Resolved, therefore* that the General Assembly of this Colony have the only and exclusive Right and Power to lay Taxes and Impositions upon the inhabitants of this Colony and that every attempt to vest such power in any person or persons whatsoever other than the General Assembly aforesaid has a manifest tendency to destroy British as well as American Freedom."

The burgesses immediately began to squirm and the room buzzed with talk over such a brash statement. But Patrick Henry wasn't finished.

"He isn't stopping at number five!" Nigel whispered hoarsely, gripping Liz's arm. "Here come the two sparks for the colonial fire!"

"*Resolved,* That His Majesty's liege people, the inhabitants of this Colony, are not bound to yield obedience to any law or ordinance whatever, designed to impose any taxation whatsoever upon them, other than the laws or ordinances of the General Assembly aforesaid."

Richard Bland, Robert Carter Nicholas, George Wythe, and the old guard burgesses were on their feet, shouting, "How dare you suggest that Virginians do not have to obey any law not passed by this Assembly! You are defying the Crown with such slander!"

Patrick ignored them and locked eyes with the painting of King George III. His anger rose and his voice boomed out the seventh and final resolve:

"*Resolved,* that any person who shall, by speaking or writing, assert or maintain that any person or persons other than the General Assembly of this Colony, have *any* right or power to impose or lay any taxation on the people here, shall be deemed an enemy to His Majesty's Colony."

404

Immediately the chamber erupted into a violent debate, as one member after another jumped to their feet, shouting their opposition. Fleming, Johnston, and other Henry supporters such as Colonel Robert Munford and Paul Carrington countered with shouts of solid arguments while the onlookers packed in the doorway stood there in awe of what was happening.

"I have never heard *anything* like this," observed Thomas Jefferson, his jaw hanging open at hearing the words coming out of Patrick's mouth. "Henry speaks as Homer wrote."

It was as if a verbal bloodbath were unleashed in the House of Burgesses as the representatives fought over the audacity of Patrick Henry. Not only were Patrick's resolves viciously attacked, but the opposition sought to destroy Patrick's personal character and reputation.

"The unmitigated gall!" Nigel screamed in response to the personal attacks against Patrick Henry.

But Liz sat there calmly and smiled. She knew that her Henry would have the final, overpowering word that would cut like a knife through the shouts of the pompous elitist burgesses who sought his political demise. She knew he would carry the day with the same supernatural zeal and power in his voice that he had used in the Parson's Cause. "Wait for it, *mon ami.*"

Patrick Henry held up his hand and a hush fell over the House, as members slowly turned one by one to see what he had to say. He allowed an excruciating pause to continue until each and every burgess was under his control and gave him their full attention. He slowly pushed his spectacles atop his head.

"Caesar had his Brutus . . ." Patrick finally said in a firm, resolute voice, looking around the room. These men well knew their Roman history of the assassination of the tyrant, Julius Caesar. ". . . Charles the First his Cromwell," he roared in a louder voice, pausing again to allow the image of Oliver Cromwell toppling the king of England to fill their minds, "and George the Third . . ." he thundered with fiery eyes as he pointed to the portrait of King George III.

"TREASON! THE MAN HAS SPOKEN TREASON!" Speaker Robinson bellowed, pointing a pudgy finger at Patrick.

"TREASON!" the other conservative burgesses shouted in agreement.

". . . may profit by their example," Patrick finished with a bone-chilling, eerie calm in his voice that brought a hush over the room. He slowly lowered his accusing finger and looked piercingly at each and every man in the chamber. "If *this* be treason, make the most of it."

Stunned silence. Patrick slowly walked back to his seat and sat down, crossing his legs, resting his hands on his knees and nodding with a grin to Fleming and Johnston.

405

THURSDAY, MAY 30, 1765

"By God, I would have given one hundred guineas for a single vote!" Peyton Randolph exclaimed as he stormed out of the hall of the House of Burgesses, blazing past Thomas Jefferson, who had returned to hear the vote on Patrick Henry's resolves. Randolph hurried down the Duke of Gloucester Street together with a group of old guard burgesses.

Liz and Nigel cheered and hugged one another outside where MizP stood. "In addition to the first four resolutions, the fifth one passed!" Liz exclaimed. "Oh, it passed!"

"Just barely, my dear, by a vote of twenty to nineteen!" Nigel replied, wiping his brow. "If there had been a tie on the vote for the fifth resolution, Speaker Robinson would have cast the deciding vote to defeat it in the favor of the Crown."

"Why was Pahtrick's fifth resolution so controversial tuh everyone?" MizP wanted to know.

"Because it was the very first time a colony declared independence from taxation by Parliament," Nigel explained.

"Well, it sounds like those old field nags got their noses smacked by Pahtrick and his high-blooded colts," MizP opined proudly. "It's always the young ones who buck the system and start new movements while the old ones try tuh hold hands tuh stop them."

Liz giggled. "I could not have given *mon* Henry a better birthday gift if I tried! Now he can celebrate with his friends tonight."

"Pahtrick has different plans, Liz," MizP replied. "He told Fleming and Johnston he was heading home this afternoon after the vote, as he figured the Governor will dissolve the House once he hears about what happened today. We'll be getting on the road soon."

Liz and Nigel looked at one another in surprise. "Maybe he is concerned that Governor Fauquier will come after him for his treasonous speech, so feels like he should depart," conjectured Liz.

"I'm not sure what Patrick is thinking, but I can imagine what *those* gentlemen are thinking," guessed Nigel, pointing to Peyton Randolph, George Wythe, and Speaker Robinson. They were hurriedly walking up the Palace Green to the Governor's Palace. "What do you suppose they are up to?"

Liz's mind raced. "Do they know that Patrick is leaving Williamsburg?"

"I suppose so," MizP answered, watching Patrick walking toward them, now dressed in rustic leather breeches, and with saddle bags draped over his arm. "Here he comes now, chatting with that young Paul Carrington, one of his greatest admirers."

"Yes, that young man was quite mesmerized with Patrick's fiery voice during the debates," Nigel agreed. "I've never seen such a visible display of enthusiasm from a burgess. Like Patrick, young Carrington was also elected late to the House and arrived after this session had already begun."

"Nigel, hurry and get to the Palace and see if those men meet with the Governor about what happened today," Liz instructed the mouse as she hid behind a tree. "Something tells me that as soon as *mon* Henry rides out of town on MizP, those men are going to try to undo everything he just did in the House."

━━━

FRIDAY, MAY 31, 1765

"WHY THOSE ARROGANT OLD FIELD NAGS!" Nigel ranted, borrowing MizP's expression for the old guard burgesses. He paced back and forth across the green tablecloth on the clerk's table, raising his fists angrily. "They actually went through with it! They convinced Governor Fauquier to postpone dissolving the House tomorrow until they have reversed the vote on Patrick's fifth resolution today! This is preposterous!"

"Steady, Mousie," Liz told the outraged mouse as she looked through the Journal of the House of Burgesses. The assemblymen had left the Capitol for the day, and Liz and Nigel stayed behind under the table to wait and see exactly what had been recorded in the official record of the House of Burgesses. "We will figure out a way to make this right. The truth must always find a way to come out, no?"

After Patrick Henry left town, Peyton Randolph, Speaker Robinson, and others met with the Governor and told him of what had happened with the Stamp Act Resolves. They all agreed that it was in their best interests in the eyes of Parliament to have the fifth resolve reversed, so looked for a way to "erase" the vote.

Thomas Jefferson had arrived early that morning at the House of Burgesses and spotted his cousin Peter Randolph hurriedly searching through the Parliament books before the burgesses arrived. Peter was a member of the Governor's Council, and was sent to find a precedent that would allow them to reverse the vote or "expunge" (remove) the vote entirely from the record. When the rest of the burgesses arrived and the assembly was called into session, Speaker Robinson and the old guard members moved to strike all five of Patrick's resolves. When that failed, they concentrated on striking down the fifth resolution alone, since it had only passed by one vote the day before. They succeeded in voting again to accept or reject the fifth resolution. Now that Patrick Henry was gone, the vote was finally a tie, and Speaker Robinson cast the deciding vote. The fifth resolution was promptly struck from the Journal, leaving only four resolves approved by the House.

"Look here, Nigel," Liz said, pointing to that day's official journal page of the Virginia House of Burgesses. "Not only did Speaker Robinson cast the deciding vote to erase Patrick's fifth resolution, it

407

appears that he even had the erasure *itself* erased! The original page showing the motion to expunge the fifth resolution has been torn out and rewritten!"

Nigel looked at the freshly inked journal entry in the place of the removed page. It showed that only four resolutions had ever been passed. There was no mention of what had transpired that day. "Why, those sneaky, stuffy burgesses! They have tampered with the truth! Blast it all, there weren't four, but *five* resolutions that first passed this House! And there were seven resolutions presented, if you count the two that were rejected as out and out treasonous."

Chills suddenly made Liz's fur stand on end as she remembered the fiddle's riddle. *"A voice in the house makes five words, two short.* Five words *plus* two words. Seven words in all were proposed, but now only four are officially in the record."

"Indeed!" Nigel replied with a scowl. He suddenly remembered something. "My dear, Clarie said you and I would need to act quickly after we figured out the rest of the riddle. What do you suppose we are meant to do?"

"Well, Patrick's resolutions were powerful but they did not lay out a course of action," Liz replied, her mind quickly formulating a plan. "They only denied the right of the king to tax the colonies. What good are words if they are not followed by actions?" She then smiled and looked at her mouse friend. "Nigel, since the sneaky burgesses want to silence Patrick's voice in their Journal for Parliament to read, then we need to make sure his resolutions are printed in the newspapers for all *America* to read."

"By Jove, you're right!" Nigel cheered, but then his face fell. "But the *Virginia Gazette* simply will not publish Patrick's resolves. That cheeky Robinson not only controls the House of Burgesses, but he also controls what that loyalist printer Joseph Royle puts in the paper. Even if the *Virginia Gazette* did print the resolves, they would only print the four that were officially passed."

"If the *Virginia Gazette* will not print *mon* Henry's resolutions, then we will make sure that the other colonial papers do," proposed Liz, twitching her tail defiantly. "We shall make copies of his resolutions that you and Cato can then deliver to the northern papers. I am certain the other gazettes will print them, but we must do this quickly and strike while the iron is hot."

"Brilliant! We shall burn the midnight oil and make copies of the resolutions so Cato and I can take flight in the morning," Nigel agreed, taking a blank sheet of paper from the clerk's desk. He dipped the quill in the ink and hesitated. "But should we copy the five resolutions that were originally passed, or the four that were *officially* passed?"

"Neither," Liz answered with a gleam in her eye, picking up Patrick's handwritten resolves. "Before they destroy this piece of evidence, we shall send copies of all *seven* of Patrick's resolutions, plus the preamble. Since those pompous burgesses have seen fit to silence *mon* Henry's 'treasonous' voice so the people will not hear, then we shall not hold back a single word he spoke. We are the Order of the *Seven*, no?"

Nigel's eyes widened behind his spectacles and he put a paw over his mouth to stifle his shock. "My dear, this is quite the scandalous move! I suppose if we simply send the original seven resolves as they were *proposed* to the House of Burgesses, then the papers will indeed still be printing the truth."

"*Oui,* of course we must print what is true. But we will do exactly as *mon* Henry instructed," Liz asserted with a determined face and a sly grin. "If this be treason, make the most of it."

409

The Beast of the Gévaudan

46

LES HUBACS, FRANCE, JUNE 30, 1764

*A*llons-y!*" Jeanne Boulet shouted to the grazing sheep as she prodded them along with a stick. Her few sheep nibbled a bare patch of ground, having stripped it of grass near the tree line at the edge of the forest. The fourteen-year-old shepherd girl turned to head back toward the village. She looked to the horizon and shielded her eyes from the bright sun to gauge the time of day, about five o'clock. "Hurry now. I wish to be home for supper."

Jeanne wrinkled her nose at the strong odor of the sheep that huddled close as they walked along behind her. "Pfft! You sheep smell worse than usual today." She leaned over to pick another wildflower to add to her small bouquet. She held the flowers up to her nose, hoping for a fragrant whiff to mask the odor. No such luck. The stench was too strong. She lowered the bouquet and dangled it by her side as she walked ahead of the sheep, singing a French folk tune:

> *"Au clair de la lune,*
> *Mon ami Pierrot,*
> *Prête-moi ta plume*
> *Pour écrire un mot.*
> *Ma chandelle est morte,*
> *Je n'ai plus de feu.*
> *Ouvre-moi ta porte*
> *Pour l'amour de Dieu."*

As she finished singing the last line, the sheep suddenly scattered in all directions, bleating in a feverish pitch. Jeanne quickly turned around and was suddenly hit in the chest, falling hard to the ground with the wind knocked out of her. Terror filled her eyes as her attacker lunged for her throat. There was no time to cry for help. It would not have made a difference, even if she had. No one would have heard her out here on the isolated hillside.

Some local peasants from the village found her the next day, a withered bouquet of flowers by her side.

CHÂTEAU DE CHAVANIAC-LAFAYETTE, FRANCE, JUNE 1765

"There was once a very rich merchant, who had six children, three sons, and three daughters; being a man of sense, he spared no cost for their education, but gave them all kinds of masters. His daughters were extremely handsome, especially the youngest. When she was little everybody admired her, and called her "The little Beauty;" so that, as she grew up, she still went by the name of Beauty, which made her sisters very jealous."

Gilbert stopped reading and glanced at his cousin, Marie, who sat on the stone steps below him with her arms wrapped around her knees, eagerly listening as he read. He paused and smiled at the nine-year-old girl who turned around to see why he had stopped reading. She twisted her mouth and pointed to the book he held, urging him to continue. Her light brown hair and hazel eyes made her quite the little beauty, and Gilbert was happy his Aunt Charlotte had brought her to live with them after Marie's father died. Marie was more like his sister, and was his closest childhood friend. Gilbert's mother had gone to live in Paris when he was two, and only returned occasionally to visit him. So Gilbert lived with his grandmother, two aunts, and his cousin Marie—surrounded by three generations of women who loved and doted on him. The red-haired, blue-eyed, freckle-faced boy was proud to be the "little lord of Chavaniac," man of the house and protector of the Lafayette family, all at the tender age of eight.

"Should I start calling you 'the *impatient* little Beauty,' cousin?" Gilbert teased. He turned his gaze to follow a hawk that flew high above the lush gardens of the Lafayette estate to the distant forest. He didn't feel like reading on this breezy summer morning. He wanted to put down the book and walk down these stone steps and through the tree-lined path that led to the green woods beyond. He wanted to go

411

exploring in the forest or swimming in the pond lined with weeping willow trees and filled with lily pads.

The young marquis did love to read, especially history books about ancient Roman and Greek warriors such as Julius Caesar and Alexander the Great. And he never tired of hearing the exciting stories of his Lafayette ancestors, asking his *grand-mère* to repeat them over and over again. Gilbert adored real stories of action and peril, war and conquest, but his cousin Marie preferred fiction stories like *Beauty and the Beast* and any of the new *genre* of books called "fairy tales."

Their tutor, Abbé Fayon, assigned summer reading for the children, and daily had them read aloud to each other to practice their diction and storytelling. Today it was Gilbert's turn. He lowered his hand to rub Kate under the chin. His beloved white dog never left his side. She wagged her tail as she lay next to him on the cool stone steps.

"I don't care what you call me, cousin. Just keep reading, *s'il vous plaît!*" Marie insisted, tipping the book back up to face Gilbert.

Gilbert nodded and found his place to keep reading. A curly lock of red hair danced on his forehead from the soft breeze. *"The youngest, as she was handsomer, was also better than her sisters. The two eldest had a great deal of pride, because they were rich. They gave themselves ridiculous airs, and would not visit other merchants' daughters, nor keep company with any but persons of quality. They went out every day to parties of pleasure, balls, plays, concerts, and so forth, and they laughed at their youngest sister, because she spent the greatest part of her time in reading good books."*

412

"Just like me and *this* book!" Marie said happily.

"Oui, but let's skip to the exciting part," Gilbert suggested as he flipped over a few pages. He put his finger on the section he was looking for. *"He was within thirty miles of his own house, thinking on the pleasure he should have in seeing his children again, when going through a large forest he lost himself. It rained and snowed terribly; besides, the wind was so high, that it threw him twice off his horse, and night coming on, he began to apprehend being either starved to death with cold and hunger, or else devoured by the wolves, whom he heard howling all round him . . ."*

Gilbert closed *La Belle et La Bête* and offered up a howl like a wolf. "AH-OOOOO!"

Marie put her hands over her ears. "Stop, Gilbert! I hate the sound of wolves, especially lately."

"I'm not afraid of wolves," Gilbert replied boldly, putting his hand on his cousin's arm. "Besides, I'll protect you, Marie. We Lafayette knights must protect our ladies from beasts." He reached over and held up another book Marie had brought to read, *Les Contes de ma Mère l'Oye*, or *The Tales of Mother Goose* by Charles Perrault. "But you should heed this advice."

Gilbert flipped through the book, reading the story titles. "*Cendrillon* (Cinderella), *Le Chat Botté* (Puss in Boots), *La Belle au bois Dormant* (The Sleeping Beauty). Ah, *voila, Le Petit Chaperon Rouge.*" He cleared his throat and animated his voice as he read aloud, first as Little Red Riding Hood, and then as the big, bad wolf:

> *"'Grandmother, what big arms you have!'*
> *"'All the better to hug you with, my dear.'*
> *"'Grandmother, what big legs you have!'*
> *"'All the better to run with, my child.'*
> *"'Grandmother, what big ears you have!'*
> *"'All the better to hear with, my child.'*
> *"'Grandmother, what big eyes you have!'*
> *"'All the better to see with, my child.'*
> *"'Grandmother, what big teeth you have got!'*
> *"'All the better to eat you up with.'*
> *"And, saying these words, this wicked wolf fell upon Little Red Riding Hood, and ate her all up. Moral: Children, especially attractive, well-bred young ladies, should never talk to strangers, for if they should do so, they may well provide dinner for a wolf. I say 'wolf,' but there are various kinds of wolves. There are also those who are charming, quiet, polite, unassuming, complacent, and sweet, who pursue young women at home and in the streets. And unfortunately, it is these gentle wolves who are the most dangerous ones of all."*

Gilbert closed the book and gave a self-confident nod as he held up both books. "Beauty's Beast turned out to be a prince, but some men can be wolves, especially to beauties like you."

Marie folded her arms over her chest and frowned. "Well, I do not want to hear about any kind of wolves today. I overheard the adults talking this morning. There's been another attack."

Gilbert's eyes widened and he leaned forward, alarmed. "Where?"

"Thirty miles from us, just like Beauty's father in the story," Marie replied, with growing fear in her eyes. "Gilbert, I'm frightened."

413

Gilbert reached his arms out and enveloped his cousin in a gentle hug. "Don't be afraid, Marie. I won't let anything happen to you."

An' neither will I, lass! Kate barked, standing up attentively.

"You see? Bibi is here, too," Gilbert said with a smile to his little dog. "We've read enough for this morning. Let's go back inside and see if *grand-mère* has some *chocolat* for us."

Marie nodded and Gilbert gathered up the books. As they turned to walk inside the château, Gilbert's smile faded as he looked back at the forest behind them. He knew full well that wolves roamed under that dark canopy of trees, but there was a monster that had been terrorizing the Gévaudan and Auvergne regions of southern France for more than a year.

After it first struck a fourteen-year-old shepherd girl, a hideous beast had gone on to attack more than sixty young women and children who were out tending sheep and cows, or gathering wood. It killed some of its victims on the spot, and dragged others away to a grisly death. People from one hundred miles around were terrified, as the killer beast seemed to be everywhere, but nowhere. It eluded hunters. There were brief sightings and even shots fired at some kind of animal, but the creature somehow always managed to get up and retreat into the dark woods, evading capture. Rumors began to spread that the beast was invincible to bullets.

This volcanic, mountainous region of rugged terrain in the south of France was dotted with little villages spaced far apart. The population was small, and peasants tended not to travel far from their homes, keeping people somewhat isolated from one another. Poor peasants worked from dawn until dusk, struggling to put food on their tables by the sweat of their brow. They had few possessions, and those who were fortunate enough to own a few sheep or cows guarded them with their very lives. These peasants were concerned only about the immediate world around them, so news spread slowly at first in this region. But as a French writer noted, the "marvelous" is a "seductive poison," and gazettes quickly discovered the power of this monster story over the masses. Newspapers and broadsides began pouring into the villages and towns, and they were filled with account after gruesome account of the attacks by the Beast of the Gévaudan. The people of France couldn't get enough of the news. They were poisoned with marvelous terror.

The French administrator of the region, Etienne Lafont, was tasked with organizing hunts of eight to ten people in each village, but fear kept most of the villagers from venturing out to try to kill the beast. In January, a brave group of seven children fought off the beast with sticks and makeshift spears as they guarded the cattle of Chanaleilles. The beast had grabbed one of the youngest in their group, and their leader, twelve-year-old Jacques Portefaix, spurred them on, telling them they had to "save their comrade or perish." The children surrounded the beast until it released their friend, who suffered a wound to his face but survived. The brave band of heroes gained the attention of France and even praise and rewards from King Louis XV. The French king then called upon the mightiest wolf hunter in France to hunt down the beast. With 1,200 kills to his name, the hunter from Normandy brought men and trained hound dogs, but after four tiresome months, the hunters had only captured and killed ordinary wolves. This killer beast was no ordinary wolf—some even questioned whether it was a wolf at all.

Some said it could be a hyena or a panther. Since it couldn't be killed with bullets, some wondered if it could be a dragon with a hide of scaly armor. Perhaps it was a new breed of wolf, crossed with another natural predator. Reports by those who had encountered the beast claimed they had almost been knocked over by the stinking, rotten smell of the beast. Eyewitnesses claimed the beast was the size of a calf, had massively sharp teeth, long claws, a black stripe down its back, a long tail it could swing like a weapon, and menacing, glowing eyes. Whatever it was, the monster of the Gévaudan was thirsty for blood.

As Gilbert and Marie walked by the Libertas statue and into the house, Kate also looked back toward the forest, furrowing her brow and shaking her head. The white Westie then followed the children inside, staying close by and comforting them in the safety of the château.

From the hedge near the stone steps, a pair of dark eyes looked on, having heard the entire conversation.

"Bonjour, Monsieur le Marquis," some local boys said as Gilbert walked down the cobblestone street of the village of Chavaniac. They tipped their hats out of respect to the village lord and their local aristocrat. Gilbert nodded and smiled back at them, returning the greeting as he marched steadily on with a determined gait.

Gilbert's smile faded as he continued on his quest to the center of the village, furrowing his brow. Kate stayed near his heels, keeping an eye out for anyone or anything. Marie was too upset to leave the château, but Gilbert wanted to learn all he could about the threat that neared his home and village. They soon came to the place where broadsides, or large sheets with news, were pinned to a wooden board for the villagers to read. Gilbert stood with his hands on his hips and scanned the postings for any news about the beast, who had struck again.

Kate sniffed and looked up to see a greasy-looking village peasant suddenly standing next to them. She wrinkled her nose. He smelled awful. His clothes were dirty and worn, and he wore a wide-brimmed, crumpled hat low over his eyes. He had obviously been working hard in the fields or in some dirty occupation.

Gilbert turned and nodded at the man. *"Bonjour, monsieur.* I understand there was another attack by that beast."

"Oui, an especially horrible one at that," the man replied. "The whole village is terrified. If only someone were brave enough to go find that beast and kill it once and for all."

"But the king did send hunters to seek out the beast," Gilbert replied.

The man crossed his arms over his chest and smirked. *"Oui,* but they failed!" He shook his head. "Ever since we lost the Seven Years' War to the British, France just doesn't seem to have brave heroes to triumph anymore—men like you nobles who are supposed to protect us since we peasants aren't allowed to own guns. And the leaders wonder why the people won't go on the hunts. What are pitchforks or even swords going to do against a beast that can carry off its victims?"

Gilbert furrowed his brow and nodded somberly. Only those in the aristocracy had the right to bear arms. *"Oui,* I think it is wrong that you cannot have guns to defend yourselves. But what about those children who beat off the beast? They didn't kill it, but at least they saved their friend and drove it away."

"Ah, true, *Monsieur le Marquis!* When King Louis first heard about those five boys and two girls, he wanted to reward the 'firm courage and intelligence' their leader showed in the battle against the beast." The man smiled and walked over to the broadsides. The odor as he moved caused Gilbert to wrinkle his nose. The man wiped off his grimy finger and pointed to a broadside with a new engraving showing Jacques Portefaix and the other children attacking a dragon-like beast with sticks. It was the latest depiction of the amazing story that continued to fill the news. With each new telling of the story, the details became even more fantastic, and the story grew more marvelous in the minds of the people. "Have you heard what the king has done now for Portefaix?"

Gilbert walked closer to study the picture, putting a hand over his nose against the man's body odor. "No, what?"

417

"Not only did the king send money to him and the other children, now the king has sent him to school in Montpellier to learn how to read. He hasn't been privileged to go to school before now," the man explained with a sneer. "After Portefaix finishes school, he will go on to military training and be assigned to the king himself! That brave boy not only protected his friends, but he achieved *glory* for himself. His fame has spread all the way to America! Word has it that the people in Boston have read about the brave Jacques Portefaix. He's been called 'Hercules in the cradle.'"

Gilbert's eyes widened with this news. He admired the local boy hero even more, amazed by the glory and fame he had achieved. "He's only four years older than me."

The man pointed to an article from the *Courrier d'Avignon* newspaper, pinned to the board. "Look what the Governor, Comte d'Eu, said about the small band of heroes."

Gilbert leaned in and read the quotation. "If their strength had matched their bravery, the hardy band now would be reaping the glory due to the eventual conqueror of the monster." He paused and nodded. "Glory."

"And did you hear about the mother of six who protected her children from the beast farther south? That Madame Varlet? Look how a playwright praised her!" enthused the man, pointing to another article.

"'Let us imitate the ancients!'" Gilbert read aloud.

"Can you imagine, *Monsieur le Marquis?* Simple peasants likened to the warriors of ancient Greece and Rome?!" the man exclaimed. He pointed a thumb back at his chest and wore a resentful expression. "We may be peasants, but we are inspiring patriotism and national pride for France, even if you nobles won't," he said, looking down his nose before leaning in to whisper, "or *can't.*"

Kate cocked her head at the man and narrowed her eyes. For a peasant, this man seemed to know a great deal, not only about history but about Gilbert. And he had all but challenged Gilbert to go out and take on the beast himself. She gave a low growl and the man shot her a sinister glance.

"*Monsieur, merci* for telling me this news," Gilbert said, giving a respectful bow. "Let us hope the beast will soon be caught so the people will no longer have to be afraid. *Bonne journée.*"

As Gilbert turned to leave, the man kicked Kate and she gave a yelp. Gilbert didn't see what had happened, but turned around to see the man looking innocently at the broadsides. "What's wrong, girl? Come on, let's go home."

Kate looked behind them and growled. The man smiled before turning to walk away.

I wonder if Gilbert realizes that stranger were the second kind of wolf he warned Marie aboot, Kate thought as she followed the young marquis down the street. *But he were mean an' he smelled bad, too.* Suddenly a fearful thought entered her mind. She shot a glance back over her shoulder but the man was gone. *The beast of the Gévaudan might not be a wolf after all!*

47

Marquis and
the Beast

bbé Fayon lit a few candles on his desk and sat down to read
by the dim light. Soon he heard a soft knock on the door, followed by the voice of Gilbert. "Abbé Fayon? May I come in?"

"Of course. Come in, Gilbert," the tutor replied in his cheery voice.
"You are up late."

Gilbert walked in and set his brass candleholder on his tutor's desk.
He smiled weakly, put his hands behind his back, and slowly paced
across the room. "I cannot sleep." He walked over to look at the world
map on the wall, gazing at the eastern seaboard of North America. "May
I ask you something? Why do you think the Lafayette men have always
been so brave?"

Abbé gave a curious smile. "Well, bravery runs through the blood
of your ancestors, Gilbert. They have always been warriors to answer
the call to fight and defend those who need them. They have sought to
honor their country, and both sides of your family have always received
glory for their achievements." He picked up a French dictionary and
opened it to the G's. "Here, read me the definition of *la gloire.*"

Gilbert walked over and put his finger on the word. "*Glory.* A reputation garnered through virtue, merit, great qualities, good actions, and
beautiful works. Synonyms: honor, esteem, praise."

Abbé leaned back in his chair and smiled at the young marquis.
"Once earned, glory is its own reward. This is proved time and again
by the heroes of history, both real and mythical." He picked up a book
about King Arthur and the Knights of the Round Table. "Knights must
be fearless and loyal to accomplish great things. Arthur was an orphan,

but he became the father of a new nation as he led his brave knights."

"And the *French* knight was the bravest one of the Round Table!" Gilbert exclaimed, drawing an imaginary sword. "Launcelot du Lac is my favorite!"

"Lancelot was King Arthur's most loyal friend." The kind tutor chuckled at Gilbert's quick enthusiasm. "I love your passion, Gilbert. You truly live up to the Lafayette family motto, '*Cur Non?*' which means what in Latin?"

"Why not?" Gilbert answered, swinging his imaginary sword across the room. He looked up at the large map. "I want to be a knight and fight like my father and grandfathers. I want to go to exciting, faraway lands someday."

"Saint Catherine of Siena once said, 'Be who God meant you to be and you will set the world on fire,'" Abbé Fayon said with a finger raised in the air. "If God means for you to follow in the footsteps of your Lafayette ancestors, you will do just that. I have no doubt, young Gilbert."

420

Gilbert smiled but then remembered what was weighing heavily on his mind. "But what about now? I'm the lord of Chavaniac. Shouldn't I be the one protecting the people from the beast that threatens them?"

Abbé's face grew serious. "Your day will come. For now, leave that fight for those who are stronger and older than you. This is a serious matter."

Gilbert nodded and looked down at the floor. "It's just that Marie is upset. And the people are so very frightened by the beast of the Gévaudan."

"*Oui,* but again, this is not your battle, Gilbert," Abbé reminded the lad. "Why don't you go to bed and put the beast to rest for tonight? It is late." The man stood and handed the candle to Gilbert as he escorted him to the door. "We'll talk about this tomorrow."

"Very well, Abbé Fayon. *Merci,*" Gilbert replied, obediently going to the door. "*Bonne nuit.*"

"*Bonne nuit,*" Abbé replied with a smile. "*Beaux rêves.*"

Gilbert walked along the stone corridor of the château. The light from his candle flickered, and his footsteps echoed off the walls. He was headed for his bedroom but then stopped and turned to go to the grand hall. He slowly walked along the wall lined with portraits of brave Lafayette warriors. The light from his flickering candle animated the faces of his ancestors, who gazed back at him. He stopped in front of the suit of armor that had belonged to his father. Gilbert ran his hand along the cold, smooth metal. How he wished he could have known his father and seen him dressed in this magnificent armor!

A pair of silver swords mounted on the wall caught his eye. He walked over and lifted the candle high to study the intricate carving on the handles. Underneath the swords was hung a plaque with the Lafayette family crest. A red and gold shield was decorated with a field of blue and silver castles. On the top was a crown with a reined horse head and the family motto, *"Cur Non?"*

Gilbert furrowed his brow, proud of his rich family ancestry. He understood what Abbé Fayon had tried to tell him about leaving the fight with the beast to those stronger and older than he. But he still felt responsible. And other children were out there fighting off the beast with sticks! The man in the village earlier had given him much to think about. He was right. France had lost its pride after their defeat by the British. And Gilbert had lost his father in the process. France needed its brave young knights to rise and meet the current challenge to protect its people.

Gilbert's eyes then landed on his father's musket mounted on the wall. He walked over and the light from his candle gleamed off the beautiful, dark wood of the weapon—a weapon afforded not to the village peasants, but to the nobility of the Lafayettes. He ran his hand along the handle and his face grew determined as he glanced back at the family crest.

"CUR NON?!" he exclaimed with a bold voice. His voice echoed in the grand hall, and he could almost hear the approval of his forefathers, cheering him on. He knew what he needed to do. He set his candle on the floor and lifted the musket from the wall mount. His heart raced as he raised the musket to his shoulder and imagined shooting the beast. The words he had read earlier that day about the seven brave children filled his mind: *If their strength had matched their bravery, the hardy band now would be reaping the glory due to the eventual conqueror of the monster.*

Gilbert smiled. "Glory due to the conqueror of the monster." He took in a deep breath and put the musket over his shoulder. "Why not, indeed!"

Kate sat in the shadows and frowned as she listened to the boy. Her heart raced to see the young marquis pick up his candle and walk out of the grand hall with the musket. "The wee lad thinks his strength will match his bravery against the beast, but he has no idea wha' he's facin'!" The white dog scurried out of the room and down the corridor. She wasn't about to let Gilbert out of her sight.

———

Gilbert woke up early and tiptoed to the kitchen with its arched ceiling, cozy fireplace, and long, mahogany farm table. His grandmother was up and had prepared a pot of hot *chocolat.* She poured him a bowl of the sweet drink, and he hurriedly ate his breakfast of baguette, jam, and boiled egg. He gulped down his last sip of *chocolat* and smiled as he wiped his mouth. *"Merci, grand-mère."* He rose from the table and kissed his grandmother on the cheek. "I am going for a walk with Bibi. Please tell Marie and Abbé Fayon I will be back. À *bientôt."*

Madame de Chavaniac tilted her head and studied her young grandson with a grin. "You are such a child of nature, *cher* Gilbert. Be safe and stay near. À *bientôt."*

422

"Allons-y, Bibi," Gilbert called to Kate, who immediately trotted along after him down the stone corridor. He picked up the musket he had left in the hall and slung it across his shoulder as they went out the door. As they passed the Libertas statue, Gilbert gazed at the face of the Roman goddess of liberty. Little did he know that her face belonged to his distant *grand-mère. "Liberté* for the people of Chavaniac," he whispered.

Kate gazed into the face of Liz, who was carved at the base of the statue. Somehow seeing her friend gave her courage. She smiled and trotted along behind the young marquis, who was out to kill the beast.

A pillow of fog covered the green grass on this overcast morning. By the time they reached the woods, Kate's fur and Gilbert's shoes were already damp. Kate's heart raced. She kept a watchful eye as she followed Gilbert down the well-worn path he had made from hundreds of walks into the forest. All was unusually quiet. Kate looked up at the canopy of trees and didn't see any birds. She didn't hear them, either. Something wasn't right.

Suddenly they heard a twig snap to their left and quickly looked over in that direction. "Hello? Anyone there?" Gilbert called out. There was no reply. His heart was pounding in his chest and he swallowed back his fear. He proceeded slowly, carefully cocking the hammer of his musket. Kate was right behind him.

After they had walked another ten yards, they heard another twig snap, this time to the right. Gilbert sucked in a quick breath and broke out in a sweat. He didn't call out but gripped his gun tighter with his sweaty palms, staying still for a moment as he looked all around them. Nothing. No movement anywhere.

As Gilbert started walking ahead once more, something reached out and touched Kate on the back. She jumped and quickly looked behind her, ready to pounce on whatever it was. Two big, black, triangle ears were sticking out of a fern.

What big ears you have! was the first thing that popped into Kate's head. She closed her eyes in relief as she came to her senses. "Ye aboot scared me out of me fur!" she whispered.

The two big, black, triangle ears rose to reveal a big, square head with two dark eyes. It was Max. "Sorry, lass. I were tryin' not ta do that. I didn't want ta scare the lad."

"It's alright, Max. Have ye seen anythin' this mornin'?" Kate whispered as she ducked under the fern with the Scottie dog.

Max had kept out of sight from Gilbert and the others at Chavaniac for the past year and a half, but he was always nearby. Little did Gilbert, Marie, or any of the women of the château know, but Max and Kate had been defending Gilbert from wolves for months now. Between the two of them, they were able to scare off a lone wolf or two that ventured near Chavaniac. They knew that the attacks happening in the south of France were not just due to one beast, but an unusual infestation of wolves in the region. But they also knew there was indeed one larger beast that was responsible for some of the attacks. They were yet to encounter the powerful beast of the Gévaudan.

"Haven't seen anythin' yet, but somethin' in me gut tells me we need ta be on high alert," Max whispered.

"Aye, me, too. Gilbert met a stranger in the village yesterday who kept tauntin' the lad aboot fightin' the beast," Kate explained. "Max, I think he were no ordinary stranger."

Max frowned. "Wha' do ye mean, lass?"

"Not only did he say things ta Gilbert that made him want ta pick up his papa's musket today, but he smelled bad for a human," Kate answered. "He even kicked me when the lad weren't lookin'."

Max growled at the thought of anyone hurting his lass. "How dar-r-re he! Are ye alr-r-right?"

423

"Aye, I'm fine. But listen, Max. That stranger made me feel the way we felt when Judas turned traitor—when the evil one got a hold of him," recalled Kate gravely. "I think the Enemy is out ta get the wee marquis."

"Jest like it tr-r-ried ta get young Patrick Henry with the panther. I smelled somethin' r-r-rotten then, too," Max grumbled. "If it is the Enemy, it's goin' ta take both of us ta handle the monster wolf."

"If it even *is* a wolf," Kate added.

All of a sudden, they both smelled it. A foul stench wafted through the air.

"The beastie be here!" Max shouted, lifting his nose in the air to determine where the smell was coming from. "Come on, lass! There's no time ta lose!"

Together Max and Kate darted out from the fern and ran in the direction of the stench, leaving Gilbert alone. They came to a small clearing of trees where water had formed a mucky bog in the dark, black soil. These bogs were common in this region of France, and had captured animals, horses, and even humans like quicksand. The two Scottish dogs were well familiar with such bogs, which were also common in Scotland. They carefully ran around the edge of the bog and in the direction of the stench that grew stronger with each step.

When they had run a half-mile, they suddenly saw the source of the stench. Max and Kate stopped in their tracks and assumed a posture of defense. There before them was a massive wolf. It was six-feet long and almost three-feet tall, weighing at least 130 pounds. It bristled its fur and snarled to show its fangs.

"Out of my way, whelps," the beast growled, a string of thick saliva hanging from its mouth.

"Ye're not goin' this way, ye stinkin' beastie," Max growled back. He and Kate stood with their fur raised and tails up, but looked pitifully small in front of this monster wolf.

The beast's snarl faded and it chuckled. "What are you going to do? Charm me to death with your cuteness?"

Kate took a step forward. "We've handled bigger beasties than ye—includin' a lion! We're not afraid of ye!"

The beast's eyes widened. "Impressive. A lion, you say?" It calmly walked toward them, getting just inches from Kate's face. "Well, *I'm* the king of the beasts in *this* forest." The wolf snapped at her, and immediately Max lunged for its throat.

Kate ran to the back of the wolf and grabbed its tail while Max kept his powerful jaws locked around its neck, refusing to release the beast. The wolf rose up and tried to sling Max and Kate off as they fought viciously in a chaotic encounter. The beast fell hard to the ground and rolled over onto its back, sending Kate flying off from the impact. She hit a nearby moss-covered boulder and had the wind knocked out of her for a moment. Max and the beast tumbled and rolled along the ground when suddenly Kate heard a sickening sound. Another wolf howled in the distance, in the direction of where they had left Gilbert.

"Max! Another wolf!" Kate cried. She didn't know what to do. Max was too small to defeat this monster wolf alone, but she knew that Gilbert's life was in grave danger. "Maker, help us!"

She took off running back toward the young Marquis de Lafayette.

***

"*Bonjour.* Where's Gilbert?" Abbé Fayon asked as he took his seat at the breakfast table. Marie, Aunt Madeleine, and Aunt Charlotte were seated there. Madame came over to pour him some *chocolat.* "*Merci.*"

"He came down early for his *petit déjeuner,*" Madame explained. "He seemed to be in quite a hurry to take Bibi on a walk this morning. But he said to tell you and Marie he would be back soon."

Abbé tapped his boiled egg on the pewter plate to crack the shell and slowly peeled it away. "Gilbert came to chat with me last night. We talked of knights and glory." He smiled, admiring the passionate spirit of the boy. "But he also seemed to be quite upset about the latest beast attack. He feels responsible to protect the people as lord of Chavaniac."

Aunt Madeleine smiled. "He's such a dear boy. If only our sister realized how loyal her son is to uphold the Lafayette family honor."

"*Oui,*" Aunt Charlotte said, spreading some fresh raspberry jam on her baguette. "Gilbert has such a big heart to wish to protect others like that."

Marie cupped her yellow and blue ceramic bowl of delicious *chocolat* with both hands and took a sip. "My cousin is very brave. He said he would always protect me. Even from the beast of the Gévaudan." She smiled, remembering how he had embraced and comforted her the day before. Suddenly her face fell and she set the bowl down on the table. She quickly got up and ran down the corridor.

Madame frowned. "Where is she going? She did not finish her *pétit dejeuner.*"

Abbé dipped his peeled egg into the salt and shrugged his shoulders. The other ladies looked at one another but continued eating.

"It's not there!" Marie cried, running back into the kitchen.

"What is not where?" Madame de Chavaniac asked with a worried expression as she slowly rose to her feet.

"Uncle Lafayette's musket," Marie answered with alarm. "Gilbert must have taken it!"

It suddenly dawned on everyone.

"Mon Dieu! He's gone to hunt the beast!" Madame cried as she put her hands to her cheeks. "Gilbert!"

Together everyone fled the kitchen and ran down the corridor to leave the château. They just hoped they wouldn't be too late.

Kate growled and snarled at the wolf, which was now a short distance from Gilbert. "Ye will *not* take another step!"

The wolf was rather small and skinny, but he was large enough to kill a small dog—or boy. "Don't make me hurt you, little dog."

Anger rose up in Kate as none she had ever known before. Her mate was in the fight of his life with the monster wolf, and now this other wolf threatened Gilbert. She was sick and tired of the dark fear that surrounded them and bullied the humans. Suddenly she snapped and lunged for the wolf, grabbing it by the ankle and puncturing its tendon. The wolf cried out in pain with a loud howl as Kate shook her head back and forth. Just as the wolf reached down to bite her, Kate let go and spun around to sink her teeth into its other leg. She barked and growled between bites, moving so fast the wolf couldn't catch her.

Just then they heard Gilbert fire his musket and shout, "Bibi! Bibi!"

Fear filled Kate's mind as she let go of the wolf. Was there a third wolf? "Gilbert!"

The bloodied wolf also filled with fear to hear the gunshot, and took off running away through the forest to make his escape.

Kate ran as fast as she could back towards Gilbert. "I'm comin'! Hang on, me wee marquis!"

"That was his gun! Do you think he spotted a wolf?" Marie cried as she and the adults ran through the gardens, reaching the entrance to the woods. "Gilbert! Come back! Come back!"

"Don't go in there!" Abbé warned, grabbing Marie by the arm. "You stay here with the ladies."

Immediately Madame, Aunt Charlotte, Aunt Madeleine, and Marie all began shouting and crying for Gilbert to return as Abbé stepped into the woods.

———

It didn't take long for Kate to reach Gilbert, who dropped to his knees as soon as he saw her. He scooped her up in his arms. "I thought I lost you!"

I thought I lost ye, too! Kate barked, relieved to see that there was not another wolf. She proceeded to lick his face while he held her close.

"Oh, Bibi! I heard you barking and shot my gun by accident. Let's get out of here," Gilbert said, now hearing his family calling for him. "They must be worried sick."

Gilbert set Kate on the ground, picked up his musket, and ran back toward Chavaniac. He soon met Abbé coming from the other direction.

"Are you alright, Gilbert?" Abbé cried. "We've been so afraid for you!"

427

"I'm fine, Abbé. I'm so sorry," Gilbert answered as they hurried out of the woods to meet the ladies. "I thought I could go after the beast myself. I disobeyed and did what you had instructed me not to do."

"That you did, but I am relieved you are unharmed," Abbé answered.

When they reached the clearing, Marie ran up to Gilbert and embraced him. "Oh, you are alright! We heard the gunshot. What happened? Did you see a wolf?"

"No, I didn't see a wolf or any kind of beast. My gun went off by accident," Gilbert explained. "I'm sorry I worried you all so."

"Well, no more going off deep into the woods until this beast is caught, understood?" demanded Madame as she wrapped the boy up in a hug. "I could not bear to lose you, *cher* Gilbert."

"*Oui, je comprends,*" Gilbert nodded. "I promise."

"What happened to Bibi?" Aunt Madeleine shouted, pointing to Kate. "She's bleeding!"

Gilbert dropped to his knees and saw the blood smeared on Kate's fur. "Bibi? Where are you hurt?" He frantically looked her over but found no wounds. Kate stood there, wagging her tail.

"I'm fine, lad. That's not me blood then," Kate barked. *"Jest the blood of a wolf beastie."*

"I don't see that she's hurt," reported Gilbert, turning to look at the women. "It doesn't appear to be her blood." Suddenly it dawned on him what could have happened. "I heard her barking." He turned and cupped her face in his hands. "Did *you* see the beast?"

"I'm sure if she had, she would not have made it back here," Abbé answered for the little dog. "Maybe she bit a squirrel or a chipmunk in the woods."

"Come, let's all get back to the château," Madame ordered. "This is all the blood I wish to see today."

Gilbert wrapped his arm around Marie and together they walked with the adults back to the château. Kate breathed a deep sigh of relief to see Gilbert walking away safe in the company of his family. But immediately her heart caught in her chest. "Max!" She took off running back into the forest.

———

428

Max was lying on his stomach, panting heavily. He was covered with blood and mud. Kate ran up and fell over him. "Max! Are ye alright? Wha' happened?"

Max nodded and let go a heavy sigh. "Aye, I be fine, lass. After ye left, that beast an' me tangled somethin' fierce. I knew I couldn't hold him for long, so I had ta turn him loose."

Kate's face grew fearful and she looked into the woods. "So the beast be out there runnin' free?"

"No, lass, he's not r-r-runnin' anywhere at the moment," Max assured her with a grin, drawing a confused look from Kate. "I did the only thing I knew ta do. I had the beastie chase me ta the bog where he pr-r-ro-ceeded ta get nice an' stuck. He's there now, up ta his chest in muck."

Kate smiled with her perky grin and plopped down next to Max. "Thank the Maker! That were quick thinkin', me love."

"Aye, an' ye saved the lad fr-r-rom a second wolf?" Max wanted to know.

"Aye. I went on a bitin' frenzy an' nipped the beastie over an' over until Gilbert accidentally shot his gun, scarin' the wolf away," Kate explained. "The lad never saw the wolf. It's a shame he'll never know that he really did help ta scare away the beastie."

"That's me br-r-rave lass," Max boasted with a broad smile. "I'm pr-r-roud of ye!"

"Whew, well at least all be safe for now," Kate sighed, resting her head on Max's shoulder. "Gilbert's grandmother told him he can't venture deep inta the woods until the beast be caught. I suppose we best go check on the big, bad wolf an' make sure he can't get free."

"We've got time, lass," Max answered. "Jest r-r-rest for now. That beastie will be bogged down for quite a while. But ye know wha's odd? When I were fightin' that beast, it were almost as if the stench weren't comin' fr-r-rom it. It's like the smell were comin' fr-r-rom somethin' else."

Kate wrinkled her brow. "Somethin' else? Wha' in the world could it be?"

The massive wolf strained against the muck in the bog, but the harder it struggled, the lower it sank. After a while it grew very calm and just sat there, breathing heavily.

"It was so easy. So . . . very . . . easy," came the sinister voice from behind the wolf. "I set up everything for you so well. I poisoned them with fear and attacked the imagination of the people until they believe you are some sort of mythical creature. I've adored watching their confusion and mass hysteria over the carnage I've caused. But no, you just couldn't get the job done, could you?"

The wolf's eyes filled with fear, and the fur on the back of its head stood on end. It tried to move, but couldn't budge. "I . . . I wasn't expecting this. Get me out of here, and I'll try again."

"My, what big *eyes* you have!" mocked the voice. "No, you had your chance and failed. If you desire second chances, you joined forces with the wrong side. I'll have to find another big, bad wolf to take your place," the voice angrily replied, growing in its ferocity. "How could you *not* expect the WHELPS!? I warned you about them! I said not to be deceived by their small size. That other useless back-up wolf even failed with the little white whelp. I HAD IT SET UP SO PERFECTLY AND YOU BOTH FAILED!"

The monster wolf swallowed back its fear as the voice shouted into its ears. The smell was overpowering, even for him. "But I didn't fail with the seven children. I let them beat me, just as you instructed me to do. Doesn't that count for something?"

"THEY WERE THE BAIT to convince the little marquis he could

fight the beast, too," the voice whispered into the wolf's flattened ears. "I made sure their story brought them glory and fame. I knew he would want it, too. But this time, HE WAS THE PREY, AND YOU FAILED! His dear *grand-mère* will see to it he doesn't venture into these woods for now."

"So what are you going to do next?" the wolf asked fearfully.

"I'll think of something," the voice replied. "Meanwhile, I'm not completely heartless. Let me give you something to ease your discomfort while you sink into the abyss."

The wolf's eyes filled with terror as its mouth was forced open and the bitter powder was shoved down its throat. It started to gasp for breath and became paralyzed as something pushed its head down into the muck. The wolf slowly slipped deeper into the bog until it completely disappeared.

<hr>

"Do ye suppose it got away?" Kate asked when she and Max eventually returned to the bog and did not see the huge wolf.

Max frowned. "It's hard ta say. The beastie could be stuck down in that muck. At least King Louis be sendin' a new hunter down here ta catch the beast."

"Aye, hopefully the only thing we'll have ta protect the marquis from will be the other kind of beast he seeks, at least until he's a wee bit older," Kate said.

"Wha' kind of beast, lass?" Max asked.

"A beast that needs ta be tamed first," Kate smiled. "Glory."

PART FOUR

LIBERTY OR DEATH

SONS OF LIBERTY

NOVEMBER 1, 1765

I'll sooner die than pay a farthing for a single stamp!" a man cried in the tavern of Newcastle, Virginia. He looked around the room and lifted his pewter mug. "I am *sure* all my countrymen will do the same!"

"Aye, a toast to our very own noble patriot, Mr. Patrick Henry!" called another man, lifting his mug.

"To Mr. Henry!" another fellow added, lifting his glass. "If the governor or any of his kind comes up here to hurt him, I'll stand by Pat Henry to my last drop of blood!"

"Aye! Even if we have to call the French back to help us fight!" another answered.

"The voice in the House has now been heard 'round the world," Clarie reported proudly.

Gillamon and Clarie stood in the midst of the IAMISPHERE, gazing at panel after panel of scenes in time since May that showed the effects of the fire ignited by Patrick Henry in the House of Burgesses. Word of what had happened blazed first throughout Virginia to the gazettes in the northern colonies, southward to the papers in the Carolinas and Georgia, and in letters and papers across the Atlantic all the way to London. Colonists were toasting Patrick Henry and the Virginia Assembly far and wide while King George and Parliament gritted their teeth at the firestorm raging against the Stamp Act up and down the Atlantic seaboard.

"It didn't matter that Patrick and the young burgesses were unable to get all Henry's resolves passed in the House. Liz, Nigel, and Cato were able to get them all passed *unanimously* in the papers throughout the colonies," Gillamon remarked with a broad grin. "They have indeed made the most of 'treason.' Well done."

Clarie pointed to a panel where a group of people clustered around a copy of the June 24 *Newport Mercury* paper in Rhode Island. "The smallest colony of all was the first to boldly print Patrick's resolves. But their Assembly took it even further, being the only colony to approve outright resistance. I'm proud of little Rhode Island for standing up to Parliament. They remind me of David standing up to Goliath." She smiled and then pointed to a scene in Boston. "So by printing Patrick's resolves, Rhode Island made Virginia appear bolder than they actually were. The colonies just *assumed* that the Virginia House of Burgesses had passed all seven resolves. Once the *Boston Gazette* printed them, Massachusetts was ashamed of how their colony had backed down timidly when the Stamp Act was passed. Their governor wrote to London that the Virginia Resolves were 'an alarm bell to the disaffected.' And another Massachusetts man on his deathbed exclaimed, 'Oh! Those Virginians are men!'"

"Perception *is* reality." Gillamon smiled and his goatee blew in the rushing wind of their time portal. He pointed to another article, this one from France, in the *Boston Gazette*. "For the seven resolves and for the Beast of the Gévaudan."

"Unfortunately it's also too true for Boston's James Otis, who seems to be going a bit mad, changing his mind and acting strangely. He went from early on proposing a Stamp Act Congress for the colonies to meet, to backing down after the Act was passed, to calling Henry's resolves 'treasonous'," Clarie recounted with a frown. "None of the colonies was interested in attending the Stamp Act Congress in New York until Patrick's resolves had been printed throughout the colonies. That spurred on nine of the colonies who were able to send delegates to meet and draw up petitions to send to Parliament."

"Very, *very* good," Gillamon said, nodding in approval. "Do you realize that besides the Great Awakening, this Stamp Act Crisis is the first thing to unite the colonies on anything? It's amazing how Jesus and taxes can move the hearts of people to action," he declared with a chuckle as he pointed to another panel. Twenty-seven delegates were meeting in New York for the Stamp Act Congress. "Virginia indeed rang the alarm bell for the continent."

"Yes, and not just in the Stamp Act Congress, but with the Sons of

434

Liberty groups that have popped up throughout the colonies," Clarie added as a violent mob scene in Boston came into view. "Massachusetts made up for feeling ashamed about its cowering. Although Virginia first suggested resistance, Boston was the first to turn words into action. In fact, they went a bit overboard with violence in protesting the Stamp Act! Their 'Loyal Nine' resistance group soon grew and took the name 'Sons of Liberty.' They *loved* Barré's nickname for American patriots!"

"Boston has always seemed to love violence for its own sake—it's a powder keg there. And that Samuel Adams is a feisty leader to watch," Gillamon said with a slight grin as he pulled the panel for August 14 into view. They watched as the Sons of Liberty hung an image of their appointed stamp distributor Andrew Oliver in effigy from their "Liberty Tree." They sent a clear message, threatening the man if he dared follow through with his job of enacting the Stamp Tax come November 1. "Liberty Tree. The original liberty tree was violent as well."

"Look what they did next!" Clarie exclaimed as the hotheaded Bostonians cut down the effigy and paraded it through the streets. "They marched and shouted 'Huzzah!' all the way to Oliver's newly built Stamp Office building where he was planning to distribute the stamps. The Sons of Liberty proceeded to burn and stomp all over the effigy before they entered the building and destroyed everything in sight, including all the furniture. Then they pulled down the building itself."

435

"Poor Andrew Oliver was first. Their next target was Lieutenant Governor Thomas Hutchinson," Gillamon said, pointing to the panel for August 26. The mob also destroyed his house. "This behavior has spread across the colonies, with some poor souls being tarred and feathered. All colonial stamp distributors appointed by the Crown have received the same 'encouragement' to quit their jobs before the Act goes into effect. The good news is that after the most violent riots in Boston and Rhode Island, only mere *threats* of violence were needed in the other colonies to get the stamp distributors to give up their posts. Only the colony of Georgia has a stamp distributor now, and his job won't last long."

"Meanwhile in London, Grenville didn't last long as Prime Minister," Clarie quipped as she pointed to a panel of the royal palace. King George threw a copy of the August *Gentleman's Magazine* across the room, barely missing Al, who darted under the settee. "David Henry's paper printed his cousin's seventh resolve under the heading of *Remarkable Events.*

It didn't take long then for *The London Chronicle* to print *all* Patrick's resolves, along with news of riots against the Stamp Act blazing through the colonies. The people of London can't get enough of this news!"

"So King George fired Grenville as Prime Minister and replaced him with Charles Watson-Wentworth, Marquis of Rockingham," Gillamon noted. "His *third* Prime Minister so far, and he's just getting started with musical ministers. It won't take long for more heads to roll once the London merchants petition the king and Parliament. Not only are the colonists refusing to put the Stamp Act into effect, but they are now boycotting British goods. The ports and the courts are closing, as merchants and lawyers prepare to halt business until the Stamp Act is repealed. Ships cannot clear their cargo without the stamps, nor can lawyers proceed without stamped legal documents. Meanwhile the other hardest-hit group, the *printers,* keep fanning the flames of this Stamp Act Crisis in the papers." Gillamon breathed in deeply and let go a sigh of satisfaction. "Everything is falling into place, just as it was supposed to."

436

"You were right, Gillamon. The *voice* started the ball of revolution rolling, and it's come all the way to London and into the halls of Parliament," Clarie observed happily. "Parliament now knows the name behind the voice—Patrick Henry."

Gillamon smiled. "Indeed." He touched another panel, which showed Governor Fauquier writing to London about Patrick in explanation of what had happened in the House of Burgesses. *"In the course of the debate, I have heard that very indecent language was used by a Mr. Henry, a young lawyer who had not been above a month a Member of the House, who carried all the young, hot, and giddy members with him."* Gillamon continued, "Patrick's fiery words have set the colonists on a path from being Englishmen to becoming Americans."

"For the first time, the colonies have found common ground to learn how to communicate and come together to take action as one unified force," Clarie agreed. "This is all so exciting, Gillamon!"

"The Stamp Act Crisis is the colonies' dress rehearsal for Revolution. Speaking of dress rehearsals . . ." Gillamon said. He put his hoof into another panel and the village of Chavaniac in the south of France came into view. Gillamon smiled affectionately as he watched the nine-year-old Marquis de Lafayette enthusiastically lead a parade of admiring young boys through the streets of Chavaniac. They were celebrating the news that the king's royal armor bearer had killed a massive wolf and had it stuffed and sent to Versailles. Gilbert led the boys in a pretend wolf hunt in the gardens of the château, with wooden swords and sticks, to reenact the victory, followed by a pretend battle with the British.

"Max and Kate have done well in protecting Gilbert from the wolves, but they know the Enemy will not let up," Clarie said. "They must remain vigilant until the young marquis leaves the south of France."

"The youngest Son of Liberty is enjoying his victory dress rehearsal. Maker willing, his victory parade will someday be the real thing," Gillamon predicted, then grew more serious. "But first must come the *real* battles he will have to fight."

437

HARD ACTS TO FOLLOW

I f we yield to them in this particular manner, by repealing the Stamp Act, it is all over; they will from that moment assert their freedom."

"I say, I rather like this 'Anti-Sejanus' fellow," Nigel chuckled, tapping the *London Chronicle*. He twirled his whiskers as he read the Englishman's rant. "I doubt the old boy realizes how prophetic he was while wielding his perturbed pen."

Liz and Nigel sat by a lantern in the brand new Henry home of Roundabout in Louisa County. Newspapers from London and the colonies were spread across the table, filled with letters, cartoons, and the glorious news of the repeal of the hated Stamp Act. All London had remained in an uproar as merchants brought pressure on Parliament to repeal the Stamp Act. After the colonial boycott of British goods had reduced trade by a staggering one million British pounds, Parliament at last voted to repeal the Stamp Act by a vote of 249-49. But to send a clear message to the colonies that Great Britain remained sovereign over them, Parliament passed the Declaratory Act on the very same day.

Patrick's busy four-county circuit-riding law practice led him to Hanover Courthouse, where he once more was celebrated by the people with a huge celebration in Hanover Tavern. Word reached the colony in May that the Stamp Act had been repealed in March, and the local people could scarcely contain their pride over their hometown hero. Patrick Henry had become a household name as his fame spread throughout the colonies for sounding the alarm about the Stamp Act. Toasts were made in his honor along with toasts to those in Parliament who had supported the colonies in repealing the cursed Act, including William Pitt and Isaac Barré. The colonists believed that King George III must have stepped in for them as well, putting his foot down on an overreaching Parliament. Surely their beloved young king was innocent of having caused such tension with the colonies, and desired harmony with his loyal subjects once more. So the colonists drank toasts to their king as celebrations erupted up and down the Atlantic seaboard. Houses were lit with candles, fireworks were set off in grand illuminations, balls were held in Williamsburg and other cities, and songs were composed for the festive occasions.

At Hanover Tavern, the newspapers were passed around and then sent home with Patrick to share the happy news with his family. Today Sallie had cooked a special meal and invited their family and close friends to join them in their own celebration. They were especially happy to have Samuel and Elizabeth Crowley attend, as the young couple was visiting Hanover from the frontier of Virginia. Patrick played his fiddle and everyone danced jigs. The Henrys' new four-room, one-and-a-half-story home was filled with the aromas of delicious food, joyful music, laughter, and exuberant hearts.

Patrick proudly showed everyone the grounds of Roundabout, with its 1,900 acres where he would grow tobacco, wheat, and other crops. The house sat on a hill with gently sloping fields away from it on all sides. There was plenty of room for the children to run barefoot and free, exploring the woods and nearby Roundabout Creek, just as Patrick had done as a boy. The house was made with hand-hewn lumber, with three rooms downstairs and a long room lit by dormer windows upstairs. All around the house were outbuildings such as the overseer's cabin, slave quarters, tobacco sheds, horse stable, barn with farm animals, carriage and wagon sheds, blacksmith shop, well house, and smokehouse.

439

"The Sons of Liberty have vowed to stage this Stamp Act repeal celebration each year, to remember America's victorious stand against tyranny," Liz reported joyfully, gazing over a *Boston Gazette*, her tail slowly curling up and down. "They also plan to keep the colonies writing to one another to watch this new Declaratory Act. The pride of Parliament simply would not allow them to repeal the Stamp Act without *declaring* that they have the right to tax and make decisions for the colonists 'in all cases.'" She furrowed her brow. "Anti-Sejanus was indeed right. The colonies may have just won the battle but the war over making decisions for the colonies has just begun. Parliament may *claim* they have the right to tax the colonies, but the colonies will only rise up again if they try to do so. And the entire world will be watching to see what happens, no?"

"Indeed, Great Britain realizes that the colonies are an important source of strength, but colonies in *rebellion* can only strengthen Britain's enemies," Nigel agreed. "Well, for now the colonies can resume a happy relationship with their king and the Mother Country despite that irritating Declaratory Act. Until Parliament does more than puff up its chest with fighting words, the colonies shall ignore it."

"*Oui,* and with the imminent departure of Rockingham, and William Pitt coming back to the helm of Great Britain, perhaps things will remain calm for a season," Liz added.

"Pitt will be King George's *fourth* Prime Minister to form his *fifth* new government in *six* years!" Nigel added. "The king loves to play Musical Prime Ministers as much as our Patrick loves to play his fiddle!"

"And he played it with such joy tonight! Things are going so well for *mon* Henry!" Liz cheered with dancing eyes. "He has built this new home for his happy family, and his law practice is booming. He is able to invest in western lands, help his father and in-laws, and is now even a vestryman at the Trinity Parish Church. His reputation continues to soar. The people love him, no? So what is next for Patrick?" Her eyes narrowed, staring at Patrick's fiddle and thinking about the next part of the riddle. "Hmmm. *A voice that is hungry.* That sounds more like a riddle about my Albert."

"I quite thought the same thing, my dear! How can a voice be hungry?" Nigel wondered. He scurried over to the fiddle and held up his tiny bow with a broad smile. "Shall we see if Gillamon can give us a clue?" The mouse proceeded to pull his bow across the fiddle, and once more musical notes lifted into the air, magically growing larger with glowing words inside them:

Good evening, little ones.
Tonight was a happy celebration in the Henry home. You
should be very pleased with how your mission is going
with the VOICE.

Liz's eyes glowed, reflecting the rising, golden musical notes that evaporated into the ceiling without a trace. She smiled with renewed wonder as the animals reconnected with Gillamon through Patrick's fiery fiddle.

"Oui, the Henry family *fête* celebrated the Stamp Act repeal!" Liz exclaimed. "Gillamon, we are so very happy about this news, but we already wonder about the Declaratory Act and what it could mean for the colonies."

"Yes, and what about the next part of the fiddle's riddle? How can a voice be *hungry,* if we might ask?" Nigel chimed in.

Well, it does not have to do with Al, Liz.
Britain imposed the Sugar Act, the Stamp Act, and now
the Declaratory Act on the colonies, but there will be
harder Acts to follow.
And those hard Acts will make the voice
hungry to act in response.

Liz and Nigel glanced at one another with perplexed looks. "Gillamon, the colonies wish to remain loyal to King George. Even Patrick sang his praises tonight. The humans believe that the king supports them and that Parliament is the true problem. But is this true?"

441

The colonies are sadly mistaken. Young King George was
not led astray by Parliament and his cabinet. He supported
Grenville's plan for the Stamp Act. When that plan failed,
he replaced Grenville with Rockingham, who is another
failure. Soon King George will bring back Pitt as prime
minister, but he is not finished shaking up his cabinet.
The truth about King George will eventually become clear
to Patrick, to Virginia, and to the other colonies with the
hard Acts to follow. A shakeup of leadership is also
coming in the Virginia House of Burgesses.

"Patrick Henry *himself* is a hard act to follow!" Nigel quipped. "That nervous Governor Fauquier is not taking any chances with calling the Assembly back to Williamsburg any time soon, not after the effect Patrick had on the House. It has been an entire year since the governor dissolved them."

Liz's eyes widened, as a distant memory from long ago London filled her mind. "Gillamon! I understand it now! *C'est ça!*" She turned to Nigel. "Do you remember when we were on mission at George F. Handel's house in London and read the letter John Henry sent to his cousin David, congratulating him on his wedding?"

Nigel tapped his chin and then snapped his fingers. "I do indeed, my pet! We were gathered around the flickering fire and Max brought us the letter from which we first learned that David had family in the colony of Virginia."

"*Oui,* and in that letter we also first heard the name of Patrick Henry," Liz replied, her eyes bright with understanding. "I immediately had a feeling he was destined for greatness. Do you remember what I said his name meant?"

"Noble ruler of the house," Nigel replied. "But *which* house?" Suddenly Nigel understood and popped his paw on his forehead. "Of course!"

"Noble ruler of the House *of Burgesses!*" Liz announced happily. "We knew he was the voice in the House, but not until now did I grasp the full meaning of Patrick's name. He is a noble ruler of his own house, but *mon* Henry must be destined to live up to his name in the House of Burgesses as well. Is this correct, Gillamon?"

Very good, Liz. I knew the meaning would become clear to you with time. Patrick Henry will indeed now, with the changing of the guard, take the lead as noble ruler of the House of Burgesses. And as things become clear to him about King George and the direction of Parliament, he will nobly lead the Assembly through these hard Acts to follow. The ball of the Revolution will pick up speed with every Act that comes.

"I cannot wait to see what happens!" enthused Liz.

"Since shake-ups are coming with Great Britain and the House of Burgesses, might I inquire as to any shake-ups coming with the Order of the Seven and our respective posts?" Nigel asked.

Max and Kate have succeeded in their protective mission with Lafayette. Kate will remain with the young marquis while Max returns to America. Max will go directly to Boston and join Clarie for a while. Nigel, you will eventually join Al in London to assist in matters with Benjamin Franklin.

Nigel furrowed his brow, continuing to pull his bow across Patrick's fiddle. "Understood, Gillamon. But I had quite expected to encounter Dr. Franklin again sooner."

You shall encounter Dr. Franklin soon ... in a way.
A SHUCCSHESSHFUL trip to Williamsburg awaits you
and the Noble Ruler of the House.

As the last notes drifted away, Liz and Nigel knew that Gillamon was gone.

"Shuccshessful?" Liz asked, drawing a chuckle from Nigel as she tried to pronounce the funny word with her French accent. "What could he possibly have meant by that?"

Nigel preened his whiskers and remembered the funny flying squirrel he and Cato had met in Philadelphia. "My dear, if our trip is anything like Philadelphia, then it shall indeed be a hard act to follow."

443

THREATENING SKIES
AND SEIZING LIBERTY

WILLIAMSBURG, NOVEMBER 1766

For the Entertainment of the
CURIOUS,
Will be exhibited at the Huſtings court-houſe,
in this City,

A courſe of EXPERIMENTS,
In that inſtructive and entertaining branch of
Natural Philoſophy,
CALLED
ELECTRICITY,
To be accompanied with lectures on the nature and properties
OF THE
Electrick Fire.
By *WILLIAM JOHNSON.*

A dvance tickets are available here at the Coffee House, but the lectures and demonstrations are to be held at the Courthouse on Monday and Tuesday," Patrick Henry remarked, holding the *Virginia Gazette*. He read aloud the advertisement for the upcoming demonstration on electricity and lighting. "*Those who desire to have their habitations effectually guarded from the fatal violence of one of the most aweful powers of nature (with which this colony in particular has been often dreadfully visited) may learn, from these lectures and experiments, more of the nature and properties of lightning than has been known to mankind until within these few years.*"

"That sounds like a fascinating way to spend an evening after a long day in the Assembly. Do you plan to attend, Patrick?" Richard Henry Lee asked, setting down a steaming mug of coffee on their table in Charlton's

Coffeehouse. He adjusted the black silk handkerchief that he kept wrapped around the palm of his maimed right hand, leaving his thumb free. Richard Henry Lee was a burgess from Westmoreland County. Tall, brilliant, well-educated, and four years older than Patrick, the sophisticated young man became fast friends with Patrick as soon as they met in Williamsburg for the newly elected Assembly. Last time, Patrick Henry hardly had a friend in the House. This time, all of that had changed.

After eighteen long months, Governor Fauquier had finally called the burgesses back in session, but only after his hand was forced. The governor had written to London that *Virginians are so heated as to shut up all avenues of reason. The colonies reciprocally inflame each other, and where the fury will end I know not."* He was much happier without the burgesses around, but after the sudden death of Speaker John Robinson, the governor had no choice. The colony needed a new treasurer, and the House of Burgesses was responsible for electing one.

Governor Fauquier had hoped that the "cool old members" of the House would regain power after Patrick Henry had taken the Assembly by storm in the last session. But his hopes were dashed as new, young faces showed up in Williamsburg after the elections across Virginia. Many of the old burgesses who had opposed Patrick Henry's Stamp Act Resolves were replaced by young representatives who joined those returning members who had been Patrick's most ardent supporters in the Stamp Act debates. Virginians not only celebrated Patrick Henry after his boldness with the Stamp Act Resolves, but they elected burgesses who would represent them in the same way. The makeup of the Virginia House of Burgesses had changed radically, with one third of the delegates new to the Assembly for this session. Patrick Henry had quickly become the leader of the new force of power surging through the Capitol at the end of Duke of Gloucester Street. And Speaker Robinson—the man who had shouted "Treason!" against Patrick Henry and then sneakily reversed Patrick's fifth resolution—was not only dead, but his memory would soon fall into disgrace and scandal.

Peyton Randolph was elected new Speaker of the House, and at the suggestion of Richard Henry Lee and Patrick Henry, the role of treasurer was separated from the speaker's chair. This move soon proved wiser than anyone could have imagined. Robert Carter Nicholas was elected treasurer and Patrick Henry made a motion for a select committee to make a thorough report on the state of the treasury. They soon

445

discovered that something wasn't right about the late Speaker Robinson's accounts. He had loaned £100,000 of public money to friends, and his vast estate would soon be sold off to pay for it.

"Perhaps I will attend the lectures," Patrick replied, taking a sip of coffee. "Now that I've built a house, I'd like to know how to protect it." He raised his eyebrows as he read more of the advertisement. "Listen to this: *As the knowledge of nature tends to enlarge the human mind, and give us more exalted ideas of the GOD of NATURE, it is presumed that this course will prove to many an agreeable and rational entertainment.*'"

"Isn't it amazing that man has found a key to unlock one of God's secrets of nature?" Richard asked, taking a sip of coffee. "Dr. Franklin's discovery has certainly taken the world by storm."

Nigel preened his whiskers proudly as he listened in on their conversation. *"Hear, hear! It's utterly splendid to see the results of our kite-flying storm in Philadelphia shared here in Williamsburg."*

"Yes, and Dr. Franklin *himself* has taken the world by storm," Patrick replied, putting down the paper. "I'll never forget first reading about how he received praise from the king of France for his discovery. I was told that great things would come from it. Now Benjamin Franklin is an international celebrity, both in France and England."

"A celebrity, an inventor, a printer, a postmaster, and now a colonial agent in London," Richard replied, shaking his head in wonder at the amazing man. "I, for one, am glad to have Dr. Franklin representing colonial interests before Parliament, even though they would not listen to him about not passing the Stamp Act. Dr. Franklin was able to summon lightning, but not the common sense of Parliament!" He leaned in close, smiled, and pointed a finger at Patrick. "It took a freshman representative to summon patriotic lightning in the House of Burgesses to knock some sense into the Mother Country."

Patrick took another sip of coffee and smiled humbly. "Well, I am glad the Crown finally felt the heat and repealed the Stamp Act."

"I truly regret I was not present during your Stamp Act speech, Patrick," Richard said. "Tell me, what gave you such confidence to assert your resolves?"

Patrick furrowed his brow and tightened his lips. "I believed that a united sentiment and sound patriotism would carry us safely to our wished-for port. If people will not die or be free, it is of no consequence what sort of government they live under."

446

"Well, *you*, my new friend, are already seen here in Williamsburg as an *aweful power of nature* yourself with such new, bold ideas. Why, they've even installed a balcony in the House chamber for spectators to listen in on our sessions! That should tell you the people are eager to come hear your ideas," Richard replied with a chuckle, pointing to Patrick. "To come hear *you*, Mr. Henry."

Patrick twisted up his mouth. "Come now, Richard! Don't be absurd. That balcony was not installed on my account."

Richard smiled and waved off his comment. "Either way, the Roman patriots thought that good citizens should serve their country every seven years, and it is good to see young patriot citizens like you who have not only joined our ranks, but quickly become leaders."

"Most kind, Richard. I'm grateful for your support. Now to wait and see what Parliament will do next," Patrick replied. "We defeated the Stamp Act, but the Declaratory Act is hanging over us like a dark cloud. It's only a matter of time before a gale sweeps over the colonies from Britain to strike us with another tax."

"Agreed," Richard answered. He smiled and tapped the *Gazette*. "But just as Dr. Franklin found the key to protecting houses against lightning, we colonies have found the key to protecting our Houses from the next storm—by working *together*."

And the Noble Ruler of the House will no doubt be the lightning rod that protects the House of Burgesses when Parliament strikes again, Nigel cheered to himself.

447

LONDON, JUNE 29, 1767

A torrential storm pelted the windows of the palace with fat rain drops. Al was sprawled out on a golden velvet cushion in a window box, fast asleep with drool running down his chin. He dreamed he was walking across a long banquet table spread with silver trays of bountiful food, sampling each and every delicacy. He lifted a piece of fish to his mouth and licked his chops when BOOM! A loud clap of thunder rattled the windows and Al's fur stood on end as he sat straight up, now wide awake. "I'll put it back!" he screamed. His heart was racing as he looked around the room, only to realize he had been dreaming. All he saw was King George and his headstrong Chancellor of the Exchequer, Charles Townshend, smiling and talking with great satisfaction.

"I wonder what cheeky Charles be up to now," Al said, studying the smug man in his forties standing behind the king, who was seated at the desk.

Prime Minister William Pitt fell ill soon after he took charge of the government and was unable to attend Parliament sessions. Charles Townshend quickly moved in to fill the void of power in the House of Commons. He had been plotting something secretly for months, ever since Great Britain's demeaning repeal of the Stamp Act.

Charles Townshend lifted his chin proudly and wore a smug expression as King George pressed the great royal seal into a glob of hot wax. "Excellent, Your Majesty! With this seal of approval, the colonies will once more be put in their place."

"Indeed. Right . . . under . . . *my heel,*" King George answered, punctuating each word with a smile as he looked over the parchment. He smacked the desk happily with the palm of his hand and rose from his seat. "Well done, Townshend. I have great faith that your Townshend Acts will make the Americans once more treat the Crown with respect. I know some in Parliament think I've been in a state of humiliation since the Stamp Act was repealed. I'm glad *you* stepped in to oversee things in the House of Commons while Pitt is away from his post. This calls for a toast."

Al's eyes lit up with joy to see servants bringing in trays of refreshments. "No, this calls for investigatin'." The plump kitty jumped off the window seat and made his way over to stand under the men.

Townshend bowed, feigning humility, then took a glass from the tray. "Thank you, Your Majesty. I am delighted you approve of the Townshend Acts. With several measures we will regain control of the colonies *and* raise money. Although I had to keep my plans secret from the Cabinet until I was ready to present them to Parliament, I look forward to this news finally reaching the colonies. Boston will be the first city to hear of the new *'customs duties'* the colonies will need to pay in order to obtain British glass, lead, paint, paper, and, of course, *tea.* The Americans complained about internal versus external taxes, so we'll take their money with a phrase they can more easily handle: *'regulating commerce.'* The distinction is ridiculous in the opinion of everybody except the Americans!"

"What, what?! Ridiculous!" the king agreed. He held up his clenched fist. "Those American smugglers will feel the grip of the new American Board of Customs Commissioners when they *enforce* the customs duties once and for all. Boston is the perfect place for their headquarters. They

448

will be able to stay right on top of those hot-headed Americans. There will be no more 'cozy accommodations' in colonial seaports." King George smiled and lifted his glass. "There is a reason you are called the cleverest fellow in England."

Townshend lifted his glass. "Most magnanimous of you, my liege. There are those who have their doubts, like Edmund Burke. 'You will not see a shilling from America!' he shouted, but I intend to prove him wrong. We'll keep the colonial governors loyal by taking the power of the purse away from the colonial assemblies to pay them. And for those hot-headed troublemakers who choose to defy the Townshend Acts, we'll haul them away to stand trial outside the colonies. And if we must, there is an old pre-colonial law from the time of King Henry VIII we can dust off and apply to the colonies. If malcontents like that Patrick Henry who spoke out against the Stamp Act try to defy us again, we'll seize them and bring them to England for trial. And we'll try them for *treason.*"

"Brilliant!" King George cheered, lifting a tasty *hors d'oeuvre* from the silver tray. As he took a bite, a clap of thunder and a flash of lightning caused him to jump, sending part of the delicacy to the floor. He looked down to see Al sitting there, not making a move to retrieve it. "What, what?! Leo, I'm surprised at you! This is a day for British lions to celebrate. Aren't you going to snatch up that morsel? What, what?!"

"I jest lost me appetite for yer British goodies, that's what," Al meowed in reply, flattening his ears in disgust over what he had heard the men say. He turned up his nose and walked out of the room. *Jest wait 'til the colonies lose theirs.*

449

———

BOSTON, JUNE 10, 1768

Click-click-click-click went Max's toenails as he trotted along a darkened cobblestone alley that led to Boston Harbor. The Scottie kept his ears up and his eyes open, following the muffled sound of angry voices. "Sounds like tr-r-rouble," he muttered under his breath. "But at least they be words I can make out instead of them Fr-r-rench words then." He had just said farewell to Kate in Chavaniac and traveled through the IAMISPHERE to reach Boston. Clarie was to meet him there.

Suddenly Max smelled something burning and saw the sky growing brighter up ahead. He turned a corner and there before him was an angry mob setting fire to a boat in Boston Harbor. Their torches were raised high in the air and they cursed the customs officer as they cheered the destruction of his boat. Max furrowed his brow and watched a mob of five hundred people at the water's edge throwing stones they had torn from the very streets they walked to reach the wharf. In the distance a fifty-gun British man-o'-war, the *Romney*, towed a beautiful sailing sloop named *Liberty* out of the range of the angry mob.

"Welcome to Boston, where *Liberty* has been seized," came a voice next to him.

Max looked up to see a young man dressed in brown breeches, an open-collared white shirt with rolled-up sleeves and a blue knit cap. Sweat dripped down his cheeks, and in his hand he gripped a stone. "Clarie? Have ye been thr-r-rowin' stones with the r-r-rest of the mob?"

Clarie plopped down on the curb next to Max. "Not throwing stones, but *catching* them, Max." She held up the stone. "This one almost hit a young ten-year-old boy in the head. His name is Christopher Seider and he got caught up in the street mob. I've tried my best to protect the children out here tonight, but I can't be everywhere at once. I told him to hurry back home, but I fear he won't stay there long."

"Well I'm here now ta help ye, lass! Tell me wha' in the name of Pete all this Boston hullabaloo be aboot," Max inquired with his tail up, poised for action. "I've been dealin' with wolf beasties so I don't know wha's happenin' here in Boston."

Clarie put her hand on Max's wiry black fur. "I'm glad you're here, Max. You and Kate did an excellent job protecting the young Marquis de Lafayette. Now that he's attending school in Paris, he's safe for the time being. Kate will enjoy her time there." She wiped her forehead with the back of her arm. "What you're seeing is the response to the Townshend Acts passed by Parliament last year. The Acts involve more taxes on the colonies for British goods, tough enforcement of customs duties on ships bringing imports, enforcement of quartering troops, and so on. Al was in the room when King George put his royal seal on the document that led to this." She pointed to the mayhem and shook her head.

"So the king jest couldn't leave the colonies well enough alone," Max huffed. "Whose gr-r-reat idea were this?"

"Charles Townshend, but he suddenly died before his Acts could even take effect!" Clarie answered. "Once more, King George's government is a mess. Pitt is too sick to run Parliament and 'Do-Nothing Rockingham' is trying to fill in since Townshend died. Now the inept

Lord Hillsborough has been made Secretary of State for Colonial Affairs but is quickly making things worse by sending threatening letters back to the protesting colonies. When word of the Townshend Acts reached Massachusetts, their legislature sent protests to London, saying they weren't fooled by Townshend's 'duties'—they know they are taxes and claim they are unconstitutional. James Otis, Samuel Adams, John Hancock, and other leaders in the Sons of Liberty have called for the colony to stop importing British goods. And they have once more taken to the streets to protest." She pointed to the ships in the harbor. "That sloop out there named *Liberty* belongs to John Hancock, and it was seized by that British warship after Hancock refused to report and pay the full customs duties for goods he brought here from overseas. Now the British are threatening to haul John Hancock over to London to stand trial for treason, so John Adams is going to defend him in court."

"TR-R-REASON? Aye, tr-r-rouble be a br-r-rewin', lass!" Max growled.

"Just wait, Max. It's only going to get worse," Clarie cautioned him. "The Massachusetts Assembly petitioned the king to repeal the Townshend duties and Samuel Adams sent a circular letter to the other colonial assemblies, asking them to join Massachusetts's efforts. Britain ordered the Massachusetts Assembly to recall the letter. When they refused, Governor Bernard dissolved them. The other colonial assemblies have been instructed to ignore the circular letter or be dissolved as well. Meanwhile, Governor Bernard has panicked and written to London that Boston is in open rebellion. He's requested that British troops be brought here to Boston."

"Ye mean them Lobsterbacks will be r-r-roamin' the str-r-reets with muskets while all these angr-r-ry people be thr-r-rowin' stones an' burnin' ships?" Max asked. He shook his head as another cheer arose from the crowd as the customs official's ship burst into flames. "If the colonies don't nip this Townshend mess in the bud like they did with the Stamp Act, the R-r-revolution could be here sooner than they think."

Clarie nodded. "Massachusetts started the protests against the Townshend Acts, but it will be again up to Virginia to lead the charge to make the British lion back down."

"Well, I hope Patr-r-rick Henr-r-ry an' the boys get ta work soon," Max said somberly.

Clarie frowned as Christopher Seider went running by, laughing with a group of boys. "Yes, before innocent blood is spilled."

COACH AND SIX OR
TEN-SHILLING JACKETS

W ill you look at *that?*" Cato said to Nigel. They perched high in the trees above the Governor's Palace. There standing in front of the palace was a gleaming white coach trimmed in elaborate gold with bright red wheels. Six immaculate cream-colored horses stood two by two to pull the coach, adorned with ornate silver bridles that reflected the early morning sun. "That looks like something the king of England himself would ride in!"

"It is precisely *that,* old boy," Nigel replied. "This coach was actually built for King George III but given by his uncle, the Duke of Cumberland, to Virginia's new royal governor. That coach once bore the royal crest of the king, but now it displays Virginia's coat of arms. It is *resplendent* in detail, and those white Percheron dray horses were imported from Hanover, Germany." Nigel crossed his arms over his chest. "After Governor Fauquier's death, clearly King George is attempting to woo and awe his loyal subjects here in Virginia with the appointment of his personal friend as the elegant new governor."

The front doors of the palace opened and servants dressed in the finest livery lined the steps and walkway leading to the palace's front gate, which bore the British lion and unicorn. Shortly there emerged walking down the palace steps the new royal governor of Virginia, Norborne Berkeley, Baron de Botetourt. He was dressed in a luxurious red coat lined with gold thread, plum-colored breeches, silk stockings, silver-buckled shoes, and a large, powdered wig. A charming man in his early fifties, Lord Botetourt exuded confidence and wore a broad smile with every regal step. After the governor ascended the steps to sit in the coach, the coachman snapped the reins, and the horses pulled away from the palace. As they rode along the Palace Green and turned left on Duke of Gloucester Street to head to the Capitol, Lord Botetourt waved to the common people who stood in the streets looking at him with wide eyes, gaping at the royal presence gracing their dusty street. Never had the citizens of Williamsburg seen anything such as this.

"So the new governor is a bachelor, just like us? It's a shame, though. He has all that pomp and no one to share it with," observed Cato as they watched the coach drive away. "I've been thinking I need to settle a nest and have eaglets, maybe when we go back to Philadelphia. Patrick now has two more little girls. He's so happy with his family of *five* children. What about you, Nigel? Do you think you'll ever find the right mouse and settle down?"

Nigel wiggled his whiskers with a chuckle. "I seldom have time to think of such things, old boy. I doubt I shall ever settle down to the wistful pursuit of romance." The mouse tapped Cato on his wing. "But you go right ahead and allow Cupid's arrow to pierce your soaring heart. For now, however, please transport me to the Capitol to watch the regal arrival of Lord Botetourt."

453

Patrick Henry stood under a shady tree with Richard Henry Lee as the coach pulled up in front of the Capitol. As Lord Botetourt climbed down from the coach, Patrick studied the effect this regal show was having on the people. "It appears the king is using a far different approach with his Old Dominion of Virginia than the heavy hand he's used on the Bostonians. While the Massachusetts Assembly sits dissolved in the shadow of the king's guns, we are called to meet in the brilliance of the king's splendor."

Richard Henry Lee nodded and watched the smiling men bow and the admiring ladies curtsy as Lord Botetourt entered the Capitol. "Indeed. We shall soon see if the heavy hand of the king remains hidden beneath the royal cloak of the governor."

Patrick nodded and then smiled, spotting a tall, red-headed, twenty-six-year old young man in a royal blue coat and breeches walking briskly to the Capitol. "We shall also see if Edmund Pendleton and the old guard try to get newly elected burgesses like Tom Jefferson there to succumb to the charms of the king. With their powers to dissolve legislatures at will, I submit that royal governors remain a threat to liberty behind their gilded coach and six."

"Agreed. Shall we get to business and see if Lord Botetourt wishes to extend his noble favor on our humble assembly?" Richard questioned with a smile, motioning with an outstretched hand. Together the two burgesses joined the others filing into the Capitol. It was time to swear in new members like Thomas Jefferson from Albemarle County, for Speaker Peyton Randolph to take his formal oaths for the new assembly, and to see exactly what this new governor desired for Virginia once they decided what to do about the Townshend Acts—pomp or punishment.

MAY 16, 1769

Following the formalities of the opening assembly, Lord Botetourt entertained some fifty burgesses at the Governor's Palace. He lavished them with fine food and drink while an ensemble of chamber musicians filled the ballroom with the heavenly sounds of Peter Pelham's harpsichord and accompanying violins. Nigel was in ecstasy in the beautiful candlelit room, closing his eyes as he swayed to the music of Handel, Bach, and Telemann. He applauded and cheered for Peter Pelham at the conclusion of the evening. "Bravo, Mr. Pelham! Another exquisite performance! Bravo!" The little mouse didn't want to leave the palace.

454

Subsequent evenings found the governor being wined and dined in the fine homes of the Tidewater gentry or dancing in the Apollo Room of the Raleigh Tavern. It seemed as if things between the new royal governor and the House of Burgesses were off to a stellar beginning. But after handling many routine business matters for the colony, attention was finally turned to the Townshend Acts. The House met in the Committee of the Whole to discuss what Virginia would do next.

"The Townshend Acts are a flaming sword pointed at the people's liberties that has to be removed by all means!" Richard Henry Lee exclaimed.

"Hear, hear!" answered many of the burgesses, pounding their hands on the benches.

"How pitiful that Parliament would actually think we are such simpletons that do not see these Townshend duties for what they really are—a tax!" Patrick Henry railed. "We must denounce them, just as we did the Stamp Tax. If we make a united stand to oppose them, they will be repealed as well."

"Listen to these telling words about the Townshend Acts from *Letters from a Farmer in Pennsylvania*," John Blair offered, holding up the *Virginia Gazette*. "It is a snare worthy of Nero to disguise taxes as trade regulation."

Nigel sat up high in the new balcony, pleased to be able to sit and watch the proceedings of the entire House rather than peeking from beneath the tablecloth of the clerk's table. "And Nero was more revolting than a rat, I assure you!" he squeaked. He looked over to see the governor's messenger take his seat in the balcony, so slipped under a bench out of sight.

Richard Henry Lee reached into his pocket and unfolded a letter. "My friend John Dickinson is that farmer in Pennsylvania, and he sent me these words: *Virginia, sir, has maintained the common cause, with such attention, spirit, and temper as has gained her the highest degree of reputation among the other colonies. It is as much in her power to dishearten them, as to encourage them.*" He looked around at the men and lifted his hand in Patrick's direction. "Gentlemen, Virginia led the other colonies before with Mr. Henry's Stamp Act Resolves. It is time to lead them again with resolves against these despicable Townshend Acts."

455

The usually quiet George Washington spoke up. "Agreed. Massachusetts has implored each colony to join her in the fight against these Acts. Now that she has come under the thumb of the king, our sister colony looks to Virginia to lead the way. As the largest and oldest colony, I feel we have a duty to take the lead in this matter. However goes Virginia, so goes America."

Nods of agreement and murmurs of approval rippled through the chamber.

"Let us then draft the Virginia Resolves against the Townshend Acts. Our resolves must obviously uphold the exclusive right of taxation by our own assembly, just as we stated in the Stamp Act Resolves," Patrick Henry offered. "But we must especially address the grievous threat to colonists who would be sent to England for trial. Imagine the horror that awaits any wretched American who offends those in power: he could be dragged from his home, thrown into prison, shackled with iron chains in the bowels of a ship for weeks, and carried off to a distant land where no friend or family can reach him to provide assistance. With no witness to testify to his innocence, I submit he would rot in the Tower of London or meet the hangman's noose, the next ship sailing for

America with the news of his demise! No, we cannot allow this, gentlemen! It is the undoubted privilege of British subjects to have a trial by a jury of their peers in their home locale. Liberty herself is in danger of being seized, shackled, and thrown into the holds of a ship bound for England."

"Hear, hear!" Nigel cheered with a fist raised in the air. The little mouse watched the faces of the burgesses, who considered that such a fate as Patrick Henry described could await each and every one of them if they displeased the Crown.

After a lengthy discussion, four resolves were unanimously adopted. A committee was then formed to draw up the formal response to the king to be presented the following day, chaired by John Blair, Jr., with members Patrick Henry, Richard Henry Lee, Treasurer Robert Carter Nicholas, Thompson Mason, and Benjamin Harrison.

"Not a single shout of treason was uttered in this chamber today! How splendid to see such calm and unity this time in the House of Burgesses," Nigel noted with a smile. He then spied the governor's messenger leaving the balcony. "Outside of this chamber, however, things may be anything but calm."

456

———

GOVERNOR'S PALACE, MAY 17, 1769

"I shall put an end to this abominable business immediately," Lord Botetourt said. He calmly dabbed the corners of his mouth with his napkin and looked up at his messenger, who had brought word of the resolves the House of Burgesses had adopted yesterday and would finalize this morning. "Thank you for your report. Please go and inform the burgesses to meet me immediately in the Council Chamber," Lord Botetourt instructed, taking one more sip of tea and scooting back his chair. As his messenger left the room, he looked out the front window of the palace onto Palace Green and shook his head. "I had hoped it would not come to this."

———

"This is a closed session of the Assembly. Keep the door locked," Patrick Henry said with a firm voice at hearing the knock of the messenger on the chamber door. "The governor's messenger can wait until we've finished our business here."

Thomas Jefferson raised his eyebrows. He leaned over and whispered to another burgess. "Mr. Henry's boldness astounds me!"

Speaker Randolph motioned to Mr. Blair. "Mr. Blair, please continue reading from the fourth resolve."

"Resolved, *nemine contradicente* (with no one speaking against) that an humble and loyal address be presented to His Majesty to assure him of our inviolable attachment to his sacred person and government, and to beseech his royal interposition, as the father of his people, however remote from the seat of his empire to quiet the minds of his loyal subjects of this colony, and to avert from them those dangers and miseries which will ensue, from the seizing and carrying beyond sea any person residing in America suspected of any crime whatsoever, to be tried in any other manner than by the ancient and long established court of proceeding," John Blair reported, looking around the room to gauge the response of the assembly to the committee's resolutions and address to the king. Another unanimous vote was taken to approve the resolves.

Patrick eyeballed the burgesses and a half-smile appeared on his face as he saw this time not a boisterous debate as with the Stamp Act Resolves, but a unanimous House standing together against the tyranny of the Crown. Even the old guard members like Edmund Pendleton and Peyton Randolph realized the dangerous waters the king had sailed into with the Townshend Acts. While the House of Burgesses expressed its opposition to the Acts, it maintained its steadfast devotion to the king. No one desired anything but unity with Great Britain, but not at the loss of liberty.

"Very well, Mr. Speaker, I move that copies of these resolves be sent immediately to the other colonies," Richard Henry Lee declared.

"Second," Thompson Mason added.

"Bravo!" Nigel cheered from the balcony, preening his whiskers. "Not only was there harmony in the House to easily pass *these* resolves, but the humans do not require the services of Liz or myself to have them printed and forwarded to the other colonies. This was almost too easy!"

The chamber door was unlocked and a wave of fresh air filled the room as the door opened, followed by the governor's messenger. He walked right up to Speaker Randolph's chair. "Mr. Speaker, the governor demands the immediate attendance of your House in the Council Chamber."

"Very well," Speaker Randolph responded, standing up to walk to the door. "Gentlemen, follow me."

"The honeymoon is over," Patrick Henry murmured to Richard Henry Lee.

As the burgesses filed out of the room to climb the wide staircase to the upper floor, Nigel held a paw to his mouth. "Oh, dear." He scurried along behind them.

Lord Botetourt sat confidently in his ornate chair at the head of the table in the imposing Governor's Chamber, his other counselors sitting on either side of him in their seats of prominence. As Speaker Randolph entered the room, Patrick Henry stood beside him as the other burgesses clustered around them. Once the entire Assembly had quietly gathered, Lord Botetourt lifted his chin and gazed into their faces. Instead of the smiling, pleasant man they had wined and dined the past week, here sat a man with serious intentions.

"I have heard of your Resolves, and augur ill of their effect," Lord Botetourt announced coldly. "You have made it my duty to dissolve you, and you are dissolved accordingly."

No one said a word for a moment, but looked at one another uncomfortably. Nigel planted his face in his paw and shook his head.

458

Speaker Randolph bowed respectfully and the burgesses nodded politely as they somberly left the chamber. As they exited the building, Thomas Jefferson came alongside Patrick Henry.

"What do we do now?" Thomas asked.

Patrick Henry grinned and patted the young burgess on the back with a wink. "We continue our meeting. At The Raleigh."

―――――――

RALEIGH TAVERN, MAY 18, 1769

Ninety ex-burgesses filed into the elegant Apollo Room with its rich pine floors, pink marble fireplace, and rich blue paneling. Sunlight poured into the room from six tall windows, and Speaker Randolph took his seat in front of the fireplace. Above his head was carved the motto of this lively meeting place, *Jollity is the offspring of wisdom and good living.* Nigel couldn't help but grin at the change of venue and the brave determination of these men to stand in defiance to the Crown. The burgesses were here to resume their meeting from yesterday afternoon, and George Washington was to present plans for a Non-Importation Agreement.

"Colonel Washington, the floor is yours," Peyton Randolph said, no longer in his formal robe and speaker chair, but now called 'Moderator' in this gathering of ex-burgesses. "We, the late representatives of the people, are eager to see what your committee has prepared."

George Washington stood to his feet and bowed humbly, towering over the men with his broad-shouldered stature. "Thank you, Mr. Randolph. Gentlemen, as you know, I seldom rise to speak in your midst. I leave oratory to those who are far more equipped than I." He smiled and nodded at Patrick Henry. "But I have discussed the challenge before us with our wise friend, Mr. George Mason, who is not here. He penned a series of prudent measures that combine with other measures proposed by merchant groups in the northern colonies. Our committee proposes that we form a new Virginia Association to promote a Non-Importation Agreement for the citizens of Virginia. If I may," he said before opening up the document and glancing around the room.

Some of the ex-burgesses cast uncomfortable glances at one another. Others sat up in their seats, eager to hear what Washington would propose.

459

"We hereby propose that the good people of Virginia cease importing from Britain the following list of items," Washington began. "We ask you to join the Association and pledge to import none of the goods taxed by Parliament for the purpose of raising revenue through the Townshend duties with the exception of cheap paper, which we will need for correspondence. Gentlemen, we propose a complete ban on British goods until the Townshend Acts are repealed."

Washington proceeded to read the long list of items that the good people of Virginia would be asked to no longer import. Instead of luxurious silk fabric, colonists would wear rough clothes made from homespun linsey-woolsey. Instead of delicious, superb British tea, colonists would make do with drinking sassafras tea. As Washington read, some of the ex-burgesses got up and left the room. They would not be party to the new Association, either unwilling to sacrifice or fearing the backlash from the Crown. Once Washington finished reading, the four Virginia Resolves were once more confirmed, and those remaining were asked to sign the Non-Importation Agreement.

Patrick Henry was among the first of the ex-burgesses to sign his name on the Agreement. He handed the quill to the next man in line and went to give George Washington an affirming handshake. "No ministerial mandate can make us buy ten-pound coats when we prefer to warm ourselves by the fire of liberty in ten-shilling jackets."

"A toast!" one of the ex-burgesses exclaimed as servants brought in cups filled with punch. These bold men would celebrate this momentous occasion with a rousing series of traditional toasts—eleven in all. They toasted the king, the queen, and the royal family, the governor, the speaker, the treasurer, and to prosperity in Virginia. They even toasted their English allies and "the Farmer" whose words had encouraged Virginia to lead the charge as the voice for the colonies against the Townshend Acts.

During the celebration, Patrick Henry, George Washington, and Richard Henry Lee joined the toasts but maintained their caution over what was to come.

"I wrote to one of my London merchants that the Parliament of Great Britain has no more right to put their hands in my pocket for money, without my consent, than I have to put my hand into yours," George Washington said, pointing to his friends.

"Clearly Parliament disagrees, as they have now stationed two regiments of British troops in Boston," Richard Henry Lee added. "Boston is now a garrisoned town. Troops have taken over Faneuil Hall and the Massachusetts State House for their military headquarters. Soldiers have set up camp in Boston Common and taken over the Parade Grounds."

"Armed redcoats fill the streets of Boston, and hot-headed men led by the likes of Samuel Adams and John Hancock are standing on every street corner with clenched fists," Patrick Henry reported gravely. "Gentlemen, despite our stand against the Crown, I fear it's only a matter of time before red *coats* are not the only source of red filling the streets of Boston."

"Oh, dear!" fretted Nigel as he scurried out of the Raleigh Tavern. "I need to tell Liz all that has happened. Heaven help Max and Clarie in Boston! If Patrick's prophecy comes true, the fight with England will move beyond words. It will turn bloody."

COMFORT AND JOY

The whole continent from New England to Georgia seems firmly fixed; like a strong, well-constructed arch, the more weight there is laid upon it the firmer it stands.

L iz and Nigel sat reading the *Massachusetts Gazette* and other newspapers from the colonies for the latest news about the colonial resistance to the Townshend Acts. The smell of hot Christmas wassail spiced with cinnamon and oranges wafted through the Henry house. Liz smiled to see Nigel reach for his tiny thimble full of the warm drink, taking a mindless sip as he scanned the paper.

"I am happy to see such unity among the colonies following the passage of Virginia's resolves against the Townshend Acts," commented Liz. "North Carolina, Rhode Island, and New York adopted them in full, while others like Massachusetts and Maryland at least copied the essence of them. The Association seems to be working well, no? Imports are down throughout the colonies."

"Indeed, my dear! Great Britain is feeling a painful pinch in its pompous purse." Nigel adjusted his spectacles, admiring his own alliteration. He read from the *Essex Gazette* of Salem, Massachusetts. "Listen to this praise for Virginia's resolves to inspire the movement: 'Virginia's resolves have *the same sense of justice and value for the constitutional rights of America, the same vigor and boldness, that breathed through the first Resolves of that truly Honorable House, and greatly contributed to form the free and generous spirit in which the Colonies are now one.* '"Huzzah!"

Liz beamed with pride. "*Mon* Henry's influence continues to spread, from his Stamp Act Resolves now to these Townshend Acts Resolves."

She scanned the paper for any word of trouble between citizens and soldiers in Boston. "But I am relieved things appear to be calm in Boston despite his concern about British soldiers being stationed there."

"Yes, things are calm in Boston for *now,*" Nigel replied, taking another sip of wassail, then chuckling as he read from the *Virginia Gazette.* "But there is quite a tempest brewing in London! That cheeky Junius fellow continues his anonymous barrage in the London papers against the chaotic government of King George and Parliament. I wish I knew who he was."

"As do King George and the rest of London," Liz noted with a wink. "Perhaps he is a long lost cousin of yours, writing with the pen of *Anonymouse.*"

Nigel chuckled and wiggled his whiskers. "Perhaps." The little mouse's eyes widened behind his spectacles. "By Jove, what if it's David Henry?! He frequently writes anonymous items for the paper."

Liz's eyes brightened at the thought. "Well, if it is David, then his cousin Patrick is most pleased with his work."

462

"Well, *I* am most pleased that Lord Botetourt called the House of Burgesses back into session in November, offering hopeful promises of Parliament repealing at least some of the Townshend Acts in the new year," Nigel told Liz. "The governor wished to 'kiss and make up' after dissolving the Assembly last May. And the festive ball he held at the Palace was splendid! While the music was exquisite and the cuisine delicious, the governor got the clear message that the Virginians would keep up their resistance to importing fine British goods. His guests were dressed in homespun gowns and breeches. I daresay, even Uncle Langloo would have blended in well with the attendees at this ball!"

"I am certain *mon* Henry enjoyed himself and felt more at home with the plainly dressed guests at the Palace," Liz posed. "But of course he feels *most* at home back here at Roundabout."

Just then they heard the Henry children laughing and rambunctious noises coming from the other room. Patrick's voice cried out playfully, "Help, Sallie! They've got me!" Liz and Nigel shared a smile and peeked into the room. Patrick was rolling around on the floor, laughing and wrestling with his boys piled on top of him. John was now twelve, and William was six. Annie, who was two, was not about to be left out, and jumped onto the pile of Henry boys.

Sallie bounced five-month-old Betsey on her hip. "I'm afraid you are on your own, Mr. Henry," she teased. "You can always offer to soothe the savages with a little fiddle music."

Patsey, now a young lady of fourteen, finished stringing a garland of cranberries to add to their mantle of simple Christmas decorations. She draped the garland across fresh cut pine boughs, cinnamon sticks, and candles. "Please, Papa, play some Christmas music for us!"

"As you wish, little girl!" Patrick exclaimed as he allowed little Annie to pin his arm to the floor. "I surrender."

"Got you!" Annie cheered before giving her father a kiss on his forehead.

· Patrick sat up and briskly patted John and William on the leg as they sat back laughing, resting their elbows on the hardwood floor. "If Virginia needs strong militia men to defend her, I have great confidence in you two. Well done, boys. And as for you," Patrick teased through gritted teeth as he scooped up Annie into his arms, "you have captured your papa's arm *and* his heart!" He gave her butterfly kisses as she giggled until her face turned red.

"They are so happy to have their father back home, no?" Liz beamed. "He has to be away from his family so very much with his successful law practice and now legislative business as well. I am quite proud of his appointment to the highest court in Virginia, the General Court. Although he now handles fewer cases' than before, he is handling the most important ones, and receives much more money for his work. But because of this, he has to be in Williamsburg even more now."

"Right. Let's add this up," Nigel replied, counting on his upheld fingers. "Patrick's time in the General Court requires two weeks in April and October for civil cases plus two weeks in June and December for criminal cases. On top of his busy law practice schedule, the House of Burgesses meets twice a year in May and November for several weeks on end. When one adds his travel time betwixt Williamsburg and Roundabout, Patrick must be away from home at least four, possibly even five, months out of the year!" The little mouse held his thimble of wassail to his lips and took a sip. "Whilst our Mr. Henry works and serves the colony, he also has a farm to manage and must travel to inspect other properties he has invested in out west on the Virginia frontier. Surely MizP must have worn out a dozen pair of horseshoes by now! Cato has certainly logged countless miles on our trips to Williamsburg."

"*Oui,* Patrick must do all of this, plus serve in the vestry of his church

463

and teach law students here at Roundabout. His current students, Isaac Coles and William Christian, show great promise as lawyers," Liz added, marveling at the heavy responsibilities on Patrick Henry's shoulders. "*Mon* Henry is indeed living up to his name. The noble ruler of the house takes care of his growing family with the farm and land, defends the powerless in court, serves his church, teaches young lawyers, and tirelessly serves his country." Liz frowned as she studied Sallie's face. There was a heaviness in her eyes and a melancholy look about her. "But I am concerned about Sallie, Nigel."

Nigel looked at the weary young mother of five with the wildly successful young husband, now picking up his fiddle to play for his family. "Concerned how, my pet? From her lack of sleep? She does have another baby to care for."

Liz's tail slowly curled up and down as she watched Sallie take a seat with Betsey on her lap. "Not just that. Something is simply not right with her. More and more she has days where she is sad and blue. I am glad I am here to comfort her while Patrick is away. While Roundabout is a wonderful place to live, it has grown quite crowded with five children plus the law students residing here as well. And Sallie is somewhat isolated out here in the country. I think she misses her family and friends, and the bustle of Hanover."

"I'm sure she is just suffering from missing her husband, and the demands of running such a busy household," Nigel tried his best to assure her.

Liz smiled sadly. "Perhaps you are right, *mon ami.* But I shall keep a close watch on her." She smiled to hear Patrick's music filling their humble home with joy. She walked back over to read the *Virginia Gazette,* scanning the advertisements. "Nigel, what if we found a larger place for the Henry family to live? Someplace where Sallie could be closer to her family as well as the Henrys? Patrick can certainly afford a larger house now."

Nigel came over to see what Liz was reading. "Have you spied something of interest?"

Liz pointed to the ad. "A large, commodious dwelling-house built of wood with eight rooms on one floor, and a very large passage pleasantly situated, and all convenient outhouses, also a good water grist mill," she read excitedly. "It's a plantation called Scotchtown, with 960 acres. It is located quite close to Mount Brilliant and would be a more convenient location for Patrick's trips to Williamsburg."

Nigel looked at the advertisement, preening his whiskers as he pondered. "Not only that, but *this* house is part of the estate that belonged to none other than the late Speaker John Robinson. Your 'Noble Ruler of the House' has already moved into Robinson's House *of Burgesses*. Now Patrick could move into Robinson's *estate* house as well!"

"*Oui,* and Scotchtown will likely sell for a reasonable price," Liz noted, her tail whipping back and forth excitedly. "*Bon.* I shall explore this possibility. I believe Scotchtown would give Sallie more room to breathe, and make her happy to be near her family and friends again."

"God rest ye, merry gentlemen, let nothing you dismay; remember Christ our Savior was born on Christmas Day; to save us all from Satan's power, when we were gone astray," came the sound of happy carolers singing in the other room.

Nigel peered into his empty thimble. "I must refill my wassail and join in the Henry Christmas revelry." As he scurried off, Liz turned her gaze back to the advertisement for Scotchtown.

"O tidings of comfort and joy, comfort and joy," Liz mouthed along with the Henry family singing the Christmas carol while Patrick played his fiddle. "Maker, please give Sallie comfort and joy this Christmas. And help *mon* Henry make this move to Scotchtown in the coming new year." She smiled as she thought of Max and Kate. *Scotchtown is a perfect place for a Scottish dog. I know Kate would be a great comfort and joy to Sallie, if trouble is coming.*

Liz suddenly remembered what Patrick had said about Boston and her smile faded. *If* mon *Henry's words about trouble in the streets of Boston come true, Max will be in the middle of it.*

53

INNOCENT BLOOD

BOSTON, FEBRUARY 22, 1770

TORY IMPORTER! TORY IMPORTER! SHAME! SHAME!" a group of boys shouted, hoisting a large, crudely carved effigy head on a pole into the air. "LILLIE IS A TORY IMPORTER! DON'T BUY FROM HIM! SHAME!"

"Wha's all the r-r-ruckus aboot this mornin'?" Max asked as he and Clarie walked up to view the scene of thirty or so boys shouting, laughing, jeering, and throwing lemon peels at the merchant shop of Theophilus Lillie. By their dress, most of them were from the lowest class of society. "An' why aren't these laddies in school?"

"It's Thursday, and school lets out by ten o'clock for boys to attend a public lecture in Boston, but they never do. It's also market day, with farmers in town to sell their produce, so it's naturally a perfect day for assembling a mob," Clarie explained. She was dressed as a worker from the dock yards of Boston. "The Sons of Liberty have recruited these young boys as apprentices to stir up trouble with merchants in the area who have refused to sign the non-importation agreements over the Townshend duties. Theophilus Lillie was among the loyalist merchants whose names were printed in the paper and listed as 'Enemies of Their Country.'"

"Aye, so the patr-r-riots be puttin' pr-r-ressure on Parliament ta r-r-repeal them Townshend Acts by not buyin' anythin' fr-r-rom England," deduced Max, watching the boys in the street. "An' for the merchants who tr-r-ry ta sell Br-r-ritish goods, this is wha' they get."

"Or worse. They could be tarred and feathered if the mob gets out of control," Clarie pointed out.

Suddenly a gruff-looking man by the name of Ebenezer Richardson came walking up to the crowd, trying to get the mob of boys to stop marching on the merchant and to take down the effigy of Lillie's head.

"That Ebenezer Richardson is a scoundrel," accused Clarie with a frown as her eyes followed the man. "His bad reputation followed him here to Boston. When he couldn't find a job he signed up to be a Customs Informer." She looked down at Max. "Meaning he squeals on anyone who smuggles or doesn't pay the Townshend duties."

"He's a r-r-rat then!" Max scowled.

Some "Whig" or patriot gentlemen standing on the corner laughed at Richardson's attempts to call off the mob. The irritated Richardson held up his fist in the air and shouted, "Perjury! Perjury!" He then stomped off toward his house, followed by the mob of boys who decided to turn their protest on the informer.

"Wha' in the name of Pete does he mean by that?"

"I don't know but he's made matters worse with these boys," Clarie worried, growing alarmed as she spotted Christopher Seider in the crowd, laughing. This was the boy she had protected and sent home the night the mobs stormed the wharf when British soldiers captured John Hancock's ship, the Liberty. "We better follow them."

467

"INFORMER! INFORMER!" the boys shouted angrily, pointing at Richardson as he reached his front door.

Richardson's wife, Kezia, opened the front door, and the couple tried to shoo the boys away. "Get out of here!"

"We will not!" Christopher shouted, cupping his mouth. "King's highway!"

Max looked up at Clarie. "King's highway?"

"He means they have every right to be out here on the street," Clarie explained.

Suddenly Richardson grabbed a walking stick from inside his house and held it up, threatening to hit the boys. He gritted his teeth. "Get away from my house, you street urchins!"

Someone hurled an egg and hit Kezia on her face, sending runny egg yolk down her cheek. "Oh! Look what they did!" she exclaimed, wiping away the egg and running inside.

Some of the boys threw lemon peels and other harmless rubbish at the open front door. Some of it landed in the foyer, as Richardson continued to angrily shout at them. The crowd was quickly growing, as now some working men and sailors from the docks joined the rambunctious mob of about seventy encircling Richardson's front door, shouting, "INFORMER! SHAME!"

One of the Richardsons' daughters stood inside the house and threw a brickbat into the mob, hitting one of the sailors on the arm. The sailor angrily picked up the brick and threw it back through their front window, shattering the glass and sending shards flying everywhere.

"This is getting out of control!" Clarie screamed in alarm.

Suddenly Max lifted his nose and sniffed the air. "That r-r-rotten stench. I've smelled it before!"

One of Richardson's fellow Customs workers named George Wilmot pushed his way through the crowd and shoved Richardson inside the house, slamming the door behind them.

"Do you have any guns?" Wilmot asked, out of breath and wiping his brow. "You better protect your family and your house before they destroy it like they did them Stamp Collectors'!"

Richardson set down his stick and grabbed two muskets mounted on his wall, handing one to Wilmot. Once he had loaded his gun with powder, Richardson opened his front door and shouted, "As sure as there is a God in heaven, I'll blow a lane through all of you!" He suddenly fired, filling the air with smoke and the smell of gunpowder.

Clarie and Max ducked as the boys scattered. "No bullet! Thank the Maker, he's just trying to scare them," Clarie sighed with relief as Richardson slammed the front door shut and disappeared again. But her smile faded as she saw a dirty man shouting instructions to the boys to pick up any heavy rocks and bricks they could find. The man pointed to Richardson's house and threw a stone. "Oh, no! They're returning!"

"Aye, this time with stones!" Max growled, sniffing the air and frantically looking around. "This isn't good, lass! Somethin' bad's aboot ta happen!"

"Try to pull any boy you can away from here, Max!" Clarie shouted as the mob started to throw the objects at the windows of the house. She ran into the mob, grabbing the boys right and left, telling them to get home before they were hurt.

"OH!" Kezia cried as a rock flew into the house and hit her on the arm. Her daughter screamed and ran to her side.

"Quickly, get to the back of the house!" Richardson shouted to his family, who scurried to the back bedroom. Turning to Wilmot, he instructed, "You stay down here while I go upstairs." He pulled out a paper cartridge of pea-sized buckshot pellets and proceeded to load his musket.

The dirty, smelly man picked up a rock and hurled it back at the house, and the boys followed his lead. Clarie's eyes suddenly fell on the blonde-headed Christopher Seider, who was leaning over to pick up another stone. As she ran to grab him, everything seemed to unfold in slow motion.

Richardson fired his musket from the open window, but this time he lowered his aim, spraying the crowd with pellets. A sailor named Robert Paterson felt the pellets rip through his baggy trousers but miss his leg. Nineteen-year-old painter Sammy Gore was hit in his right hand and thigh and fell back into the street, screaming as he held his hand in agony.

But suddenly, eleven-year-old Christopher Seider's white shirt turned red as eleven pellets found their mark in his chest. He fell back onto the cobblestone street just as Clarie reached him. "NO!" she screamed as she quickly scooped Christopher up in her arms and started running toward the home of Dr. Joseph Warren.

469

Max ran after Clarie as the crowd dispersed, but glancing over his shoulder he saw the dirty, stinky man tossing a rock up and down in his hand, smiling.

54

BLOODY BOSTON

WHARTON AND BOWE BOOKSELLERS, BOSTON, MARCH 5, 1770, 1:00 P.M.

Henry Knox's lips moved silently as he read from a book about European military strategy. The six-foot-tall, burly nineteen-year-old leaned his elbows on the counter, so engrossed in the book he didn't hear the little bell ring as the door to the booksellers' shop opened. In walked Captain John Preston, a grenadier serving with the 29th Regiment of Foot, one of the regiments sent to Boston from Ireland to restore order. The forty-year-old British officer stomped the ice from his black boots and brushed the snow off his red coat.

"Good day, Mr. Knox. That must be an engaging read," Captain Preston noted with a grin, walking over to the counter.

Henry started and then stood up abruptly. "Good day, Captain Preston. Yes, indeed. I'm reading about siege warfare."

"Big guns?" Captain Preston asked, tipping back the book to see the cover.

"Yes, sir. I've always been interested in artillery, ever since I joined 'The Train' militia company of artillery in 1768," Henry answered, closing the book. "I've loved reading about military history and warfare since I started working here as a nine-year-old boy. I think I've read every book in this shop!"

"Ah yes, didn't you tell me The Train drilled with a British regular artillery unit the winter of '66?" Captain Preston recalled.

"Indeed! The British regulars were delayed from leaving Boston for Quebec, so Captain Mason had The Train benefit from that bad winter weather by learning from the best artillery soldiers. I was only sixteen at the time, but one of the Sergeants allowed me to watch them up close. Would you believe his name was Sgt. Jock Frost?" Henry asked with a grin.

"*Jock* Frost? Not Jack Frost?" Captain Preston asked.

"No, sir, Sgt. Jock Frost," Henry confirmed. "Well, what can I help you with today, sir?"

Captain Preston pointed to a can of snuff on the shelf behind Henry. "One can, and the latest *Gazette*. I'm the officer of the day, but it will soon be a cold night. Simple comforts."

"Very good, sir," Henry answered, reaching for the snuff. As his back was turned, he heard the bell on the entrance door sound, announcing another customer. He turned to see the old sergeant from The Train step inside, and at his feet was a little black dog.

"Sgt. Frost! What a strange coincidence! I was just talking about you to Captain Preston here," Henry told him, setting the box of snuff on the counter.

"Good day, lad. Aye, 'tis a cold, snowy day, jest like the day we trained with those guns," the old, white-haired soldier answered, his blue eyes twinkling with a knowing grin. He nodded to Captain Preston and put a finger to his black tricorn hat. "Sir."

"And who is this fine dog?" Henry asked with a big grin, kneeling to pet the Scottish terrier. "Aren't you the sturdy fellow?"

"His name is Max, and he's been one of me best soldiers, always barrelin' through the snow and ice," Sgt. Frost answered with a grin. "Never was there a finer breed ta have by yer side in winter, Mr. Knox. Ice and snow don't seem ta bother Scotties a bit."

"I'd love to have a dog like this," Henry agreed, rubbing Max behind the ears, then standing with his hands on his hips, grinning broadly.

"Aye, of course ye would, bein' a fine Scot yerself," Sgt. Frost answered. He winked at Max. "Maybe ye'll be lucky enough ta have a son of a gun from Max here one day."

Captain Preston put his coin on the counter, picked up the *Boston Gazette* and frowned. Sprawled on the front page was the horrible news covering the massive funeral for Christopher Seider a week before. "Such a senseless tragedy."

"They say it was the largest funeral ever held in America. Some 2,000 people lined the streets of Boston," Henry reported with a wrinkled brow.

"If only Dr. Warren could have saved the boy," Sgt. Frost added sadly, shaking his head. His eyes brimmed for a brief moment as he looked down at Max, who looked up at him with sad eyes.

Captain Preston folded the paper and snapped it on the counter. "I know that hothead Sam Adams and his kind roused up those boys to go after the Customs official. Then he roused the crowds to line the streets for the boy's funeral," he surmised angrily. "He played on the people's emotions by having three hundred children dressed as angels in white to walk behind the casket! The situation was sad enough without Adams making it worse! Tensions have been high all week and until those hotheads learn to respect British authority, things are only going to get worse for the people of Boston."

"One thing ye must always keep in mind, Captain Preston, is that Bostonians are passionate aboot their liberty, and they'll fight ta the last drop of blood in their veins if they have ta," Sgt. Frost warned, stopping the man as he turned to leave. "They do wish ta remain loyal ta the Crown, but not at the expense of their freedom. But understand also that there are those who *wish* ta cause trouble for the sake of trouble. The scuffles between yer soldiers and the citizens at the Rope Walk the other day could lead ta more heated conflict. Keep a close watch on yer men, Captain. It's a powder keg on the streets of Boston. We don't want any more innocent blood spilled out there. Let the frosty chill of the night remind ye ta cool yer tempers."

Captain Preston stared into the penetrating blue eyes of this old soldier and felt a sense of urgency to get back to his men. "Agreed, Sgt. Frost." He nodded to Henry. "Mr. Knox."

As Captain Preston left the bookshop, Sgt. Frost turned to Henry Knox and tapped the book about artillery sitting on the counter. "Be on yer guard as well, lad. Remember, it only takes a single spark ta fire a cannon, much less a musket."

"Thank you, sir," Henry replied. "Even though you're retired, you're still on guard for Boston and for me."

"May the same be said of *ye* one day, lad," Sgt. Frost answered, leaning in with a knowing grin. "Ye may not always just *read* books aboot firin' cannons. Ye may command an artillery unit of yer own someday. Once a soldier, always a soldier."

"Well, right now I'm saving money to open my own bookstore next year, but I appreciate your confidence in me," Henry replied. "What was it you came in for, sir?"

"Just ta say hello. We'll be going now," Sgt. Frost said, turning with Max to walk to the door. A rush of cold air came inside as the bell jingled. "Keep yerself safe, lad. It may be a frosty night ahead, but things are heatin' up in the streets of Boston."

"Will do, Sgt. Frost. Goodbye, Max. Thanks for stopping by," Henry told them, rubbing his upper arms against the blast of cold air. He closed the door behind them and went back to pick up his book. He smiled. "Jock Frost."

When the old soldier and Max were outside walking down the street, Max looked up. "Wha' did ye mean with that 'son of a gun' comment, lass?"

Clarie grinned. "Oh, just planting a seed, Max." Her smile faded as she pulled her collar up around her neck against the chill. "You needed to meet Henry Knox and Captain Preston. We must make sure they are both kept safe tonight. Get ready, Max. Things will happen quickly here in Boston."

BOSTON, MARCH 5, 1770, 7:30 P.M.

Captain John Goldfinch of the British 14th Regiment of Foot turned to walk hurriedly down King Street in the center of town. A brawl had erupted between some Boston dock workers and British soldiers outside Murray's Barracks, and Goldfinch was headed there to break it up.

Goldfinch passed a wigmaker's shop belonging to John Piemont. Standing in front of the shop was one of the wigmaker's teenage apprentices named Edward Garrick. The boisterous teen recognized the captain as one of their slower-paying customers. His hands were covered in grease from having worked on shaping some wigs. He wiped his greasy palms onto his apron and pointed a finger at the captain. "You, there! You haven't paid your bill to Mr. Piemont!"

Captain Goldfinch happened to have a receipt from the wigmaker in his pocket. He had paid his bill earlier, but was not about to even acknowledge the presence of some ignorant, lowly wigmaker's boy rudely shouting accusations at him in the street. He walked on, ignoring Edward's taunts.

"Greasy Lobsterback! You're all alike!" Edward called after the silent captain.

Standing within earshot of Edward's shouting was Private Hugh White of the 29th Regiment. The thirty-year-old soldier stood guard at his sentry post in front of the nearby Customs House, a mansion that had been rented to house the Customs Office where the king's treasury was collected and used for the colony of Massachusetts. As an eleven-year veteran serving in His Majesty's army, Private White was not about to ignore the insults hurled at an officer of the Crown. He was weary of the continual disrespect that the people of Boston had for the troops stationed there, and today he had had his fill of their hot-headed remarks.

Private White pointed a finger at Edward. "You, there! That officer is a gentleman, and if he owes you anything, he will pay it."

"Ha! There are no gentlemen in the 14th Regiment!" Edward snapped back before turning to see his fellow apprentice Bartholomew Broaders walking up to him with a young lady on each arm. He bowed low with his arm over his chest, putting on his best 'gentlemanly' gesture. "My dear ladies. Shall we enjoy some refreshments?"

474

Edward joined the three other teenagers and together they walked past Private White and into the Customs House. The two girls worked in the kitchen, and frequently invited the boys in for a meal. This only irritated Private White even further, to have such an insolent youth dining inside the place he was obliged to guard.

CUSTOMS HOUSE, BOSTON,
MARCH 5, 1770, 8:30 P.M.

Edward and Bartholomew left the young ladies and stepped back out onto King Street, patting their stomachs after enjoying a warm meal. Edward spied Private White and grinned, nudging Bartholomew with his elbow. It was a bitter cold night, and the soldier stomped his feet in place, trying to keep warm.

Edward spat on the ground as he walked in the shadows near Private White. "Filthy, stealing Lobsterback Goldfinch better pay his bill or we'll rip his wig from his head when we see him next." The teenage boys laughed as they shuffled through the snow.

Private White lifted his chin and clenched his jaw. "Come over here, boy, unless you're afraid to show your face," he challenged, icy puffs of breath rising into the air. He was standing next to a small lantern hung by his sentry alcove placed by the Customs House steps. The light from the flame danced off his fixed bayonet as he gripped his musket tight.

"I'm not afraid to show my face," Edward answered, walking over with his hands on his hips. He leaned in close to the soldier, the glint of the lantern illuminating his defiant sneer. "Especially to a Lobsterback."

Private White's eyes filled with fury and he raised his weapon high, quickly hitting Edward on the side of the head with the butt of his musket. Edward staggered backward and gripped his head, crying out in pain. Bartholomew grabbed Edward by the arms and shouted angrily at Private White, "What do you mean by abusing the people?!"

A redcoat sergeant ran over, having seen what happened. "Get out of here, vermin!" he shouted as he chased the young men away with his sword. The teenagers ran off into the darkness, shouting about what had happened, drawing alarmed bystanders closer to the sentry's post.

Henry Knox was heading home after visiting with friends when he turned a corner and bumped into the shouting teenagers who continued to rant about what the sentry had done. "Dear God," he muttered under his breath, hurrying to the Customs House. When he arrived, Henry saw Private White removing his bayonet to load his musket. He ran up to the soldier and gripped his arm, shaking his head. "If you fire, you will die!"

Private White shook Henry Knox off his arm and roared back, "I don't care! If they touch me I will fire!"

The small gathering of bystanders started to grow, as more boys and men flocked to the scene. "You rascally scoundrel lobster!" they shouted. One of the boys made a snowball and threw it at the Customs House door, followed by more volleys of snowballs from other boys.

One of the town watchmen named Edward Langford hurried to stand between the sentry, the flying snowballs and the grumbling crowd. "Come now, and let the sentry alone." He turned to Private White and held his hand out to the crowd. The image of dead Christopher Seider was still fresh in his mind, and he feared for the boys. "Don't be afraid, private. They are only boys. They won't hurt you."

Just then a couple of young boys started running after a teenage boy toward the church. "Come on, some stinky man said he'd pay us to ring the bell!"

475

DOCK YARD, BOSTON,
MARCH 5, 1770, 8:30 P.M.

A group of sailors warmed their hands around a fire outside by John Gray's Rope Walk. They had finished an exhausting day of making ropes for the tall ships in the harbor. They passed a small flask of rum to warm themselves as they sat in a circle to rest for a while.

"I can hardly feel my hands," complained Samuel Gray, one of the ropeworkers. He moaned and rubbed his sore, cold fingers.

"Keep your mouth shut, Gray!" another ropeworker named Samuel Bostwick snapped back. "If Mr. Gray hears you complaining, he might hire one of them Lobsterbacks that Green picked a fight with last week."

"Listen to him," Crispus Attucks added. He was a mulatto slave turned sailor who knew these ropeworkers. "You may share Mr. Gray's last name, but you're not related to the boss, so your job is on the line."

Samuel Gray took a swig and nodded. "Green didn't show up to work today."

476

Suddenly a dirty, smelly man dropped a bundle of thick sticks on the ground by the fire, and proceeded to barge in on their conversation. "Didn't you hear what happened to William Green?" He stoked the fire as the ropeworkers looked at one another in alarm.

Samuel Bostwick wrinkled his nose and squinted his eyes at the smelly man. "What happened, stranger?"

"Mr. Gray made a deal with the colonels of the 29th and 14th Regiments. He told them he'd fire Green, who had caused the fight with his big mouth that insulted that Lobsterback and set off that brawl with those thirty soldiers," the man explained. He neglected to tell the sailors that Mr. Gray also had the colonels agree that soldiers would not enter his property without his permission, and each side would try to calm their own men. "I tell you, the Customs Office is behind *all* of Boston's troubles. If it weren't for them, there would not be Lobsterbacks in Boston stirring things up and threatening to steal our jobs!"

Crispus Attucks frowned and rose to his feet in anger. "He's right! How much more of this are we going to take?"

"Brawl at Murray's Barracks!" someone shouted in the streets. "Now there's trouble at the Customs House!"

Startled, the men all got to their feet. "Speak of the devil! We should go see exactly what the trouble is!" Samuel Gray grumbled.

The dirty man picked up two of the thick firewood sticks and handed them to Crispus Attucks and Samuel Gray. "Better take some clubs just in case you meet up with any of those Lobsterbacks."

"Come on!" Crispus agreed, gripping a stick and stomping off toward the Customs House.

Soon a group of twenty sailors were marching in the darkened, snowy streets, with Crispus Attucks in the lead. The dirty man cupped his ear playfully, as if anticipating a sound. A moment later came the sound of church bells ringing rapidly, which usually sounded the alarm for fire. "Ah, there we are." He picked up a large, heavy stick and grinned. "But there is no fire, is there?"

CUSTOMS HOUSE, BOSTON, MARCH 5, 1770, 9:00 P.M.

The crowd now swelled to two hundred people, many of whom arrived at the city center with fire buckets in hand after hearing the alarm bells. When it soon became clear there was no physical fire, an angry blaze of news quickly spread through the crowd about the earlier brawl outside Murray's Barracks, and about the scene now unfolding at the Customs House. Private White sent two messengers to the Main Guard located by the Town House, calling for reinforcements. The senior officer there was none other than Captain Thomas Preston, who immediately sent a force of seven privates from the 29th under Corporal William Wemms. He told them he would follow them shortly.

"Stand out of the way!" shouted the soldiers as they poked bystanders with their bayonets to make a path through the crowd. They quickly surrounded Private White, forming a semicircle in front of the Customs House steps. The angry mob started throwing oyster shells and snowballs.

"This isn't good. Three of those privates were in the brawls at the Rope Walk last week," Clarie told Max, eyeing the group of now thirty sailors making their way to the front of the crowd, clubs in hand. She then spotted Henry Knox. "I'll get to Knox. You get to Preston."

"On it, lass!" Max agreed, weaving through the legs of the crowd to reach the soldiers.

477

Henry Knox saw Captain Preston making his way to his men and grabbed him by the coat, "For God's sake, take care of your men! If they fire, you will die!"

Captain Preston clenched his jaw and calmly looked Henry in the eye. He removed Henry's hand from his coat. "I am aware of it." The two men shared a brief moment of unspoken alarm, recalling Sgt. Frost's words earlier that afternoon: *Cool yer tempers!*

When Captain Preston left Henry standing there in the street, Sgt. Frost rushed up to the young man, grabbing his arm. "Step back, lad. Ye don't want ta get tangled up in this mess."

Henry Knox, startled to see his old sergeant suddenly next to him again, nodded. Sgt. Frost pulled Knox firmly by the elbow back into the crowd.

Max poked his head out in front of the crowd, seeing the soldiers arrayed in a semicircle, holding their muskets chest-high, their bayonets fixed. Captain Preston walked in front of his men and shouted to the crowd. "Go to your homes! Clear the streets!"

478

A local innkeeper named Richard Palmes was carrying a club, having just come from the scuffle with soldiers and citizens in front of Murray's Barracks. He walked right up to Captain Preston and got in his face. "Are your men's weapons loaded?"

"They are, but they will not fire unless they are ordered to do so," Captain Preston replied, not taking his eye off the crowd.

Palmes gripped his club angrily. "Without a magistrate, you have no legal authority to order your men to fire! I hope you do not intend these men to fire upon the citizens."

"Sir, by no means," Captain Preston replied calmly. "As you can see, I am standing in front of my men."

The crowd pressed in closer around the soldiers, taunting them with jeers and threats. "We did not send for you! We will not have you here! We'll get rid of you! We'll drive you away!" They continued to angrily hurl oyster shells, snowballs, and other small objects at the soldiers.

"It wasn't enough that a Customs informer killed young Christopher Seider!" came the voice of Robert Paterson, the sailor whose trousers had been torn by Richardson's gunshot that day. "Now this Customs sentry seeks to kill another of Boston's youth?!"

Seeing one of the same soldiers they had fought with days ago,

Crispus Attucks stepped up and grabbed his bayonet, jerking it back and forth. "Have you come back to finish what you started, Lobsterback?"

Suddenly Max looked up to see the same dirty man from the street where Christopher had been shot. The man was pushing his way to the front of the crowd. He lifted his arm and threw a club that struck Private Montgomery in the head, knocking him to the snowy street, all the while screaming, "FIRE! FIRE, YOU BLOODYBACKS, YOU LOBSTERS! I DARE YOU TO FIRE!"

Montgomery dropped his musket and scrambled in the snow to quickly retrieve it. Max ran over to Captain Preston and Richard Palmes as chaotic shouting broke out all around them.

"FIRE! YOU DARE NOT FIRE!" other angry voices echoed from the crowd. "KILL THEM!"

Montgomery got to his feet, cocked his weapon, which was loaded with two musket balls, and angrily shouted, "FIRE!" He fired into the crowd although no command had been given. Both musket balls hit Crispus Attucks in the chest.

479

Palmes immediately swung his club at Montgomery, hitting the soldier's arm. Max quickly jumped up and grabbed Palmes by the trousers, causing the man's right foot to slip on the ice and pulling him down on one knee just as he tried to swing again at Captain Preston's head. Palmes's club struck Preston's arm instead, causing the commander to fall.

After a brief pause but in the midst of growing chaos, the other soldiers randomly started shooting their muskets, some which also held two balls of shot. As the smoke cleared, screams rang out from the crowd as eleven men had been hit. Crispus Attucks, Samuel Gray, and James Caldwell lay dead in the street. Samuel Maverick and Patrick Carr were mortally wounded and six others lay writhing in agony.

Time seemed to stand still as the smell of gunpowder filled the air. Captain Preston rose to his feet and held his sword under his men's muskets to stop them from firing again before ordering them to march back to the Main Guard. The crowd fell back as the town's Constable Burdick started barking orders for the people to disperse and carry the wounded and dead away. Palmes and the others moved off. The dirty man slunk off into the shadows, smiling with grim satisfaction.

Max remained in the middle of King Street, looking around sadly at the blood-splattered snow covering the cobblestones of Boston.

The BLOODY MASSACRE perpetrated in King—†—Street BOSTON on March 5th 1770 by a party of the 29th REGT.

Unhappy Boston! see thy Sons deplore,
Thy hallow'd Walks besmear'd with guiltless Gore
While faithless P——n and his savage Bands,
With murdrous Rancour stretch their bloody Hands;
Like fierce Barbarians grinning o'er their Prey,
Approve the Carnage and enjoy the Day.

If scalding drops from Rage from Anguish Wrung,
If speechless Sorrows lab'ring for a Tongue,
Or if a weeping World can ought appease
The plaintive Ghosts of Victims such as these;
The Patriot's copious Tears for each are shed,
A glorious Tribute which embalms the Dead.

But know, Fate summons to that awful Goal,
Where Justice strips the Murd'rer of his Soul:
Should venal C——ts the scandal of the Land,
Snatch the relentless Villain from her Hand,
Keen Execrations on this Plate inscrib'd,
Shall reach a Judge who never can be brib'd.

The unhappy Sufferers were Messrs. Saml Gray, Saml Maverick, Jams Caldwell, Crispus Attucks & Patr Carr
Killed. Six wounded two of them (Christr Monk & John Clark) Mortally

480

"*Unhappy Boston! See thy Sons deplore, Thy hallow'd walks besmear'd with guiltless gore,*" Clarie read aloud. She and Max were poring over the news following the horrific events of March 5, studying the etching Paul Revere had published about the event.

"'The Bloody *Massacre?*' While it were sad, I wouldn't call five dead patriots a massacre," Max grumbled. "This picture shows Captain Pr-r-reston standin' *behind* his men, orderin' them ta fire. That's not wha' happened, lass," Max lamented, shaking his square head. "That Paul R-r-revere sure did str-r-retch the tr-r-ruth with this picture, includin' how he drew *me!* I don't look *anythin'* like that!"

"Yes, this is what 'propaganda' looks like—stretching the truth to inspire others to join your cause." Clarie pointed to the little moon etched in the upper left-hand corner, a hint that the Boston Massacre had happened at night. "Well, it *was* dark and hard to see that night, Max. At least Paul Revere got one thing right in this picture. A dog was indeed there. So what, if history doesn't know that it was a Scottish terrier? At least we know the truth about you and about what really happened that night. I protected Henry Knox, and you protected Captain Preston."

After the crowd moved away from the Customs House, Captain Preston had immediately called out most of the 29th Regiment to stop the growing mob before things spiraled completely out of control. Red-coated soldiers lined up in defensive positions in front of the State House, while acting Governor Thomas Hutchinson stood on its balcony, promising a thorough investigation of the shootings. Calm was restored, and the next morning, Captain Preston and the eight involved soldiers were arrested to stand trial. At the insistence of Boston's citizens, all British troops were removed from the city to Castle Island. Samuel Adams staged an even larger funeral for the five victims of the Boston Massacre than he had for Christopher Seider. This time ten thousand citizens lined the streets.

"We know that if we hadn't been there it r-r-really *would* have been a massacre in Boston," Max agreed. "So wha's goin' ta happen ta Captain Pr-r-reston?"

"I have to make sure no one takes his case," Clarie answered as she scanned the *Boston Gazette.*

Max's eyes widened with shock. "CLARIE LASS! How can ye do such a thing? The lad be innocent!"

481

Clarie smiled and put a hand on Max's back. "Don't worry, Max. I need to make sure no one takes his case so I can arrange for a special young lawyer to handle Captain Preston's defense. He's only a year older than our Patrick Henry. This case will be important not just for Captain Preston and the soldiers, but for this lawyer's reputation and future leadership in America. Just as 'Sgt. Frost' helped Captain Preston remain calm and collected, this lawyer will seek to have the same effect on hotheads like Samuel Adams going forward."

Max blew out his breath, relieved. "That's a r-r-relief. Who's the lawyer then?"

"He just so happens to be Sam Adams's cousin," Clarie shared with a smile. "His name is John. John Adams."

55

A Darkness Begins

T he response of the colonists to the Townshend Acts was so predictable. Even Al knew what would happen when the colonies stopped importing British goods!" Clarie reported to Gillamon. "British exports to America dropped 30 percent over-all, 50 percent to Massachusetts, and a whopping 80 percent to New York." Clarie stood with Gillamon in the IAMISPHERE, observing key moments in their unfolding mission on both sides of the Atlantic. She pointed to a frame showing Britain's new Prime Minister: Frederick, Lord North. "Do you think he'll last longer than the five who came before him?"

"As the king's *sixth* Prime Minister, Lord North has been tasked with forming the *sixth* government so far in King George's ten-year reign," Gillamon replied, watching Lord North take a seat at his desk. "Twelve is the biblical number of governmental perfection, but the number six means incomplete, falling short and the number of man without God."

"Unlike *seven,* which means complete," Clarie interjected with a smile. "Like the Order of the Seven."

Gillamon nodded and smiled. He pointed to the crest of Great Britain with its lion and unicorn. "The British lion seeks to dominate the colonies. How interesting that the lion was only given six names in the Old Testament."

"But the British unicorn doesn't look anything like the ones in Old Testament times," Clarie jested. "So time will tell if this *sixth* Prime Minister will make the British lion fall short in dominating the colonies."

Lord North reviewed a letter from King George III. His finger followed the words on the page to make sure he fully understood the wishes of his sovereign:

I am clear that there must always be one tax to keep up the right, and as such I approve the tea duty.

Lord North sat back in his chair with his elbows resting on its arms, propping up his chin with tented fingers. *"Keep up the right.* A tax on tea. Repeal the rest," he said aloud to himself, gazing out the window as cold rain pelted the glass. "Surely this will put an end to the rebellion and restore trade."

Gillamon walked up to the panel and shook his head as Lord North took out paper and dipped his quill into the inkwell. The man in his late thirties began writing instructions for Parliament to repeal all the Townshend duties except for the tax on tea. "Lord North will last a while, but his constancy of mediocrity will not help King George. He lacks the vision and the strength needed to combat the self-seeking, blind interests of Great Britain."

Gillamon touched two panels of concurrent time that swirled into view, side by side for the same date: March 5, 1770. One panel showed Parliament in London. The other panel showed the Boston Massacre. Gillamon pointed to Clarie ushering Henry Knox away from the scene while Max stood by Captain Preston. "You and Max did well in Boston, little one. It was a tragedy but it could have been far worse. What a shame the people didn't know what was happening on that very same day on the other side of the Atlantic—that Parliament was repealing the Townshend duties."

"Except for the tax on tea," Clarie added. "Do you think keeping this tax will cause more trouble in Boston and the colonies?"

Gillamon gave Clarie a knowing look. "What do *you* think, given all that you've seen in Boston so far?"

"Bostonians aren't ones to back off from a fight," Clarie replied. "Patrick Henry and Virginia may have led the charge to oppose the king with words, but the Sons of Liberty in Boston have led the charge to oppose the king with violent protests."

"If these young colonies truly wish to become a new nation that seeks to not abuse but preserve liberty, they must learn to do so without mob rule and anarchy," Gillamon explained. "There will ever need to be counterbalances for such behavior to bring things into proper perspective. And in this case, one cousin had to be the counterbalance for the other. I think you can expect things to calm down for a while in the streets of Boston." He pointed to another panel from November 1770, with John Adams defending Captain Preston and his men in the Boston courtroom. *"Facts are stubborn things; and whatever may be our wishes, our inclinations, or the dictates of our passion, they cannot alter the state of facts and evidence,"* spoke John Adams, slowly tapping the bar as he looked into the eyes of his frustrated cousin, Samuel Adams.

"I was glad that John Adams was able to clear Captain Preston and his men, except for the two charged with manslaughter," stated Clarie, wincing as they watched the two guilty men branded on the thumbs. "Still, a brand on the thumb was a small price to pay to avoid the gallows. So Max and I are to stay in Boston for the time being?"

"Yes, and when the tempest in the Boston teapot boils, Nigel will need to join Al on mission in London," stated Gillamon, pointing to a panel showing Benjamin Franklin playing chess with David Henry. "They will need to help turn the key to Benjamin Franklin's future."

"And Liz is to remain with Patrick?" Clarie asked. "I know there is no place she would rather be than with her Henry."

484

"Yes, she and Kate will be crucial to Patrick and the Henry family in the coming years." Gillamon tapped another panel and the scene of New York Harbor came into view.

Patrick Henry and Richard Bland slowly rode their horses down Wall Street on a hot summer day in July 1770. Patrick pulled on MizP's reins to walk her toward the water's edge. He gazed out across the water lapping the shoreline. "New York is a beautiful colony, indeed. Although this trip did not accomplish its intended purpose, it has broadened our horizons, Mr. Bland."

"Yes, Mr. Henry, we have been able to see well beyond the borders of Virginia," Richard Bland agreed, looking out to the shoreline of New Jersey. "We've now seen Maryland, Delaware, Pennsylvania, New Jersey, and New York, so nearly half the colonies. Although the intercolonial convention to discuss the Indian trade was cancelled, this trip has been of value nonetheless."

Patrick Henry gazed out to Upper New York Bay at the few Oyster Islands that dotted the middle of the harbor. "My eyes have been opened to see firsthand the results of liberty and the common sense of the working freeman. These northern colonies were settled by European immigrants and laborers. And they have prospered with free labor over slave labor," he said, wrinkling his brow and shifting his weight in MizP's saddle.

Gillamon smiled and thought, *Little does Patrick know what will someday stand out there on one of those islands in the middle of New York Harbor.*

"Religious toleration helped the value of land in Pennsylvania to rise five times greater than ours in Virginia! Their colony is filled with hardworking freemen, not hapless slaves. A Dutch, Irish, or Scotch emigrant finds there his religion, his priest, his language, his manners, and everything but that poverty and oppression he left at home," Patrick suggested. "I submit to you that most Virginians have nothing more than a trifling concern for religion. If Virginia would wish to bring in such pious, immigrant artisans of Europe to lead Virginia to manufacture by the hands of freemen, I submit that a general toleration of religion appears to me the best means of peopling our country. And if Great Britain will not allow the colonies to end the evil slave trade, we must make it wither on the vine. Freedom and liberty naturally lead to happiness and prosperity for all."

Richard Bland nodded quietly. "I have no doubt but that you will fire up those debates in the House of Burgesses when we return to Williamsburg, Mr. Henry. It's time for us to be on our way."

Patrick Henry nodded and patted MizP on the neck. "Agreed. Back to Williamsburg, MizP." Together Patrick and Richard left the water's edge to depart New York City.

485

"Little did Patrick know all the changes that were coming after that trip," foretold Clarie, pointing to several panels of time. "Governor Botetourt's death in October, the horrific flood in the spring of 1771, and moving his family to Scotchtown." She smiled sadly. "The birth of his sixth child, Neddy. Sallie hasn't been the same since that precious baby was born. In spite of the joy, there is a cloud of darkness over her, Gillamon."

Gillamon furrowed his brow as they watched Sallie curled up in bed while Neddy cried in the small wooden cradle on the floor next to her. She turned over, pulled her legs up into her chest and covered her ears, sobbing. Liz sauntered into the room and saw what was happening. She walked over to the cradle and started rocking it with her paw, looking into Neddy's face as she whispered words of comfort to the infant. "It's time for Kate to join Liz at Scotchtown to help her with the children and Sallie. Gilbert will be safe and secure at the Military Academy in Versailles. Kate has seen him through his time of loss, and she cannot go with him there."

"I will let her know. The Marquis de Lafayette is now the richest orphan in France," Clarie said, watching another panel of young Gilbert attending the funerals of both his mother and grandmother. "He's inherited wealth and land, and now will be trained to serve as one of the king's musketeers. He has such a bright future ahead of him, despite his sadness now. But Gillamon, I dread the darkness for Sallie!"

"I know, little one, I know. But we will help Sallie and the Henry family through as best we can. The Maker's grace will be sufficient," Gillamon replied. "There is darkness coming, not only in Patrick's house but also for the entire colony of Virginia." He frowned and pointed to another panel of a forty-year-old Scotsman having a temper tantrum in New York.

"Who is *that?*" Clarie asked in disgust.

"*That* is Virginia's next royal governor: John Murray, Lord Dunmore," Gillamon replied.

"But I thought Dunmore was the governor of New York," Clarie stated, confused.

"He was, but has been replaced. Dunmore was governor for only one month before Lord Botetourt died. As soon as word reached London about Botetourt's death, King George picked Dunmore here to replace him as Virginia's governor, moving North Carolina's governor to New York to replace Dunmore."

"Curse Virginia—did I ever seek it? Why is it forced upon me?" Dunmore scowled, taking a big gulp of whiskey from a crystal glass. He looked around the room at his drunken companions. "I asked for *New York*—New York I took, and they have robbed me of it without my consent!"

Clarie's eyes widened as Dunmore threw down his glass and ran out of the Governor's Palace with his friends. It was midnight, and they snuck up to the coach house belonging to New York Chief Justice Horsmanden. "They're destroying the coach!" Clarie put her hands to her mouth in shock. "Now they're cutting the tails off those poor horses!"

"Yes, Dunmore is a wild one. He's a burly, avid hunter with a coarse personality and not a shred of religion. He tends to drink and act impulsively," Gillamon agreed. "He loves everything about New York, including the land he's been scheming to acquire while there. He's so obsessed with owning land that he cheated the system to get 51,000 acres of land for himself under the guise of granting land to others. Since he was prohibited from granting more than 1,000 acres of land to any one individual, he granted fifty-one land grants of 1,000 acres each to fifty-one 'friends.' Then he turned around and bought those grants from those 'friends' for five shillings each."

"Why that schemer! And HE is going to govern VIRGINIA?!" Clarie shouted in alarm.

"Don't fret, little one. It's all part of the plan," Gillamon reassured her with a smile. "He'll despise not only Virginia but especially Patrick Henry. But Dunmore will do more to help the cause of American Independence than Virginia could ever have hoped for."

"*Help* the cause of Independence?" Clarie asked in surprise. "How?"

Gillamon leaned in with a wink. "By trying to do the exact opposite."

487

56

Gasping for Liberty

SCOTCHTOWN PLANTATION, VIRGINIA, JANUARY 18, 1773

The house was finally quiet, as everyone had finally gone to bed. But Patrick Henry could not sleep. Many things were weighing heavily on his mind and his heart, and he desperately needed these quiet moments to sort through them all.

Sallie seemed to be slipping away from him, withdrawing mentally and emotionally into a deep, dark pit. Ever since Neddy's birth she had steadily become more and more depressed. He was worried not only for her welfare, but for the welfare of his children, as she had acted violently toward them. Of course, she didn't realize what she was doing, but the children couldn't understand why their mother acted the way she did. Sallie's condition was a source of sadness but also of shame. The family needed to keep her illness a secret, as many regarded mental illness as a curse. Only the family physician knew about Sallie's state and had confidentially recommended that Patrick consider putting Sallie into an asylum for the insane, which would be opening by the fall in Williamsburg. This was a thought he could scarcely fathom. Thus far he had not been able to bring himself to visit the place, but with each day he realized he had to do something.

Patrick's father, John, was ill, and Patrick knew it would probably not be long before he would die. What would become of his mother then? She and his unmarried sisters couldn't stay at Mount Brilliant with the bad state of his father's finances. Perhaps he could bring her here to live at Scotchtown. That might be the biggest blessing to the family, given the sadness that pervaded their lives because of their mother's condition. Patrick's thriving law practice required him to spend so

488

much time away at the General Court in Williamsburg, and having his mother at Scotchtown would be a tremendous help. He was gratefully able to press on with excellence in pursuing liberty for the people in court, but no one knew the personal weight he carried on his shoulders.

While things were relatively peaceful between the colonies and the Mother Country at the moment, there was trouble stirring in Rhode Island that had Patrick greatly concerned. In June, a group of angry citizens had lured the H.M.S. *Gaspée* into shallow waters, and in the middle of the night rowed out to scuffle with the captain and crew to bring them to shore before setting the ship ablaze. Not that the arrogant Lieutenant Dudington didn't deserve their wrath—he had mightily earned it. Dudington constantly interfered with shipping, seizing cargo and bullying honest merchants by forcing passing ships to dip their colors in salute to the *Gaspée* and firing his cannon if they refused. He despised Americans and exploited his royal orders to patrol for smugglers, but he had passed a tipping point with the citizens. The *Gaspée* incident naturally brought an angry response from London with orders to find and bring those responsible to stand trial not in Rhode Island, but in London. Everyone knew that anyone suspected and put on a ship bound for England was as good as dead.

489

A mysterious epidemic of amnesia evidently swept through Newport, as not a single citizen could be found who saw or knew anything about what had happened to the *Gaspée*. A frustrated inquiry commission looking for someone to punish came up empty. While Rhode Island was off the immediate hook, Patrick Henry was deeply concerned about this threat that once more reared its ugly head to violate the constitutional right to a trial by a jury of one's peers. He knew it was only a matter of time before another incident occurred in one colony or another. The colonies must find a way to communicate between themselves beyond reading gazettes for news. Patrick knew the colonies needed to be prepared for the inevitable clash with the British lion that loomed on the horizon. He also was greatly concerned that violent uprisings such as those in Boston could lead to simply trading one form of tyranny for another—from a king trampling on the people's rights to mob rule trampling on level-headed liberty and the law.

On top of all these things was the issue that continually weighed heavily on Patrick's mind and heart—slavery. Liz sat on Patrick's desk as he thumbed through a book a Quaker friend named Robert Pleasants had sent to him. He sighed deeply and nodded with a furrowed brow. The light from the candle flickered and he reached out his hand to wave over the flame, just as he had done since he was a boy. He looked at Liz, whose golden eyes glowed, catching the low light of the flickering candle. "The king has ignored the latest appeal from the House of Burgesses to cease the slave trade. But I cannot justify it."

Patrick cleared his throat and pulled back his hand, picking up a quill to dip into the ink. He took a deep breath and began writing a letter to Mr. Pleasants:

Dear Sir:

I take this opportunity to acknowledge the receipt of Anthony Benezet's book against the Slave Trade. I thank you for it.

It is not a little surprising that the professors of Christianity, whose chief excellence consists of softening the human heart, and in cherishing and improving its finer feelings, should encourage a practice so totally repugnant to the first impressions of right and wrong.

What adds to the wonder is that this abominable practice has been introduced in the most enlightened ages. Times that seem to have pretensions to boast of high improvements in the arts and sciences and refined morality, have brought into general use, and guarded by many laws, a species of violence and tyranny which our more rude and barbarous, but more honest, ancestors detested.

Is it not amazing that at a time when the rights of humanity are defined and understood in a country, above all others, fond of liberty, that in such an age and country we find men professing a religion the most humane, mild, gentle,

490

and generous, adopting a principle as repugnant to humanity as it is inconsistent with the Bible and destructive to liberty. Every thinking, honest man rejects it in speculation, how few in practice from conscientious motives!

Would anyone believe I am the master of slaves of my own purchase! I am drawn along by the general inconvenience of living here without them. I will not, I cannot justify it. However culpable my conduct, I will so far pay my devoir to virtue, as to own the excellence and rectitude of her precepts, and lament my want of conformity to them.

I believe a time will come when an opportunity will be offered to abolish this lamentable evil. Everything we can do is to improve it, if it happens in our day; if not, let us transmit to our descendants, together with our slaves, a pity for their unhappy lot, and an abhorrence of slavery. If we cannot reduce this wished-for reformation to practice, let us treat the unhappy victims with lenity. It is the furthest advance we can make toward justice. It is a debt we owe to the purity of our religion, to show that it is at variance with that law which warrants slavery.

I know not when to stop. I could say many things on the subject, a serious view of which gives a gloomy perspective to future times.

Your Most Obedient and Humble Servant to Command,

T. Henry

491

Patrick stopped and blew on the ink. "A gloomy perspective already hangs over our nation. And until we can secure liberty in general for all, we will secure it for none."

———

MOUNT BRILLIANT, FEBRUARY 2, 1773

A bitter wind whipped across the sloping meadow and down into the small clearing of trees behind the Henry home, sending a chill through the family members gathered around the freshly dug grave. The family was dressed in black bombazine clothes and wore black buckles of mourning on their shoes.

Patrick Henry held his mother Sarah in a tight embrace as she sobbed against his shoulder. He clenched his jaw and fought back his emotion as his brother, William, and his sisters tossed handfuls of soil onto the pine coffin that had been placed with such tender care into the grave. He swallowed the lump in his throat, and the icy wind stung his eyes as tears escaped onto his cheeks. Uncle Patrick Henry read from the *Book of Common Prayer:*

492

"Forasmuch as it hath pleased Almighty God of his great mercy to take unto himself the soul of our dear brother, John Henry, here departed: we therefore commit his body to the ground; earth to earth, ashes to ashes, dust to dust," Uncle Patrick recited with a trembling lip, tossing his own handful of soil onto his brother's coffin. The aging parson's voice cracked with emotion, and he paused to regain his composure before beginning again. "In sure and certain hope of the Resurrection to eternal life, through our Lord Jesus Christ; who shall change our vile body, that it may be like unto his glorious body, according to the mighty working, whereby he is able to subdue all things to himself." He closed his book and nodded to the family. "Amen."

"Amen," the family repeated solemnly. Everyone proceeded to quietly hug one another and then slowly turned to walk back to the house. William came over to Patrick and took Sarah from his embrace, allowing him a moment to pay his last respects to their father.

Patrick stood over his father's grave and allowed the tears to flow freely. "Oh, Father. Thank you. Thank you for instilling in me a love for God, a love for family, and a love for my country. I hope I have made you proud. I will take care of mother. She will come to live with us at

Scotchtown now, and she will worry for nothing." He paused and blew his nose on a handkerchief. He thought back to the last conversation he had with his father before he died.

"*Remember what I've always told ye about that priceless jewel of liberty, Pat. A jewel is simply a handful of ordinary earth that has endured a long, difficult ordeal. The pressure, the sorrow, and the pain are necessary ta turn ordinary things into priceless gems. As it is with bits of earth, so it is with us. Anything of value will cost us dearly. Never let it go, Pat,*" John Henry, clenching his fist, had instructed Patrick. "*Hold on ta that precious jewel of liberty until ye also reach the end of yer days.*"

Patrick scooped up a handful of soil and gripped it tightly in his hand. "I will, Father, I promise." He tossed the dirt onto the coffin and allowed a silent moment to pass, brushing off his hands in the air.

Suddenly he felt a warm presence by his leg and looked down to see a small, white dog standing there. He looked around and saw no one. "Where did you come from?" He knelt down and looked Kate in the eye.

"*I jest came from France, but it were fittin' ta make sure ye had a fellow Scot here with ye today, lad,*" Kate whimpered. "*An' I'll be with ye in the days ta come.*"

493

SCOTCHTOWN, MARCH 1, 1773

Kate was eager to understand everything she could about Patrick Henry. When Patrick moved his mother and unmarried sisters to Scotchtown, he naturally brought along the little white dog who had shown up at his father's grave. No one knew where she had come from, but he knew that this little dog would provide comfort for everyone, especially Sallie. Liz and MizP were thrilled to have her here, and she quickly became a beloved member of the family. Nigel had left for London to help Al on the mission with Benjamin Franklin, so the lassies were left to watch over Patrick and Sallie.

"How does he capture the humans he speaks ta?" Kate wanted to know.

"'Study, men!' Pahtrick always tells his law students," MizP answered quickly. "He knows people as well as he knows his own reflection in a mirror."

"Oui, so he has a way of getting a jury to agree with him, no matter which side of a case he represents," Liz explained. "For the jury members he knows, he already has knowledge of what and how they think. For jury members he does not know, he studies them carefully, watching their body language and expressions as he begins to speak." Liz smiled and walked, head down and tail low to the ground, in front of the Westie. "He likes to begin in a humble posture and speak slowly, as if he does not know what he is talking about, or is unsure of himself."

"That don't seem like a promisin' strategy, Liz," Kate noted with a frown.

"Ah, but once he tests how the jury responds to what he first says, he will stand up straight, his eyes will suddenly blaze with passion, and his melodic voice will fill the courtroom!" described Liz, now rising up tall and proud with her tail high in the air.

"And if Pahtrick then pushes his spectacles tuh the top of his wig, those opposing him better watch out!" MizP exclaimed. "That's his declaration of war, and they're in for a lengthy speech."

494

"Oui, but he does not need to shout, for his passion, charm, and hypnotic delivery keep the jury glued to his words." Liz paused and stared at Kate, allowing the silence to linger until the little dog leaned in, expectant for Liz's next words. "Patrick's carefully timed pauses make the humans lean in to hear what he will say next. His audience feels he has read the minds of each and every one of them as he makes eye contact around the room with his signature 'Patrick flash' and half-smile."

"So much so that some of those in Pahtrick's audience cannot contain themselves," MizP quipped. "One fella sitting in the balcony in Williamsburg became so lost in Pahtrick's oration that he forgot where he was and spit out his tobacco juice onto the heads of the poor people below! He then almost toppled over the railing himself!" MizP snorted with a chuckle. "If Pahtrick can make the people laugh on purpose, he'll even twirl his wig! People come tuh court just tuh hear—and see—him speak."

Kate's eyes lit up and she grinned her perky grin as she wagged her tail. "He twirls his wig? That's funny!"

"But above all, *mon* Henry is always very humble and respectful to everyone in the courtroom," Liz assured her. "He has the ability to convince others of how to do the right thing, and so he is winning endless numbers of cases. He is the master at disarming those with power and empowering those with none. He is the champion for the defenseless, like the Baptists and other Dissenters."

"Dissenters. Those be the people who don't worship as does the Church of England, right?" Kate asked.

"Precisely, *mon amie*," Liz answered. "As a boy, Patrick was witness to the very first Dissenter movement of Presbyterians here in Hanover County. Interestingly enough, Hanover has once again been the cradle where the Dissenter movement among *Baptists* has been birthed."

"Yes, but as they've grown, the poor Baptists have suffered incredible persecution," MizP added sadly. "The Baptists are the most vocal about deliberately disobeying the law tuh get a license tuh preach. They claim they do not need a license tuh preach the Word of God, and that they have as much right tuh preach as the Anglican parsons."

"So wha' happens when they preach without a license?" Kate asked.

"Oh, it's simply dreadful!" MizP lamented, shaking her head and stomping her hoof in the dirt. "These poor souls have been violently jerked off the stage while preaching, shoved into the dirt, pelted with apples and stones, dragged away, and beaten tuh a bloody pulp, all the while violently cursed and threatened tuh stop preaching!"

495

"Oh, me!" Kate exclaimed in horror. "How can this be? I thought America had more religious freedom than in France, but it don't sound like it. Wha' happens ta the poor preachers then?"

"Well, most of them get right back on their feet, singing and praising God," Liz replied.

Kate smiled sadly. "They sound jest like Paul an' the other apostles. We saw the same things happen ta them. Jesus must be so proud of these preachers as well."

Liz smiled, fondly remembering their mission of helping the early church spread the gospel in the midst of horrific persecution by the Roman Empire. *"Oui,* and just like Paul and the others, these Baptist preachers have been thrown into prison. They face charges of 'disturbing the peace.' When ordered to pay a fine, they refuse to pay and continue to preach through their prison bars!"

"They really *do* sound like Paul an' the apostles!" Kate cheered, wagging her tail.

"Crowds even gather outside the prison windows tuh listen," MizP reported. "And even when the constable makes the humans leave, they come back anyway, just like a gnat that won't stay away from my ear."

She shook her head, tossing her mane side to side. "Some of those preachers even get their hands cut with knives by hateful humans as they stick them outside those prison bars. All of this has of course *not* set well with Pahtrick. He and I have ridden miles out of our way tuh represent these poor preachers, many times at considerable time and at Pahtrick's own expense."

"You see, Kate, Patrick's father, uncle, and their Anglican Church taught him that the king and church are flawless. But Samuel Davies and his mother's Presbyterian Church taught him that the king and church are as flawed as they come," Liz explained. "He has long been torn between the two belief systems. He will not abandon the Anglican Church, but he'll fight against it to protect the liberty of the Dissenters. A godly nation must support religion—not run or control it, but support it. There is a difference."

"What is that 'Lord of the conscience' thing Pahtrick quotes from the Presbyterians, Liz?" MizP asked.

496 *"God alone is Lord of the conscience, and hath left it free from the doctrines and commandments of men; and that the rights of private judgment, in all matters that respect religion, are universal and inalienable,"* Liz replied. "Patrick's mother first taught that to him, and he frequently says, 'To be silent would be treason to God.'"

MizP nodded. "Whether those preachers pay him a farthing or not, Pahtrick says he must speak up for them."

Kate grinned broadly. "I love our Patrick more an' more! So how does he help the preacher laddies then? Wha' does he say in court?"

"Allow me to relay this story," Liz insisted, holding up her paw and giggling. "His finest moment I believe was when he sat in court and listened to the charges of disturbing the peace read aloud. He asked if he could see the paper with the written charges and slowly rose to his feet." Liz did her best Patrick Henry impersonation, wearing a grave expression and speaking softly. "Did I hear it distinctly, or was it a mistake of my own? Did I hear an expression, as of a crime, that these men, whom your worships are about to try for misdemeanor, are charged with—with—what?—preaching the Gospel of the Son of God?"

Liz paused, walking slowly in front of Kate, who looked back at her, wide-eyed with her jaw hanging open.

The sleek black cat held up the imaginary paper in the air and slowly waved it three times over her head. Then she lifted her face and raised her paws to the sky, as if imploring the heavens to hear her. "Great God!" she exclaimed loudly. "Great God!" she repeated. "Preaching the gospel of the Son of God—Great God!" She then calmly slinked away and sat down.

"And the case was dismissed!" MizP concluded. "Pahtrick not only shuts up those uppity lawyers, an' doesn't charge those preachers a farthing, but I've even seen him pay the bail for those preachers without letting them even know."

"I should mention that Patrick Henry never curses or takes the Maker's name in vain," Liz clarified. "If he ever utters God's name, he means it with respect and reverence."

Kate jumped for joy and wagged her tail furiously. "I love this story! Wha' a bold lad he be!"

"So you see, *mon amie,* our Patrick Henry has a large heart for those who are gasping for liberty, whether they be slaves, preachers, or the colonies themselves," Liz explained. "And Patrick's voice will only grow louder to speak up for that precious jewel of liberty itself in the days to come."

497

Liz paused as they watched Patrick coming over to saddle up MizP to ride to Williamsburg. "Now it's time for Patrick to decide on what to do for Sallie. Lord Dunmore has finally called the House of Burgesses to meet, but while he is there, *mon* Henry will visit the asylum."

Suddenly they heard the shrill cries of Sallie from inside the house. "She's getting worse, isn't she?" MizP asked sadly.

Liz's eyes brimmed with tears. *"Oui.* Oh, Kate, how I wish you could have known Sallie when she and Patrick were young! They've had such a happy life together, despite all the hardship they have faced. And it was Sallie who supported Patrick as he found his voice as a lawyer. But now, she is imprisoned inside a darkened mind."

"So Sallie now be the one gaspin' for liberty," Kate noted somberly.

"But the asylum is not the answer," offered Liz. Cato's shadow appeared as he circled overhead and landed in a nearby tree. Liz started walking over to meet him. She told Kate, "Stay here and look after Sallie, *mon amie.*"

"Where are ye goin'?" Kate asked, calling after her.

"To do what I have never done before." Liz looked up at Cato and let go a deep breath. "I am flying to Williamsburg."

57

TROUBLING LETTERS

LONDON, DECEMBER 10, 1772

"Joy to the world, the Lord is come!
Let earth receive her King;
Let every heart prepare Him room . . ."

Al happily swished his tail back and forth and he held back his head to belt out the Christmas carol. He was decorating the frame of his royal cat bed with sprigs of holly he had found in the parlor. And on the holly's thorny points he carefully skewered cubes of cheese. He animated each and every word by rapidly bobbing his head as he sang:

"And heav'n and nature sing,
And heav'n and nature sing,
And heav'n, and heav'n, and nature sing."

Nigel was about to die from laughter, wiping away tears from behind his spectacles to see the large orange cat singing and decorating his "room" for Christmas. Al was unaware his little mouse friend had arrived, and blissfully continued to howl at the top of his lungs. *If the humans were around, they would surely think the old boy was bellowing out in pain,* Nigel thought with a chuckle.

Nigel looked around the room festooned with garlands of holly, ivy, pine boughs, and berries. He ran over to pull off a few stringed cranberries and slowly walked up behind Al, joining in singing the Christmas carol.

"He rules the world with truth and grace,
And makes the nations prove
The glories of His righteousness . . ."

Al stopped singing and looked up. "Now that sounds like Mousie." He slowly turned to see his little mouse friend walking up behind him, smiling broadly with the berries raised in the air. Al and Nigel proceeded to finish the Christmas carol in unison, both bobbing their heads excitedly to punctuate each word:

> *"And wonders of His love,*
> *And wonders of His love,*
> *And wonders, wonders, of His love."*

"MOUSIE!" Al exclaimed, dropping the holly and picking Nigel up in a smothering embrace. "I'm so happy, happy, happy to see ye! Clarie said ye'd be comin' so I wanted to surprise ye with me Christmas decorations! Look, I decorated with *cheese.*"

Nigel struggled to pop his head out from Al's fluffy orange fur. "I am happy to see you as well, old boy. May I add these berries to your festive array?"

"Sure!" Al answered happily, setting Nigel down.

Nigel stuck the cranberries onto some of the holly thorns and smiled. "I must say, you've made quite the bountiful, delicious garland . . ." he started to say before Al snatched a piece of cheese from the garland and popped it into his mouth. "But something tells me it will not last long."

499

Al smiled. "Aye, that's the hazard of decoratin' with food."

Nigel wiggled his whiskers and chuckled. "Well, Christmasing would not be complete without the merriment of food to enjoy."

"That's what I always say!" Al picked off another piece of cheese. "That's why I think we should celebrate Christmas all-l-l year long."

"Indeed," Nigel replied with a smirk. "Well, now that I am here in London, let us discuss the mission at hand, shall we?"

"I'm all ears," Al agreed, lying back on his red velvet cat bed pillow, pulling off one of Nigel's cranberries and popping it into his mouth.

"Right. We need to acquire some important letters and get them into the hands of Benjamin Franklin," Nigel began, pacing back and forth with his paws clasped behind his back as he detailed their mission. "Clarie indicated that we would locate these letters in the possession of a William Whately. The letters were sent to his late brother, Thomas Whately. He was a Member of Parliament and Secretary to the Treasury for the Prime Minister."

"Which one?" Al asked, picking his teeth with a sprig of holly.

"Which one, what?" Nigel asked.

"Which Prime Minister? King George be on his sixth one now, Lordy North," Al explained. "That king goes through them PMs as fast as I do me Christmas decorations."

Nigel chuckled. *"Indeed.* Thomas Whately worked for PM George Grenville, and was a huge supporter of that dreadful Stamp Act business. Anyway, these letters were written by then-Lieutenant Governor Thomas Hutchinson of Massachusetts in 1768–69, in which he detailed the riots in Boston following the passage of the Townshend Acts and suggested some rather drastic measures for Parliament to take against the colony. Hutchinson was made governor of Massachusetts in 1770, and his brother-in-law Andrew Oliver became lieutenant governor. Oliver also penned some of the letters in question, so you and I must find them and get them to Dr. Franklin, posthaste. Clarie said you have become well acquainted with the ins and outs of London and the men about our mission. Where do you propose we begin?"

"At the bank," Al responded, standing up and walking toward the door. "But we best get there before they close then."

Nigel wrinkled his brow in confusion. "The bank? Whatever for?"

Al kept walking. "That Whately lad be a banker, on Lombard Street."

500

"Ah, how splendid to be back in London!" Nigel cheered, taking in the sights and sounds of the bustling Lombard Street. Horse-drawn carriages clip-clopped down the cobblestone street and people from all walks of life filled the sidewalks, from wealthy merchants to sailors, to children playing on the corner. Storefronts were decorated with ample items for shoppers, and street vendors called out their goods for sale to passersby.

"Did ye know that this very street were one of the original roads them Romans made when they called this place 'Londonium'?" Al remarked, proud to share something he had learned.

"Fascinating! I recall our visit when Londonium was just an idea," Nigel remembered. "Clarie brought us here when our Roman soldier, Armandus, came here on mission to meet with the tribal kings. My, how this city has grown since ancient times!"

Al pointed to a coffee house. "And there be the famous Lloyd's Coffee House. I like their scones, but they talk aboot borin' stuff in there, like insurance. Sometimes Benjamin Franklin pops in there to get the latest shippin' news."

"Good to know," Nigel replied, gazing up at the tall buildings as they walked along. "There are so many banks here, Al. Where shall we find Whately?"

"Ri-i-ight there," Al replied, sitting down and pointing with his chubby finger to a grey building. "So how should we go aboot gettin' the letters?"

"We shall slip inside and find the letters after the humans have left for the day," Nigel explained. "Then we can exit with the letters in tow and deliver them to Dr. Franklin."

Al furrowed his brow and then put a paw up to his mouth in alarm as he stared up at the bank entrance. "Oh, no! Do ye realize what this means?"

"What is that?" Nigel asked, studying the front door to the bank.

"We'll be bank robbers!" Al cried.

"We most certainly will *not* be bank robbers! We are *not* here to steal money, but to find letters that were simply passed on to Whately after his brother's death," Nigel explained, adjusting his spectacles. "See here! Whately gave an American agent named John Temple access to the letters so he could find some of his *own* letters mixed in the pile of correspondence. We are simply *reclaiming* a few select letters as well. Since they were written by and to public officers, they are not private and are already well known to officials here in England. So you can put that image of bank robbers out of your mind this instant!"

"Okay, that makes me feel better," Al replied. "I'd hate to become a criminal. What's so important aboot these letters anyway?"

Nigel furrowed his brow. "That, my good fellow, is something I do *not* yet know."

501

The fire crackled and Benjamin Franklin took a sip of his hot toddy while wiggling his toes against the warmth of the fireplace. He immediately started feeling revived after trudging home in the snow. "Ah, much better," he murmured to himself, shaking off the December cold of London. He reached over and picked up the packet left for him while he was out. It was addressed to him, but there was no sender's name. "Hmm, I wonder who sent this."

Al and Nigel hid in the shadows of the room behind the curtains, watching as Benjamin Franklin opened the packet. "Not bank robbers," Al whispered.

"*Hutchinson* is the one who called for British troops to be sent to Boston!" Ben exclaimed with wide eyes. He leaned forward, reading one of the letters with surprise. "'*It is impossible for colonists to have the full rights they would have in the home country. There must be an abridgment of what are called English liberties.*' Hmmmmm. This explains the harsh treatment of the colonies by Parliament—not all the troublemaking is happening here in London. Much of it is happening right there in Boston from the pens of loyalists such as Hutchinson!" he said aloud to himself. He kept reading through letter after letter until he reached the bottom of the pile. Finally he slapped them on his knee, got up from the leather chair, and walked over to his desk, taking out quill and ink. He proceeded to pen a letter to Thomas Cushing, speaker of the Massachusetts Assembly:

502

There has lately fallen into my hands part of a correspondence that I have reason to believe laid the foundation of most if not all our present grievances.

Nigel snuck up to read over Ben's shoulder as he wrote, explaining that the Massachusetts Assembly should read the letters but not make them public by any means. Ben was of the opinion that England's unwise actions toward the colonies were due to bad advice they had received from leaders like Hutchinson. A few bad apples were spoiling the relationship between England and her colonies. Ben hoped that by reading these letters, the men of Massachusetts would be able to move toward reconciliation with the Mother Country when they saw that it was their "siblings" who had complained to their "Mother" behind their backs.

Ben signed and sealed the letter and enclosed it with the packet of letters to go out in the morning mail. After he went to bed, Nigel looked at Al with concern. "Oh, dear. I'm beginning to wonder if we should have been bank robbers after all, stealing money instead of acquiring those letters. It may have caused less harm."

"Mousie! What do ye mean?" Al reacted in shock.

"I'm afraid Dr. Franklin is about to unknowingly ignite another fuse in Boston," Nigel explained. "And we've supplied him with the powder."

━━━━

RALEIGH TAVERN, WILLIAMSBURG, MARCH 11, 1773

Patrick Henry, Richard Henry Lee, and his brother Francis Lightfoot Lee, and Thomas Jefferson and his brother-in-law Dabney Carr gathered around the candlelit table in a private room at the Raleigh. The House of Burgesses had met for a week so far, having been called to a special session to address an alarming situation involving counterfeiters that threatened Virginia's flow of paper money. Governor Dunmore requested that the Assembly take measures to shore up the public credit. A ring of counterfeiters had been caught, but the way Dunmore handled them raised red flags in Patrick's mind. Patrick harshly criticized the new governor and embarrassed some of the older members of the House.

503

"You've certainly made the worst possible first impression on Lord Dunmore that you could, Pat," Francis jested. "At least he knows you mean business."

"I *do* mean business, as should we all," Patrick replied, looking around the table at the men. "Dunmore proceeded to round up counterfeiters in Pittsylvania County and bring them directly here to Williamsburg for trial, bypassing their proper, *due* right of trial first in the county court. And he did so with the private blessing of the old guard members of the House! We need to jealously guard our liberties, gentlemen." He tapped the table with his finger. "If Dunmore can round up citizens for trial here, what is to prevent him from sending citizens directly on to London for trial? That's exactly what Parliament has ordered for any Rhode Islanders involved in the *Gaspée* incident. No, this must be addressed not just here in Virginia, but with our brethren to the northward and all of our sister colonies."

Richard spoke up. "Agreed! Gentlemen, the time has come for us to establish a Committee of Correspondence with the other colonies. We must communicate in a timely manner about incidents like the recent events in Boston, the *Gaspée*, and Dunmore violating our ancient, legal, constitutional liberties."

"When Governor Hutchinson announced last year that he would

now be paid by the Royal Treasury and not by the Massachusetts Assembly, the alarm quickly arose in that colony. If their leader was not dependent on the people, he could order unpopular measures without consequence," Thomas reported. "So, Sam Adams proposed this very thing you are suggesting—a Committee of Correspondence with towns throughout Massachusetts. He requested that local citizens share their grievances and threats to their liberties, and the people have quickly responded. They are sending letters, attending town hall meetings, and seeking to learn all they can by reading the gazettes."

"This Committee of Correspondence must not exist just within a single colony but between all the colonies, so we can respond quickly on a united front. And these committees must function year 'round, not just when the assemblies are in session," Patrick suggested. "I would go even further, to suggest a meeting of committee representatives from each colony to meet in a central location to discuss our findings."

I believe mon *Henry just suggested a Continental Congress of some sort,* Liz thought as she sat in the shadows, soaking in this astonishing meeting. She listened as the men worked late into the night on their resolves to be read in the House the following day. She pondered, *They no longer sound like Englishmen. They are becoming Americans.*

504

———

WILLIAMSBURG, MARCH 16, 1773

Once the resolutions were adopted by the House of Burgesses to form the Committee of Correspondence, eleven members were chosen, including Patrick Henry. Lord Dunmore promptly dismissed the House after having been presented the resolutions, saying they had no more work to do. On the contrary, they had plenty of work to do. The Committee of Correspondence promptly met and drew up a circular letter to send to all the other colonies, urging them to bring the Virginia resolutions before their respective assemblies and also each to form their own Committee of Correspondence. Peyton Randolph was instructed to send express couriers to deliver the letter and resolutions as quickly as possible. As the couriers rode out of Williamsburg, Patrick Henry needed to take care of one more matter before heading home.

Liz frowned, watching Patrick Henry walking along South Francis Street on this raw, overcast day. "This is when I need Nigel, to slip in the door unnoticed."

"You can do it, Liz," Cato encouraged her.

"Absolutely you can," MizP added. "You need tuh see what Pahtrick is facing."

"*Oui,* I will figure something out," Liz agreed. "Be ready to leave when we come out, Cato. Patrick is eager to return to Scotchtown, so we will follow MizP from above. I wish Nigel were also here as the one to ride on your wings, *mon ami.* I know I am difficult for you to carry."

Cato stretched his wings and flapped them to warm up. "It's okay, Liz, but if you weren't so light we'd both be grounded! Thankfully you are such a little thing. I'm sorry it's not very comfortable for you."

"Well, you needed tuh be here these two weeks tuh see all that happened in Williamsburg," MizP added. "I'm glad you both were willing tuh be uncomfortable."

"*Merci,* but our discomfort is nothing compared with what *mon* Henry is experiencing." Liz sighed and started following Patrick at a distance.

Patrick Henry slowly walked toward the newly constructed two-story brick building topped with a cupola. It was almost finished, and would begin accepting patients in a few short months. Patrick stopped in the middle of the brick path and read the sign for the building, the first of its kind in North America: *Public Hospital for Persons of Insane and Disordered Minds.* He lowered his gaze to the ground and clenched his fists, looking behind him as if thinking about turning around. Liz dodged behind a tree. He took in a deep breath, pulled the brim of his hat lower over his eyes, crossed his arms over his chest, and pressed on. His feet were heavy as he climbed the few steps leading to the asylum. Thankfully, the door was propped open as workers carried building supplies inside. Liz slipped in behind him, breathing a prayer, "*Merci,* Maker."

505

"Yes, sir. Can I help you?" one of the workers asked as Patrick stood in the foyer of the hospital. The young man held a bucket of paint in one hand and a brush in the other, and didn't realize he was talking to Patrick Henry.

"I . . . I wanted to see how the hospital is progressing. I understand it opens soon, and was curious to see the inside," Patrick replied. "Governor Fauquier dreamed of building this hospital years ago to provide for . . . for those who suffer so terribly."

"I was getting ready to paint one of the rooms and can show you, if you wish," the young man replied. He led Patrick down a hallway that led to a series of twenty-four cells. "As you can see, each cell has a heavy wooden door with a barred window so the patients are isolated and secure. We've got one room all set up that I can show you."

Beads of sweat appeared on Patrick's forehead as he followed the young man down the dim corridor. He followed him to a completed room but hesitated at the entrance while the man stepped inside. It was sparse and cold, with whitewashed walls. "Patients will have a mattress and a chamber pot," he said, pointing to those items. He then grasped an iron ring in the wall, "And their wrist or leg fetters will be attached to this ring. Of course, when they need to have their icy plunge baths or bleeding treatments, they'll go to another room. I can show you that, too, if you wish."

Patrick's eyes filled with horror. This was more a prison than a hospital. He thought he was going to be sick. "No! No . . . thank you. I've seen enough. Thank you for your time." He quickly turned and made his way down the corridor and outside, gasping for fresh air. He walked briskly down the brick walkway to a nearby house. He leaned against it, his heart seemingly beating out of his chest. His hands were shaking from the trauma of even having considered putting Sallie in that place. He clenched a fist and set his jaw. "Not this, Sallie, I promise you." He slammed his fist against the wooden boards of the house and started walking toward Duke of Gloucester Street.

Liz wiped away her own tears of heartache mixed with relief that Patrick refused to put Sallie in such a horrible place. *"Cher* Patrick. We will think of something to care for her, do not worry," she promised as she watched Patrick walking away with hunched shoulders. "He carries the weight of the world on those strong shoulders—his beloved Sallie and his beloved Virginia. Yet who would ever know?"

Lord Dunmore gazed out the window of the Governor's Palace and narrowed his eyes at the thought of the troublemaker from Hanover County. He tossed the Virginia resolves concerning the Committees of Correspondence onto his desk and sat down. He took out a quill and dipped it in the ink to draft a letter to Parliament. "Enclosed is a copy of the resolves, and the list of men who were primarily involved, including . . ." Dunmore muttered as he scowled and again dipped his quill in the ink, "Patrick Henry."

While Dunmore was writing his letter about Virginia's Committees of Correspondence to send to London, Benjamin Franklin was writing his *second* letter to Thomas Cushing in Boston.

The fuse had indeed been lit when Franklin's packet of Hutchinson letters had been opened by the clerk of the Massachusetts Assembly, who happened to be none other than Samuel Adams.

507

BREWING TROUBLE
WITH THE CAT'S-PAW

I knew it! I knew this would happen!" Nigel roared (at least as much as a mouse can roar), pulling on his whiskers as he paced back and forth in front of a bench in Hyde Park. "I knew sending those Hutchinson letters to Boston would lead to trouble!"

Al sat on top of the bench next to Clarie, who was dressed as an old woman sitting there feeding the pigeons. He was drooling as she calmly tossed pieces of stale bread to the ground while pigeons fluttered all around them.

"We knew it, too. That's exactly why Benjamin Franklin needed to send them," Clarie answered calmly, tossing another handful of bread. "Max and I delivered the packet to Sam Adams."

Nigel's eyes widened behind his spectacles as he stood in the middle of the flapping pigeons. "What? Has your mind become completely *unhinged?!* Why on earth would you do such a thing? This will only lead to trouble for Dr. Franklin and the colony of Massachusetts!"

"Steady, Mousie," suggested Al before jumping down among the pigeons. He batted at pieces of bread and scrambled as did the birds.

"Samuel Adams opened the packet and shared the letters immediately with Thomas Cushing," Clarie began to explain. "He honored Dr. Franklin's request that the letters be shared only with a few people and not published. But when they shared the letters with the Massachusetts Committee of Correspondence the alarm immediately rippled through those men, including John Adams and John Hancock. They feel that the people should be told the truth of the content of Hutchinson's letters, so Cushing wrote back to Franklin, asking if they could share the letters more widely. By the time they receive Ben's second letter, the uproar led by Sam Adams will be uncontainable. Leaks of the existence of the letters are already out to the press. It's only a matter of time before everything will be printed in the *Boston Gazette* for the world to read. Then Hutchinson, along with most of London, will be a tempest in a teapot."

Nigel and Al stood side by side with mouths open, in shock. Nigel threw up his paws, speechless over the turn of events in Boston. Al happily caught a piece of bread.

"AND?" Nigel finally said. "What is the good that will come of this?"

"The good that will come of it is this," Clarie began to answer, leaning forward on the bench, throwing her last few breadcrumbs on the ground. Al and the pigeons chased after them. "While the colonies are acting less like Englishmen and more like Americans in every clash with Great Britain, Benjamin Franklin is not. He will play a vital role in securing American Independence, but he cannot do so without being pushed, like a baby eagle out of its nest. The discomfort of this issue with the Hutchinson letters is going to get worse for Dr. Franklin, but chin up, Nigel. In the end, it will be for the highest good of all. It will also play into other events coming to Boston."

509

Nigel clasped his paws behind his back and tightened his mouth gravely as he considered the scenario for a moment. He shook his head, unsure of things.

Clarie got right in Nigel's face and smiled. "This is just the second phase of your mission with Dr. Franklin and the key he holds to the future. You helped him *make* the key with the stormy kite experiment. Now the storm of these Hutchinson letters will *insert* that key into the door. Everything will make sense in time."

Nigel lifted his chin, preened his whiskers, and adjusted his spectacles. "Right, then. I shall endeavor to see Dr. Franklin through *this* storm with electrifying success."

"That's the spirit!" Clarie cheered, tickling Nigel under the chin. "You'll need to be strong for Dr. Franklin, because he will soon be 'steeped' in greater trouble than he realizes."

"Steeped, as in tea?" Nigel asked.

Just then Al came running up to them. "I jest gathered some intelligence! Am I supposed to do somethin', Clarie lass? One of them pigeons jest told me the news they overheard on Parliament's windowsill."

"What news?" Nigel asked in alarm.

"Some of those Lordy Lads said something aboot needin' a 'cat's-paw' for the colonies," Al reported.

"*Cat's-paw* is a figure of speech from a fable," Nigel offered. "It means that someone is used unknowingly by another to accomplish the other's own purposes. Whatever could this mean?"

"Well, that Lordy North jest made Parliament pass some Tea Act," Al further offered. "Does that help?"

Nigel put a paw to his mouth. "Tea Act! Oh, dear! The *tea* is going to be the cat's-paw to tax the colonies! I heard rumblings about this from Dr. Franklin's discussions with friends, but I was unsure how it would play out. There are eighteen million pounds of unsold tea sitting in London's warehouses this very minute. They have been discussing how they can get rid of it and save the East India Company from bankruptcy. They have now found a way, by some scheme of sending the tea to the colonies with this Tea Act."

"But I still don't understand how tea can be a cat's-paw," Al wondered, scratching his head. He poked out his iron claw and wore a goofy grin. "But I could use this to stir some milk into tea."

"We'll explain things a little better for you, Al," offered Clarie. "Since Parliament repealed the Townshend duties except for the tax on tea, the colonies have refused to buy tea from England. They've either smuggled it in from other countries or made do with homemade sassafras tea. So, British tea has piled up in the warehouses as Nigel said. To get rid of it, Parliament is going to allow the East India Company to sell tea directly to new dealers in the colonies and cut out the colonial merchants doing business in London. These new tea dealers will be like those Stamp Distributors they assigned to collect the Stamp Tax. The tea will be shipped to them in the port cities of Boston, New York, Philadelphia, and Charleston. They'll reduce the tax on tea from twelve pennies per pound to three, which will make it cheaper than smuggled tea."

"*Ergo,* the East India Company tea will become the 'cat's-paw' to make the colonies pay the tea tax," Nigel added. "But it's all under the guise of returning to the happy days of having a steaming good hot cup of British tea! England will tempt the colonies with cheap tea, thereby making them *admit* that Parliament indeed has the right to tax them." Nigel's eyes widened and he pulled on his whiskers. "By Jove, they'll set up a monopoly in the tea market while they are at it! If this conspiracy

510

works with tea, England could try it with other imports. Why, those schemers are steeped in mischief!"

"Sounds like those Lordy Lads be brewin' trouble," Al noted, holding up his paw. "So ye won't be needin' me cat's-paw to make the tea then, Clarie?"

"No, Al, not to make tea," Clarie answered with a smile.

"Good, because I don't like tea," Al replied.

"Just keep your paws on King George's desk to gather intelligence of any news about the colonies and Benjamin Franklin to share with Nigel." Clarie rose to her feet. "I need to get back to Max. Between the Hutchinson Letters and the Tea Act, trouble will soon reach its boiling point in Boston."

<hr />

ROYAL PALACE, LONDON, JULY 15, 1773

"Bring my tea out on the veranda," King George said hoarsely, rubbing his throat. "I need some fresh air."

"Honey or milk with your tea, sire?" the royal servant asked.

"Make it honey. My voice is strained," King George answered, glaring at Lord North. He proceeded to walk out of the room with the Prime Minister trailing along sheepishly.

"Aye, no wonder it's strained," Al muttered under his breath, finally removing his paws from his ears after George's temper tantrum. He shook his head. "Now let's see what all that yellin' were aboot. But first, a snack."

After the servant prepared the tea, he left the room carrying a silver tray. Al jumped up on the serving table and stepped in a glob of honey the servant had spilled. He snatched a scone and proceeded to jump down to the floor where King George had tossed some papers, sticking to the rug with each step. He tried to shake the honey off his paw while he scanned the pages of the *Boston Gazette*. "Looks like them letters got printed, jest like Clarie predicted. And here's somethin' from Lordy Dunmore," mentioned Al, scanning Dunmore's letter about the Virginia Assembly and their resolves. He spotted Patrick Henry's name, along with Richard Henry Lee, Thomas Jefferson, and the others who had come up with the Committees of Correspondence. Al ate the crumbly scone and then proceeded to mindlessly lick the remaining honey from his paw. "Uh-oh. Looks like they be in as much hot water as them

Boston lads." He moved a few pieces of paper around and grew quickly worried as he read a letter from the Lords of Trade about the Virginians.

"I gotta tell Mousie!" Al exclaimed, his mouth covered in honey and crumbs. He shook his paw but the paper was stuck to it. As he fought with the paper, he proceeded to get more pieces stuck on all four paws and noisily ran out of the room. "Guess I'll be *showin'* Mousie, instead."

As these proceedings of the House of Burgesses of Virginia appear to us to be of an extraordinary nature, and we think that inviting the other colonies to a communication and correspondence upon such matters as are stated in these proceedings is a measure of the most dangerous tendency and Effect, we humbly submit to Your Majesty to take such measures thereon as Your Majesty, with the advice of Your Privy Council, shall think most proper and expedient.

512

"No wonder King George was upset! Those Committees of Correspondence look like they are organizing for Revolution!" Nigel worried, reading the nervous letter from the Lords of Trade to the king. The little mouse then scanned the *Boston Gazette*. "And Parliament must be about to explode! The Massachusetts Assembly is calling for the removal of Hutchinson and Oliver. In London everyone is wondering *who* leaked the Hutchinson letters, but interestingly enough, no one has yet mentioned Benjamin Franklin."

"Do ye think they suspect me, Mousie? I be the sticky thief . . ." Al announced, grinning as he licked his honeyed paws, ". . . with *four* cat's-paws to gather intelligence."

"Indeed, you have taken far more than the *biscuit,* my good fellow," Nigel quipped with a jolly chuckle. "I say, with all this trouble brewing with letters and tea in the colonies, no telling what will happen when that British tea makes it to American ports, especially Boston. And what will become of Benjamin Franklin, I wonder?"

"If the Lordy Lads are out to make the tea their cats-paw for taxing the colonies, then they best remember that cats like milk more than tea anyway," Al offered. "Maybe Ben Franklin will stop drinking tea and start drinking milk."

"Hmmm. *Milk*. Benjamin Franklin was actually born on Milk Street in Boston, right across from the Old South Meeting House. But that's neither here nor there," Nigel decided, with a wave of his paw, to get back on topic. "The colonies are shifting their talks from Parliament's right to *tax* to Parliament's right to *govern*. It would appear the colonies are finally weaning themselves off of milk. *Mother Country's* milk, that is."

———

BOSTON, DECEMBER 16, 1773, 5:00 P.M.

"So wha' happens at midnight?" Max wanted to know. "An' why are ye puttin' that stuff on yer face, lass?"

"Midnight marks the twenty-day deadline for the tea to be unloaded and taxes paid for the first of the three tea ships that arrived in Boston, the *Dartmouth*," Clarie explained, smearing black coal dust on her face. She was in the form of a young man. "Otherwise the Customs officials can seize all the cargo on the ship. The people have been meeting by the thousands for almost three weeks, demanding that Governor Hutchinson send the tea ships back to London without unloading them. So tonight Sam Adams has called the citizens to gather at Old South Meeting House to hear the governor's final word on the matter. If Hutchinson doesn't allow Captain Rotch and his unloaded ships to leave Boston Harbor, the people are going to do something drastic." She slipped on a fringed shirt, styled her black hair up in a quasi-mohawk, sloppily stuck feathers in her hair, and stood with her hands out. "How do I look?"

"Like a r-r-really badly dr-r-ressed Indian. Are ye headin' ta a costume party or somethin'?" Max asked, looking her up and down with his head cocked to the side.

"Perfect! I'm *supposed* to look like a really badly dressed Indian," Clarie explained, sticking a hatchet in her belt. "And yes, it *is* a costume party of sorts. A costume *surprise* party."

"An' wha' am I supposed ta go as—a kitty?" Max grumbled. "Don't tell me I have ta put cinnamon on me fur ta look like Al."

Clarie giggled. "No, Max, Al has already contributed to the party with his cat's-paw. I'll take it from here. You can go to the party just as you are. In fact, you don't have to do anything but show up and observe the festivities." She mussed the fur on his head. "Get to the Old South Meeting House and wait for Sam Adams to give the signal. When you hear the commotion outside, get out of there and run to Griffin's Wharf."

513

Max gave her the most perplexed look and then shook his head. "An' jest wha' will they be servin' at this party, lass?"

"Why, the perfect drink to toast the start of a revolution!" Clarie answered with a wink before turning to disappear into the night. "Tea!"

"This has ta be one of her str-r-rangest missions yet. She's dr-r-ressed as an Indian, goin' ta a tea party at night in the middle of Boston," Max muttered as he started to trot down the cobblestone street toward the Old South Meeting House. Suddenly he realized what she had just said. "R-r-revolution?!"

———

MILK STREET, OLD SOUTH MEETING HOUSE, BOSTON, DECEMBER 16, 1773, 6:00 P.M.

"Here he comes!" shouted John Hancock, parting the crowd so Captain Rotch could enter the church. He proceeded to escort the man to the front of the overflowing sanctuary.

More than five thousand people had gathered, packed into the church before spilling out onto Milk Street. Max easily scooted under the legs of the people to slip inside. He poked his head out to see Samuel Adams standing at the front of the church, banging on the lectern. A debate had been raging for an hour over what to do about the tea sitting on three ships in Boston Harbor. They had threatened the newly appointed East India Tea agents with tar and feathering, just as they had the Stamp Distributors. While not everyone approved of such treatment, the people did agree on one thing. They were not going to pay the tax.

"Order! Order! Let Captain Rotch through!" Sam Adams shouted.

The wealthy American captain walked to the front of the church and turned to face the crowd. "I've just returned from meeting with Governor Hutchinson at his house in Milton. He has denied my request for a pass to leave Boston and plans to unload the *Dartmouth* in the morning."

A cry from the crowd quickly rose to a deafening pitch as Captain Rotch held up his hands in a futile gesture. He tried to shout above the noise, but finally walked down the middle aisle to exit the church. The people were on their feet, shaking their fists in anger at Governor Hutchinson's decision. "First, Hutchinson's letters called for England to reduce our liberties, now the governor is forcing us to pay a tax on tea! Hutchinson must go!"

Sam Adams banged on the lectern and called the assembly to order. Suddenly a hush fell over the crowd and the patriot looked around the room, making eye contact with John Hancock, Josiah Quincy, and other prominent men from the Sons of Liberty. "This meeting can do nothing more to save the country." He locked eyes with a man in the back of the church who immediately slipped out the door. Within minutes the people heard the whooping war cries of Indians followed by the roar of people outside the church.

That must be the signal! Max thought, waiting for Sam Adams to move, but the patriot leader stayed where he was. Other prominent Sons of Liberty members took their seats. They weren't going anywhere. Max furrowed his brow and ran underfoot of the people who were exiting the back of the church. "Now let's see wha' that little Indian lass does at this party."

A sea of people with torches marched down the packed streets of Boston to Griffin's Wharf, where the *Dartmouth*, the *Beaver*, and the *Eleanor*, were moored. More than one hundred men in Indian dress and others with blackened faces split into three groups and boarded the ships.

515

Max stood at the edge of the wharf and watched in stunned disbelief as the *faux* Indians took their hatchets and broke open 340 chests of tea while the crowds yelled and cheered. But they took great care not to harm any of the crew members or touch any of the rest of the cargo. It was an organized, efficient group of poorly dressed Indians tossing tea and only tea.

"Well, I'll be a Scottie's uncle! They're dumpin' the tea into the harbor! An' there be no Br-r-ritish soldiers ar-r-round ta stop 'em!" Max couldn't see Clarie anywhere, so he just sat there, watching the harbor fill with tea. "If the colonies wanted a r-r-revolution, they sure have br-r-rewed up one now."

LONDON, JANUARY 19, 1774

"WHAT? WHAT? EIGHTEEN MILLION CUPS OF TEA ARE FLOATING IN BOSTON HARBOR?!" King George screamed, spitting out his mouthful of tea, spraying Lord North in the face.

Lord North took out a silk handkerchief and dabbed his face, trembling as he stood in front of the angry king. "I'm afraid so, Your Majesty. The Bostonians protested the Tea Act by dumping 340 chests of tea worth more than 9,000 pounds sterling into the harbor. But thankfully there was no other damage done to the ships or cargo. In fact, the criminals even swept the ship decks clean and made sure everything was back in its proper place before they left."

King George clenched his fist and set his jaw. "You dare to tell me that we can be thankful that they were *tidy* vandals?" His face turned red and he threw his cup against the wall, splattering tea and sending shards of fine china flying across the room. "WHO WERE THEY? I WANT THEM ALL ARRESTED AND BROUGHT HERE FOR TRIAL!"

Lord North dabbed the handkerchief to his sweaty upper lip and cleared his throat uncomfortably. "We don't know exactly who they were, your Majesty. They were dressed as Indians so no one recognized them."

"INDIANS?!" King George roared. "What about those hotheaded Sons of Liberty—Sam Adams, Paul Revere, and John Hancock? You *know* they were behind this!"

"Evidently they were seen by witnesses at Old South Meeting House and elsewhere at the time, so we cannot arrest them," Lord North explained.

516

"Well, *someone* needs to stand trial for what happened!" the king shouted.

"Agreed, and we may have just the person. Those ungrateful Bostonians dressed as Indians not only to disguise themselves. They chose a symbol of something completely native to America to send a clear message they see themselves distinctly as *Americans,* not Englishmen," Lord North said, picking up a copy of the *London Chronicle.* "Why not allow the one Englishman here in London to give an account for the Americans he has chosen to represent?" He waved the paper in the air.

King George rolled his eyes impatiently at the prime minister. "Get on with it! Whom do you mean?"

"Benjamin Franklin finally admitted *he* sent the Hutchinson letters to Boston. William Whately accused John Temple of stealing the letters and challenged him to a duel, but was wounded. In order to prevent a second duel, Franklin stepped up and published his full confession in the *London Chronicle* on Christmas Day," Lord North explained, handing the paper over.

King George snatched the paper out of Lord North's hand and read Franklin's entry: *"I alone am the person who obtained and transmitted to Boston the letters in question."* The irate monarch turned to scowl at Lord

North. "But the man did not apologize for doing so! The Massachusetts Assembly has sent a petition to have Hutchinson removed, which I'm actually inclined to agree with after this tea business in Boston! What are *you* suggesting?"

"Parliament has called Dr. Franklin to stand before the Privy Council to answer for his actions with the Hutchinson letters, actions that he claims he took to *help* matters," Lord North replied. "Since Benjamin Franklin is the agent representing Massachusetts here in London, let him give an account for the letters *and* receive the Council's fury for the actions of the Bostonians."

King George watched Al pawing at a tray of cookies. "We'll let *Franklin* be the cat's-paw to take the heat for all of Boston's trouble. Then I'll appoint a strong military commander to take over as governor of Massachusetts."

"General Gage is due back to England any day," Lord North offered with a smile.

"Bring General Gage to me as soon as he arrives," King George replied. "If Massachusetts won't yield to the pen of her old governor, we'll make her yield to the sword of her new one."

517

LONDON, JANUARY 28, 1774

"Boston, what have you done? It was wrong to destroy private property," Benjamin Franklin said as he pulled his fingers through his long, silvery hair. He shook his head, yawned, and tossed the latest correspondence about Boston onto his desk. "Now to give an account for *your* act of violent injustice, and for *my* reasons for sending those letters to you. Tomorrow we'll both be in the Cockpit."

As Franklin went to climb into bed, Al and Nigel came out from behind the curtains. "It don't sound like he's ready to become an American yet, Mousie. He's pretty mad at Boston for dumpin' all that cat's-paw tea."

"Indeed. His love for our beloved homeland of England has him grasping for ways to set things right betwixt the Mother Country and her naughty colonies. He has always been proud to be an Englishman," Nigel lamented. "But Clarie said that somehow these events will make Dr. Franklin have a change of heart. Everything shall come to a head tomorrow and I predict that Benjamin is in for a brutal day."

"Why's he goin' to be in a cockpit?" Al asked. "I thought he were goin' to meet with all the king's men."

"The Cockpit is the famed room of the King's Privy Council, so called because cockfights were held there during King Henry VIII's time," Nigel explained in a whisper. "Such a dastardly business. I wish I knew how to encourage Dr. Franklin as he stands in the Cockpit tomorrow."

"Is Ben goin' to have to fight like a mad rooster with all the Lordy Lads?" Al asked, worried. "They be the powerful-est British lions the king's got, ye know. They've got the *big* cat's-paw claws."

"No actual fighting, but the king's newest lion *will* try to verbally tear Benjamin Franklin to shreds. Ben will have to stand in front of Lord North and the Privy Council while Solicitor-General Alexander Wedderburn throws everything he has at him," Nigel predicted, furrowing his brow. "Ben will be just like Daniel thrown into the lion's den."

Al put his paw over his chest. "Do ye need me to go with ye to shut the mouths of those lions like I did for Daniel?"

"I seem to recall it was the *angel* who shut the mouths of those lions," Nigel replied with a slight grin to the orange cat.

"Oh, aye. That's right," Al sheepishly replied with a goofy smile. "Sometimes I should jest keep me own mouth shut. Now *that* I know I can do." He put both of his fluffy paws over his mouth.

Nigel crossed his arms and tapped a finger on his mouth. "Keep your mouth shut, like a lamb." Suddenly his face brightened. "Brilliant, old boy! I know how I can encourage Dr. Franklin as he enters the lion's den!"

"Happy to give ye an answer with all me questions, Mousie," Al quipped as he removed his paws from his mouth. He stretched out on the floor while Nigel ran over to Ben's desk to scribble a few words on a piece of paper.

"Now what will he wear to the Cockpit tomorrow?" Nigel asked as he jumped to the floor and scurried into Ben's bedroom. He saw Ben's plain suit made of blue Manchester velvet hanging there, pressed and ready for his important day. "Perfect."

WHITEHALL, "THE COCKPIT," LONDON,
JANUARY 29, 1774

Benjamin Franklin spoke in hushed tones with his two lawyers while thirty-six English lords eagerly entered the prestigious chamber. They quickly filled all the seats at a long table in the center of the room. A roaring fire in the fireplace warmed the room at one end against the cold coming from the windows that looked out on St. James's Palace—the king's residence. Nigel was well hidden up on the windowsill before the humans arrived, and Al stayed behind in the palace rather than enter this British lion's den.

"Check your pocket, old boy," Nigel muttered to himself. He kept his gaze on Benjamin Franklin, who looked cool yet felt the heat already filling the room. They were waiting on Lord North to arrive so they could get started.

After a moment, Benjamin Franklin put his hand into his pocket to lift his handkerchief and felt the piece of paper Nigel had placed there. He unfolded the paper and read while Nigel grinned with anticipation. Benjamin wrinkled his brow and turned the paper over, as if to see where it had come from. The paper was filled with quotations he himself had penned and published long before in *Poor Richard's Almanack*:

> The things which hurt, instruct.
> A slip of the foot you may soon recover,
> but a slip of the tongue you may never get over.
> Think of three things: Whence you came, Where you are going,
> and to whom you must account.

519

Benjamin clenched his jaw as he then read the verse Nigel had penned from Isaiah 53:7:

> He was oppressed, and he was afflicted,
> yet he opened not his mouth.

Nigel nodded hopefully as Benjamin put the note back in his pocket and patted it, as if to tell himself to remember the words he had read.

Suddenly Lord North entered the room yet couldn't find a chair, as they were all taken by the other lords. He stood beside the chair of the seated council president and nodded for the hearing to begin. After Franklin's two lawyers presented the petition by the Massachusetts Assembly that Governor Hutchinson be removed, Solicitor General Wedderburn moved in for the attack.

"Governor Thomas Hutchinson has only acted and spoken as a loyal minion of the king. If he has lost the confidence of the so-called *people,* then I submit it is Franklin's doing! Furthermore, Franklin parades as a doctor and a scientist but he is a *thief!* I hope, my lords, you will mark and brand that man, for the honor of this country, of Europe, of mankind!"

The Cockpit rocked with laughter and the lords of the Privy Council studied Franklin with mocking, haughty eyes. Nigel's heart sank to hear such vitriol hurled at the brilliant man. But Nigel lifted his chin with pride as he saw Benjamin Franklin standing there as solid as a statue, unmoved and not showing a shred of emotion nor offering a single word of objection.

"Hutchinson has been the victim of Franklin's unscrupulous schemes to incite rebellion. And I submit that Franklin schemed in this manner primarily in order to have himself made governor!" Wedderburn continued. For a solid hour, his Scottish brogue filled the chamber with scathing personal attacks on Benjamin Franklin. Wedderburn not only shouted but pounded the council table, bringing out all the British fury to bear against the Bostonians for the letters and the destroyed tea.

"These British lions look like the Romans attending the games in the Colosseum. They are actually *enjoying* these proceedings as entertainment," Nigel muttered in disgust as the lords frequently burst out in loud applauses and howls of laughter. "This is madness!"

"Letters might certainly be conveyed, without any electrical shock," Wedderburn snidely remarked, making fun of Dr. Franklin's fame for his electrical experiments. "They have, it is true, given a *shock* to their friends; but our Correspondent knows of no conductor that will convey a shock to themselves. Against the Transmitter of certain letters to America . . . the whole Fire seemed to have been extracted from his Frame!"

"OF ALL THE NERVE!" Nigel squeaked. He could not contain himself any longer and shook his fists in anger while he ranted up on the windowsill. "I'll have you know, you pompous little Wedderburn, that those electrical experiments are the KEY to the future for Benjamin Franklin and the colonies you are railing against!" The little mouse then turned to look down at Benjamin Franklin, who was doing exactly as Nigel had hoped. He didn't utter a single word in response. Nigel cleared his throat, preened his whiskers, and tried to regain his own composure. "Steady, old boy."

Finally, Wedderburn stopped his rant and called Franklin as a witness but Franklin's lawyers replied that he did not choose to be

520

examined. Eventually the hearing concluded with the Privy Council denying the petition to remove Governor Hutchinson, expressed with as much scorn as had been heaped on Benjamin Franklin. Then he was summarily dismissed from the Cockpit.

"Brilliant, Dr. Franklin! I have no doubt that *you* will someday shut the mouths of these lions," Nigel cheered as he applauded Ben's astounding strength, courage, and self-control.

Little did King George, Lord North, Wedderburn, or the Privy Council know, but *they* had unwittingly been used as the cat's-paw to insert the key of American Independence into the lock.

When Benjamin Franklin set foot in the Cockpit, he was an Englishman. When he walked out the door, he was an American.

A Voice That
Is Hungry

SCOTCHTOWN, APRIL 28, 1774

"A Lady's Adieu to her TEA TABLE.
FAREWELL the Tea Board, with its gaudy Equipage,
Of Cups and Saucers, Cream Bucket, Sugar Tongs,
The pretty Tea Chest also, lately stor'd . . ."

P lease skip to the bottom, *mon amie,*" Liz asked Kate, who was
reading from the *Virginia Gazette.* It was one of many patriotic expressions about the need for the colonists to stop drinking
their beloved English tea.

"Aye, let's see," Kate answered as she moved her paw down the page.
"Here then:

"Because I'm taught (and I believe it true)
Its Use will fasten slavish Chains upon my Country,
And LIBERTY'S THE Goddess I would choose
To reign triumphant in AMERICA."

"And Liberty's the Goddess I would choose to reign triumphant in
America," Liz repeated aloud with her paw raised in the air, impersonat-
ing how Patrick had read it aloud this morning. "They speak of course
of *Libertas.* How amazing, no? *Libertas,* here in America! I still cannot
believe that you saw our statue in France at *Chavaniac* with the Marquis
de Lafayette."

"Aye, with *yer* smilin' face also carved there at her feet," Kate
answered with her peppy grin. "It made me happy ta see ye there every
day, Liz, especially when I were lonely for Max an' me friends."

"All this time, and Libertas remains," pondered Liz. "But Liberty is timeless, no? The Maker instilled the longing for freedom in the beating hearts of His creation." She gazed out to the garden where Patrick sat with Sallie, playing his fiddle for her. She sat there quietly, as if she didn't hear the music, but at least she was calm. Patrick's mother had taken the Henry children for a ride in the countryside to visit family, giving the weary couple a quiet day. "*Mon* Henry is torn over whether he is doing the right thing, building a daylight basement for Sallie. He, more than anyone, hates to think of confining her."

Kate nodded sadly. "Aye, but puttin' a hedge around someone isn't jest ta keep them from gettin' out, but ta keep harm from gettin' in. That airy basement room with the cozy fireplace an' big windows lookin' out at the garden is the best solution ye helped Patrick ta see, Liz. Since noise an' bein' around the children an' other people upsets Sallie, she *needs* a calm, quiet place, even if she'll be away from her family. And she'll be safe an' snug with someone always watchin' out for her down there—especially *us.*"

"*Oui,* you are right. I know it is the best for Sallie," Liz replied, tilting her head in admiration as she studied Patrick setting his fiddle aside. "Sometimes Patrick is the only one who can reach her, but he is gone so very much."

523

Patrick leaned over and picked a white daisy from the patch he had planted there in the garden, just for Sallie. He handed the flower to her and tenderly cupped Sallie's face in his palm as he spoke softly to her. He longed for his sweetheart to mentally and emotionally return to him, even for a moment.

Liz smiled sadly, seeing Patrick's calm way with Sallie. "He is so gentle with her. The way he brushes her hair and feeds her like a child is sad yet so very beautiful, no?"

Kate let go a heavy sigh. "But the lassie doesn't seem ta want ta eat when he's not around, which will be happenin' more an' more in the days ta come. I worry she'll be hungry without saying a word aboot it."

Liz's eyes widened. "*A voice that is hungry.* That is the next part of the fiddle's riddle. We are long overdue for the next part of the riddle to unfold, especially with all that is happening with Boston and other unrest in the colonies." Her tail whipped back and forth as she saw Patrick help Sallie to her feet. He put his arms around her to guide her back to the house, leaving his fiddle sitting on the bench. "It is time we received an update from Gillamon."

Once Patrick had taken Sallie inside, Liz and Kate quickly ran through the hedge of aromatic boxwoods to reach the bench on the far end of the garden. Liz picked another daisy and looked around to make sure no other humans were nearby. She then softly pulled the flower stem across the strings of the fiddle. Musical notes rose into the air as they had done since Patrick Henry's childhood.

Hello, Liz and Kate. I've been expecting you ladies.

Kate's eyes widened to see the magical, golden notes rising with the words inside. "Good day, Gillamon. I've never got ta see this! If only Patrick knew wha' his fiddle could really do."

Liz smiled to see Kate enjoy the wonder of the magic fiddle. "*Bonjour*, Gillamon. It has been a long time, but can you please tell us about the next part of the riddle? Does it have to do with Sallie not eating?"

*It does have to do with not eating, but not just for Sallie.
Patrick needs to get all of Virginia to not eat when
he gets to Williamsburg.*

Kate and Liz shared confused looks. "Wha' a strange idea, Gillamon! Ye mean like a fast? Wha's happenin' in Williamsburg?"

*That's right, little Kate. Lord Dunmore is calling the
House of Burgesses back in session to deal with the matter
of the war he set off with the Indians.
In his zeal to pursue land out on the frontier and settle
the boundary dispute between Virginia and Pennsylvania,
he made things worse.
A military force he sent to the area ended up
killing some friendly Indian allies.
The Indians are now on the warpath,
attacking and killing settlers.
Governor Dunmore wants the Burgesses to approve funds
to raise an army to send to the frontier.
So after a year he has reluctantly called them back
to Williamsburg.
Patrick will be leaving in a couple of days.*

Liz wrinkled her brow. "Lord Dunmore has set off a war with the Indians on the frontier? I hope it will not drag on like the last war. Does fasting have something to do with this war, as when Samuel Davies called for prayer and fasting in the French and Indian War?"

You have the exact right idea, Liz, but prayer and fasting will not be for Dunmore's War. While the burgesses are in Williamsburg, word will arrive about London's harsh response to Boston's "tea party." Patrick will need to lead the charge for how Virginia will respond.

Liz's mind raced. "Then I must return to Williamsburg. Kate can stay here with Sallie."

Kate, you will be able to reach Sallie while Patrick is gone. She will respond to you. Liz, Nigel will meet you in Williamsburg to fill you in on all that has happened with Benjamin Franklin in London. Share with him what I've told you here. You and Nigel must make sure Patrick meets a man by the name of George Mason. It is time for things to unfold rapidly now in your mission with Patrick Henry. The rest of the riddle will all come to pass very soon.

525

"How do ye mean Sallie will respond ta me?" Kate wanted to know. "Am I supposed ta talk ta her?"

Liz continued to pull the daisy stem across the fiddle, but the notes stopped rising. "He is gone, *mon amie.*" She turned to Kate and smiled with a paw on the Westie's shoulder. "If you feel led to talk to Sallie, do not be afraid to do so. I know she will be in good paws with you." A shadow passed overhead. It was Cato. "For now, I must ask Cato to allow me to be in good wings with him."

WILLIAMSBURG, MAY 19, 1774

"Have you read today's *Virginia Gazette*?" Richard Henry Lee exclaimed, holding up the paper as he met Patrick Henry outside Charlton's Coffee House. "England is going to close the port of Boston."

"What?" Patrick Henry gasped, reaching for the paper as the men stepped inside and sat down. He immediately started reading the details of the rumored Boston Port Bill. "The port will close on June 1 and remain closed until Boston pays for the destroyed tea. Only military supplies are to be shipped to Boston, along with troops to administer them no doubt." He leaned back in his chair and frowned. "Britain is going to strain the Bostonians like tea for every penny of damages while redcoats fill the streets of Boston once more."

Richard nodded and pulled out a letter he had received from London. "My brother writes that Lord North told the House of Commons that he *would not listen to the complaint of America until she was at his feet.*' Members of Parliament even joked of sending *'gunpowder tea to be taken with a smack of British spirit.'"* He slapped the letter on the table. "The colonies are being viewed in open rebellion and we should expect more coercive measures soon. Also, it is rumored King George may replace Governor Hutchinson with General Gage."

"John Hancock, Samuel Adams, and two others have been ordered to be returned to England in iron fetters!" Patrick further read, looking up at Richard in stunned disbelief. "Closing the port of Boston. A military governor with troops in the city. Threats of carrying citizens to England in irons. Virginia must respond immediately to these actions against Boston." He glanced over to see George Washington at another table.

526

Seated next to Colonel Washington were two other burgesses, also colonels who had served under his command in the French and Indian War. Fifty-three year old Andrew Lewis represented Botetourt County in the southwestern part of Virginia. His thirty-eight year old brother Charles was from Augusta County, representing the northwestern part of the state.

"Can you imagine redcoats marching through Williamsburg?" Richard asked.

Patrick folded his arms over his chest and shook his head. "The *last* thing we should do is give Dunmore a regular army under his control for the Indian crisis on the frontier. County militias will keep military control with *American* citizens, not the royal governor." He pointed to the three colonels. "When troops were needed in the French and Indian War, Reverend Samuel Davies rallied the able-bodied young men to swell the county militias."

"Virginia's toughest fighters and those most knowledgeable about Indian warfare are those Scots-Irish long-riflemen out on the frontier," Richard added.

"Aye. The time I spent with my Uncle Langloo in the wilderness taught me that," Patrick replied, remembering that experience with fondness. "My uncle even showed up at my wedding with two young men he was training. One of them, Samuel Crowley, ended up marrying Sallie's friend Elizabeth. They moved out to the frontier, and Samuel has become one of Andrew Lewis's best scouts."

"Perhaps Dunmore doesn't realize Virginia already has the finest warriors to meet the Indian threat," Richard offered.

"On the contrary. I wonder if Dunmore realizes it *all too well.*" Patrick thought a moment. "When we take a stand against England's treatment of Boston, Dunmore will be threatened again by political opposition and dissolve the House of Burgesses. But he can't dissolve *military* opposition as easily. If England were to come down hard on Virginia as it has on Boston, the militias under the command of the Lewis Brothers would be a formidable fighting force. I wonder. Would Dunmore feel *threatened* by Virginia's own militia without British redcoats here to protect him?"

Richard's eyes widened and he furrowed his brow. "What are you thinking, Pat?"

527

"I'm thinking Virginia first needs to be alerted to the threats against Boston. I predict we will soon need to be ready to take up arms. Lord North has singled out Boston to make her pay for her crimes, and he likely underestimates how the other colonies will respond. But if the British Lion can come after one colony, it can and it *will* come after all the colonies," Patrick replied. "We need action, but the conservative burgesses will only want to send more weak petitions to London to protest the Boston Port Bill."

"We should call for a General Congress of all the colonies to meet," Richard answered enthusiastically. "I say we go beyond just banning imports. We should ban *exports to* Britain as well."

"Agreed, but the burgesses aren't ready for such drastic action. They first need to be pushed by the popular sentiment of the people they represent." He leaned over to rest his elbows on the table. "Reverend Davies did a remarkable job of alerting the people and patriotically inspiring young men to sign up to fight in the French and Indian War. But he also called on the people to pray and humble themselves before God. What if we were to call on the people to do the same for Boston, to show Virginia's support for our sister colony?"

"Sound the alarm, oppose British tyranny, rally the people of

Virginia, but appear as harmless as doves," Richard said, nodding. "I like it. After all, who could object to prayer?"

"Lord Dunmore," Patrick quipped with a flash of his eyes. "Especially after we make the people hungry for the *goddess of liberty* to reign over them—not a tyrannical king or a scheming governor."

———

COUNCIL CHAMBER, CAPITOL BUILDING, WILLIAMSBURG, MAY 23, 1774

Patrick Henry, Richard Henry Lee, Thomas Jefferson, and a few of the younger, more liberal burgesses were seated around the table of the Council Chamber, poring over law books and precedent journals by the dim candlelight. Together they sought to come up with Virginia's resolution against the Boston Port Bill and head off another round of spineless petitions to Parliament. Thomas Jefferson had just found an old Puritan precedent they could use, and the men were busy drafting a resolution for a day of fasting, humiliation, and prayer. George Mason from Fairfax County was not a current burgess but had arrived in Williamsburg on business the day before. He was delighted to get word that Patrick Henry was speaking that day, and sat in the balcony of the House of Burgesses, listening with undivided attention to the famed 'Ruler of the House.' Afterward he introduced himself to Patrick and they immediately bonded as they talked at length about the situation in Boston. Patrick was so taken with Mason's keen intellect that he invited him to attend tonight's secret meeting.

528

"Well, George Mason is here," Nigel whispered to Liz as they sat in the dark shadows of the hallway. "I am not certain why Gillamon wanted us to ensure their meeting, but he and Patrick seem to have hit it off quite splendidly."

"Gillamon always has his reasons," Liz answered. "You may wish to keep tabs on Mason to shed any light on their relationship."

"Will do, my dear," Nigel assured her, clasping his paws behind his back. "It is good to see these brilliant men taking action. Al and I overheard King George declare, *'The die is now cast. The colonies must either submit or triumph.'*"

"*Oui,* the die is cast. It is clear that these men will *not* submit. But I cannot believe that more trouble is coming beyond the Boston Port Bill," Liz lamented. "When Patrick learns about the other Coercive Acts passed by Parliament, *ooh-la-la!* He will be even more furious!"

"Those acts are beyond coercive! They are utterly *intolerable!*" Nigel ranted, clucking his tongue and shaking his head as he recalled all he had learned before leaving London. "The *Massachusetts Government Act* will take away the colony's charter. The *Impartial Administration of Justice Act* will send royal officials charged with capital crimes to trial in *England,* not in the colonies—like Captain Preston and his men after the Boston Massacre. The revised *Quartering Act* will allow British soldiers to take over *private homes* to house troops! The *Quebec Act* will set up a permanent administration in Canada and extend Canadian borders, taking away land earmarked for the colonies. Intolerable, all of them!"

"And once General Gage takes over as a *military* governor and lands *eight* regiments of troops, Boston will suffer greatly." Liz slowly shook her head. "I know *mon* Henry wants immediate action, but this will take a little while. His idea of a day of fasting, humiliation, and prayer will move the people, and the people will then move the burgesses."

"But first, the *Voice That Is Hungry* will no doubt move Lord Dunmore."

529

COUNCIL CHAMBER, CAPITOL BUILDING, WILLIAMSBURG, MAY 26, 1774

Governor Dunmore picked up the morning's *Virginia Gazette* and his face turned red as he saw what the House of Burgesses had passed two days earlier, right under his nose. Robert Carter Nicholas was chosen to present the resolution to the House, and it was unanimously adopted with no discussion.

"They dare to call for a day of fasting, humiliation, and prayer on June 1 to coincide with the closing of the port of Boston '*to implore heaven to avert from us the evils of civil war, to inspire us with firmness in support of our rights, and to turn the hearts of the King and Parliament to moderation and justice,'*" Dunmore read aloud. He slammed his fist on the table and glared at his clerk. "Bring me those burgesses this instant!"

As they had done before, Patrick Henry and the rest of the burgesses climbed the steps of the Capitol building and crowded into the Council Chamber upstairs to receive the wrath of Virginia's royal governor. Lord Dunmore scowled and held up the *Gazette*. "This paper is conceived in such terms as reflect highly upon his Majesty and the Parliament of

Great Britain, which makes it necessary for me to dissolve you; and you are dissolved accordingly."

The burgesses quietly turned and walked down the stairs. Thomas Jefferson leaned over to Patrick Henry with a grin. "I know where we're going this time to continue the discussion on the Boston Port Bill. On to the Raleigh for a bite, Mr. Henry?"

Patrick smiled, patted Thomas on the back, and held out his hand as they stepped out the door of the Capitol onto Duke of Gloucester Street. "After you, Mr. Jefferson. I'm famished."

RALEIGH TAVERN, WILLIAMSBURG, MAY 26, 1774

Eighty-nine former burgesses met and signed another agreement to halt the import of British goods, but stopped short of calling for an annual intercolonial meeting, as Patrick Henry and Richard Henry Lee wanted. George Mason joined in the extra-legal meeting of the former burgesses as they made plans to proceed with the day of fasting, humiliation, and prayer. Flags would be lowered to half-staff, bells would toll, businesses would close, and the people would call on Almighty God to help the people of Boston.

That evening, George Mason retired to his room, took out paper and quill, and proceeded to write to a friend about how the plans to protest the Boston Port Bill had been quietly made in Williamsburg by a handful of men, with Patrick Henry leading the way:

> *He is by far the most powerful speaker I have ever heard. Every word he says not only engages but commands the attention; and your passions are no longer your own when he addresses them. But his eloquence is the smallest part of his merit. He is in my opinion the first man upon this continent, as well in abilities as public virtues, and had he lived in Rome . . . Mr. Henry's talents must have put him at the head of that glorious commonwealth.*

"I couldn't agree more, old boy, seeing how I was *there* to observe that glorious Roman commonwealth." Nigel beamed with pride from the shadows. "Now to see what happens as the voice that is hungry is heard throughout Virginia. I believe the first man upon this continent will no doubt get his First Continental Congress indeed."

To Philadelphia

WILLIAMSBURG, AUGUST 6, 1774

Things moved quickly through Virginia following the day of fasting, humiliation, and prayer. Churches collected food and supplies to send to weary Boston. Dissenting pastors and even parish rectors preached stirring sermons on liberty. Taverns filled with the sounds of toasts and liberty songs, and effigies of General Gage were burned as citizens railed against the British lion. Patriotic fervor was roused against the Coercive Acts, or the "Intolerable Acts" as they were now called by the colonists. The Virginia Committee of Correspondence called for an intercolonial congress, and by June, letters of approval were pouring in from sister colonies with sentiments such as those from the Philadelphia Committee that "all America look up to Virginia to take the lead on the present occasion."

Counties across Virginia mobilized to send representatives to attend an extra-legal convention on August 1 in Williamsburg. Lord Dunmore had departed the city in mid-July to take personal command of the war with the Indians out on the frontier, calling up the frontier militia commanders like Andrew and Charles Lewis to meet him out west. The Governor planned to call the dissolved burgesses back in session in November, after he had secured a peace treaty with the Indians—and secured popularity for himself by being a hero. Patrick Henry, George Washington, and Andrew Lewis were in favor of Dunmore's move as they each had land interests on the frontier of Ohio and Kentucky. Patrick Henry's sister, Anne, who was married to Colonel William Christian, and their friends Samuel and Elizabeth Crowley, lived in that hazardous region, so Patrick also had a personal interest in keeping the Indian threat at bay. But with Lord Dunmore gone, the ex-burgesses could meet freely in Williamsburg, and not at the Raleigh Tavern. While the cat was away, the mice would play—right inside the Capitol building while the portraits of King George and Queen Charlotte looked on.

On July 20 in Hanover County, the freeholders gathered on the steps of Hanover Courthouse to select Patrick Henry and his half-brother John Syme, Jr., to attend the extra-legal convention in Williamsburg. They read an eloquent statement and list of instructions for the men as they represented the people of Hanover. The instructions indicated they were in no position to judge Boston in regard to the tea incident:

> *But this we know, that the Parliament, by their proceedings, have made us and all North America, parties in the present dispute, and deeply interested in the event of it; insomuch, that if our sister colony of Massachusetts Bay is enslaved, we cannot long remain free ... We will never be taxed but by our own representatives ... We judge it conducive to the interests of America, that a general congress of deputies from all the colonies be held, in order to form a plan for guarding the claims of the colonists and their constitutional rights ... UNITED WE STAND, DIVIDED WE FALL.*

More than one hundred men, minus the frontier delegates, gathered in Williamsburg on August 1 for the First Virginia Convention. They debated about what they should do in regard to halting imports from, and exports to, Great Britain. They agreed to cancel the importation of slaves, something Patrick Henry had pressed for. They also passed resolutions denying the import of British goods, and especially banning the consumption of British tea. Some sought to gain sympathy from the British people with correspondence while the more militant Patrick Henry and the Lees sought a clear demonstration of strength in response to the Intolerable Acts. But after a week, they did at least agree on seven delegates to send to the Congress in Philadelphia to find a solution with the other colonies: Speaker Peyton Randolph, Richard Henry Lee, George Washington, Patrick Henry, Richard Bland, Benjamin Harrison, and Edmund Pendleton. While there was disagreement between these liberals and conservatives, they were the most brilliant, experienced minds Virginia had to offer. The Virginia Convention instructed them to express their loyalty to the king, to express concern for the unconstitutional measures against

Massachusetts, to put an end to arbitrary taxation, and to offer aid to the people of Boston.

George Washington, who rarely spoke in public, offered up an inspiring pledge to the hearty cheers of the men of the Convention: "I will raise one thousand men, subsist them at my own expense, and march myself at their head to the relief of Boston."

When the convention adjourned, George Washington walked up to Patrick Henry, as the representatives exited the Capitol. "Mr. Henry, why don't you come to Mount Vernon on your way north? We'll ride to Philadelphia together."

"Nothing would please me more, Colonel," Patrick answered with a broad smile and a handshake.

"Splendid. Martha and I will look forward to hosting you," Washington answered. "I'll invite Mr. Mason to join us from Gunston Hall. We will have much to discuss by then, I am sure."

"I have no doubt. I look forward to it," Patrick replied, spotting Edmund Pendleton walking toward them.

George Washington tightened his lip. "Mr. Pendleton will also be joining us at Mt. Vernon, and mentioned riding with you from Scotchtown. I know you two do not see eye to eye on a great many things. It could make for a tense journey."

"I will keep a bridle for my mouth as well as for my horse when riding with Mr. Pendleton," Patrick said with a wry smile, patting MizP. "United we stand, divided we fall."

"Including falling from your horses," MizP whinnied.

533

———

SCOTCHTOWN, AUGUST 29, 1774

Liz and Kate sat on the brick floor of Sallie's bedroom, watching Patrick and Sallie. He was gently brushing her long hair with the silver brush he had given her that first Christmas so long ago. He recounted happy stories and memories of their life together but Sallie didn't respond. They sat there for a few minutes in silence as Patrick continued to brush her hair.

"They talk to me," Sallie suddenly muttered in a faint whisper, staring at the animals.

"Who, my love?" Patrick answered eagerly. Sallie rarely said anything now, so he grew animated to hear her speak. He put two fingers under her chin to lift her eyes to his, searching her face for signs of his Sallie. "Who talks to you?"

"Them," Sallie replied, pointing to Liz and Kate. "They told me not to be afraid." She looked Patrick in the eye and gave a slight smile. "I'm not alone." Just as quickly as her lucid moment came, it vanished. The blankness returned to her eyes and her smile faded into an emotionless expression.

Patrick glanced over at Liz and Kate. A lump grew in his throat. He clenched his jaw against such a mad thought from his mentally lost wife. How he wanted to believe her! Suddenly the story of Balaam's talking donkey filled his mind. *If a donkey talked to a human, why not a dog or a cat?* Tears quickened in Patrick's eyes and he wore a sad smile. He kissed the top of Sallie's head and wrapped his arms around her. "That's right, my love. You are not alone," he said as his voice cracked with emotion. He set the brush down on the table and cleared his throat. "I'll be back soon."

534

Liz's eyes brimmed with tears as Patrick walked over to pet her and Kate before he left the room. It was time for him to mount MizP and ride to Philadelphia. "Thank you, little ones. Take care of my girl," he whispered in a broken voice. He gave one last glance at Sallie, who sat quietly in the chair by her bed, now gazing up to the window as her children ran past outside. Patrick put on his hat and left the room.

BOSTON, SEPTEMBER 1, 1774

"Looks like General Gage might be thinkin' differently aboot these patr-r-riots now," Max pointed out with a stout grin. He and Clarie watched the British Redcoats stand their ground as the Massachusetts Minute Men dispersed without violence. General Gage had ordered seizure of the military stores and gunpowder from the arsenal in Boston, and thousands of militia troops had marched on the town, but their leaders had urged calm. No incident took place.

"Yes, the rumors in London of American 'cowardice' led the British to think that the presence of their famed Redcoat army would effortlessly put a stop to any rebellion." Clarie smiled. She was in the form of a militia soldier. "They believed that with a few regiments, the Redcoats could 'advance from one end of America to the other, and at the first sound of English muskets the Americans would run for their lives.'"

"But that ain't the case now, is it?" Max growled, wagging his tail. "These Minute Men showed them that the Amer-r-rican laddies won't back off fr-r-rom a fight!"

Clarie's smile faded, and she furrowed her brow, rubbing Max on the scruff of his neck. "And when they won't back off from a fight, patriot blood will be spilled. But that is the price of liberty."

Max turned and looked at Clarie with grave concern. "When's it goin' ta start, lass? An' where?"

"Soon. Out on the frontier. Lord Dunmore is leading two forces of militia to fight the Indians. He himself commands the Northern Army, with Colonel Adam Stephen as his first officer. Dunmore has assigned Colonel Andrew Lewis to command the Southern Army, and to meet him at the mouth of the Kanawha River. From there Dunmore has told them they will pursue and subdue the Indians north of the Ohio River."

Max cocked his head in confusion. "Indians? But I thought this comin' fight were goin' ta be with the Br-r-ritish."

535

"It will be," Clarie answered, not offering up any explanation beyond that. She let go a heavy sigh, picking up her musket. She pulled out a piece of parchment with the Order of the Seven seal, ready to send Max through the IAMISPHERE. "I've got to get going while you join Gillamon, Nigel, and Cato in Philadelphia. The Enemy will try to break up the unity of the First Continental Congress. Gillamon will give you further instructions when you arrive."

"Philadelphia? But don't ye need me on the fr-r-rontier with those Virginia laddies?" questioned Max.

"Not for this first battle, Max," Clarie answered, ready to break the Seven seal to open the IAMISPHERE.

Max frowned, not understanding what this could mean. "So where're ye goin' then?"

As Clarie broke the Seven seal, she exclaimed, "To meet Colonel Andrew Lewis's Southern Army, at a place called Point Pleasant."

A Voice Unified

PHILADELPHIA, SEPTEMBER 4, 1774

S o, when Cato said, *'It is not now a time to talk of aught, but chains or conquest; liberty or death,'* he was telling Juba that greater things were happening at the moment?" Cato asked Nigel. "Now was not the time to talk about love that the young man had for his daughter, is that right?" The eagle had asked the little mouse to recite the play *Cato* on their journey to Philadelphia.

Patrick Henry and Edmund Pendleton had arrived at Mount Vernon the evening of August 30, and spent the night dining and discussing matters with George Washington and neighbor George Mason who joined them. The next day after lunch, Martha Washington had sent the men off on their journey: "I hope you will all stand firm. I know George will."

Cato, with Nigel aboard, had followed Patrick Henry, George Washington, and Edmund Pendleton as they rode on horseback from Mount Vernon. It had taken four days to travel the 150 miles, and the men had stayed in taverns and inns along the way. Nigel had recited and explained the entire play *Cato* to the eagle, who had grown more thoughtful about the origin of his name.

"Precisely, dear boy," Nigel replied, scanning the green countryside of Pennsylvania.

Cato thought for a moment. "How long do you think we'll be in Philadelphia?"

"I would imagine several weeks, why?" Nigel asked.

"Well, like Juba, I'm thinking about love, Nigel," Cato answered with a grin. "I'd like to finally find a mate, build a nest, and have some eaglets. That is, if it would be okay with you. I would need to stay here for five months at least."

Nigel wiggled his whiskers happily and patted Cato on the neck. "My dear boy, this is glorious news! Of course, you *should* have a family here in the city of your birth, although I do not see the Congress meeting for five months. Why, that would be utterly preposterous! If the representatives cannot finish their business for the people in a matter of several weeks, then they clearly need to be replaced!"

"Thank you, Nigel," Cato replied happily. "I didn't want to let you or the team down. Liz said I'm to do something special for the Maker, so I don't want to let Him down, either. I don't want to be like Juba and talk about love if greater things are at hand."

"You shall not let anyone down, old chap. I am certain the Maker will let us know when greater things such as liberty or death spring up. You go find that special she-eagle and build that nest." Nigel gave a jolly chuckle. "I can always return to Virginia via pigeon, although I've become rather accustomed to flying first class courtesy of your impressive wingspan."

537

"There is nothing wrong with flying pigeon-class," Cato answered with a laugh. He scanned the ground below. "What is happening down there?"

"Will you just *look* at that grand reception for our merry trio of delegates? Why, it's still six miles until they enter Philadelphia!" Nigel enthused, surveying the road below.

"Looks like the people are excited to see the Virginians' arrival," Cato answered with a smile. "Someone must have told them Patrick Henry and George Washington were coming."

Suddenly Nigel spotted a distinguished gentleman in the middle of the crowd wearing a magnificent red cloak. A black Scottie dog was at his side, wagging his tail. "I believe I know exactly who that was." Nigel waved at Gillamon and Max. Gillamon held out his arms and bowed in welcome as he smiled up at them.

"Looks like delegates from other colonies are arriving, too," Cato added, spotting other men on horseback, shaking the hand of Edmund Pendleton. They were men from North Carolina, Maryland, and Delaware. "This is exciting to see, Nigel!"

More than five hundred people lined the streets, cheering the men who would make up the First Continental Congress. A band of fifes and drums played music, Philadelphia riflemen and infantrymen stood at attention, and gentlemen on horseback tipped their hats respectfully to Colonel Washington, hero of the French and Indian War. The people shouted huzzahs for the man whose Stamp Act Resolves had first set the colonies ablaze in defiance of British tyranny and gave rise to the Sons of Liberty: Patrick Henry.

Patrick and George exchanged surprised looks, and a broad smile appeared on Patrick's face as something dawned on him. "Please keep this between us, Colonel, but I just realized that you and I are in quite the exclusive club."

George Washington lifted a hand in greeting to some soldiers and turned with a puzzled look toward Patrick. "What do you mean, Mr. Henry?"

"Well, technically *you* started the French and Indian War, did you not?" Patrick asked, waving at some cheering patriots as MizP clip-clopped along. She winked at Max as they passed, but Patrick didn't see Max or Mr. Gillamon.

538

"Technically, yes," George replied with a frown, followed by a growing realization coming to his mind. "Not that I desired war."

"And if this emerging Revolution leads to war, as I certainly believe it will . . ." Patrick started to say.

"Then *you* will have technically started a war with your Stamp Act Resolves—a Revolutionary War," George interjected. He gave an uncharacteristic, singular laugh. "An exclusive club indeed, Mr. Henry."

Patrick nodded. "Not that I desire war either, Colonel. But that precious jewel of liberty is worth fighting for."

"That it is, Mr. Henry," George Washington replied. "That it is."

While Nigel and Cato soared above, and Gillamon and Max cheered below, the delegates were escorted into Philadelphia and to the finest establishment in America: the City Tavern. With its large club rooms and fifty-foot-long dining room, the City Tavern quickly became the gathering place for the fifty-six delegates, assembled from every colony except Georgia. Georgia was seeking assistance from the British with the Indian problem out on its frontier, and opted not to attend the Congress so as not to adversely affect that matter.

After dinner, the Virginians were escorted to the home of Dr. William Shippen, brother-in-law of Richard Henry Lee. Lee had arrived earlier from Virginia, along with Peyton Randolph, Benjamin Harrison, and Richard Bland. The Congress was to have opened on Thursday, September 1, but with the late arrival of many delegates, especially these Virginians, they had to postpone. They hoped enough representatives would be present by tomorrow, September 5.

Richard met Patrick at the door with an enthusiastic handshake and a broad smile. "Welcome to Philadelphia!" He quickly gave them the news of the men they had already met, including the famous Boston men—John and Sam Adams—who instantly took a liking to the Virginians. Letters of encouragement and support had arrived for the delegates, and before they turned in for the night, Richard handed Patrick a letter from a Colonel Adam Stephen from Virginia. Colonel Stephen had served as second in command under George Washington in the French and Indian War, and now headed up Lord Dunmore's northern army. Colonel Stephen had long corresponded with Richard Henry Lee about the frontier, ever since the French and Indian War.

"A gentleman wearing a striking red cloak delivered Colonel's Stephen's letter to me here in Philadelphia, as it had arrived after I left Virginia," Richard explained. "He said he hoped you would also read it before the convention. He also said to tell you he will host a dinner soon and welcomes us to be his guests. Mr. Gillamon was his name, I believe."

539

Patrick's eyes widened with surprised delight as he took the letter. "Mr. Gillamon? He's here, in Philadelphia?!"

"Yes. He's quite the distinguished gentleman, I might add. And he spoke highly of you," Richard answered with a smile and a hand on Patrick's shoulder. "Good night, Pat. Sleep well. We have a big day tomorrow."

"Good night, Richard. Yes, we do," Patrick answered. He closed the bedroom door, kicked off his shoes, and sat on the edge of the bed, tossing his wig on the nightstand. He smiled to think of his old friend Mr. Gillamon who still took an interest in him. He couldn't wait to see the older gentleman here in Philadelphia.

Patrick unfolded the letter and held it up to read by the light of the small candle. He nodded as he read Colonel Stephens's words, which encouraged the colonies to prepare militarily.

"Lord Dunmore orders me to the Ohio with his lordship to endeavor to put matters on a footing to establish a lasting peace with the brave natives. This prevents my attending the general Congress. The fate of America depends upon your meeting; and the eyes of the European world hang upon you,

waiting the event . . . let us be provided with arms and ammunition, and individuals may suffer, but the gates of hell cannot prevail against America.

Patrick then reread one sentence that gripped his heart:

The fate of America depends upon your meeting; and the eyes of the European world hang upon you, waiting the event.

Patrick furrowed his brow with the weight of that sentence. "The fate of America," he said to himself. "Not just Virginia. *America*. Not just one colony. One nation. May God guide our steps." The exhausted patriot set the letter down, blew out his candle, and quickly fell asleep.

"One nation under God, my good fellow," Nigel muttered from the shadows, there to confirm that Patrick had read the letter, which he would report back to Gillamon. "It is time for the next part of the fiddle's riddle to unfold: *A Voice Unified.* The fate of America indeed depends upon this meeting."

———

540

PHILADELPHIA, SEPTEMBER 5, 1774, 10:00 A.M.

"HUZZAH! We count forty-five delegates present! We have a quorum! We can finally open the Congress!" the men cheered in the club rooms of the City Tavern. Several more delegates were due to arrive, but there were enough present to begin proceedings. Together they walked outside and excitedly marched two blocks up the street, over Dock Creek Bridge, took a left onto narrow Whalebone Alley, and entered a beautiful courtyard. There before them was a two-story brick building in the shape of a cross, called Carpenters' Hall. Patrick Henry, George Washington, and Richard Henry Lee exchanged expectant smiles and ascended the stone steps into the newly completed building.

Carpenters' Hall was owned by The Carpenters' Company of Philadelphia, the oldest craft guild in the colonies. Founded in 1724 in the tradition of the Worshipful Company of Carpenters in London, the guild was made up of carpenters, bricklayers, masons, painters, and other artisans. When construction of a house was contracted for, it was the carpenter who oversaw every step of the process, from design to construction to completion. The master carpenter was the force behind building something from nothing; he was the Master Builder.

The Carpenters' Company of Philadelphia was made up of the cream of the crop of immigrants who had come to America to build a new world. They weren't bewigged aristocrats, but neither were they street rabble. They represented the common people, the backbone of America. These artisans had built The Pennsylvania State House, Christ Church, St. Peter's Church, and now, Carpenters' Hall. Benjamin Franklin's Library Company found its home on the second floor in this newly constructed building, which thereby was housing the first library in America. The Hall was intended as meeting space for the guild, as a place to conduct business, and as a source of rental income.

Robert Smith, who designed the building, had also coincidentally designed America's first insane asylum in Williamsburg—where Patrick Henry had visited when he was exploring options for a way to care for Sallie. Smith served on the Philadelphia Committee of Correspondence. He had offered up the Hall as the meeting place for the First Continental Congress after a certain "Mr. Gillamon" paid him a visit with the idea of using the Hall as neutral ground for the delegates.

Rather than meet in the Pennsylvania State House—the seat of government of the host colony, owned by Great Britain and heavily guarded by conservatives loyal to the Crown—the delegates could meet and freely discuss their ideas on neutral ground, in a privately owned meeting room in Carpenters' Hall. While Smith's work in Williamsburg did not meet Patrick's personal needs for Sallie, it perfectly met Patrick's professional needs in Philadelphia for the Congress. Here conservatives like Joseph Galloway from Philadelphia and John Jay and James Duane of New York could meet on a level playing field with radicals such as John and Sam Adams, Patrick Henry, and Richard Henry Lee. Here they could seek unity in the midst of their differences.

Robert Smith proudly opened the doors to the large twenty-by-thirty-foot east room. The delegates entered to the smell of fresh paint and the gleaming heart-pine floors. Sturdy Windsor chairs awaited them in a semicircle. The clean fireplace would not be needed in the sweltering heat of this September morning, but everything else was perfect.

Nigel awaited them from the rafters of the library, pleased with this clever choice of meeting space. Carpenters' Hall had been secured by John Adams and Richard Henry Lee before the delegates had all arrived in Philadelphia. "Bravo, Gillamon. There could be no more appropriate place for the Master Carpenter to build a new nation."

The first order of business was to elect Peyton Randolph as president of the Congress, and Charles Thomson as secretary. After hearing the commissions read by each colony's delegation, there arose a problem that started the first debate in Congress: How would they vote? By a majority rule? What about the differing population sizes of the colonies? This question could already undermine their unified beginning. Conservative James Duane and radical John Adams were already debating the answer, but soon the room grew uncomfortable. Everyone looked around in silence until, finally, Patrick Henry took the floor.

Patrick was wearing a dark gray suit and a plain, unpowdered brown wig. With his characteristic stoop and grave appearance, he looked more like a humble parson than the fiery orator from Virginia. Charles Thomson looked him over from his secretarial seat, not knowing who he was. *He must be some Presbyterian clergyman, used to haranguing the people. How sad that a country parson should so mistake his talents and audience.*

As usual, Patrick started off slowly with a humble voice. But soon his eloquence rolled off his tongue, and members began to turn to each other, asking, "Who is it? Who is it?"

542

Patrick Henry soon made his identity unmistakable.

"We are met here in a time and on an occasion of great difficulty and distress," Patrick began. "Our public circumstances are like those of a man in deep embarrassment and trouble, who calls his friends together to devise what is best to be done for his relief. One would propose one thing, and another a different one, while perhaps a third would think of something better suited to his unhappy circumstances. This he would embrace, and think no more of the rejected schemes with which he would have nothing to do.

"This is the first general congress which has ever happened; no former congress can be a precedent. I submit that we will have occasion for more General Congresses, therefore a precedent should be established now," Patrick suggested. "It would be a great injustice if a little colony should have the same weight in the councils of America as a great one."

New Hampshire delegate John Sullivan quickly rose to his feet. "A little colony has its all at stake as well as a great one."

Immediately the assembly began debating the issue. Patrick Henry took his seat after suggesting that a committee devise a plan for fair and equal representation.

Nigel raised his eyebrows as he stared at Patrick's furrowed brow and pensive state as the debate continued throughout the afternoon, with no answer in sight. "I say, it appears the master orator has been given pause to think this through a bit more before his is truly a voice unified."

———

CARPENTERS' HALL, PHILADELPHIA, SEPTEMBER 6, 1774

The Congress convened again at 10:00 a.m. and picked up where they had left off the previous day. It wasn't long before Patrick Henry once again took the floor. He had indeed thought how to better clarify what was needed in this First Continental Congress.

"By the oppression of Parliament, all government is dissolved. Fleets and armies and the present state of things show that government is dissolved," Patrick Henry declared, drawing surprised looks from the assembly. "Where are your landmarks, your boundaries of Colonies? We are in a state of nature, sir. I do propose a scale should be laid down; that part of North America which was once Massachusetts Bay, and that part which was once Virginia, ought to be considered as having a weight. Will not people complain? Ten thousand Virginians have not outweighed one thousand others. I will submit, however; I am determined to submit, if I am overruled."

543

Patrick looked around the assembly room and walked calmly a few steps, glancing at John Sullivan. "A worthy gentleman near me seems to admit the necessity of obtaining a more adequate representation." He walked a few more paces and locked eyes with Richard Henry Lee, who gave him an affirming nod. He lifted his chin and slowly, quietly clapped his hands. "I hope future ages will quote our proceedings with applause. It is one of the great duties of the democratical part of the constitution to keep itself pure. It is known in my province that some other colonies are not so numerous or rich as they are. I am for giving all the satisfaction in my power."

Patrick's voice began to rise in its urgency, causing the assembly to hang on every word. "The distinctions between Virginians, Pennsylvanians, New Yorkers, and New Englanders, are no more." He paused and raised a fist of unity and victory in the air and exclaimed loudly and proudly, "I am not a Virginian, but an *American.*"

"Hear, hear!" John Adams exclaimed, pounding his fist on the table in approval, along with other members of the Congress who agreed with

Patrick. He marveled at what he had just heard. *Patrick Henry is the only man in this Congress who appears to understand the precipice on which we stand. And he has the candor and courage enough to acknowledge it. I will have to write Abigail about this insightful man.*

Richard Henry Lee quickly raised a practical question of whether Congress was even capable of knowing the importance of each colony. There were no exact facts and figures on population, after all. After a bit more debate, it was finally decided that each colony would have one, singular vote in this First Continental Congress. But all the delegates agreed that this voting method would not be locked in as the precedent for future sessions, as circumstances might dictate a better way to ensure fairness.

"A voice unified at last," stated Nigel, preening his whiskers proudly. He breathed a deep sigh of satisfaction, but was then startled as he heard loud voices shouting outside.

Suddenly the doors to the meeting room burst open and an unknown messenger exclaimed, "Boston has been attacked! The city was shelled by the British navy!" Quickly the messenger left the hall as the assembly got to their feet.

544

The Massachusetts men rushed out to the streets, eager to confirm the story and get more information of what was happening back home. Patrick Henry and the rest of the Congress filed out onto the streets after them.

"WAR! WAR! WAR!" the people cried as they ran down the streets.

The delegates looked at one another in alarm. But from the shadows, a sinister pair of eyes filled with delight.

GOD BLESS AMERICA

Geneneral Gage tried to seize the gunpowder from a magazine in Cambridge," one man shouted in alarm.

"I heard six citizens were killed in the fight!" another man added. "It's another Boston Massacre!"

"People have taken up arms all the way to Connecticut!" still another declared.

Panic filled the streets as the bells tolled, but something wasn't quite right. The men quickly saw that the stories were conflicted. The rumor mill fueled chaos, and it soon became clear that the information had come from an unconfirmed source. They would need to wait for more reliable news to verify what had happened in Boston.

Gillamon stood by with Max and Nigel and tightened his mouth. "There has been no attack in Boston. Someone is trying to create panic and break up the Congress with this false news." He looked down at the two friends. "Someone who is the author of chaos. We must keep a keen eye out for other such maneuvers. Max, I need you to keep that keen *nose* of yours on the alert to sniff out trouble."

"Aye! I'll r-r-root out any smelly minions," Max barked, sniffing around. "Gillamon, I smell somethin' foul in the air."

"Heaven help them," Nigel lamented, watching the delegates who huddled together, trying to bring calm back to the situation and return the Congress to Carpenters' Hall to resume the meeting.

"Heaven help them, indeed. War is coming, but not yet. Not until they are prepared with the proper armor—and not dependent on their own strength to fight. Excuse me while I have a little chat with Mr.

Adams and Mr. Cushing," Gillamon said, his eyes following the round-faced Boston firebrand Sam Adams as he made his way back toward Carpenters' Hall with the speaker of the Massachusetts House, Thomas Cushing. "I need to offer an encouraging word to this doubting Thomas, and drop a little heavenly name in Sam's ear."

Max and Nigel looked at one another and shrugged their shoulders. They never knew what Gillamon was going to do, but one thing was certain. He always found a way to impact the tiniest of details, which in turn would impact the grandest of moments in history.

———

Once back inside, the Congress attempted to reign in their emotions to focus once more on the task at hand. They decided that from here on they would need to keep their meetings secret, allowing no one to enter unless approved by the Congress. The door to Carpenters' Hall would be bolted shut each day. They would not reveal any of their discussions or decisions until they were ready to publish the whole of their work. They decided to form two committees, one to draft a statement of colonial rights and grievances, and one to halt trade with England.

As the afternoon close of the session neared, Speaker Thomas Cushing of the Massachusetts House rose to his feet and addressed President Peyton Randolph. "Sir, given the uncertainty of the news from Boston, and the gravity of these proceedings, I humbly request that we open up tomorrow morning's session with prayer."

"If I may, sir, wouldn't private devotions be adequate?" John Jay offered above the murmuring in the room. "Our members are divided in religious sentiments, so formal worship might cause friction."

Sam Adams cleared his throat and got to his feet. Peyton Randolph nodded with a hand out for him to speak. "I am no bigot. But I could hear a prayer from any gentleman of piety and virtue, who is at the same time a friend to his country," Sam offered. "Although I am a stranger in Philadelphia, I have heard about an Episcopal minister, a Mr. Jacob Duché from Christ Church, who is deserving of such character. Might we hope that he could come tomorrow and read prayers for our assembly?"

Nigel stood high in his windowsill perch, smiling as the assembly grew calm and agreed to Sam's suggestion. "A heavenly name in his ear," he said, knowing it was Gillamon who had suggested Duché.

546

CARPENTERS' HALL, PHILADELPHIA, SEPTEMBER 7, 1774

The bells were still ringing in the city, anxious for the truth about the situation in Boston. The fifty-six delegates filed quietly into the hall, wearing anxious looks and murmuring amongst themselves: "Has any reliable news arrived?" "Is it really war?" They knew they were not yet ready to face that reality. The gentlemen found their way to their Windsor chairs and sat down. Once Peyton Randolph called them to order, Reverend Duché entered the hall, wearing his full formal rector attire. Patrick Henry locked eyes with Samuel Adams and nodded.

Reverend Duché lifted his hands in greeting with a warm smile and opened the *Book of Common Prayer*. Those delegates who remained loyal to the Church of England were pleased. "In His divine wisdom, God has provided a timely word from today's reading. Hear now, the word of the Lord, from the Thirty-Fifth Psalm:

"Plead *my cause*, O LORD, with those who strive with me; Fight against those who fight against me.
Take hold of shield and buckler, and stand up for my help.
Also draw out the spear, and stop those who pursue me.
Say to my soul, 'I *am* your salvation.'"

547

Nigel's heart swelled with joy to watch the First Continental Congress hear the blessed assurance that God would arm them with strength. They hung on every word of the Psalm as Reverend Duché read it in its entirety. When he reached the end of the Psalm, he paused and turned the page to read the prayer in the little book that followed the daily reading. Then he looked around the room at the men, closed the book and set it on the table. The Quakers and other Dissenter delegates shared approving glances. They were delightfully surprised. He wasn't going to simply read a prayer; he was going to pray from his heart. Reverend Duché held up his hands and quietly requested, "Let us pray."

Slowly Patrick Henry slid off his Windsor chair and got to his knees, turning to rest his face atop his folded hands as he leaned his elbows on the seat of the chair. Many of the other delegates did the same while others sat or stood in humble reverence. At that holy moment, the Reverend filled the room not with a general, pre-written prayer in a book, but with a prayer from the deep recesses of his soul.

"O Lord our Heavenly Father, high and mighty King of kings and Lord of lords, who dost from Thy throne behold all the dwellers on Earth and reignest with power supreme and uncontrolled over all the kingdoms, empires and governments; look down in mercy, we beseech Thee, on these our American States, who have fled to Thee from the rod of the oppressor and thrown themselves on Thy gracious protection, desiring to be henceforth dependent only on Thee. To Thee have they appealed for the righteousness of their cause; to Thee do they now look up for that countenance and support, which Thou alone canst give. Take them, therefore, Heavenly Father, under Thy nurturing care; give them wisdom in council and valor in the field; defeat the malicious designs of our cruel adversaries; convince them of the unrighteousness of their cause, and if they persist in their sanguinary purposes, of own unerring justice, sounding in their hearts, constrain them to drop the weapons of war from their unnerved hands in the day of battle!

"Be Thou present, O God of wisdom, and direct the councils of this honorable assembly; enable them to settle things on the best and surest foundation. That the scene of blood may be speedily closed; that order, harmony, and peace may be effectually restored, and truth and justice, religion and piety, prevail and flourish amongst the people. Preserve the health of their bodies and vigor of their minds; shower down on them and the millions here they represent, such temporal blessings as Thou seest expedient for them in this world and crown them with everlasting glory in the world to come. All this we ask in the name and through the merits of Jesus Christ, Thy Son and our Savior. Amen."

"Now THAT is the way to start a Congress," Nigel opined, lifting his gaze following the astounding prayer. The delegates rose to their feet with heads held high and now wore expressions of confident eagerness. The entire room was transformed, and the fear and anxiety from yesterday's news from Boston evaporated, even before they had received word that the information was false. "And THAT is exactly the kind of prayer the Maker will answer."

A messenger did in fact arrive from Boston the day after the Congress opened up with prayer with the news that there had been no bloodshed and no bombardment in Boston. But the false rumor had driven the delegates to their knees in prayer. After that day, they were driven to accomplish the task given them by the people they represented—the *American* people, as Patrick Henry now called them.

The weeks passed, and the committees trudged along to accomplish their work. Max patrolled the two blocks between Carpenters' Hall and the City Tavern, watching and smelling for any signs of trouble. Patrick Henry was lodging at the City Tavern for the duration of the Congress. Max checked in with MizP to see if she had seen anything suspicious. Nigel attended the daily sessions of Congress, as no bolted door could keep out the brilliant mouse. He gave daily updates of any progress to Gillamon, Max, and MizP. Gillamon waited until the right time to approach Patrick Henry, and invited him as well as Richard Henry Lee, George Washington, and John and Sam Adams to dinner at the house where he was residing while in Philadelphia.

They would be dining with Mr. Gillamon the following evening, but this night, as he frequently did, John Adams sat down to write to his wife, Abigail, about the things happening in the Congress. Little did he know, but he was being watched in the dimly lit room. He muttered aloud as he wrote with his quill.

549

"We go to Congress at nine, and there we stay, most earnestly engaged in debates upon the most abstruse mysteries of State, until three in the afternoon. The business of the Congress is tedious beyond expression. This assembly is like no other that ever existed." With twenty-two of the delegates being lawyers, and all the others being at least great orators, critics, or statesmen, every bit of business was drawn and spun out to consume a miserable length of time as each man made his opinion known.

But when Paul Revere delivered the Suffolk Resolves from Boston on September 18, there was great excitement in the Congress. Dr. Joseph Warren had called a meeting of patriots in Suffolk County, including the city of Boston, and drafted the strongest resolutions yet adopted by any American assembly. The Suffolk Resolves plainly stated "that no obedience is due from this province to . . . the recent act of Parliament, but that they should be rejected as the attempts of a wicked administration to enslave America." No taxes or monies from trade should be sent to the Crown until all grievances were redressed and Massachusetts was restored to a constitutional basis. Americans should not riot but act in an orderly way "so as to merit the approbation of the wise, and the admiration of the brave and free, of every age and country." Still, each town should be well armed for defense and trained in the manner of war. The day Congress ordered the publication and support of the Suffolk Resolves was one of the happiest days of John Adams's life. He wrote in his diary: *This day convinced me that America will support Massachusetts, or perish with her.*

The conservatives in Congress, however, became uneasy with such bold, radical, treasonous talk. Ten days after Congress approved the Suffolk Resolves, they had a strenuous debate to defeat Galloway's "Plan of the proposed Union between Great Britain and the Colonies," which was a British-styled parliamentary government that would have maintained the Crown's grip on the colonies. Patrick Henry and the Virginians would have no part of it, and defeated the plan.

Adams yawned and shook his head before dipping his quill in the ink to tell Abigail about the other side of life in Philadelphia. "Our tedious days are relieved with festive dinner parties nearly every day. It is a perpetual round of feasting. After Congress adjourns each day at four in the afternoon, the delegates go to dine with some of the nobles of Pennsylvania . . . and feast upon ten thousand delicacies, and sit drinking Madeira, Claret, and Burgundy till six or seven, then go home fatigued to death with business, company, and care." He yawned, patted his growing belly and gave a hearty chuckle, thinking about the dinner party he would attend the next night with Patrick Henry at the home of Mr. Gillamon. "I am being killed with kindness in this place."

As John Adams set down his quill and blew out his candle, the pair of eyes gleamed in the shadows. *Why thank you, Mr. Adams. Why hadn't I thought of that?*

550

Unjust Desserts and Passing the Mantle

W elcome, friends," greeted Gillamon as the servant opened the door for Patrick Henry, Richard Henry Lee, George Washington, and John and Sam Adams. "I'm so glad you could come."

"Thank you for having us, Mr. Gillamon," responded Patrick happily as he shook Gillamon's hand. "My friend, you never cease to amaze me! How is it that you have been there for so many key moments of my life's journey?"

Gillamon smiled and placed his hand on Patrick's shoulder. "I had a feeling about you from the time I met you as a boy, Patrick. I told you long ago that I have a special interest in young people." He leaned in to stare Patrick in the eye. "I believe in investing in lives, for they are the only things that are eternal."

"That you did, sir, and I hope the investment you have made in my life is paying off handsomely in your wise eyes," Patrick answered humbly.

Gillamon gave a firm nod and a wink. "More than you realize, Mr. Henry."

As Gillamon welcomed Richard, George, John, and Sam, Patrick spotted Max sitting in the corner. He walked over and crouched down to pet the Scottie. Max wagged his tail happily.

"Hello there, boy. I used to have a dog like you when I was young," Patrick reminisced.

Not jest like me, lad, Max thought with a grin as he licked Patrick's hand. *It were me. It's gr-r-rand ta see ye!*

"Mr. Gillamon, if you recall, I had a Scottie who looked just like yours here," shared Patrick, rising to his feet. "His name was Max."

Gillamon smiled. "Indeed I do remember what a fine animal he was, so I named mine 'Max' as well."

Patrick's face lit up with delight. "Remarkable!"

"I, too, have a special fondness for this breed. A Scottie kept me warm one frigid night before the war with the French. I attempted to cross an icy river and fell in, and out of nowhere a Scottie and a little Westie were there by my side," George Washington recounted, stooping to scratch Max under the chin, making his back foot scratch on reflex.

Aye, that were me then, too, lad, Max thought as he licked George Washington's hand.

Patrick immediately thought of Kate, who appeared out of nowhere at his father's funeral. *Remarkable, indeed.*

"I would welcome such a good breed to have on my farm. Rodents keep infesting my crops," George said, getting to his feet. "Scottish terriers are well bred to round them up."

"Indeed, there is no finer breed to protect humans and round up pests," Gillamon answered with a broad grin, winking at Max. "Gentlemen, shall we?" He held up his hand to usher his guests into the dining room.

As the men took their seats, servants bustled about, bringing in trays of delicacies and filling the guests' crystal goblets. Max stood guard watching the humans as they were being served.

"How have you enjoyed your stay here in Philadelphia, Mr. Gillamon?" John Adams asked. "I understand you hail from London."

"It's been a splendid stay, as always," Gillamon answered. "Although it is the largest city in America, its 25,000 inhabitants cannot, of course, match the million souls residing in the crowded city of London. But Philadelphia is a beautiful city, filled with so much activity, culture, and commerce. The theater here is especially grand."

"I do enjoy plays so would very much like to attend the theater while we are in Philadelphia," George Washington interjected. "What is currently playing?"

Gillamon smiled and looked at Patrick. "*Cato* will be performed soon. Perhaps we could attend together?"

Patrick tapped the table excitedly. "Mr. Gillamon, I would be delighted to go see *Cato* with you! I am not so fond of plays as is Colonel Washington, but this play I definitely would like to see." He turned to the other gentlemen at the table. "Mr. Gillamon actually sent me a copy of the play *Cato* when I was a youth. My father had just begun tutoring me, and quickly introduced me to *Plutarch's Lives*. I recall giving a report on Cato the Younger."

"*Cato* is a riveting story of patriotism," George Washington said as he nodded thoughtfully. "And it is undoubtedly my favorite play."

"I believe it is a favorite of many patriots gathered here at the Congress," John Adams added. "We may fill up the theater with delegates!"

"Let's make a night of it, shall we?" Richard Henry Lee suggested happily.

"Huzzah, it sounds as if you shall have an entourage to attend *Cato* with you, Mr. Gillamon," Patrick enthused.

"Nothing would please me more," Gillamon answered, with a good-natured glance at Max.

553

He's been plannin' this all along, Max thought with a grin.

"I'll make the arrangements," Gillamon offered. "My neighbor has actually done some work on theatrical costumes."

"I noticed the boarding house next door had a sign out front for a seamstress," Sam Adams noted.

"Yes, that seamstress is the *star* seamstress of Philadelphia, I assure you. In fact, I was so impressed with her work that I commissioned her to make me a new cloak," Gillamon answered, rising from the table to retrieve the new cloak to show the men. He handed it to George Washington. "Of course with the new non-importation of British goods, she made my cloak from homespun fabric."

George Washington raised his eyebrows. "I am quite impressed with her workmanship and will have to keep her in mind. What is her name?"

"Her name is Betsy Ross," Gillamon answered with a knowing grin.

"It is indeed a wonderful cloak, Mr. Gillamon, but I cannot imagine you not wearing that magnificent red cloak of yours," Patrick Henry added. "I've always admired it."

Gillamon smiled but didn't answer. Soon the servants brought in the first course of dinner and the men got into a lively discussion about the issue of the Indians out on the frontier. Lord Dunmore and his armies should have been engaged in battle by then, but the delegates had not heard any news from the Ohio country. Max sat and listened, catching Gillamon's eye occasionally and thinking about Clarie out there in the midst of the conflict.

"My compliments to your cook," Richard said, dabbing the corners of his mouth as the servants cleared their plates following the last course of dinner. "What a splendid meal!"

"Thank you, sir. Our regular cook suddenly took ill this afternoon, so we had to bring in a new cook this evening," the servant girl explained. "I'll pass on your kind compliment. Dessert will be out shortly."

Patrick Henry patted his stomach. "I don't know if I can eat another bite."

Max looked at the company of men gathered there. They were some of the most important men attending the First Continental Congress. Then Max grew concerned to hear that the regular cook "suddenly took ill." He growled and decided to make sure everything was secure. He followed the servant back to the kitchen, which was in a separate building behind the grand house.

554

"NOT THAT WAY!" the bossy cook screamed at the young girl assisting her. She grabbed the bowl and wooden spoon and beat in the sugar at a feverish pitch. "You must beat it into the cream without mercy. Now do it right before I box your ears again."

"Yes, Miss Charlotte," the servant girl replied fearfully. She took the bowl and spoon and did as she was told.

"And you, put the cakes and berries on the plates and set them on the tray," Charlotte ordered another girl. "I'm going to deliver the desserts myself, and need to change into something more presentable."

Max's eyes narrowed as he stared at the substitute cook, "Miss Charlotte." She was wearing a great deal of perfume that left a heavy waft of fragrance in the air as she stomped around the kitchen, barking orders at the servants. But it was anything but pleasant. It smelled sickly sweet, as if it was meant to cover up a heavy bad odor.

When Charlotte stepped out the back door of the kitchen to change, all the servants murmured against her.

"She is so *mean!* How did we get stuck with her?" one girl spat.

"And why would our usual cook send *her?*" another girl questioned. "I hope she's not here tomorrow. I don't think I can handle staying here another minute."

"What happened to our usual cook anyway?" a third girl asked. "She seemed fine yesterday."

"I don't know. Maybe it was something she ate," the first girl answered. "I don't care how good a cook this Charlotte is, or how much the guests like her meal, I hope she is gone tomorrow."

Somethin' she ate? Max growled. *I think this Charlotte ain't who she seems ta be.*

As Charlotte came back into the kitchen, she had tidied up her hair and slipped on a nicer dress. She inspected the silver serving tray to make sure the little cakes were topped with berries as she had ordered. When the servant girl with the bowl of cream came over to top the desserts, Charlotte snapped the bowl from her hands. "I'll do this. It needs to be done *right*. Go clean up the dishes," she grumbled. "All of you!"

The servant girls turned to take the dirty dishes out back to wash. When they were gone, Charlotte pulled a vial from her pocket. She smiled and poured it into the batter of cream. "Last but not least, my secret ingredient." She mixed in the liquid and poured the cream on top of the cakes. "Now to serve them their just desserts." She chuckled darkly and picked up the tray to leave the kitchen.

"Where do ye think ye're goin' with that tr-r-ray?" Max growled, standing in her way in the courtyard. "Ye can't hide yer foul stench, ye vile beastie."

Startled, Charlotte stopped in her tracks. She fumed and tried to kick Max. "Get out of my way, you pathetic minion."

As Charlotte attempted to walk on to the house, Max nipped at her ankles, grabbing the folds of her dress. "YE'RE NOT GOIN' ANY-WHERE!" he growled through his clenched jaws as he tugged and tugged.

"YOU PARASITE! GET OFF OF ME!" Charlotte screamed as she desperately tried to keep the tray from toppling over while struggling to get free of Max's grip.

Suddenly Max shook his head wildly and Charlotte lost her balance. The silver tray went flying through the air, sending the fine china plates crashing onto the brick courtyard.

"NO!" she screamed as she sat in the middle of the mess of broken dishes and dessert.

As Charlotte scrambled to her feet, Gillamon appeared at the doorway of the house to see what had happened. "BE GONE. You have no authority here."

555

Charlotte wore a grotesque expression but Max detected her shivering at Gillamon's rebuke, as if she was afraid. She scowled and ran off into the night.

"Gillamon, she were goin' ta poison those lads with them tainted tr-r-reats!" Max cried.

"Well done, Max. She's gone now," Gillamon answered with a frown. "I'll let our guests know there will be no dessert, which I don't think they will mind." He turned to go back in the house. "I'm sure they would prefer no desserts to unjust desserts."

———

CITY TAVERN, PHILADELPHIA, OCTOBER 20, 1774

At the end of six weeks, the First Continental Congress had accomplished a great deal besides passing the Suffolk Resolves. They drafted a Declaration of Rights and Grievances for the repeal of the thirteen acts Parliament had passed since 1763. They wrote a memorial to the American colonies and a petition to the king. They voted to halt all imports of British goods and exports of American goods to England, to be enforced by the Continental Association. This would be a network of committees formed in every city and town throughout the colonies to enforce non-importation and non-consumption of British goods, along with non-exportation of American goods to England. And they called another Continental Congress to meet in May of 1775. A week still remained to wrap up some of the business of the Congress.

Patrick Henry and the Virginia delegates had worked hard with men from other colonies these last few weeks, but they had also enjoyed many dinners and social events, including attending the play *Cato* with Mr. Gillamon. Nigel had arranged for Cato the eagle to also come to the theater to celebrate the birth of his baby eaglets. Nigel and Cato peeked in from a window high above the theater rooftop to watch the play. Nigel had never seen an eagle weep, so it was a touching moment for the little mouse as well. Cato was so moved after seeing the play come to life that he decided to name one of his eaglets "Plutarch." He named the other two eaglets "Veritas," meaning *truth,* and "Alexander," meaning *greatness.* Cato would remain in Philadelphia until the eaglets were old enough to be on their own, then he would return to Scotchtown.

Gillamon left Max at the City Tavern for George Washington with a note on his collar that his upcoming travels would not permit him to take the dog along. He hoped Max would serve Colonel Washington well at Mount Vernon. George was thrilled, and couldn't wait to take the Scottish terrier home to Martha. Little did he know he was taking home the same Scottie who had protected him before and during the French and Indian War. Nigel decided he would go with Max to visit Washington's plantation.

Some delegates such as Patrick Henry would be heading home the next day to make the tentative November assembly of burgesses in Williamsburg, while others stayed behind to tie up loose ends. But tonight there was a grand dinner hosted by the newly elected, more radical Pennsylvania assembly at the City Tavern. It was an evening of elegant entertainment with music, dancing, and bountiful food. Toasts were raised to the First Continental Congress as the delegates congratulated one another on a job well done. One of the Quaker delegates offered up a solemn toast: "May the sword of the Parent never be stained with the blood of her Children."

John Adams and Patrick Henry sat together in a corner to have a private farewell. The two men had grown close in these past few weeks. They differed in their backgrounds, temperaments, and talents, but they shared the vision that America not only needed, but likely would see become reality.

557

"I fear that however necessary or expected by the American people our resolves, declarations of rights, remonstrances, and non-importation agreements might be to cement the union of the colonies, they will be nothing but waste paper in England," stated John Adams in his low, gravelly voice.

Patrick Henry pursed his lips and nodded gravely. "They might make some impression among the people of England, but I agree with you they will be totally lost upon the government." He sighed deeply. "Richard Henry Lee and the other Virginia delegates besides Washington and myself believe that our work here will be victorious and carry our points forward without war. Colonel Washington is in doubt as to what will happen, and I feel we will have no choice but to fight."

John pulled an envelope from his pocket. "My friend from Northampton, Major Joseph Hawley, sent me this short and hasty letter. Herein he gives a few broken hints as to the course he feels the colonies should take. Allow me to share some of his sentiments." He opened the letter and Patrick leaned in to listen as John read portions aloud. "We must fight, if we can't otherwise rid ourselves of British taxation, all revenues, or the constitution, or form of government enacted for us by the British parliament. It is evil against right—utterly intolerable to every man who has any idea or feeling of right or liberty. America's salvation depends upon an established, persevering union of the colonies. Every grievance of any one colony must be held and considered by the whole as a grievance to the whole. This will be a difficult matter but it must be done. It is now or never that we must assert our liberty. After all, we must fight."

Patrick Henry snapped his head up in a burst of energy and vehemence and exclaimed, "By God, I am of that man's mind!"

John Adams nodded and folded the letter, understanding Patrick's bold and solemn declaration. He knew that Patrick was making a sacred oath, not cursing.

"You may not know this yet, but you are being likened to Demosthenes while Richard Henry Lee is being likened to Cicero for your oratory and leadership, both in Virginia and in this Congress," shared John Adams with a warm grin.

Patrick wore a resolute smile. "I shall endeavor to live up to such a commendation." He leaned forward. "Plutarch penned the following in his biography about Demosthenes: 'When Demosthenes was asked what was the first part of oratory, he answered, "Action," and which was the second, he replied, "Action," and which was the third, he still answered, "Action!"' Mr. Adams, it is time for us to return home and take our oratory to action."

"Agreed," John Adams replied as the men stood and shook hands in farewell.

"Farewell, John," Patrick said. "Stay safe in Boston. May God bless the work of the Congress, and may God bless America."

"Thank you, my friend," John replied. "Godspeed. Until May, keep speaking boldly for liberty."

Patrick bowed and smiled. "Indeed I will, sir."

As Patrick turned to leave, a servant from the tavern approached him. "Mr. Henry, this package was left for you earlier today." He handed Patrick the package wrapped in brown paper and tied with twine.

"Thank you," Patrick said, taking the package in hand. He looked for a note on the outside but didn't see anything attached. He wore a puzzled expression as he ascended the wide staircase of the City Tavern to reach his room and turn in for the night. He set the package on the table and pulled on the twine. His eyes grew wide as he saw that it was Mr. Gillamon's magnificent red cloak. Sitting on top was a note:

Dear Patrick,

It seems only fitting that I pass on my red cloak to you, now that I have a new cloak. Consider this a symbolic gesture of passing the mantle of responsibility on to you, the next generation of leaders for the people. I am extremely proud of all you have accomplished as a lawyer, a burgess, and now a delegate to the First Continental Congress. You have become the Voice of the Revolution for the people of America. Never stop speaking the truth that the people need to hear in the fight for liberty. Many dark days lie ahead, but I know that you will be a light on the path to freedom for America.

I also have placed an item of priceless value within the cloak. Use it well.

Godspeed,
Mr. Gillamon

559

"Thank you, Mr. Gillamon," Patrick whispered as he wiped away a tear of gratitude. He reached his hand into the pocket of the red cloak and his hands felt something curious. He pulled out the item and ran his finger along its edge.

It was an ivory letter opener.

64

WINDS OF WAR

The early morning dew had already drenched the fringed moccasins of the two scouts who walked along the upper banks of the Ohio River. Dressed in rugged buckskin clothes with wide-brimmed hats and carrying their long rifles, the men moved quietly along. They smelled the air for the aroma of cooking fires and listened for the sound of any Indian activity. The stars were slowly beginning to fade into the light gray sky as sunrise approached.

"Let's look up there," one of the scouts whispered, pointing to a ridge. The other scout nodded silently and followed him to the crest of the hill where a brisk wind hit them, as did the view.

The two men's eyes widened, and their hearts started pounding at what they saw in the valley below. Like a snake uncoiling from its perch to seek its prey, hundreds of Indian warriors were leaving their campsite and moving onto the warpath. The scouts looked at one another in alarm. "We've got to warn Colonel Lewis!"

As the scouts began running along the ridge, they were spotted by an Indian scout who fired his rifle, hitting one of the men in the side. The scout fell to the ground, while the other man kept running back to camp. The Indians began beating their war drums, and a few warriors filled the air with blood-curdling war cries.

The scout who was shot lay on the ground, blood trickling from the corner of his mouth as he held a bloodied hand over his abdomen. Clarie, in the form of a frontiersman, ran over to him and knelt by his side, grief-stricken that she was too late, although Gillamon had told her he would not survive. She put her hand on his forehead, trying to calm the dying man. "Shhhhh, Samuel. Have no fear of leaving this earth, for glorious heaven awaits you. Your wife and children will be well cared for. And your legacy will touch generations to come."

Samuel looked up at Clarie but could only communicate with his eyes. A single tear rolled down his cheek to the cold ground, and he suddenly grew calm. As the first pink streaks of color filled the morning sky, Samuel let go a shallow breath and was gone.

Clarie closed his eyes with the palm of her hand and tenderly kissed his forehead. "Well done, good and faithful servant." She picked up her rifle and stood over Samuel, gazing at the Indians heading to war against the Virginians. "Maker, please arm us for battle, and make our aim sure." She hurried away and ran as fast as she could back toward Andrew Lewis and his men.

———

HANOVER, NOVEMBER 2, 1774

Patrick Henry had rushed back from Philadelphia early for nothing. Lord Dunmore had not yet arrived from the frontier, so the assembly of burgesses would be delayed once again. News was beginning to trickle in about Dunmore's War and his victory over the Indians, but the people of Hanover were also eager to hear the news of what had happened in Philadelphia at the First Continental Congress.

One evening, Patrick sat around with some prominent gentlemen at the home of Colonel Samuel Overton.

"Please tell us, Pahtrick, do you think there is any hope for reconciling with England?" Colonel Overton asked.

Patrick wore a grim expression and slowly shook his head. "Great Britain *will* drive us to extremities." He looked around the room at the men gathered there to gauge their response. "No accommodation will take place—hostilities will soon commence—and a desperate and bloody touch it will be."

"But see here, can the colonies successfully oppose Great Britain's navy and army?" another man asked worriedly, followed by murmurs of doubt from the others.

"I doubt we can do it alone," Patrick replied, suddenly getting to his feet to zealously face the men. "But where is France? Where is Spain? Where is Holland?" he asked them urgently, punctuating the air with his hands. "Do you suppose they will stand by, idle and indifferent spectators? Will Louis the Sixteenth be asleep all this while? Believe me, *no.*"

The gentlemen looked at one another in alarm to consider the possibility of international powers getting in the middle of their quarrel with the Crown.

"Did the Congress go so far as to already suggest foreign alliances?" Overton asked.

Patrick crossed his arms over his chest and looked at his toes for a moment. "Not as a whole, but I believe it to be inevitable that they will. They must, if the winds of war continue to blow in as has the gale from the north."

Little did Patrick know that the winds of war were blowing not just from the north in Boston, but from the west in Point Pleasant.

SCOTCHTOWN, NOVEMBER 15, 1774

562 "William, I'm glad you are here, safe and sound," Patrick told his brother-in-law as he ushered him into his office and shut the door.

"It's good to be safe and sound, Pat, thank you," Colonel William Christian answered. He was married to Patrick's sister, Anne.

"Mother was visiting Anne out west when the hostilities began," related Patrick, "so they both came here to Scotchtown for safety. I'm just sorry I was in Philadelphia and not here to comfort them. They anxiously awaited word, and shared with me the little news they received about Point Pleasant, but I'd like to hear it firsthand from you." Patrick wore a grave expression and gripped his brother-in-law's arm. "Please, tell me everything. What happened out there?"

"I will tell you what I learned from Colonel Lewis, as I and my men did not arrive until the evening of the bloody battle." William removed his tricorn hat and set it on the table as he took his seat. "It was a long day of hand-to-hand combat with the Shawnee and Mingo Indians. Chief Cornstalk brought 1,200 Indian warriors against Colonel Lewis's army of 1,250 militiamen. Our Virginia long-riflemen won the victory despite heavy losses, and the Indians retreated across the Ohio. Dunmore did secure a peace treaty with the Indians, and is now marching home with a victory under his belt. The western frontier is secure from Indian threats for now. Dunmore will no doubt be hailed as a hero, Pat. But *how* the Battle of Point Pleasant came about is troubling."

Patrick rested his elbows on his knees, and leaned in, listening intently. "What do you mean?"

"Well, Dunmore had mapped out a simple plan. His northern army was to rendezvous with Colonel Andrew Lewis and his southern army at the mouth of the Kanawha River, and then they were to march as one force to cross the Ohio and face the Shawnee," William began. "Colonel Lewis arrived at the meeting place of Point Pleasant on October 6, but Dunmore wasn't there. They found a note from Dunmore left in the hollow of a tree, telling Lewis and his men to meet him many miles upstream in Fort Gower, and there they would proceed against the Indians. But Lewis's officers and men were tired, and their horses needed rest before pressing on. Colonel Lewis felt it wise to wait for me and my men to arrive from Fincastle with gunpowder and supplies."

"Andrew Lewis is a wise man. What happened then?" Patrick asked.

"Lewis sent messengers up the Ohio to find Dunmore and tell him of their arrival at Point Pleasant and his decision to rest and wait for reinforcements and supplies, especially black powder, before marching on to Fort Gower. Dunmore sent a message back to Lewis on October 9 with an old Indian trader named William McCulloch." William leaned in toward Patrick. "McCulloch hinted that Lewis might soon expect some 'hot work,' but he didn't explain."

"Hot work?" Patrick asked, narrowing his eyes. "Go on."

"On the morning of October 10, Colonel Lewis wisely sent several two-man teams to scout out the area," William relayed. "One team proceeded along the upper banks of the Ohio River. Suddenly they came over the crest of the hill to see the main body of Cornstalk's force moving in a three-quarter-mile-long column toward Point Pleasant. The scouts immediately turned to run back to warn Lewis, but they were spotted. One of those men was killed, and the other scout made it back to camp to warn Lewis. The battle erupted soon after. We lost eighty men and one hundred-forty were wounded. Sadly, Andrew's brother Colonel Charles Lewis was killed, and your brother-in-law Colonel William Fleming was wounded."

Patrick clenched his jaw. "What a tragic loss of Charles Lewis and those brave men. I pray Fleming will recover quickly."

William paused and drummed his fingers on the arm of his chair.

"The Indians were well armed, with tomahawks, but also powder, lead, and guns including *British* flintlock muskets and rifles. Dunmore supposedly was meeting with the Indians to work out a peace treaty, and had invited the Shawnees, but they would not come. Delaware Chief White Eyes informed Dunmore that seven hundred Shawnee warriors had gone southward to 'speak' to the army there, and would be joined by another Indian nation. He said 'they would begin with the Virginians there in the morning, and their business would be over by breakfast.' Not only that, but the Indians themselves taunted our men and mocked our fife-playing, shouting, 'Don't you whistle now' and making very merry about a *treaty*. Dunmore knew the attack was coming, Pat. Andrew Lewis suspects that Dunmore may have arranged for or at the very least *allowed* the Indians to attack us at Point Pleasant."

"This is hard to believe." Patrick's face grew ashen with the shock of this news.

"I know," William agreed with a frown. "Following the battle, Lewis attempted to head north to meet up with Dunmore, but Dunmore *three* times demanded that he return to Point Pleasant, as he was in the middle of a treaty. Lewis wanted to attack Dunmore himself after that. Why keep Lewis away after he had secured a victory?"

"Was Dunmore working on a treaty . . . or *treason?*" Patrick asked gravely, standing to pace about the room. "If Dunmore knew the Indians would be attacking in the morning, why didn't he go to Lewis's aid?"

William thought a moment before answering. "If we wish to consider him in an innocent light, perhaps Dunmore knew he couldn't reach Lewis in time to be of any help, or perhaps he had great confidence in our fighting men to handle the Indian attack. Or maybe he was put out with Lewis for not following his orders to head immediately to Fort Gower. But if Lord Dunmore did in fact *allow* those Indians to wipe out Andrew Lewis's southern army, it would remove a military threat against him."

"Dunmore has already felt the sting of Virginians opposing him politically, and has repeatedly dissolved our House of Burgesses. But he knows that this has not stopped us from meeting and taking action, such as sending delegates to Philadelphia for the Congress," Patrick detailed.

"So if Virginia were to rise up in arms, as the people of Massachusetts have, against the British, Lord Dunmore knows there are no regiments of Redcoats here to squash a rebellion of the most populous colony in

America," William realized. "He hasn't been able to stop Virginia politically, so was he trying to stop us militarily?"

"What if the Crown ordered Dunmore to quickly end the war with the Indians and secure an alliance with them in favor of England *against* the colonies, should the mounting revolution come?" Patrick asked rhetorically. He folded his hands and propped them over his mouth with his thumbs under his chin as he paced about the room, thinking. "Andrew Lewis and his men thought, as did we all, that this war with the Indians would be a battle of *Colonists* versus Indians," Patrick reasoned as he continued to pace. "But it is only *after* the conflict that Dunmore's War appears to have been a battle between *Rebels* versus Indians armed and *used by* the British. If Lewis claims that Dunmore not only failed to come to his aid, but actually aided the Indians, then this is inconceivable treachery. Beyond that, if the British allied with the Indians against the colonists, or *rebels* as Dunmore sees us, this would make the Battle of Point Pleasant the first conflict in a revolutionary war." He stopped, looked at William, and crossed his arms over his chest. "And we cannot do anything about it—yet."

565

William Christian's eyes widened. "But why? Colonel Lewis intends to notify Colonel Washington of everything that happened at Point Pleasant, and has vowed to refuse any future orders from Lord Dunmore."

"Because we are not yet sufficiently armed to face the British army and navy," Patrick explained, sitting down next to William. "Since we cannot really *prove* anything, we must not allow the general population to know of Dunmore's possible treachery until we are well armed and have solid evidence. Otherwise, the people of Williamsburg will storm the Governor's Palace and drag Dunmore through the streets."

"Then the British navy would arrive off our coast and Redcoats would descend on Williamsburg and spread through Virginia like a swarm of red locusts," William slowly predicted as he realized the gravity of the situation.

"Virginia needs to take up arms in each and every town and county, with a well-armed militia ready to fight at a moment's notice. You and I shall call a gathering of men here in Hanover, and when you return to Fincastle you can rally the militia there," Patrick told him. Still fresh in his mind were the images of his Uncle Langloo standing on a tree stump to rally soldiers to the cause of the French and Indian War, and

Reverend Samuel Davies pleading with brave young men to fight. "You can rally the men with the heroic account of the Virginia militia defending the frontier against the Indians at Point Pleasant, and inspire them with the sacrifice that our brave men gave in shedding their blood. We shall affix urgency in the hearts of the people to be ready for armed conflict from *anyone* hostile to our liberty, including the British."

"Very well, I shall do as you wish, Pat," William answered. "I need to share one more bit of information with you about the Battle of Point Pleasant. The scout that the Indians killed, who shed his blood before anyone that day—it was Samuel Crowley."

Patrick's face fell. "Oh, no, not Samuel! Poor, dear Elizabeth. She and Sallie were such close friends." Patrick shook his head sadly. "She has several small children."

William nodded. "Not only has she lost her husband, but Elizabeth is pregnant, Pat. Her baby is due in the spring."

Grief rose in Patrick's throat, and his eyes flashed in anger to think of Samuel's death coming as a result of Dunmore's actions. "I count Samuel Crowley as the first patriot to die in this revolutionary war, which will also soon be birthed. Virginia owes this first war widow assistance for her sacrifice. I will write to Elizabeth about filing a wartime pension in Samuel's name for this battle. And I will do all I can to assist her."

Liz locked sad eyes with Kate as they heard this news. The men then made plans to rally the Hanover militia at Smith's Tavern. Patrick would seek the formation of a voluntary expeditionary force that would select its own officers once enough men had signed up to serve.

When William at last left the room, Patrick took out paper and quill and wrote a letter to Elizabeth. He also enclosed some money for her immediate aid. Liz and Kate made their way outside to sit by the boxwoods. The air had turned cold.

"Quel dommage! I cannot believe Samuel was killed!" Liz cried. "But I am grateful *mon* Henry will make sure his family is cared for."

Kate lowered her head. "Aye, 'tis sad ta think of Elizabeth left alone with all those wee lads an' lassies."

"No one is sadder than I," came a voice from the boxwoods. It was Clarie. She was in the form of a courier. "I was with Samuel when he died."

Liz rushed over to Clarie. "We are so very sorry, *mon amie.*"

"Wha' will happen ta his widow?" Kate worried.

"I'll take Patrick's letter to Elizabeth and then stay a short while to help her with the house and the children," Clarie explained. "She will be well taken care of by family and friends like Patrick. Gillamon told me that one of Samuel and Elizabeth's children will play a crucial role for the Order of the Seven in the future, but how he doesn't yet know. I will be looking out for the boy in the years to come. He's only two years old." Liz and Kate shared a look of puzzlement mixed with sadness. "What is the boy's name?

"His name is Littleberry," Clarie answered. "Littleberry Crowley."

"I like his name," Kate said with a ray of hope in this melancholy moment. "I wonder wha' he'll do that's so grand."

"Time will tell. It always does," Clarie answered.

"Clarie, I fear that Elizabeth is not the only one who will be widowed and left with small children like Littleberry," Liz lamented. "Sallie is growing worse by the day."

Clarie softly petted Liz and nodded. "I know, Liz. There are hard days ahead for Patrick and the Henry household. You and Kate will need to stay strong and bring them comfort in the midst of it all."

"We shall," promised Liz, locking eyes with Kate. "But we are also worried about all that has happened with Lord Dunmore and the mounting tensions Patrick discussed with William."

"The winds of war have started ta blow," Kate added.

A heavy gust of wind blew, and Clarie tightened her hat on her head. "Yes, the Revolution is coming, but you've known this all along. For now, there is nothing you need to do but stay here with Patrick through the cold months ahead. I'll see you soon." She stood up, ready to walk to the house. "And just to let you know, Max went to Mount Vernon with George Washington from Philadelphia, and Nigel decided to go with him to explore the farm. Cato will remain in Philadelphia until February and pick up Nigel on his way back to Scotchtown."

"Why's Cato stayin' in Philadelphia?" Kate asked.

Clarie smiled. "You'll be glad to hear that Cato found a mate and had three baby eaglets: Plutarch, Veritas, and Alexander."

"*C'est bon!* Oh, what happy news!" Liz cheered.

"Aye, we needed some happy news," Kate agreed, wagging her tail. "Wee ones always give us hope for the future."

"And what is the news of my Albert?" Liz wanted to know.

567

"He is happy and well, Liz. Al recently completed an important assignment in London," Clarie told her. "He arranged for a man named Thomas Paine to meet Benjamin Franklin in order to help the man with introductions in Philadelphia. Paine just arrived in the city and will pick up his pen soon."

"Oh? What will Thomas Paine write?" Liz asked.

"A lot of common sense," Clarie replied with a grin. "Now, I must be going."

"À *bientôt, mon amie,*" Liz said.

Clarie reached down and scratched Kate under the chin. "Take care of Sallie, and keep talking to her. It helps."

"Aye, that we'll do," Kate answered, trotting along with Clarie as she headed to the house to retrieve Patrick's letter to Elizabeth.

Liz sat a moment to consider all the news she had heard: alarming news about Lord Dunmore and the coming Revolution; sad news about Samuel and Elizabeth; hopeful news about Littleberry; happy news about Cato's eaglets; and crushing news about Sallie. Life was ever filled with all manner of sad and happy things, happening at once.

568

Another gust of cold November wind blew Liz's fur and sent a chill up her spine. She walked over to the patch of daisies Patrick had planted for Sallie. They were now withered and dead. Liz's eyes brimmed with tears as she thought of the words from Ecclesiastes. "There is a time for everything, and a season for every activity under heaven—a time for war and a time for peace, a time to be born," Liz recited aloud with a broken voice, picking up a brown daisy stem, "and a time to die."

FAREWELL, MY LOVE

Dinah hummed a Christmas song and rocked as she sat in the basement room outside Sallie's bedroom, finishing her work. She bit off the thread with her teeth and held up the off-white linen straight-dress to look it over. She set down the needle and thread and frowned, pursing her lips and sadly shaking her head. "I hope Missus Sallie will be comfortable in this." She held out the sleeves, which were twice the normal length of regular shirtsleeves, and had drawstring wrists with long, thick strings dangling from them. She looked into the bedroom where Sallie lay sleeping on her bed next to the wall under the windows. "That poor child."

Liz and Kate sat on the cool brick floor and watched as Dinah worked. Dinah stayed down here with Sallie all the time, making sure Sallie had everything she needed, and was never alone. She even had a bed on the wall opposite Sallie's bed, so even in the night she could tend to Sallie. Lately Sallie had become violent, and had nearly harmed herself. It was decided she would need to be restrained by wearing this straight-dress.

"*Chère* Sallie, I am so sorry it has come to this," Liz murmured softly. Suddenly they heard Patrick's booming voice upstairs, and heard his footsteps making their way to the trap door where he came down to the basement from the hallway above.

Patrick made his way over to where Dinah worked, and she stood to lay the dress out on the table. "I just finished it, Mister Patrick."

"Thank you, Dinah," Patrick answered quietly.

Dinah nodded and gathered a few sticks of firewood to go add to the fireplace in Sallie's room.

Patrick clenched his jaw and haltingly reached out his hand to touch the string attached to the sleeves. "Not all fetters are made of iron," he muttered, his voice breaking with emotion. He cleared his throat and stepped over the threshold of the doorway leading into Sallie's room. He watched her as she slept. He walked over and picked up the patchwork quilt at the foot of her bed. Sallie had labored on the quilt over the years, filling it with squares of cloth from the children's clothing.

"Do you think she remembers her children anymore?" Patrick asked.

Dinah placed the straight dress on her own bed and walked over to touch the quilt. "I surely do. Missus Sallie sleeps under her babies' clothes, and they hold her close."

Patrick held the quilt up to his face to breathe in the scent of his children. He placed the quilt on top of his sleeping wife and turned to see his daughter Patsey standing in the doorway. Dinah quietly left the room.

Patsey walked over to the fireplace to stoke the fire. She then went and quietly touched the straight-dress laid out on Dinah's bed. Neither Patsey nor Patrick said a word for a moment, but listened to the crackling fire. Patsey sat down on Dinah's bed, holding up a sleeve of the straight-dress. Patrick came to sit beside her.

"Have I done the right thing, putting your mother down here?" Patrick wanted to know, looking around the room with the pink brick floor, curved fireplace, and ceiling with the heavy exposed wooden beams.

A bird called from outside the window. "Blue jay," Patsey said. A crow answered back. "And a crow. Mama can hear the birds talking. That's a happy thing."

Patrick looked out the basement window and smiled to hear his daughter name the birds she heard, just as he had taught her so many years ago. He looked at Liz and Kate. *Among other animals.* He didn't tell his daughter that Sallie had told him they spoke to her. No need to cause more heartache for Patsey. She was now married to John Fontaine, but had come to live at Scotchtown so she could take care of her younger siblings and manage the household, along with Patrick's mother, Sarah.

Patsey put her hand on her father's back and leaned her chin on his slumped shoulder. "Sometimes the right things are the hardest things, Papa. Other people would have locked Mother away in that horrid asylum in Williamsburg. That might have been the easier thing to do, but it would not have been the right thing." She picked up the straight-dress. "This will swaddle her and bring her comfort."

"I hope so," Patrick answered, standing to walk over to Sallie's bedside table. He gently touched the looking glass and brush he had given Sallie that first Christmas after they fell in love. "I'm sorry I do not feel much like celebrating Christmas. It is hard for me to be merry these days." He picked up the mirror and frowned as he gazed at his reflection. "I look like an old man."

Patsey walked over and took the mirror from his hand. She held it up to him. "Look again. I see a man who has been a knight in shining armor to his childhood sweetheart, and who will take care of her until her last breath."

Patrick smiled sadly and enveloped his eldest daughter in his strong arms. Together they stood there and watched Sallie sleeping. "Thank you, Patsey. She will always be my sweetheart."

———

571

GOVERNOR'S PALACE, WILLIAMSBURG, DECEMBER 24, 1774

Lord Dunmore heard the cries of his newborn baby as he sat at his desk. He looked up for a moment, but then dipped his quill once more in the inkwell to continue writing a long-overdue letter to Lord Dartmouth. Dunmore had to explain what he was doing out on the frontier in the war with the Indians, and why he had not responded to Dartmouth's letters from the fall. Dunmore told of Andrew Lewis's stubborn refusal to obey his orders, and how ultimately Dunmore's forces won the battle, secured a peace treaty with the Indians, and how he had returned to Williamsburg a hero. His wife Charlotte had just given birth to a new baby, and the festivities of the Christmastide had consumed his time since his return three weeks before.

Dunmore was briefed on what had transpired in Philadelphia with the Continental Congress, and the aftermath of action spreading across his colony. *Every county is now arming a company of men whom they call an independent company, for the avowed purpose of protecting their committees, and to be employed against government if occasion requires,* he wrote. He scowled as he thought about what the men of Virginia had done while he was out defending them on the frontier.

These undutiful people should be made to feel the distress and misery, of which they themselves have laid the foundation, as soon as possible and before they can have time to find out ways and means of supplying themselves. Their own schemes should be turned against them and they should not be permitted to procure underhand what they refuse to admit openly, and above all they should not be permitted to go to foreign ports to seek the things they want. Their ports should be blocked up and their communication cut off by water even with their neighbouring colonies, and this could be done effectually with only one ship of force and a frigate of a couple of tenders. With this, and without any other force or expense, no vessel could stir out of the Bay of Chesapeake or approach any port of Virginia.

The functions of every department of government, which in fact are now entirely obstructed, should be suspended and the governor and all other officers withdrawn. The people, left to themselves and to the confusion that would immediately reign, would I cannot believe soon become sensible from what source their former happiness flowed and prostrate themselves before the power which they had so lately considered as inimical and treated with contempt.

572

Once he finished his letter, Lord Dunmore tossed his quill on the table. He stared up at the map of the colony that hung on the wall, and his eyes narrowed at the misery of his assignment there. "Cursed Virginia."

Dunmore didn't know he would soon receive another October letter from Lord Dartmouth to all the royal governors in the colonies, instructing them to seize all the gunpowder. Given the tensions in Virginia, Dunmore would have to wait for just the right moment. Then he would raid the gunpowder magazine in Williamsburg.

———

LONDON, JANUARY 12, 1775

King George held the resolves from the First Continental Congress up to his face as he read them. All that Al could see were his pudgy fingers and the snug gold signet ring that dug into his finger. The king tightened his grip on the parchment before slowly lowering it to reveal a cynical smile. "How . . . eloquent," he commented sarcastically, allowing the resolves to fall to the floor. His eyes bored into Lord North who stood there before him. "I demand that Parliament reject these grievances, halt trade with the colonies, give protection to loyalists with our army, and arrest those colonial protestors as traitors."

"As you say, Your Majesty," Lord North replied with a respectful bow as the king left the room. Lord North scooped up the colonial resolves and grievances to the king and slapped them in his hand. "Exactly as you say."

Al's eyes widened. "Uh-oh. Them lordy lads will be writin' up more trouble now. I sure hope Benjamin Franklin gets outta London soon. There's nothin' left for him here."

LONDON, FEBRUARY 5, 1775

Benjamin Franklin sat up in the balcony of Parliament, listening to the futile attempts of William Pitt to convince Parliament to avoid bloodshed with the colonies. He had suggested that General Gage remove his troops from Boston. But rather than withdraw Gage, the Parliament selected three more British generals for duty in America, and passed a bill to restrain trade and commerce with the New England colonies. The House of Commons discarded the petitions from the colonies, claiming they were "pretended grievances." Ultimately, Pitt's efforts were rejected, and Parliament set a course Ben knew would ultimately lead to war. He stood up, put on his hat, and went home.

573

As Ben sat by the fire sipping his hot toddy, he sighed deeply. Even after he had been humiliated over the Hutchinson letters, he remained in London all these months, hoping that somehow things could take a turn for the better. But after watching the response of Parliament to the Continental Congress, he knew there was no longer any hope. He went to his desk and took out a piece of paper and wrote:

I cannot but lament . . . the impending calamities, Britain and her colonies are about to suffer, from the great imprudencies on both sides. Passion governs and she never governs wisely——anxiety begins to disturb my rest.

He looked around at his apartment and then up at the map of Great Britain hanging there on his wall. He knew it was time for him to make preparations to leave London and go home—to America. It was time for him to join his fellow Americans in their fight for liberty. He touched the map with a sorrowful expression. "My dear England." He shook his head, rubbed his eyes, and blew out the candle on his desk.

SCOTCHTOWN, FEBRUARY 25, 1775

Sallie sat quietly in the chair by her bed, looking up at the birds perched in the tree outside the basement window. She was wearing her straight-dress but she didn't struggle against it. It had a calming effect on her, much to everyone's relief. Patrick walked into the room with a plate to feed her some lunch. He pulled up a chair in front of her and sat down.

"Okay, my love, let's see if we can get you to eat something," Patrick whispered, piercing a carrot with the fork. He held it up to her mouth and noticed a tear rolling down her cheek. He pulled back the fork and leaned in to search her eyes. She appeared to be having a lucid moment. "Sallie?"

She turned her gaze to him. "I wish to be free."

Patrick clenched his jaw and slowly set the fork on the plate. He set the plate over on the table and sat back down. He placed his hand on her arms that were bound to her waist. "From this dress?"

Sallie shook her head "no" and uttered a faint whisper. "Let me go." Her face then went blank once more and she turned her gaze back to the birds.

"I . . . cannot." Patrick swallowed the lump in his throat. He knew she wasn't talking about the straight-dress. "Perhaps you need to rest. Come, let me help you into bed and I'll play the fiddle to soothe you." He wrapped his arms around her waist and lifted her to the bed. He put the quilt over her. "I'll be right back."

As Patrick left the room to retrieve his fiddle, Liz and Kate noticed that Sallie was gazing up at the ceiling, smiling. "Oh, how beautiful," she marveled. Her eyes darted from one corner of the ceiling to the other, as if she was watching a scene unfold before her eyes.

"She's slipping away!" Liz cried, watching as the room was suddenly drenched in bright light as the sun poured in through the window.

"Aye." Kate ran over and put her paws up on the bed while Liz jumped up to sit by Sallie's legs. "We're here, lass."

Sallie smiled at Liz and Kate. "I'm not afraid." She looked back up to the ceiling. "How beautiful it is there!"

"Get Patrick!" Liz begged Kate.

Kate started barking and ran to the other basement room. They soon heard Patrick's heavy footsteps coming down the stairs, and he hurried into the sun-drenched room. He set down his fiddle and rushed to Sallie's side, taking her face in his hands.

"Sallie? Sallie?" Patrick cried in a panicked voice, fearing he was losing her. "Don't leave me!" He started to furiously untie her straight-dress to free her arms. He then draped her arms around his neck and held her close. "Please don't leave me, Sallie."

Liz joined Kate on the floor, and they looked at one another as their eyes filled with tears.

Sallie breathed out a quiet whisper in Patrick's ear. "Farewell, my love." Her arms slowly went limp.

Patrick buried his face into her hair and rocked her back and forth, sobbing. "Oh, Sallie. My Sallie!"

Liz and Kate stepped into the other room to allow Patrick complete privacy as he let her go.

"She's finally free," Kate whispered tearfully.

Liz nodded and struggled to speak. "It took death to give her liberty."

CLOAK AND DAGGER

The fire popped on the hearth in Patrick Henry's bedroom, startling Liz. She had been sitting next to the fire, watching Patrick sleep. The weight of the world was on his shoulders, and Liz had heard his quiet sobs as he drifted off to sleep. The pallor of Sallie's death still hung in the air over Scotchtown. Sadness filled the eyes of his children, and everyone spoke in hushed tones around the plantation. No laughter, no dancing, and certainly no fiddle music had filled the halls in the three weeks since Sallie's death.

Patrick had lost his best friend—his first and only love. He was now a widower with six children, and yet he was needed to serve his country by attending the Second Virginia Convention in Richmond in just a few short days. He didn't even have time to grieve properly. Duty called, and Patrick had learned by watching those who had run the race before him that life was no respecter of heartache. Like Samuel Davies, who had pressed on to the task of fighting for religious freedom after he lost his wife and baby—his *entire* family—so, too, must he put one foot in front of the other to fight for all the freedoms at stake for the people of Virginia, and ultimately, for America.

Today is St. Patrick's Day, Liz thought to herself. *If there ever was a saintly servant, it is you, my Patrick.* She glanced over at Patrick's desk where sat his open Bible and a scattering of documents. His work had become a blessing in disguise, for in it he found a strange solace and a distraction from his unresolved grief.

Liz walked over and jumped up on the desk, her cat's eyes glowing with the reflection of the hearth's fire. She saw that Patrick's Bible was opened to 2 Chronicles 14. She had heard him mutter aloud verse 11:

"Lord there is no one like you to help the powerless against the mighty." He was reading about Judah's King Asa facing the Cushite army, a foe far too powerful to defeat with its vast army and hundreds of chariots. But God's forces intervened and crushed the enemy against impossible odds. In his nightly hour of Scripture reading this evening, Liz also had heard him flipping through Jeremiah, softly quoting verses 5:21, *"Hear this now, O foolish people, without understanding, who have eyes and see not, and who have ears and hear not,"* and 6:14, *"Peace, peace; when there is no peace."*

Earlier in the day Liz sat and watched Patrick break the wax seals off several letters with his ivory letter opener. Those letters contained news from fellow delegates around the colony about growing tensions among the people. The iron heel of the British army was already pressing its might against the necks of the people of Boston. What was to prevent them from coming southward to do the same in Virginia? Liz moved Patrick's ivory letter opener out of the way with her paw, and read the resolutions he was preparing to offer at the upcoming Convention. She scanned his resolutions, muttering quietly as she read.

577

Resolved, That a well-regulated militia, composed of gentlemen and yeomen, is the natural strength and only security of a free government; that such a militia in this colony would for ever render it unnecessary for the mother country to keep among us, for the purpose of our defence, any standing army or mercenary soldiers, always subversive of the quiet, and dangerous to the liberties of the people, and would obviate the pretext of taxing us for their support.

Liz grinned, catching Henry's humorous jab at the British monarch, who claimed to keep a standing army for the purpose of "protecting" the colonists. Protect them against whom exactly? The king further dared to dip his hands into the pockets of the people to pay for this "protection"? *Even in such a serious situation, you know how to add humor to lighten the moment,* mon *Henry.*

He went on to pen that since Virginia's militia laws had expired, and Lord Dunmore refused to call the House of Burgesses to convene a legislative session, the Second Virginia Convention itself should essentially act as the government of Virginia in this crisis. Liz's eyes widened. *Mon Dieu, he wishes to bypass the Royal Governor! Once the king sees these resolves, they will be seen as treason. This could launch the entire war!*

Resolved, therefore, That this colony be immediately put into a state of defence, and that a committee to prepare a plan for embodying, arming, and disciplining such a number of men as may be sufficient for that purpose.

On another sheet of paper where he had worked out his thoughts was scribbled in Latin: *Igitur qui desiderat pacem, praeparet bellum*— "Therefore, whoever wishes for peace let him prepare for war."

Liz looked over at Patrick, in awe of what she had just read. "No one will ever realize that a man carrying such silent grief and the weight of the world on his shoulders could rally a nation in such a powerful, decisive way. *C'est incredible.*"

"Ps-s-st! Liz, you are wanted downstairs, my dear!" came Nigel's voice in a whisper as he peeked around the slightly cracked door. He and Cato had recently returned to Scotchtown.

Liz jumped down to the floor and went to the door. "What is this about, *mon ami?*"

"Patrick's fiddle is no longer silent," Nigel answered with a knowing grin.

578

———

"There ye be, lass," Kate said, greeting her as she and Nigel entered Sallie's bedroom in the basement. "Gillamon wants ta have a word with all of us."

Patrick had left his fiddle down here in Sallie's room the day she died. There had been no reason to play it since, so he had left it where it was.

Nigel picked up his bow and pulled it across the strings of Patrick's fiddle. Once more, the magical notes rose into the air with words from the group's wise leader, Gillamon.

Good evening, Liz. How is Patrick resting tonight?

"Good evening, Gillamon," Liz replied. "He is sleeping, but it must be from exhaustion. I just read the resolves he will present to the Second Virginia Convention. I do not know how he can sleep with all that is on his heart and mind these days."

Indeed. But Patrick is drawing strength from the Maker, and he will accomplish what the Maker has long purposed for him to do—to rally a nation to Independence.

Kate, Liz, and Nigel looked at one another in alarm.

"Are ye sayin' it's finally time for the Revolution ta begin?" Kate asked.

The time has been coming for over a decade, as you know. Patrick's voice has been leading the charge in speaking the truth that the people of this nation need to hear. And now they need to hear it again, but this time with even greater urgency and with a call to action. Like an eagle forced out of its nest, VERITAS—truth—will fill the hall of that Convention when he speaks, despite those who do not wish to hear it and will have to move from their comfortable, infantile perches. The Enemy always desires bondage, not freedom, for the human spirit. The last thing he wants is freedom for an entire nation of God-fearing souls.
For the first time in history, one nation of people under God has the opportunity to form a free republic with a government beholden to THEM, instead of those people being beholden to the government. So be vigilant and on the alert. There will be danger in Richmond to stop Patrick.

579

"Will Max be there ta keep him safe?" Kate asked. "I feel I best stay with the children."

Yes, Max will shadow George Washington from Mount Vernon and be there to protect both him and Patrick Henry in Richmond. Kate, you are indeed most needed here with the children, but Liz, you need to go to Richmond. Clarie will transport you after Patrick rides off on MizP to Richmond. You will keep watch for danger en route. Nigel, you need to fly on Cato to keep watch from above.

"Understood, Gillamon," Nigel answered with a frown, still pulling his bow across the strings. "I've been reviewing the fiddle's riddle and we have reached the final line about the voice, after which 'something new will begin.' I must say, it troubles me deeply: *A voice that is dying on the out- and inside.*"

"Please do not tell me that my Henry will die!" Liz cried.

Dying happens in far more ways than just when breath leaves the body. Remember there are always deeper shades of meaning to my riddles, Liz. You must protect Patrick from the evil forces coming against him, indeed, but also understand that this is when all of the layers of history I gave you at the beginning of this mission finally come together. And that includes Plutarch and Cato.

"Please give me something specific to help me understand, Gillamon," Liz pleaded. "I can better help my Henry if I have *some* idea of what to expect."

Always expect the unexpected when it comes to the Maker's assignments. But I will grant your request, with as much as I know, for even I do not know everything that will come. The ivory letter opener that I left in the red cloak I gave to Patrick is the key to the speech he will give in six days. He will use it at a crucial moment, but even he will not know it until that time. You must ensure that it remains in his cloak pocket when he enters the fourth day of the Convention.

"Do you mean the one sitting on his desk?" Liz asked. "Why is that particular letter opener important, Gillamon? Where did you get it?"

You have seen it before, Liz, but it was in a different form. I will leave you with the same clue as I left you with when you started this mission. Focus on Plutarch, and remember, you will connect all the dots for this mission down to the letter, just as you always do.
It is time. Godspeed.

The notes ceased floating into the air and Gillamon was gone.

"It is time indeed," came the voice of one peering in at the basement window. "Time for some cloak and dagger."

SWAN TAVERN, RICHMOND, MARCH 22, 1775

Everyone had arrived safely in Richmond from Scotchtown. Clarie gave Liz a ride in her saddlebags, while Nigel flew on Cato's wings. Max met up with them after George Washington rode into town. Upon their arrival, the animals stayed out of sight so Patrick wouldn't know they were there. Tonight, as every night, Max stood guard outside the tavern, while Liz and Nigel crept upstairs to the room where Patrick Henry was staying. They had tried their best to keep an eye on the letter opener, which was in Patrick's cloak pocket when he left Scotchtown. Patrick was sharing a room with his half-brother John Syme, Jr., and with George Washington. The room filled with the snores of the tired men who had been at the Convention for three days. Liz and Nigel jumped up onto a bench at the foot of Patrick's bed, and whispered, so as not to wake the men.

"Gillamon said I would figure this mission out *down to the letter*— now I see that this means not only the letters we have arranged over the years, but Patrick Henry's ivory letter *opener* as well," related Liz. "It all began on Plutarch's desk. Of course! Ivory!"

581

"I'm not following you, my dear. Do you mean when you ensured that Plutarch would write about Cato the Younger?" Nigel asked. "How is Patrick's letter opener related?"

"Layers of history, one on top of the other, *mon ami*. Just as Gillamon said," Liz marveled. "When I sat on Plutarch's desk for my mission to ensure that he wrote about Cato the Younger, something strange happened. I accidentally knocked Plutarch's ivory statuette of Winged Victory onto the floor. A fragment of the wing broke off." She looked at Nigel in disbelief and smiled. "That ivory fragment was in the shape of a feather from Victory's wing."

Nigel's eyes widened behind his spectacles. "And that 'feather' fragment became Patrick's ivory letter opener that Gillamon left in the red cloak for him to find! My dear, this is extraordinary! All these years, Patrick has wanted an eagle feather. If only he knew he held in his hands an *ivory* feather from the very desk of Plutarch!"

"*Oui!* So I have figured out one part of Plutarch that Gillamon wanted me to see, but there still must be more layers of history to connect for what my Henry is getting ready to do," Liz realized.

Nigel straightened his spectacles. "Well, my pet, let us think this through, step by step. Right, so Plutarch wrote about Cato the Younger. And *who* would have benefitted most by reading the historical account of the Roman patriot, besides young Patrick Henry in his studies?"

Liz thought a moment and brightened. "Joseph Addison, who wrote the play *Cato!*"

"And *who* then has benefitted most from the play *Cato?*" Nigel posed.

At that moment George Washington let a loud snore rip through the room. Liz giggled. "Well, it *is* George Washington's favorite play."

"*Precisely,* as it is for most of the ardent patriots gathering at this Convention," Nigel added, followed by a jolly chuckle. "Our dear eagle, Cato, also adores his namesake play since we saw it together through the roof in Philadelphia."

"I am glad Cato was able to see the play," Liz replied with a smile. "*C'est magnifique!* Just look at all that has happened from the stroke of Plutarch's pen that night on his desk! But I still do not see why Gillamon insisted Patrick's letter opener be in his cloak tomorrow." Suddenly another memory from that night on Plutarch's desk entered her memory. She reached for Patrick's red cloak, which was draped across the bench, and put her paw into the pocket, searching for the letter opener. "It's not here! And I think I know who took it—someone who has tried to take it before."

"Whatever do you mean, dear girl?" Nigel asked, scurrying up the cloak and down into the pocket to make sure the letter opener wasn't hidden deep inside. He popped his head out as he hung on to the pocket. "Who could *possibly* have taken it?"

"The one time I didn't believe the meaning of a name. I didn't *want* to believe it. I've been so blind!" Liz shook her head at herself. "That night with Plutarch, after I had broken the statue, we heard another crash outside on his terrace. We ran outside to find that Plutarch's oleander plant had crashed to the tile floor. He thought it must have been the wind, but now I know it was not the wind."

"What was it?" Nigel implored, impatient to understand.

"I saw the footprints of a creature in the scattered dirt on the terrace, but before I could identify the creature they belonged to, the wind snatched them away," Liz explained. "Plutarch called to me, warning me not to touch the oleander, as it is poisonous to cats."

582

Nigel looked up in alarm. "Poison! There have been mysterious poisonings surrounding Patrick and the other young patriots ever since . . ."

"Ever since I rescued Kakia from the Tower of London," Liz finished Nigel's train of thought. "Those footprints were *hers* on Plutarch's terrace. She is not a mortal being. Do you know what her name means?"

"Oh dear," Nigel answered, with a paw up to his mouth. "Kakia in the Greek means 'evil, trouble, and desire to injure.'"

Liz nodded. "And Kakia comes from the root word 'Kakós', which means 'bad, evil in the widest sense, inwardly foul . . .'" She paused and looked Nigel in the eye. "And poison. *She* poisoned the guard in the Tower before we arrived. She was trying to get to Cato then! I didn't think it mattered, so I did not tell Gillamon that I had freed her!"

"Oh dear, what about George Washington?" Nigel said with a paw to his mouth.

Liz drew in a quick breath and nodded. "Clarie said someone intentionally poisoned young George on Barbados with the smallpox virus. Gillamon allowed it, since it would provide him with immunity protection later on."

583

"Yes, but there was *another* attempt on George Washington and Patrick Henry with poisoned food in Philadelphia!" Nigel added worriedly. "Could she have made other attempts on Patrick and other humans that we simply don't know about?"

Liz closed her eyes as her mind raced to recall other instances where Kakia could have been involved. She suddenly opened her eyes. "The panther that failed to kill Cato and Patrick was found *poisoned!*"

Nigel gulped. "Max told me that when he went looking for the panther in the woods, he smelled a foul stench. He smelled it again in France with the wolves, in Boston, and again in Philadelphia, but those encounters involved *humans.*" The little mouse put a paw to his forehead. "Max said it was a stench he had not smelled since before ancient Egypt."

"Since the Ark . . . since *Charlatan,*" Liz answered in shock, with a shiver down her spine as it dawned on her who they were dealing with here. "Kakia is not the discarded, bitter cat who was abused and named by humans. She is something completely different, and wicked."

"If Kakia is immortal, that means she is one of the Enemy's minions," Nigel said gravely.

"But not just *any* minion—she is clearly a leader or one of the

Enemy's generals in the animal kingdom," Liz answered gravely. "Snakes are the only creatures who can shed their skins and not die."

"Do you mean to say she could be like Gillamon is for the Order of the Seven?" Nigel wondered as the blood drained from his face. "Can Kakia change form like Gillamon or Clarie?"

"It is a theory we must consider." Liz wrinkled her brow. Something deeper than she could comprehend was going on here. She shook her head with this revelation. "For now we must find out immediately what she is up to."

Nigel gulped. "What could she possibly be doing with Patrick's letter opener?"

Liz's mind was racing. She looked over at Patrick, who was sleeping with his right hand wrapped in a cloth. He had cut it on a small, jagged piece of metal mysteriously lodged in his saddle bag after today's session at the Convention. "When Patrick searched for a copy of the last petition to the king of England in his saddle bag, he cut his hand. Nigel, can poison be absorbed through the skin?"

584

"Certain poisons can. Arsenic and cyanide come immediately to mind, but an open wound is necessary," Nigel answered. His face fell and he shot a glance at Patrick, now understanding Liz's train of thought.

"And if the letter opener were laced in poison and stuck inside Patrick's cloak?" Liz asked.

"Oh dear, just like mythological Hercules!" Nigel exclaimed in alarm. "Hercules was killed by poison smeared on his cloak!"

"A *Greek* tragedy, no less," Liz realized. "Just the poetic type of death message that the Greek cat would send! Nigel, I believe she somehow stole the letter opener by slipping inside the Convention and that she plans to lace it with poison to then slip into Patrick's cloak. She also knows he is supposed to use the letter opener in his speech tomorrow!"

"Then we must intercept it before she gets that far," Nigel answered determinedly.

"We must go tell Max. He can help us find Kakia with that nose of his," Liz suggested. "We'll have to spread out in order to spot her. If only we could know where she will appear."

"Eagle eye!" Nigel exclaimed. "On our flight here, I told Cato about Gillamon's message that Patrick would use the letter opener in his speech. Cato said he would stay nearby, as he could not wait to see what Patrick would say and do. Our eagle can search from the skies above."

"Then we must find Cato as well!" Liz looked over at Patrick who breathed deeply in his sleep. "I will not allow Kakia to succeed, *mon* Henry." She jumped down from the bench at the foot of the bed where Patrick's cloak was draped, and nudged Nigel. *"Allons-y!"* There is no time to waste."

RICHMOND, MARCH 23, 1775,

Cato circled back over the falls of the James River and caught the thermals to remain aloft as he scanned the ground below for any sign of Kakia. His anger at hearing the threat to Patrick Henry launched him immediately into flight, and he called back to the others that he would find her, if it was the last thing he did.

The skies were overcast, which actually helped Cato's search, as he did not have to look against the glare of the sun. He could see Max and Liz out searching for the enemy cat below. Nigel had agreed to stay hidden down in Patrick's cloak pocket to intercept the poisoned letter opener if Kakia got that far. As Cato circled Church Hill, where Henrico Parish Church sat, he suddenly saw catlike movement coming up from the south side of the city. He soared downward to get a closer look and saw that it was Kakia, with the letter opener in her mouth.

Cato came swooping in and startled the cat, screeching and reaching out with his talons to grab her. She immediately tossed the letter opener on the ground and swiped back with her claws, hissing violently at the eagle. Her speed caught Cato off guard as they wrestled on the ground for a moment, tumbling down the hill as they fought against one another. Horrible sounds filled the air with the guttural growls and hisses of this sinister cat against the screams of the eagle. Cato knew he couldn't pick her up, but he knew he didn't need to. All he needed was the letter opener. He broke free and made his way back to where Kakia had dropped it. Just as he was about to pick it up, he heard her chilling voice behind him.

"Pick it up and you're dead," Kakia screeched. "It's laced with poison. I'm immune to it, of course, but you're NOT."

Cato paused with his talon perched over the letter opener. "I'm not going to carry it in my mouth like you, wicked cat. I've got my talons to carry it."

"You'd better look at that little eagle foot of yours," Kakia teased with a wicked grin.

Cato looked down, and drops of blood were on the grass under his foot. He lifted his other foot and saw that it was cut as well, sliced by Kakia's razor-sharp claws in the fight. He looked at her with fierce anger.

Kakià walked up to Cato and slowly circled him, speaking in a mocking tone. "So, you have a choice to make, *Cato.* But there are plenty to choose from. Let's see, shall I name them for you?" She sat down in front of him, and calmly curled her tail around her feet, looking at him with sinister eyes. "You can pick up the letter opener with your mouth, and you're dead. Or you can pick it up with your talons, and you're dead. Or, you do nothing and I slip it into Henry's cloak, and *he's* dead. Or you can stop me from delivering it at all, and your precious Patrick never utters the most important words he will ever say to change the course of history." She laughed coldly. "My, what a poetic moment. You actually get to choose to live up to your name! OR NOT. You can fly away and save yourself." She got right in his face and whispered. "You can choose to be free from this situation by just *leaving.*"

Cato lowered his head as he realized the impossible situation before him. He was immobilized by fear. He stared at the letter opener, which was so close yet emotionally out of his reach. Kakia was enjoying watching his struggle of indecision and rolled on the ground playfully.

"Poor you. Can I help you decide?" Kakia offered in a sarcastic voice, stretched out on the ground next to the letter opener. She popped out her pointer claw and scraped it along the ivory. "How about I tell you what will happen to you if you pick up this letter opener? I've laced it with aconite, a personal favorite of mine. This poison works splendidly on wolves who fail me." She laughed, recalling the dead wolves who failed to kill the young Marquis de Lafayette. "First you'll notice tingling and numbness in your mouth, and a sensation of ants crawling all over you. Your body temperature will drop, followed by your pulse. Then your heart rate will become deliciously irregular, as if you're about to have a heart attack. Then you'll feel nauseous, you'll vomit, and your stomach will be wracked with pain. You'll have difficulty breathing and then—I love this part, especially for *you,* my eagle-eyed friend—your pupils will dilate causing blurred vision. Then the *real* fun begins! Your face will become paralyzed, and anxiety and tremendous fear will set in as the sense of suffocation consumes you." She rose to her feet and crept over to whisper in Cato's ear. "Death comes in a few short hours." She chuckled softly.

Cato's heart raced and terror held him in a vise as he heard the fate that awaited him should he pick up that letter opener—or the fate that awaited Patrick should he do the same.

"Our time here is short, so you must decide. What will it be, Cato?" Kakia asked him. "Liberty or death?"

Those words immediately touched the deep recesses of Cato's soul. The eagle snapped his head up and glared at the wicked cat. The words from the play echoed in his mind. *It is not now time to talk of aught, but chains or conquest, liberty or death.* "I *know* what course I must take." He flapped his wings, picked up the letter opener with his talons, and soared off into the sky, leaving Kakia screaming on the ground below.

———

Patrick Henry pulled his red cloak tightly around his shoulders, wincing at the wound on his hand. He had removed the cloth wrapped around the cut. He didn't wish to appear weak on any level today. As he turned the corner to walk up the dirt path leading to the Henrico Parish Church, a chilly, easterly wind hit him in the face, sending shivers through him. He looked up at the cloudy sky. It looked as if it might snow. Regardless of the cold weather outside, he knew things would heat up quickly once he took to the floor of the Convention inside the church.

587

The Henrico Parish Church stood on the highest point of Richmond, a small trading town built by William Byrd II. He named it Richmond, for it reminded him of Richmond-on-Thames in England. The town was located at the seven-mile rapids and roaring falls of the mighty James River, separating the Piedmont and Tidewater regions of Virginia.

Peyton Randolph had called this Second Virginia Convention to elect delegates for the Second Continental Congress in Philadelphia in May, but everyone knew there were other pressing security matters at hand. Lord Dunmore had refused to call the assembly of the House of Burgesses to order since his return from the Ohio country in December. Randolph wisely proposed that this second "illegal" Convention meet far from the eyes and ears of Dunmore in Williamsburg. Putting sixty miles of distance between them, the Virginia delegates could meet in safety and have plenty of warning should Dunmore make a move to force them to disband and then incur his wrath.

The layers of history surrounding this chosen location and building were not lost on the delegates. It was in this same area, a century before Richmond was founded, that Nathaniel Bacon had led his rebellion against the royal governor. And it was in a church in Jamestown that America's first legislature met in 1619. The cause of liberty could find no better sanctuary than a church, for liberty itself was born on its altar of grace.

The Henrico Parish Church was the only building large enough in the market town of Richmond to house the one hundred twenty delegates. It was a small, wooden building with fifteen-foot ceilings and a peaked roof. A recent addition made it into the shape of a "T" with doors at each end and semicircle-topped windows running along the sides.

Many delegates had ridden for a week over muddy roads to reach Richmond; for others, their journey only took a day or two. Patrick Henry had ridden only a day from Scotchtown to reach Richmond. He quickly joined his circle of friends and family whom he knew he could count on to support his resolutions, including his half-brother John Syme, Jr., his Uncle Anthony Winston, and his brother-in-law William Christian, who was with Colonel Andrew Lewis, commander of the troops at Point Pleasant. Other ardent young patriots in Virginia he could count on included Richard Henry Lee, George Washington, Thomas Jefferson, and Paul Carrington (who had been his ally in the Stamp Act fight.) The "old guard" of Virginia, who were reluctant to stir up any trouble, thereby arousing the king, but would oppose Patrick Henry in a heartbeat, included Richard Bland, Benjamin Harrison, Archibald Cary, Edmund Pendleton, Robert Carter Nicolas, and Carter Braxton.

Patrick Henry knew most of the delegates at the Convention, as most of them had served with him in the House of Burgesses. Together they exchanged the latest news from around the colony. They discussed the movement afoot in the northern colonies to form militias, as had been done in Delaware, Maryland, and even closer to home in Fairfax County across the Potomac River. George Washington himself had presided over the Fairfax meeting where George Mason authored the Fairfax resolutions, declaring they were prepared to defend their rights and privileges as Englishmen under the British constitution. Things in Boston remained tense, according to reports from Samuel Adams, and they remained alert to the very real possibility that General Gage would strike at their provincial militia at any moment. News from London confirmed the king's harsh tone in Parliament and the unlikely possibility he would ever answer the petitions sent by the colonies. Peyton Randolph relayed the disturbing news, quoting a report that the patriots "are to be treated as rebels and Enemies without any ceremony."

The Second Virginia Convention opened on March 20 and had spent the last three days getting formally organized and reviewing the proceedings of the First Continental Congress. Peyton Randolph was selected and referred to as "president" rather than "speaker." Reverend Miles Selden of Henrico Parish was named chaplain, and John Tazewell was selected as clerk. Everything so far in this Convention had been expected. But now it was the fourth day.

And Patrick Henry was about to do the unexpected.

589

LIBERTY OR DEATH

L iz sat behind a tombstone in the graveyard near the main door to Henrico Parish, which was their designated meeting spot. They had decided that once they retrieved the letter opener, she would be the one to sneak inside the church, as Max was too big and would clearly be seen. Her heart pounded as she saw the stream of delegates filing into the church. She looked through a group of stockinged legs until finally she saw the unmistakable square head of a Scottish terrier trotting along behind them. She strained to see his full face when suddenly relief flooded into her spirit. In his mouth Max carried the ivory letter opener.

"Max! You have it!" Liz cried as he ran up to her, dropping it on the ground.

"Aye, Cato gr-r-rabbed it fr-r-rom that evil kitty, cleaned it off in the James R-r-river, an' dr-r-ropped it ta me," Max explained. "He didn't have time ta explain, but said ta meet him by the falls later. The eagle lad did it, lass. The letter opener's here an' clean as a whistle."

Liz's face beamed as she placed her dainty paw on the letter opener. "Well done, *cher* Cato! But how will I enter the church?" she asked. "Before I can slip the letter opener into the pocket of my Henry's cloak, I first must get inside."

"Leave that to me," came the voice of Clarie behind them. She was dressed as a man in the silk breeches and coat of a delegate, with buckled shoes and tricorn hat. "Max, you get to the opposite side of the church. I've positioned a crate under a window where you'll be able to listen and observe everything. Liz, you take the letter opener, and be ready for my signal. Go!" She walked off to open the door just as Patrick Henry and a group of men approached the entrance to the church.

Max kissed Liz on the cheek. "Okay, yer Henry's safe inside, with Mousie in his pocket. Now he jest needs that letter opener, an' all will be set. Ye can do it, lassie. R-r-remember wha' Gillamon always says."

Liz nodded and smiled. *"Oui.* Know that you are loved, and you are able."

"Aye!" Max agreed with a wink. "I'll see ye an' Mousie after the meetin'."

With that the Scottie trotted away, leaving Liz there alone behind the tombstone. She took a deep breath and exhaled slowly. *"Mon Dieu,* make me swift and unseen, *s'il vous plaît."*

———

The heat in the room was rising, not just from the one hundred twenty men packed into Henrico Parish Church, but from the heat of argument that was building in the room as well. After opening the fourth day of the Convention with a prayer asking God to protect the king and hearing a series of reports, Patrick Henry asked to be recognized by President Randolph. As he read his resolutions, calling for the colony of Virginia to immediately be put into a state of defense, cries of treason echoed off the walls of the church, and an animated debate ensued. Men were gathered around the outside of the church, straining to hear the arguments coming from inside.

It was during that heated debate Clarie made her way to the front of the church and whispered in President Randolph's ear, requesting that she be permitted to open the windows and doors to allow fresh air into the church. Thinking that this "man" was a delegate from one of the counties in Virginia, or perhaps a parishioner of Henrico on site to help with anything the Convention needed, he nodded in agreement with Clarie's request.

Clarie proceeded to open the window and winked at Max, who smiled back at her with a wide grin. Then she opened the far door on the opposite side of the church from the window, and motioned for Liz with a finger to her tricorn hat. Fresh air poured into the church, a welcome relief from the stuffy, hot air inside.

Edmund Pendleton raised his hand to be recognized by President Randolph.

"Jest in time, lass," Max muttered under his breath. "Here comes more hot air."

591

"The gentleman from Caroline County!" Peyton Randolph bellowed, pounding his stick and pointing to call attention to the speaker. "Mr. Edmund Pendleton."

"Sir," Mr. Pendleton said, nodding in respect to Mr. Randolph. Turning to Patrick Henry, he furrowed his brow and exclaimed, "We must arm, you say; but gentlemen must remember that blows are apt to follow the arming, and blood will follow blows, and sir, when this occurs the dogs of war will be loosed, friends will be converted into enemies, and this flourishing country will be swept with a tornado of death and destruction!"

"Wha' were I jest sayin' aboot hot air?" Max grumbled. "Dogs of war, humph."

Patrick Henry raised his hand to be recognized.

"The gentleman from Hanover County, Mr. Patrick Henry," Peyton Randolph bellowed, nodding that the floor was now his.

Patrick rose from his seat on the third pew near the window where Edward Carrington looked on. He hadn't noticed Max in the window as he walked by. Carrington was amused by the little dog jumping up next to him, but the young patriot was so caught up in the anticipation of hearing Patrick Henry speak that he just stood there, mesmerized, unconcerned that a dog was interested as well. Max wagged his tail, eager for what was about to unfold.

Nigel was sweating inside Patrick's cloak pocket. Patrick had gotten so chilled on his walk to the church that he had kept the cloak on until he warmed himself. *Do please cooperate and remove your cloak, old boy!* Nigel thought, praying that Patrick would do his bidding.

Liz peeked in the door through the legs of bystanders in the doorway, her heart beating wildly as she also prayed for Patrick to remove his cloak. Patrick walked to the front of the church, bowed with his foot forward and his arms outstretched respectfully. He turned around and his red cloak swirled behind him. He cleared his throat and started speaking in a low, halting voice of humility as he slowly walked along the front of the church, lifting a hand to acknowledge his worthy opponents scattered in pews around the church.

"No man thinks more highly than I do of the patriotism, as well as abilities, of the very worthy gentlemen who have just addressed the House. But different men often see the same subject in different lights; and, therefore, I hope it will not be thought disrespectful to those gentlemen if, entertaining as I do opinions of a character very opposite to theirs, I shall speak forth my sentiments freely and without reserve." George Washington stood by the open door, having got up for a moment to stretch his legs and whisper a word to one of Henry's late-arriving supporters. Patrick made his way to the front pew box and shared a nod and knowing look with Washington. He quietly removed his red cloak and draped it over the pew box.

Finally! Liz, Nigel, and Max all thought from their various vantage points. Liz quickly slipped into the church unnoticed as all eyes were on Patrick, who started walking in the opposite direction across the front of the church. She glided under the cloak just as Nigel slid out of the pocket onto the floor. They were hidden by the folds of the red cloak.

"Bravo! You have it!" Nigel whispered.

Liz smiled with the letter opener in her mouth and then proceeded to slip it into Patrick's pocket in the middle of the rolled-up petition he had tucked away there. She exhaled in relief. *"Oui,* it is done. Now we wait." They peeked out and saw George Washington standing right next to them for a moment before he took his seat a couple of rows behind them.

"This is no time for ceremony," Patrick said. "The question before the House is one of awful moment to this country. For my own part, I consider it as nothing less than a question of freedom or slavery; and in proportion to the magnitude of the subject ought to be the freedom of the debate. It is only in this way that we can hope to arrive at truth, and fulfill the great responsibility which we hold to God and our country. Should I keep back my opinions at such a time, through fear of giving offense, I should consider myself as guilty of treason towards my country, and of an act of disloyalty toward the Majesty of Heaven, which I revere above all earthly kings."

Patrick turned and addressed Peyton Randolph, who remained seated in his chair at the front of the church. "Mr. President, it is natural to man to indulge in the illusions of hope. We are apt to shut our eyes against a painful truth, and listen to the song of that siren till she transforms us into beasts. Is this the part of wise men, engaged in a great and arduous struggle for liberty? Are we disposed to be of the number of those who, having eyes, see not, and, having ears, hear not, the things which so nearly concern their temporal salvation? For my part, whatever anguish of spirit it may cost, I am willing to know the whole truth; to know the worst, and to provide for it."

"Veritas," Liz whispered.

Nigel nodded. "Truth."

Patrick then held out an imaginary lantern over his feet as he walked back across the front of the church toward the opened door. "I have but one lamp by which my feet are guided, and that is the lamp of experience." He paused and pointed one hand ahead of him and one hand behind him. "I know of no way of judging the future but by the past." He walked over to his red cloak draped over the pew rail. Liz and Nigel pressed their backs against the pew box. They held their breaths, hoping Patrick wouldn't see them. He reached into his pocket to pull out a copy of the latest petition to the king. Liz and Nigel both exhaled and looked at one another.

"That was close!" Nigel whispered.

"Oui," Liz quickly whispered back. "I wonder if he realizes he has the letter opener."

"And judging by the past," Patrick continued, "I wish to know what there has been in the conduct of the British ministry for the last *ten* years to justify those hopes with which gentlemen have been pleased to solace themselves and the House." He smiled coyly and slowly waved the petition in the air. "Is it that insidious smile with which our petition has been lately received? Trust it not, sir; it will prove a snare to your feet. Suffer not yourselves to be betrayed with a kiss." He allowed the image of Judas betraying Jesus in the Garden of Gethsemane to hover before the mind's eye of his listeners while he walked back across the front of the church to the open window.

"Ask yourselves how this gracious reception of our petition comports with those warlike preparations which cover our waters and darken our land," Patrick continued, pacing around the front of the church. He proceeded to fix his eyes on the men in the audience who wanted to keep pleading with the king, darting his gaze from one to the next. They knew he spoke not only of the closing of Boston Harbor, but of the British warship stationed in the waters near the Virginia capital of Williamsburg. "Are fleets and armies necessary to a work of love and reconciliation? Have we shown ourselves so unwilling to be reconciled that force must be called in to win back our love?" He leaned over with his spectacles perched firmly atop his head as he bored into their eyes with a look that arrested their best arguments. "Let us not deceive ourselves, sir. These are the implements of war and subjugation; the last arguments to which kings resort."

Patrick held his arms out wide and slowly turned as if the church itself was surrounded by cannon and British warships. "I ask gentlemen, sir, what means this martial array, if its purpose be not to force us to submission? Can gentlemen assign *any other possible* motive for it?" He slowly shook his head, willing his audience to agree with him. He gradually elevated the volume of his voice. "Has Great Britain any enemy, in this quarter of the world, to call for all this accumulation of navies and armies? No, sir, she has none." He pointed to himself and then to the audience. "They are meant for us: they can be meant for no other. They are sent over to bind and rivet upon us those chains which the British ministry have been so long forging."

"Hear, hear!" Edward Carrington cheered from the window.

"And what have we to oppose to them? Shall we try argument? Sir, we have been trying that for the last *ten* years. Have we anything new to offer upon the subject? Nothing. We have held the subject up in every light of which it is capable; but it has been all in vain." He unrolled the petition against the hazy light coming in from the open window. It was then he saw his ivory letter opener wrapped in the parchment. He slipped it into his right hand while he rolled the petition back up and gripped it tightly with his left hand.

"He's got the letter opener!" Nigel cheered.

"Now to see what he will do with it," Liz answered.

Patrick continued to increase the volume of his voice while he pointed with the petition, grilling the opposing men, one by one: "Shall we resort to entreaty and humble supplication? What terms shall we find which have not been already exhausted? Let us not, I beseech you, sir, deceive ourselves. Sir, we have done *everything* that could be done to avert the storm which is now coming on. We have *petitioned;* we have *remonstrated;* we have *supplicated.*" He bowed low and spread out his arms. "We have prostrated ourselves before the throne, and have implored its interposition to arrest the tyrannical hands of the ministry and Parliament."

He then stood up tall, pursed his lips, and shook his head. He allowed his voice to grow louder as he recounted each result from their efforts. "Our petitions have been *slighted;* our remonstrances have produced additional violence and *insult;* our supplications have been *disregarded;* and we have been spurned, with *contempt,* from the foot of the throne!" He threw the petition to the floor and stomped on it with his foot.

595

A chorus of "Hear, hear," echoed around the room as men thumped on the church pew railings, and used their canes to pound the wooden floor. Murmurings were heard all over the church until President Randolph struck the floor with his stick to silence the onlookers. "Order, order!"

Patrick bowed slightly in respect and appreciation to Mr. Randolph. He then stood in the middle of the church and turned his voice to one of hopeless resolve. "In vain, after these things, may we indulge the fond hope of peace and reconciliation. There is no longer any room for hope." It was as if Patrick had just pronounced the sentence of death over a dying patient. He then began to slowly raise the volume of his voice with each successive sentence until he reached a deafening crescendo. "If we wish to be free—if we mean to preserve inviolate those inestimable privileges for which we have been so long contending—if we mean not basely to abandon the noble struggle in which we have been so long engaged, and which we have pledged ourselves *never* to abandon until the glorious object of our contest shall be obtained—we must fight! I repeat it, sir, we must fight! An appeal to arms and to the God of hosts is all that is left us!"

"Treason! Treason against the king!" shouted the group of men opposing Henry.

"Aye! We must fight!" shot back those supporting him.

"This is utter madness! Even if we followed such treasonous measures, we have no arms that can oppose the might of the British army, and no ships to oppose her navy!" argued the opposition.

Once again, the attendees erupted into shouts of opposing voices. Men pounded the church pews until President Randolph rose to his feet and struck the floor repeatedly with his stick. "Order, order! Allow the gentleman from Hanover County to continue! Order!"

The murmuring subsided and Patrick once more gave a nod of respectful gratitude to Mr. Randolph.

"They tell us, sir, that we are weak; unable to cope with so formidable an adversary. But when shall we be stronger?" He shrugged his shoulders and used his hands to punctuate each question. "Will it be the next week, or the next year? Will it be when we are totally disarmed, and when a British guard shall be stationed in every house? Shall we gather strength by irresolution and inaction?" He leaned back and then wrapped his arms around his chest. "Shall we acquire the means of effectual resistance by lying supinely on our backs and hugging the delusive phantom of hope, until our enemies shall have bound us hand and foot?" He stood up straight and balled his hand into a fist. "Sir, we are not weak if we make a proper use of those means which the God of nature hath placed in our power. Three millions of people, armed in the holy cause of liberty, and in such a country as that which we possess, are *invincible* by any force which our enemy can send against us. Besides, sir, we shall not fight our battles alone." He looked up toward heaven and held out his hands. "There is a just God who presides over the destinies of nations, and who will raise up friends to fight our battles for us."

"Oui, the French will come, *mon* Henry!" Liz cheered quietly.

Nigel preened his whiskers proudly. "Franklin's electric key has already turned the lock in *that* door."

"The battle, sir, is not to the strong alone; it is to the vigilant, the active, the *brave,*" Patrick continued, holding out his arms. "Besides, sir, we have no election. If we were base enough to desire it, it is now too late to retire from the contest," Patrick continued, allowing the volume of his voice to reach its maximum. "There is no retreat but in submission and slavery! Our chains are forged! Their clanking may be heard on the plains of Boston! The war is inevitable—and let it come! I repeat it, sir, let it come."

597

Yet again the chorus of protests erupted from the floor of the Convention over the mention of war. Above the din of voices, Patrick suddenly heard the unmistakable voice of an eagle—little did he know it was *his* eagle. In a split second he saw Cato fly by the open window, crying out, *"Liberty! Liberty! Liberty!"* Patrick gripped the letter opener in his hand and a flood of childhood memories filled his mind— Whitfield, Davies, *Cato:* his eagle, Plutarch, and the play.

Liz's heart raced as she saw Patrick look at the letter opener in his right hand. "This is it, *mon* Henry!"

Patrick bellowed in a loud voice and immediately regained command of the audience. His eyes were flashing and his face flush with passion as he held his arms out wide. "It is in vain, sir, to extenuate the matter. Gentlemen may cry, 'Peace, Peace'—but there is no peace." He directed his gaze and nodded at Colonel Andrew Lewis, who had already experienced first blood drawn at the Battle of Point Pleasant. "The war is actually begun!" He then pointed north with his hand extended in dramatic form. "The next gale that sweeps from the north will bring to our ears the clash of resounding arms!" He clenched his fists and his voice grew to such a pitch that men began rising to their feet. "Our brethren are already in the field! Why stand we here idle? What is it that gentlemen wish? What would they have?" He then crossed his wrists as if they were manacled by heavy chains, with his gaze lowered to the floor. He closed his eyes and the fresh image of his beloved Sallie bound up in the "chains" of her straight-dress flashed across his mind. A lump formed in his throat, followed by a wave of anger at the thought of America also now bound by the tyranny of the British lion.

Patrick clenched his jaw and tightened his right fist around the letter opener. He opened his eyes that now blazed with fury and the piercing question posed to every man in the room. "Is life so dear, or peace so sweet, as to be purchased at the price of chains and slavery? Forbid it, Almighty God!" Patrick cried, throwing back his head as he gazed up to heaven, the tendons in his neck protruding as he strained against the imaginary fetters weighing him down. He then lowered his

fiery gaze to the timid men opposing him, making them squirm with the notion that they were allowing him to remain in such a state. He then hunched his shoulders forward and allowed his gaze to drift to the floor. He willed the assembly to envision him as the embodiment of the humiliated, oppressed colony of Virginia under the iron heel of the British monarch. "I know not what course others may take," he groaned through clenched teeth, slowly raising his gaze, "but as for me, give me lib-er-ty," he cried, belting out each syllable with a roar and strain-ing with every muscle to cast off the imaginary chains from his arms. He stood there fearless and defiant, the pure embodiment of freedom, allowing the word 'liberty' to reverberate off the walls as he gripped the letter opener in his fist. The unconquerable spirit of Cato possessed him and flashed before the eyes of every man in the room, causing the hair on the backs of their necks to rise. He then pretended to plunge the letter opener into his patriot heart, and in an electrifying, triumphant cry exclaimed, "Or give me death!"

Deafening silence filled the room. No one uttered a word. In that moment, the entire assembly was instantly transported to the bluffs of Utica. They were listening to the cries of Cato, the last citizen of the Roman republic, beseeching them to never give up their liberty no mat-ter the cost. The gravity of a decision fell onto each soul as the piercing question was pressed to each breast like a dagger—what then will *you* choose? Liberty or death?

Liz closed her eyes tightly, allowing the tears to stream down her cheeks from the enraptured moment. The destiny-filled influences, hardships, and resolve that had poured into her Henry throughout his entire life came together in that one, eternal moment.

"Boys, bury me here on this spot!" came the cry of Edward Carrington, who pointed at the ground below where he stood at the window. He was energized by the urgency of the ancient Roman tragedy revived against the backdrop of history's current stage of events.

Max jumped as Carrington enthusiastically hit the wooden crate that he had been sitting on to also peer in the window next to the excited patriot. *"Steady, lad!"* he barked.

"TO ARMS! TO ARMS!" came the cry from trembling lips as the emotion of Patrick's sentinel call rippled throughout the assembly. Patrick slowly walked back to take his seat on the third row near the window where Carrington and Max were stationed.

Richard Henry Lee raised his hand to be recognized. "I wish to second Mr. Henry's resolutions, that the colony of Virginia be immediately placed in a state of defense."

Thomas Jefferson quickly lifted his hand in agreement. "I echo the motion by the gentleman from Westmoreland County."

Wealthy, young Thomas Nelson, Jr., was on his feet. His family home in Yorktown was situated overlooking the York River where British warships could anchor. He slammed his fist on the pew box and declared, "If any British troops land within my county of York, I will wait for NO orders, and will obey none which would forbid me, to summon my militia and repel the invaders at the water's edge!" He turned and looked at his fellow wealthy aristocrats. "To shrink away from this challenge now would mean dishonor."

Opposing shouts continued until Peyton Randolph pounded his stick on the floor at the front altar of the church to call the men to order one more time on this immortal day. "It is time to take a vote on Mr. Henry's resolutions." He looked around the room and maintained a grave expression as he furrowed his brow. "Think carefully about what you will be putting your name to. If you vote 'aye' you will be potentially accused of declaring war against the king of England."

The men of the assembly cast anxious glances at one another. Those who were certain of their decision to support Henry's resolutions nodded with vigorous resolve. They were eager to vote. Those opposed were just as eager to voice their opinion, but their motivation was to block Henry's resolves. Those who were uncertain wavered as they looked around the room to see who was on what side of the decision.

Peyton Randolph perched both hands atop his stick. "Very well. All those in favor? Say, 'Aye'!"

"AYE!" came a resounding chorus of voices ready to take up arms.

President Randolph paused a moment as Clerk Tazewell counted the upraised arms. Then he followed with, "All those opposed?"

"NAY!" shouted the fearful voices siding with the king.

"This is goin' ta be close," Max muttered to himself, catching Clarie's eye across the room.

"Do you suppose the 'ayes' have it, my dear?" Nigel asked Liz.

She looked up and saw Clarie standing in the open door, urgently motioning them to exit. "*Je ne sais pas,* but we cannot stay to find out."

"No time to explain," Clarie said as Max, Liz, and Nigel joined her outside. She squatted down behind a tombstone. "You need to get to Cato at the falls. I'll meet you there shortly and fill you in on what happens with the vote. Now hurry! Get to Cato!" She quickly rose to her feet and rushed back inside the church.

Max, Liz, and Nigel looked at one another, stunned and confused.

"Wha's happened, ye think?" Max asked as they started walking in the direction of the falls.

"No . . . no . . . NO!" Liz shouted as it slowly dawned on her what was happening. Her heart suddenly caught in her throat. "Cato!" she cried as she took off running ahead of the others.

ON EAGLE'S WINGS

The sound of rapids grew louder as the animals neared the water's edge. Max ran a distant stride behind Liz, who had not slowed her pace since they left the churchyard. Nigel rode on Max's back, holding on tightly to the dog's fur. He shouted into Max's large triangle ear, "I've never seen our girl run so fast!"

Max huffed as they neared the meeting spot at the James River where the cascading falls churned the water into a foam against the massive boulders peppered along the shoreline. "She's never had such an urgent message ta get her movin' like this!"

Liz stopped when they reached the riverbank and looked both ways, panting heavily to catch her breath. "CATO! CATO! Where are you?!" Her face was riddled with anguish when she turned to Max and Nigel, who had caught up with her. "Where is he?" Before they could answer she took off again, running along the riverbank and calling out to the eagle.

Max shouted after her, "Shouldn't we be lookin' up in the sky?"

"I'm afraid that this time we shall find him on the ground," Nigel answered gravely.

It wasn't long before Liz spotted the distinct white head of the eagle up ahead on the riverbank. He was lying on his side next to a boulder with his talons curled under him, breathing heavily. She rushed up to him and her voice broke as she spoke his name, "Cato. Oh, *cher* Cato."

The eagle struggled to lift his head, which trembled from the simple effort. His eyes were glazed over and he blinked, unable to see clearly. "Liz?" he called softly. "Did . . . Patrick . . . ?"

Liz placed her paw on the eagle's wing. *"Oui,* he used the letter opener, Cato," she replied with tears falling from her face onto his feathers. "It was in his hand when he saw you fly by, and at that moment I believe he knew what to say. His words carried the day." She smiled sadly and sobbed, wiping away her tears. "You did it, Cato."

Max stopped a few yards behind them, and Nigel climbed off his back to the ground. "We've got ta save him!" Max said as he saw Cato's condition, taking a step forward.

Nigel placed his paw on Max's leg to stop him. "I'm afraid it's too late," the mouse murmured softly. "He's been poisoned. It won't be long now. Give them this moment."

Max looked at Nigel with sadness in his eyes and didn't know what to say. Together he and Nigel stood back, allowing Liz the space she needed to speak to her old friend.

Cato closed his eyes and shuddered, relieved. "What . . . words?"

Liz tenderly placed her paw on the eagle's head, gently smoothing back his feathers. "'Liberty or death.' From *Cato*. Patrick acted out the scene from the play, *mon ami*. The humans were moved beyond words and were eager to support his resolutions. Thank you, Cato, for your bravery . . ." she forced out, looking down at his talons. She saw that they were cut and her mind pieced together how he had been poisoned. "And for your sacrifice."

The eagle took in a shallow breath and shivered. He managed a slight nod, relieved to hear the news. "'Despair . . . not . . . the . . . tragic . . .'" he struggled to say, quoting the end of Gillamon's riddle.

Liz swallowed the lump in her throat and softly finished the line. "'Each pain is a key, to unlock the next door for the voice to be free.'" She sobbed and put her head near his. "But this pain I do not think I can bear."

"I . . . am old. My . . . time is short on Earth . . . either way," Cato gasped, breathing even more heavily now. "My sons . . . Plutarch . . . Veritas . . . Alexander . . . tell them they must be . . . the next generation . . . to fight . . . for liberty."

Liz nodded through eyes blinded with tears. "It will always be up to the next generation to keep a nation free," she uttered with a broken voice.

"'What a pity . . . that we can die but once . . . to serve our country,'" Cato said softly with a sad smile.

Nigel wiped the tears from behind his spectacles and leaned over to whisper to Max. "He's quoting another line from the play, *Cato*."

602

Cato's eyes opened wide as if startled by something unseen in front of him. He started breathing rapidly, and tried to lift his head.

Liz tried to stop him from moving. "Shhhhh. I am here."

"One . . . thing," the eagle struggled to say as he reached down to his shoulder. He gripped his beak around a feather and pulled it out with all his remaining strength. "For . . . Patrick."

"Oh!" Liz cried out, falling on the dying eagle as she accepted the feather with her paw. She wrapped her arms around her friend and rocked him back and forth, weeping uncontrollably. She held him close to her heart until he slipped away.

Max and Nigel sat quietly by for a long time, allowing Liz time to grieve the loss of their friend. The James River seemed to hold but a tiny drop of water compared with the river of tears flowing from their eyes.

Clarie came walking up to them and squatted down next to her friends on the riverbank. "Did she get to say goodbye?" she asked softly.

"Aye," Max replied. "This were a shock ta all of us. I hope the lass can handle it."

Clarie nodded and looked over at Liz. "She can. She will. She must."

"The price of being immortal is having to tell those we love farewell while we remain behind," Nigel said, "whether it be tragically like this, or whether it be naturally."

"Cato was not going to live much longer," Clarie pointed out. "He was thirty years old, so he had lived longer than most eagles."

"It still don't make it any easier," Max moaned, looking at Liz still draped over Cato.

"Come, let's go to her," Clarie prompted them, standing to walk over to Liz.

Liz heard them behind her but kept her head on Cato. "He wanted Patrick to have his feather. I will take it to him, but he will never know where it came from."

Clarie knelt down, and she, Max, and Nigel surrounded Liz and Cato. "Someday he will," Clarie said with a smile. "I will take care of Cato from here." She put her hands on Liz's small form and pulled the grieving cat to her chest to hold her for a moment. "You and Cato accomplished your mission, Liz. Patrick's resolutions passed, 65-60. He is already leading the committee to set things in place for Virginia's defense."

Liz sniffed and nodded gratefully. "Thank you for this good news, *mon amie*. But I feel too weak in my spirit to do anything else for the cause of liberty right now."

"Remember what you helped Isaiah to pen so long ago about eagles?" Clarie whispered into Liz's ear. "'Those who wait for the LORD will gain new strength; they will mount up with wings like eagles.'"

Liz's eyes brimmed and her voice filled with emotion as she finished the verse from Isaiah 40:31: "'They will run and not get tired. They will walk and not become weary.'"

"Wait for the LORD," Clarie said as she kissed Liz on the head and placed her on the ground next to Max and Nigel. They enveloped her with hugs. Clarie then gently scooped up Cato's lifeless form in her arms, hugging him close. "Remember, for those who love the Maker, it is never a final goodbye. Only a temporary farewell. Take comfort in the fact that you will see Cato again." She rose to her feet and started to slowly disappear before their eyes, but they could hear Clarie's voice over the rushing waters of the James. "And know this. Cato now soars with the angels in heaven."

Liz closed her eyes to imagine the beautiful scene of Cato, young again and very much alive, forever flying freely around the Majesty of Heaven. She let go a laugh of bittersweet joy. "*A voice dying on the out- and inside,*" she recited to Max and Nigel, understanding the final part of the fiddle's riddle. "So many layers of meaning, but I never thought Cato would be part of the riddle."

"I guess it meant both Catos—the play an' the eagle," Max suggested. "Jest like yer Henry acted it out as if he were dyin'."

Nigel clasped his paws behind his back and shook his head in wonder. "Extraordinary. While Cato was dying on the *outside* of the church, Patrick was 'dying' on the *inside* of the church."

"My Henry has also been dying on the *inside* from the weight of a grieving heart . . ." Liz added.

"Yet the Voice of the Revolution threw off his own chains of grief to exclaim Cato's words and rally a nation to Independence," Nigel replied in awe.

"And so must we," Liz replied, wiping her eyes. "Time for something new to begin."

604

"Aye. Amazin' wha' this mission finally led ta," marveled Max. "Jest seven little words."

"Give me liberty, or give me death," recited Liz, echoing Patrick's words.

Nigel nodded. "I do believe the power of those seven little words will forever soar through the air of freedom."

"Oui," affirmed Liz, with tears of joy mixed with sadness, softly touching Cato's feather, "on eagle's wings."

A Word from the Author

"GIVE ME FACTS, OR GIVE ME DEATH AS A CREDIBLE HISTORICAL AUTHOR!"

It is vitally important to me that I share with you background information on my research that fills the pages of my books, and the liberties I take to tell the stories. The genre I write is historical fiction fantasy, in that order. This means the first layer I begin writing is the *history*. This foundation layer must be rock solid historically, down to the most minute detail. I exhaust my sources of books, online research, site visits, and interviews with historical experts on people, places, and events. Once the bedrock history is laid, I then add the layer of *fiction* which must be *plausible*. For instance, the fictional words I put into Patrick Henry's mouth, as well as his actions, must match his character and the cultural setting. Once the historical fiction is as pure as I can make it, I add the layer of *fantasy* where the animal characters come into play. I look for those "unknowns" in the story of things that did happen (but we don't know how or why) or that *could* have happened. I allow my animals to affect the events of the story without ever giving away their true identities, which makes it fun. Once all three layers are set, the book is an accurate, educational, enjoyable (I hope) read intended to make history come alive for the reader.

Below is a great deal of background information that I hope you will find fascinating and that will fill in some details I cannot possibly cover with an already lengthy manuscript. I encourage you to further pursue any aspect of this amazing historical period to increase your understanding of and appreciation for the life and times of Patrick Henry and the Revolution.

PART ONE: CHAPTERS 1–16

Scottish terriers weren't introduced into America until the 1800s, but I had to allow Patrick to know about them in order to help his argument to keep Max.

David Henry's letters are fiction. He and John Henry were first cousins, and he was indeed the editor of *Gentleman's Magazine* in London.

The Romans celebrated with birthday cakes, and it is thought that even the ancient Greeks put lit candles on cakes.

The New England Primer – The excerpts in Chapter 9 are from the actual book used to teach children in America's first three centuries. Isn't it amazing to see the unashamed moral and religious instruction children received in schools?

Patrick's Fiddle – The description Nigel gives of its Flemish design and features is taken from the appraisal of Patrick's fiddle on display at the Patrick Henry National Memorial of Red Hill in Brookneal, Virginia. No one knows when he acquired the fiddle or how. The fact that Flemish fiddles ceased being made in that design around 1740 made it very plausible that he acquired it as a boy. He did attend the St. Andrew's Day festival with his family, where a fiddle was awarded to the best fiddler.

Hey, Diddle, Diddle was written around 1765, but parts may have come from the 1500s, so I used it anyway in 1745.

Cato: **A Tragedy** – *Cato* was written by Joseph Addison in 1712, and was based on the last days of Cato the Younger in Rome. Cato was known as the last citizen of the Roman Republic who railed against the coming dictatorship of Julius Caesar. The theme of the play deals with liberty versus tyranny. Addison would have read *Plutarch's Parallel Lives* for the historical background to inspire the play. Addison did have Pope write the Prologue; however, the night of the play's dedication to Pope in memory of his passing is fiction on my part, as well as David Henry writing an article for *Gentleman's Magazine*. The play was wildly popular in the colonies leading up to the Revolution. It was George Washington's favorite play, and he and others including Nathan Hale quoted from the beloved work. Patrick Henry knew how to "push people's buttons." So that day in the Henrico parish (now known as St. John's Church) Henry was putting every man in that assembly on a bluff overlooking the sea at Utica, awaiting the armies of the tyrant Julius Caesar. He harkened back to the words of Cato to emote the exact feelings of the ensuing threat to liberty.

Molly's Collar – The inscription on Molly's collar are the exact words Alexander Pope had inscribed on the collar of a dog he gave to his good friend, Frederick, Prince of Wales. We don't know the kind of dog that was given, but I patterned Molly after a real Corgi named Molly that belongs to my friend Beth Woods, in Greensboro, North Carolina.

608

I was inspired to write about Molly when I stayed with Beth, and her daughter joined us to brainstorm about the letter opener and Plutarch the eagle, and to create the evil Kakia as my villainess.

Plutarch's Parallel Lives comprises forty-six biographies, but the compilation of these lives vary by publisher. My copies are in two volumes, but other editions may have nine volumes. For simplicity, I had Liz dealing with two volumes like mine.

Tower of London Menagerie – Everything you read about the menagerie is actual historical fact, including the possession of American animals such as a sea eagle. For our purposes, I made that eagle a bald eagle.

PART TWO: CHAPTERS 17–32

George Whitefield did visit Hanover and Reverend Patrick Henry's St. Paul's Parish in October 1745, just as I detailed. It is very likely that Patrick Henry attended this historic event; however, we don't know the exact sermon Whitefield preached. If Patrick Henry did not hear Whitefield's famed *Method of Grace* (quoted verbatim here), he most certainly read it in pamphlet form, as did half of the colonists at that time. This would be another "connection point" of well-known vernacular for Henry to use "Peace, peace, when there is no peace" in his Liberty or Death speech.

Samuel Davies had a greater impact on Patrick Henry than any other speaker, according to Henry's own words: "He taught me what an orator should be." Davies's voice was second only to Whitefield in the minds of America during the Great Awakening. He truly launched the Presbyterian Church in the colony of Virginia, and I wish I could have expounded more on his amazing story. I couldn't find a definitive account of the first sermon he preached at Polegreen, so I had Patrick "re-preach" Davies's sermon *Divine Government, the Joy of Our World*. If you'd like to learn more about Davies, I recommend the book *Living on the Borders of Eternity* by my friend, Dr. Robert Bluford, Jr., which is a novelized account of Davies's life. Patrick Henry knew Davies from Patrick's ages 11 to 23, so this eloquent man of God played a huge role in helping Henry to find his voice, both from a religious and a political standpoint. Davies was one of the most significant recruiters for the Virginia Militia during the French and Indian War, and inspired passionate patriotism. He later went on to briefly serve as the president of what would become Princeton University, before dying at the

609

early age of thirty-seven. Please visit the Historic Polegreen Church Web site to learn more about Davies and the Great Awakening movement in Virginia at http://www.historicpolegreen.org. I'm grateful for Dr. Bluford's book, and patterned my fictional scenes with Patrick and Davies after his wonderfully imagined encounters. I'm grateful to Bob for his gracious help in taking me to see the Patrick Henry sights of Studley, Pine Slash, Polegreen, and Hanover Courthouse, and of course his good humor when we set off the alarm while visiting Rural Plains together one rainy afternoon! The Sherriff's deputies came and . . . well, it's a long story.

Patrick's Broken Collarbone/Flute – Patrick Henry did break his collarbone when he was twelve, and he taught himself how to play the flute. We don't know how he broke his collarbone, so I was able to weave in some exciting fiction as well as a life lesson that touches on his character development. We also don't know the origin of his flute, so I incorporated Samuel Davies into the story. Patrick's flute is on display at Red Hill, but we don't know if it is the same flute he had as a child. The flute's description: wooden, made possibly in France, eighteenth century, ebony, 26 inches long in two parts with six finger holes. Key rings are shiny metal, possibly silver.

Benjamin Franklin/Peter Collinson/David Henry/Handel – I could not believe the actual, incredible connections of these men and the plot lines from my fourth book, *The Roman, the Twelve, and the King*, converging with this book seven. The timing of Handel's concert and David Henry's article detailing Franklin's experiments in *Gentleman's Magazine* in May 1750, with Peter Collinson as the link between the two, was uncanny. Ben and David did meet as struggling young printers in London, and it indeed set them up to electrify the world together decades later.

Handel's *Messiah* – You may be surprised to learn that it took seven years for *Messiah* to really take off after its 1743 premiere in London, due to the controversy surrounding the setting for performing the sacred masterpiece. In 1749, Handel became actively involved with the Foundling Hospital, which was an orphanage in London, offering to perform a benefit concert of *Messiah* to raise money to build a chapel there. The concert on May 1, 1750, was a sellout, as the setting and cause seemed to resolve any conflicts that the "good people of London" had about the work being performed outside a church. This benefit concert became an annual event continuing past Handel's death in 1759 all the way to 1777, and was the key to *Messiah's* growth in popularity and lasting success.

Handel willed a gift to the Founding Hospital in the third codicil (a document that adds to or changes something in a will) to his will: "I give a fair copy of the Score and all the parts of my Oratorio called *The Messiah* to the Foundling Hospital." Handel died on April 14, 1759, and within two weeks, that score was copied and delivered per his request. While researching for book four, *The Roman, the Twelve, and the King*, on March 2, 2012, I was privileged to hold that actual score in my hands with the gracious permission of Librarian Katharine Hogg and the Foundling Museum in London. I encourage you to visit www. foundlingmuseum.org.uk to learn more. To see pictures of me (and Nigel) with that 1759 score and of me writing the scene of *Messiah* in Handel's composing room, please visit my Web site: www.epicorderofthe-seven.com/Books/Roman.

George Washington's Near Misses – Yes, George Washington did get smallpox while on Barbados, which immunized him against the dreaded disease. (Of course, I needed to frame my villain as the culprit who exposed him to the virus.) He was fired upon by an Indian scout fifteen feet away in "the Murdering Town," but let the Indian go that night. He did cross the icy Allegheny River at night on the raft with Gist, stayed on the island, and walked across the ice in the morning completely fine while Gist suffered frostbite. He escaped harm at Fort Necessity and did not realize what he was signing in the surrender documents with the French that said he had murdered Jumonville. Until his dying day, he believed that the French scouting party was spying, and he was justified in defending his position. He was untouched in Braddock's failed battle, with four bullet holes in his coat and two horses shot out from under him.

Samuel Crowley and Elizabeth Strong were my sixth great-grandparents. Elizabeth was from Hanover County, but the friendship she had with Patrick and Sallie is unknown. Samuel was indeed the scout who died at the Battle of Point Pleasant, and he is buried there with his name on the historic marker. If one considers that battle as the beginning of the Revolutionary War, then it explains why I am so passionate about this period of history. My ancestor's blood was the first to be spilled in the Revolution. Elizabeth was the only widow who received a wartime

611

pension from the Battle of Point Pleasant by the authority of the Virginia House of Burgesses, and Governor Patrick Henry (stay tuned for the next book!) himself went to bat for her years later to increase the amount of money, which she needed to care for her seven children. I have to believe he did this to help the first widow of the Revolution, and I believe in my heart that he and Sallie indeed were friends with Elizabeth and Samuel.

PART THREE: CHAPTERS 33–47

Hanover Courthouse still stands and is a treasure on the Road to Revolution trail. I do not know if portraits of the kings hung in the courthouse, but I needed to take the liberties to have Patrick gaze at their tyrannical faces for inspiration. Likely the crests of the British monarchs were hung there, but it is plausible that the courthouse had the portraits as well.

Patrick's Horse – MizP is none other than my dear friend and Patrick Henry genealogist, Edith Poindexter. This amazing woman first toured me around Patrick Henry's Red Hill in Brookneal, Virginia, and has helped me with my research all these years. Jack Poindexter was her husband, so of course I had to make him the owner of MizP. I'm grateful to Edith, whom everyone loves and affectionately calls "MizP" at Red Hill. She worked as Red Hill's genealogist for decades, and her son, Cole Poindexter, now carries on the charge to help descendants of Patrick Henry trace their lineage.

Patrick's Law License in Williamsburg – We know that Patrick presented his law license to the Goochland County Courthouse on April 15, 1760, in order to take the necessary oath and be admitted to the local bar to practice there. That license bore two signatures: George Wythe's and John Randolph's. But history is silent on what happened during his interview with George Wythe, other than Thomas Jefferson's later (incorrect) report that Mr. Wythe had refused to sign the license. (Jefferson also gave an incorrect account that Nicholas and both Randolph brothers had signed the license.) We do not know what transpired with Robert Carter Nicholas or Peyton Randolph, so my scenarios with the first three gentlemen are fictionalized. We do know that John Randolph at first refused to interview Patrick based on his appearance, but *somehow* came to misunderstand that he had already received two signatures (enter Clarie). We do know he indeed pretended to disagree with Patrick's correct position and then led him to his library to exclaim the words I relayed at the end of chapter 38. Patrick did stop in and see Thomas Jefferson while he was in Williamsburg but I did not add that scene to an already lengthy chapter.

Coronation of King George III – The king's mother supposedly did tell him to be a king, and supposedly a jewel did fall out of his crown during the coronation, which some later saw as having been an omen of King George losing the colonies.

The Parson's Cause – Patrick Henry's debut on the public legal stage happened with this, likely one of the most important legal cases in American history. It was a precursor to the American Revolution, for Patrick Henry set the tone for every legal battle with the king that followed.

Here are the highlights of how the drama unfolded, but there was far more nitty-gritty infighting in the process. I encourage you to study this fascinating case on your own.

On October 12, 1758, the House of Burgesses passed the Two Penny Act, providing that all public and private debts contracted on a tobacco basis could be paid in coin instead of tobacco at two pennies per pound, for one year. Governor Francis Fauquier signed the Act.

613

The Clergy met in Williamsburg and decided to send Reverend John Camm to London to lay their grievances before the king in his Privy Council. Thomas Sherlock, bishop of London, supported the Virginia parsons, even calling the Two Penny Act an act of treason and an attack on the church.

On August 10, 1759, the king disallowed not only the 1758 Act but also those of 1753 and 1755. However, word didn't reach Virginia until June 27, 1760, eight months after the 1758 law had expired.

In May 1759, when payment was due the parsons for the 1757–58 year, was the Two Penny Act of 1758 a valid law in Virginia? The real issue was when the law was made invalid—at its passing on October 12, 1758, or on August 10, 1759, when the king struck it down. Since the Privy Council in London did not explicitly say on paper, the decision would be made in the courts in Virginia.

The parsons were asking the courts to make the 1758 Act unconstitutional, as violating higher law. There was no precedent for this. Five suits were brought. First, Rev. Alexander White filed suit in King William County, but the jury decided for the collectors and against White. He appealed to the General Court. The second suit was filed by

Rev. Thomas Warrington in York County. Although the jury decided for the parson and awarded substantial damages, the justices held that the law of 1758 had been valid and refused to allow the damages paid. Since Rev. John Camm's parish was in Williamsburg, his suit was brought in the General Court on October 10, 1759, but the decision would be dragged out and delayed until April 1764. He was denied, and Camm appealed again to London, but was struck down by the precedent made in Hanover in 1763.

The third case was brought by Rev. James Maury on April 1, 1762, and it came to court on November 5, 1763, in Hanover County. Mr. John Lewis was the defense attorney for the two collectors. Mr. Peter Lyons was the prosecuting attorney for Maury, and argued that the law had never been valid. The presiding justice, Mr. John Henry, sustained the argument and declared the Two Penny Act as invalid from its beginning. He called a jury to decide the damages due Reverend Maury, and set the date of the trial for December 1, 1763. John Lewis turned the final part of Maury's case over to Patrick Henry. All Patrick was supposed to do was keep the fine amount as low as possible, and he technically had no place to argue the validity of the law or to cry out against the actions of the parsons and the king. After the embarrassing outcome of one penny awarded to Maury, the other parsons realized pursuing their own lawsuits would likely be in vain.

It is interesting to note that an even more dramatic episode could have unfolded in this saga, but never took place. Despite the outcome of the Parson's Cause (or perhaps *because* of it), Reverend Patrick Henry filed his own suit in 1764, with Peter Lyons to represent him, and with his nephew, Patrick Henry, to oppose him. But the case was continued until the General Court gave its ruling on the general issues involved with Camm's case, and was later dismissed. Can you imagine the heated discussion around the Henry dinner table, if John Henry had to preside over a battle between his brother and his son?!

We don't know if Patrick was sitting in the courtroom for the November 5 case with John Lewis, but it seems natural he would have made every effort to be there for such a monumental case. We also don't know exactly when or how John turned the case over to Patrick, so a little help from Liz to spur them along couldn't hurt. Were portraits of the kings hanging on the walls of Hanover Courthouse? The royal crest certainly was, but we don't know about the paintings. It makes plausible sense to me, and served as perfect inspiration for "my Henry" in this case.

The scene of Uncle Patrick arriving and Patrick asking him to leave is traditionally accepted. However, Uncle Patrick's return to the courtroom has only recently been uncovered as a possibility by Patrick Henry historian, Mark Couvillon. I'm deeply indebted to Mark for helping me to craft this scene from his wealth of details.

As with all of Patrick Henry's speeches, we only have small bits of his words and the general outline of what he said recalled by those who were there, but not a complete script of the actual words he spoke. I formulated his opening remarks and the use of the "mathematics equation" analogy from my own mind. And the bit about him walking over to put the penny on Maury's table was all me. When possible, I used snippets in the original wording from William Wirt Henry's account of the Parson's Cause, including delicious morsels such as, "Curiosity was on tiptoe." Henry's biographer also noted the following as the lasting effect of this historical case: "It is said that the people who heard this famous speech never tired of talking of it, and they could pay no higher compliment to a speaker afterward than to say of him, 'He is almost equal to Patrick Henry when he pled against the parsons.'"

615

Stamp Act Crisis   Okay, so Al didn't really inspire the Sugar Act or Stamp Act. Britain had used the Stamp Tax measure in the past, and it had already been considered for the colonies years before Grenville began looking at proposals in 1763. Parliament underestimated the violent response this tax would generate as the first direct tax imposed on the colonies. Grenville's unstable series of missteps (announcing the coming Stamp Tax, withdrawing the idea to gather more information on colonial procedure, telling the complaining colonial agents to come up with their own way to raise the money without giving them an amount, ignoring colonial petitions and pleas) all added fuel to the fire smoldering from the other threats to American liberties. Patrick Henry's Stamp Act Speech was the spark that set the fire ablaze across the already dry wood piled on top of colonial patience.

I have simplified the two days of argument that took place May 29 and 30 when the "bloody, violent debate" filled the House of Burgesses. For the most detailed account of what took place, read Henry Mayer's *A Son of Thunder.* Patrick Henry read his resolves in the Committee of the Whole, and they argued over them. The arguments continued once

Speaker Robinson resumed his seat in the General Assembly the following day. The preamble was struck and each resolution was revised to
make it palatable for inclusion in the official record. Then came the vote
for each resolution. Originally, the first five resolutions were approved,
with the fifth passing by only one vote. It was expunged the following
day after Patrick Henry had left Williamsburg thinking his work was
done and secure. Resolutions six and seven never had a chance of being
accepted, and were not recorded. Details on the debate itself come from
a few eyewitness accounts, including those of Thomas Jefferson and a
mysterious "French Traveler" who penned them in his diary. Recent
discoveries have revealed that the mystery traveler was not French, but
actually a Scottish madeira wine merchant named Charles Murray, and
several things he penned were found to be inaccurate. So we are left with
mysteries and uncertain holes in the story (which, of course, are perfect
for the Order of the Seven to fill in).

The only thing Patrick Henry cared to be remembered for was his
Stamp Act Resolves. He enclosed a copy of the first five resolves with his
will, and wrote the following on the other side of the paper:

616

*The within resolutions passed the House of Burgesses in May 1765.
They formed the first opposition to the Stamp Act and the scheme of taxing
America by the British Parliament. All the colonies, either through fear, or
want of opportunity to form an opposition, or from influence of some kind
or other, had remained silent. I had been for the first time elected a Burgess
a few days before, was young, inexperienced, unacquainted with the forms
of the House, and the members that composed it. Finding the men of weight
averse to opposition, and the commencement of the tax at hand, and that
no person was likely to step forth, I determined to venture, and alone, unad-
vised, and unassisted, on a blank leaf of an old law-book, wrote the within.*

*Upon offering them to the House violent debates ensued. Many threats
were uttered, and much abuse cast on me by the party for submission. After
a long and warm contest the resolutions passed by a very small majority,
perhaps of one or two only. The alarm spread throughout America with
astonishing quickness, and the Ministerial party were overwhelmed. The
great point of resistance to British taxation was universally established in the
colonies. This brought on the war which finally separated the two countries
and gave independence to ours. Whether this will prove a blessing or a curse,
will depend upon the use our people make of the blessings which a gracious*

God hath bestowed on us. If they are wise, they will be great and happy. If they are of a contrary character, they will be miserable. Righteousness alone can exalt them as a nation. Reader! whoever thou art, remember this; and in thy sphere practise virtue thyself, and encourage it in others.
- P. HENRY

I have been privileged to hold this exquisite document that is kept with the Special Collections of the Rockefeller Library in Colonial Williamsburg. It is believed that these five resolutions may have been penned by John Fleming, as the penmanship appears to be similar to his. However, no one knows for certain, nor does anyone know why Henry did not include the sixth and seventh radical resolves with his will. Was a second page containing them lost? Did Henry think it didn't matter to include those resolutions since they were not passed or even recorded? What happened to his original resolves written on the leaf torn from his *Coke upon Littleton?* Who knows?

We also don't know who sent the full text of Patrick Henry's preamble and all seven resolutions to the northern colonies (besides Liz and Nigel.) But they indeed spread like wildfire in the papers, and spurred on the colonial legislatures to the Stamp Act Congress, the Sons of Liberty to form and take violent action, and eventually to the repeal of the Stamp Act. This indeed set the ball of the Revolution in motion, for nothing was the same after these events. Not only had the colonies stood up against tyranny, but for the first time, the colonies came together and learned how to communicate and take action. When the Revolution began in earnest, the colonies knew how to move together for Independence. The Stamp Act Crisis was the dress rehearsal for the colonies declaring Independence in 1776, eleven years later.

So I can see why Patrick Henry considered his Stamp Act Speech and not his Liberty or Death Speech to be the most important words he ever uttered. Without the Stamp Act Resolves, he may never have even had the opportunity to utter, "Liberty or Death." And maybe we would still be affixing British stamps to our "gazettes" today.

Marquis de Lafayette and the Beast of the Gévaudan – For centuries, wolves have roamed the forests of France and other parts of Europe, causing widespread panic from grisly attacks on animals and humans. Surprisingly, historians estimate there have been more than nine thousand wolf attacks since the 1600s. During 1764–67, there was an unusual outbreak of wolf attacks in the south of France in the Auvergne but more so in the Gévaudan region, beginning with the fourteen-year-old shepherd girl, Jeanne Boulet. The details I have given about the events, including the varying descriptions of the beast, the heroism and widespread fame and rewards for Jacques Porterfaix and the seven children, the efforts by the king, authorities, and hunters to capture the beast are all true. And the young Marquis de Lafayette wrote in his memoirs that he fetched his father's musket to go hunt the beast. He wrote, "My heart pounded when I heard of the beast, and the hope of meeting it made my walks very exciting." He was called back by his tutor and the ladies of Chavaniac and never saw the beast.

King Louis XV's royal armor bearer by the name of Antoine did in fact shoot and kill a massive wolf and had it stuffed and sent to Versailles so the king and his court could celebrate the triumph over the beast in late September of 1765. Things were quiet for two months, when another rash of attacks happened again, although fewer in number. Eventually, a local hunter named Jean Chastel killed another beast in June of 1767 and the attacks finally ceased. No one knows for sure what happened, but due to the widespread nature of the attacks, a serious infestation of wolves was suspected, along with a few actual massive wolves that were culprits as well. This phenomenon was one of the first instances for people to experience the power of "mass media" in the press. Given the superstitious mindset of the masses, still coming out of the Dark Ages, those who wished to stir up the frenzied imagination and fear in the people were easily able to do so. Still, the fear was real because the attacks were very real. For an in-depth, fascinating read about these events, I recommend *The Monsters of the Gévaudan* by Jay M. Smith.

PART FOUR: CHAPTERS 48–68

Townshend Acts/Raleigh Tavern – Charles Townshend died in September 1767, just three months after King George III approved his hated Townshend Acts. In his "wake" Townshend left a mess, both in Parliament and in the colonies. The unraveling of Great Britain's government through its mercurial leadership played a huge role in the miracle of American Independence. One misstep after another led the colonies to Revolution. The events following the passage of the Townshend Acts are quite remarkable. While Massachusetts was the first to react in protest and riots, all eyes looked to Virginia for what they would do in response. I had to compress time and content. The discussion on the floor of the House of Burgesses for the 1769 session is made up partially of my words for Patrick Henry, including his directive to keep the doors locked when the governor's messenger knocked. The doors were indeed locked, as the burgesses needed to officially finish their business before Lord Botetourt dissolved them, as they had anticipated he would. A balcony was indeed built in the House of Burgesses chamber in 1766, a year after Patrick Henry's famous Stamp Act Speech. (*Of course,* I give him credit for it! I'm certain the crowds wanted to gather to hear what Patrick Henry had to say next. The famous painting by Rothermel of a red-cloaked Patrick Henry for the 1765 Stamp Act Speech shows a soaring balcony, but the artist was off by a year in depicting the scene. This painting hangs in the splendid museum at Red Hill.) The words I have Patrick Henry say in the Raleigh Tavern (*"No ministerial mandate can make us buy ten-pound coats when we prefer to warm ourselves by the fire of liberty in ten-shilling jackets."*) are not mine but were cleverly penned by Henry Mayer in his brilliant book, *A Son of Thunder.* I absolutely loved Mayer's wordsmithing, and to me it sounded like what Mr. Henry would say.

619

Patrick's Letter Opener – No one knows the origin of the ivory letter opener that Patrick Henry used during the Liberty or Death speech, but you can see it for yourself at Patrick Henry's Red Hill. Could it have come all the way from Plutarch? As Lafayette would say, *"Cur non?"*

Liberty or Death Speech – It has been called the second most famous speech in American history, second only to Abraham Lincoln's Gettysburg Address. It was delivered on March 23, 1775, in the Henrico Parrish Church, now known as St. John's Episcopal Church, in Richmond, Virginia. But we have no idea if Patrick Henry actually spoke every word I've dramatized. Why? Because Patrick Henry never wrote his speeches down. He always spoke "extemporaneously from his mother wit," as I often hear my friend and Patrick Henry interpreter Richard Schumann say. The text I presented is the historical record, published in Patrick Henry's first biography in 1817 by William Wirt. However, Wirt pieced together the speech from eyewitness accounts of men who were there, thirty years after the event. (For a detailed analysis of how Wirt compiled the speech, and the best argument I've seen for the authenticity of its contents, see Robert Meade's excellent biography, *Patrick Henry.*) We do know that the battle cry of "Liberty or Death" spread like wildfire and was soon stitched on militia hunting shirts and flags, and we know that Henry used those words to press the "Cato button" of his audience. Addison's play, *Cato*, was wildly popular and Henry knew how to emote the same passionate response of his audience, both with words and with his dramatic gesture of plunging the ivory letter opener into his heart, portraying the ancient Roman who chose death rather than life under the tyranny of Julius Caesar.

I had the distinct and surreal experience of penning the Liberty or Death chapter while sitting in Patrick Henry's seat in St. John's Church on the 241st anniversary of the speech, March 23, 2016. But more divinely inspired things happened in the process. The fantasy side of this entire novel involves a bald eagle named Cato who serves to inspire Patrick's LOD speech. I didn't plan on this new character—he just showed up on my pages as I started writing the book. I quickly grew to love him. Well, when I got the "Carpe Diem" nudge from God the week before to get to Richmond and write, I suspected that in addition to the incredible honor of sitting sit there all day and writing, something magical would happen. It did. When I arrived in Virginia the day before, a bald eagle circled over my car as I boarded the Surry ferry to cross the James River. That night, I dreamed a bald eagle built a nest over my doorway but I couldn't place where it was (when I later got to the church, it was the doorway of St. John's Church that I had seen in my dream). As I got on the interstate to drive from Williamsburg to Richmond, a bald eagle circled over my car. As I walked around the front of the church I noticed an old, ornate chair carved with a bald eagle. They don't know where it came from, but use it as Peyton Randolph's chair in their reenactments. And finally, while I was sitting in Patrick Henry's seat after writing the last words of the book, my friend Raymond Baird told me a bald eagle had just that moment circled over the church—only seen twice in eight years. I've been researching Patrick Henry for eight years. For icing on the cake that day, Raymond allowed me to ring the bell of the church as they started the reenactment of the Second Virginia Convention. Guess how many times you are supposed to ring the bell. SEVEN!

So, was Cato the eagle real? I know not what course you may take, but as for me, he *was*, both in 1775 and in 2016, as he flew over me all the way to the church. Was there a mad dash to retrieve Patrick Henry's ivory letter opener to slip into his red cloak? Well, I'll let you decide that one.

BIBLIOGRAPHY

Adams, John Quincy, Daniel Fenton, Moore Baker, and C. W. Fenton. *Oration on the Life and Character of Gilbert M. de Lafayette: Delivered at the Request of Both Houses of the Congress of the United States, before Them, in the House of Representatives at Washington. December 31, 1834.* Trenton and Princeton: D. Fenton, Moore Baker, 1835.

Andrlik, Todd. *Reporting The Revolutionary War: Before It Was History, It Was News.* Naperville, IL: Sourcebooks, 2012.

Appleby, Joyce Oldham. *The American Republic to 1877.* New York: Glencoe/ McGraw-Hill, 2005.

Army, Officer in the Late. *A Complete History of the Marquis de Lafayette: Major-General in the American Army in the War of the Revolution Embracing an Account of His.* Memphis, TN: General Books, 2010.

"Attributions of Authorship in the Gentleman's Magazine, 1731–1868: An Electronic Union List." Attributions of Authorship in the Gentleman's Magazine, 1731-1868: An Electronic Union List. Accessed April 6, 2016. http://bsuva.org/bsuva/gm2/GMintro.html.

Auricchio, Laura. *The Marquis: Lafayette Reconsidered.* New York: Vintage Books, 2015.

Barton, Thomas Frank, and Mel Bolden. *Patrick Henry, Boy Spokesman.* Indianapolis: Bobbs-Merrill, 1960.

Bass, Robert D. *The Green Dragoon; the Lives of Banastre Tarleton and Mary Robinson.* New York: Holt, 1957.

Bearce, Stephanie. *The American Revolution.* Waco, TX: Prufrock Press, 2015.

"Beauty and the Beast." Beauty and the Beast. Accessed September 13, 2016. http:// www.pitt.edu/~dash/beauty.html.

Bell, J. L. "Boston 1775." Boston 1775. Accessed November 03, 2016. http://boston1775.blogspot.com/.

Bennett, Michael Jesse. *Patrick Henry's Comments on Life, Liberty (or Death), and the Pursuit of Happiness.* Brookneal, VA: Descendants' Branch, Patrick Henry Memorial Foundation, 1991.

"Ben's Big Idea." Ben Franklin's Kite Experiment. Accessed April 13, 2016. http:// www.codecheck.com/cc/BenAndTheKite.html.

Bernier, Olivier. *Lafayette: Hero of Two Worlds.* New York: E. P. Dutton, 1983.

Bluford, Robert. *Living on the Borders of Eternity: The Story of Samuel Davies and the Struggle for Religious Toleration in Colonial Virginia.* Mechanicsville, VA: Historic Polegreen Press, 2004.

Boston and the American Revolution: Boston National Historical Park, Massachusetts. Washington, DC: Division of Publications, National Park Service, U.S. Department of the Interior, 1998.

Bris, Gonzague Saint, and George Holoch. *Lafayette: Hero of the American Revolution.* New York: Pegasus Books, 2011.

Bull, John, and John Farrand. *The Audubon Society Field Guide to North American Birds: Eastern Region.* New York: Alfred A. Knopf, 1994.

Carson, Jane, and Edward M. Riley. *Patrick Henry, Prophet of the Revolution.* Williamsburg, VA: Virginia Independence Bicentennial Commission, 1979.

Carter, Hodding. *The Marquis de Lafayette, Bright Sword of Freedom.* New York: Random House, 1958.

Clary, David A. *Adopted Son: Washington, Lafayette, and the Friendship That Saved the Revolution.* New York: Bantam Books, 2008.

Collins, Kathleen. *Marquis de Lafayette: French Hero of the American Revolution.* New York: Rosen Central Primary Source, 2004.

Couvillon, Mark. *The Demosthenes of His Age: Accounts of Patrick Henry's Oratory by His Contemporaries.* Brookneal, VA: Patrick Henry Memorial Foundation, 2013.

Couvillon, Mark. *Patrick Henry's Virginia: A Guide to the Homes and Sites in the Life of an American Patriot.* Brookneal, VA: Patrick Henry Memorial Foundation, 2001.

Cowman, Charles E., and James Reimann. *Streams in the Desert: 366 Daily Devotional Readings.* Grand Rapids, MI: Zondervan Pub. House, 1997.

Davies, Samuel. "Religion and Patriotism the Constituents of a Good Soldier. A Sermon Preached to Captain Overton's Independent Company of Volunteers, Raised in Hanover County, Virginia, August 17, 1755. / By Samuel Davies, A.M. Minister of the Gospel There." Religion and Patriotism the Constituents of a Good Soldier. A Sermon Preached to Captain Overton's Independent Company of Volunteers, Raised in Hanover County, Virginia, August 17, 1755. / By Samuel Davies, A.M. Minister of the Gospel There. Accessed April 28, 2016. http://quod.lib.umich.edu/e/evans/ N05830.0001.001/1:1?rgn=div1%3Bview.

"Divine Government the Joy of Our World - Sermon Index.". Accessed March 08, 2016. http://www.sermonindex.net/modules/articles/index. php?view=article&aid=27299.

Eckenrode, H. J. *The Revolution in Virginia.* Hamden, CT: Archon Books, 1964.

"Experiments and Observations on Electricity: Made at Philadelphia in America." Experiments and Observations on Electricity : Made at Philadelphia in America. Accessed April 06, 2016. https://archive.org/stream/ experimentsobser00fran#page/n7/mode/2up.

Fontaine, Edward, and Mark Couvillon. *Patrick Henry: Corrections of Biographical Mistakes, and Popular Errors in Regard to His Character. Anecdotes and New Facts Illustrating His Religious and Political Opinions; & the Style & Power of His*

Eloquence. A Brief Account of His Last Illness & Death. Brookneal, VA: Patrick Henry Memorial Foundation, 2011.

Fritz, Jean, and Ronald Himler. *Why Not, Lafayette?* New York: Puffin Books, 2001.

"George Whitefield." Christian History. Accessed March 02, 2016. http://www.christianitytoday.com/history/people/evangelistsandapologists/george-whitefield.html.

"God the Sovereign of All Kingdoms - Sermon Index." God the Sovereign of All Kingdoms - Sermon Index. Accessed April 28, 2016. http://www.sermonindex.net/modules/articles/index.php?view-article&aid-27312.

Grote, JoAnn A. *Lafayette: French Freedom Fighter*. Philadelphia: Chelsea, 2009.

Hannings, Bud. *Chronology of the American Revolution: Military and Political Actions Day by Day*. Jefferson, NC: McFarland, 2008.

Hayes, Kevin J. *The Mind of a Patriot Patrick Henry and the World of Ideas*. Charlottesville, VA: University of Virginia Press, 2008.

Henrickson, Beth. *The Marquis de Lafayette and Other International Champions of the American Revolution*. New York: PowerKids Press, 2016.

Henry, Patrick, and James M. Elson. *Patrick Henry in His Speeches and Writings and in the Words of His Contemporaries*. Lynchburg, VA: Warwick House Publishers, 2007.

Henry, William Wirt, and Patrick Henry. *Patrick Henry: Life, Correspondence and Speeches*. Vol. 1-3. Whitefish, MT: Kessinger Publishing, 2006.

Henry, William Wirt. *Patrick Henry; Life, Correspondence and Speeches*. New York: Charles Scribner's Sons, 1891.

"History." The Great Bell 1702. July 23, 2013. Accessed April 06, 2016. https://thegreatbell1702.wordpress.com/history/.

"History." Papers of George Washington. Accessed April 06, 2016. http://gwpapers.virginia.edu/history/biography-of-george-washington/.

"History.org: The Colonial Williamsburg Foundation's Official History and Citizenship Website." Of Sharpers, Mumpers, and Fourberies: The Colonial Williamsburg Official History & Citizenship Site. Accessed June 08, 2016. http://www.history.org/Foundation/journal/Spring05/frauds.cfm.

Hoffer, Peter Charles. *Benjamin Franklin Explains the Stamp Act Protests to Parliament, 1766*. Oxford: Oxford University Press, 2016.

"Home." Historic Royal Palaces. Accessed March 02, 2016. http://www.hrp.org.uk/.

"Isaac Barré: Advocate for Americans in the House of Commons - Journal of the American Revolution." Journal of the American Revolution. August 11, 2015. Accessed August 08, 2016. https://allthingsliberty.com/2015/08/isaac-barre-advocate-for-americans-in-the-house-of-commons/.

Isaacson, Walter. *Benjamin Franklin: An American Life*. New York: Simon & Schuster, 2003.

"The Journal of Major George Washington." DigitalCommons@University of Nebraska - Lincoln. http://digitalcommons.unl.edu/cgi/viewcontent.cgi?article=1033&context=etas.

"Journals of the House of Burgesses of Virginia." Digital image. Journals of the House of Burgesses of Virginia. Accessed August 25, 2016. https://archive.org/stream/journalsofhouseo17611765dvirg#page/330/mode/2up.

Kelly, C. Brian., and Ingrid Smyer-Kelly. *Best Little Stories from the American Revolution: More than 100 True Stories*. Naperville, IL: Cumberland House, 2011.

Kidd, Thomas S. *Patrick Henry: First among Patriots*. New York: Basic Books, 2011.

King James Bible. Nashville, TN: Holman Bible Publishers, 1973.

Kukla, Amy, and Jon Kukla. *Patrick Henry: Voice of the Revolution*. New York: PowerPlus Books, 2002.

Kukla, John. "Two Penny Acts (1755, 1758)." Two Penny Acts (1755, 1758). January 18, 2012. Accessed April 28, 2016. http://www.encyclopediavirginia.org/Two_Penny_Acts_1755_1758#start_entry.

Lafayette, Marie Joseph Paul Yves Roch Gilbert du Motier. *Memoirs of General Lafayette*. New York: Robbins, 1825.

Latzko, Andreas, and E. W. Dickes. *Lafayette: A Life by Andreas Latzko*. New York: Literary Guild, 1936.

"Little Red Riding Hood." Little Red Riding Hood. Accessed September 13, 2016. http://www.pitt.edu/~dash/type0333.html.

Litto, Fredric M. "Addison's *Cato* in the Colonies." JSTOR.org. http://www.jstor.org/stable/1919239?seq=1#page_scan_tab_contents.

Loker, Aleck. *Patrick Henry: The Spark That Ignited a Revolution*. Williamsburg, VA: Solitude Press, 2006.

MacCants, David A. *Patrick Henry, the Orator*. New York: Greenwood Press, 1990.

Mayer, Henry. *A Son of Thunder: Patrick Henry and the American Republic*. New York: Grove Press, 2001.

McGaughy, J. Kent. *Richard Henry Lee of Virginia: A Portrait of an American Revolutionary*. Lanham, MD: Rowman & Littlefield Publishers, 2004.

McPherson, Stephanie Sammartino, and Nicolas Debon. *Liberty or Death: A Story about Patrick Henry*. Minneapolis: Carolrhoda Books, 2003.

Meade, Robert D. *Patrick Henry: Patriot in the Making*. Philadelphia and New York: Lippincott, 1957.

Meade, Robert Douthat. *Patrick Henry: Practical Revolutionary*. Philadelphia: Lippincott, 1969.

"The Method of Grace." The Method of Grace. Accessed March 02, 2016. http://biblehub.com/sermons/auth/whitefield/the_method_of_grace.htm.

Meyer, F. B. *Christ in Isaiah*. Grand Rapids, MI: Zondervan, 1950.

Morgan, Edmund Sears, and Helen M. Morgan. *The Stamp Act Crisis: Prologue to Revolution*. Chapel Hill: Published for the Institute of Early American History and Culture by the University of North Carolina Press, 1995.

Morgan, George. *The True Patrick Henry: With Twenty-four Illustrations*. Philadelphia: Lippincott, 1907.

Morrow, George, and Roger Hudson. *The Day They Buried Great Britain: Francis Fauquier, Lord Botetourt and the Fate of Nations*. Williamsburg, VA: Telford Publications, 2011.

Morrow, George. *A Cock and Bull for Kitty: Lord Dunmore and the Affair That Ruined the British Cause in Virginia*. Williamsburg, VA: Telford Publications, 2011.

Morrow, George. *The Greatest Lawyer That Ever Lived: Patrick Henry at the Bar of History*. Williamsburg, VA: Telford Publications, 2011.

Payan, Gregory. *Marquis de Lafayette: French Hero of the American Revolution*. New York: PowerPlus Books, 2002.

Reische, Diana L. *Patrick Henry*. New York: F. Watts, 1987.

"Research Library." George Washington's Mount Vernon. Accessed May 03, 2016. http://www.mountvernon.org/library/research-library/.

"Robinson Crusoe." By Daniel Defoe: Text, Ebook. Accessed April 15, 2016. https://americanliterature.com/author/daniel-defoe/book/robinson-crusoe/summary.

Sabin, Louis, and Bill Ternay. *Patrick Henry, Voice of the American Revolution*. Mahwah, NJ: Troll Associates, 1982.

"Samuel Davies: The Curse of Cowardice." Samuel Davies: The Curse of Cowardice. Accessed March 08, 2016. http://www.lexrex.com/informed/other-documents/sermons/davies.htm.

"A Short Narrative of the Horrid Massacre in Boston, Perpetrated in the Evening of the Fifth Day of March, 1770, by Soldiers of the 29th Regiment, Which with the 14th Regiment Were Then Quartered There; with Some Observations on the State of Things Prior to That Catastrophe : Boston (Mass.) : Free Download & Streaming : Internet Archive." Internet Archive. Accessed October 13, 2016. https://archive.org/details/shortnarrativeof00inbost.

"A SMALL SELECTION OF HEROES, KINGS & VILLAINS." Heroes of Greek Mythology THEOI.COM. Accessed March 02, 2016. http://www.theoi.com/greek-mythology/heroes.html.

Smith, Jay M. *Monsters of the Gévaudan: The Making of a Beast*. Cambridge, MA: Harvard University Press, 2011.

Spivey, Larkin. *Miracles of the American Revolution: Divine Intervention and the Birth of the Republic*. Chattanooga: AMG Publishers, 2010.

"Stamp Act." Stamp Act. Accessed June 06, 2016. http://www.stamp-act-history.com/.

Strum, Richard M. *Henry Knox: Washington's Artilleryman*. Stockton, NJ: OTTN Publishing, 2007.

"The Time Benjamin Franklin Tried (and Failed) to Electrocute a Turkey." Mental Floss. Accessed April 06, 2016. http://mentalfloss.com/article/31225/time-benjamin-franklin-tried-and-failed-electrocute-turkey.

Translation, Bible English. New Living. *Holy Bible, New Living Translation*. Wheaton, IL: Tyndale House Publishers, 1996.

625

Troy, Anne, and Phyllis Green. *Where Was Patrick Henry on the 29th of May?: Jean Fritz*. Palatine, IL: A. Troy and P. Green, 1988.

UK. National Archives of the UK. *CO 5/1353 Correspondence, Original – Secretary of State Virginia Part I*.

Unger, Harlow G. *Lafayette*. New York: Wiley, 2003.

Unger, Harlow G. *Lion of Liberty: Patrick Henry and the Call to a New Nation*. Cambridge, MA: Da Capo Press, 2011.

United States. National Park Service. "Tobacco: Colonial Cultivation Methods." National Parks Service. Accessed April 15, 2016. https://www.nps.gov/jame/learn/historyculture/tobacco-colonial-cultivation-methods.htm.

Walbert, David. "6.5 The Value of Money in Colonial America." The Value of Money in Colonial America. 2007. Accessed July 30, 2016. http://www.learnnc.org/lp/editions/nchist-colonial/1646.

Weitzman, David M. *Living a Life That Matters: A Memoir of the Marquis de Lafayette*. Place of Publication Not Identified: Liberty Flame, 2015.

Welch, Catherine A. *Patrick Henry*. Minneapolis: Lerner Publications, 2006.

"Welcome to Our Online Collections Database!" Christ Church Preservation Trust: Online Collections. Accessed April 06, 2016. http://christchurchphila.pastperfectonline.com/.

Wells, James M., and Carris J. Kocher. *The Christian Philosophy of Patrick Henry*. Concordville, PA: Bill of Rights Bicentennial Committee, 2004.

Willison, George F. *Patrick Henry and His World*. January 21, 2017. Accessed February 23, 2017. http://www.worldcat.org/title/patrick-henry-and-his-world/oclc/712607.

Wilson, Hazel Hutchins, and Edy Legrand. *The Story of Lafayette*. New York: Grosset & Dunlap, 1952.

Wirt, William. *Sketches of the Life and Character of Patrick Henry*. Philadelphia: Published by James Webster, No. 24, S. Eighth Street. William Brown, Printer, Prune Street, 1818.

Glossary

French Terms

À *bientôt*	See you soon
Au contraire	On the contrary
Ami/amie	Friend
Allons-y!	Let's go!
Beaux rêves	Sweet dreams
Bien sûr!	Of course!
Bon	Good
Bon appétit	Enjoy your meal
Bon vol	Good flight
Bonjour	Hello/Good day
Bonne journée	Have a nice day
Bonne nuit	Good night
Bonsoir	Good evening
C'est ça	That's it!
C'est extraordinaire	This is amazing
C'est incredible	It is incredible
C'est magnifique	It is magnificent/incredible
Ce n'est pas bien	This is not good
C'est tragique	It is tragic
Cher/chère	Dear
Déjà vu	This has happened before
Dieu	God
Exactement	Exactly
Fête	A grand party or celebration
FEU!	Fire!
Grand-mère	Grandmother
Je comprends	I understand
Je ne comprends pas	I don't understand
Je ne sais pas	I don't know
Je suis désolée!	I am sorry
Je suis très heureuse	I am very happy
Je vous en prie	You are welcome

Joyeux Anniversaire	Happy Birthday
La gloire	Glory
L'amour	Love
Le petit prince	The little prince
Liberté	Liberty
Livre des Conquérants	Book of Conquerors (for William the Conqueror)
Ma/Mon	My
Merci	Thank you
Mes amis	My friends
Moi aussi	Me, too
Mon ami/amie	My friend (masc./fem.)
Mon Dieu	My God
Mon professeur	My teacher/professor
Monsieur	Mister
Oui	Yes
Quel dommage	What a pity
Petit déjeuner	Breakfast
Pour vous	For you
Réveillez-vous	Wake up
S'il vous plaît	Please
Touché	Used to acknowledge a clever or witty remark in an argument
Toi aussi	You, too
Très jolie	Very pretty, very nice
Tu n'es pas encore more, mon père	Thou are not yet dead, my father
Un chat	A cat
Une chienne	A dog
Un moment	Just a minute
Voici! L'ennemie	The enemy is here!

French 18th Century Folk Song: Au Clair de la Lune

"Au clair de la lune,	"By the light of the moon,
Mon ami Pierrot,	My friend Pierrot,
Prête-moi ta plume	Lend me your quill
Pour écrire un mot.	To write a word.

Ma chandelle est morte,	My candle is dead,
Je n'ai plus de feu.	I have no more fire.
Ouvre-moi ta porte	Open your door for me
Pour l'amour de Dieu."	For the love of God."

Kakia's Greek

Efcharistó!	Thank you!
Misó tous anthrópous	I hate humans
Ýpoulos	Sneaky

Latin

Ab initio	From the beginning
Alis aquilae	On eagle's wings
Carpe diem	Seize the day
Capta est optimus mundus creatus vitas hominum historia	The world of man is best captured through the lives of the men who created history
Dormi bene	Sleep well
E pluribus unum	Out of many, one
Ego te provoco	I dare you
Ex tempore	From this moment; this instant
Ficta voluptatis causa sint proxima veris	Fictions meant to please should approximate the truth
Historia vitae magistra	History, the teacher of life
Hoc est bellum	This is war
Igitur qui desiderat pacem, praeparet bellum	Therefore whoever desires peace, let him prepare for war
In absentia luci, tenebrae vincunt	In the absence of light, darkness prevails
In omnibus requiem quaesivi, et nusquam inveni nisi in angulo cum libro	Everywhere I have searched for peace and nowhere found it, except in a corner with a book (Quote by Thomas à Kempis)
In pace ut sapiens aptarit idonea bello	In peace, like the wise man, make preparations for war
Ita vero	Thus indeed

629

A useful phrase, as the Romans had no word for "yes," preferring to respond to questions with the affirmative or negative of the question (e.g., "Are you hungry?" was answered by "I am hungry" or "I am not hungry", not "Yes" or "No").

Ite, missa est	Go, it is the dismissal
Longissimus dies cito conditur	Even the longest day soon ends
Non operae pretium est elit	Nothing worthwhile comes easy
Perfer et obdura; dolor hic	Be patient and tough;
tibi proderit olim	someday this pain will be useful to you.
Sic infit	So it begins
Sic semper tyrannis	Thus always to tyrants

Attributed to Brutus at the time of Julius Caesar's assassination. Shorter version from original sic semper evello mortem tyrannis ("thus always I pluck death from tyrants"). State motto of Virginia, adopted in 1776.

630

"Veni, vidi, vici"	I came, I saw, I conquered

Rat's Cockney Slang

Fisherman's daughter	Water

Terms in Patrick Henry's "Liberty or Death" Speech

adversary	enemy; foe
anguish	suffering; pain; great distress
arduous	hard; very difficult
avert	avoid; prevent
basely	dishonorably
beseech	beg; request; appeal urgently
brethren	brothers
comports	agrees with
contending	competing; challenging
delusive	misleading; deceptive
effectual	effective; successful
election	choice
entertaining	thinking
entreaty	appeal; earnest request
extenuate	stretch out

forged	made
formidable	powerful
gale	strong wind
implements	tools; devices
implored	pleaded; begged desperately
indulge	gratify; yield to desire
inestimable	beyond measure
irresolution	indecision
insidious	sneaky; crafty; deceitful
interposition	influence
in vain	without success; uselessly
invincible	unbeatable
inviolate	unbroken; unaltered; undisturbed
magnitude	greatness
martial array	warlike display
moment	importance
petition	formal request
phantom	ghost
prostrated	totally submitted
remonstrated	forcefully protested; argued; objected
resounding	loud; booming
revere	highly respect; admire
rivet	fasten firmly; hold; attach
slighted	insulted; offended; snubbed
snare	trap
solace	comfort
spurned	rejected
subjugation	conquest; defeat; suppression
supinely	passively
supplication	plea; meek request
temporal	worldly
tyrannical	harsh; oppressive; unjustly cruel
vigilant	watchful; always alert

631

ABOUT THE EPIC SCRIBE . . .

Award-winning author and speaker Jenny L. Cote, who developed an early passion for God, history, and young people, beautifully blends these three passions in her two fantasy fiction series, The Amazing Tales of Max and Liz® and Epic Order of the Seven®. Likened to C. S. Lewis by readers and book reviewers alike, she speaks on creative writing to schools, universities, and conferences around the world. Jenny is excited about making history fun for kids of all ages, instilling in them a desire to discover *their* part in HIStory. Her love for research has taken her to most Revolutionary sites in the United States, to London (with unprecedented access to Handel House Museum to write in Handel's composing room), Oxford (to stay in the home of C. S. Lewis, 'the Kilns', and interview Lewis's secretary, Walter Hooper, at the Inklings' famed The Eagle and Child Pub), Paris, Normandy, Rome, Israel, and Egypt. She partnered with the National Park Service to produce Epic Patriot Camp, a summer writing camp at Revolutionary parks to excite kids about history, research, and writing. Jenny's books are available online and in stores around the world, as well as in multiple e-book formats. Jenny holds two marketing degrees from the University of Georgia and Georgia State University. A Virginia native, Jenny now lives in Roswell, Georgia. To schedule a talk, book signing, or interview please visit her Web site at www.epicorderofthe seven.com and the official Jenny L. Cote Facebook page

. . . AND HER BOOKS.

The Amazing Tales of Max and Liz® is a two-book prequel series that begins the adventures of brave Scottie dog Max and brilliant French cat Liz. Book One: *The Ark, the Reed, and the Fire Cloud* introduces Max and Liz, who meet on the way to the Ark and foil a plot by a stowaway who is out to kill Noah and stop his mission. Book Two: *The Dreamer, the Schemer, and the Robe* brings Max, Liz, and friends to work behind the scenes in the life of Joseph in the land of Egypt. The Epic Order of the Seven® series picks up where the Max and Liz series left off. Book One: *The Prophet, the Shepherd, and the Star* gives Max, Liz, and the gang their most important mission yet: preparing for the birth of the promised Messiah. Their seven-hundred–year mission takes them to the lives of Isaiah, Daniel, and those in the Christmas story. Book Two: *The Roman, the Twelve, and the King* unfolds the childhood, ministry, and passion of Jesus Christ with a twist – his story is told within the story of George F. Handel as he composes his *Messiah*. Book Three: *The Wind, the Road, and the Way* covers Acts 1 through 18 and Paul's first two missionary journeys. Book Four: *The Fire, the Revelation, and the Fall* concludes the story of Acts to the fall of Rome, showing the miraculous birth of the church amidst persecution by the Roman Empire. Book Five: *The Voice, the Revolution, and the Key* begins a Revolutionary War trilogy featuring Patrick Henry and the Marquis de Lafayette. Upcoming books: *The Declaration, the Marquis, and the Spy* (2020), *The Sword, the Thunder, and the Jewel* (2022), and C. S. Lewis and World War II. Jenny's books have been developed into VBS curriculum (*Heroes of HIStory*) with animation and original music. Future plans include an animated TV/DVD series, feature film adaptation, and school curriculum.

RESOURCES
ON PATRICK HENRY AND
THE AMERICAN REVOLUTION

Please visit the following places to see where the EPIC history in *The Voice, the Revolution, and the Key* happened!

 Would you like to see THE ivory letter opener that Patrick Henry held in his "Give me liberty, or give me death" speech? How about Patrick's "magic" fiddle and flute? These priceless items and more are housed in the museum at Red Hill, Patrick Henry's final home and burial place. Visit the beautiful place that Patrick called "the garden spot of the world," and see seven historic buildings, the Patrick Henry grave site, and the grounds overlooking the Staunton River Valley, which appears much as it did in Henry's time. Red Hill holds special annual programs including Living History Days for Homeschool Students (with Jenny L. Cote as speaker) and the July 4th fireworks celebration. Red Hill is located in Brookneal, VA. www.redhill.org

 For an excellent, comprehensive guide to all of the Patrick Henry sites mentioned in *The Voice, the Revolution, and the Key*, pick up *Patrick Henry's Virginia: A Guide to the Homes and Sites in the Life of an American Patriot* by Mark Couvillon (2001). Illustrated and filled with biographical information. Includes driving directions to each of the 23 locations. (available at www.redhill.org)

 "Where Liberty Found Its Voice!" Visit St. John's Church in Richmond, Virginia, the place where Patrick Henry made his "Give me liberty, or give me death" speech. Take a tour and attend a re-enactment of the 2nd Virginia Convention to see the speech brought to life in the very room where it happened. www.historicstjohnschurch.org

Located twelve miles from Richmond, see where young Patrick Henry learned "what an orator should be" as he listened to Reverend Samuel Davies at Polegreen Church. This was the epicenter of the Great Awakening and Dissenter movement in Virginia. www.historicpolegreen.org

Dine where Patrick Henry served guests when he brought his family to live at Hanover Tavern. Located across the street from Hanover Courthouse, where Patrick cut his teeth as an orator in The Parsons Cause case. Enjoy a tour to learn more about the colorful history of this place. www.hanovertavern.org

Patrick Henry's Scotchtown – Visit the original home where Patrick Henry lived when he lost his first wife, Sarah. It was from here that he rode to Philadelphia for the First Continental Congress, and where he resided when elected as Governor of Virginia. preservationvirginia.org/visit/historic-properties/patrick-henrys-scotchtown

Colonial Williamsburg – See where the American Revolution got its start! Visit the home of George Wythe, where Patrick Henry applied for his law license, and sit in the Capitol, where he served as a Burgess in the Virginia Assembly and gave his famous Stamp Act Speech. Tour the Governor's Palace, where Patrick lived as the first elected Governor of Virginia. And meet Patrick Henry (and the Marquis de Lafayette) in character on the streets of Williamsburg! www.history.org

American Revolution Museum at Yorktown – See one of the few full-size statues of Patrick Henry in his "Liberty or Death" stance at this fantastic new museum in Yorktown, VA. You will gain a comprehensive understanding of the pre-Revolution years—all the way to Victory at Yorktown and on to the Constitutional years. Enjoy interactive exhibits and films, including "The Siege of Yorktown," with a 180-degree surround screen and dramatic special effects. Step outside for a living-history experience with artillery demonstrations, a re-created Continental Army encampment, and a Revolution-era farm. http://www.historyisfun.org/yorktown-victory-center

George Washington's Mount Vernon – Visit the beautiful home of our first President that overlooks the Potomac River in northern Virginia. Both Patrick Henry and the Marquis de Lafayette stayed here as guests of George and Martha. www.mountvernon.org

Museum of the American Revolution, Philadelphia – Look no further than the new Museum of the American Revolution in Philadelphia, PA for a hands-on, comprehensive, multimedia experience to understand how America achieved Independence. See incredible artifacts, including George Washington's amazingly preserved wartime tent. www.amrevmuseum.org

City Tavern, Philadelphia – Tour Carpenter's Hall and then dine where Patrick Henry and other founding fathers stayed while attending the First Continental Congress. www.citytavern.com

Château Lafayette, France – If you want to see where the Marquis de Lafayette was born and raised, you can visit his childhood home in the Haute-Loire region in the south of France. For pictures and videos, visit www.chateau-lafayette.com.

American Friends of Lafayette – If you would like to learn more about "America's favorite fighting Frenchman," the Marquis de Lafayette, please visit https://friendsoflafayette.wildapricot.org/

This is by no means an exhaustive list of resources. Please visit the many museums and National Parks in Boston, Philadelphia, and in each of the original thirteen colonies of America. Go see where history happened, and while you're at it, make some history yourself.

The Declaration, the Marquis, and the Spy

COMING 2020

"THE BRITISH ARE COMING!"...
but so is the MARQUIS DE LAFAYETTE!

Opening with Paul Revere's heart-pounding midnight ride, Book Two in the EPIC Revolutionary Trilogy will leave your heart pounding until the last page. Who will fire the first "shot heard 'round the world" and be responsible for launching the American Revolution at Lexington and Concord? Ride with Patrick Henry to the Second Continental Congress where George Washington must be appointed Commander in Chief of the Continental Army. Witness the bloody Battle of Bunker Hill and Washington's impossible struggle to form and supply his undisciplined, rag-tag army. Patrick Henry picks up his gun as Colonel but is quickly branded an outlaw by Lord Dunmore and strives to avoid capture. His voice is needed once more—this time for a resolution to vote for American independence. But the exuberant cries of "Liberty!" are soon dampened by patriot losses in New York. Only a miracle can save what's left of the Continental Army. Meanwhile, the Marquis de Lafayette must disobey his king and slip out of France unnoticed in order to join the glorious cause of America's struggle for Independence. He faces a perilous journey, with a stowaway watching his every move and snipers waiting for him when he arrives. Patriot blood will spill until the Order of the Seven team leads Washington to a secret weapon that will mean the difference between defeat and victory: a spy ring. A glimmer of hope from the victory at Saratoga is all but extinguished by bloody footprints in the snow at Valley Forge. The Enemy seeks to crush the patriots and their commander before the spring thaw, but which will be the most dangerous—the enemy without or the enemy within?